KEIRITH'S POWER SURGED, FED BY FURY
and shame so intense that he thought he would scream if he couldn't release it. His blood pounded in his ears, a frenzied drumbeat that urged him to let go, to obliterate that mocking smile and shatter his enemy's spirit.

Screaming, he hurled his power at his tormentor. The man staggered backward, tripping over the step. Keirith touched shock and disbelief. A savage joy filled him. He pushed harder, wanting to destroy that sneering spirit, to send it hurtling out of the man's body into Chaos, to feel his scream, to taste his helpless terror.

Instead he felt . . . nothing. As if the connection between them had abruptly been severed The Zheron slowly raised his head and grimaced—not in pain, but as if the touch had contaminated him.

Keirith swayed, drained by the release of energy and the long interrogation and his sense of failure. When the guards released him, he collapsed to the floor.

Until now, he had never felt such an overwhelming desire to kill. This was what the Tree-Father had feared. This was why his father had reacted with such horror. They had known he possessed this potential for violence, that one day, he would turn his power on someone with the deliberate intent to destroy.

"Merciful Maker," he whispered. "Help me. . . ."

BARBARA CAMPBELL'S

Trickster's Game Series:

HEARTWOOD (Book One)
BLOODSTONE (Book Two)

BLOODSTONE

Trickster's Game #2

BARBARA CAMPBELL

DAW BOOKS, INC.

DONALD A. WOLLHEIM, FOUNDER

375 Hudson Street, New York, NY 10014

ELIZABETH R. WOLLHEIM
SHEILA E. GILBERT
PUBLISHERS

http://www.dawbooks.com

First Printing, August 2006
1   2   3   4   5   6   7   8   9

Acknowledgments

The gang at The Never-Ending Odyssey 2005, who helped me celebrate the publication of my first novel and reviewed the opening chapters of this one. Special thanks to Bob Cutchin, Geoffrey Jacoby, Laurie Lemieux, Susan Sielinski, and Susan Winston.

Laurie Lanzdorf and Michael Samerdyke, who critiqued the first draft, asked the tough questions, and pointed out the occasional horrifying gaffe like having a character die in one chapter and show up, alive and well, in the next.

The experts: Professor Ellis Underkoffler for insights into earthquakes and tsunamis and Joe Abene, keeper of the Bronx Zoo Reptile House, for advice on adders.

Susan Herner, my agent and friend, who helped keep me calm and focused when deadlines loomed.

Sheila Gilbert, my terrific—and terrifically patient—editor. Her feedback shaped the story and her comments and questions helped me manage this large cast of characters without losing my mind. Too often.

And finally, David Lofink, my husband, my first reader, and my best friend. Whether discussing characters, bringing home takeout food, or demonstrating how a "loose-limbed wolf on the prowl" *really* moves, he kept me going during the writing of *Bloodstone* and I dedicate it to him.

PART ONE

The remains of his body are scattered and lost,
But his name shall be remembered forever:
Morgath the False.
Morgath the Destroyer.
Morgath the Eater of Spirits.
His deeds shall be cursed by gods and men,
And his fate, the fate of all who subvert the laws of
   nature.

—The Legend of Morgath

Chapter 1

HE WAS FLYING. Not the dizzying whirl of emerging from a trance or the effortless drifting of dreams. He was flying with the eagle.

Keirith wanted to laugh, to shout with the joy of it, but he was voiceless now. His body still sat on the boulder. He could see it far below, face upturned to the sky, eyes closed, hands resting lightly on his knees. He could even feel the sun-warmed rock under his thighs and the breeze that stirred his hair. The core of his being still rested there while his spirit reached skyward, a spider's spinneret that connected him to the eagle.

They soared over Eagles Mount, great wings scarcely moving despite the cool gusts of air that ruffled the tips of their dark feathers. Below them, shadowed by the overhanging shelf of rock, the female perched on her nest of sticks and bracken. As long as Keirith could remember, the pair had nested on this crag. The tribe regarded them with awe; most eagles preferred the open moors of the north to the dense forest that surrounded the village.

They rode the air currents up, banking around the circle of huts. Each was the size of a man's fist from this height, and the lake looked small enough to jump across. Their eyes—keen enough to pick out the blossoms on a gorse bush—swept over the glistening thread of the river as they searched for prey. With their hooked talons and muscled legs, they could easily carry off one of the newborn lambs frolicking on the rocky slopes of Eagles Mount, but the shepherds and their dogs would be watching. Aye, there was Conn, one hand raised to shade his face from the sun as he followed their flight.

Keirith yearned to call out a greeting to his milk-brother. Surrendering to his eagerness, the eagle gave a soft chirrup, a silly, weak sound for such a majestic bird.

A wolf howls. Even a hawk screams. You should have a cry the whole world can hear.

As if the thought were his own, he heard the eagle's response: <*Your mate hears your cry during courtship. Why warn your prey when you hunt?*>

May I hunt with you?

<*Another day.*>

Disappointment shadowed the joy of the flight, but he knew the eagle was wise; the experience of flying together was still too new for them.

He had always loved the eagles. During his vision quest last spring, he had climbed far up Eagles Mount, to the special place he had discovered as a child. All night, he had sat there, shivering with cold. As dawn approached, he'd watched the sky lighten to a deep blue and Bel's first rays paint the treetops gold.

At first, all he could make out was a faint shadow against the sky. He knew at once it was not a real eagle, for the outspread wings flapped with otherworldly slowness as the bird descended. His heart slammed against his ribs at the thought of finding his vision mate so quickly; his father had waited three days and nights in the forest before he heard the she-wolf's howl.

Only when the eagle swooped lower did he see the wriggling serpent in its curved talons. The adder's head reared back. Red-brown eyes gazed down into his. A tongue flicked out and a voice, dry and rasping as autumn leaves rubbing together, whispered his name.

The adder's choice had shocked him. He'd been so certain his power was leading him along the shaman's path and every shaman in the tribe's history had found a bird during his vision quest, a bird that became his guide to the spirit world. When Tree-Father Gortin agreed to take him as an apprentice anyway, he had been relieved and thrilled, but he could not resist the urge to seek communion with a real eagle.

Three moons ago, the male had permitted his touch, such a fleeting brush of spirits he had wondered if he'd imagined it. Since then, they had touched many times, but only today had the eagle allowed them to fly together.

And already, it was time to separate; Keirith could feel his weariness mingling with the eagle's hunger pangs.

Thank you, brother, for allowing me to fly with you.

<We will fly again, fledgling.>

Slowly, carefully, he began the process of returning to his body. The separation must be done gently lest he injure his host, the energy furling as gently as the morningstar closed its blossoms at twilight.

"Keirith!"

The voice startled them both. His spirit tore free. For one terrifying moment, he was lost between bodies, falling helplessly through space. And then his spirit hurtled back into his body with a jolt that left him gasping.

When he came to himself, he was lying on the ground, looking up into the Tree-Father's worried face. The Tree-Father was speaking in a low, urgent voice, but it took Keirith a moment to understand the words. When he did, he whispered his name three times to seal his spirit's return. Then he ran his hands over his body to reestablish the boundaries of his physical self. But when he tried to sit up, the Tree-Father pressed him back.

"Just lie still and breathe."

He closed his eyes, allowing the dreamy lassitude to relax his body and mind.

"What were you doing out here by yourself?" the Tree-Father scolded in his mild way. "You should know better than to attempt a vision on your own."

"It wasn't a vision. I was flying."

"What?"

"With the eagle. I touched his spirit. And we flew together." His triumph faded when he opened his eyes and saw the Tree-Father's expression. "What is it?"

"You touched his spirit?"

Keirith nodded, still trying to understand why the Tree-Father looked so horrified. When he realized the truth, relief left him breathless. "I was careful. I never hurt him. Not even the first time."

"How many times have you done this?"

"I . . . not many," he lied.

"*How* many? Twice? Three times?"

"I can't remember. Please. Tell me what's wrong?"

"Merciful gods." The Tree-Father stumbled away, rubbing the empty socket of his left eye. He drew a trembling breath as he turned to face Keirith. "To subvert or subjugate the spirit of any creature is a violation of our laws. Worse, it is an abomination in the sight of the gods."

Keirith scrambled to his feet. "But I didn't subvert his spirit. He welcomed me. And next time—"

"There will be no next time! You must never do this again."

"But why? You touch the spirit of every person in the tribe. You touched mine when I came back from my vision quest. Tree-Father Struath touched the spirit of the Holly-Lord himself."

"A shaman spends years honing his power and understanding its limits. When we touch a human spirit, we receive permission first. Animals cannot offer that."

Guilt filled Keirith when he recalled how long it had taken him to overcome the eagle's panic.

"And there's another reason why riding the spirits of animals is forbidden. That was how Morgath began."

"You think . . ." Keirith could hardly force himself to speak the words. "You think I'm like Morgath?"

The Tree-Father's expression softened. "Nay. But what you did was wrong. Perhaps Morgath began in innocence as well, but in time, he used his power to cast out the spirits of the animals he touched. For that, his body was sacrificed to appease the gods and his spirit consigned to Chaos."

If the Tree-Father knew how many times he had touched the eagle, he would condemn him as surely as the elders of the Oak and Holly Tribes had condemned Morgath. His chest would be cut open and his still-beating heart ripped out. His body would hang from the lowest branches of the heart-oak to be devoured by scavengers. His bones would be scattered in the forest, never to lie in the ancestral cairn. That was Morgath's fate—and his if he flew with the eagle again.

It was forbidden. It was an abomination. *He* was an abomination.

"This power is dangerous. You must swear never to use it. Or I shall be forced to call you before the council of elders."

Never to fly with the eagle again. Never to share that terrifying, giddy exhilaration of flight. But what choice did he have? Helpless, Keirith nodded.

"I must have your spoken oath."

"I swear. I will never fly with the eagle again."

"That is not enough. Swear that you will never touch the spirit of any bird or animal."

"I . . . I swear."

Keirith sank down on the rock, numbed by the sacrilege he had unwittingly committed and the loss of his link with the majestic bird that soared overhead. The Tree-Father's hand came up as if to pat his shoulder, but fell back to his side.

For who would want to touch an abomination?

"I'm sorry, Keirith. I'd hoped that one day . . ." The Tree-Father shook his head impatiently. "I'll speak to your parents tonight."

"Can't we just keep this a secret? Between you and me?"

"I must offer some sort of explanation for releasing you from your apprenticeship."

Keirith could feel his mouth working, but no words emerged.

"I thought you understood. I cannot permit you to continue with your studies."

Gortin had been his guide and teacher for nearly nine moons. In the space of a few moments—hardly longer than his flight with the eagle—he had severed him from both his gift and his life-path.

"It's my fault. I should never have accepted you as my apprentice. But you had such a desire. And since the eagle appeared during your vision quest as well as the adder, I thought . . ." The Tree-Father sighed, his face sorrowful. "I was wrong. Forgive me."

"Please."

"If I was wrong to take you as an apprentice, I would be more at fault for instructing you further in the mysteries."

Keirith went down on his knees. He seized the Tree-Father's hand and pressed his lips to the tattooed acorn.

"Stop this. Get up." The Tree-Father yanked his hand free. "I'm sorry. Truly. And I will tell your parents that when I speak to them."

"Nay. I'll tell them." He didn't know why it was important to him to have that much control over his future, but it was. "At least let me do that."

The stones bit into his knees while he waited for the Tree-Father's decision. Finally, he said, "Very well."

Fingers brushed the top of his head in blessing. Then the Tree-Father left, taking Keirith's hopes for the future with him.

A fortnight later, he was still seeking the courage to break the news to his parents. He told himself that he hadn't wanted to ruin his father's last days at home before leaving for the spring Gathering. Then, of course, he had to wait for him to return. In his heart, he knew the truth: he was a coward. The son of the great Darak Spirit-Hunter was a coward and an abomination.

For ten long days, he had kept up the pretense that he still went to the Tree-Father's hut for his lessons. Instead, he crept out of the village before dawn to roam the forest and the hills to the north. But today, he had returned to Eagles Mount, to his special place near the top of the crag.

If I had come here that afternoon, the Tree-Father would never have found me.

But the afternoon had been waning and he'd been too eager to touch the eagle to waste time climbing here. Such an unimportant decision at the time, but one that had ruined his life.

He flung himself onto the grassy ledge, panting. Boulders shielded him from the women sowing barley and oats in the fields. The ground was too rocky to lure the sheep away from the eastern slopes. Even the fishermen out on the lake would be unable to say for sure whose figure they spied scrambling up the steep ridge. His only companions were the rocks and the sun and the eagles.

He knew it was foolish to come. Like picking at an unhealed scab. It only reminded him of everything that had gone wrong—and tempted him to fly again.

How could an experience so wonderful be wrong? He hadn't dared ask the Tree-Father that or reveal how many other creatures he had touched with his power.

Keirith shuddered, remembering that first time. He had practiced with the sling for moons before his father took him into the forest to hunt. Gods, he'd been excited. And scared that he might shame himself before the man who had once been the greatest hunter in the tribe.

He missed his first two shots completely and stunned the wood pigeon with his third. Cheeks burning, he waded through the underbrush; his father always emphasized the importance of a clean kill. When he crouched to wring the bird's neck, the wood pigeon screamed. He screamed, too, scuttling back in shock.

"What is it, son?"

When his father knelt beside him, the bird screamed again. Even with his hands over his ears, he could hear the screams, high and shrill and terrified. Only when his father twisted the bird's neck did they stop.

"Keirith. Tell me."

"It . . . it screamed. Inside my head. I heard it, Fa. I swear."

His father patted his shoulder and wiped his cheeks. But when Keirith asked if he'd heard the dying screams of his prey when he was a hunter, his father slowly shook his head. "Perhaps you're meant to follow another path."

But he refused to give up so easily. He practiced shot after shot, aiming at clumps of grass, at pebbles on the lakeshore, at a groove in a tree stump. He whirled the sling until his arm ached, until he was sure he would always make a clean kill. But inevitably, it happened again, this time with a rabbit he had snared. He managed to control himself long enough to end its misery before he doubled over and vomited.

He offered extra sacrifices to the spirits of the animals he failed to kill cleanly. He prayed to the gods, begging them to take away the curse. When he mastered the bow, he accepted his father's praise and pretended not to see the doubt that shadowed his expression. But the first time he sighted down an arrow at a doe, his hands began to shake and sweat broke out on his forehead. His father's hand came down on his shoulder, gripping him hard despite the missing fingers.

"Let it go, son."

That was the last time they went hunting together. If his father was disappointed, he kept it to himself. Somehow, that was worse.

He continued to set snares and bring down game with his sling. All boys were expected to do that, and he refused to let this weakness—or power—keep him from doing his share. He taught himself to block some of the terror of the wounded animals before it overwhelmed him. Later, it seemed only natural to reach out to their spirits and calm them. He'd never imagined it could be wrong. Touching the eagle's spirit . . . that had been different, of course, but even if the impulse was selfish, it wasn't evil.

With an effort, he quelled the resentment that rose in him. Throughout his studies, the Tree-Father had praised his ability to fall into a trance, his close communion with his spirit guide Natha. Now he used the same gift to condemn him.

He couldn't keep his dismissal a secret forever. Someone was bound to find out the truth. As soon as his father returned from the Gathering, he would have to tell his parents.

That confrontation would be far worse than the one with the Tree-Father. For if Morgath was the most evil man in tribal legend, his father was the greatest hero. The man who had survived the torture of his body and spirit to destroy Morgath. Who had rescued the spirit of the Oak-Lord from Chaos. The man who had saved the world. How was he going to stand before such a man and admit that he was a failure—again?

Perhaps he could tell his parents he had erred in believing the way of the shaman was his life-path. Other boys changed their minds, discovering new talents after their vision quests. Not everyone was like Conn. For generations, his family had tended the village flock and he was happily following that tradition.

A shout made him jerk his head up. As if the thought had conjured him, Conn was scrambling up the slope. Keirith waved back without enthusiasm and when Conn neared the ledge, thrust out a hand to pull him up. The effort left them both panting; he was half a head taller, but Conn was more solidly built. On the other hand, he was starting to

get his whiskers in—a few, anyway—while Conn's round
face was still as smooth as a babe's.

"What are you doing here?" he asked as Conn flopped
down beside him.

"I followed you. Why aren't you at your lessons?"

"Why aren't you with the sheep?"

"I saw you sneaking off. What's wrong?"

"Nothing's wrong. I just . . . sometimes a man wants a
little peace and quiet."

Conn's features screwed up in The Ferocious Scowl.
After their vision quests, they'd spent many evenings prac-
ticing manly behavior. Their efforts were less than successful. When Conn's father observed The Dignified Walk, he
inquired if they had sat on nettles. When they tried out
The Ferocious Scowl, Keirith's mam demanded to know
the last time they had moved their bowels.

"You haven't heard a word I've said."

"Sorry. I was thinking about my mam's reaction to The
Ferocious Scowl."

Conn laughed. "Well, that's what comes of being the son
of a healer. Still, it's better than being the Grain-Mother's
son. Everyone expects you to be so pious." A wistful expression stole over his face. "At least your mam's there.
When you go to sleep, when you wake up. It's hard sometimes. On the little ones, I mean."

"It's not like she's living miles away."

"But it's not the same. Mam living with the other priestesses while the rest of us live with Fa." Conn sighed.
"Sometimes I wish we had a normal family like yours."

"My father's the greatest hero in the world, my mother's
kissed the Trickster-God, and my uncle's a tree. You call
that normal?"

"Well, when you put it that way . . ." Conn offered an
exaggerated version of The Thoughtful Nod and Keirith
had to laugh. Then Conn's expression turned serious again.
"So are you going to tell me or not?"

Keirith told him. Not about flying with the eagle, but about
his apprenticeship. Even to his best friend—especially to his
best friend—he couldn't bring himself to reveal that he was
an abomination.

"But a moon ago, everything was fine."

"It's . . . gotten more difficult."

"It's Uncle Gortin, isn't it? I'll get Fa to talk to him. Maybe—"

"Nay! I haven't even told my parents yet. I tried before Father left for the Gathering, but . . ." His voice trailed off as Conn's eyes went round with shock.

"You've known that long?"

"I was going to tell you," Keirith mumbled.

"When? At the Ripening? 'Oh. Sorry,' " he mocked. " 'I guess you're wondering why I'm not wearing my ritual robe.' "

"Conn . . ."

"I'm your best friend."

Keirith nodded, miserable.

"Your milk-brother."

"I know," he said, misery deepening. When his mam was in one of her moods, she'd remind him how difficult his birth had been, how for the first moon of his life, the Grain-Mother had nursed him at one breast and her own son at the other.

"Why didn't you tell me?"

"I was ashamed."

"Why?" Conn persisted.

"Because I failed."

"Is that what Uncle Gortin said? Gods, I could murder him."

"It's not his fault."

"I bet it was Othak. That little sneak. He's always been jealous of you."

"Can we please not talk about this?"

"What did Uncle Gortin say? Exactly."

"It doesn't matter."

"What aren't you telling me?"

In all his life, this was the one secret he had kept from Conn. But after seeing the horror on the Tree-Father's face, he couldn't bear to witness it on his milk-brother's.

"It can't be that bad." Conn peered into his face. Whatever he saw must have shaken him, for he swallowed hard. "And even if it is, you know I'll stand by you." He thrust out his right hand, revealing the old scar at the base of his thumb.

They had been eight when they'd made the oath: "To be friends through this life and brothers in the next, spirit linked to spirit and heart bound to heart." Keirith had thought up the oath, but it was Conn who had insisted they seal it with blood.

If Conn knew about his forbidden gift, the Tree-Father might punish him as well. He could not let that happen.

"Please. Just trust me." Keirith clasped Conn's hand, just as he had when they made their blood oath. Shepherd's hands, strong but soft from the grease in the wool.

Conn jerked his hand free. "Why should I trust you when you won't trust me?"

Before he could say anything, Conn scrambled off the ledge. Keirith got down on his hands and knees to follow his descent, wincing each time Conn stumbled, each time he swiped at his cheeks.

First he had failed his father, then the Tree-Father. Now he had failed his best friend. But he would find a way to make it up to him. Somehow. His gaze swept the horizon, seeking inspiration. Instead, he found the eagle winging downriver.

If only I could fly away with you. Fly away and never come back.

He leaned forward, squinting at the small, dark objects that marred the glistening expanse of the river. His stomach lurched. They weren't expected till the morrow. He had counted on having this one last day to prepare. But there was no mistaking the fifteen coracles moving slowly up the river.

His father was home.

Chapter 2

GRIANE DIPPED HER finger into the sticky sap and slipped it into the babe's mouth. Even before she tasted her mother's milk, she must have sap from the ash tree to make her strong. The babe's face screwed up in outraged protest and she began to howl. With those lungs, she'd make a fine healer.

"Don't be afraid to shout," Mother Netal had always told her. "It inspires confidence. And don't let anyone order you about. Except me, of course."

Fifteen years since her mentor had died, and Griane still missed her earthy humor, her grumbling, her wisdom. Especially her wisdom.

Three generations of priestesses were in the birthing hut today, along with Griane and her apprentice. Sali crouched by the fire pit, frowning into the stone bowl. "Be sure to add some honey to cut the bitterness of the thistle," Griane instructed.

Sali squeaked at the sound of her voice and then nodded nervously. She was clever with plants, but had about as much spirit as the rabbitskins Lisula lay upon.

This was the fourth time Griane had helped ease a child from Lisula's womb, but their friendship had begun after the Long Winter. Both of them elevated too soon into positions of authority—Griane to healer, Lisula to Grain-Mother—they had started by sharing their concerns and ended up sharing confidences about their men and later, their children.

The Grain-Grandmother and Grain-Sister began the chant to welcome the newborn into the tribe, Muina's voice cracking with age, Bethia's high and light. Griane joined the two priestesses at the fire pit, lightly pressing the babe's face to her breast to shield her from the peat smoke. Twice, they circled sunwise before Griane passed the babe across the low flames to Muina.

"That your mind should be wise. That your heart should be full. That your body should be strong." With a bony thumb, Muina sketched a circle upon the babe's brow, chest, and belly. "Maker, bless this child."

Bethia touched the babe's left hand with an acorn and her right with a sprig of holly. "Oak and Holly, bless this child."

Together, they anointed the babe, Muina sprinkling earth upon her toes, Bethia drizzling water over her head, Griane brushing a feather across her body. Although it was not part of the ritual, she tickled the babe's belly, smiling when her cries changed to surprised hiccups.

Alone, Muina circled the fire pit a final time. "Earth and air, fire and water. Bless this child, the daughter of our tribe."

The babe waved her fists in the air.

"I've birthed a warrior," Lisula said, smiling.

"More likely, she's still angry about the ash sap," Griane replied.

"Are you sure she's the last?"

"Did you hear a pop when I threw the afterbirth on the fire?"

"Nay. But Muina coughed just then, so I was hoping . . ." Lisula sighed, her face forlorn. "I suppose it's only a matter of time now before my moon flow stops."

"Well, of course it is," Muina scolded. "Just like it's only a matter of time before these old bones are resting in the tribal cairn. But you have years left to serve the tribe. I was Grain-Mother for seventeen years."

"Eighteen," Griane corrected.

"And I came to it far later than you. You're only . . . what? Twenty-nine?"

"Thirty-one."

Lisula laughed. "Griane should be Memory-Keeper instead of Darak."

"The things I remember never get into the legends."

Muina held the child up and gave a dry chuckle. "Well, Lisula may be done with childbearing, but you're not, Griane. 'If a babe should spy you between its legs, 'tis you who'll be nesting on the eggs.' "

"My nesting days are over."

"Don't be so sure," Lisula replied. "What do you wager, Muina? A count of ten or a count of twenty after Darak's coracle touches the beach before Griane has him out of his breeches?"

"A count of ten. By twenty, she'll be yowling loud enough to rattle the bones in the cairn."

Heat flooded Griane's face. She hoped the others would think it came from the fire. She was a matron, the tribe's healer, the mother of three children, but her kinfolk never tired of reminding her of her enthusiastic response to married life.

For three moons after her wedding, she'd been puzzled by the giggles that followed her each time she emerged from their hut. Lisula had finally broken down and told her. Apparently, old Sim had given a memorable performance: a frown, a puzzled shake of the head, a rheumy look of bewilderment. "I was that frightened. Thought sure poor Darak had trapped a wildcat in his hut. Judging from those bite marks on his neck, I guess he did."

Trust a Memory-Keeper to create a story that would live forever.

"Look at her smiling," Lisula said. "The poor man doesn't stand a chance."

"Grain-Mother, I have a rite to perform."

"Aye, Mother Griane," Lisula responded with mock solemnity. "Give Ennit my love."

Griane took the babe back from Muina and ducked through the low doorway of the birthing hut. She straightened to find Ennit shaking the stiffness out of his bandy legs.

The other men in the tribe would expect her to make the presentation at their huts, but Darak and Ennit always waited together outside the birthing hut, in fair weather and foul. This was the first time Ennit had to keep vigil alone; Darak had been confident he'd be back from the Gathering before the birth.

As tradition dictated, she held the babe out to Ennit. "I bring you Lisula's daughter."

Only when the man took the newborn was the child acknowledged as his. Ennit immediately stretched out his hands for the squalling babe, cradling her in the crook of his arm with the ease that bespoke many years of practice.

"I accept my daughter, Mother Griane." He peered down at her. "She's beautiful."

Griane smiled. Ennit said that every time. And every time, the same foolish grin softened his homely features. The little shepherd was a treasure. Father and mother both to his children, for the babe would remain with Lisula only until she was weaned. After that, she would live with Ennit and the other children.

Hard enough to be separated from Darak while he attended the Gathering; she could not imagine living apart from him. She shot a quick glance at the lake, but the only coracles she spied belonged to the fishermen.

"He's not due home till the morrow, Griane."

The telltale heat flooded her cheeks again. Why did her face have to be as transparent as water?

"Let me have the child. She's hungry."

"Is that it?" With obvious reluctance, Ennit relinquished his daughter, but he couldn't resist drawing his hand across the dark fuzz on her head. "I was afraid my ugly face scared her."

"Oh, hush. You're not ugly. You're not handsome, but you're not ugly."

Ennit laid his hand over his heart. "Ah, Griane. I always wondered how Darak remained humble in the face of his accomplishments. Now I know."

"Get back to your sheep before they fall off Eagles Mount."

"Conn'll mind them. And Trian," he added as an afterthought.

At fourteen, Conn was already more responsible than his uncle. A strange assortment of brothers had come out of that womb—Gortin so dour, Ennit dour of face but merry of heart, dreamy Trian. And Pol, of course. A blessing when his spirit had finally flown to the Forever Isles. Neither Mother Netal nor Struath had been able to heal the poor lad after the ram kicked him in the head.

"How is Conn? I've hardly seen him since the lambing began."

"Tired. Happy. Lambing time's always busy. But the newborns are sweet." Ennit cast a fond look at his daughter. "And Keirith?"

"I don't know. He's turned broody again."

"It's a broody age. Gods, I wouldn't be fourteen again for anything."

"I wouldn't mind fifteen. Or sixteen."

"Oh, aye." He threw back his head and yowled.

Griane punched him. "I'll give Lisula your love."

"I'll do that myself. Lisula!"

Startled by his bellow, the babe began to wail again. Griane glared at Ennit and tried to soothe the poor mite.

"I love you, Lisula. As long as the sun rises and sets. As long as the moon waxes and wanes. As long as—"

"As long as you have breath to shout with," Griane said, "which will be forever, I'm sure. Now stop scaring the child."

"I love you, too, you wonderful, silly man." Lisula's answering shout made Ennit laugh. "And I can't wait to get out of this stuffy hut and hold you in my arms again."

"Well, you'll have to wait," Griane replied. "Seven days and seven nights. That's the law."

"It's a stupid law," Ennit muttered, then continued shouting endearments to Lisula.

Not so stupid, Griane thought. The law decreed that no man should touch or see a woman at the magical times of birthing and bleeding. Magical or not, those were the only times a woman was freed from the endless demands of work and family. The placing of the birthing hut near the fields to ensure the fertility of crops and women alike was only common sense. But the tradition that dictated both the birthing and moon huts be built within sight of the Death Hut . . .

A man surely invented that tradition, thinking to reinforce the endless circle of life, death, and rebirth, but totally oblivious to the feelings of the women who had to walk past the Death Hut to deliver their babes or celebrate their moon flow. She could still remember her rite of passage, the women's chanting vying with the raucous croaks of the crows and ravens feasting on poor Giti. Even the spicy tang of the burning herbs had failed to disguise the sweet-rotten stench of his corpse.

Belatedly, she realized Ennit had ceased his shouting. "What is it?" Then she heard the high, thin voice of a child. They both spun around, searching for the source of the cry. In the fields, women and girls straightened to do the same. In a tribe as small as theirs, everyone looked out for the safety of a child.

"Mam!"

Through the alders that screened the birthing hut from the lake, she glimpsed the small figure racing down the beach.

"Mam! They're coming!"

The children in the fields took up Callie's shout and surged toward the lake. The women dropped their bone spades and hurried after them. Other children, too young to be of help with the planting, scampered down the gentle slope from the village. Their mothers trailed behind, chattering, laughing, and pausing occasionally to dust off a toddler who stumbled and fell.

Peering through the alders, Griane spied the first coracles emerging from the narrow channel between Eagles Mount and Stag's Leap.

He's home.

"Ennit . . ."

"Go."

She kissed his cheek, then remembered she was still holding the babe. Bethia ducked out of the hut and Griane quickly deposited the child in her arms. "Tell Lisula I'll be back tonight. And tell Sali—"

"Go, Mother Griane. We can manage."

Maker bless her. So calm, so capable. She'd make a fine Grain-Mother someday. And here she was, nearly ten years Bethia's senior and as flustered as a girl. It was unseemly. She hurried toward Callie, then abandoned decorum and ran.

"Fa's home!" His cheeks flushed with excitement, Callie seized her hand and pulled her toward the lake.

"You go. I want to change out of these clothes first."

Callie's face screwed up in a frown as he studied her. She smoothed her untidy braid, rubbed a splotch of blood on the sleeve of her worn doeskin tunic, but there was no

help for the patched skirt spattered with faded bloodstains
that all the scrubbing in the world couldn't get out. You
didn't wear your best clothes to a birthing, after all.

"But you look pretty."

She pulled him close. Keirith was broody like his father
and Faelia was just plain difficult—the gods only knew who
she took after—but her baby had inherited his sweet nature
from his uncle Tinnean.

Callie squirmed and pulled away. Her baby was six now,
too old to endure his mother's fussing—in public, anyway.

"You go," she repeated. "I'll just be a moment."

Callie rolled his eyes. He'd picked that up from Faelia.
She was forever rolling her eyes and blowing out her breath
in exasperation. Though never at her father, of course.

Griane hurried toward her hut, praying that Faelia had
remembered to put the stew on the fire and prepare a fresh
batch of oatcakes. Her prayers—as usual—were not answered; the unbaked oatcakes sat on plaited withies, the
stewpot beside them.

She shoved the baking stone atop the peat bricks and
vented her anger on a bunch of wild onions. She tossed
them into the stew, hefted the pot into the fire pit, and
thrust a handful of dead twigs under it, watching to be sure
they caught. At this rate, it would be dark before the stew
was hot.

Squatting beside their pallet, she threw back the wolfskins. For a long moment, she eyed her best tunic, the
one she wore only on feast days. Shaking her head at her
foolishness, she pulled out her everyday tunic and skirt.
Her fingers fumbled with the drawstrings of her birthing
skirt.

*Like a girl on her wedding night. Except Darak was more
nervous than I was.*

She kicked her birthing clothes under the wolfskins; time
enough on the morrow to wash them. No time, alas, to
rebraid her hair. A splash of water on her face, a quick look
around the hut. Was it so much to ask that the children tidy
their sleeping places instead of leaving the furs strewn
about? It looked like a storm had blown through. She spent
a few precious moments smoothing furs and folding clothing, then abandoned the effort and raced down to the lake.

Everyone was there, hugging family members, shouting

greetings, waving to those whose coracles had yet to reach
the beach. Darak was easy to find, a good head taller than
most of the men. He'd caught Callie up in his arms, but
freed one as Faelia flung herself on him. Keirith must still
be with the Tree-Father.

*You'd think he could abandon his lessons long enough to
welcome his father home.*

Darak's lips moved, still talking to the children, as his
gaze swept the crowd. "It's like you carry the sunset on
your shoulders," he'd once said in a most uncharacteristic
burst of poetry. Her hair had been brighter then, even
brighter than Faelia's. Age and worry had streaked the sunset with white, but still he found her.

The milling throng, the babble of voices, the glittering
water of the lake all faded away. There was only that cool
gray gaze and that slow smile and the ridiculous thumping
of her heart. He walked toward her, Callie clinging to one
hand, Faelia to the other.

"We didn't expect you so soon."

"We were eager to get home."

"No trouble at the Gathering?"

He shrugged, his glance straying to the children, letting
her know without words that they would talk later.

"You were probably trying to seduce Seg's wife again."

"Aye. Well. I've a great fondness for scolds."

He freed his hands from the children to brush wisps of
hair off her cheeks with his thumbs. Then he cupped her
face and kissed her lightly. She hugged him hard, abandoning herself to the feel of that broad back under her fingertips, the familiar smell of leather and peat smoke and that
indefinable something that was Darak and only Darak.

"I missed you, too, girl," he whispered.

"Did you bring us presents from the Gathering, Fa?"

With a rueful grin, her husband slipped out of her arms
and back into his role as father. "Maybe."

"Fa . . ." Callie danced from one foot to the other in
impatience.

"Callum. Give your father a moment to catch his
breath."

"Fetch my pack and we'll see about presents." Darak
scanned the thinning crowd. "Where's Keirith?"

"Praying, probably," Faelia said. "I snared twelve rabbits

while you were gone and brought down four wood pigeons and three—"

"It's awful heavy." Callie's face was mashed into a frown of concentration as he staggered toward them, dragging the pack. "You must have brought a lot of presents."

"Enough, both of you. Your father's probably starving. There's rabbit stew. And oatcakes. If they bake in time." Griane spared a quick glare for Faelia who predictably rolled her eyes.

Hand in hand, she and Darak started up the slope. Suddenly, he pulled away. "Urkiat. Forgive me. I'm a poor host."

For the first time, Griane noticed the hawk-faced stranger. He smiled at Darak's words, but his rapt gaze remained fixed on her. Perhaps she looked better than she imagined.

"Griane, this is Urkiat. He's going to be spending a few days with us."

Griane smoothed her hair, the vision of their untidy hut making her wince.

"Urkiat, this is my wife. My daughter, Faelia. And this one . . ." He bent down to retrieve the pack that Callie was attempting to drag up the hill. "This is my younger son, Callum."

Urkiat bowed. "Griane. I can't tell you . . . It's . . . I am honored."

Merciful Maker, another of the worshipful young men. Every summer brought one or two to the village, slack-jawed and stammering, to meet the great Darak Spirit-Hunter. Their own tribe had long since accepted their roles in the quest to find the spirit of the Oak-Lord, lost during that long-ago Midwinter battle. Even those who still remembered Darak's brother seemed to view the story of Tinnean's transformation from boy to tree as if it had happened to a stranger. And no matter how many times they heard the story of her interval in the Summerlands with the Trickster, it was hard to worship the woman who dosed you with dandelion root and yellow dock to loosen your bowels.

"Best close your mouth," Faelia said. "Else you'll be having flies for supper."

Urkiat flushed and snapped his mouth shut. Darak

tugged Faelia's braid, unsuccessfully hiding a grin. As usual, it was left to her to preserve the proprieties. "Forgive my daughter's rudeness, Urkiat. You are welcome to our village."

Gods grant the rabbit stew would stretch to feed another. He didn't look like a big eater, but the skinny ones invariably surprised you.

Faelia and Callie hung on their father as they walked back to the village, leaving her to make polite conversation with Urkiat. "I judge from your accent that you come from the south."

"Aye. I grew up by the sea."

"You're a fisherman?"

"I was."

Clearly, there was a story, one the young man didn't want to tell. She'd get it from Darak later.

"Was this your first Gathering?"

"Nay. I went once before. When I was young."

Griane suppressed a smile. Despite the white scar that curved like the waxing moon from cheekbone to jaw, Urkiat couldn't be much older than twenty.

"How did you meet Darak?"

"I spoke at the convocation."

"You're a chief?"

"Nay."

"Oh. The chiefs invited you to speak?"

"Not exactly."

Easier to pull a bullock from a womb than to get words out of this one. She considered him, frowning. After the Long Winter, the chiefs had broken generations of tradition to ask Darak to join the convocation they held at the twice-yearly Gatherings; only at their invitation could anyone else address the circle.

"So. How did you find the convocation?"

"Worthless."

The savagery in his voice stopped her.

"The northern tribes don't understand what it's like."

"The raiders, you mean." He glanced at her, clearly surprised. "We've all heard the tales."

"But you've never lived them."

"Nay. We're fortunate."

"So far. Forgive me, I shouldn't be burdening you."

"Bel's blazing ballocks. I'm not a child. How bad are things?"

"Bad." He lowered his voice. "Many of the coastal villages are deserted, the people murdered or fled inland."

"Your people?"

He looked away, his face bleak.

"Forgive me, Urkiat. I'm the one burdening you by forcing you to speak of such things."

"I have to speak. But no one seems to hear."

"Darak did." Again, that surprised look. "He's not in the habit of inviting strangers home."

"The Memory-Keeper . . . Darak . . ." He breathed the name with prayerful reverence. ". . . encouraged me to speak and tried to calm the chiefs after, but—"

"Calm them? Good gods, man, what did you tell them?"

"The truth. That the northern tribes have abandoned us. That they don't care what's happening in the south. That they must be foolish or stupid or both to believe they'll be safe from the raiders forever."

"That must have gone over well."

"Not as well as I hoped."

His glower gave way to a reluctant smile and Griane decided she might like him, after all.

"Darak and your chief—Nionik? They called a meeting of the chiefs from the tribes along your river. I spoke better there. A little. But they all said they had enough to do with the planting and the peat cutting. And after that, of course, there was the thatching and the shearing. Time enough come the harvest to worry about the raiders." With a visible effort, he calmed himself. "I came to speak to your council and the elders of the Holly Tribe across the lake. Gods grant I have better luck with them."

"You're tired and hungry and heartsore. You'll tell the tale soon enough, but for now, try and let these matters go." She drew back the bearskin that hung across the doorway of their hut. "Urkiat, you are welcome to our home."

Instead of offering the ritual response, he just stood there. "This . . ." He took a deep breath. "This is where you live."

"Aye, Urkiat," Darak said, his voice dry. "It's a hut. Come in and sit down."

Urkiat dropped his pack and seated himself beside Darak.

"Faelia, put the oatcakes on the fire. Callie, stop rummaging in your father's bag and fetch the brogac." Darak dipped his little finger into the stew, deftly avoiding the smack she aimed at his hand. "Enjoy the brogac. The stew will be a while yet."

"We could open the presents," Callie suggested.

"Best wait for your brother," Darak said.

Faelia tossed her braid. "Who knows when he'll appear? Half the time he doesn't even come home for the midday meal."

"He'll be home," Griane said with more assurance than she felt.

"I could fetch him," Callie said. "After we open the presents."

Darak laughed and pulled Callie into his lap for a hug. "All right. We'll have the presents."

He'd brought a new shell for Callie's collection and a dagger for Faelia who squealed when she saw the bronze blade. Griane gave Darak a long look. The gift was far too expensive and offering her a dagger would only feed her illusions of becoming as great a hunter as her father had been.

With an apologetic shrug, Darak held out the dagger to Faelia, carefully cradling it in both hands. Over the years, he'd become skilled at manipulating objects, but it still hurt Griane to see the stumps where Morgath had severed the forefinger and middle finger of each hand, to watch him holding a weapon and remember how skillful those hands had once been with dagger, with sling, with bow. The tribe still valued his hunting instincts and many fathers sent their boys to him for instruction. He taught them with the same quiet patience he showed when teaching the children the legends of the tribe, but since he had taken the path of Memory-Keeper, he had abandoned the hunt.

"The oatcakes are burning, Mam."

"Well, turn them over, Faelia. If you can tear yourself away from your gift."

Faelia sniffed. "You're just jealous."

"Faelia."

Although Darak's voice was quiet, Faelia flushed. Griane wished she had the gift of controlling their volatile daughter with a single word.

"What did you bring Mam?" Callie asked, oblivious to the undercurrents.

"What do I always bring your mam?"

He fumbled in his bag and pulled out several small packets made of that wonderfully light woven material the southerners called "flaxcloth." She unwrapped the first, bending her head to sniff the small blue-violet buds.

"Mmm. They're lovely."

"They're called sweet spike. The trader said ladies put the packets in their clothes to keep them smelling nice. They're also supposed to relieve headaches and irritability."

I'll dose Faelia with them tonight, she thought.

Callie leaned over her shoulder, his soft hair tickling her cheek. "What are these little ones, Fa?"

"Flea seeds. Good for the bowels—tightening *and* loosening, the trader claimed. And those are sunburst, sun blossom . . . sun something or other. Fine Memory-Keeper I am. Anyway, you make the flowers into an ointment for skin rashes, cuts, and scrapes. The trader said it was especially good for babes—scalp itch and arse rash—and also for a woman's nipples when they get sore from breastfeeding."

The children were used to such conversations, but Urkiat's mouth hung open. Again. She was about to tell him Darak had picked up a good deal about healing from her, when she realized she'd completely forgotten to pass along the news of Lisula.

"And Ennit?" Darak asked, after she'd told him about the birth.

"Plumped up like a partridge, of course."

"I wish I could have been here. Well, I'll visit him after supper." He glanced toward the doorway, thumb drumming an impatient tattoo on his thigh. "What's keeping Keirith?"

She had been wondering the same thing. Darak had urged her to give Keirith time to work out whatever was troubling him. Well, he'd had time. Tonight, they would sit him down for a talk. It wasn't the way she had planned to spend Darak's first evening at home, but the sooner they got this matter into the open, the better.

" . . . how he can spend all day there," Faelia was saying. "Well, the visions might be interesting, but the praying and the chanting . . ." She gave an exaggerated shudder, then glanced at Urkiat. "You're not studying to be a shaman, are you?"

"Nay."

"I didn't think so. With that scar on your—"

"See to the oatcakes, Faelia."

"We can't eat without Keirith," Callie said.

"Your father and our guest need something in their bellies."

"I could go to the Tree-Father's and fetch him."

Faelia gingerly plucked the oatcakes off the baking stone and dropped them into a reed basket. "I'd just as soon he stayed away. He's been so difficult lately."

"Should I go, Fa? I could go."

"Fine. Go. Fetch him."

Before Darak finished speaking, Callie was dashing out. Griane sighed. "Do you have children, Urkiat?"

"Nay."

"Are you married?" Faelia asked.

"Nay."

"Really? Oatcake?" She held out the basket, favoring him with a wild fluttering of her pale lashes.

From hunter to whining child to flirt. Griane couldn't keep up with her daughter's transformations. If she was this difficult at eleven, gods preserve them—and whatever quarry she sought—when she became a woman.

Since Faelia was in a helpful mood, Griane let her scoop the cheese into a bowl and pass it around. It was good to sit and sip her elderberry wine while the men regaled them with tales of the Gathering: the trader with the brightly-colored bird that could curse in three languages; the tribes-man from the north who shot four arrows through a gourd resting on a rock one hundred paces away; the boy who could keep three apples in the air at the same time.

She had hoped to attend this year's Gathering with Darak; they'd had such fun at the others, giggling like young lovers in their furs at night. After she weaned Callie, she'd expected to share more times like that, but there were always birthings to attend, bones to set, illnesses to monitor. Hard to believe the girl who had braved the First Forest had left her village only four times since she had returned.

Darak still went to the grove with the priests for the spring and fall rites of Balancing. Never at Midwinter or Midsummer; he couldn't bear to witness the battle between the Oak and the Holly. As for her, she would never go there again. Although it was the place where they had found love, there were too many painful memories. The quest had left Darak's spirit as badly scarred as his body. It was moons before he could sleep through the night without jolting awake, sweat-sheened and shaking. Longer still before the shadows left his face.

The shadows were there now, this time conjured by their son. Although Darak nodded his head and exclaimed over Faelia's exhaustive description of every snare she'd set in his absence, his thumb continued its relentless tattoo.

Griane tested the stew, scowled, and laid out some smoked salmon. She was considering whether to send Faelia to a neighbor to augment their meager fare when Callie slipped back inside. To her surprise, Gortin followed.

Darak rose and bowed. "Tree-Father. Your presence honors us."

Neither his words nor his manner betrayed the lie. Nor, to his credit, did Gortin's. His square face had never been handsome, but as a young man, there had been a certain softness, an eager light—sweet and pitiful at the same time—that illuminated it. That disappeared after Struath died. Tonight, the scars around the shadowed eye socket gave him a particularly sinister look.

She chided herself for her silliness. Gortin couldn't help the scars. The Tree-Father from the Holly Tribe had been too sick and too old to conduct the rite properly. All the poultices in the world couldn't undo the damage that shaking dagger had inflicted. She still remembered Gortin's screams.

Darak and Gortin were just staring uncomfortably at each other. "Please. Join us," she said. "We were just about to have some supper."

"Thank you. I've eaten." Gortin hesitated, his gaze lingering on Urkiat. "There is a matter we need to discuss, but I fear this is not the best time."

Urkiat turned to Faelia. "After hearing so much about the rabbits you snared, perhaps you'd show me the best spots. We might even have time to set some snares before the light goes. If Callum will help us."

"Callie's too little—"

"I am not. I helped the other day. I sprinkled dirt over the snare and everything."

"Fa . . ."

Before Darak could speak, Griane said, "It's too late to be wandering about the lakeshore. Take Urkiat to Ennit's. Both of you."

Urkiat had eaten their food; he was honor-bound not to violate the laws of hospitality. And Darak must trust the man if he'd brought him home. Still, his angry outbursts made her reluctant to send the children off with him.

As Gortin sat down, Darak said, "I take it Keirith's not with you."

"Nay."

"Is there a problem? Has he been neglecting his lessons?"

"He hasn't told you?"

Griane's stomach lurched. Darak shot her a quick look and she shook her head, as puzzled as he was.

"Keirith assured me . . . I'm sorry. I should have told you myself."

"Aye. Well." Darak's voice was calm enough, but she could hear the edge in it. "Suppose you tell us now."

Chapter 3

B Y THE TIME KEIRITH neared the village, the sun had disappeared behind Eagles Mount. He endured some good-natured chaffing from the returning peat cutters who marveled that he could have ripped his tunic during a vision, and silently blessed the women who herded the begrimed men and children toward the lake to wash.

He paused at the little stream that flowed into the lake to assess the damage the gorse bush had inflicted during his headlong flight down Eagles Mount. The dim light in the hut might hide the scratches on his bare legs, but his mam would surely spy the hole in the elbow of his tunic; her eyes were as sharp as the eagle's. Maybe if he kept his arm straight . . .

Kneeling under the big willow, he splashed water in his face and smoothed his hair. Hoping his meager ablutions would suffice, he hurried toward the village.

A few children scampered past, heading home for supper. The usual group of old women sat outside Jurl's hut, scraping hides and gossiping. Old Erca looked up as he walked by, and, in her penetrating screech, demanded to know if he'd been wrestling with a gorse bush.

"For shame. Scampering around the hills instead of welcoming your father home."

"Darak'll take his belt to him."

"More likely Griane. She'll have to mend the tunic."

"Boys are so hard on their clothes. I could scarcely keep up with my two when they were that age."

"My Jurl—thank the Maker he's settled down now—but

the scrapes that rascal used to get into! I still remember
that Midsummer . . . oh, he couldn't have been more than
ten or eleven . . ."

Mercifully, they lost interest in him, chuckling and nodding over the oft-heard tales of their own children and
grandchildren.

He'd have to find a way to get Callie and Faelia out of
the hut. It would be bad enough to break the news to his
parents without Faelia rolling her eyes and Callie interrupting with a hundred questions.

His footsteps slowed, stopped. He scuffed his big toe in
the dirt.

Just get it over with, Keirith.

As he strode toward the hut, he heard his father shouting.
When he recognized the Tree-Father's voice, also raised in
anger, the wave of nausea made sweat break out on his forehead. He took one step forward, then another, determined
to ignore his pattering heart and churning stomach.

A hand lifted the bearskin. The Tree-Father ducked outside. His expression grew even grimmer when he saw him.
"Callum came to my hut to fetch you."

His parents knew. And because of his stupid, endless
delays, they'd had to hear the truth from the Tree-Father.

"Forgive me," he said. "I failed you."

"Talk to them, Keirith."

Expecting a stern reproof, the sympathy on the shaman's
face brought a thick clot to his throat. He swallowed it
down as the Tree-Father walked away. All his life, he'd
heard the slighting comments about Gortin, how he was a
"good man" but a far cry from Struath. That had only
convinced him of their kinship; Keirith, too, knew what it
was like to live in the shadow of a great man—the one who
was waiting inside for him now.

As he reached for the bearskin, his father shouted, "Why
didn't you just get down on your knees and kiss his arse
while you were at it?"

"You and your pride! You'd attack Gortin for—"

His mam broke off. Had she seen the bearskin move?
Resisting the urge to slink away, Keirith slipped inside and
found his father watching him with eyes as cold as storm
clouds in winter.

He'd smacked their bottoms a few times when they were

little. Occasionally, he raised his voice. But when he went quiet and cold like this, they knew he was really angry.

"I'm sorry."

His father just stood there, watching and waiting. If he no longer hunted, he still possessed a hunter's patience.

"I was going to tell you."

"When?"

His mam tugged on his father's arm. "I think we should sit."

"When were you going to tell us?"

His father's voice was flint grating on bone. Keirith told himself it was the smell of the stew that made his gorge rise, but he knew it was fear. "I tried. I did." Gods, he sounded like a whining child. "Right after the Tree-Father dismissed me from my apprenticeship."

"Damn your apprenticeship."

"Darak . . ."

"I'm talking about the other. This . . . power . . . to communicate with the eagle."

"Oh. That."

"Aye. That."

The savagery of those two words made him wince. Perhaps his mam saw; she clutched his father's arm with both hands. "Enough."

He yanked his arm free without deigning to look at her. "How long have you had it?"

He could lie. Tell them only the part about flying with the eagle and hide the rest. But sooner or later his father would realize the truth. "The wood pigeon," he whispered.

His father went very still. His mam's gaze darted back and forth between them. "What wood pigeon?"

For some reason, his father refused to look at her. "Keirith brought the bird down with his sling. When he went to finish it off, it . . . he said it screamed."

"Screamed?"

"Aye."

"When was this?"

His father hesitated. "Seven years ago."

"Seven years?" his mam echoed.

"Griane . . ."

"And you never told me?"

"I thought—"

"I had a right to know, Darak!"

"You'd just lost the babe!" In a much softer voice, he added, "I didn't want to worry you."

The same day he had heard the wood pigeon scream, he and his father had returned from the forest to discover Ennit waiting for them. Faelia was too young to understand, but his father's stark expression told Keirith something was terribly wrong. He'd waited and waited in Memory-Keeper Sanok's hut until the tension became unbearable. Then he ran to the birthing hut.

He saw his father pacing in the moonlight. Heard his mother's anguished cry, as terrible and shrill as the wood pigeon's. His father caught him up in his arms, held him so tight the breath was squeezed out of him. Then the Grain-Mother came out of the birthing hut and told them the babe was dead.

Ennit tried to stop his father from going inside. That was the first time Keirith had seen that cold rage on his face. He waited with Ennit, listening to his mother's sobs and the low murmur of his father's voice.

Later, after his father had tucked Faelia under her wolf-skins, he asked if it was his fault, if the gods were angry because of what had happened in the forest. His father grabbed his shoulders, the thumbs digging in so hard it made tears come to his eyes, and said his little brother had come into the world too soon. Too small to live, his spirit would fly to the Forever Isles to be reborn in its proper time.

Two moons later, when he heard the rabbit scream, he had offered prayers and sacrifices to avert another death. Later, he realized his ability to feel an animal's pain did not foretell a death in the village, but he still couldn't bring himself to speak of his power; in his mind, it would always be linked with the death of his baby brother.

He wished he could explain that now, but his parents seemed to have forgotten him. His mother was staring at the rushes. His father kept reaching for her, then letting his hand drop to his side.

"And later?" she finally asked.

"I thought he imagined it. I was wrong. I'm sorry, girl."

She held his gaze a long while. Then, as if they exchanged some signal he couldn't see, they both turned to him.

"I thought it would stop. If I didn't hunt. And it wasn't always bad. Sometimes I could make things better."

"How?" his father demanded.

"The ewe. Three springs ago. It was her first lambing and she was having trouble. And I helped her."

"So it's not just birds."

He shook his head.

"But you didn't tell Gortin that."

"I couldn't. Not the way he was looking at me. Like I was . . . something awful."

He waited for one of them to tell him he wasn't awful, that he'd done nothing wrong, but his mam only said, "And you use this power to touch their spirits."

"I don't hurt them. I would never hurt them. I'm not like Morgath."

His father's breath hissed in. "Do not speak that name in my home."

"That's what you're thinking, isn't it? That I'm like him. An abomination."

"If I thought you were anything like him—"

With an effort, his father choked back his next words, but Keirith knew what they were: *"I would kill you as surely as I killed him."*

He must have made some sound, for his mam stopped chewing her upper lip and said, "Struath always claimed magic was neither good nor evil. It was what people did with it. And Morgath—aye, I will say his name if only to curse it and condemn him to Chaos for all time—he used his power for evil. I know . . . we both know . . . you're not like that."

She paused, glancing at his father, waiting for him to speak. But he didn't. He hesitated. And finally nodded. And in that terrifying pause—only the space between one heartbeat and the next—something inside Keirith died.

"You should have come to us," his mam said.

His father refused to look at him.

"You should have told us the truth."

His father loathed him. His father thought he was as evil as the man who had tortured and mutilated him.

"I thought . . . I hoped it would go away."

Finally, his father looked up. "And when it didn't?" His voice was hoarse, as if it hurt him to speak to the abomination he had spawned.

"I don't know. I just . . ."

"You lied."

"Darak . . ."

"You lied to the Tree-Father when you told him that you'd only flown with the eagle a few times. You lied to us every day you sneaked out of this house and pretended to go to your lessons."

"I tried—"

"Gortin dismissed you a fortnight ago. You could have told us then. You could have told us years ago. Instead, you hid this power. Because you knew it was wrong."

"It's not wrong. It can't be."

"So now you know more than Gortin," his father said, his voice heavy with sarcasm.

"Maybe he's just jealous. He can only fly with his spirit guide, and half the time it doesn't come to him. Besides, he hates you." Keirith overrode his mam's vehement denial. "That's what you say. I've heard you. Both of you."

"Gortin does not hate your father. What happened with Struath . . . that was a long time ago. And whatever flaws Gortin may have, he would never punish you because of his . . . differences with your father."

Again his mam's eyes sought his father's for confirmation.

"We're talking about your behavior," he said, "not the Tree-Father's. You think we'll shrug this off because you're too young to know better? When you heard the wood pigeon, aye. Even when you helped the ewe. But you're supposed to be a man now."

He was a man. It was his father who insisted on treating him like a child, who stubbornly refused to understand. "You think I asked for this power? That I want it?"

"Don't you?" his father shot back. "It's one thing to help with the birthing of a lamb. It's another to fly with an eagle. That you did for your own pleasure."

And because he knew it was true, Keirith lashed out. "At least the eagle welcomes me! He wants me. Which is more than you do."

His father's head snapped back. "Stop talking nonsense."

"Do you know what it's like? Everyone watching you, tallying every mistake, every failure. Shaking their heads and thinking 'He'll never measure up to his father.' "

"That's not . . . no one says that."

"You think I don't see the way they look at me? The way *you* look at me? Your firstborn son who can't make a kill without puking up his guts. Who can't keep his apprenticeship with the Tree-Father. Who's as evil as Morgath!"

He felt the power roaring through him. Not the gentle unfurling that came when he sought the eagle's spirit, but a wild, uncontrollable current that left him breathless. He spun around, but before he could reach the doorway, his father caught his arm. Even with only three fingers, it hurt.

He didn't mean to do it. He only wanted to free himself from that punishing grip, to escape his father and his accusations. He only wanted to get away.

The energy poured out of him, a raging torrent that slammed into his father's spirit and sent him reeling backward. Too late, Keirith pulled it back, gasping as the unleashed power crashed into him, gasping again as he careened into the wall of the hut. From a great distance, he heard his mam cry out. There was a brilliant burst of light—red, orange, gold—that faded into shimmering black dots. Had he done that, too? Or was it because he'd hit his head against the wall?

His legs folded under him, and he slid to the ground. Something glinted among the rushes. Callie's quartz charm, the one he had mislaid a sennight ago. He'd snapped at Callie for going on and on about it and felt awful when tears welled up in his brother's eyes. He reached for the charm, but his hand was shaking so badly that he dropped it. The charm lay there, mocking him. Even this one simple act he couldn't do right.

His father was on his knees. His mother crouched beside him, stroking his hair. Neither of them would look at him.

It seemed to take forever to get to his feet. He had to dig his fingers into the turf that filled the chinks between the stones. Only by leaning against the wall did he manage to stay upright. He didn't know how he found the strength to speak.

"Father."

His mam's head came up. He hoped it was the fire that made her eyes so bright. If he had made her cry, he would never forgive himself.

"Father."

His father's shoulders rose once and fell.

"Please."

Any explanation, any words of apology died when his father finally raised his head and Keirith saw the horror on his face.

Half blinded by the tears welling up in his eyes, Keirith groped for the bearskin and staggered outside. He thought he heard his father shout his name, but he didn't turn back. He raced through the village and splashed across the stream, ignoring the icy water that soaked him to the knees. He didn't know where he was going. He didn't care. He just had to get away—from the village, from his family, most of all, from his father.

Only during his vision quest had he spent a night outside the village. But why should he be afraid? The night belonged to unnatural creatures.

Chapter 4

FEAR IS THE ENEMY.
   Darak had lived by those words as a young man. In the years after the quest, he had repeated them sometimes: when Griane was in labor, when Callie took sick three winters ago. Little wonder they came back to him now.

Eagles Mount shrouded their valley in gloom. Would Keirith have gone there, back to the one place where he felt accepted and wanted? Or fled from it because it held too many painful memories?

Eagles Mount at night. Barefoot. Clad only in a tunic. This early in the spring, it would be miserably cold up there. Easy enough to miss your footing in the daylight. At night, you could tumble all the way down those treacherous slopes unless a ledge broke your fall—or your back.

Control the fear.

He picked his way across the stream. Dark clouds seethed over the hills to the north, and a freshening breeze chilled him as he headed up the hill. Behind him, tree limbs rubbed against each other, groaning. Although he knew it was just a storm coming on, his hand reached up to clutch the bag of charms he wore around his neck. It was too much like those final moments of his dream-journey through Chaos. When he reached the lone oak at the summit of the hill, he half expected the ground to split open, to fall helplessly into that endless black tunnel that had taken him to Tinnean, to the Oak, to the World Tree itself.

When the power of the World Tree flooded him, Tinnean

had helped him understand he could surrender to the song without losing himself. When Struath sought to learn whether Morgath had taken his body, the assault was brutal but brief. Morgath's invasion was so gentle he'd scarcely been aware of it. The terror came later.

And now Keirith had attacked him. His son had invaded his spirit.

Control yourself.

He squinted into the distance, cursing the failing light and his aging eyes. He could see no signs of movement among the clumps of gorse and moor grass that studded the rocky terrain.

He hadn't ventured onto Eagles Mount since he was a boy. The northern slope was less steep, but hidden from Gheala's feeble light. If he circled up from the south, he'd face a more difficult climb. He was still trying to decide the best course when he heard the hoarse panting. He whirled around, shouting Keirith's name.

Conn pulled up so quickly he nearly dropped his torch. "Nay, it's me, Memory-Keeper."

"What is it?"

"Mother Griane. She came to our hut. She said . . . well . . . there'd been a fight. About Keirith's apprenticeship."

"You knew?"

Conn took a hasty step backward. "He only told me today." His head drooped. "We had a fight, too. Because he hadn't told me before and because . . . I think there's more to it than he's letting on."

Conn gave him a searching look, but Darak just nodded. "I can take you. To the place he goes. On Eagles Mount."

Blessing Griane's foresight and Conn's loyalty, he squeezed the boy's shoulder and nodded again.

As they trotted toward Eagles Mount, he kept going over the confrontation with Keirith. He could still feel the lingering ache in his head, still hear his son's voice screaming inside him.

Let me go!

Instinct. That was all it was. The same instinct that impelled a trapped animal to flee or to fight. He had prevented Keirith from fleeing, so he had to fight, throwing that power at him with mindless strength.

One look at Keirith's face told him he was horrified by what he'd done. His son hadn't set out to hurt him. He was just scared and angry. He could have no idea of the memories the attack would evoke.

His children knew the story, of course. Every child did. But he never spoke of Morgath. Even Griane, whom he trusted more than anyone in the world . . . even to her, he had never confessed the helpless terror he'd experienced while he hung on that twisted tree in Chaos.

Now, he was equally helpless to withstand the memories: Morgath wearing Yeorna's body, her beauty only amplifying his evil; Morgath smiling as he severed the fingers, one by one; Morgath stroking his body, oozing through his spirit, staining him forever with his touch.

"If I thought you were anything like him—"

"Memory-Keeper? Watch the footing here. It's tricky."

Even with Conn's guidance, he slipped twice, but the bruises and scrapes wouldn't matter if they found Keirith. Instead, the ledge was empty. If he'd come here, he hadn't stayed long; the grass was cool, the blades springing straight up under his questing palm.

When he slipped again on the way down, Conn urged him to go home. Reason told him they could search all night without finding Keirith, that they would never find him unless he wanted to be found, that he would have a far better chance of tracking him in the morning. And then he imagined the broken body of his son lying in the cold and the dark.

Conn's piece of deadwood burned down to a stick no longer than his thumb as they searched the places where Keirith might have gone: the tumble of boulders on the eastern slope of Eagles Mount where the boys used to pretend to be wolves stalking the flocks; the sheltered strip of beach where they had made their blood vow; the small stand of alders where they spied on the girls bathing in the river.

"Don't tell him I brought you here," Conn said. "He'd kill me. So would my fa."

It was the only time that night Darak smiled.

They found no signs of Keirith in any of the familiar places, but near a tiny grotto under the exposed roots of an oak, Gheala's fleeting light revealed a footprint in the damp earth. It was at least a day old, certainly made before he had come home. The thought of his son hiding there, too ashamed to face him, sickened him.

He knew what it was like to grow up in a father's shadow. His had been the best hunter in the tribe. He'd spent his youth and early manhood trying to best him. Until he discovered his father's spirit in Chaos, he had preserved the memory of him as a cold man, distant and critical. He had sworn to be a different sort of father. Yet Keirith's words and actions bespoke far deeper problems than the natural pulling away that occurred when a boy became a man. Long before this night, he had failed his son—and he wasn't even sure how.

The night was waning by the time they headed back to the village. The threatened storm had blown past with only a few fat raindrops. Seeing him eyeing the sky, Conn repeated his promise to help him search again at daybreak.

"He won't have gone far, Memory-Keeper. I know him. He gets in these moods sometimes, but they always pass."

Darak patted the exhausted boy and told him to go home, but Conn lingered. "If he comes home . . . if you see him before I do . . . just . . . tell him I'm sorry."

"I will. And thank you, Conn. Keirith's lucky to have you for a friend."

Thankfully, the children didn't stir when he entered the hut, although Urkiat jerked awake. One look at Griane's face told him Keirith had not come home.

She cleaned his cuts and scrapes without fussing, a sure sign that she was worried. Before he undressed, he bent over Faelia and then Callie, kissing each lightly on the forehead. Later, lying next to Griane under the wolfskins, she told him in a halting whisper that she had gone to the Tree-Father for help. He was surprised and ashamed when she told him that Gortin and Meniad had promised to use their vision to search for Keirith if he was still missing in the morning.

Darak winced, remembering his words to Gortin: "If you're making up this story to hurt my son—if you're using him to wreak some kind of twisted vengeance on me because you believe I caused Struath's death—then by the gods, I will destroy you."

He had always dismissed Gortin as Struath's weak suc-

cessor. Yet Gortin cared enough for Keirith to overlook
those awful words, proving himself the better man.

He pulled Griane into his arms, grateful for the comfort
of her body nestled against his. Long after she'd finally
drifted into sleep, Darak lay awake, staring into the darkness.

Fear is the enemy.

The only way Keirith managed to stay warm was by moving. All night he wandered through the foothills north of
the village, never daring to go too deep into the forest for
fear of losing the path or encountering one of the creatures
that roamed the night—the wolves and wildcats of this
world, the demons and restless spirits of the other. Despite
his earlier bravado, he was no more prepared to face a
demon than he was to face his father.

Whenever he thought about what he had done, the shaking started. Sometimes it got so bad he had to kneel until
he could force his legs to bear him again. He devised a
dozen wild plans to escape his home forever. Cursed the
roots and stones that seemed to rear up, determined to trip
him. Cursed the gods. Prayed. Cursed himself. Wept. Cursed
himself for weeping.

And always, his thoughts returned to his father. When
he skirted the path that led to the heart-oak, he remembered the first time his father took him into the forest.
When he searched the cloudy sky for the Archer, he remembered his father telling him the point of the constella-
tion's arrowhead would always guide him home. When he
spied the open expanse of the lake, he remembered his
father teaching him to swim, the big hands supporting his
belly, the soft voice instructing him, the sputtering laugh
when his clumsy efforts doused him with water. Every
thought, every memory conjured up that awful moment
when he attacked his father and felt his spirit's horror echoing inside him.

Dawn was nearing when he finally collapsed on the beach,
a mere bowshot from the village. Mist shrouded the lake,
enveloping him in a dense white cloud, like an insect
wrapped in a cocoon. His trances always began like this,

his vision clouded by mist. One day, the Tree-Father had promised, he would be able to cross the barrier between worlds. So far, he had only succeeded in parting the mists long enough to See farther into this one.

He had not called upon Natha since his apprenticeship ended. He wasn't even sure a spirit guide could still hear someone who was no longer on the path of the shaman. But Natha was both vision mate and spirit guide, the one relationship forged during his quest to manhood, the other evolving as he learned to access his powers.

Keirith called his name three times, asking Natha to help him conquer the terrible gift that had brought him to this moment and lend him the courage to return home. For he knew he must return. Much as he dreamed of escaping, he had nowhere to go. Even if he did, how could he just disappear, leaving his mam to wonder if he was alive or dead? He could not keep running like a scared animal. A man faced the consequences of his actions.

The mist swirled around him. His body swayed in rhythm to the mesmerizing dance. He sucked in a great gulp of cold air and let it out slowly, steadying himself. He breathed again. In. Out. Slow. Deep. The first skills the Tree-Father had taught him. Controlling your breath. Emptying your mind. Seeking the inner stillness that would allow the spirit to surrender to the gods-given vision.

A long tendril of mist floated toward him. It curled sinuously around his ankles. It rose to encircle his knees, his waist, his chest. Cool and damp, it licked his neck, kissed his cheeks, tickled his eyelashes. Mist filled his vision, blinding him with white. And then a pair of red-brown eyes blinked open so close to his that he gasped.

Natha flowed around him, as insubstantial as the mist. Yet he could clearly see the black scales that zigzagged down the adder's green back, the dark "X" on the back of his head.

"Where have you been?" Natha whispered.

"Lost."

Natha sighed, his body dissolving, leaving only the large eyes gazing steadfastly into his. "And now you have found your way."

"Aye."

"Good. But first you must See."

Natha curled around his shoulders, his small body as
heavy as a wet mantle. Just as the weight grew oppressive,
the mist thinned. Keirith glimpsed the trees on the far side
of the lake, the faint outline of Stag's Leap. Then, as if
sucked away by the mouth of a giant, the mist vanished.

Although the valley still lay in shadow, Bel's light illuminated the summit of Eagles Mount. Just below it, he could
make out the female perched on her nest. His heartbeat
quickened when he spotted the small blotch of white nestled under her dark breast feathers. A chick had hatched.
And he was the first of his tribe to see it.

"Thank you for this gift, Natha."

His spirit guide hissed. "Foolish boy. Would I waste my
time showing you what you could see with your own eyes?"

Puzzled, he let his gaze drift. He spotted the eagle, soaring through the narrow channel between Eagles Mount and
Stag's Leap. Only then, did Keirith See.

The wooden boats were huge, ten or twelve times longer
than a man's height. Above them, giant squares of cloth
flapped in the breeze. Even their paddles were enormous,
long and slender as saplings. There had to be twenty on
each side, like the legs of a crawling insect, only these legs
dipped rhythmically into the water, driving the boats swiftly
up the lake.

Men clustered together on the wooden planks of the
boats, but most wielded the long paddles, their bodies rocking back and forth in a stately, seated dance. He could See
their breath steaming in the cool morning air, their muscles
bunching under the sleeves of their tunics, the sweat dripping down their backs.

Two boats slowly turned away from the others. On the
windcloths, black ovals stared out of circles of red like malevolent, bloodshot eyes. Natha hissed a warning, but he
could not look away. The eyes grew larger, filling his vision,
mocking his puny gift, pulling him down into twin pools
of darkness.

Keirith's spirit slammed back into his body with such
force that he slumped onto the pebbles, as helpless to stop
the convulsions as he had been to withstand those all-seeing
eyes. Through chattering teeth, he managed to gasp out his
name, once, twice, three times. When the convulsions ceased,

he patted his body with shaking hands. Then he lay back, exhausted.

Gortin and Meniad always cautioned that visions were unreliable; even they sometimes struggled to make sense of what they saw. Visions could carry you to a familiar place or one that didn't exist at all, offer glimpses into the past or warn of what might happen far in the future.

He couldn't ask Natha; his spirit guide had vanished as soon as the trance ended. Mist once again enveloped the beach, muffling the sound of the groaning tree branches and the small splashes made by fish rising to feed. Judging by the number of splashes, the fishermen would have a fine catch.

The splashing ceased. A low rumble broke the silence, as if dozens of clubs drummed against tree trunks. Despite his lethargy, he sat up.

Two naked spars rose gray and ghostly out of the mist, looming above the giant boats.

Keirith staggered up the slope toward home, screaming a warning. "Raiders!"

Chapter 5

IN HIS DREAM, he heard Keirith shouting something, but he couldn't make out the words. Only when he heard answering shouts did Darak realize he wasn't dreaming.

"Griane. Wake up."

He flung back the furs and groped for his breeches. Griane sat up, clutching the wolfskin to her breasts. Urkiat was already reaching for his quiver and bow.

"What's happening?" Faelia asked, her face groggy with sleep.

Before he could answer, Keirith appeared in the doorway, breathless and disheveled. "Raiders. On the beach. Two boats."

Griane's eyes locked with his. Then she snatched up her tunic and pulled it over her head.

"The forest," he told her.

He strapped on his belt, the sheathed dagger bouncing against his thigh as he grabbed the ax. When Keirith bent to retrieve his quiver and bow from beside his pallet, Darak said, "Go with them."

"I'm staying with you."

"I said—"

"I'm a man now. That's what you said last night."

The words were a stark reminder of all the other things he had said and had failed to say and had no time to say now. "All the more reason to go with them. Protect them."

"I've got my sling," Faelia said.

"Nay! Just run."

"Stay or go," Urkiat said. "Don't waste time arguing."

Griane herded the younger ones to the doorway. Urkiat peered outside and nodded. She looked back at him, her face stricken. "Lisula."

"Ennit will go." Darak prayed the raiders would be too intent on the pickings in the village to notice the birthing hut.

She nodded, her eyes huge in her narrow face. For a heartbeat, they stood there: his wife, his children. Then they fled.

"A spear."

He heard Urkiat's words, but all he could do was stare after his family.

"A spear, Darak. Arrows will be useless up close. And their swords are twice the length of our daggers."

Keirith handed the hunting spear to Urkiat and grabbed the smaller two-pronged one the boys used for fishing. Darak hefted the ax. "Tie it to my wrist, Keirith. Use Callie's belt."

Keirith bound the ax handle to Darak's wrist with the narrow strip of braided leather. Such beautiful hands, despite the scraped knuckles—the fingers clever and quick like Griane's, long and slender like Tinnean's. Nothing of him in those hands, except maybe the dirt under the fingernails.

"Can you see them, Urkiat?"

"Not yet." He left off peering out the doorway to glance back at them. "Hurry up."

"I'm trying," Keirith muttered.

"You're doing fine, son."

Keirith's eyes met his, then returned to his task. Darak tested the bindings and nodded. He'd have less freedom of movement, but at least it diminished the risk that the first blow would send the ax flying out of his hand.

He paused long enough to gaze around his home for what might be the last time, then ducked outside. Griane and the children had already vanished into the mist. Ghostly figures of women raced past, children clinging to their hands, screaming babes clutched to their breasts, all racing for the fields and the safety of the forest beyond. Boys lingered to help the old folks who followed slowly, so slowly in their wake. Men poured out of the nearest huts, some in breeches, others wearing nothing but their belts and daggers. Somewhere in the mist, he heard Nionik frantically shouting for the men to cover the women's retreat, but those he could see were already running toward the lake, clutching whatever weapons came to hand: spears, axes, hoes, peat cutters.

Sanok stumbled out of the next hut, looking dazed. Alada flung a mantle around her father's shoulders. When Darak sprinted toward them, Sanok peered up at him as if he were a stranger.

"I don't understand," he said, his voice querulous with shock. "I thought they only came in the autumn."

Darak seized his arm. Together, he and Alada half-dragged the old man through the village. They had just made it to the edge of the circled huts when they heard a deep-throated roar, like the howl of a giant beast. It crescendoed to an unnatural ululating shriek that sent shivers crawling down Darak's spine. The sudden silence that followed was even worse.

For a moment, the world seemed to stop, frozen in anticipation and terror. Then the beast roared again, and this time it was everywhere.

Griane and the children stumbled through the furrows in the newly plowed earth. When they heard that awful roar, Callie whimpered once. She hissed at him, and he choked back a sob. After that, he didn't make a sound; even when he fell and she and Faelia yanked him to his feet, her brave little boy gave only the smallest gasp, quickly stifled. But when she heard the women's screams, even Griane moaned.

She veered north—what she thought must be north; the familiar landmarks were lost in the mist. The raiders might have spread out from the lakeshore, but surely they couldn't have encircled the village already.

She tripped over a rock and went down hard, dragging Callie with her. She gave him a quick kiss as she pulled him to his feet. Pain lanced through her right knee at every step, but fear drove her on. If they could make the higher ground north of the village, they would find plenty of hiding places among the trees and scrub. The raiders would never search so far afield.

As the ground rose, the pain in her knee slowed her to a lurching trot. She stumbled and careened into a boulder. Stunned, she clung to it until Faelia's urgent tug forced her to move again.

The mist thinned as they climbed. If it was easier to pick their way through the clumps of gorse, it also made them clear targets. Clinging to rocks and scraggly bushes, they clawed their way up the slope.

Behind them, Griane heard a terrified shriek. Callie screamed and Faelia immediately clapped her hand over his mouth. Griane whirled around to see a woman sliding to the ground as slow and loose-limbed as if she were dancing. Her gray hair swirled around her, obscuring her face, but it could not hide the blood pouring down the back of her tunic.

She dragged her gaze from the woman's body to find the raider watching them.

"Run." Although she screamed the word in her mind, only a hoarse whisper emerged.

The raider stood there, the bloodstained dagger—longer than her forearm—resting against his thigh. And then he smiled.

Rage churned in her belly, overriding the terror, fury that this man could enjoy their fear and savor the anticipation of killing them.

Just like Morgath in the clearing that morning.

Still smiling, the raider started up the slope.

"Your sling. Faelia, your sling."

Her daughter just stood there, watching the raider stalk toward them. Griane spun Faelia around, fingers fumbling with the leather straps looped through her daughter's belt. Only when she ripped it free did Faelia come out of her daze.

"Take Callie and run," Griane told her.

Instead, Faelia dropped to her knees, scrabbling in the loose earth. Before Griane could shout at her to get her brother to safety, Faelia rose, a stone clenched in her fist.

It had been fifteen years since Griane had used a sling. Faelia brought down game nearly every day. She passed the sling to her daughter and unsheathed her dagger.

As Faelia slipped the stone into the leather pouch, the raider's pace quickened. One shot—that's all she would have time for. If she missed, Griane would have to attack him with her dagger and hope that she could steal enough time for the children to escape.

Faelia planted her bare feet and swung the sling in a slow circle over her head. The raider's smile vanished and he broke into a trot. The sling whirled faster, Faelia's slender body swaying with the rhythm.

Maker, guide her arm.

A dozen steps and he'd be on them. She could see the sweat gleaming on his forehead, the bloodstains spattering his cheeks.

Kill him. Kill him now!

Out of the corner of her eye, Griane saw Faelia's body flow forward in the smooth, powerful release Darak had taught her. She could barely follow the stone's flight. She only heard the hollow crack as it struck the raider's forehead, saw his brief look of shock as he staggered backward. He tumbled down the slope, rolling over and over before he slid into a boulder.

For a long moment, they stared at his motionless body, one arm outflung as if reaching for them.

"Is he dead?" Callie whispered.

"I think so," Griane replied. "But he might only be stunned."

"I hope he's dead."

"So do I."

Griane stole a look at Faelia. Her daughter was as motionless as the raider, her eyes huge and glittering in her white face.

"Mam?" Callie said in the same whisper.

"What?"

"I think I pissed myself."

For the first time, she noticed the stain on his tunic.

Faelia giggled.

"I didn't mean to."

"It doesn't matter, love."

Faelia's giggle became a shriek. Her face crumpled, wild laughter changing to hysterical sobs. Griane pulled her daughter into her arms. She couldn't remember the last time Faelia had permitted such an embrace, but now her daughter clung to her, her body shaking.

Eleven years old. Eleven years old and she's killed a man.

Darak barely had time to shove Sanok and Alada inside
the hut before the raiders came screaming out of the mist.
Two went down, clutching the shafts of the arrows embedded in their chests. The others never slowed.

An arrow hissed past, bouncing harmlessly off the stone
wall of the hut. Keirith and Urkiat took down two more
and then the raiders were on them. Darak sidestepped the
first thrust, twisting to hack at his attacker's arm with his
ax. Screaming, the raider lurched sideways, blood spurting
from his severed wrist.

A sword slashed downward. Darak ducked under it and
drove the head of his ax into the man's belly. The raider
doubled over, his face so close that Darak felt the spray of
his spit. As he raised the ax for another blow, the raider
seized the haft. Darak stared up into eyes as dark as a
winter night. Yellow teeth flashed. Trapped, Darak rammed
his forehead into his attacker's, stunning them both. The
raider stumbled back, knocking over a comrade who was
swinging a net. They fell, tangled together, but another
dodged their struggling bodies and veered toward Darak.

The shock of Keirith's attack, the fruitless search, the
gut-churning fear for his wife and children . . . all coalesced
into the bloodlust that flooded his legs and burned up
through his belly and chest to pour out of his mouth in a
full-throated bellow of defiance.

The raider's steps faltered. Darak bent to rip the sword
free from the severed hand at his feet. Ferocious joy filled
him. These hands could wield any weapon. These hands
could cut down a charging boar. These were hunter's hands,
sure and strong and whole again.

The ax caught his prey where the neck joined the shoulder. He wrenched it free, laughing as the blood sprayed
him, laughing as his sword slashed open another's belly,
laughing, breathless, panting, as his prey dropped his weapon,
fingers scrabbling to hold in the guts spilling onto the
ground. Red mist filled his eyes. The thrum of his blood
filled his ears, pounding in rhythm to his heartbeat, louder
than a drum, louder than the screams of the dying, louder
than his own wild howling.

The raiders scattered before him. Like a wolf eager for

the kill, he raced after the slowest. The earth rose beneath
his feet, as if Halam herself carried him over the rutted
field, sending him flying swift and sure as an arrow. His
prey glanced back once and stumbled, his shriek mingling
with Darak's triumphant shout.

On hands and knees, the man crawled through the furrows. Darak fell into an easy trot as he pursued him. He
could already feel the shock of flint on bone radiating
through his arms, the warmth of spurting blood bathing his
body. He could taste the kill. He wanted it.

A dirty face glanced up at him, eyes white-rimmed with
terror. The raider rolled over, slashing wildly with a dagger,
but when Darak advanced, he dropped it and raised both
hands.

Darak let the sword fall to the ground. The raider babbled something, a plea perhaps, or a curse. Gripping his ax
with both hands, Darak raised it over his head. His prey
screamed once before Darak buried the blade in his upturned face.

He planted his bare foot on the man's neck, slipping
twice in the blood before he managed to pry the ax free.
His legs trembled, every muscle burning from the chase.
Panting, he retrieved the sword. As the thrumming of his
blood faded, he could hear again, but the screams and
shouts seemed muffled as if they came from a great distance.

The deep blast of a horn shattered the illusion. He
looked up, surprised to find himself in the middle of the
fields. A few raiders stood frozen, as if uncertain whether
to obey the summons. Others were already racing toward
the lake.

He glanced back at the village. Through the shreds of
mist still floating across the fields, he saw Urkiat and Keirith, their backs to the hut, fighting off three raiders. Even
before he started running, Urkiat went down.

Keirith planted himself in front of Urkiat, slashing at the
raiders with his fishing spear. Always, they remained just
out of reach.

Urkiat lay tangled in the net. Blood oozed from a cut on his head. The screams of the dead and dying filled the air, echoing with nauseating intensity in his spirit. Shaking with frustration and fear, Keirith lunged at the greasy-haired man on his right who sidestepped, deflecting the blow with the flat of his sword.

"What do you want?" he screamed at them. "Why don't you kill me?"

The big one in the middle muttered something. The other two nodded and stepped away from him. Keirith's gaze darted from one to the other. Even if he managed to wound the big man, the other two would sweep forward from either side and overpower him.

They wanted him alive. That was his only advantage.

Urkiat couldn't help him. He didn't know where his father was or if he was even alive. He'd caught only a glimpse of him racing after his attackers, screaming like a demon escaped from Chaos.

That awful bellow sounded again from the beach. The raiders exchanged glances. Alone, he could never fend them all off. They were older, stronger, more battle-wise. But he had a strength none of them possessed.

Frantically, Keirith summoned energy from the blood-soaked earth beneath him and the misty air above. He sought power from the newly risen sun and the sweat rolling down his face. He pulled the energy of all the elements into his body, fueling the power he summoned from his spirit. And he sent them all hurtling toward the big one.

The raider reeled backward, clutching his head. Before the others could react, Keirith lunged at the gap-toothed one, but the release of magic had drained him. The spear wobbled in his hands, the points merely grazing the man's side. Numbness crept up his arms and legs. The spear slipped through his fingers. He fell to his knees, groping for it.

An agonizing shaft of pain ripped through his head. Something scraped his cheek as he hit the ground. A leather shoe appeared, then another, the toes spattered with blood. Hands gripped both arms. His belly heaved as the ground swung away. A hot stream of vomit poured out of him, burning his throat. Black dots swirled before his eyes,

crowding his vision, shrinking the world to a jolting circle
of earth that grew smaller and smaller until finally, there
was only darkness.

Darak was still racing toward the village when the raiders
trotted away, dragging his son's body between them. That
meant Keirith had to be alive. He glanced briefly at Urkiat
who was struggling to throw off the net. Alada emerged
from the hut as he ran past. He saw no other signs of life
in the village at all, although bodies lay everywhere.

The horn boomed a third time. Desperate, he charged
down the slope. Slipping on the dew-slick grass, he barely
caught himself before he stumbled over the bodies: Meniad,
his arms outflung as if beseeching the raiders to stop, and
Onnig, his head nearly sheared off, sprawled atop him.

Shouts from the beach drove him past other bodies,
raider and kin alike. Elathar lay crumpled beneath an alder,
still clutching his fishing spear. Red Dugan slumped against
him, his lips twisted in a snarl of defiance.

When he finally skidded to a halt, the two boats were
already pulling away from shore. A few stragglers splashed
through the shallows. Nionik led a group of men in pursuit,
but deadly flights of arrows drove them back.

He searched the chaotic scene for Keirith. When he spied
a limp body being hauled over the side of a boat, he
charged into the water, knowing he was already too late,
knowing he could never reach him in time, knowing that
his son was lost because he had allowed himself to be seduced by bloodlust and the thrill of being a hunter once
more. But still he ran, plowing through the knee-deep
water, heedless of the arrows hissing past, screaming his
son's name until his throat was raw.

He stumbled and fell, choking as water splashed into his
mouth. He tried to push himself to his feet, but the head
of the ax kept slipping on the pebbles and his left arm was
oddly weak. Looking down, he found an arrow embedded
in his bicep. He felt no pain, only a numbing cold that
spread up his arm to envelop his entire body.

Darak sat in the shallows, watching the rise and fall of
the giant paddles, watching the windcloths crawl up the

spars and grow big-bellied. Even when Nionik knelt beside him and repeated his name, he sat there, watching the boat that carried his son grow smaller and smaller until it entered the channel and disappeared from view.

Chapter 6

THE CROWS AND RAVENS came first, soaring in patient circles over the fields. Women emerged from the forest, wary as deer, but when they saw the bodies, they started running. Some fell to their knees beside a loved one, their high-pitched keening shattering the stillness that had fallen when the raiders left. Others walked dazedly toward the village, children clinging to their legs.

Skirting the raider's body, Griane led the children home. She paused beside Jurl's mother long enough to offer a prayer that Erca would continue to share gossip and advice with the other old ones whose spirits had flown to the Forever Isles. And there were many. Frustrated by the flight of the younger women, the raiders had vented their fury on the old folk, hacking the bodies so many times that they were barely recognizable. Callie buried his face in her tunic, but Faelia paused as if to burn the image of each mutilated body into her memory.

Sanok sat outside his hut, clinging to Alada's hand. Men staggered past carrying bodies; already, more than a dozen lay side by side in the center of the village. Gortin crawled from one to the next, his body shaking in silent sobs as he pressed the back of his left hand to a forehead, blessing each with the tattoo of the acorn. Griane scanned each face, relief mingling with guilt when she failed to find Darak or Keirith among the dead.

When she saw Ennit walking toward her, she froze in

horror. Then she realized he cradled Trian in his arms, poor Trian who would never again daydream among the flocks.

As he passed her, she caught his sleeve. "Is Lisula safe?" Ennit just stared at her. "Ennit, what's happened to Lisula? And the children?"

"Conn took the girls. I stayed with Lisula and the babe." His face crumpled as he stared into his brother's face. "They cut him to pieces. He couldn't even bring himself to castrate a lamb, and they cut him to pieces."

"Griane!"

She tore her attention from Ennit to discover Nionik staggering toward her, carrying his son. Nemek's moan assured her he was alive, but the wounds to his shoulder and leg bled profusely.

"Thank the gods you're all right," Nionik said. "We're taking the wounded to the longhut. Bring your medicine bag and—"

"Darak? Where's Darak?"

Before he could answer, Callie screamed, "Fa!"

He tottered toward them, moving like a man in a dream. An arrow protruded from his left arm, but he was alive, Merciful Maker, alive. He fell to his knees, burying his face in Callie's neck, pulling a sobbing Faelia into the curve of his good arm. Then he looked up at her, his face empty of all expression.

"They took him. They took Keirith."

The morning passed in a daze of shock and numbed grief. She couldn't mourn her lost son. She could scarcely spare the time to comfort her remaining children. Too many others needed her.

She sent Faelia and Callie to Sanok's hut where Alada was caring for some of the little ones. Outside the longhut, women were cutting up nettle-cloth and doeskin to use as bandages and slings.

Mirili entered the longhut with her and began feeding the fire. "I thought of keeping the men outside where there's more light, but they'll be better here, I think, than lying in the open."

Griane nodded; after all the horror their families had witnessed, they didn't need to watch her sew their loved ones back together.

Sali was waiting for her, bless the child, her healing bag clutched in one hand and an overflowing basket of medicinal supplies in the other. Griane paused long enough to give her a quick hug before issuing orders: stone pots of water for cleaning wounds, tallow for ointment, greenwood to splint broken bones. A few eyes went wide at the last instruction, but Bethia stepped forward, offering to make the necessary prayers and sacrifices so they could cut living branches from the trees.

At some point, Faelia joined them, fetching water and cleaning up the vomit and blood and urine that slimed the rushes. White-lipped but determined, Sali applied poultices of yarrow and hartstongue, stitched flesh wounds, and replaced soiled bandages with fresh ones.

Griane held out little hope for those with belly wounds. Mother Netal had taught her to ease suffering and preserve life, and when that was not possible, to use her skill to offer a clean and speedy death. For now she stanched the bleeding, numbed them with brogac, and prayed.

Even her prayers were brief; as soon as she finished tending one person, another needed her to splint a bone or dig an arrowhead out of a shoulder. By midday, she was soaked with sweat and blood, her legs trembling with exhaustion. She sent those with minor injuries home. A dozen still remained in the longhut, most deeply unconscious, a few tossing restlessly with fever. Half might survive if the wounds didn't turn putrid. The next two or three days would tell.

When she paused for a sip of water, Mirili whispered, "They took Owan, too."

"Oh, gods." Duba had lost her husband last winter. Now Owan. He was only a year older than Faelia. "I'll go to her. Will you stay with the wounded?"

Mirili nodded, her gaze lingering on Nemek.

"He's young, Mirili, and strong."

Mirili nodded again, her face haggard; Nemek was her only son.

Keirith. My son. They have taken my son.

Mirili touched her cheek. The silent sympathy of the gesture brought tears to Griane's eyes. She blinked them back. Tears were useless.

Outside, she gulped great lungfuls of air, so clean and cool after the smokiness of the longhut and the stench of blood and death. She would go to Duba first. Then she had to find Darak.

After those first few words, he had not spoken. When she knelt beside him, when she pushed the broken shaft of the arrow through his arm, when she stitched and bound his wound, he simply sat there. His silence chilled her, conjuring up memories of the days after Tinnean's transformation when he'd huddled between the roots that had once been his brother's feet, his spirit slowly drifting away. She had brought him back then; she could—she would—now.

There were more bodies in the center of the village. Some were already hidden under mantles. Women squatted beside others, helping Bethia and Muina strip and wash them. Tradition dictated that only priestesses could prepare a body for burial, but with Lisula still recovering from the birth and with so many bodies—dear gods, nearly a quarter of the tribe lay there—the women had forsworn tradition so that their dead could be ready before sunset.

Her breath caught when she saw Jani. Griane knelt next to her and stared down at her uncle Dugan's body. Red Dugan they still called him, although the hair had long since gone white. She'd hated him as a child, fought with him as a girl, avoided him after his return from the First Forest. Things changed after he married Jani. Perhaps her uncle had mellowed; more likely, Jani insisted he make an effort. Whatever the reason, Griane and her uncle had learned to tolerate each other, and Jani and Dugan had enjoyed a good marriage for more than ten years.

Dry-eyed, Jani drew the mantle over his face. "He wouldn't listen. Had to go with the other men. Old fool." Her voice broke, and Griane hugged her hard.

He would lie here with the others tonight while the priestesses kept vigil with Gortin. On the morrow, they would make the journey to the Death Hut. How many more might be taking that journey if Keirith had not sounded the alarm? How many more might have been stolen?

Keirith. My son. They have taken my son.

She found Duba rocking back and forth beside the fire pit. Her parents watched with bleak faces until Griane motioned them outside.

"She hasn't spoken," Petha said. "Not since she found out."

"It's the shock. It takes some like that." Griane leaned close to Mintan so she wouldn't have to shout; Duba might not be speaking, but she could still hear. Even with Mintan cupping his hand behind his right ear, she had to repeat herself twice. "You're sure Owan's not just missing?"

Mintan shook his head. "Jurl saw them," he said loudly. "Pulling poor Owan into the boat." He broke off and abruptly turned away, his thin shoulders shaking.

"It was his hair," Petha said. "That's how Jurl knew. Bright as your Faelia's."

Griane passed the tiny bundle of herbs to Petha. "This will help her sleep. Use half in a bowl of hot water. Let it steep until the brew turns golden." If only she had the magical heart-ease from the Summerlands. For Duba. For herself. For all those who had lost children today.

Keirith. My son. They have taken my son.

Petha touched her arm gently. "We shall pray for your Keirith."

Griane nodded and hurried away before the last shreds of her self-control vanished.

Darak was not in their hut. The fire was dead. The furs lay in scattered heaps. Only Keirith's sleeping place was tidy, his mantle folded neatly atop his pallet. She fell to her knees and clutched it to her breast. For the first time that awful day, Griane allowed herself to weep.

She didn't know how long she knelt there before she heard the shouting. She wiped her face and carefully refolded the mantle before hurrying outside.

Jurl and Rothisar passed her, dragging a struggling man between them. A group of men trailed in their wake, some shouting curses, others waving weapons. The two men halted by the bodies and shoved the man to his knees. Jurl seized the skinny tail of black hair that hung down the man's neck and yanked his head back.

It shocked her to see how young he was—a beardless boy,

only a year or two older than Keirith. Droplets of sweat oozed down cheeks the color of pine bark. He screamed curses at Jurl, his dark eyes rolling wildly.

Jurl tugged the boy's head to the left. "You see this woman? That's my mother. And this . . ." Another vicious tug jerked the boy's gaze to the right. "This is my brother Onnig."

"My father!" screamed Rothisar, his face contorted in rage. "My grandmother!"

"Murdering bastard!" a man shouted.

"Coward!"

"Child stealer!"

Women and children poured out of neighboring huts, as caught by the spectacle as she was. Jani rose from Dugan's corpse and spat in the boy's face. Even mild-mannered Lorthan was screaming for blood.

Jurl drew his dagger. "Do we sacrifice him at the heart-oak or kill him here?"

The shouting crescendoed to a roar. In a moment, they would tear the boy apart with their bare hands.

Darak shoved his way through the crowd. Only when people moved aside, did she see Nionik and Gortin behind him. Gortin used his blackthorn staff to clear a path; Nionik's air of command was enough to make his kinfolk back away.

The shouting died down as the three men strode toward Jurl and Rothisar. Jurl turned to face them without releasing his grip on the boy's hair. "We found him trying to steal a coracle."

"Let me kill him, Oak-Chief," Rothisar begged. "Let me avenge the deaths of my father and grandmother."

Nionik raised his hands, silencing the roar of approval. "We have all lost family this day." Grim-faced, the chief turned to Gortin. "Is it fitting to sacrifice an unbeliever at the heart-oak?"

"Nay. His blood would pollute our sacred tree. Nor will I have it shed here to mingle with the blood of our people. On the morrow, we will burn our dead. But before—"

Howls of protest rose from the crowd. Gortin raised his staff, demanding silence. "Would you allow your loved ones to lie in the Death Hut, stacked like . . . like peat bricks?" he asked, outraged. "Nay, we will construct a pyre on the beach. I will go with the men to the forest this afternoon so that I might make the appropriate offerings to the spirits of the trees we must injure. As for this monster . . ." He gestured to the kneeling boy with his staff. "Let him be taken to the standing stones. Let him watch us honor our kinfolk. After the fire has consumed their bodies, let each family exact retribution for their dead from his living flesh."

The tribe cheered, howling like wolves.

Darak leaned close to Nionik. After a brief exchange, the chief nodded. He held up his hand and waited for the cheering to die down. "The Memory-Keeper has requested that the council of elders question this man before he is killed."

"You can't even understand his barbarous tongue," Jurl said.

Again, Darak whispered something to Nionik, although his gaze remained fastened on the prisoner. The dazed look had vanished. Now his face was as cold and hard as stone.

Nionik said, "Urkiat—our guest from the south—will translate."

At his words, Urkiat squeezed through the press of onlookers to stand beside Darak. With all that had happened, she'd had no time to learn much about him. Had Urkiat been stolen by the raiders? Is that how he came to know their language?

"But what's the point?" Jurl persisted.

"The point," Nionik said in a sharper tone, "is that this man may have information." The chief said something in an undertone to Darak who stared at the prisoner, his eyes glittering. Nionik spoke again, more urgently. Without taking his gaze from the kneeling boy, Darak gave a curt nod.

Jurl scowled and spat. "Just you remember, Darak. I want him alive on the morrow."

"He'll be alive," Darak said in a calm, terrible voice.

She had to run to match Darak's long stride, but she caught up with him and Urkiat at the edge of the village.

"Urkiat. Give us a moment."

He hesitated, glancing toward Darak for instruction, but

quickly retreated when she turned on him in a fury. Darak stared up at the lone oak on the hilltop.

"You mean to torture him, then?"

A muscle twitched in his jaw. "I mean to do whatever is necessary."

"He's just a boy."

His head jerked toward her, eyes blazing. "So is my son."

"He's my son, too!"

"Then you should worry more about him and less about that murdering raider."

She drew back her arm and struck him as hard as she could across the face. His breath hissed in, but he barely flinched. She struck him again and yet a third time, and still he stood there. Only when she raised her hand for another blow did he grab her wrist.

"Enough."

She kicked him in the shin and gasped, wondering if she'd broken a toe. He jerked her toward him, pinioning her against his bare chest.

"Griane."

She struggled futilely, heedless of Urkiat's shocked stare.

"Stop. Please."

It was the "please" that caught her. She went still, the sound of her panting loud in her ears. A tremor shuddered through her body; only when she looked up did she realize it came from Darak.

"Don't do this."

His expression hardened. "You still plead for him?"

"Nay. For you." The mask slipped ever so slightly, enough to show her a glimmer of the man she had loved for so many years. "I would not have you do to him what Morgath did to you."

His head snapped back as if she had slapped him again. "You think this is the same? That I do this for my pleasure?"

"Don't you? What can he possibly tell you? The raiders will come or they won't. Knowing the number of men on one of their boats or how fast they travel cannot help us."

And then she realized. Darak didn't care about that. He wanted to know where they had taken Keirith. He meant to go after him. What a fool not to have realized it immediately.

"I must go," Darak said.

"Please. If he must be tortured, let it be someone else. I can't bear to see you do this."

"Then don't watch."

With Urkiat at his heels, he splashed across the stream. Sanok passed her, supported by Nionik and Gortin. When she felt a light touch on her shoulder, Griane turned to discover Muina beside her. She would not have thought it possible for the Grain-Grandmother to look any older, but the meager flesh on her cheeks sagged and grief had carved deeper grooves around her mouth.

"The elders mean to question him at the oak," Muina said. "Will you come?"

Griane hesitated. If she couldn't stop the torture, she could make sure the boy didn't bleed to death. But perhaps it would be more merciful if he did. It would spare him the lingering death that awaited him on the morrow.

They stole my son. They killed my kin. Why should I care how he dies or what he suffers?

But she did care. She had never killed a man, although she had been prepared to do so this morning. But it was one thing to kill someone who threatened her children, another to slice flesh off a helpless man and listen to his screams. That would not bring back Keirith. Or Owan. Or any of their dead.

"Will you come?" Muina repeated.

Could she watch the torture? Aye. She was strong enough for that. But she could not watch her husband wreak the same vengeance on the body of this nameless boy that Morgath had wreaked on him all those years ago.

Slowly, Griane shook her head.

She went back inside the longhut to check her patients. She dribbled water between a pair of cracked lips, changed a bandage over a seeping wound. She gave her strength and her skill and her concentration to the men and women who needed her. But it was not enough to drown out the high-pitched scream that drifted down from the hilltop.

The babe's whimpering woke her. Still half-asleep, she rolled toward him, guiding her nipple to his mouth. With a small

animal growl, the toothless gums clamped on it and sucked greedily.

She shifted position, cupping her son's naked bottom with one hand and his head with the other. Too soon to know if the soft fuzz would darken or remain as unrepentantly red as hers.

Her eyes closed, blissful with the suckling. Tiny fingers kneaded her breast. Bigger ones closed on her thigh. She opened her eyes to look into Darak's. For a long while, he simply watched them while his fingers stroked her thigh, as rhythmic and sensual as the babe's suckling but slower than the insistent tug at her nipple.

"What does it feel like?"

She smiled; how to explain such a thing to a man? "It tingles. As if all the energy in me is being pulled into that greedy little mouth."

"It doesn't . . . drain you?"

"Nay. It feels good."

"I wondered . . ." Even in the predawn gloom, she thought he was blushing. "Maybe it was like . . . well, when you . . ."

Her smile widened. "It's not at all the same as when I drain you."

Now she knew he was blushing. She loved to make him blush. Even after a year, there were moments like this when he would turn unexpectedly shy. Whether it was his natural reserve or the lingering effects of his first marriage, she never knew.

The babe lay limp and heavy in her arms. She shifted him to her right nipple, but no amount of gentle urging would rouse him. With a sigh, she lay back.

"He's finished already?"

"I'll wake him in a bit and see if he'll take some more." She cupped her swollen breast, wincing.

"Does it pain you?"

"A little. But if he won't feed again, it'll ache something fierce."

His fingers covered hers, gently tracing the curve of her breast. She eased her right arm behind his head and pressed him closer. His lips fastened on her nipple and she moaned. He started to raise his head, but she pulled him back. His mouth was gentle, nothing like the babe's relentless tug.

"Harder," she whispered.

His mouth obeyed, while his fingers brushed her body, gentle as fern fronds. Her hand wandered over the scarred shoulders and back. Locked together, they drifted, dreamlike, until the gentle rocking of their bodies carried them into another rhythm, fiercer than the first and even more ancient.

"Mam?"

Griane jerked awake to find Faelia squatting beside her. "You were dreaming."

"Aye."

The shreds of the dream still clung to her, her nipples swollen, her body flushed with unsatisfied desire. Even as she noted the sensations, others intruded: the groans of the wounded, the smoky stench of the longhut.

"I heated up the stew," Faelia said. "Shall I fetch it here, or will you come home?"

Griane got to her feet, shaking the stiffness out of her limbs. She cast a quick look around the hut. Sali was sprawled near her, sound asleep. Mirili still sat by Nemek. Griane frowned when she saw Catha had joined her; the longhut was no place for a woman so big with child, but she could no more send Catha away than the others who had come to keep watch over their wounded.

"Go home," Mirili said. "We'll send to you if we have need."

Griane nodded. She couldn't have slept for long; the heaviness of exhaustion still lay on her. Judging from the dark smudges under her eyes, Faelia was equally exhausted. She rested her hand briefly against her daughter's cheek. "Thank you. For helping."

"I had to do something." Her voice cracked, and she swallowed hard. "I tried to sleep, but every time I closed my eyes . . ."

"You saw him."

Faelia nodded.

"I can mix you something to help you sleep."

"It won't help me forget," Faelia said, her voice soft but savage.

"Nay." She took her daughter's shoulders, the bones sharp under her fingers. "Only time can do that. For all of us."

"Can we forget this?" Faelia gestured around the hut. "Or the dead lying outside?"

"We will never forget. Nor should we." Griane heard the sharpness in her voice and softened it. "But we will learn to bear it. Because we must."

Callie was waiting outside the longhut. His tremulous smile of greeting changed to a look of horror. When she realized he was eyeing her bloodstained tunic, she got down on her knees and took his hands. "The blood is from the men and women who were injured. I had to stitch their wounds and bandage them."

"Will they be all right now?"

She hesitated, then gave him the truth. "Most of them. But some of the wounds were very bad."

"Then we should pray for them."

"Aye."

"And for Keirith."

Not trusting her voice this time, she just nodded. Callie studied her, his face puckered with concern. "Don't worry, Mam. Fa will find him."

Young as he was, Callie knew.

"Of course he will." Shielding her eyes against the sun's glare, she saw Nionik and the other elders making their way toward the village. "Children—go home. As soon as I find your father, we'll join you."

"Where is he?" Callie asked, his voice gone shrill with fear. "Did the bad men come back?"

"Nay, love, nay. He went with the elders to . . . to talk to the man they captured. I'll find him. I'll bring him home. All right?"

Callie nodded, blinking back the tears that welled in his eyes.

"That's my good boy." She hugged him hard. "Go with your sister. We'll be there soon."

"Promise?"

"I promise."

Gortin and Muina trailed behind the other elders. Urkiat strode past them, but stopped when Muina called his name. His stormy expression only heightened Griane's anxiety.

"Is he still up there?" she asked.

Gortin nodded. "We'll set a watch tonight in case he—"

"He went toward the lake," Muina interrupted.

"Who? Oh. Darak. Aye. He handled the questioning well—" Urkiat's inarticulate exclamation made Gortin break off, frowning. "He only had to break—"

"Tree-Father."

Gortin looked offended at Muina's second interruption.

"I know you must gather men to cut wood for the pyre. We shouldn't be keeping you. Or Urkiat," she added pointedly. "I'm sure you could use his strong arms."

"You're right. Thank you, Grain-Grandmother."

"I'm going after Darak," Urkiat said.

"Nay," Muina replied. "You're going to cut wood." Her head barely reached Urkiat's shoulder, but he was the one to back down. With a muttered oath, he strode after Gortin.

"Dear gods, what happened up there?" Griane asked.

"Urkiat is young and thirsty for blood."

"Damn Urkiat! Is Darak all right?"

"Nay. But he hides it well. Wait!" Muina's hand shot out to clutch her arm. "Give him a moment."

"Was it that bad?"

"The boy pissed himself before Darak even touched him. Two broken fingers and he was babbling so fast Urkiat could hardly keep up with him." The keen blue eyes gazed up into hers. "As for Darak? Well. You know him better than anyone."

So she had thought—before this morning.

"He holds things close. Always has, ever since he was a lad. When he went back to the First Forest, there were those who thought he'd gone for good. 'Twas Darak's love for you that brought him back and 'twas your love that healed him. And I don't mean love of the spirit, Griane. 'Twas the comfort of your body he needed then and it's what he needs now. And you could do with the comfort of his as well."

Muina pressed a light kiss to her forehead and walked away.

He stood in the lake, water lapping around his waist. His skin looked very white. Whiter still were the scars on his back where the thorn tree in Chaos had torn his flesh.

He bent down to scoop up water in his cupped hands,

then straightened and threw it over himself. The droplets sparkled in the sunlight, creating little rainbows around his head before streaming over his shoulders and back.

He shifted position so that he stood in profile to her and repeated the ritual, shivering a little as the water dripped over him. Again, he turned, this time facing her. Blood stained the bandage on his arm. His eyes were closed, and his lips moved although she heard no words. His shivering was more pronounced now; even from her hiding place in the thicket, she could see the bumps of cold on his arms.

When he bent a fourth time, she knew this was no simple act of bathing. So might a shaman cleanse himself before conducting a ritual or a hunter before going into the forest. Facing each direction, seeking the power of the four winds, the strength of earth and air, fire and water. Not only washing the body, but cleansing the spirit as well.

A cloud drifted across the sun, leaving him in shadow as he waded back to the beach. He squatted beside his discarded breeches, his wet hair hanging in snarled tangles. When he rose again, he held his dagger. His lips moved as he raised his hand. Blood blossomed in a thin line across his wrist. He waited a moment, then snapped his wrist, flinging droplets of blood into the water. Twice more he repeated the gesture.

Three times for a charm—or a curse. Every child knew that.

He stood very still, head raised as if listening. She held her breath, listening with him. Her heart thudded loudly, nearly drowning out the soft lapping of the waves and the faint rustling of a small animal in the underbrush.

Tree limbs moaned in a gust of wind. A shaft of sunlight emerged from a break in the clouds. For a heartbeat, Bel's rays burnished his body. Then the trees fell silent and Bel ducked back behind the cloud, leaving the beach in shadow again.

He sat down on a rock, arms folded across his knees. His body tensed when he heard her approach, but he didn't raise his head.

She pulled off her tunic and walked toward the lake. The shock of the cold water made her gasp. She sifted through the pebbles for a handful of sand, scrubbing the blood of the wounded from her body, washing the stench of death from her hair. By the time she was finished, she was shaking so hard she had to clench her jaw to keep her teeth from knocking together.

He watched her come out of the water, but his gaze never reached her eyes. She stopped in front of him, willing him to look at her. When he refused, she reached out very slowly, as if to touch a wild creature, and laid her hand on his hair.

A strangled cry escaped him. He flung out a hand blindly, fingers closing around her wrist in a punishing grip that would surely leave bruises. She eased between his legs and pulled his face to her breasts, but he kept shaking his head, refusing the comfort she offered.

His mouth brushed her nipple. A moan shuddered through his body and into hers. Then his lips closed and his arms came around her and he laid his head against her breast. Gently, she stroked his hair and held him until the shaking stopped.

"Griane . . ."

"Hush."

She led him into the thicket and pulled him down beside her. Blessing Muina's wisdom, they shared the wordless comfort of their bodies and a respite from the wounds of their hearts.

Chapter 7

HE HAD FOUND OUT as much as he could from the boy. He had washed off the raiders' blood and offered his to the gods for their blessing and their guidance. He had spent a few precious moments with his son and daughter. Only one thing remained for Darak to do.

Meniad was dead. Gortin must keep vigil over the bodies. And so, in defiance of shame and ancient taboo, Darak made his way to the birthing hut to ask a woman, newly delivered, to rise from her childbed and open the way to the First Forest.

He found Ennit sitting outside with Muina. Before he could speak, Ennit rose. His mouth worked. "I heard. About Keirith. Oh, Darak . . ."

Darak held him as he wept. His eyes were dry. He had shattered once, when Griane touched him. Then, in her wisdom, she had taken all his emotions—rage, fear, disgust, shame—and transmuted them to a more primitive need. In her flesh, he found forgiveness and understanding and—for a few moments—oblivion.

He felt as distant from Ennit's grief as his own. He had experienced the sensation often when he was a hunter, the strange separateness of being in the moment yet standing apart, observing the prey, the surroundings, and his reactions. His dangerous tangle of emotions had been consumed in the fire of that brief, violent lovemaking, leaving him calm and hollow. But somewhere in the charred remains, an ember of shame flickered.

He comforted Ennit. He asked after Lisula and the babe. And then he turned toward home, knowing he could not ask Lisula for help.

He had nearly reached his hut when the shouting penetrated his mind. "Are you deaf, boy?" Muina said by way of greeting.

"Forgive me. Come inside and sit a moment."

She slapped away his hand. "There's no time to sit. 'Twill be sunset soon. If you're going to the grove, you must hurry." Between pants, she managed a hoarse chuckle at his look of surprise. "That's why you came to Lisula, wasn't it? To ask her to open the way?"

He simply nodded without bothering to ask how she knew; little that happened in the village escaped Muina's notice.

"Well?"

"I couldn't ask. It seemed . . . wrong."

"She would have done it. She's a good girl—loyal and true to those she loves."

Another ember blazed to life in the carefully banked fire of his emotions. He took a moment to master his voice before he said, "Aye. She is."

"It never occurred to you to ask me?"

Excitement, hope, fear . . . too many embers to stamp out this time. "You still possess the power?"

Her face creased in a smile. "Let's see, shall we?"

Old as she was, Muina set a brisk pace, although she allowed him to take her arm and guide her through the rutted fields. As they hurried along the narrow forest trail, the familiar peace stole over him—and with it the familiar melancholy.

This was his place. This was where he belonged.

He scanned the shadowy depths of the forest as a man home from a long journey might study the face of his beloved. He noted the changes since he had walked the trail at the Spring Balancing: the ducklike quacks of the wood frogs and the distant whistles of the peepers in the wetlands; the raw slashes on the trunk of a pine where a bear had clawed it; the violets and starflowers that now vied with primroses and snowdrops to decorate the forest floor.

He led Muina past the boulder, past the partially uprooted birch, and stepped into the glade of the heart-oak.

As many times as he had stood here, he still felt the same awe when he stared up at his tribe's sacred tree. Here, his kin had offered sacrifices in celebration and propitiation, honoring their tree-brothers and their gods and a way of life that had survived plague and famine and the near-destruction of their world. Here, Tinnean had been initiated into the priesthood. And here, too, he had first glimpsed his nemesis after Morgath returned to the world in the body of a wolf.

Today, no such threat lurked. There was only the wind in the trees and the cooing of wood pigeons roosting in the branches. Through the thin canopy overhead, a few shafts of late afternoon sunlight burnished the uppermost branches of the heart-oak. Shadows cloaked the lower branches, adding an air of mystery to the aura of peace that pervaded the glade.

Tokens from past rites hung from the branches and nestled among the exposed roots. Birds and animals had long since devoured the gifts of food and berry wine, but the flint arrowheads and bone fishhooks remained.

He had brought no gifts with him. Instead, he took his dagger and reopened the wound at his wrist. Kneeling before the heart-oak, he allowed his blood to drip upon its roots as he had so many years ago. Then, he had offered his blood so that he—a hunter who had turned his back on the gods—might be permitted to enter the sacred forest and seek his brother's spirit. Today, he sought only the wisdom and comfort of the spirits who dwelled in the One Tree.

"Darak. It's nearly time."

Only at sunrise and sunset, when the barrier between the worlds was thinnest, could the crossing be made. He retrieved the thin strip of nettle-cloth Griane had tied around his wrist, but in his haste, he fumbled it. He could feel his face flush as Muina knotted the bandage for him; he hated for others to see his clumsiness.

Muina, bless her, merely took his hand and led him sunwise around the heart-oak. Three times, they circled the sacred tree, Muina's chants mingling with the rustle of the dead leaves underfoot. In a strong voice, she spoke the ancient words of permission. Hand in hand, they stepped forward.

When Fellgair opened the way, it was like stepping from one world into another. The transition was less tranquil with a human guide. The forest blurred, trees melting into smears of gray and brown and green, color and light hurtling past him and around him, and only Muina's hand to tether him to his body and Muina's voice telling him that she would return at dawn.

Her hand slipped free. The nauseating sense of rootlessness faded as the world slid back into place: earth beneath his feet; a circle of giant trees; and in the center of the grove, the heart of this ancient forest, the One Tree.

Once it had dwarfed the others, a giant among giants. Now all but the birch towered over it. Morgath had destroyed the Tree that had stood in this grove since the world's first spring. As the world measured time, this one was just a sapling. Yet from the moment of its conception, it had proclaimed the miracle: the One Tree that was forever Two. From those roots, from that slender trunk, two branches forked, one studded with the dark red buds of the Oak and the other drooping under the weight of the spiny leaves of the Holly.

Darak stepped between the gnarled roots that had once been his brother's feet and placed his palm on the trunk. In the days following Tinnean's transformation, the bark had been supple, retaining the faintest warmth. Now only its creamy color gave evidence that this had once been the flesh of a man.

Not even a man. Just a boy. Keirith's age.

Even before his brother's body underwent its transformation, Tinnean's spirit had altered. Darak had merely touched the World Tree; Tinnean had dwelled in it. No man could remain unchanged after hearing its song, a song that had echoed in the blood and bones and spirits of every being since the creation of the world. The gods who dwelled among its silver branches, the creatures who lived in the middle world, the spirits of the dead in the sunlit Forever Isles that floated in its roots—the World Tree linked them all. And now Tinnean's spirit dwelled with the Oak and Holly, forever bound to the Tree-Lords and to the ancient being that was the consciousness of the world.

Tinnean Tree-Friend, the tale named him. And Darak

Spirit-Hunter and Griane the Healer. When they had first crafted the tale, he and Sim clashed repeatedly, the old Memory-Keeper arguing that people needed a hero, while he argued just as fiercely that people needed to know that a hero was only a man—a man who had suffered frostnip and hunger, whose stomach had churned when he first encountered the Trickster, who had screamed in agony when Morgath mutilated his body.

"They know you froze your arse off," Sim said, dragging his fingers through his sparse white hair. "Everyone freezes their arses off in winter. That's not a tale worth telling."

"Are we telling a tale or the truth?"

"We're telling a tale that conveys the essence of the truth. There's a difference."

"Perhaps we could say your breath froze upon your lips," Sanok suggested.

"But it didn't. Our snot did."

Old Sim scowled. "I'll never make a Memory-Keeper of you."

"Then why are you trying?"

And as he did at least once a day in those first moons, he had jumped to his feet and marched to the doorway of their hut, only to be stopped by Sim's voice. " 'Tell the tale,' Tinnean said."

Darak glared at the Tree. "You might have whispered. Once Griane heard—and the Trickster . . . well, without that, I might have gone on being a hunter. Or a shepherd. Or something other than a gods-cursed Memory-Keeper!"

The drooping boughs of the Holly moved, stirred by the faint breeze. "And don't you start, Cuillon. If I didn't love you both, I'd swear it was a conspiracy. To make the man who didn't like talking choose the one life-path—the only one, mind you—that relied on words."

He stroked the pale trunk of the Tree. "Aye. Well. When Sanok dies, and it's left to me to tell the tale at Midwinter, I'll tell my version. And Sim can howl all he wants in the Forever Isles."

Old Sim and Sanok. The one had chivvied and chided him as he struggled to master the legends and chants and bloodlines preserved by generations of Memory-Keepers. The other had been infinitely patient, gently correcting his mistakes. It had taken both of them to shape a hunter into a Memory-Keeper. Like chipping flint with a hammerstone, bits of his old self flaking off little by little.

Darak shook his head. He had not come here to relive the past, but to seek help for his son.

In a halting voice, he told Tinnean and Cuillon about Keirith's abduction. It led naturally to the tale of their awful confrontation and spiraled back over the years, one tale intertwining with the next. By the time he finished speaking, his voice was hoarse and the light had died. The trees were indistinguishable in the gloom, but out of the corner of his eye, he caught the flicker of movement as the Watchers darted in and out among them. "The rootless ones," Cuillon had called them, the spirits of trees long dead who guarded those still living. Once, he had feared them; now he only wished Keirith had such guardians to watch over him.

He sat down, his back against the Tree. "Can you see beyond the First Forest, Tinnean? Can you see our boy?"

As always, his brother remained silent.

When they had embarked upon the quest to find Tinnean and the Oak, Cuillon had guided them. All he had to guide him now was the information he'd gotten from the captured boy and Urkiat's knowledge of the raiders.

Five days and nights for their giant boats. Four times that—maybe more—by coracle. Due south under the third star in the curving tusk of the Boar. Due south to the place called Pilozhat, Beloved of the Gods. Pilozhat, the holy city of the people who called themselves Zherosi, the Children of Zhe. A city of stone nestled beneath a great mountain, where the lucky ones were sold as slaves and the unlucky ones—those with red hair like Keirith and Owan—were sacrificed to their sun god at Midsummer.

Darak forced his hands to relax. If he could rescue his brother from Chaos, he could rescue his son from Pilozhat.

At least, he would not be alone; Urkiat had guessed his intention and eagerly volunteered to go with him. He'd accepted immediately. He needed Urkiat's gift of language and his knowledge of the Zherosi. If he had to curb Urkiat's desire for vengeance, that was a small price to pay.

And a small pack for such a journey; Wolf would be displeased.

He closed his eyes, conjuring the image of his vision mate. Together, they had hunted the Oak and Tinnean in that dream-journey through Chaos. He had never reached for her since then. Once he turned his back on hunting, he no longer believed himself worthy of her. But he'd thought of her often in the intervening years, and sometimes he woke from dreams with her howl echoing in his spirit.

"Wolf," he whispered, the name evoking the same longing and melancholy that had touched him when he entered the forest. Twice more he whispered her name and felt peace stealing over him.

Darak opened his eyes. Gheala peeped between the branches of the trees, spilling shafts of moonlight into the grove. A Watcher darted past the rowan. Bolder than the others, it abandoned the safety of the trees and approached him. For a heartbeat, he was transported back to that moment when he confronted Morgath. Then he heard the familiar yip, and his heart lurched again.

He was still scrambling to his feet when she launched herself at him. He fell backward, his joyous shout cut off in a gasp as his injured arm struck the ground. She butted her head against his, her rough tongue bathing his cheek. When he buried his, fingers in the thick fur at her neck and scratched behind the tattered left ear, her whole body wriggled with pleasure.

He tried to sit up, and she butted him again. The breath whooshed out of him as the huge forepaws landed on his chest.

"Mind my arm," he managed to wheeze.

She jumped off, only to swerve and lunge forward as if to attack. He fended her off with a laugh and she dodged away again, yipping excitedly as she raced around the grove. Finally, she trotted toward him and sat down, tongue lolling.

Wincing a little, he pushed himself onto his knees so they could be face-to-face. Her golden eyes stared into his. He couldn't resist touching her, savoring the soft-rough feel of her fur. He was startled to discover white hairs among the black on her muzzle. Because she was not a creature of his world, he had always assumed she was ageless.

"Wolf."

"Little Brother."

"I've missed you."

"And I, you. It has been too long since we hunted to-gether."

He hung his head. "I've thought of you. Dreamed of you."

"I know. But until this moonrise, you did not call."

"I thought . . . I wasn't sure you'd come."

"I will always come, Little Brother. We are pack."

"But I . . . I don't hunt."

She cocked her head. "You are a hunter."

"No longer."

"Always. That is your nature. As it is mine." The golden eyes regarded him for a long moment. "That is why you called me. So we could hunt again."

He sat back on his haunches, conscious of his thudding heartbeat. "The place I seek . . . it's not in this forest or the one we traveled in Chaos. It is in my world."

"I have crossed the stream between our worlds. I came to you when you were little more than a pup."

"Aye, but . . . not like you are now. Not . . . real."

"In your world, I am a creature without fur or fangs. But I will always be real. To you."

"You'd really come with me?"

"We are pack." Her tongue flicked out to lick his face.

"My son. My . . . pup. He is the one we seek."

"He has wandered from the pack?"

"Stolen. Taken. By a strange pack."

"We will find the pup. And kill the others." Her lips drew back, baring the yellowed fangs. Then she butted him gently in the chest and darted away, black fur blending instantly with the darkness.

"Thank you." He wasn't sure if he was thanking Wolf or the gods or Tinnean and Cuillon. Perhaps all of them. He had come here seeking Tinnean's love and Cuillon's wisdom and the Oak's strength. Wolf embodied all those qualities. Twice before he had lost her, once through simple ignorance, and later, through his own stubborn pride. Never again. She was with him always—just as Tinnean and Cuillon were.

He rested his hand on the gnarled root and closed his eyes. "Keep him safe, Tinnean. If you have that power. Keep our boy safe until I can find him."

It was nearing moonset before Griane dared to leave the hut. She hesitated outside the doorway, her eyes on Gortin and Bethia who kept vigil beside the bodies. Abandoning her original plan, she walked openly through the village. They would see her healing bag clutched in her arms. They would watch her walk toward the longhut. They would believe she was going to check on the wounded. And she did, but only long enough to assure herself that none needed immediate attention. Then, safely cloaked by darkness, she made her way across the stream and up the hill.

She made out only one form—Jurl's by the size of it. She heard Rothisar's snores before she spied him, sprawled on the side of the hill. Even in the darkness, she could feel Jurl's eyes. He rose into a crouch as she approached, then settled back when he recognized her.

"What do you want?"

She squatted beside him and pulled the waterskin out of her bag. "I brought you something to help you stay awake."

Steam rose as he opened the waterskin and sniffed at the brew. "What's in it?"

"Herbs. Bitter blossom. Oats."

He handed it back. "You'd have done better to bring brogac."

She pulled a clay flask from the bag and held it out. With a soft chuckle, Jurl unstoppered it and drank deeply.

"Save some for Rothisar."

"He's had enough. He finished most of the one we brought. Greedy little bastard."

She watched him take another long swig before venturing, "It doesn't seem fair."

"What?"

"The two of you, up here alone all night. I could send one of the other men—"

"Don't want anyone else. It's our right. And our brogac."

Tentatively, she touched his sleeve. "I'm sorry. About Onnig. And Erca."

"Onnig fought well. But my mam . . ." He drank, slopping brogac down his chin. "Bastard'll pay."

"The boy didn't kill her."

"Doesn't matter."

"I . . . I saw the raider who did."

His hand darted out and seized her wrist. When she gasped, his fingers relaxed just a little. "Tell me."

His voice was thick, perhaps with emotion, more likely, the brogac. By the time she finished, his hand had fallen to his knee. "Faelia, eh? She's tough. Like you."

"I'm not so tough."

"Five people went into the First Forest. You and Darak came back."

"I was lucky."

"Maybe." He nudged her. "Did you lie with him?"

"Darak?"

"The Trickster."

"Nay. Nay!" she repeated in a fierce whisper.

"Always figured you did. To get him to help you. But if that's your story—"

"It's not a story. It's the truth."

"As you will."

When he took another deep drink, she said, "You'd best go easy."

"You think I can't hold my drink?"

"I think you'll have a raging headache on the morrow."

"I'll still be sober enough to cut off his ballocks."

"Well, don't come to me for a tonic."

She rose out of her crouch and found her ankle snagged by rough fingers. "Why'd you come tonight?"

"I told you."

He jerked her off balance and she sat down hard. Glaring at him, she said, "I thought you'd kill him."

"And spoil the fun?" He leaned close, the scent of brogac mingling with his unwashed body. "I know why you really came."

She turned her head away. "Then why bother asking?"

He released her ankle, but only to run his fingers up her leg. She slapped his hand away.

"All these years, married to a cripple. I've got all my fingers, Griane. And a spar that'll make you squeal when I plough your sweet furrow."

"Be quiet! You'll wake Rothisar."

It was the wrong answer. Moving far too quickly for a man who had consumed so much brogac, Jurl seized both ankles and yanked her flat. She fought him silently as he spread her legs and shoved between them.

"I remember how you screeched when you first married him. The whole village could hear you. Not lately, though."

He shifted his weight. His fingers groped between their bodies. Hoping to catch him off balance, she shoved him hard in the chest. He rocked backward, then held her down with one hand while the other continued its persistent fumbling at the waist of his breeches.

Her fist grazed his cheek. He chuckled as he caught her wrist. "I saw you slap him this afternoon. Guess that's what it takes to straighten Darak's twig."

With her free hand, she flailed for her healing bag, a rock, something to use as a weapon. Her fingers found the discarded flask. Gripping it by the neck, she swung it as hard as she could. It shattered against the side of his head.

Jurl smiled. Then his eyes glazed and he slumped over.

She managed to shove herself out from under him. Too angry to be frightened, she lay back, panting. Then she cautiously raised her head. A few trickles of blood, black in the moonlight, marred his face, but his breathing was deep and regular. Clumsy ox hadn't even managed to unlace his breeches. She felt his pulse, then got to her feet and kicked him once in the ribs.

She retrieved the waterskin and slung her healing bag over her shoulder. Rothisar was still snoring. As she approached the oak, she heard the boy's quick intake of breath. She squatted next to him, wrinkling her nose at the faint stink of urine. Her fingers found his right hand. He gasped when she touched the broken fingers, grotesquely swollen now. Patting his arm, she rose.

The knots were tight. It took a long while to work them free, using her teeth as well as her fingers; she didn't dare cut them with her dagger. As it was, Jurl might accuse her. Still, it would be her word against his and he wouldn't want her to add the tale of attempted rape to her story because Darak would kill him.

Even after the rope fell to the ground, the boy just sat there, staring at her. Realizing he would never manage one-

handed, she loosened the knots at his wrists. Then she
backed away, sucking her chafed fingers, and motioned him
to rise.

It took him three tries before he managed it. She pointed
toward the lake, made a paddling gesture, and then pointed
downriver. He nodded but continued to stand there even
after she shooed him away. Cocking his head, he whispered
something in his language. Even without the words, it was
not hard to imagine what he was asking.

Why?

*Because I'm a healer. Because I have a son. Because I
don't want another mother to experience this grief, to imagine her waiting for your boat and scanning the faces of the
men as they land, anticipation changing to uncertainty and
then to panic when she finds you're not among them. And
never knowing, through all the years remaining to her, if
you're alive or dead.*

Griane folded her arms as if cradling a baby. Then she
laid one hand over her heart and placed the other on the
boy's chest. His heart thudded wildly beneath her fingers.
He moved suddenly and she stumbled back, safely out of
reach. He shook his head and said something else in his
horrible-sounding language. Then he sketched a spiral on
his chest and bowed very formally. Not knowing what else
to do, she bowed, too. By the time she straightened, he
had vanished.

In giving him his life, she had also given him the opportunity to kill to preserve it. She hoped she had made the
right choice. She hoped that if a woman—a mother—
encountered her son, she would show him the same measure of mercy and kindness. She hoped—she prayed—that
Keirith was still alive.

Keirith, my son, my firstborn, my child.

The first time, Keirith woke to pain.

The throbbing in his head radiated down his neck to his
stiff arms and finally to his wrists. Only then did he realize
they were lashed together and tied to some kind of wooden
beam. He heard the rhythmic creak of paddles from above
and the splash of water against the sides of the boat and

then a soft moan. He lifted his head and discovered Owan lying near him. Chinks of light filtered through the planks, enough to tell him they were lying in the bowels of the boat, but too dim for him to make out the extent of Owan's injuries. He whispered his name, but got no response. After a while, the moaning ceased.

He dreamed of flying with the eagle. All of his kinfolk gathered by the lakeshore to watch. When he soared overhead, they shouted his name over and over to the rhythmic pounding of a drum.

He came awake in joy and bit back a moan when he realized where he was. The light was nearly gone, but the drumming was real—the same rumble he had heard before the boats came out of the mist. Pebbles crunched against the bottom of the boat as it shuddered to a halt.

Tense and alert, he listened to the sounds from above: the tramp of boots, the creak of wood, men calling to each other and laughing. And then silence. A square of gray light appeared and the blinding flare of a torch. A rope ladder was flung into the hole and two men climbed down. He shrank back against the beam when he recognized the Big One and Gap Tooth.

The Big One scowled at him. Then Gap Tooth whispered something that made him smile. The Big One picked up Owan's limp wrist, then flung it down with a sound of disgust. He gestured to Gap Tooth who heaved Owan over his shoulder. Crouching to keep from bumping their heads against the planks, they made their way back to the rope ladder, hauled Owan out of the hole, and slammed the wooden door shut behind them.

Keirith struggled briefly, but only succeeded in pulling the rope tighter. The air was close and dank and smelled of pine resin, but he also caught the faint scent of woodsmoke. The growl of distant thunder proved too rhythmic and regular; he guessed he was hearing the crash of waves against the shore.

The boat must have reached the place where the river emptied into the great sea. Only days earlier, his father had been here for the Gathering. Was he still alive? Had his mam escaped with Faelia and Callie? How many of his kinfolk had been killed? How many others had been stolen?

He struck his head against the beam, allowing fresh pain

to drive away thought. As the pale light faded to darkness, he succumbed to the lulling rhythm of the waves and slept once more.

The third time, he woke to terror.

Hands dragged him from sleep. There seemed to be dozens of them, shoving a piece of cloth into his mouth, fumbling with the rope around his wrists, digging into his armpits to lift him. He kicked and heard a grunt as his foot struck flesh. A fist punched him in the belly and he doubled over, retching dryly into the gag.

He heard whispers. A scratch. A spark flickered and died. Another scratch, another flicker. This time, the spark caught. A light flared, steadied, swayed back and forth. He raised his head. The light swung across the three faces: a gap-toothed smile, a greasy forelock, and the dark, glittering eyes of the Big One.

He flailed uselessly as they forced him onto his hands and knees. Wasn't it enough that they had dragged him from his home? What more could they want?

His forehead was shoved onto the wooden planks. Booted feet kicked his legs apart. Hands seized his thighs and spread them wider. His tunic was flung over his waist. A man spat. Another chuckled. Fingers dug into his naked buttocks.

Keirith screamed.

Chapter 8

THE PROCESSION WAS already making its way to the lakeshore when he and Muina joined it. Darak took his place beside Griane who looked very pale but composed. But when he touched her arm, he could feel tremors coursing through her body. He tightened his grip, but she refused to look at him.

As he passed the birthing hut, he heard Lisula singing the death chant. Gortin could lead the rite of Opening, freeing the spirits of their dead to fly to the Forever Isles, but Lisula's sweet voice would help ease the grief of their kinfolk.

His footsteps faltered when he saw the pyre. It stood nearly chest high and, although narrow, was the length of four huts. He realized why it was so narrow when they began laying the bodies on it. Even the tallest men struggled to accomplish the task with grace and dignity; had the pyre been any wider, they would have had to fling the bodies of their loved ones atop it.

A greasy sheen covered the doeskin garments. Tallow, he realized, smeared on tunics, breeches, and skirts to help the bodies burn. The greenwood at the top of the pyre had been anointed in a similar fashion, while deadwood and brush had been stacked at the bottom where it would burn—please, gods—hot and fast.

Although it was the right and responsibility of the family members to prepare the dead for their final journey, he stepped forward to help. In a tribe as small as theirs, all of the bloodlines were intermingled. And if his hands were a liability, his height and strength gave him an advantage in lifting the bodies into position.

He felt no revulsion when he clutched bony shoulders or a pair of cool, stiff legs, only grief and a sense of shame that they must endure his greasy fingers fumbling with their limbs. And even that faded as he concentrated on maintaining his grip lest the tallow-smeared garments slip through his maimed hands.

In spite of the morning chill, sweat ran down his sides. His arms trembled from the effort of lifting bodies. Surreptitiously, he wiped his palms on his breeches before reaching for Callie's hand. The ceremony would be hard enough for him to witness without the memory of his father's greasy hand clasping his.

Family members stepped forward to lay gifts of food beside their loved ones to strengthen them for their journey. They lay in rows of three, heads nearly touching the shoes of their kinfolk, feet facing southwest so they could follow the sun to the Forever Isles.

The chanting ceased. Gortin circled the pyre sunwise, reciting the names of the dead. Two more had died in the night. No wonder Griane had trembled.

Callie's grip tightened as Gortin approached. Although he had witnessed other rites, Gortin's appearance must still frighten him. The right side of his face was blackened with soot, signifying life's dark passage into death, while the left bore a spiral, painted in blood.

He squeezed Callie's hand and then gripped it so hard that his son whimpered. Out of the corner of his eye, he saw Griane's head snap toward him, but he couldn't take his eyes from Gortin.

In an ordinary rite, the bodies would be left in the Death Hut until scavengers cleaned the flesh from the bones. Always, the Tree-Father retained a finger bone of the deceased, braiding it into his hair before interring the rest of the bones in the tribal cairn. For this morning's ceremony, Gortin wore twenty-three braids, one for each of the dead, just as tradition dictated. At the end of each plait hung a severed finger.

A part of him realized that Gortin probably intended to lay each in the Death Hut, preserving one small part of the rite. But all Darak could see was Morgath sitting cross-legged before him on the parched earth of Chaos, smiling and humming as he braided each of his severed fingers into Yeorna's golden hair.

Sweat drenched him. Bile rose into his throat. He clamped his lips together, choking it down, but even with his eyes closed, Morgath's smiling face remained. He concentrated on controlling his body, on Griane's fingers digging into his forearm. In the end, though, it was his father's words that kept him from shaming himself before his tribe.

"You've fought so hard, son. Don't let him beat you now."

Morgath's face receded, replaced by his father's, his expression stern but sorrowful.

"The scars on your body you'll carry forever. It's the wounds to the spirit and the mind that are harder to heal."

He opened his eyes to find Griane watching him, her thin face pinched with worry. He couldn't manage a smile—she wouldn't have believed it anyway—but he nodded once and saw the taut lines of her face ease a little.

Gortin's voice rose, dispelling Darak's memories. Torch held high, he shouted the final words of the rite: "We have carried Death out of the village."

Together, they intoned the response: "Let it not return to us soon."

Gortin's eye swept the circle gathered around the pyre. "The fire may eat their flesh. The wind may scatter their ashes. But their spirits shall fly on the wings of eagles to the sunlit shores of the Forever Isles."

As he thrust the torch into the pyre, a great wail rose from the women. It crescendoed to a high keening as the brush caught. Some beat their breasts. Others fell to their knees, tearing at their hair. As the frenzy grew, a few began to sway, then to whirl and spin, all the while shrieking their grief. The shaman could open the gateway to the otherworld, but the women's voices would announce the arrival of these new spirits.

Griane and Faelia screamed with the others. Faelia's red hair whipped around her as she danced. Like most of the men, Darak stood in silence. A man was permitted to weep or roar the name of a loved one, but the shrill death-song belonged to the women.

The flames reached higher, embracing the bodies. Hair ignited, shrouding the faces in a blaze that quickly died. Doeskin burned more slowly, the stink of tallow and leather gradually overwhelmed by the appalling stench of burning flesh.

Callie bent over, retching. Darak wiped his mouth with the hem of his tunic. Other parents did the same for their children. Even a few of the adults had to leave the circle, then stumble back to bear witness.

No amount of tallow could speed the flames. The death-song ebbed, choked by grief and smoke. In silence, the tribe watched the pyre collapse. Ashes fell like dirty snow. Darak wiped his mouth with the back of his hand and stared, sickened, at the greasy gray stain. The thick smoke slowly dispersed, revealing the sun high above the trees to the east.

He was surprised to hear Gortin summon the people back to the village. For the first time, he glanced toward the standing stones. "Where is the boy?" he whispered to Griane.

"Escaped."

"What?"

"Last night."

"But that's—"

"Not now."

He'd watched Jurl lash him to the oak. The boy could not have wriggled free.

As they neared the village, his stomach lurched. It was customary to feast after any rite, but the smell of the roasting meat sickened him. What he wanted—and needed—was a drink. Others clearly felt the same; although it was only midmorning, men were passing jugs of brogac and skins of wine.

Urkiat trailed after him as he followed his family into the hut. Faelia rushed to the stone basin and plunged her hands into the water, scrubbing her face, her neck, her arms. One by one, they did the same, cleaning the ashes of the dead from their bodies.

Callie shivered as Griane wiped his face. "I'm sorry," he said. "For getting sick."

"Other folk got sick. Even grown-ups."

"Faelia didn't. You didn't. Fa didn't."

Darak crouched before his son. "I had your hand for strength—and your mam's. Otherwise . . ." He shrugged. "It was hard today. For all of us."

"Try and remember them as they were," Urkiat said. "That helps. A little."

Callie thought a moment. "Tree-Brother Meniad—he was always kind."

"Aye," said Darak. "And remember the stories Trian used to tell? And what a good fisherman Elathar was? And the way Erca's voice carried through the village, no matter how hard you tried to get away from it?"

Callie's eyes went wide and then his lips curved in a smile so much like Tinnean's it made him ache. "Even if you covered your ears."

"Aye. Even then."

"She always knew if you'd done something wrong," Faelia said.

"And never hesitated to tell you," Griane added.

They were all smiling now. Relieved, he got to his feet.

"Callie, take the pot of cheese." Griane's voice was brisk. "Faelia, bring the skin of elderberry wine. I'll put some oatcakes on the fire before I check on the wounded. Urkiat . . ."

"I'll see if the men need any help with the fish traps."

Darak waited until they left. Even then he hesitated, watching Griane knead the melted dripping into the oats. She was the first to break the silence. "You asked about the boy?"

He nodded, relieved to postpone the discussion of his departure.

"Jurl and Rothisar roused the village before dawn. He'd stolen a coracle, but Nionik sent out search parties anyway. Jurl wasn't sure how he got free. He must have loosened the ropes somehow. Apparently, the boy taunted him. When Jurl went over to the tree to teach him to mind his tongue, the boy grabbed his ankle. He fell and hit his head on a rock."

"And Rothisar?"

"Slept through it all. They'd both been drinking."

"How do you know?"

Without looking up, she said, "I was there." Her hands never faltered as they shaped the dough into flat circles.

"Did you free him, Griane?"

This time she did look up. "Aye."

Darak took a deep breath and let it out slowly. "Does anyone suspect?"

"Jurl. But he won't say anything."

"How can you be sure?"

Her smile was mirthless. "Better to be overpowered by a half-grown boy than a woman."

"*You* hit him? Sweet Maker." He rubbed his eyes and finally asked, "Why, Griane?"

She tested the baking stone, frowned, and went back to patting the oatcakes. "I kept thinking how his mother would feel. If her son didn't come home to her."

"He might have attacked you or—"

"Nay." Her hands fell still and she stared into the fire. "He bowed to me. And put his hand over his heart."

Darak stalked to the doorway and back. "You're sure Jurl will keep his mouth shut?"

"Aye." She gnawed at her lip. "Do you hate me?"

"What?"

"For freeing him."

"Nay. They would have torn him apart. I couldn't have stopped it. And I'd . . . I would have hated having the children witness that. Still . . ." He sighed. "Aye. Well. It's done now."

There was something she wasn't telling him, but before he could question her, she said, "I packed. Food, extra clothing." She gave him a weary smile as she laid the oatcakes on the baking stone. "I guessed. When you wanted to question the boy."

"You don't mind?"

"You went to Chaos and back for your brother. You could do no less for our son." Briskly, she dusted meal off her hands. "Ennit will take the children. I'll speak with Sali before we go. Make sure she knows what to do."

It took him a moment to realize what she was saying.

"I need to make up some more decoctions. That will give us a little time with Callie and Faelia."

"Griane . . ."

"I know you want to leave as soon as possible, but for the children's sake—"

He grabbed her by the shoulders and jerked her to her feet. "Listen to me!"

She reared back, her eyes enormous.

"You cannot come."

"I've done all I can for the wounded. And Sali—"

"Sali's an apprentice."

"So was I when I returned from the First Forest!" She shoved past him, breathing hard. "You can't go alone."

"I'm not. Urkiat's coming with me."

"Good gods, Darak, you barely know him."

"He speaks the language. He knows the land."

"There's a darkness in him. A violent streak."

"The raiders wiped out his family. Of course, he's dark-natured. But I need him."

"And not me."

"You know I need you. But our children need you more. A quarter of their kinfolk are dead. Their brother has been stolen. They can't lose both their parents as well. If anything should happen—"

She whirled around and slapped her fingers against his mouth. "Don't say that. Don't even think it."

Obediently, he swallowed his words before they could reach the ears of the gods. Then he took her hand. "The children have lost their brother. Now they're losing me. They need you to keep them strong."

"Ennit . . . or Alada . . ."

"They need you, Griane. You know I'm right."

"And why should you be the one to go? I guided Cuillon back to the grove. I kept him alive. I chose the trail. I marked it for you to follow."

"I know."

"And yet you claim I'm not strong enough or clever enough—"

"I didn't say that."

"Then why must I remain behind?" When he didn't answer, her mouth twisted. "Because I'm a woman."

"Nay."

"And a woman's place is by the hearth. Or grubbing in the fields. That's all we are fit for, isn't it? To bear your children and cook your meals and harvest your crops."

"That's not true."

"Isn't it? A girl isn't permitted to find a vision mate. Or to hunt. If she's lucky, she might become a healer or a priestess, but never a hunter. And yet you teach Faelia, encourage her to dream of becoming the one thing she can never be. What happens when she comes to you to learn to draw a bow and you refuse? How will you explain to her that slings and snares are one thing, but a bow is only for men? Will she thank you for your wisdom and your teaching then?"

"She would have thanked me yesterday when her skill saved your lives!" Angry now, he paced. "What do you want me to say? That it's unfair that women cannot do everything that men can? You're right. It is. It's unfair that a girl doesn't have the same choices as a boy. It's unfair that our son has been stolen, that our kinfolk have been slaughtered. It's unfair that I lost my life-path and can only teach others to do what I can't. Life is unfair, Griane."

Again, he seized her shoulders, staring down into her resentful face. "There is no one—no one—I would rather have guarding my back. If it were only you and me, we would already be gone. It's not because you're a woman, Griane. It's because you're a mother."

Deliberately, he softened his voice. "And that, too, is unfair. But the fact remains that I have a better chance of finding him. I'm stronger than you. A better tracker. And if I can no longer draw a bow, I can use sling and snare to feed myself and a dagger to gut the man who attacks me. I can trade a story for a meal. And when I reach this city where they've taken him, I can wander into places a woman cannot without risking rape or death."

He caught her pointed chin between his thumb and little fingers and tilted it up. "I know what I'm asking. And I know it's not easy. Especially for you. You were never much good at waiting." He gave her a bleak smile. "I need to know that you're here. Watching over our children, keeping our tribe strong. I need you guarding my back."

Although he was desperate to leave, he knew his limits. He'd slept little in the last two nights, had eaten even less. He took his leave of Nionik and Sanok, asked Elathar's oldest boy for the loan of two coracles, asked Ennit to look after his family. He sat beside Duba and promised he would search for Owan, but she just stared at him as if his words made no sense. Then he made his way to the birthing hut. Standing outside, he told Lisula his plans and asked for her blessing.

He heard the low murmur of voices from within and then Muina emerged. "Since you cannot look upon Lisula or touch her, I will help perform the rite."

Lisula spoke the words, while Muina sketched the signs of protection on his forehead and over his heart. "May the wind be at your back and the sun upon your shoulders. May the moon chase away the darkness and the stars guide your feet. May your path be smooth, your journey swift, and your homecoming joyous."

Muina pulled his head down. "The blessing of the gods upon you." She pressed a kiss to his forehead. "The blessing of the Oak and the Holly upon you." Her lips brushed one cheek, then the other. "The blessing of your Grain-Mother. And your Grain-Grandmother." Hands cupping his face, she kissed him twice on the mouth. Finally, she folded his hands between hers. "It's the strength of your spirit that will carry you on this journey, not the strength of these hands. Remember that, boy. And hurry back to us."

He returned to his hut and found Urkiat silently chipping the flint of his dagger to a sharper edge. Griane and the children crouched near the fire pit, their heads close together. His eyes widened when he saw the pile of supplies.

Everyone in the village must have contributed: arrowheads and sinew, bone hooks and fishing line, stone bowls and turtle shells, a bag of oatmeal, a coiled braid of nettle rope, and most valuable of all, a bundle of furs to trade. With shaking hands, he unwrapped doeskin packets containing strips of dried venison, smoked salmon, and suetcakes.

Had Ennit passed the word? Or Nionik? Or had they all realized from the beginning that he would go after his boy?

Carefully, Darak rewrapped the food and packed the supplies into the bag that had once carried his hunting gear. The children helped him make up fire bundles to carry embers from one camp to the next. He talked quietly to them as they worked, explaining the route he and Urkiat

would take, their hope of staying with other tribes for the
first part of the journey. Much of it he simply made up;
even Urkiat didn't know how many villages remained along
the coast.

Callie stuffed flints, tinder, and straw into the small belt
pouch. Faelia wrapped his firestick in his extra tunic. As
he added it to his bag, he heard a choked sound and looked
up to find Griane holding Keirith's folded mantle. Tenderly, he took it from her and laid it beside his hunting bag.

Then he took his children's hands and led them outside.
He sang with his kinfolk, adding his memories to theirs,
sharing laughter and tears and stories as the afternoon
waned. By the time the sun was gone, most of the men
were drunk and a few of the women as well. Tired beyond
words, he let Griane lead him back to the hut.

He kissed the children, told them he and Urkiat would
be up before dawn so they must say their good-byes now.
Faelia threw her arms around him, her face fierce despite
the tears. Callie promised to be good. He tucked them in
and sat beside them until they slept. Then he stripped off
his clothes and crawled under the wolfskins next to Griane.
Urkiat had not returned; Darak wondered if he had chosen
to sleep elsewhere to allow him time alone with his family
or if he had sought comfort in a stranger's arms.

Griane had hardly spoken to him since their argument.
He wanted her badly, needed her even more, but feared
she would turn away. He knew his refusal had wounded
her; even if she understood his reasons, he wondered if she
would forgive him.

He was groping for her hand when she rolled toward
him. They came together, fierce and wild and silent. It was
over in moments, Griane biting down hard on his shoulder
at the last to stifle her cry, while he shook in her arms,
tasting the blood from his bitten lip. Only then, need satisfied and punishment exacted for the hurts each had inflicted
on the other, could they come together again, hands and
mouths and bodies seeking forgiveness and forgetfulness,
promising that this parting would be temporary, that this
joining was not the last.

It was still dark when he abandoned the warmth of the
wolfskins and his wife's body to dress and gather his supplies. He held back the bearskin just enough to admit the

faint half-light that heralded the dawn, just enough to make
out the sleeping forms of his family. He watched them a
long while, imprinting the moment on his memory. Then
he slipped outside and found Urkiat waiting.

His last quest had begun in the darkness of a winter night.
As they made their way to the lake, the first streaks of
violet and rose tinted the sky to the east. A promise of
dawn, of a new day, of hope.

Darak looked back only once, just before his coracle entered the channel. His heart thudded unevenly when he
saw the three figures standing at the water's edge. He raised
his paddle, but he never knew if they saw him. He wasn't
even sure if they were real or if their beloved forms had
been conjured by the desire in his heart and the sun in his
eyes and the tears blurring his vision.

PART TWO

By these signs shall you know him:
His power shall burn bright as Heart of Sky at
  Midsummer.
His footsteps shall make Womb of Earth tremble.
Speechless, he shall understand the language of the
  adder,
And wingless, soar through the sky like the eagle.

No pageantry shall attend his arrival.
No poet shall sing his name.
No mortal woman shall know his body.
No mortal man shall call him son.

Hail the Son of Zhe, the fire-haired god made flesh.
Welcome him with reverence and with dread,
For with him comes the new age.

Zherosi Prophecy

Chapter 9

THE STENCH WAS A living presence, as real as any captive. A reek of sweat and vomit and piss and shit so overpowering that Keirith could taste it, could feel it burning his eyes, staining his lungs, poisoning his skin. All the scrubbing in the world could never clean this boat; the very air reeked of misery and hopelessness.

But the confinement was even worse. Shoulders rubbed against his, bare thighs brushed his legs, elbows dug into his ribs. Even the gentlest touch made him flinch, recalling the terror of those unseen hands that had seized him in the dark.

The first day, the constant pitch of the boat made everyone sick and there were always hands, some light as butterfly wings, others impatient, all groping their way toward the small open space at the far end of the hole that served as a slop area. Those who were too sick to move simply fouled the planks—and the people—around them.

They measured the passing of time by the opening of the door above them. Morning and evening, the raiders tossed down skins of lukewarm water and sacks of food. Keirith choked down the hard flatbread, but the saltiness of the dried meat only made him more desperate for water.

The raiders had moved him to this boat the morning after the rape. He'd made a feeble attempt to escape, but after one lurching step, the halter around his neck jerked him to his knees. After that, he'd splashed through the shallows after his captor, obedient as a bullock about to be slaughtered.

Numbly, he'd observed details: the salty semen stink of the tide pools; the cold water burning every scrape and cut on his body; the man floating facedown in the water, gray hair rippling like lakeweed. And the red-haired men and boys being herded toward two of the boats.

After the worst of the seasickness passed, his fellow captives spent much time discussing that.

"It might mean we'll be given special treatment," someone speculated.

"It might mean we'll be sacrificed," another muttered.

"They cut down the forests for their fields," a voice intoned. "They dug stone out of the earth for their altars. They stole the children of The People to sacrifice to their gods."

"Shut up!"

Only those sitting closest had names. By the second day, he'd come to recognize Sinand's whimpers and Roini's muttered curses. Brudien was the voice of calm; Temet, the voice of reason; Dror, the incessant whisper of vengeance.

Although Keirith dreamed of revenge and escape, he grew impatient with Dror's plotting. They were unarmed, weak from lack of food, and sick from the rough seas. How could they ever overpower their captors? The raiders never entered the hole. They never allowed them to leave it. And when they beached the boat at night, they left guards on board.

Like dogs worrying a bone, the captives spent part of every day sharing stories of the raids on their villages. No one, it seemed, had any warning.

"Normally, our currachs would have been out to sea," Brudien said. "We could have spotted their boats. But we were still cleaning up after the Gathering. How could they have known that?"

Roini cursed. "The traders. They'd sell their mothers if there was profit in it."

"Or one of the southern tribes." That had to be Dror. When he wasn't plotting escape, he was assigning blame, whether to the neighbor who elbowed him or the chiefs who had failed to take the threat of the raiders seriously.

Talk of home always ended in muffled tears or frightened speculations about the fate awaiting them. The hopeful predicted slavery, the gloomy, death, but the doomsayers spoke only in whispers lest they frighten the others.

Keirith tried to shut out the voices. He didn't want to share their pain or their memories; he had enough of his own.

In every village, the reek of decaying bodies and clouds of black birds atop the Death Huts gave mute testimony to disaster. In every longhut, survivors told Darak the same tale: families awakened before dawn by raiders storming into their huts; men and women clubbed and dragged to the boats, others snared with nets as they stumbled from their homes. A few managed to slip away in the darkness, their freedom bought with the lives of the men and women who fought back. Once any resistance was crushed, the raiders looted what they could and left, their departure accompanied by the wails of those either too young or too old to be considered valuable as slaves.

Keirith's warning had spared them from that fate. Their death toll was higher, but perhaps a swift death was better than a life of slavery. It was certainly better than death upon a Zherosi altar.

When their coracles scraped ashore, the hollow-eyed inhabitants straggled down to greet them; even tragedy could not dispel the ancient tradition of hospitality. They shared dried fish, dried venison, stale oatcakes—whatever the raiders had overlooked. Invariably, their hosts apologized for the meager fare. If the great Darak Spirit-Hunter and his friend would remain another day, they would slaughter a sheep and feast him as he deserved. Always, Darak thanked them and declined.

When they heard his mission, the men shook their heads, but after the meal, the women surrounded him, timid hands plucking at his sleeves.

"Please, Memory-Keeper. If you should see my Sinand—he's thirteen, but small for his age, with bright red hair . . ."

"They took my husband, Memory-Keeper. Varon. You'll know him by the scar on his chin . . ."

"My daughter Urna. She's three moons gone with child, Memory-Keeper, and she hasn't been well . . ."

"My sister Larina . . ."

"My brother Bosath . . ."

On and on it went, the litany of the lost. Darak repeated each name, the weight upon his spirit growing. Urkiat suggested they simply paddle past the villages, but he refused. He might have accepted the position of Memory-Keeper reluctantly, but he had fulfilled his duties: committing the bloodlines of his tribe to memory, teaching the children the legends and songs of their people, sharing those same legends and songs at the rites. But he also had the responsibility of carrying news—good and ill—to and from the Gatherings.

This year, he'd never gotten the chance to tell Erca about her new grandson or comfort Barima with the news that her mam had gotten over the cough that always plagued her around the Freshening. And although he had brought the tale of Rordi's first tooth and Mela's first moon blood to their grandparents before he left, the old couples were too shattered by the deaths in their families to do more than nod.

He had left his village with only one goal: to bring his son home. But he could not ignore the anguish of the other parents who had lost children or waited anxiously for news of a daughter who had married into another tribe. The living deserved to know the truth and the lost deserved to be mourned.

Sinand. Varon. Urna. Larina. Bosath. Owan. Keirith.

Each night, they pursued him in dreams. Some nights, it was only formless hands pushing him down. Other nights, it was the Big One's mocking smile and the faint whiff of sour wine on his breath as he crouched there, holding his wrists, while the others took their turns. The remembered agony of that first brutal penetration always catapulted him to wakefulness, but other dreams stretched out endlessly, filled with rhythmic animal grunts, the frenzied slap of flesh on flesh, the warm ooze of blood and semen down his thighs, and always, the soft chuckles that mingled with his muffled screams.

Each night, Keirith jolted awake, terrified he had made some sound that would reveal his secret to the others. On the fourth night, he awoke with the Big One's hands on his shoulders and shrank back, flailing.

"Hush," Brudien whispered. "It's all right. No one will hurt you."

Shame flooded him. He pushed the gentle hands away, hating himself for crying out, hating Brudien for hearing him.

Darak gazed at the promontory overlooking the mouth of the river. A sennight ago, he had deliberated with the chiefs on trade agreements and intertribal grievances. The beach below had teemed with visitors haggling with traders, cheering on those participating in contests of archery, wrestling, and footraces, sharing food and songs come the evening. Now it teemed with carrion eaters.

They had hoped to exchange their coracles for one of the village's fishing boats, but every currach was hacked to pieces. Even with the help of the survivors, Urkiat guessed it would take three days to build the skeleton, cover it with hides, and seal the seams with pine resin. And even then, he refused to vouch for its seaworthiness. Darak argued for going on in the coracles, but bowed to Urkiat's emphatic assertion that the little boats would capsize in the rough surf.

So the next morning, they shouldered their packs and headed south on foot. Girn's village was only a few days' walk. If it was still standing. Darak refused to believe the raiders had attacked every village along the coast, but he had never imagined the massive scale of destruction he had already seen. Even Urkiat, who had lived under the threat of the raiders for years, was shocked.

Everything Darak had known—or thought he'd known—about the raiders had been proven false. The southern chiefs had always claimed the attacks were haphazard, one village plundered while another a scant ten miles away escaped harm. Although a few reported raids during the spring

and early summer, the vast majority came after the harvest
was in.

But the last years had seen fewer and fewer southern chiefs
at the Gatherings and they only ventured north in the
spring. Those from the far south had not attended in more
than five years. How could he have been so blind as to
believe it would never happen to his folk?

"Why now?" he asked Urkiat as they picked their way
along a stream bank, looking for a place to ford. "Why in
force? Just because they needed . . . sacrifices?"

"Likely, they needed slaves to work in their fields, too.
And their mines."

"Mines?"

"Great pits they gouge in the earth where they dig for
copper or tin. They need those to make bronze."

He plied Urkiat with questions, but it had been four
years since the raiders had destroyed his village. Since then,
he'd been living inland with a small group of survivors from
various coastal tribes. They'd been so shattered by the loss
of their kinfolk and homes that only this year had they
dared send someone north to tell their story at the
Gathering.

If only we had listened. If only we had acted at once.

"Why not try and exact tribute from us?" Darak asked.
"As they did your folk."

"That was only after they'd attacked us and we were
too weak to fight anymore." Urkiat's expression darkened.
Darak knew he hated to talk about what had happened,
but he needed information.

"So they'll come back."

"They always come back," Urkiat replied. "Sooner or
later."

Although Urkiat's facility at learning their tongue had
encouraged the raiders to use him as an interpreter, he
knew little about the land they came from. He could only
repeat the tales told by the other survivors in his village,
and pass along the scraps of information they'd gleaned
during their visits to the coast to trade pelts for grain.

The afternoon was waning when the reek of decay reached
them. They discovered the first body as they emerged from
the trees—an old woman lying facedown with three arrows
protruding from her back. Eight more bodies lay tangled

together at the water's edge. Crows rose up in a squawking black cloud as they approached.

Most of them were young, little more than Faelia's age. Although the birds and crabs had been busy, it was clear their skulls had been crushed. When he spied the red hair, he fell to his knees.

"Thirteen, but small for his age, with bright red hair."

But when he turned the body over, he discovered it was not Sinand, but Owan. A tiny crab scuttled out of the boy's open mouth. With an oath, Darak flung it away.

"Is it the boy from your village?"

"Aye." He brushed the wet sand from the beardless cheeks. "Why club them to death? Could they have tried to escape?"

"They probably died on the voyage downriver. I'm surprised there aren't more, given how many captives they took."

Darak folded Owan's hands across his chest and made the other bodies decent. And all the while, the guilty thought echoed in his mind: thank the Maker it isn't Keirith.

He rose to find Urkiat examining the deep furrows that gouged the beach from waterline to grass. "From their ships. A dozen of them, at least. They must have beached them here."

But Darak was already walking toward the fire pits. The bones of roasted sheep lay among the ashes. His gaze drifted from the charred logs to the forest. Even from this distance, he could see the fallen trees, the heartwood of the stumps raw and pale.

Urkiat crouched beside a fire pit, sifting through the ashes. "Four days old at least," he said, wiping his fingers on his breeches.

Numbly, Darak walked toward the forest, passing scattered fragments of lives: a woman's shoe, a torn strip of doeskin, a tooth crusted with dried blood. The trees lay in miserable heaps, delicate branches of birch peeping out from the ancient oaks. Jagged shards, still bleeding sap, reared up from the scarred trunks. They hadn't bothered chopping them into logs, simply sheared off the limbs to use as fuel.

The sacrilege was even more appalling than the sheer waste. Dozens of saplings had been felled along with five older trees, the spirits that had dwelled within murdered as brutally as the children on the beach. If the raiders had so little regard for life, how would Keirith ever survive?

"We'd best get moving," Urkiat said.

"We have to gather the bodies and build a cairn."

"The light will be gone by the time we finish."

"We can't just leave them."

After a moment, Urkiat shrugged.

Darak swept his arm across the beach. "Doesn't this affect you at all?"

Urkiat's expression hardened. "Aye, Memory-Keeper. But I've seen it all before."

Keirith came to hate Brudien's voice, always so calm, always so hopeful, forever singing the old songs, forever telling the old tales. Forcing him to remember his home, his family. Reawakening the fears that they might have been hurt or killed.

When Brudien sang the song of farewell, hot tears prickled in Keirith's eyes. Every autumn at the full Goose Moon, his father sang it to honor their ancestors' long journey north, fleeing the invaders who had driven them from their homeland.

He blinked back the tears, but he could not suppress the memories. Memories of days in the forest, drinking in the lessons his father taught. Any child, his father claimed, can observe something in the forest simply by using his eyes, his ears, his nose. A hunter augmented those senses with his skill with bow and arrow, sling and snare. A great hunter not only understood his prey's habits and feeding patterns, but learned to anticipate their reactions. A great hunter remembered.

Keirith took strength from those early lessons. He promised himself to watch his enemies. Observe their behavior. Remember any detail that might help him stay alive.

Each time Brudien sang the song of farewell, more voices joined in. "The Oak and the Holly are with us," the song promised, but Keirith knew better. The gods hadn't saved his people during the Long Winter and they couldn't save him now. He couldn't trust them any more than he could trust these strangers. If they found out what the raiders had done to him, they would scorn him. If they discovered his gift, they would revile him.

The Oak and the Holly weren't with him. He was alone.

Chapter 10

SOMETIME IN THE MIDDLE of the sixth day, Keirith heard a flurry of activity from above. Instead of the inevitable scrape of pebbles, the boat thudded against something and settled into a gentle rocking. Anxious speculation gave way to silence as the door swung open. The dark form of a raider stood silhouetted against brilliant light. He flung the rope ladder into the hole, drawing startled curses from those below.

For a long moment, no one moved. Finally, Brudien spoke. "We are the children of the Oak and the Holly. Like them, we know what it is to fight and suffer defeat. And like them, we will remain strong to fight again—if we have the courage to face the coming days."

A few murmured assent, but one man shouted, "The coming days will bring death. Better to fight now."

"Against armed men?" Brudien shouted back. "Twice our number?"

"Should we go forth like sheep to the slaughter?" Dror demanded.

"Nay! Like proud men. Let them see our strength and wonder at it."

Bent almost double because of his height, Brudien edged through the closely-packed bodies and seized the rope ladder. People muttered prayers of protection as he climbed up. Then Dror pushed forward. "If there's a chance to make a break, I'll shout. When I do, take out the nearest guard."

"Good gods," Temet said with weary disgust. "Half of us can barely walk, never mind 'take out the nearest guard.'"

"And where would we run?" someone cried.

"Make for the forest," Dror replied.

Weak from the days of confinement, Keirith's legs betrayed him, and he had to let the raiders pull him out of the hole. The heat made him gasp; if the air smelled better, it was just as stifling. A raider bound his wrists. Another looped a rope around his neck, tethering him to Temet. A shove sent him stumbling forward.

Images formed before his dazzled eyes: sunlight striking sparks on the blue-green water; a treeless cliff silhouetted against the sun-bleached sky. Below him, a long tongue of stone rose nearly as high as the side of the boat; the line of captives trudged down it toward a beach of white sand. Fishing nets lay stretched like giant spiderwebs across the snowy expanse. Beyond it, clusters of people shouted and waved. Some of the raiders called out greetings in return. Of course, they must have families. Families who greeted their homecoming with the same joy and excitement his folk displayed when a loved one returned from a Gathering.

Make for the forest, Dror had said. But there was only a sprawling mass of white buildings marching up the side of a hill, row upon row of small, square houses that reflected the merciless sun back into his eyes. In the distance, a dark crag thrust out from the hills, its peak obscured by a haze of yellowish dust or smoke. On its slopes, Keirith made out a few patches of green. There was Dror's forest, those pitiful clumps of trees.

A shout saved him from tripping as the stone tongue gave way to sand.

Watch, Keirith. Watch. Observe. Remember.

Bare-chested men with whips and clubs. The snap of a whip when a captive faltered. Snowy sand sifting through his toes like hot ash.

The world blurred, then re-formed to show him heads bobbing up and down along the line as captives hopped from foot to foot to escape the burning sand. One of the raiders mimicked them, drawing roars of laughter from his comrades.

Keirith kept a wary eye on the raiders hurrying toward their loved ones, but he couldn't see the Big One. Did he have a wife? Would she rush forward to fling herself into his arms? Would she hurry him home, eager for the touch of those calloused hands, the thick fingers knotted in her hair, pushing her down, shoving her skirts up . . .

Stop it stop it stop it!

He forced himself to breathe, sucking in deep gulps of the hot air. When the black dots cleared from his vision, he spied a pathway of smooth stone and sighed with relief as he left the burning sand behind.

The path twisted between rows of buildings too low to provide shade from the midday sun. He heard snatches of muffled conversation from within. More tantalizing were the smells: frying fish, roasting meat, and spicy scents he couldn't identify. Saliva filled his dry mouth and he swallowed it gratefully.

Steps led them past more houses that clung to the slope of the hill as if they might tumble off. Those at the top rose up two or three times a man's height, offering brief patches of shade.

Up ahead, a man shouted. Answering shouts echoed down the line as a man lurched away from the other captives. Good gods, was it Dror? Where did he think he could go?

Whips cracked. Clubs rose and fell. A boy screamed. He saw guards dragging someone away. And then the line began moving again.

He stepped in something wet. Blood, he realized, when he saw the trail of red footprints. They grew steadily fainter as the procession approached another set of steps, steeper than the first. By the time he reached the top, he was panting. His head ached. His legs quivered. The sweat oozing down his sides evaporated before it could even dampen the waist of his breeches. If it was this hot now, what must it be like at Midsummer?

He heard the clamor of contending voices before he saw the open square. Small knots of people lingered before wooden stalls. Women hurried past, clutching baskets brimming with vegetables he couldn't even recognize. Few bothered to give the captives more than a cursory glance, although one or two pulled their children back.

It must be some kind of market, he thought dully.

As the procession wound its relentless way upward, the

world narrowed to the gray stones before him and Temet's grimy heels, rising and falling in a slow but ceaseless rhythm. Only when he felt the sun beating down on him again did he look up. The guards led them up another flight of steps toward an enormous building. Gods, they could put ten villages inside it. Giant pillars, tall as pines, marched along the path, but the line veered away toward a section of the building that jutted out. Craning his neck, he saw two wooden gates swing open in the wall.

When he passed through, he found himself in yet another open area. Instead of stalls, this one had flimsy shelters lining the walls. He glimpsed fair skin and dark, red hair and black, but before he could guess at the number of captives, the guards brandished their whips and herded his group forward.

He had thought they were all roped together. Now he realized they were tethered in small groups. Just so they could fall into the neat lines their captors required.

Some forty or fifty other newcomers had already been arrayed in the center of the compound. Nearly all were men and most had red hair. He wondered why there were so few; he'd seen ten or twelve boats at the mouth of the river. Had the other raids failed or did those boats have different destinations?

He tried to think, to remember, but he was so tired. He heard moans around him, voices begging for water. A shout silenced them.

Four men in loincloths trudged through the gates, clutching the ends of two long wooden poles that supported a box big enough for three men to lie in. Sweat streaked the bearers' naked chests and the muscles in their straining arms. Grunting, they carefully lowered the box to the ground. Two open-toed shoes thrust through the bright blue fabric on the side of box. Beringed hands reached out. Two of the bearers seized them and pulled.

A heavyset man emerged, clad in baggy knee-length breeches. Bracelets decorated his arms and a bronze collar adorned his neck. A man hurried forward to greet him. He was dressed in the same odd half-breeches, but his only adornment was a sheathed sword belted around his waist. Three boys trotted behind him. One unfolded a small stool.

Another proffered a cup. A third waited until the heavyset man seated himself before holding up a short pole topped by a fringed canopy that shaded the man from the sun.

Keirith didn't even realize another man had emerged from the box until he began speaking. "Slaves of the barbarian north. You are blessed to have come to Pilozhat, holy city of the Zherosi."

He spoke the tribal tongue with an odd guttural slur, but the word "slaves" was clear enough. And now his enemies had a name: Zherosi.

"You live to serve the pleasure of the gods and the pleasure of the Jhef d'Esqi—the Slave Master." He gestured to the heavyset man. "A few of you will be selected to serve in the great houses. The rest go to our temples. It is an honor to be chosen for such service. Others must toil in the fields or in the mines."

Keirith had no idea what mines were, but it might explain where the rest of the captives had been taken.

"If you obey, you will be treated well. If you disobey, you will be punished. The punishment for the first act of insubordination is the loss of a day's water. The punishment for the second act of insubordination is the loss of a day's food. The punishment for the third act of insubordination is ten lashes." The litany of punishments rolled on, climaxing with, "The punishment for attempted escape is death."

No one spoke. No one moved. Keirith hardly dared to breathe. Who knew what these people would consider insubordination?

The Slave Master heaved himself up from his stool and slowly walked between the lines of captives. Each time he pointed, the captive was untethered and led off to the side. Keirith's heart pounded when the Slave Master paused in front of him, but after a moment, the man moved on. At the end of the inspection, seventeen people—mostly girls and boys—had been chosen.

The Slave Master climbed back into his box, while the Speaker said, "Now you will clean yourselves. You will drink. You will eat. You will rest. When Heart of Sky descends, you will be inspected by the Jhef d'Esqi and the Jhevi of the great houses."

The welter of strange names and titles immediately fled his mind with the promise of water. Impatiently, he waited for the Slave Master to take his leave, and licked his dry lips when he spied guards trotting forward with buckets and long wooden dippers. The other guards edged closer, whips and clubs at the ready, as the water bearers moved between the lines of captives. The man in front of him elbowed his neighbor aside and grabbed for the dipper. A club crashed down on his hands and he cried out, dragging those roped to him to their knees as he fell. The guards jerked him to his feet, cut him free, and dragged him over to a wooden stake. Ignoring his pleas, they tied his hands to the stake and returned to the lines.

After that, no one attempted to take water out of turn. Keirith watched the bearer in an agony of anticipation, cursing him for giving each captive two drinks, cursing each captive for taking so long. When his turn came, he seized the dipper with trembling hands and swallowed the luke-warm water in three gulps. Licking his dripping fingers and lips, he waited for the guard to raise the dipper again. Too soon, he moved on. Keirith could only watch as the precious water dribbled down Roini's stubbled chin.

To his amazement, the guards then handed out bulging waterskins to each of them. Keirith drained almost half the skin before Temet whispered, "Save some for later. This may be all we get today." Reluctantly, he lowered the skin, nodding his thanks. But why go through the ritual of the buckets and the dippers if they intended giving each person a skin of water? Then he glanced at the man tied to the stake: they had just been given their first lesson in obedience.

His mouth tasted sour. He wondered if it was the aftertaste of the water or the lesson.

The guards herded a group of captives toward two wooden troughs. Keirith's stomach lurched when they began to strip off their clothing. Were there marks on his body? Scratches or bruises that would testify to the rape?

When his turn came, he kept his back to the trough as he shed his tunic. He accepted a dirty round of soap from Temet and picked up one of the scraps of cloth dangling from the edge of the trough. The rough fabric abraded his skin, but it was a relief to wash some of the filth away. If only he could scour away the memories as easily.

Boys in loincloths trotted forward with new clothes. Their

noses wrinkled with disgust as they picked up discarded tunics and breeches. After some experimentation, Keirith figured out how to wind the long strip of wool around his hips and through his legs, tucking one end in at his waist.

He followed the others to a long slab of wood supported by two crosspieces. Here, a guard handed each person a bowl and another ladled soup into it—fish soup, by the smell. He gulped it down where he stood. After a moment's hesitation, he followed Temet to one of the canopied shelters that lined the walls of the compound. One man raised himself on his elbow, but the others dozed, oblivious to the newcomers. Keirith seated himself at the far corner of the shelter. He would rather endure the sun's glare than another night of bodies brushing against him.

To his dismay, Brudien walked toward him, one arm around Sinand's shoulder. Carefully balancing his bowl, Brudien helped Sinand sit and coaxed him to eat. Sinand just curled up on the ground. Brudien sighed and nodded to the man propped up on his elbow. "I am Brudien, Memory-Keeper of the Holly Tribe."

"Soriak."

"You're a child of the Oak and Holly, too?"

"Oh, aye."

"How long have you been here?"

Soriak shrugged. "Half a moon. Or so."

"How many others were taken with you?"

"Not so many as that." His gaze drifted to the line at the feeding station.

"Where are they now?"

Again, Soriak shrugged. "Gone. Mostly."

"To the great houses? And the temples?"

"It's only the young, pretty ones who go to the houses."

When Soriak turned that sleepy smile on him, Keirith felt heat rise into his cheeks. He glanced at the group selected by the Slave Master; they huddled together under one of the shelters near the gate.

"What about the others?" Brudien asked. Soriak gave a languid wave and flopped down on the hard-baked earth. Brudien shook his shoulder, his voice sharp. "Soriak. Where do the others go?"

"Big gates. Little door. Pretty ones out the gates. Other ones out the door."

"Where does the door lead?"

"Not the ones with red hair."

"What happens to them? Soriak!"

Roini cursed and spat. "He's drugged. Or bespelled. They want to keep us docile. If we're going to make a break for it, it'll have to be soon. Else we'll all end up like him."

His comment sparked renewed discussion about escape, but for every man like Roini who favored action, there was another who cited Dror's foolhardy attempt. No one had seen him after the guards had dragged him off, but everyone suspected he was dead.

Keirith fell asleep to the drone of men's voices and dreamed of cool rain and the rumble of thunder. When he awoke, the sun hung atop the western wall of the compound and all of the men were sleeping; even the guards on the walls seemed content to doze, heads drooping, bows held loosely in their laps.

The headache that had plagued him since his arrival had become a persistent throb. The equally persistent howling of dogs only made it worse. His bag of charms seemed like a great weight around his neck. All he could do was lie on his side watching the ants marching past his nose. They streamed across the compound in long lines; in Pilozhat, even the ants were orderly.

Shouts roused them. The gates slowly creaked open under the combined efforts of eight guards. A line of curtained boxes swayed into the compound, stopping before a large canopied shelter the guards must have erected while he slept. Men emerged, as richly adorned as the Slave Master. As they settled themselves on brightly colored cushions, boys trotted forward with jugs and platters of food. The smells made Keirith's mouth water.

Two guards pulled a girl forward. An animated discussion followed, the voices of the five Jhevi—for surely that was who they were—as shrill as women. They punctuated their arguments with groans and shouts and dramatic shaking of fists. When the voices fell silent, the Slave Master clapped his hands twice and the Speaker scratched something on a clay tablet. The girl was shoved to one side and, after the Jhevi paused for meat and drink, the process began again.

The sun sank below the wall while they haggled. Lightheaded from hunger and heat, Keirith watched and hated them: their clacking speech and callous laughter, the jewels on their greasy fingers and the bracelets clattering on their wrists, the oily sheen of their black hair and the pretty cushions beneath their pampered arses, and their utter and appalling disregard for the starving captives who watched every bite, every sip with mingled torment and longing.

Finally, it was over. The Jhevi crawled into their boxes. Their chosen captives lined up behind them. The gates creaked open.

A shout from a neighboring shelter made the Slave Master freeze. The guards on the walls drew their bows. Those in the compound hefted their clubs. Instead of a mass attack, a lone man leaped up and staggered out of his shelter. As the guards moved in, more men poured out from under the canopy, knocking over slower comrades crawling on their hands and knees. One man untied his bulky loincloth and swatted the ground with it. He looked so silly that Keirith laughed.

He was still laughing when someone seized his arm and yanked him to his feet. Temet pushed him out of the shelter. Sinand screamed. Roini shoved past, screaming even louder.

The snakes seemed to come from everywhere, wriggling out of the walls, slithering across the parched earth, slipping over the legs of men who blinked sleepily at the commotion. Keirith backed away, stumbling in his haste. In horrified fascination, he watched the snakes converge on him.

He bumped up against the serving table. Heedless of the greasy platters, he hopped onto it, drawing his feet up in the air. The snakes streamed past. They were adders, he realized, with the same distinctive markings as Natha.

Only then did he remember the rest of his dream, when the rain and the clouds gave way to bands of shimmering blue lights. They arced across the sky like rainbows, then spiraled in on themselves and slithered earthward, hissing his name with Natha's voice.

Mercifully, none of these adders hissed his name. They simply slithered past the screeching Jhevi, and through the open gates.

For a moment, guards and captives alike simply stood there, staring after the adders. The last screams faded. Even the howling of the dogs ceased. As if by magic, his headache vanished as well. He experienced a moment of pure relief. And then the screaming began again.

Not the voices of frightened men and women, but howls, bleats, squeals, squawks. As if every animal in the world were crying out in terror. Instinctively, Keirith covered his ears, although he knew that he couldn't shut out the sounds, that it was the spirits of the birds and beasts screaming inside of him. He tried to block them out, but there were too many. Their terror lanced through him, ripping him open until he was screaming, too, begging them to stop, begging the gods to silence them, please, Maker, stop the screaming.

The earth rumbled like the thunder in his dream. The table shuddered beneath him, rattling the bronze platters. A clay jug danced off the edge and shattered. The wine spread like a bloodstain and the greedy earth sucked it up. Ladders tilted off the walls and clattered to the ground. The poles of the shelters swayed like saplings in a storm. Captives staggered drunkenly and fell to their knees. The guards planted their feet, bracing themselves. Human shock mingled with animal terror, crashing over him in ceaseless waves.

And then, as suddenly as it had begun, it was over. The shaking of the earth, the rattling of the platters, the screaming of the animals—it all just stopped. The terror of the men and women in the compound faded more slowly, vibrating inside of him until it was no louder than the drone of bees.

He didn't know when he had fallen. He was only aware of dusty earth beneath his cheek and dusty toes in front of his face. A voice spoke, but he closed his eyes, too exhausted to respond. Water splashed his face. He licked his lips greedily. His eyes fluttered open, but instead of Temet or Roini or Brudien, he looked up into the flat black eyes of the Slave Master.

The Speaker's face loomed into view. "Why did you scream?"

Keirith shook his head, then gasped as a whip stung his legs.

"Why did you scream?"

"The earth. It was shaking—"

"You screamed before the earth shook. Why?"

"The snakes . . ."

"You screamed after the snakes fled. Why?"

"Please . . ."

"Why did you say the animals were screaming?"

"The dogs. I heard the dogs."

Again and again, the same questions and then the pause while the Speaker translated his answers. And throughout it all, the Slave Master's eyes never left him.

"Which animals screamed?"

"All of them!"

"If you lie, you will be punished."

"Punish me, then! Just leave me alone!"

Keirith let the guards pull him to his feet; he was too tired to struggle. Then he realized they weren't taking him to the stake; they were marching him toward the little door.

Terror gave him the strength to break away. He could see guards closing in, but still he ran, knowing he could never reach the gates before the arrows cut him down, not even caring if they did, for at least he would be free of the heat and the pain and the shaking earth and the screaming animals and the Big One pursuing him in his dreams.

But the arrows never came. Instead, something snared his ankles. The breath whooshed out of him as he hit the ground. The last thing he heard amid the babble of strange voices was someone shouting his name.

Chapter 11

THEY DROPPED THEIR packs in the lee of two large boulders. A storm had blown through that afternoon, drenching them, and the wind had turned colder. Darak sent Urkiat to collect deadwood and dug his firestick out. His palms were still raw from four days of paddling, but he'd always found the ritual of making fire strangely soothing. He was kneeling before the fireboard, ash rod cradled between his stiff palms, when he heard Urkiat's shout.

Grabbing his spear, he raced toward the trees, but his footsteps slowed when Urkiat appeared, smiling.

"What is it?" he asked.

"An old acquaintance."

The raider lay in a thicket near the base of a rocky outcrop. He must have dragged himself there after he'd fallen. The Maker only knew how he'd managed it with two broken legs. The right was twisted at a grotesque angle. The left was even worse. A white shard of shinbone protruded through a rent in his baggy breeches. His beardless face was deathly pale beneath the dirt, but when Darak crouched beside him and pressed his thumb to the boy's wrist, he felt a faint, irregular pulse.

"Sweet Maker, he's still alive."

"Not for long."

He'd probably lain here a night and a day. Even with a healer's care, he wouldn't survive.

Darak folded the cold hand with its hideously swollen fingers over the boy's chest and rose. When Urkiat unsheathed his dagger, he said, "He's beyond pain. And blood will only attract predators."

The odds had always been against the boy—hundreds of miles from his homeland, alone in the forest, probably starving. In the end, a chance misstep had kept him from reaching his destination. It could happen just as easily to them.

When he realized Urkiat was not following him, he glanced over his shoulder and found him crouched beside the boy, carefully slitting open his breeches.

"What are you—?"

Urkiat seized the bulb of the boy's limp penis and pulled it. His dagger slashed downward, slicing the penis off at the root. But only when Urkiat thrust the bloody member into the boy's half-open mouth did Darak finally recover from his shock.

He strode forward and seized Urkiat's wrist. After a momentary flash of surprise, his features relaxed. "Don't worry. I'll save the fingers for you."

Darak backhanded him across the face. The blow flung Urkiat to the ground. Cursing, he stumbled to his feet and slowly backed away, one hand wiping his mouth, the other still gripping the dagger.

"Are you mad?" Darak demanded.

"You attack me and ask if *I'm* mad?"

Darak eyed the bloodstained blade pointing at his belly. Urkiat noted the direction of his gaze, but did not lower the dagger. "This is what your folk would have done if he hadn't escaped. I'm giving them the vengeance they deserve. The vengeance *you* deserve."

"The boy's dying. Isn't that vengeance enough?"

Urkiat's fury gave way to bewilderment. "They stole your son. They killed your kinfolk."

"Mutilating this boy won't change that. For mercy's sake—"

"What mercy did they show your people? Or mine?" Urkiat's hand fell to his side. "I don't understand you."

Because you saw me with the bloodlust still burning hot. I wanted to do it then. Would have if Griane hadn't stopped me. Instead, I only broke his fingers. And I enjoyed his pain and fear as much as Morgath enjoyed mine.

When he was sure he could speak calmly, Darak said, "I'm sorry I struck you." He waited for Urkiat to nod before adding, "We'll camp farther down the coast. Pack up our things. I'll be along in a moment."

After Urkiat stalked away, he pulled the bloody stump from the boy's mouth, laid it between his legs, and covered him with the torn flaps of his breeches. With a handful of wet leaves, he wiped the blood from the narrow lips. He didn't bother checking for a pulse; he'd seen enough dead bodies to recognize that the boy's spirit had fled.

He was wiping his fingers when he felt the presence of another. He looked up, expecting to see Urkiat, and caught a flicker of movement among the shadowy trees. He reached for his spear as a form slipped soundlessly through the underbrush.

Wolf padded forward, hackles and ears erect. Her bushy tail was as rigid as her body, but her gaze was directed toward the beach.

"Wolf?"

At the sound of his voice, her ears pricked forward and her tail relaxed. When she poked him in the chest with her muzzle, he was shocked to feel only the faintest brush of air. It was like touching his father when he'd found him in Chaos. A creature without fur or fangs, she had said. But the fur was still there and the fangs. His father's body had been insubstantial, but Wolf's still looked completely real.

"I was afraid for you, Little Brother. That is why I did not wait for your call."

"Afraid?"

"I have watched you. With the young one." A growl rumbled in her chest.

"His name is Urkiat. He goes with me on the hunt."

"He is not-pack."

"He's all the pack I have."

Her ears went back. "You have me."

"Aye. Forgive me."

"The young one is dangerous. He kills for pleasure, not for food, not to defend the pack."

"He is . . ." How to explain revenge to a creature that did not understand the concept? "His pack was killed by this boy's. That's why he attacked."

"The pup was no threat."

"This is something men do. Hurt another whose pack has hurt them."

"Even if the other is dying? This makes no sense."

Darak tried again. "Foxes. Wildcats. They sometimes play with a kill."

"Foxes. Wildcats. These are not-pack."

Her disapproval was so plain he had to smile. "I need this young one."

"Then you must teach him the ways of the hunt. Or he will fail you when it is time to make the kill."

Her tongue slid over his cheek. He missed the warm, wet roughness of it.

"I must leave now. But I will be with you, Little Brother."

Before he could thank her, she had vanished into the deepening shadows of the forest.

Darak headed back to the beach. He made himself smile at Urkiat whose troubled expression cleared. "I scouted a little ways down the beach. There's a good place to camp—sheltered from the wind by a cliff."

"Good work."

Urkiat looked as pleased as Callie when he praised his flute playing. Darak let him chatter on about the prospects of good weather on the morrow. And all the while, Wolf's warning echoed in his head.

Chapter 12

COOL STONE INSTEAD OF warm earth beneath his cheek. The scent of burning oil. Men's voices, one loud, the other two softer, uncertain.

Keirith opened his eyes and found himself staring at a neat row of feet, two pairs in boots, two in open-toed shoes. Something nudged him in the back. When he made a feeble movement, the voices broke off. Hands pulled him to his knees. The sudden movement made his head throb. He fell forward, his bound wrists knocking painfully against a stone step. The same hands jerked him upright again, seized his hair, and yanked his head back.

He gasped as much from astonishment as pain. Soaring walls rose four, five times as high as the venthole of their hut. They were brilliantly painted with gold suns, black serpents with crimson feathers, white fish swimming through blue seas. More serpents slithered up the milk-white pillars, tall and broad as oaks, that flanked the stone platform in front of him.

Atop it, a bald man and a white-haired woman sat on a low bench. Another man stood beside them. All three wore robes that bared their left shoulders, the seated man in gold, the younger in red, and the woman in brown. The younger man was also bald, but he sported bracelets and tattoos on his arms. Was he the chief? And the seated couple a priest and priestess?

This must be one of the stone temples the legends spoke of. That could only mean they meant to sacrifice him. Keirith glanced around wildly and discovered the owners of the feet: the Slave Master and the Speaker, and next to them, the grizzled older man he had seen briefly when they moved him onto the second boat. Standing beside him was the Big One.

An inadvertent whimper escaped him and he clamped his lips together. The younger man leaned down to whisper something to the older one who responded with a negligent wave. Then the younger one barked out a command. The Slave Master frowned, but bowed and backed away with the others.

Keirith's mouth went dry. He tried to get to his feet, but was shoved back to his knees. Two guards scowled down at him. Then they glanced to their left and their expressions changed.

The girl looked to be about his age. She walked with a slight limp, favoring her right leg. She kept her eyes downcast and her hands folded demurely over her stomach. Her shapeless tunic hung to her calves. Hair the color of the newly risen moon fell over her shoulders.

Among the black-haired, fawn-skinned Zherosi, she looked strange and exotic. Was she a child of the Oak and Holly? A slave, he guessed, as she knelt beside him and touched her forehead to the floor. But why would they summon a foreign slave?

She listened intently to the younger man's short speech, murmured something in reply, then settled back on her heels. The man fixed him with a cold stare and spat out a question.

"What is your name?" she translated.

Her voice was deeper than he would have expected and she spoke the tribal tongue with just a trace of an accent. A little like that man—what was his name?—Urkiat. When he didn't answer immediately, she lifted her head. Her eyes were as hard and blue as the Pilozhat sky.

"The Zheron asks your name. You must—"

The younger man interrupted. The girl flinched, then said, "Are you deaf, boy? What is your name?"

"Keirith. My name is Keirith."

She translated this, then paused while the Zheron asked another question.

"How old are you?"

"Fourteen summers."

Slowly, patiently, she translated the questions. Like the tattoos on the Zheron's arms, they twisted back on themselves, a seemingly innocuous question about his village followed by a swift probe about him. On and on it went until his knees ached as much as his head. He gave them the truth when he suspected they already knew it, but kept his answers short, determined to reveal as little about his tribe as possible.

"Who is your mother?"

"A healer."

"And your father?"

"A Memory-Keeper."

The girl spoke at length to the Zheron, obviously explaining what a Memory-Keeper was. She showed no visible emotion when describing his village, a village that must have been like hers. How long ago had she been stolen? She had clearly been here long enough to speak their language effortlessly—and long enough to be trusted to interpret for her masters. Why use her instead of the Speaker? That must have been why the Slave Master had frowned before he acquiesced. Did the Zheron want to check to see if the girl's translation matched what the Speaker had told him? Was there any way he could use that suspicion to his advantage?

Think, Keirith.

"Your father's name?"

Did they know the tale of the Long Winter? Perhaps not. But the girl would. She might be a child of the Oak and Holly, but he could not count her as an ally. If she told the Zherosi that his father was the hero who rescued the Oak-Lord from Chaos, they might return to the village, capture him, kill him.

"Ennit," he blurted out. "My father's name is Ennit."

"How many people in your village?"

"Before or after your raiders attacked?"

Before he could take back the words, she had translated them. The Zheron took two steps forward, then halted at a soft murmur from the older man.

"The Zheron wishes me to remind you that your life depends upon your answers. You would be wise to avoid insolence."

"Your advice or his?"

Without looking at him, she whispered, "Don't be a fool."

"Ninety-seven men, women, and children. Before the attack."

And then it began again: new questions, old ones, the Zheron circling around his answers like a stalking wolf.

"Please. May I have some water?"

She hesitated and then translated his request. It was the older man who nodded. Keirith heard the soft slap of leather against stone. Then silence. The Zheron's fingers drummed against his thigh. The older woman fingered the chain around her neck, but the man beside her just watched him.

Then the footsteps returned. One of the guards thrust a wooden cup toward him. The water was cool and delicious, and he drank gratefully.

The questioning began again. He wondered why they didn't ask about the shaking of the earth or his attack on the Big One. Surely that was why they had brought him here.

"Ninety-seven," he repeated for the third time. His head jerked up. "Nay, ninety-eight. The Grain-Mother went to the birthing hut the morning before the attack."

Had she still been struggling to deliver the child when the raiders came? Nay, his mam had been at home. She would never have left the Grain-Mother unless both mother and child were out of danger. Did Conn have a little brother or sister? Was Conn alive?

Always the same questions and never any answers: Were they safe? Were they hurt? Were they dead?

Keirith lowered his head. He would not weep before these murderers. Another question jerked his attention back. "I'm sorry. I didn't hear you."

"Are you a priest?"

"Nay."

"The warrior Kha says you attacked his mind. Is this true?"

If it were just the Big One's word against his, he could lie. But the Speaker and the Slave Master could also testify to his powers.

"Is this true?" the girl repeated.

"I tried to . . . push him away. With my mind. My spirit."

A flurry of questions: How long had he possessed this skill? Who had taught him? How often had he used it? What did he take to enhance his powers?

"Take?"

"Drugs. Drinks. Herbs."

"Nothing. Well . . . water. Afterward. To clear my head."

"You take nothing to open your powers?"

"Nay."

The Zheron made him repeat his answers twice before turning to the older man for a swift, muted conversation.

Keirith let his head droop, still reeling from what he had seen on their faces, what they had revealed through their questions. They understood his power. There had been surprise, aye, but mostly that his gift was untaught. So the Zherosi—some of them, anyway—must possess the same power. And clearly did not consider it an abomination. It sickened him to realize that only among his enemies could his power be accepted.

"Do you speak to the gods?"

"What? Nay."

"Do your priests?"

"Aye. That is, a priest has a spirit guide. An animal. Who helps him cross between the worlds. Helps him communicate with the gods."

"And your mother? The healer? Does she communicate with the gods?"

"Nay. But she—"

He broke off. The Zheron was watching him, his expression eager. Keirith felt a trickle of sweat ooze down his side. He had almost told them his mam had spoken with the Trickster. He must be more careful.

"She calls on the gods. To aid her healing."

"The scribe of the Jhef d'Esqi says that you knew of the shaking of the earth before it happened. Is this true?"

He started to nod, then hesitated. "I knew something would happen. I didn't know the earth would shake."

This provoked a heated exchange between the Zheron, the Slave Master, and the Speaker. By the end of it, the Speaker's expression of satisfaction had dwindled to one of fearful appeasement.

"The Zheron says you will tell him what happened."

He told them, choosing his words carefully. Unless he

remained vigilant, he might reveal something that could endanger not only his life, but the lives of his fellow captives.

"Which animals spoke?"

"There were many."

"Did their voices sound alike?"

"Nay."

"Then you heard different animals."

"Aye, but they were all screaming. Terrified. There were dogs. And birds—I don't know what kind. And sheep, I think. And the adders, of course."

The older woman gasped. In the prolonged silence that followed, he realized he had made a terrible error. The faces of the Zherosi revealed shock, wonder, disbelief. Only the older man seemed unmoved, although he leaned forward on the bench.

The Zheron slowly descended the steps. "You heard the adders speak?"

"I . . . I think so. It all happened so fast . . ."

"What did their voices sound like?"

"Like . . . like adders. Low. Hissing."

"Many snakes hiss. You said adders."

"My spirit guide is an adder. They sounded like him."

"You said only priests had spirit guides."

Another error.

The Zheron's hand darted out and Keirith shrank away, but strong fingers seized his chin and forced him to look up. "And you claimed you were not a priest."

"I'm not."

"But you have a spirit guide. An adder."

"Because I wanted to be a priest. Once. Natha—my spirit guide—came to me. But I'm not a priest. I'm not even an apprentice anymore."

He was saying too much. They would hear the desperation in his voice, see the way he was shaking, and know he was hiding something.

The older man beckoned the Zheron, then addressed the spectators. The four men bowed and backed away. Keirith could feel the Big One's gaze, but he refused to look at him. Their footsteps receded and there was silence.

After a brief consultation with the older man, the Zheron

straightened. Slowly, he descended the steps again. "Speak to them."

"What?"

"Speak to the adders. Now."

"I can't."

The Zheron circled him like a hungry wolf. A sneer twisted his lips. "You lied."

"Nay."

"You cannot speak to the adders."

"I never said I could. I heard them. Screaming."

The Zheron bent over him and Keirith flinched. "You miserable savage. Do you think you can deceive us?"

"I wasn't . . . what do you want?"

"I want you to speak to the adders."

"I can't! It doesn't work that way."

"How does it work?"

"I don't know. I just . . . reach out. And if the bird or the animal permits me, I can touch its spirit."

"And a man? Can you touch a man?" The Zheron's sneer vanished, replaced by a smile. "Could you touch me?"

Sickened by the girl's seductive whisper, Keirith swallowed down the bile that rose in his throat and looked at the floor.

"Do you want to touch me, little savage?"

Cool fingers brushed his cheek. Keirith slapped them away, only to have the guards seize his elbows.

"Touch me. I want you to. I want to feel you inside of me."

He shook his head, fighting down the impotent fury.

"You want to. I know you do. You want it so much you're shaking."

Keirith averted his face, but he was helpless to stop the fingers that traced a cool, lingering path down his jaw. He jerked his head away, wild to escape, but the Zheron seized his face between his hands. The dark eyes stared into his, the full mouth curved in a teasing smile.

"Or shall I take you? Would you like that better?"

The power surged, fed by fury and shame so intense that he thought he would scream if he couldn't release it. His blood pounded in his ears, a frenzied drumbeat that urged him to let go, to seek the release, to obliterate that mocking smile and shatter his enemy's spirit.

"Shall I be gentle? No. You like it rough, don't you? Rough and hard and—"

Screaming, he hurled his power at his tormentor. The man staggered backward, tripping over the step. Keirith touched shock and disbelief. A savage joy filled him, more intense than any emotion he had ever known. He pushed harder, wanting to destroy that sneering spirit, to send it hurtling out of the man's body into Chaos, to feel his scream, to taste his helpless terror.

Instead, he felt . . . nothing. As if the connection between them had abruptly been severed. The Zheron lay slumped on the steps, his shoulders rising and falling in quick breaths. He slowly raised his head and grimaced—not in pain, but as if the touch had contaminated him.

Keirith swayed, drained by the release of the energy and the long interrogation and his sense of failure. When the guards released him, he collapsed to the floor and lay there, too spent and humiliated to care what they did to him.

During the raid, his arrows had brought down raiders, but until now, he had never felt such an overwhelming desire to kill. This was what the Tree-Father had feared. This was why his father had reacted with such horror. They had known he possessed this potential for violence, that one day, he would turn his power on someone with the deliberate intent to destroy.

"Merciful Maker," he whispered. "Help me."

He heard footsteps approaching and opened his eyes. A face swam into focus. The older man knelt beside him. Keirith flinched, but the man made no move to touch him.

"You are tired," he said. "You must rest. Go with the guards." His panic must have been obvious, for the man added, "No one will harm you."

The guards lifted him to his feet. He wanted very much to walk out of the chamber unaided, but his legs wouldn't support him. The Zheron had risen as well. His voice was as strong as ever as he rapped out an order. The girl rose and bowed, wrists crossed over her breasts, before walking away. Not once did she glance in his direction. Keirith was surprised how much that hurt.

"Don't be a fool."

Even if she could help him, she wouldn't. She had survived this long by obeying her masters and ignoring the plight of her people.

Keirith allowed the guards to help him from the chamber. He drew up short at the doorway and looked over his shoulder. The older man was watching him. In his exhaustion, the words had simply flowed over him. But the man had spoken to him directly, without the aid of a translator. With utter fluency, he had spoken the language of the tribes.

Malaq returned the boy's stare, absently toying with the vial of qiij that hung around his neck. As soon as the guards escorted him out, he turned to Xevhan who still looked a bit shaken from the attack. Malaq chided himself for enjoying that.

"He didn't hurt you?"

"Of course not. Once I erected the barrier, he simply . . . stopped."

"When did you take the qiij?" he asked quietly.

Xevhan hesitated. "After I received your summons. It was a wise precaution," he added defensively.

He'd guessed as much from Xevhan's restlessness and the light sheen of perspiration on his face. Of more concern was his haggard appearance. All priests took qiij—to facilitate communication with the gods, to touch the spirit of another—but there were always those who used the drug for pleasure. Xevhan was young enough—and arrogant enough—to ignore the long-term effects.

"He made no attempt to breach the shield?" Malaq asked.

"He clearly did not possess the skill."

Or had decided that he had demonstrated too much of his power. Or was simply too exhausted to try.

"How did you guess what would provoke him?" Xevhan asked.

Malaq shrugged. "The Tree People are less broadminded about sexual relations. Particularly those between members of the same sex."

"We are fortunate that you know so much about their customs."

Xevhan's voice and expression held only respect, but Malaq sensed the hidden barb.

He heard Eliaxa's slow shuffle, but before he could go to her, Xevhan vaulted up the steps with the graceful—if annoying—exuberance of youth and offered his arm. She gave him a quick smile, but her expression remained distracted. "Do other Tree People possess this power?"

No barb in Eliaxa's words. He wondered if she even remembered his former ties to the Tree People; since her illness last winter, her mind was often as uncertain as her gait.

"Their priests claim to use spirit animals to guide them into trance, rather than rely on qiij or similar brews. It is said that the shaman of each tribe has the power to touch the spirits of his people."

"But one so young? He cannot be older than sixteen."

Without correcting her, Malaq said, "Even among our first-year Zhiisti, we see varying degrees of power. Some need only a sip of qiij to slip the bonds of their bodies. Others require so much that they are rendered helpless for days."

Xevhan's breath hissed in, and Malaq gave him a mild glance. Inwardly, though, he chided himself again.

You imagine an insult and must get a bit of your own back by reminding him of his lack of skill. Childish. And foolish. Xevhan's spiritual powers may be limited, but his earthly connections are not. How else could he have risen to Zheron before his twenty-fifth summer? At that age, I hadn't even begun my training as a priest.

Eliaxa appeared oblivious to the undercurrents. Her wrinkles deepened as she frowned. "Will you conduct the testing yourself?"

"If I may speak, Pajhit . . . ?" The title dripped off Xevhan's lips like honey.

"Yes?"

"The slave Hircha may prove useful again. She could question the boy. Under my supervision, of course."

And report everything to her master, of course.

"She *was* helpful today," Malaq replied. "It was kind of you to suggest summoning her so that I might save my strength. But for now, the fewer people who come in contact with this boy, the better. And since I have some . . .

facility with the language, it should only take a day or two to resolve this matter."

"As you command, Pajhit." Xevhan bowed stiffly, both the smile and the honey gone.

"It might be advisable to remind the Jhef d'Esqi and the others that we require their silence. We do not want untoward rumors flying about the city."

"I will see to it personally, Pajhit."

Malaq turned to Eliaxa. She looked so frail. She had been priestess of Womb of Earth even before he had come to Pilozhat after the Long Winter. It was time for her to step aside and allow a younger, stronger woman to assume the responsibilities of Motixa.

"You look tired, my dear. May I see you back to your chamber?"

She nodded, still distracted. Her small hand grasped his arm with surprising strength. "Is it possible, Malaq? Could he be the one?"

Malaq patted her hand, the flesh dry and slack beneath his fingertips. "He's just a boy with red hair and a gift for touching spirits. He's no different than the others."

"The others did not speak to the adders. Or make Womb of Earth tremble."

"Neither did he," Malaq reminded her gently. "He heard their voices—along with those of other creatures—crying out in fear. Womb of Earth trembled as she has many times before. Perhaps he is more sensitive than the others, but that is all."

Her fingers dug into his forearm. "You'll make sure, Malaq? We must be sure. If he is the one and we fail to recognize him . . ."

"I'll make sure. I always do."

"Perhaps Heart of Sky will give you a sign. You are his priest, and he loves you."

In his five years as Pajhit, he'd seen little evidence of the god's love, but it would only upset Eliaxa to hear that.

Before he could assure her that he would seek the god's guidance, she began reciting the prophecy in an eerie singsong. "Hail the Son of Zhe, the fire-haired god made flesh. Welcome him with reverence and with dread, for with him comes the new age."

"Yes, dear. Please. Calm yourself. I hate to see you so distressed."

"I'm sorry. I only wish . . ." Tears filled her eyes and spilled down the deep grooves around her mouth. "All my life, I've dreamed of his coming. I pray for it every day. We need him now, so badly."

He patted her hand again. "I know. But you must rest now."

Still muttering the words of the prophecy, she let him lead her from the hall.

Just a boy with red hair and a gift for touching spirits. That's all. He's no more the Son of Zhe than he is my son.

Chapter 13

DURING THE DAY, Griane kept herself busy. She and Sali visited the convalescents, checking wounds, changing bandages, dispensing potions to aid sleep or reduce fever. They gathered watercress and nettle shoots for tonics, willow bark and yarrow for the joint-ill and fevers, mallow leaves for poultices, goose grass for straining milk, and elderflowers and violets for infusions to combat coughs.

Some days, she helped the other women in the fields, grubbing out weeds, tenderly urging the newly sprouted stalks of barley and oats to stand upright. Once, she took Callie with her to raid the nests of tufted ducks, but he preferred spending his days with the shepherds. Even a six-year-old could help, and while he was busy throwing stones at marauding foxes or trotting back and forth to Eagles Mount with baskets of food for the weary shepherds, he would not worry so much about his father and brother.

Lisula remained confident that Darak would find Keirith, and while Griane sat beside her in the birthing hut, she was confident, too. But late at night, she lay under the wolfskins, alone with her fears.

Two nights before the Ripening, she sought out Gortin. He seemed to have aged years in the sennight since the attack, but he, too, was driving himself hard, visiting the injured, offering prayers and sacrifices for the dead, even joining the men who mounted a watch every night on the summit of Eagles Mount.

"Forgive me for intruding," she said as Gortin motioned her to sit.

"You're not. I welcome your company."

For five summers, he and Meniad had shared this hut. How empty it must be for Gortin now. The sooner he accepted Othak as his initiate, the better. She didn't know whether the shy boy would make a very good priest, but at least Gortin would have company and Othak would be safe from Jurl's beatings.

"I'm glad you came tonight," Gortin said. "I've been wanting . . . I've been thinking about you. About Keirith."

A spasm of pain crossed his face. Impulsively, she touched his arm. He surprised her by clutching her hand. Immediately, he released it, clearly embarrassed.

"I had to dismiss him," he said in a low voice. "But I didn't . . . I should have handled it better. I think . . . I'm not very good. With people."

"Neither was Struath." Remembering how he still idolized his mentor, she quickly added, "Or Darak when he was younger."

"Tinnean was. Everyone loved him. And Meniad. What fine Tree-Fathers they would have made." When she nodded, the smallest smile lightened his heavy features. "Thank you for not trying to assure me that I am superior to them."

"You're a good Tree-Father, Gortin. And a good man. But . . ."

"Well? You can't stop there."

"For mercy's sake, stop comparing yourself to Struath. Or Tinnean or Meniad, for that matter. Meniad died young and beautiful, Struath gave his life to defeat Morgath, and Tinnean saved the world! You can never compete with that. Besides, Struath might have been a gifted shaman, but he was also . . . cold. Forgive me, but it's true. Tinnean was the sweetest boy I've ever known but he could be horribly impulsive, and Meniad . . . well, even when he wasn't having visions, his head was in the clouds."

She broke off, horrified at delivering such a tirade. Again Gortin surprised her, this time by laughing. "And you are refreshingly honest but a terrible scold. Mother Netal would be proud."

"Nay, it's awful. Old as I am, I should know better than to blurt things out without thinking." She hesitated, won-

dering how to turn the conversation to the purpose of tonight's visit without spoiling this rare moment of intimacy.

"And now you're thinking that you should get to the
point of your visit." He smiled. "Your face has always been
easy to read, Griane."

"Forgive me, Tree-Father. I know you have preparations
to make for the Ripening. I wouldn't ask if I weren't so . . ."

Oh, just be "refreshingly honest" and ask him, Griane.

"Could you seek Keirith with your vision? Or Darak? I
know they've only been gone a sennight, but—"

"I've tried to find Keirith. He and I share a closer connection, so I thought it would be easier than seeking Darak.
So far, I've had no success. I'll try again, but visions cannot
be commanded."

"At least I'd feel we were doing something. The waiting
is hard."

"I know."

His face clouded. He had been the one left behind on
the last quest, forced to wait and wonder what was happening to the man he loved more than anyone in the world.

"I will seek Keirith again after the Ripening."

His promise helped Griane endure the rite. Once, it had
been her favorite. The Freshening celebrated the retreat of
ice from the streams and rivers, but the world was still
locked in winter. The Balancing brought the lambing season, but was fraught with anxiety that a late winter storm
could blow in and threaten the survival of the frail newborns. By the Ripening, winter had surrendered its hold on
the land, which gratefully responded with an explosion of
color and life: green shoots thrusting out of the soil, green
leaves unfurling on the tree branches, the peat bog brightened by the pinks of cuckoo flowers and bogblossoms, and
the forest festooned with carpets of bluebells, violets, and
speedwell.

For her, the rites had a more personal meaning. The Freshening recalled their return from the First Forest, filled with
violent swings of emotions: reunions with friends and family
marred by the absence of those who had died during their
quest; the first tentative explorations of love shattered by
Darak's recurring nightmares and inability to find his place.
When Darak went back to the First Forest at the Balancing,
she wasn't sure he would ever return. But he did, gaunt

and haggard but more peaceful in spirit. Although it was customary to marry at either the Spring or Autumn Balancing, she refused to wait. They were married at the Ripening and within two moons, she was pregnant with Keirith.

Celebrating the Ripening without Darak would have been hard enough; the losses suffered by the tribe cast a pall over the rite for everyone. They still sang the joyous song to welcome spring. They repeated the prayers as Gortin blessed three sea trout, the first of those returning to the lake before heading upstream to spawn. They marched to the lake as he returned one to the goddess Lacha in thanks for her bounty. But when Gortin sacrificed the second trout, wrapped it in oak leaves, and carried it into the barrow to feed the spirits of the dead, everyone recalled the ceremony days earlier when he had interred the ashes and bones of those killed in the raid. Men and women alike wept as they added stones to the cairn in memory of those they had lost.

The ceremony at the heart-oak was equally fraught with emotion. Gortin's voice cracked when he laid the third trout between two of the gnarled roots and thanked the sacred tree for watching over their people. Lisula's hand trembled as she sprinkled the libation of water. The children who usually skipped around the tree, scattering blossoms of rowan and quickthorn, simply marched in silence behind their parents.

As she did every Ripening, Griane lingered with the children to sprinkle water at the base of a rowan. It was her way of honoring her friend from the Summerlands, one of the ancient tree-folk who had helped her return to the First Forest after Fellgair abandoned her. She still preserved the sprig of blossoms Rowan had given her when they parted, the petals brittle now and brown with age.

When she said a quick prayer and began plucking blossoms from a sprig, the children stared at her, round-eyed with surprise. She repeated her prayer, hoping the spirit of the tree would understand and forgive her.

While the others returned to their huts to prepare the feast, she led the children back to the lake. They walked west along the shore. By the time they neared the channel, the ground rose too steeply for Callie to go farther, so she stopped and held out her handful of blossoms.

"Throw a petal into the water," she told them, "and say a prayer for Fa and Keirith."

"Is that like putting a stone on the cairn?" Callie asked.

"It's like . . . we're sending our love to them. The river will carry the blossoms all the way to the sea."

"And the sea will take them to Fa and Keirith."

"That's right."

"And they'll know they're from us?"

"Aye."

"And that we're thinking of them?"

"They'll know that anyway," Faelia said.

Griane shot her a warning glance. Faelia had retreated into sullen silence after her father departed. She spent some mornings in the fields, but more often, she disappeared into the forest, returning with squirrels or rabbits or wood pigeons that she tossed beside the fire pit, as if daring her to object. Griane said nothing. Since Darak's departure, she had never seen Faelia weep, but her red-rimmed eyes told a different story.

Together, they tossed the petals into the water and watched as they rolled back to shore.

"It doesn't matter," Griane said as Callie's face puckered. "Our prayers are on the water. Lacha will make sure they reach the sea."

"Will she tell them about the petals, too?"

"Why don't you throw the last one in and ask her?"

Callie heaved the petal with all his might.

"Quick now. Before it comes back."

"Lacha, goddess of lakes and rivers, please tell Fa and Keirith about the petals and that we're thinking about them and we want them to come home soon and . . ." His voice trailed off as the petal drifted back. "Does it count, Mam?"

"Aye. It counts."

"I'll bring Lacha an offering every day. Just to make sure."

Callie smiled up at her, confident now that he had a plan. All she had was the hope of Gortin's vision.

The blossoms clung forlornly to the wet pebbles. Griane resolutely turned her back on them and led the children home.

Keirith tiptoed to the open doorway of the Pajhit's chamber. Outside, the guards continued their soft conversation. He could only hope they would remain where they were.

The Pajhit had interrogated him all morning, his manner polite but distant. He seemed almost bored by the procedure, but at least that was better than the Zheron's taunts. At midday, the guards had arrived to take him back to the small chamber where he had spent the night. The second round of questioning had scarcely begun when another priest arrived and the Pajhit left with him. Keirith had no idea how long he would be gone; he only knew he would have to act quickly.

Light seeped through the woven draperies drawn across the other doorway of the chamber. Cautiously, he padded across the cool tiles toward them. He hesitated when he passed a dim hallway. It probably led to the priest's sleeping quarters. Certainly there was no bedding in the main room, only a few stone benches against the walls and a low stone table surrounded by cushions. Tempted as he was to search for a weapon, he was afraid to linger that long.

He drew aside the draperies. Instead of freedom, he found a walled enclosure. All he could see above it was the cloudless sky. Tall spikes of scarlet flowers nodded against the wall to his left. Stone benches flanked the others.

He climbed onto the one in front of him and peered over the top of the wall. To his left, the glowering mountain thrust up into the sky. To his right, he saw a walkway flanked by giant pillars; unlike those he'd seen on his way to the slave compound, these were red. From the position of the mountain, he guessed the Pajhit's chamber was on the opposite side of this fortress—or temple—from the compound. It was hard to be sure, though; his first impressions had been so clouded by exhaustion and fear.

The walkway led to a stepped platform also flanked by pillars. A smaller rectangular slab of stone squatted atop it. Was that where they offered sacrifices?

With an effort, he shook off the disturbing thought and craned his neck to get a better view. The pillars offered some cover, but the ground was flat and open. A few scraggly bushes clung to the rocky soil. No houses and, surprisingly, no people. Perhaps they were hiding from the heat of the midday sun. With any luck, he would be gone by the time they emerged.

The rubblestone walls of the fortress rose behind him. He'd be clearly visible from the row of windows above. There were probably more on the level below; the drop to the ground was nearly three times his height. But even if he was seen, he'd be halfway across the open ground before an alarm could be sounded. Assuming he didn't break a leg when he jumped.

Whispering a quick prayer to the Maker, he gripped the top of the wall. Wriggled the toes of his left foot into a chink between the stones. Took a deep breath and started to heave himself up.

Something soft brushed against his ankle. As he spun around, he caught a blur of motion and spotted a small furry creature racing toward a bench at the far end of the enclosure. Before he could recover from his shock, a voice said, "I see you've met Niqia."

The Pajhit stood in the doorway, surveying him impassively.

Keirith's heart raced. Any moment the guards would rush in. Would they kill him on the spot or drag him, screaming and struggling, to the altar?

The Pajhit's gaze shifted to the creature crouched under the bench, lashing its tail. "An old friend suggested Niqia's name. In honor of a . . . lady he used to know. She, too, had a soft body and sharp claws. The Tree People haven't domesticated cats, have they?"

Keirith shook his head.

"Niqia's ancestors were wildcats, much like those that still roam your forests. It's been generations since any have been found in our kingdom. Did you know that you can hand rear wildcats if you take them as kittens before their eyes open? That's how the first ones must have been domesticated. They were crossbred with the Eriptean golden cat. The mix produced a creature smaller than the true wildcat and more of a reddish gold in color, but with the same dark markings. Also, the tail is less bushy."

He paused, as if expecting some response, so Keirith nodded, all the while wondering why the man was lecturing him on cats instead of killing him for trying to escape.

"Niqia's fond of this garden. Although it does get intolerably warm in the afternoon. As you will have noticed. I assume you also noticed the temple?"

Keirith finally found his voice. "Aye."

"It is sacred to Zhe, the winged serpent. The Zheron is his chief priest. I am the priest of Heart of Sky, our sun god. You cannot see his temple from here."

"Do you sacrifice captives there?" he blurted out.

"Yes."

"Including the ones with red hair?"

The Pajhit's eyes narrowed, but all he said was, "We could continue this conversation inside. Unless you prefer standing on the bench."

After a moment's hesitation, Keirith hopped down.

Someone had placed a small basket of flatbread on the table. There was also a bowl containing a brownish paste, another with creamy white stuff, and a shallow dish filled with pale green disks, each studded with a circle of white seeds. The Pajhit seated himself on a cushion and reached for a bronze pitcher.

"The brown paste is jhok. Ground chickpeas and lentils." Golden liquid flowed into a tall cup that reminded Keirith of a bluebell only it, too, was made of bronze. "Do you have them?"

"Nay."

"Beans. Mixed with spices. You dip the bread in it. This is gyrt and those are kugi. Gyrt is made from goat's milk. You don't have goats either, I believe. They're somewhat like sheep, but they have short hair instead of wool. Kugi are vegetables. They're like . . . I can't recall anything similar among your people. You dip them in the gyrt. Very refreshing."

"Are you going to kill me?"

"Not right now. Sit, please. My neck is beginning to ache from staring up at you. And help yourself to the wine."

Keirith sat. He had no appetite and he was afraid to lift the pitcher for fear the Pajhit would see his hand shake.

"Your story has been remarkably consistent. Either you're telling the truth, or you're an excellent liar. However, to assess the true extent of your gift, our spirits must touch."

Shocked by the sudden shift in conversation, Keirith could only shake his head.

"I'm not suggesting that I enter your spirit. I require you to enter mine."

"I can't do that."

"You did it yesterday. To the Zheron."

"I didn't mean to . . . I mean, I did, but only because I was . . . angry."

"Now you'll attempt to do so without anger."

"It's . . . you don't understand. My people don't do that."

"Your priests touch the spirits of their tribe mates, do they not?"

"Only the Tree-Father. For anyone else to do that . . . it's an abomination. A sacrilege."

"So yesterday you committed sacrilege. As you did when you attacked the spirit of the warrior Kha."

"He was trying to kill me. Capture me."

"So it's permitted to use this gift under duress?"

"I . . . nay . . . I don't know."

The Pajhit leaned forward. "Tell me this: if you had defended yourself with a dagger, would your people punish you?"

"Of course not."

"But you're not a warrior. You used the only weapon you had. True?"

"Aye, but—"

"You've only used this weapon against your enemies, not your own people."

His father's scream echoed inside his head.

"So," the Pajhit continued in that same reasonable voice, "as you—presumably—consider me your enemy, and since I—definitely—am inviting you to enter my spirit, explain to me how that can be a sacrilege." He leaned back, waiting.

"I don't . . . can't you test me in some other way?"

"I could enter *your* spirit. However, that would be . . . unnerving for you. It always is the first time, even when your partner is a trusted friend. To enter the spirit of another without permission, of course, would be tantamount to rape."

Keirith repressed a wince. "Why do you care if it's . . . unnerving for me?"

The Pajhit simply set his cup on the table and folded his hands.

"I could hurt you," Keirith said.

"No. You couldn't."

"I hurt the Zheron."

"Only because your attack was clumsy. Once he recovered from his initial shock—"

"He pushed me out."

"No. You would have felt that."

Keirith went through the encounter again. Slowly, he said, "He shut himself off."

A very small smile curved the Pajhit's mouth. "Yes."

"How?"

"By erecting a protective shield. So you see, you could not hurt me if you entered my spirit."

It sounded like the same thing he did to block out the cries of a wounded animal. But the Pajhit was skilled enough to get past any pathetic shield he tried to erect. And then he would be able to peer into the most hidden parts of his being and learn all his secrets—who his parents were, what had happened on the boat.

"What if I won't agree?"

"Then I'll have to arrange a different test. One that is more dangerous."

"What . . . what sort of test?"

The Pajhit sipped his wine. "I haven't decided."

Keirith studied his smooth face and recalled the whispered conversation that had prompted the Zheron to change tactics and taunt him. The Pajhit knew exactly what test he would choose. He'd known from the beginning. His casual conversation about food and cats was merely a tactic to catch him off guard, his reluctance to invade his spirit a sham, and his politeness a mask to hide his ruthlessness.

"And if I fail the test?"

The Pajhit's silence was more eloquent than any words. But better to risk failure and die than betray his people— and himself—to his enemies.

"When will you conduct this test?" His voice came out too loud, but at least it didn't crack.

"Tomorrow." The Pajhit leaned forward. "Are you certain, Kheridh?"

The priest pronounced his name with an odd slur that made it sound more guttural but strangely melodious.

"Aye, Pajhit."

As he walked to the door, the Pajhit spoke his name again. Keirith turned to find him plucking a flower from a vase resting in a wall niche, the same long-stemmed ones he'd seen in the garden.

The Pajhit walked toward him and held it out. "I believe the giving of flowers is customary among your people on this day."

The day you were condemned to die? Then he realized: it must be the Ripening.

At home, they would be feasting on sea trout and oat-cakes. Callie would run around the circle with the other little ones, showering people with petals of rowan and quickthorn. His mam's uncle Dugan would drink too much brogac, and she and Jani would have to help him home, all the while scolding him for being too old for such behavior. Couples would sneak off to make love, pursued by the squeals and giggles of Faelia and her friends. And his father's gaze would turn to the forest, and a hush would fall around the circle as he began the tale of the rowan and the alder that pulled up their roots and crossed the boundary from the First Forest to become the first woman and man in the world.

To hide his emotions, he sniffed the flower and grimaced at the tangy fragrance.

"Bitterheart," the Pajhit said softly. When Keirith looked up, he nodded at the flower. "That's what we call it."

They found a few stretches of beach that made for easy walking, but mostly, they had to pick their way through tumbled piles of boulders or reed-choked marshes. Darak knew he was not the same man who had guided his folk through the First Forest, but he'd always done his share of the physical labor around the village: cutting turf, plowing the fields, bringing in the harvest. Urkiat was half his age; it was foolish—and useless—to resent his stamina, but it still galled him that he was the one slowing the pace.

Sometimes a soaring cliff forced them inland, but they didn't dare go too deep into the forest. If the breeze was from the west, they would smell the smoke from the cook fires, but if not, it would be too easy to walk past a village and never know it was there.

By the end of each day, all he wanted to do was make a fire and curl up beside it. He had to force himself to make conversation with Urkiat. Mostly, he took refuge in trying to learn a few phrases in the Zherosi tongue. They both shied away from personal matters—and never discussed their confrontation over the young raider.

On the fourth afternoon of their journey down the coast, the sound of singing drew them up a shallow stream. The voices died when the feasting villagers spied them.

Darak called out the traditional greeting. "I am Darak, son of Reinek and Cluran, of the Oak Tribe."

"I am Urkiat, son of Koth and Lidia, of the Holly Tribe."

"We are travelers, seeking your hospitality."

A heavyset man with three eagle feathers in his hair rose. Girn had attended the Gatherings for years and the few times he'd spoken at the convocation of chiefs, his words had always been thoughtful and sensible.

"Darak and Urkiat, you are welcome to our village."

"Your welcome warms us at the Ripening."

Formalities dispensed with, Girn strode across the circle. His smile dimmed a bit when he recognized Urkiat—clearly, he remembered his outburst at the Gathering—but he clasped his arms firmly, sealing the welcome before his kinfolk.

"I had not expected to see you after the Gathering," Girn said. "What brings you to our village?"

Darak lowered his voice. "Bad times, I fear."

Girn nodded slowly. "Come to my hut. We can talk there."

Two young men trotted forward to relieve them of their packs. An older woman hurried toward one of the huts. They turned out to be members of Girn's family. His sons dropped the packs and after polite greetings, immediately left. His wife lingered long enough to pour cups of berry wine. Then she, too, departed.

As soon as the ritual toast had been drunk, Darak set his cup down. "Forgive me for spoiling the Ripening with ill tidings."

Girn waved away his words. "Tell me your news, Memory-Keeper."

That was another reason he liked Girn. Unlike so many of the chiefs, he never used the ridiculous title Spirit-Hunter when he addressed him. Without mentioning their encounter with the raider, Darak told him of the attacks along the river and the losses sustained by the villages.

"Merciful gods. So many?" For a long moment, Girn stared into the fire pit. Then his head jerked up. "And your family, Memory-Keeper?"

"My son." Darak cleared his throat; even after repeating the story so many times, the words still came with difficulty. "They stole my son."

Another man might have cursed or lamented or gripped his arm in fellowship. Girn simply asked, "What can I do?"

"We need a boat. Small enough for two men to handle."

"You're going after him."

Darak nodded.

"You'll make better time in a currach. My men will take you to Foroth's village."

"Oak-Chief, you don't have to—"

"You should reach Illait's village in ten days if the weather holds. He can advise you about the best route to take after that. We don't hear much from the villages in the far south."

"The raiders have never attacked you?" Darak asked.

"Nay. Until now, the farthest north they've ventured is Illait's village. After that attack, I ordered our huts torn down and rebuilt here where they would be hidden from the sea. But if the raiders are striking as far north as your village, I'd best mount a watch on the beach as well. Better to lose a little sleep than—" Girn broke off abruptly. "Well. You'll be tired after your journey. If you'd like, I'll have the women bring food here."

It would be rude to absent themselves from the feast, especially after Girn's generous offer of help. "Urkiat and I would be honored to share the Ripening with your folk."

Girn's smile told him it was the correct answer. After another toast, they joined the circle of celebrants. Round-eyed children watched every bite of roast venison and fish as if shocked to discover that the great Spirit-Hunter ate real food. One, bolder than the others, darted close enough to toss a handful of rowan blossoms on his head. His mother scolded, but the other women nodded their approval when he smiled. A few of the men questioned him about the reason for his visit, but subsided when Girn shifted the conversation to crops and the weather.

As the shadows lengthened, the Memory-Keeper rose to recite the legend of the rowan-woman and alder-man. Darak kept his smile carefully in place, but hearing the tale told by another only reminded him that he was far from home.

When the Memory-Keeper concluded his recitation, he motioned for silence. "Darak Spirit-Hunter."

Darak restrained a wince.

"Your presence honors our village and heightens the joy of this Ripening. Would it be too much to ask you to share a tale with us?"

Oh, gods. He should have known.

"It would give us great joy to hear from your own lips the tale of your magnificent quest."

"I do not tell that tale. Ever."

Silence fell around the circle. The Memory-Keeper's smile disappeared. Even Girn looked uncomfortable.

"Forgive me," he managed. "I did not mean to be rude. But that story . . . it's not just a legend about things that happened long ago. Those . . . things . . . happened to me. To my wife. To my brother." He realized he was rubbing the stumps of his fingers and clenched his hands together. "I do not tell that tale," he said, his voice softer now and under control. "I cannot."

He knew he should offer another tale, but each one conjured memories of other feast days. It was hard enough to be away from home when he should be sharing this day with Griane, but to celebrate it with strangers when his son . . .

Lost. Lost like Tinnean.

With an effort, he quelled the rush of fear. Later, when he was alone, he could confront it. If he had no heart for this celebration, he could at least avoid ruining it for his hosts.

He stared down at his hands. A rowan petal lay on his knee. He picked it up and rubbed it gently between his thumb and little fingers. Then he looked around the circle of expectant faces and cleared his throat.

"With your permission, I will tell another tale. It's one that rightly belongs to my wife, but it's a good tale for the Ripening, and I don't think she'd mind if I told it."

He rose and took a deep breath to steady himself. "You'll have heard how Griane the Healer led the Holly-Lord back to the grove of the First Forest. But the tale barely mentions her adventures in the Summerlands and that is a wonderful story. For in the Summerlands, Griane met the Trees-Who-Walk. One of them was a rowan-woman. Just like the one in the legend. This is how it happened."

He conjured Griane as he spoke, recalling the emotions that had flitted across her expressive face when she first told him the story: fear, awe, wonder, joy. He was surprised to feel those emotions now and find them reflected in the faces of his listeners. When he described the thunder of the tree-folk's feet as they pursued her, the children gasped. When he told how they used their own shoots and leaves to create a raft to carry her back to the First Forest, the men nodded thoughtfully. And when he described her farewell to Rowan, many women wiped their damp eyes.

"And she stood on the bank of the river and watched the raft grow smaller and smaller until it disappeared behind the wall of mist. And still she waved, for she was alone and frightened. But then she smelled the sweet fragrance of the rowan sprig and realized she carried Rowan's love with her. Griane still has those blossoms, though they are no longer soft and white like this one. And every year at the Ripening, she looks at them and remembers the kindness of the tree-folk and the tear Rowan wept when they parted."

A sigh eased its way around the circle. A little girl shouted, "Tell it again!" and the laughter warmed him. He bowed and excused himself, suddenly tired. Instead of returning to Girn's hut, he sought the privacy of the beach.

He sat by the water's edge, content to watch Bel sink into the sea, trailing a shimmering streak of orange behind him. When he heard the crunch of pebbles, he took a deep, calming breath.

"Are you all right?"

It was Urkiat, of course. Darak nodded without turning, hoping Urkiat would leave him alone. Instead, more pebbles crunched as he strode forward. "The Memory-Keeper shouldn't have made you speak."

"He didn't know what had happened."

"You should have told them."

"And spoil their celebration?" Darak shook his head.

Urkiat scuffed at the pebbles. "Doesn't it bother you? Their complacency? Their happiness?"

"Resenting other folks' happiness only adds to your misery."

But he understood. When he'd first looked around that circle of happy faces, he had resented every father who sat beside his son, every husband with his arm casually flung around his wife's shoulders.

"Sometimes I hate them," Urkiat said. "All those who don't know what it's like. Who'd rather live in ignorance than face the truth."

"And what is the truth?"

"That there's nowhere to hide. Nowhere safe. They're like a plague. A hailstorm that flattens the barley or lightning that strikes a tree. They won't be satisfied until they've destroyed us."

"Sooner or later, balance will be restored."

Urkiat spat.

"We've survived plague and hailstorms and lightning strikes," Darak reminded him. "We survived the Long Winter when the world teetered on the brink of extinction. We'll survive the Zherosi, too. Somehow."

"It took only a handful of people to restore the world after Morgath destroyed the One Tree. It'll take every child of the Oak and Holly to destroy the Zherosi."

A seabird cried overhead like a mother keening for a lost child.

Darak rose. "We'd best go back."

"I'm sorry. You wanted to enjoy the peace of the evening, and I've ruined it. I just . . . I thought I could help. Share your worries. Or talk about . . . things. I didn't want you to feel alone."

Darak considered reminding him that he had been a hunter for the first half of his life. He liked being alone. He still hungered for the quiet of the forest, the peace. And then the sudden rush of excitement when you saw the prey, the muscles tensing in your arms as you drew the bow, the moment just before you released when the world seemed to go absolutely still. And that perfect moment when your arrow found its target and the blood pounded in your ears and every fiber of your being sang.

Urkiat was watching him, his face strained.

"Thank you for your concern," Darak said, wishing he sounded less stiff and formal. He still didn't know what to make of Urkiat. He could kill with dispassion and then suddenly erupt in anger over an imagined slight. One moment, he seemed as world-weary as an old man and the next, he behaved like an awkward boy. Now he was watching him like a dog that had been beaten by its master.

"I was proud when you agreed to let me come with you." Urkiat's voice was little more than a whisper. "Proud to think you needed me."

"I did. I do."

Urkiat nodded eagerly.

Gods, he was tired. All he wanted to do was sleep. But Urkiat was his only ally, and he needed to be able to count on him. "It's hard. Being away from my family. Worrying about my son. Sharing this day with strangers."

Wasn't this obvious? Why should he have to explain it? But Urkiat kept nodding, hungry for the words, so he forced himself to continue. "I should have expected the Memory-Keeper to ask for a tale. It's customary. But to have asked for that one . . ."

"You've never told the tale? I thought you just said that. To shut him up."

"Nay."

"Not even to Griane?"

"I've told her . . . most of it." He frowned and steered the conversation away from Griane. "Sometimes, the children ask me things. 'What did you eat?' 'Were you scared when you met the Trickster?' 'Did you cry when he cut off your fingers?' "

"They ask that?"

"Those are the things they wonder about."

"And you don't mind?"

"It's . . . different with children. I remember what it was like to feel small in a big world, to feel clumsy and stupid and scared. If Darak Spirit-Hunter can admit to being afraid, they know it's all right for them to feel afraid, too."

"So you always answer them?"

"I'm their teacher. I owe them honesty."

Urkiat hesitated. "Did you . . . ?"

"What?"

"Nothing."

"Bel's blazing ballocks, man. What?"

Half-ashamed, half-eager, Urkiat asked, "Did you cry? When he cut off your fingers?"

Darak's hands closed into fists. "Nay. I screamed."

Chapter 14

NEW GUARDS BROUGHT him water and dried fruit in the morning. Keirith wondered if the others had been killed or simply relieved of their duties. He called on his lessons with the Tree-Father, seeking stillness and calm, but ended up pacing his tiny prison. Windowless and dark, it was like a small cairn; he shuddered every time he went inside.

He shuddered now as he heard footsteps. Half the morning had fled while he waited. If that was a ploy by the Pajhit to frighten him, it had succeeded.

One of his guards gestured for him to come out. The Pajhit barely glanced at him before starting down the corridor.

"Where are we going?"

The Pajhit ignored him.

Watch, Keirith. Watch. Observe. Remember.

Instead of leading him up the stairs to the interrogation chamber, the Pajhit turned left into another corridor. More than a dozen small chambers lined both sides. Pale light streamed through the doorways on the right, illuminating piles of fleece, but whoever slept on them was gone. Slaves, perhaps? Or guards?

The Pajhit turned left again, leading him away from the bright spill of light ahead that hinted at an entrance to the fortress. In less than ten steps, the tantalizing glimpse of freedom vanished. Their little procession turned right and right again before the corridor came to an abrupt end.

Against the wall to his left, narrow stone stairs led to the level above. Opposite them, an old man stood before a wooden door. Unlike the scantily clad Zherosi Keirith had seen so far, he wore a long-sleeved tunic, creased leather breeches, and stout boots that rose to mid-calf.

"You will go with the Qepo now."

He searched the Pajhit's face for some hint of what might await him, but the priest simply mounted the stairs, leaving him with the two guards and the Qepo.

Keirith forced himself to breathe deeply, pretending the air was fresh and forest-clean instead of thick with stale air and smoke from the torches, thicker still with the stink of his fear. The old man said something, but only when he pointed at the wall did Keirith spot the clothes hanging from several bronze hooks embedded in the chinks between the stones.

He pulled the tunic over his head. The stiff leather hampered his movements, but at least it offered some protection from the chill, as did the breeches he pulled over his loincloth. The Qepo knelt and held up a boot. Bracing himself against the wall, Keirith lifted his foot, the creak of leather disturbing the silence. The old man tucked the breeches into the boots and laced them tightly. That done, he rose, holding out something that looked like an enormous stuffed hand. The Qepo slipped it over his fingers and tucked the sleeves of his tunic into it, weaving the leather thongs around his wrist. His hand and forearm looked as thick as a bear's and felt just as unwieldy.

After the Qepo secured the second bear paw, he straightened. His gnarled fingers sketched a spiral on the wooden door. The guards made the same sign over their chests. Their uneasy expressions only added to his fear.

The door swung open with a dull creak. The Qepo stepped inside, gesturing for Keirith to follow.

Maker, guide me.

The open-air pit was no larger than his family's hut. The square of light illuminated a tangle of vines in the center. A single torch guttered in the draft of the open door, casting eerie shadows on the stone walls that rose up four or five times his height. Except one, he quickly realized. The Pajhit leaned over that one, flanked by the Zheron and the older priestess—the Motixa?

The Qepo backed away. The door closed behind him with another protesting creak. Bewildered, Keirith raised his head and called, "What am I supposed to do?"

"Speak to them," the Pajhit replied.

As he examined the pit again, the vines shifted with an almost imperceptible rustle. Startled, he peered at them, searching for the animal underneath.

One of the vines reared up. That's when Keirith realized that they weren't vines at all. They were snakes. Dozens of snakes.

As the boy flattened himself against the wall, Xevhan whispered, "Not a very promising start."

Malaq ignored him, concentrating on the boy whose eyes darted around the walls—seeking handholds, perhaps?—before settling on the adders.

"Well?" Xevhan asked. "What do we do now?"

"We wait," Malaq replied.

The boy slid down the wall. He sat in the pit, legs splayed in front of him, staring at the adders. Then his head fell back and he closed his eyes.

"Praying?" Xevhan speculated. "Or simply committing his spirit to his gods?"

Malaq resisted the urge to snap at him. Already, he regretted his decision to choose this test. Distasteful as it might have been to enter the boy's spirit without permission, he could have learned more about him and his gift. Once the boy failed, he would have to be sacrificed.

After yesterday's escape attempt, Malaq had expected him to show more spirit. The rush of disappointment surprised him. After all, it wasn't as if he believed he was the Son of Zhe.

The mist writhed around him, mimicking the movement of the adders. Cool air filled his lungs. He tasted subtle hints of moist earth and smooth stone. Bright sparks flashed amid the stately dance of earth and stone, the graceful swirl of air and water. His body jerked helplessly as the elemental dance possessed him. He thrust out his tongue to lap up more of the mist and sighed when his body slid to the earth, so cool and welcoming against his cheek.

The mist was softer than any cushion. The earth cradled him more gently than any arms. He sank into the womb of mist and earth, following the flashes of fire that lurked just out of reach, urging him deeper, promising . . . promising . . .

The mist gave an irritated hiss. Red-brown eyes appeared before him. A long tongue flicked out to sting his lips. Keirith's head jerked back, knocking painfully against stone.

"You are not ready to go so deep," Natha said. "You would have lost yourself."

But how wonderful to be so lost, he thought with regret.

His spirit guide slithered across his throat and Keirith shivered in delight. "Why did you call me?" Natha demanded.

Still dazed by the dance, it took him a moment to remember. "The adders. They want me to speak with them."

"I do not perform for strangers. Especially these who claim to worship us but keep us in this hole."

"Perhaps they're frightened of us."

Natha's sigh of satisfaction flowed through him, warmer than the mist but just as pleasurable. "Perhaps they are. And that is good. Come."

The mist dissipated as Natha led him toward the adders. His limbs moved reluctantly beneath their shroud of leather, the cool air no longer refreshing but a heavy weight that made each step difficult. Even his heartbeat had slowed, which made no sense, for he was frightened. But visions were strange that way and this one was the strangest he had ever experienced, every sensation both real and dreamlike.

What had seemed an undifferentiated mass proved to be a tangle of gray and buff and brown. In the north, adders blended in with grass and leaves, but in a world where green existed only in scenes painted on walls, they would naturally wear the colors of earth and stone.

"Brothers. Sisters."

Heads reared up as Natha spoke. Tongues flicked out, scenting the air.

"Why are you in this place?"

Perhaps the adders answered Natha in words. Keirith experienced their replies as disjointed images and sensations.

Cold. So cold. Huddling around the heat-stone. Basking

in the brief moments when sunlight touched them. Only the strong fed. Only the strongest mated. The young ones were too weak to compete, too sluggish to seek the light and the warmth.

Keirith sent back images of his own. Sun-warmed slabs of rock to bask upon, shady dens to shield them when the heat grew too intense. Brush piles where they could seek mice and nestlings, muddy shallows where they could hunt frogs. Stalking the prey. Fangs sinking into flesh. Following the prey's scent as it crawled or hopped away. Patiently waiting for the venom to take effect, patiently waiting for the beautiful, tremulous convulsions of death before gorging to repletion and drowsing until the next kill.

Instead of soothing them, his images roused the adders. He saw leather-clad feet walking among them, leather-clad hands reaching for them, separating each from the others, forcing open their mouths, pushing their heads down as the males pushed down the heads of their opponents when they fought for the females. Fangs sought the leather-clad hands and penetrated instead the strange, soft stone pressed into their gaping mouths.

Hatred as pervasive as the cold.

"Natha? What should I do?" His spirit guide slithered between his feet, his small body encircling a boot. "Natha?"

And then, in the way of visions, Keirith understood.

The boy bent his head over his arm.

Xevhan leaned forward. "Why is he chewing the glove?"

His head jerked back and bent again. He repeated this strange ritual several times before Malaq realized he was trying to unlace the glove with his teeth.

Xevhan groaned. "This could take all morning."

The boy's arduous progress was punctuated by such pithy observations. Finally, he tucked his hand under his armpit and tugged the glove free. He laid it carefully on the ground. The second glove took less time to remove. He placed it next to the other and went down on one knee.

"Blessed Zhe," Eliaxa breathed. "What is he doing?"

"He's unlacing his boot," Malaq replied.

"I see that. But why?"

"That, of course, is the question." As the boy tugged the heavy leather tunic over his head, Malaq beckoned the Qepo forward. "How many strikes can he withstand?"

"They were milked this morning, great Pajhit. I did it myself. And they're sluggish because I extinguished the brazier. They may not attack at all."

Malaq reluctantly withdrew his gaze from the pit.

The Qepo flinched. "I've seen a man take five strikes after a milking and live."

But this was a boy, of course, not a man.

"Shall I go down, great Pajhit?"

The boy folded his breeches neatly atop his tunic. He unwound his skimpy kharo and let it fall to the ground. Naked, he walked toward the adders.

The Qepo raced toward the stairway, moving far more quickly than Malaq would have expected for one so old. "Wait!"

The Qepo froze. Eliaxa and Xevhan stirred restively. The boy walked slowly toward the tangle of adders.

"Wait."

Unblinking eyes watched him as he stepped closer. Although he had shed the heavy leather garments, every movement was slow, as if the cold had seeped deep into his bones, rendering him as sluggish as the adders. He understood their hatred of the leather-clad feet and hands, but each step made his heart thud.

Every summer, someone disturbed an adder and had to be carried to his mam. In spite of the intense pain and swelling, all survived, but Keirith could still remember the screams. And that was one snake, not dozens.

He stopped just out of striking range. Natha wove in and out between his feet, calming his fear, steadying him. Naked, he stretched out on the cool earth.

Slender tongues flicked out, scenting him. Slender bodies slithered toward him. When he felt the dry brush of scales against his ankle, his mind told him to flee, but the dreamlike calm only deepened. Mist touched his cheek—Natha's touch. Natha's reassuring whisper echoed inside him: "Be calm. Be still."

Stillness. Emptiness. Control.

With a sigh of acceptance, Keirith offered himself to them.

An adder slid over his wrist. Another wove a sinuous track across his belly. They wriggled up his legs, around his arms. Their scales drifted across his thighs and genitals. Their tongues kissed his chest, his neck, his mouth.

Fluid as water, smoother than stone, the adders danced. Their eyes were the dull fire of the dying sun. Their voices were autumn leaves, rustling in the wind. Their bodies were vines, weaving around the trunks of trees. And he was the earth beneath them, warm and comforting and alive.

The adders swarmed over him. And the boy smiled. They covered his legs, his torso, his arms. And the boy smiled. They slithered over his neck, their bodies tangled in his hair. And still, the boy smiled.

Eliaxa whispered prayers. Xevhan traced the spiral on his chest. Malaq simply watched, his heart pounding so loudly he was sure the others must hear. All his life, he had longed to see a miracle. In the pit below, it was happening.

Could it be true? Could he really be the one?

As if they heard an unspoken command, the writhing mass of adders became still. One by one, they retreated. Only then did the boy's eyes open.

His chest heaved in a sigh as he rose. He walked toward the door and removed the torch from its bracket. Moving with the same dreamlike grace, he returned to the adders. They parted before him, allowing him to step close to the clay brazier. He touched the torch to the fuel and waited for it to catch. Then he backed away, allowing the adders to seethe toward the heat.

He returned the torch to its bracket and gathered his discarded clothing. With a last, lingering look at the adders, he pulled open the door and disappeared.

The Qepo was the first to recover. He hurried toward the stairs and this time, Malaq let him go. Still lost in the miracle, he stared into the pit.

"It's impossible," Xevhan whispered.

"He shed." Eliaxa's voice caught on a sob. "As the adder

sheds its skin, he shed his clothing. And they blessed him. The adders blessed him."

"It was cool in the pit," Xevhan argued. Already, he was regaining his self-possession. "You heard the Qepo. The adders were sluggish. They had just been milked. The danger was minimal."

"Yes," Malaq replied. "But the boy didn't know that."

"By these signs shall you know him." Eliaxa swayed as she recited the ancient words. "His power shall burn bright as Heart of Sky at Midsummer. His footsteps shall make Womb of Earth tremble. Speechless, he shall understand the language of the adder, and wingless, soar through the sky like the eagle."

Movement caught Malaq's attention. The Qepo stepped aside to allow the boy to pass. He had donned his kharo once more, but his dazed expression conveyed the lingering effects of the trial he had undergone.

"Ask him what they said," Xevhan demanded.

"Later," Eliaxa said. "The glory is still upon him. He must rest."

Malaq gestured for him to follow the guards, but he couldn't resist asking, "Why did you remove your clothes?"

When the boy frowned, Malaq wondered if he even remembered what had happened. Then Kheridh shrugged, as if the answer should be obvious.

"The adders. They were cold."

Chapter 15

MALAQ MARCHED UP the wide steps. The royal
guards thumped their chests with their fists as he
passed, then returned to blank-faced immobility. According
to the king, the original builder of the palace had boasted
that twenty men could march abreast into the throne room.
When a demonstration proved only nineteen could manage
the feat, the unfortunate builder was condemned to death.
Ten generations later, the king still giggled when he pointed
out the delicious irony of sacrificing the man on the newly
erected altar of the God with Two Faces.

The babble of voices grew louder as he entered the throne
room. He squeezed through the crowd of guests—priests,
administrators, courtiers—who had been fortunate enough
to secure invitations. What had begun as a solemn rite,
attended only by the monarchs and their senior priests, had
evolved into a prestigious social occasion. For all the elegant attire and abundance of jewelry on display, he might
be at the wedding of a nobleman's daughter.

As usual, the most favored of the king's companions
lounged on the steps of the dais. At least the queen still
insisted that her attendants stand. With flounces of blue
and gold and scarlet adorning their long skirts, they looked
like a flock of brilliantly plumaged birds. Yet they paled in
comparison to the queen.

While her ladies covered themselves with jewelry, she
wore only a golden snake coiled around her bicep and another in her hair. Instead of noticing the jewels, the eye

was drawn to the slenderness of the arms, the delicacy of
the long fingers, the glossy coils of her black hair. A shimmering sheath of imported lilmia swathed her breasts, and
her skirt flowed over her thighs like water before cascading
into a tumble of blue and green flounces.

He prostrated himself at the base of the dais. The queen
smiled as he rose, but the king's head lolled against the
back of his throne. Malaq tried to hide his shock at the king's
sickly pallor, the dark shadows under his eyes, the sunken
chest. His sojourn at the summer palace had done him no
good at all. He was always weak before The Shedding, but
never so bad as this.

The king's companions managed to bestir themselves
long enough for him to mount the steps and take his place
beside the king. Eliaxa and Xevhan performed the ritual
prostration and took their places, Eliaxa at the queen's left
and Xevhan between the thrones.

The queen raised her hand. The blast of the kankh made
everyone wince. Astonishing that a shell so beautiful and
delicate could produce a bellow worthy of a bullock. Courtiers shuffled back to create a narrow path down the center
of the chamber.

*They'll have to breathe in unison if they want to get any
air.*

The horn bellowed again as the twenty-six candidates
marched toward the thrones. Their escorts squeezed aside
to allow them to prostrate themselves. Shoulder to shoulder, given the crush. The queen leaned forward as she motioned them to rise. Even the king sat up a little straighter
when they pulled off their short flaxcloth tunics and stood
naked before the dais. This year, Malaq had made certain
only the strongest candidates were presented to him; he
refused to allow the king to choose yet another frail, willowy boy as the Host.

His thoughts drifted as the questioning began; the candidates' responses mattered little, although the queen always
preferred a young woman with wit as well as beauty. Van-
ity, really; only her beauty would remain after The Shedding.

Today's council meeting was his only opportunity to
speak to the king and queen about the boy. The banquet
later would be as much of a crush as this audience and the

moon of seclusion began at dawn. After that, no one was permitted to see or speak to them until they emerged for The Shedding; even the two attendants who waited on them must serve and dress them in silence, with eyes averted.

The problem was how much to reveal. He could claim the boy was Zhe himself and get nothing more than a disinterested nod from the king. The queen was another matter.

There had always been false prophets claiming to be the Son of Zhe; during his five years as Pajhit, he'd questioned six. A few possessed genuine power, while others were tools of the men and women who sought power through them. None had ever heard the voices of the sacred adders.

The queen held out her hand to a tall, sturdy-looking girl who fell to her knees and kissed it. A dimple graced her left cheek when she smiled. The king—gods save us—chose the smallest and slenderest of the youths, but at least this one didn't look as if a gust of wind would drop him to his knees. Doubtless he would do so tonight—before one of the king's favorites; the king was too enervated by qiij to do more than watch.

Malaq's hand crept up his chest to touch the tiny vial that hung from the gold chain, the visible reminder that only the rulers and senior priests were permitted the unsupervised use of qiij. Regular consumption of the drug robbed one of the appetite for food as well as sex, but he wondered again if it rendered one sterile as well. Otherwise, the king and queen surely would have produced one child in the ten generations they had ruled. Was that the effect of the adders' venom or the juice of the pozho plant?

Even if his speculations were unfounded, the queen had only to look at her brother to see the devastation qiij wrought on his body and mind. Perhaps that was the key to convincing her to grant him more time with the boy.

The bellow of the kankh shattered his reverie. The queen rose and took the king's arm. With a sigh of relief, Malaq left the crowded throne room for the private reception chamber.

Although it was far smaller, it was just as ornate. Thick rugs covered the floor. Colorful cushions lay scattered around the low table. Behind the two thrones, a mural depicted scarlet-winged Zhe rising from the verdant sacred mountain—a bit of artistic overstatement as Kelazhat was

neither lush nor green—bearing a golden Heart of Sky
through pink and violet clouds. Although the colors were
far too garish for his taste, Malaq still preferred it to the
mural on the opposite wall that showed Zhe devouring his
father. Blackened feathers drifted through a fiery sunset as
Zhe plummeted toward a sea that looked disturbingly like
blood. Fortunately, protocol dictated that the priests sit
with their backs to the dying gods.

Sky-wells in the two courtyards flanking the chamber admitted light and air. The slaves must have lit a brazier earlier; the smoky scent of incense still lingered, overpowering
the fragrance of the thornblossoms and bitterheart that
overflowed the vases in the wall niches.

The queen plumped the gold pillow on her brother's
throne before easing him onto it. Then she seated herself
and nodded. Malaq and Xevhan held Eliaxa's elbows while
she sank onto a cushion, then sat on either side of her.
Vazh and Besul took their places at opposite ends of the
long table. An obvious case of seating arrangements re-
flecting life: Eliaxa always the buffer and mediator, Vazh
and Besul as far apart as possible.

As if to prove that point, Vazh took one look at the
steaming mounds of bread proffered by the slaves and
glared at Besul. The winter rains had delayed the planting
of the millet; the recent drought had destroyed the barley.
While Eliaxa redoubled her entreaties to Womb of Earth,
the eminently practical Vazh had ordered grain rationing.
Clearly, Besul did not believe such restrictions applied to
the royal council.

Slaves glided in with platters of cold partridge and
smoked mussels, bowls of goat cheese and jhok, pitchers of
wine and water, then disappeared as silently as they had
come. The two royal attendants remained, kneeling beside
the thrones to proffer goblets of wine and tidbits of food
to the monarchs. The king drank thirstily, but the queen
contented herself with a single sip before passing the goblet back.

As usual, the Supplicant of the God with Two Faces was
missing. She was as mercurial as the god she served, rarely
attending council meetings, scarcely bothering to appear in
the god's temple. The Acolyte conducted most of the sacrifices. Even those were unusual. The Supplicant insisted the

god preferred flowers or small animals. But occasionally—and apparently without warning—the god demanded a human life. The Supplicant herself made those sacrifices, ripping out the throat of the man or woman who lay on the altar. Or so it was whispered.

Malaq repressed a shudder; all in all, he was relieved that the Supplicant had chosen to absent herself, although he continued to wonder why the queen permitted it.

The queen raised her hand, commanding their attention. "We have enjoyed our sojourn in the north, but always we welcome our return to our holy city. And the opportunity of speaking with our trusted counselors. We have much to discuss today and many preparations to make before we enter our moon of seclusion. Let us begin."

With difficulty, Malaq quelled his restiveness during the lengthy discussion of the upcoming trade negotiations with Eriptos, the measures being taken to alleviate the drought, and the state of hostilities in the east. Besul and Vazh wrangled with each other as always. As the senior civil authority in the kingdom, Besul oversaw trade, while Vazh supervised internal security. Unfortunately, the slave raids required their cooperation. Vazh coordinated the raids, but it fell to Besul to ensure that there were enough ships to convey the captives to Zheros, enough food to feed them during their voyage, and adequate facilities to house those who were brought to Pilozhat.

It was a pity Vazh had been wounded in Carilia. He was far better suited to the life of a general than that of administrator. Still, Malaq was glad the leg injury had brought his old friend back to Pilozhat. He only wished the press of their responsibilities allowed them more time to enjoy each other's company.

We'd probably just sit around reliving the battles we fought—like a pair of old men.

He reminded himself that he wasn't old; past his prime, perhaps, but still vigorous. It was this business with the boy that wearied him. Shutting out Besul's interminable drone, he considered again the meaning of the dream.

He'd overcome his reluctance and entered Kheridh's spirit while he slept. Although it was easiest to touch a spirit then, the results of such explorations were always difficult to evaluate. Dreams of flying were common enough. What

stood out in the boy's was the clarity of detail: the circle
of huts beside a lake, the long silver thread of the river.
Judging from the glimpses he'd caught of long, brown wing
feathers, it seemed the boy had been transformed into a
hawk or an eagle. That, too, was common, but now he
wondered. Had he actually ridden the bird's spirit in violation of his people's laws?

And wingless, soar through the sky like the eagle.

Kheridh's joy was so infectious that Malaq had to
strengthen his shield lest he be detected. Then, in the sudden way that dreams have of shifting time and place, there
was darkness and a terror even more palpable than the joy.
Footsteps. Rough hands. Men's laughter. And before the
ultimate violation, the scream that jolted the boy awake
and forced Malaq to flee.

The faces of the attackers had been invisible, but he
guessed one was the warrior who had testified during that
first interrogation. Rapes occurred on every raid. But red-
haired captives were reserved for the Midsummer sacrifice
to Heart of Sky and as such, were safe from abuse. Should
be safe.

Malaq banished a pang of sympathy. It was his duty to
learn as much from the boy as possible. Hard enough to win
the trust of a captive; harder still when he had suffered so.
And impossible if the queen refused to give him more time.

As the discussion turned to the recent raids, Malaq
forced his wandering attention back to the meeting.

"We garnered sixty-eight slaves for the altar of Heart of
Sky," Besul reported. He shot Vazh an innocent look. "It
was anticipated that we would capture the full complement
required. Was there some unexpected problem?"

"The ships that fell short had a night's journey upriver."
Ignoring Besul, Vazh addressed the queen directly. "Both
villages were already stirring when they arrived."

"A risk you pointed out, Khonsel, at the time the plan
was discussed," the queen noted. "Still, the raids brought
in more than four hundred slaves, I believe."

"Four hundred and twenty-two," Besul said; his attention
to detail was invaluable, if tiresome. "The sixty-eight pre-
viously mentioned will be reserved for the Midsummer sacrifice. Forty-five additional slaves were brought to Pilozhat
to augment the fifty-three still remaining in the slave com-

pound from previous raids. These will be used for our daily sacrifices, save for the seventeen sold to the Jhevi. The rest were taken directly to Oexiak for sale." After a quick glance at Vazh, he added, "I hesitate to recommend additional raids at this time, Earth's Beloved. We do have to feed the slaves." He sighed, obviously regretting the necessity.

"In light of our depleted granaries, it's wise to keep them for as short a time as possible." The queen waved away the basket of bread her attendant proffered.

"Yes, Earth's Beloved," Besul agreed. "But it's a delicate balance. Made even more difficult when raids do not deliver the anticipated results."

"Burn me!" Vazh exclaimed.

Malaq repressed a wince. The king's eyes fluttered open, but the queen seemed mildly amused by Vazh's blasphemy.

"You can't predict everything that'll happen in a raid. Especially one of this scale. You'd know that if you'd spent one day fighting with the army instead of counting your bales of wool."

"I am quite aware of the exigencies of war. And I resent—"

"Stuavo. Khonsel. Peace." The two men subsided, still glaring at each other. "We understand the difficulties you face and are grateful for your dedication and loyalty in carrying out your responsibilities. Do you recommend more raids on the north at this time, Khonsel?"

"The ships are needed to ferry troops and supplies to Carilia. They can bring the slaves we require for the Midsummer sacrifice on the return voyage." Vazh thrust up a hand to forestall Besul's interruption. "If we need more, I'll organize a smaller raid on the Tree People as we approach Midsummer."

"Let it be done." The queen glanced at the king whose eyes had closed. "We thank the Khonsel and the Stuavo for attending. There are a few matters pertaining to The Shedding that we must review with the priests, but we will not bore you with those."

Vazh heaved an audible sigh of relief and winced as he pushed himself to his feet. The stubborn old fool insisted on sitting on a cushion, no matter how it aggravated his leg.

The queen held out her hands and both men bent low to

kiss them. She clung to them a moment, murmuring something too soft to hear. Whatever she said made Vazh and Besul exchange a quick glance, looking as guilty as first-year Zhiisti who'd been caught raiding the kitchen for a snack. They nodded reluctantly and won a smile from the queen before she dismissed them.

The details of The Shedding were dispatched quickly; he and Eliaxa had overseen the rite enough times for it to become almost routine.

"Now. About this boy."

As always, the queen's network of spies was efficient. Malaq would have given much to have seen Xevhan's expression and gauge whether he was one of them, but short of leaning past Eliaxa, it was impossible.

"What boy?" the king asked.

"A captive from the north. He is supposed to possess . . . interesting powers. Would you like to see him?"

"I suppose. But then I want to lie down. I have a headache. That awful kankh." His voice was thin and fretful, preserving little of the sweetness that had been so admired after the last Shedding.

The queen nodded to her attendant who slipped out of the chamber. Malaq had been prepared for such a summons; he only hoped Kheridh was.

"Zheron, I believe you conducted the initial interrogation. While we wait for the guards to bring the boy, please enlighten us."

Xevhan's report was concise but accurate. When he finished, Malaq described the events in the adder pit and his subsequent conversation with Kheridh.

"'They were cold?' Those were his exact words?"

"Yes, Earth's Beloved."

"And the things he told you later. Do you believe them?"

"If he sought to curry favor, I doubt he would have told me that the adders were . . ."

"Miserable." Her fingers drummed on the arm of the throne. "Yet we have cared for them thus for generations and our people have prospered."

"I've instructed the Qepo to place additional braziers in the pit," Malaq said, "and to keep them burning at all times—save for the mornings when the adders are milked."

The queen held up her hand. Malaq glanced behind him and saw the boy hovering in the doorway, flanked by his two guards. His awed glance took in the sumptuous decorations before settling on the queen.

"Let him come forward."

Malaq rose and beckoned. Although he had personally supervised Kheridh's garbing—much to his discomfiture—he still found himself inspecting every detail of his dress; boys' clothes had a lamentable ability to fall into disarray within moments of donning them.

A lock of unruly hair had escaped the simple leather thong at the nape of his neck, but his khirta was in order. It had taken an inordinate amount of wrestling with the sheath of flaxcloth before Kheridh mastered the trick of drawing the fabric between his legs and allowing the folds of the short trousers to cascade over his hips. Knotting it at the waist proved so ineffective that Malaq had to resort to a leather girdle. His scabbed knees and hairless chest made him look even younger than his years, but there was no helping—or hiding—those.

Boys at the cusp of manhood were awkward creatures. Eventually, the gods would finish the task of putting them together, but in the meantime, there was something endearing about watching one try to cope with newly-long legs and a treacherous voice that cracked into a falsetto at inopportune moments.

Kheridh was watching him with a look of panic. Malaq realized he was frowning and quickly nodded.

He performed the ritual prostration correctly and remained motionless until the queen commanded him to rise. Malaq translated, adding a reminder to remain on his knees; a slave never stood in the presence of royalty.

"He doesn't look like the Son of Zhe," the king noted.

"Sky's Light, we don't know that he is," Malaq replied.

"Didn't he speak with the adders? Or something?"

"Yes, Jholin." The queen squeezed his hand. "Remember? They were cold."

"Oh. Yes. I think so."

"Tell us what else you know of him," the queen commanded.

Briefly, Malaq reviewed Kheridh's dream, leaving out

any mention of the rape. He also related the incidents with the slaves he'd sent to Kheridh's room, ostensibly to reward him for his success in the adder pit.

When he concluded, the king leaned forward. "Perhaps he suffers some infirmity."

"Sky's Light?"

"That prevented him from lying with the slaves."

Trust the king to fasten on that. "The girl—and the guards—swore that he was . . . aroused. He showed no interest in the male slave."

His reaction had been somewhat more dramatic. One guard described his expression as "horrified," the other said "disgusted."

"It's very strange," the king mused. "Don't you think so, Jholianna?"

"A mystery." She turned her dark gaze on Kheridh whose head had remained appropriately bowed throughout their conversation. "What is your name, boy?"

His head jerked up as Malaq translated. "My name is Kheridh," he replied in Zherosi.

"He speaks our tongue?" the queen asked, clearly startled.

"I instructed him in a few sentences, Earth's Beloved."

"What else can he say?"

At his prompting, Kheridh said, "Earth's Beloved, this slave is unworthed to kneel at your foots."

"Unworthy," Malaq corrected. "Feet."

"Forgive me. Unworthy feet."

"He means—"

"Yes. I know." The queen extended her hands, then drew back, frowning, as the boy tensed.

He doesn't even realize he's doing it.

"Take the queen's hands," Malaq ordered, thanking the gods he'd insisted on filing down the ragged nails and soaping out the dirt accumulated under them.

"Your hands are very cold," the queen said, her voice a low caress.

The boy swallowed hard. "I'm scared," he whispered in the tribal tongue.

"Your presence fills him with awe, Earth's Beloved."

"Without the decoration, please."

"He said, 'I'm scared.' "

"As he should be. Don't translate that." She favored the boy with one of her dazzling smiles. Color flared on his pale cheeks. A nervous smile came and went.

"You are so beauty," he whispered in Zherosi.

Still smiling, the queen asked, "Was that one of the phrases you taught him?"

"No, Earth's Beloved." Bad enough that he had the temerity to construct an independent thought from the standard phrases he had learned; to address the queen without her permission could earn him a whipping.

"You are bold," she said.

"Forgive me, Earth's Beloved." Fear replaced the glazed look of adoration. "Please . . ." He fumbled with the words and dragged his gaze from the queen. "Would you tell her I meant no disrespect? I'm not . . . my people . . . our chiefs . . ."

"He asks your forgiveness again, Earth's Beloved, and assures you he meant no disrespect. His people are accustomed to less formality when addressing their chiefs."

"So you tell your chief that she is beautiful?"

Kheridh laughed, then quickly controlled himself. "Earth's Beloved, our chief is a man."

"A man cannot be beautiful?"

"To a woman, I suppose."

This time, she was the one to laugh. "You may go."

The boy prostrated himself again, then rose and backed out of the reception chamber. Malaq lowered himself onto his cushion with a small sigh of relief.

"So." The queen made a minute adjustment to one of the flounces on her skirt. "A red-haired virgin of—what? Fourteen?—who refuses congress with both male and female slaves. Who possesses the ability to speak with the adders. Who has the power to touch the spirits of others without the use of qiij. And who might—might—have used that ability to ride the spirit of a bird."

"Yes, Earth's Beloved."

"But is he the Son of Zhe?"

"Impossible!" Xevhan burst out. "The Son of Zhe would never come to earth in the body of a barbarian."

"What better way to test our faith?" Eliaxa asked. "Oh, my queen. If you could have seen him in the pit. When he shed."

"He's already admitted his father is a . . ." Xevhan fumbled for the title.

"Memory-Keeper," Malaq supplied.

"He may not know his true parentage," Eliaxa said. "His mother may have kept it a secret to protect him. Perhaps she does not realize it herself."

"Not realize she was seduced by a winged serpent?" Xevhan scoffed. "I'd think few women would forget that."

"Perhaps great Zhe came to her in another guise," Eliaxa said.

"Perhaps," Xevhan conceded impatiently. "But this boy's powers are hardly unique. I'm told every priest in every village possesses them. Isn't that right, Malaq?"

"They claim to have the ability to touch the spirits of others," he said evenly. "But they spend years honing their gifts. For a boy so young to possess them is unusual."

Malaq took a deep breath. If the gods existed, he hoped they would guide him now. "Earth's Beloved. Does it matter whether or not he is the Son of Zhe? Of course, we will continue to test him, to observe. But meanwhile, we should learn more about his gift."

"A gift he calls an abomination," the queen said.

"He is afraid of it, true. But he longs to use it."

"The gift or the power it might bring him?"

"He knows the joy—and the fear—that comes of possessing it, but I doubt he perceives the power. Earth's Beloved, we have never seen such a boy before. Think of what we could learn from him. The ability to speak with the adders. To control the spirits of others—to touch them, cast them out, commune with them—without relying upon a drug that saps the body and breeds an insatiable hunger for more."

"I am well aware of the addictive powers of qiij."

"Of course, Earth's Beloved. Forgive me."

"I am also aware of the danger in allowing such knowledge to become widespread among the priesthood."

"Knowledge can be controlled. Just as the supply of qiij is now."

"He'll never cooperate," Xevhan insisted. "You said yourself he refused to allow you to touch his spirit."

"He won't cooperate if coerced," Malaq said. "But he's

frightened. Far from home. Among people who perceive his power as a gift, not an abomination."

"The same people who captured him," the queen interjected. "Hardly an incentive to win his trust."

"Among his people, the use of his power makes him an outcast," Malaq said. "I believe we should encourage him. Win him over. Seduce him."

"Your attempts at seduction have proven less than successful."

"I speak of seducing him to our ways." The queen frowned at his sharp tone. "Let us teach him our language," he continued mildly. "Educate him about our culture. Offer him a life he never dreamed of."

"To what end?" Xevhan demanded. "So he can pollute our priesthood with his foreign ways? It's bad enough that you—" He broke off abruptly, then said, "Earth's Beloved, I agree there might be value in learning more about his powers. But once we have, we must dispose of him."

"No!" Eliaxa cried. "My queen, you cannot allow it."

The queen held up her hand. "We will investigate this boy—and his gift—more thoroughly. But we should make inquiries in the slave compound as well. Perhaps we captured priests in this last series of raids who can provide additional information. I wonder we never thought to interrogate any before."

Malaq returned her limpid gaze stolidly. Until today, the queen had never cared about the fate of slaves.

"Zheron, you will investigate the remaining slaves. Pajhit, provide the Khonsel any information that would help us target these priests in future raids. And continue to study the boy."

"Thank you, Earth's Beloved."

"But enlist another to teach him our language. The Shedding is a moon away and the Midsummer rite follows hard on its heels. You have too many responsibilities to allow yourself to be distracted."

"There are several scribes who—"

"The slave Hircha," Xevhan suggested. "Who translated during the initial interrogation. She's quite capable. And the boy will be more likely to reveal information to one of his own people."

"A male slave might be—"

"No." The queen smiled. "Use the girl."

"Yes, Earth's Beloved." Malaq bowed his head, his fury carefully hidden.

The queen swiveled slightly on her throne. "Jholin. Dearest. Would you like Dax to take you to your chamber?"

The king opened his eyes. "Is the meeting over?"

"Yes, dear."

"Oh, good. What did we decide?"

"We will continue to investigate the boy. As you suggested."

"Did I?" He smiled. "You'd remember. You remember everything."

"Yes. I do." The queen's smile was pained, but when she turned back to their table, she was as composed as ever. "My brother and I thank you for your counsel and hope to see you at tonight's banquet to celebrate our homecoming."

Malaq rose with the others, but as he turned to leave, the queen's voice stopped him. "A moment, Malaq." She whispered something to her attendant who rose and left the chamber.

Dax entered and prostrated himself; he must have been waiting outside in anticipation of the summons. At the queen's gesture, he approached the throne and gently lifted the king. Cradled against the slave's broad chest, the king's body looked even more wasted. After they disappeared through the doorway leading to the royal apartments, the queen sighed.

"Do you remember how beautiful he was after last summer's Shedding?"

"Yes, Earth's Beloved."

"And will be again."

"Yes, Earth's Beloved."

She favored him with an ironic smile. "I detect your hand, I think, in the selection of the Hosts. Thank you."

Malaq bowed.

"Others pander to his tastes. Indulge him. Well. You know."

Her rare confidences no longer shocked him, but he was wise enough not to voice his agreement.

"You don't believe he is the Son of Zhe."

The sudden change in subject and tone took him aback. "Earth's Beloved, I cannot say. The gods offer the same riddles as the prophecy."

"Riddles are the gods' way of testing our faith. And our patience."

A lesser being could be put to death for uttering the last words, but she was Earth-Made-Flesh and far above the judgment of mortal men.

"You're drawn to this boy. Why?"

Since he was certain she'd seen his surprise, he must give her part of the truth. "Perhaps because of what happened in the pit. If you had seen him, covered by the adders—smiling." Malaq shrugged. "Or perhaps it is only that he's young and gifted and I . . . envy him."

"Yes. It is hard to remember what it was like to be young."

He'd rarely heard such wistfulness in her voice. It was easy to see only a beautiful woman, wise beyond her years, and forget that her spirit had lived for ten generations. How must it feel to be so ancient? To have seen everyone she had ever known die? Except, of course, her brother-husband.

"Xevhan is young as well," the queen continued. "And eager to prove himself. But he is faithful to our ways."

"As am I, Earth's Beloved."

"It was a reminder of Xevhan's character. Not a criticism of yours."

Malaq bowed his head, accepting the rebuke.

"Take care that your affinity for this boy—and your past association with his people—do not blind you to the danger he represents."

"Earth's Beloved—"

"Already you and Xevhan vie to control him. I am willing to permit this contention. It may even prove . . . fruitful. Use the moon of my seclusion to learn all you can about this boy's powers. Especially his ability to touch spirits without the use of qiij. Discover how it is done. Determine conclusively whether he is the Son of Zhe. By Midsummer, I will require a report."

"Earth's Beloved, to learn about his gift is one thing. To master it is quite another."

"We can always find other Tree People with this ability.

It's only a matter of time before we gain the knowledge we seek."

"And if we don't know by Midsummer whether or not he's the Son of Zhe?"

"If he is willing to adopt our ways and worship our gods, I will consider—consider, Malaq—letting him live. If not, he will be the first sacrifice you offer to Heart of Sky."

Chapter 16

KEIRITH SAT ON the stone bench, watching Niqia purring in the Pajhit's lap. In the sennight since his arrival in Pilozhat, he'd gone from slave to suspect to . . . what? Three days after his audience with the queen, he still wasn't sure.

His life had fallen into a routine. Mornings and afternoons, Hircha taught him the rudiments of the Zherosi tongue. Every evening, he shared a simple meal with the Pajhit. And every night, he returned to his little room and prayed the nightmares wouldn't come.

He'd found the language surprisingly easy to learn; it was similar to the ancient words the Tree-Father spoke during their rituals. Still, by the end of the day, his head ached from the effort of mentally translating every thought into Zherosi and he was grateful when the Pajhit allowed him to lapse into his native tongue. When Keirith asked how he came to speak it so well, the Pajhit said he'd grown up in the north of Zheros where there was a good deal of trading and intermingling with the children of the Oak and Holly.

They spent most evenings here in the garden. Although you couldn't describe the air as cool, it seemed almost refreshing after the sun went down. The Pajhit didn't seem perturbed by his continued refusal to demonstrate his gift or by his reluctance to talk about his home. He seemed content to answer his questions about Zherosi food and daily life and religion.

"I know you are sun-priest. And the Motixa is earth-priest. And—"

"Priestess."

"Priestess. Yes. Thank you. And Zheron is Zhe-priest. But who is Zhe? He is . . ." Keirith fumbled for the word "important" and gave up. ". . . very big god. He is your Maker?"

The Pajhit studied him for so long that Keirith wondered if he had committed another blunder. "Forgive me. I mean no disrespect."

He knew those two sentences by heart; he was always apologizing for his lack of understanding or inability to choose the correct words.

"We will speak your tongue as I want to be certain you understand." The Pajhit's hand glided across Niqia's head and down the striped back. "Zhe was born after the creation of the sky and the earth. Heart of Sky fell upon Womb of Earth and ravished her. Legend says the cataclysm of their union created Kelazhat, our sacred mountain."

Keirith repressed a shudder. It made perfect sense to him that the brooding mountain had been created as a result of rape.

"To punish Heart of Sky, Womb of Earth imprisoned him in the mountain. Nine moons later, she gave birth to Zhe, the winged serpent. The mountain split open during her birth pains—you've noticed Kelazhat's jagged peak?"

Keirith nodded; it looked like fangs.

"Zhe was seduced by his father's warmth and light into defying his mother. He rose from the mountain at dawn to carry his father across the heavens. Womb of Earth ripped open crevasses in the ground and hurled boulders down the slopes of Kelazhat. In her deep, booming voice, she called out, 'My son. My son. Why have you betrayed me?'"

The Pajhit swept his hand across the sky. "To escape his mother's voice, Zhe fled west, but the longer he flew, the hotter his father burned. His scarlet wings turned black. His body shriveled. Furious that his father should betray him after he had freed him from his underground tomb, Zhe turned on Heart of Sky and devoured him, leaving only his father's spirit-self—the moon—to light the ensuing darkness. And then he plummeted toward the Abyss."

A bitter tale of rape and betrayal and death. How much kinder the gods of his people were, with Bel chasing his lover Gheala through the skies. And how strange to believe the moon was merely the shadow of another god instead of a goddess in her own right.

"But Heart of Sky couldn't have died," Keirith said. "He rises every day."

"Womb of Earth's lamentations so moved The Changing One of the clouds that her tears flooded the Abyss before Zhe could reach its bottom. Zhe swam across the sea to our winding river—it flows through the gorge just there, beyond the temple—and finally reached the slopes of Kelazhat. Cold and sluggish, he wriggled up to the summit where, with his dying breath, he disgorged Heart of Sky whose heat restored him to life. And so it has been every sunset and every dawn. Zhe loves the cool embrace of his mother, but cannot resist his father's warmth. Each day, he rises from the summit of Kelazhat. Each night, he returns." The Pajhit scratched Niqia behind the ears. "So. What do you think of our gods?"

Keirith hesitated. "They seem to suffer so much."

"That is why we must feed them with sacrifices."

"Human sacrifices."

"As your people once did."

"Long ago."

"Until fifteen years ago, we offered human sacrifices only once a year. But then came the Long Winter."

"You call it that, too?"

"Yes." The Pajhit eased Niqia off his lap. She stretched, mouth gaping in a pink yawn, and padded inside in search of a more hospitable nest.

"The rains fell for a moon. The earth slid into the sea. We thought—as your people must have—that the world was ending. That Heart of Sky was dying or that Zhe had grown too weak to carry his father through the sky. And so we began offering daily sacrifices to Heart of Sky and to Zhe. Not slaves or captives, but strong young men who offered their lives freely so our world might live again. But still the days did not grow longer. We realized that the God with Two Faces must also be appeased if we wished to change our fortune."

"The god has two heads?"

"It refers to his nature rather than his anatomy," the Pajhit replied with a hint of a smile.

"And Womb of Earth?"

"She is the goddess of life. It would be unfitting to offer death on her altar. To her, our younger priestesses offered the blood they shed each moon. On the day we offered sacrifices to all four gods, the sun came out. The year began to turn again. And the world was saved."

"But that's not . . ." Keirith's voice trailed off. He didn't want to offend the Pajhit by denigrating his beliefs, but he felt impelled to tell him what had really happened.

"That's not the legend your people tell. You believe the Oak's spirit was lost during the Midwinter battle and a man went in search of him. Yes?"

Keirith nodded, surprised that he knew the story. The quest had occurred long after the Pajhit had left his northern village.

"This man—what do you call him?"

"Darak Spirit-Hunter," Keirith replied, careful not to give the words too much weight.

"Yes. This Spirit-Hunter went to Chaos—we call it the Abyss—and brought the Oak's spirit back."

"Not just the Oak," Keirith interrupted. "The Spirit-Hunter's brother—we call him Tinnean Tree-Friend—his spirit had been lost in the Midwinter battle, too. The Spirit-Hunter brought them both back. Tinnean Tree-Friend gave up his body. He became a tree. The One Tree that shelters the spirits of the Oak and the Holly. Only then could the Midwinter battle be completed."

"And once it was, the year began to turn." The Pajhit nodded thoughtfully; he seemed remarkably undisturbed at learning the truth. "It's interesting, isn't it? The similarities between the tales. Not the details, of course, but the necessity of sacrifice in order to restore the world."

"It's not just a tale. It happened." When the Pajhit nodded politely, he said, "It did. Darak Spirit-Hunter and Griane the Healer—they were there. In the grove of the First Forest. They saw Tinnean transform. They witnessed the battle."

"I understand."

"Then . . . ?"

"Why do we believe something different?" The Pajhit

rose and crossed toward him. To Keirith's relief, he made no attempt to sit beside him. "Every culture has its legends about the Long Winter. Your people believe that Tinnean Tree-Friend's sacrifice made the seasons turn. My people believe that human blood gave our gods the strength to live. The Eripteans built giant bonfires on their mountaintops; they believe the flames rekindled the light of the sun."

"But Darak Spirit-Hunter—"

"I'm not denying what your Spirit-Hunter did or what he claimed to have witnessed. I'm merely suggesting that it might have required the prayers and sacrifices of many people—and the will of many gods—to restore the world."

The Pajhit bent over him and Keirith tensed. Immediately, the Pajhit straightened, but his expression remained intent. "You find it hard to accept our beliefs. The necessity of offering human life to feed our gods. But we believe such sacrifices are essential to preserve our world, to honor the suffering of our gods, and to give them the strength to endure that suffering. Ours is a harsh land."

But if the legends were true, it had once been a lush paradise, where the barley grew higher than a man's head and the forests stretched to the horizon. Perhaps the ancestors had come from another part of the world. This land held little more than rocks and scrub and a relentless sun that robbed even the great river of its water.

"Our legends say our people fled from invaders," Keirith said carefully, "who cut down our tree-brothers and stole our children for sacrifice."

"And ours say that the people who lived here refused to let us build our temples and worship our gods. When they attacked us, we fought back—and in the end, they left us in peace. Which story is true?" The Pajhit shrugged. "Both, no doubt."

He was always pointing out the similarities between their peoples, their languages, their legends. No matter what Keirith said—or how hotly he spoke—the Pajhit always had a calm, reasonable reply. And every morning at dawn, this calm, reasonable man cut the heart out of another captive and offered it to his hungry sun god.

The next evening, he bluntly asked, "What's going to happen to me?"

"That depends upon you."

"You want to touch my spirit. To have me touch yours. But I've already—"

"You've made it clear you won't allow that."

"Then why—?"

"Am I wasting my time with you?"

"It's not just because you enjoy finishing all my sentences."

The Pajhit smiled. "When I was younger—before I became the priest of Heart of Sky—I was the Master of Zhiisti. I instructed the first-year apprentices."

"Did you enjoy it? Teaching?"

"Very much."

"So does my—" Keirith broke off. This time, the Pajhit waited. ". . . my father."

"Ah, yes. The Memory-Keeper. What was his name again?"

"You remember his name." The man remembered everything.

"Has Ennit always been a Memory-Keeper?"

"As long as I can remember."

The Pajhit chuckled. "Very good. I probe. You evade. I don't suppose you'd tell me if you have brothers or sisters."

Keirith considered. "One of each."

"And you are the eldest."

"How did . . . ?"

Because you just told him. In two words.

"I've lost track of the score," the Pajhit said. "Who's winning tonight?"

"Is that all this is to you? A game?"

The Pajhit's smile vanished. "No. But I'm willing to play by the rules you establish. For now."

It was easier with Hircha. She never asked any questions. But she was just as good at evasion as the Pajhit.

She was later than usual this morning, leaving him to sit in the garden and play with Niqia. Absently dangling the end of his khirta just out of reach of her questing paw, Keirith admitted that he looked forward to their lessons.

At first, Hircha had seemed as wary of him as he was of her. She'd told him that she was required to report everything he said and did, but as they grew more comfortable, he sometimes forgot her warning and found himself confiding in her. Just the frustration of being held here against his will, his anxiety about his fate. He never used the word fear; a man didn't let on such things to a girl. Still, he felt better when she confessed that she'd been scared during her first moons in Pilozhat. But when he'd asked about her capture, she'd abruptly changed the subject, leaving him to curse himself silently for his clumsiness.

He often felt clumsy around her. He'd never spent much time with girls—except Faelia. And she didn't count.

His khirta jerked in his hands as Niqia pounced. He tried to tug it free, but that only caused her to seize the fabric between her teeth. When he rose, she darted away.

"Niqia. Stop that."

She raced under another bench, leaving him to trail after her. He laughed, realizing how ridiculous he must look, down on his knees, one hand clinging to the taut length of flax-cloth, the other grabbing a fistful of material to keep the khirta from sliding off his hips. When he heard echoing laughter, he looked up to discover Hircha standing in the doorway. His face grew warm and he tugged hard enough at the flaxcloth to drag Niqia out of hiding. After a brief tussle—careful lest Niqia decide his fingers made a more tempting target than a strip of cloth—he managed to free himself.

"Stupid cat," he mumbled as he rewound his khirta and double knotted it at his waist.

"Silly boy." But her smile was kind. His face grew even warmer. "She'll never let you alone now. We'd best find another place for our lessons."

His heart raced at the unexpected opportunity to escape the confines of the Pajhit's chamber. "Is it allowed?"

"It's not like they won't be with us," she said, nodding toward the guards, just visible through the thin draperies.

To his dismay, she led him only a short way down the corridor and into an open-air courtyard. It held a few stone benches and a small "garden" composed entirely of different colored rocks, artfully arranged in a spiral.

"This is the priests' private garden," Hircha told him as she settled herself on one of the benches, "but the Pajhit has given us permission to use it as long as no one's here."

To call it private seemed an overstatement; anyone leaning on the railings above would have a perfect view of them.

"That floor has a dining hall and a classroom for the male Zhiisti as well as their living quarters."

"Do the priestesses live there, too?"

"Their wing is on the other side of the hall where you were questioned."

"Where does the queen live?"

"In the north wing. Near the throne room. The king lives there, too. Not that you'd care." Her pointed look reminded him of his enthusiastic description of the queen. He pretended to examine the rock garden while he waited for his blush to subside.

As the lesson progressed, Hircha seemed distracted, idly tracing the pattern of the tiles with her toe, jumping up to brush her fingers against a pillar. Finally, he asked, "Is something wrong?"

"I'm just restless today."

"I don't think the queen is all that beautiful."

"What?"

"I mean, she is, but it's probably because she's so . . . different. From the women at home. And the girls." To his utter shame, his voice broke on the last word.

Hircha looked completely bewildered. Obviously, she hadn't been upset about the queen at all. Desperate, he said, "Can we go someplace? Anywhere. Just walk? We could practice at the same time."

Too late, he remembered her limp.

Of course, she doesn't want to walk. Idiot.

"We'll have to stay in the palace," she finally said.

Relief washed over him. "Of course. All right. That's fine."

Shut up!

Her mouth was pursed, as if she had tasted something bad—or was trying not to laugh at him.

Please, gods, let it be a bad taste in her mouth.

He was acting like a fool. This was his opportunity to observe details about the palace instead of shambling along, casting covert glances at a girl he barely knew—a girl he'd never have a chance to know. He could trust no one. Not the captives in the slave compound. Not the Pajhit with his lessons on cats and culture. Not this girl who reported everything he said and did—and whose thin lips would curl in disgust if she ever found out what had happened on the ship.

Watch, Keirith. Watch. Observe. Remember.

He shivered as they walked through the empty interrogation chamber; it was one place he never wished to see again. The pillared entrance led to a broad stairway. Beyond it was a huge courtyard, three or four times as wide as the marketplace he had glimpsed that first day. The walls of the palace rose around it, but to his left, he noticed another smaller courtyard. He shrank back when he saw the bearers and their curtained boxes coming through it.

"Are those the Jhevi?"

"Hard to say. They're rich, though. Only important visitors arrive in litters. The merchants use the west gate." Hircha pointed across the courtyard, but he saw nothing resembling a gate. "That's the administrative wing," she said, as she limped slowly down the steps. "The kitchen and storage rooms are on the ground floor. The one above is for the scribes, the potters, the metalworkers—"

"What are scribes?"

"They keep the accounts. The merchants . . . oh, it's easier if I show you."

She led him across the courtyard, but instead of going up the steps, she ducked into the dark passageway beside them. Light streamed in from the larger entrance at the far end. That must be the gate.

Hircha came to a halt where a long corridor intersected the passageway. A steady stream of slaves hurried past with sacks of grain, haunches of meat, bundles of fleece, and hides. The aroma of fresh-baked bread wafted toward him, along with the clamor of contending voices and the sound of something shattering on stone.

"The kitchen," Hircha said, observing the direction of his gaze.

They darted past the slaves, but when he neared the gate, Hircha grabbed his arm. Reluctantly, he stopped, watching the long line of men and animals waiting to enter the palace.

"You see those men with the donkeys?"

"Donkeys? That's what you call those wooden carts?"

"Nay, the animals with the sacks. If the load is very heavy, the merchants hitch the donkeys to carts. The round things on the back of the cart—those are wheels."

Litters. Kitchen. Donkeys. Wheels. Every strange thing has a name.

Unlike the slave compound, this gate had no doors, although guards stood at attention on either side. The merchants, he noticed, did not use the kitchen corridor, but veered off into another that must parallel it.

Watch. Observe. Remember.

"When a merchant unloads his goods, they're weighed. A scribe writes down the weight of each sack or bundle. It looks like the scratches of a bird's claws to me, but they must know what it means."

So the Speaker had been a scribe. Imagine being able to record such information so that anyone—well, anyone who could read the bird scratches—understood. You could communicate with people hundreds of miles away.

"Is it always this busy?" he asked. The line of merchants seemed endless.

"Until midday. After that it's too hot to do much of anything."

"Which way is the city?" From here, he could see only a vast open expanse—fields, perhaps.

"To the south. Through the main gate."

She turned back toward the central courtyard. After a final hungry look at the gateway, Keirith followed. "And the adder pit?" he asked.

She waved vaguely in the direction of the north wing. So the adder pit was near the throne room. And the throne room was next to the chamber where he'd met the queen. His excitement grew with each new piece of information. To hide it, he asked, "Have you always been a translator?"

"Nay. I . . . mostly, I work in the kitchen."

"That seems a waste."

"I'm a member of the Zheron's household. He can use me any way he wishes."

He'd imagined she served the Pajhit. "The Zheron has a household?"

That closed look came over her face. "It's too hot to talk out here."

Obediently, he followed her back toward the priests' wing. "Do they question all the prisoners in there?"

"The hall of priests," she said, avoiding a direct answer. "Say it in Zherosi."

"Zala di Dozhiistos."

"Dozhiisti. You change the 'o' to an 'i' for the plural. So if we had two halls, it would be . . ."

"Zali di Dozhiisti." Keirith grimaced. "It twists your mouth up something awful," he said in the tribal tongue.

"Say it in Zherosi."

He did his best. His best provoked a giggle, which made the failure more bearable.

"You just said, 'You tie my tongue in bad.' "

"Well, it does tie my tongue in bad."

He glanced around, but no one was paying them any attention other than his two guards. So he hopped onto the first step and shouted, "Un." Then up to the next. "Bo. Traz. Uat." By the time he reached "Iev," he was panting. He slapped one of the massive pillars that supported the roof and jerked his hand back. A splinter was embedded in his forefinger. Carefully, he ran his hand over the pillar. Beneath the russet-colored paint, he could feel the ridges of bark.

"They're made from tree trunks. Can you guess why they're wider at the top than at the bottom?"

Fine observer he was; he hadn't even noticed.

"They sink the tops into the ground to keep them from sprouting."

More than a hundred trees had to have been destroyed to make all the pillars he'd seen. At least these held up a roof; the ones lining the walkways were merely decorative.

He sank down on the top step, then leaped up to extend a hand to Hircha who was making her slow way up the steps. Disdaining his help, she sat down, carefully tucking her right ankle behind her left. "I was shocked, too. When I first came here."

"When was that?"

She surprised him by answering. "I was nine."

Gods, she was only a child when they captured her. No wonder she'd been scared. "Was that when you hurt your leg?" Appalled at blurting out the question, he stammered an apology but she interrupted him.

"That was later. I tried to escape. After they brought me back, they cut the tendon behind my right ankle."

"Merciful Maker." He wasn't sure which was more appalling—the punishment or her calm description of it.

"The usual penalty for attempted escape is death. But the Zheron wouldn't allow it. I was lucky. It healed cleanly. And it doesn't hurt. It just . . . slows me down."

For a long while, they sat in the shadow of the great wooden pillars. The central courtyard was nearly deserted now; no one wanted to risk the heat of the midday sun.

"Do you still think about home?" he asked.

"There's no point. I'll never leave Pilozhat."

Hircha could never run far enough or fast enough to escape. But he could. He would.

But no matter how far or how fast I run, they'll still be there. The three of them. Chasing after me in my dreams.

Chapter 17

IN EVERY VILLAGE, the chief was more than happy to assist the great Darak Spirit-Hunter. For the price of a tale, they secured food and lodging for the night and, more importantly, a group of men to row two currachs to the next village.

Unfortunately, the great Darak Spirit-Hunter soon discovered he had little stomach for the sea. When he first saw the currachs that would carry them south, he eyed the sleek vessels with misgiving. True, their tapered points—prows, Urkiat called them—looked like they could easily cut through the waves, especially with the aid of the long oars. But the currachs were little wider than a coracle and so lightweight that two men could carry one on their shoulders.

Urkiat had warned him it would be "a bit rough" until they got out beyond the breakers. The men had given him a place on one of the narrow seats near the middle of the boat. Neither precaution prepared him for the wild ride that ensued.

As they fought to crest each wave, the prow reared up, dropping the back of the boat so low that Darak found himself looming above the man in the stern. Then they plunged down into the next trough, sending the stern skyward and drenching them with spray.

When Darak dared a glance at Urkiat's currach, he found him laughing as he battled the waves. Watching the rise and fall of that triumphant face made him more conscious of his lurching stomach, so he kept his gaze on his feet and his hands on the sides of the currach.

After three mornings of vomiting up his porridge, he learned to eat nothing until they reached open water. His stomach could handle the gentle rocking. His mind had more difficulty accepting that a thin skin of hide was the only thing between him and the vast expanse of water. Beautiful and awe-inspiring from the shore, the sea transformed into a splashing, probing, gurgling creature, slapping at the hide as if determined to poke a hole in it. No wonder the men kept an amulet tied to the prow.

As Girn had promised, they reached Illait's village on the evening of the tenth day. Darak staggered ashore and apologized to the men who had carried them from the last village, just as he apologized every evening for being such a useless passenger. As all the others had done, the men just smiled. One assured him that he'd come to love traveling by sea. Darak managed a sickly grin. Given eternity, he would never enjoy it. He only hoped a man could get around the Forever Isles on foot.

Illait strode down to the beach to welcome them. A small, wiry man with a face given to flushing red with either anger or delight, Darak remembered him mostly as a voluble speaker at the Gatherings, haranguing the northern chiefs about their negligence regarding the raiders. But his face creased in a smile when he saw his visitors.

"Darak. This is a surprise. What brings you to our village? Never mind. That'll wait. Come inside. You look like you could use a drink."

Illait gave him a comradely punch. Fortunately, it was his right arm; the left still ached from the raider's arrow; ten days of stinging salt water hadn't helped.

"Northerners aren't much good on the sea. No shame in it. Takes a while to get used to the pitch of the boat. Up and down. Back and forth."

Darak swallowed down his rising gorge.

"You're lucky you had such good weather. When a storm's brewing, the currachs are tossed about like barley husks at the threshing."

Darak excused himself politely and strode behind the nearest hut. When he returned, he found Illait grinning with delight.

"Holly-Chief, I think I'll have that drink now."

He let Urkiat do most of the talking. Not daring to test his stomach with brogac or wine, he accepted a cup of water from Illait's daughter Sariem and contented himself with nibbles of barleycake while Illait and Urkiat wolfed down fresh venison and salmon. The smell of the fish nearly undid him. Seeing his distress, Illait's wife shooed Sariem outside with the untouched helpings and crouched beside the fire pit to stir herbs into a steaming bowl of water. The soothing fragrance of mint made him smile.

Jirra eyed him critically, but all she said was, "Husband. These men need a good day's rest before they'll be fit to travel."

"What? Oh. Fine." Illait waved a magnanimous hand. "Stay as long as you like."

"Thank you, Holly-Chief, but we can only spare one day." He was reluctant to spare even that, but Jirra was right. "Girn said we should seek your wisdom about the route to take from here."

Illait's chest swelled visibly. "You're safe enough till you reach Ailmin's village. That's four days south of here. More if the weather turns foul. After that, though . . ." He frowned. "Most of the villages have been abandoned. We've little contact with the others. But there are rumors . . ." The fire hissed as he spat into it. "Tales of those in the far south selling off strangers to the raiders."

"Nay!" Urkiat scrambled to his feet, breathing hard. "Pelts and hides, perhaps. But no tribesman would sell one of his own people to the Zherosi."

"Sit down," Darak said.

With a visible effort, Urkiat controlled his temper. "Forgive my rudeness, Holly-Chief."

"Well." Illait spat again. "As I said, they might only be rumors, but it pays to be cautious. This holy city where you think they've taken your boy—it's to the east?"

Darak nodded.

"The passes will be open, but it's a fair climb over the mountains."

"We don't have that kind of time."

"Then keep on down the coast. If you skirt the villages by night, you should be safe enough."

"And if we go by currach?"

Illait looked skeptical. "Could you manage a two-man vessel, do you think?"

"I put in a little time at the oars. When I wasn't puking over the side."

Illait took a healthy swig of brogac. "Your best bet might be to make for the big port city. Can't remember the name. Sounds like gargling."

"Oexiak."

Illait gave Urkiat a sharp look. So did Darak. "Aye," Illait said. "That's it. Ailmin's folk used to carry furs there before the raids got so bad."

"Girn said you'd been attacked."

"Once. Last autumn. Killed my oldest girl and her husband." Illait glanced over his shoulder. "Hua never recovered."

The little boy hadn't stirred once since they'd entered the hut. Darak had assumed he was ill.

"Poor lad saw his mother and father cut down. The shock of it shattered his spirit. Even our Tree-Father can't restore him." Illait grimaced and took another swig of brogac. "Jirra and Sariem feed him. Change him when he soils himself. He doesn't speak. Doesn't move. I don't even know if he hears us. He just . . . lies there."

Like Ania after the bear mauled her. Or poor Pol who'd been kicked in the head by the ram.

Illait cleared his throat, frowning. "Forgive me. You came to me for help, and I'm burdening you with our troubles."

"We share the same troubles," Darak said. "Even the northern tribes understand that now."

"If only it didn't take a disaster to teach us wisdom. Oh, we set watches after the harvest, but they beached their boats farther down the coast and crept up on us in the dark. We nearly starved last winter. Soon as the spring thaw came, we built storage huts in the forest. If they come again, they'll go away empty-handed. And now, we keep watch for a mile around the village, day and night. Every

person over the age of ten takes a turn. It's no way to live."
Illait shook his head. "I thought Girn was a fool for tearing
down his village. Now I'm thinking he was the smart one."

Jirra supported her grandson while Sariem dribbled
broth into his mouth from a turtle shell. The boy's eyes
stared past them, unseeing.

Darak added Hua to the growing list of the lost.

Chapter 18

KEIRITH CLIMBED INTO the litter, floundering among the pillows until he managed a semblance of the Pajhit's elegant pose—half-sitting, half-reclining. The priest had given him no explanation for this excursion into the city, but he was too excited to care. Even if it meant skipping his morning lesson with Hircha, he might learn something valuable.

He pulled back the flaxcloth curtains, eager to see everything. The bearers carried them through the central courtyard and into the smaller one that led to the main gate. The soaring columns made him recall his parents' story of walking among the giant trees of the First Forest. Instead of mysterious Watchers, a stream of litters passed between the columns.

A pillared walkway branched off from the one they were following. "The temple of Womb of Earth," the Pajhit told him, mercifully keeping the language simple. Like the temple of Zhe, the altar stood on a raised platform of stone, but there was a building behind it that resembled a large cairn.

The Pajhit said something he couldn't catch and then switched to the tribal tongue. "The priestesses still offer their moon blood to Womb of Earth at the dark of the moon, but we also make daily offerings of flowers, fruit, grain, or wine. At the full moon, the Motixa offers the afterbirth of newly delivered ewes to the goddess."

Perhaps that was why the land was so inhospitable. How

could a priestess as old as the Motixa call it to fertility?
Since it would be impolite to say so, he merely asked, "Do
all your gods have temples?"

"The Changing One of the clouds has a shrine near the
top of Kelazhat. Fishermen and sailors throw their offerings
into the sea to honor and appease the Sleepless Sisters."

Just as the fishermen of his tribe offered the first of their
catch to Lacha.

"The other gods have shrines throughout the city attended by a priest or priestess." The Pajhit rapped on the
ceiling of the litter. Immediately, the bearers halted and set
them down.

The Pajhit led Keirith to the edge of the plateau. Below
them, Pilozhat was a patchwork of golden thatch and white
walls. What had seemed an endless maze of streets on that
long march to the slave compound was really an orderly
grid, with paved avenues running roughly north to south
and smaller pathways twisting between them. Low walls of
rubble created a series of stepped terraces; he wondered if
those had been built after the Long Winter to keep the
earth from sliding into the sea again.

"Oexiak lies that way." The Pajhit pointed west where a
road cleaved the browning fields like a spear. "It's our busi-
est port, far larger than Pilozhat."

Could he reach it on foot? Or did he have a better
chance striking north through the hills?

"And that is the road to Iriku."

Keirith swung his attention east where a bridge spanned
the river.

"It, too, lies on the sea. Most of its commerce comes
from trade with Eriptos."

"The place with the golden cats."

The Pajhit smiled. "Yes. The marketplaces are open every
morning except during religious festivals. The Fishmarket is
self-explanatory. The Clothmarket—there—sells woven
goods. At the Haymarket—off to the left—merchants sell
different goods. Today, barley and millet, tomorrow, wine
and ale. The craftsmen—potters, barrel makers, workers of
precious metals—keep their shops in specific sections of the
city. The tanners are on the outskirts where the stink is
less offensive. Of course, we have our own craftsmen in the
palace as well."

It was another example of the Zherosi passion for organization, but he had to admit it made sense. With craftsmen clustered together, buyers could compare quality and prices. It was a far cry from his village where the "tanners" were five old women.

He squinted at the sea. The sun made it sparkle like Callie's quartz charm.

Don't think about home. Watch. Observe. Remember.

He eyed the dozens of small boats bobbing on the water and asked, "Are there many fishermen in Pilozhat?"

"Of course. The sea supplies much of our food."

He didn't dare ask where the boats were beached at night. Instead, he pointed to another marketplace near the bottom of the steps where a large crowd was gathering.

"What's that?"

"On most days it's the Fleshers Market, selling meat, game, hides, furs. At the half moon, it serves as the Plaza of Justice. Or as it's more commonly known, Blood Court. Condemned criminals are brought there for punishment or execution. Today, I'm overseeing a punishment. Not you," the Pajhit quickly added. "Come. We're late."

Keirith scrambled back into the litter, wondering why he had to witness this punishment, too. Before he could ask, the Pajhit said, "Brace your feet against the front and grab hold of the frame."

Even those precautions failed to keep him from jostling against the Pajhit as the litter lurched down the steps. He grimaced each time their naked arms touched. If the Pajhit noticed his distaste, he had the courtesy to say nothing.

Between the swaying curtains, he caught glimpses of people. They spoke too quickly for him to understand their words, but their excitement was clear. Some goggled at their litter, others paused to sketch a hasty bow, but most rushed headlong down the steps.

The street below was clogged with pedestrians, but as soon as their litter appeared, a pathway miraculously opened. People pressed against the walls, those in back craning for a glimpse of the Pajhit. Either they recognized his litter or they were just naturally curious to see the rich folks who had come to witness the punishment. Their expressions held curiosity and awe. Keirith wondered if any of them had ever been so close to the Pajhit before.

As the close-packed street gave way to the Plaza of Justice, he tried to calm his breathing.

I'm not being punished. It's just another test. If I survived the pit of adders, I can survive this.

The litter scraped against the paving stones. As the Pajhit emerged, hundreds of voices shouted a greeting. Keirith followed him up a short flight of steps to a raised dais shaded by a scarlet canopy. More than a dozen men and women, elaborately garbed and coiffed, sat on carved wooden benches. One man glanced at him, then at the Pajhit. He nudged his neighbor. Their dark gazes flitted over him. The first man's mouth curved in a knowing smile. He whispered something that made the other man chuckle.

Stone-faced, Keirith took a seat next to the Pajhit. The spectators had left a narrow path between their dais and another at the opposite end of the plaza. Two men flanked a long slab of stone. They crossed their wrists over their chests and bowed. The Pajhit raised his hand and every voice fell silent, save for the wailing of a babe somewhere in the crowd.

The Pajhit let his hand fall. A single drum throbbed in a slow, rhythmic pulse. Heads peeped out of tiny windows in the buildings surrounding the plaza. Boys and girls sat on the flat roofs, legs dangling. Suddenly, the crowd erupted in jeers and catcalls. Here and there, Keirith spotted a waving fist, but he had no idea what had caused the outburst.

"Who's being punished?" Too late, he realized he'd spoken the tribal tongue, but no one appeared to have heard over the deafening noise of the crowd.

"Three men."

"What crime did they commit?"

The Pajhit brushed a speck of dust off his robe. "Rape."

It couldn't be the same three men. It had to be a gruesome coincidence. He realized his fingers were digging into the bench, his arms taut and trembling. He forced himself to relax, to fold his hands in his lap like the Pajhit, to calm his unsteady breathing.

A procession moved slowly through the screaming crowd into the plaza. Guards flanked the prisoners, obscuring them from view. All he could make out were three bowed heads and the rope halters that linked one to the next. As they neared the dais, his breath caught.

They shuffled forward in silence. Greasy Hair swayed and had to be shoved back in line. Gap Tooth stared dully ahead. The Big One had a bruise on his cheek and his mouth was slack.

Oh, gods, if he looks to his left, if he sees me . . .

The procession halted directly before the dais. The drum ceased its relentless pounding. The guards shoved the three men to their knees. The Pajhit rose and the crowd fell silent. Greasy Hair and Gap Tooth stared at the cobblestones but the Big One slowly raised his head.

Keirith slumped down on the bench, his gaze fastened on his shaking hands as he waited for his tormentor to speak, to raise his bound wrists and point an accusing finger, to laugh and claim that he'd only gotten what he deserved.

The Pajhit's speech washed over him. From under his lashes, Keirith dared a glance at the Big One. The man was looking right at him. He had to see him shrinking on the bench, but he just knelt on the stones, his eyes as dull and glazed as a dream-walker's.

The crowd roared. The drum renewed its beat. The men were dragged to their feet and the procession moved toward the other platform.

The Big One hadn't recognized him, hadn't noticed him at all. Through his haze of relief, he realized the Pajhit was addressing him. "Excuse me. I do not hear—"

"I said they were convicted of raping a boy," the Pajhit said in the tribal tongue. "They caught him alone. At night. He tried to fight but . . . three men against one. He never had a chance."

Keirith tasted blood and realized he'd bitten his lip.

"One of our Zhiisti. That's why I'm here. To witness on the boy's behalf."

"He . . . he told you? The boy?"

"He was too ashamed to come forward. When I discovered the truth, I went to the authorities myself."

"But how . . . ?" He licked his bleeding lip and tried again. "How did you discover the truth?"

For the first time, the Pajhit looked at him. "One night, while he was sleeping, I touched his dreams."

Keirith drew breath on a shaking sob and immediately clamped his lips together to prevent another sound from escaping. Had they raped another boy? Or had the Pajhit, after all his protestations, entered his spirit?

The Pajhit's gaze returned to the prisoners. The guards were cutting the ropes around Gap Tooth's neck and ankles. His legs collapsed under him and he had to be dragged onto the platform.

"They were lucky the boy survived," the Pajhit said in the same flat voice. "If not, the punishment would be death. Instead, they'll be castrated."

Savage pleasure shot through him. In sleep, he dreamed of the rape, but awake, he dreamed of revenge—of stalking them, catching them one by one, and exacting slow vengeance for what they had done. In those dreams, he was always the one wielding the knife. He wished he wielded it now. He wanted the Big One to look into his eyes and see him—see *him*. He wanted to watch those dark eyes widen with recognition. He wanted to see him struggle against the men holding him, to taste the sour bile of terror flooding his mouth, to scream until his voice was hoarse, to beg for mercy and weep when none was forthcoming.

The guards cut away Gap Tooth's tunic. Naked, he crawled onto the stone slab. When Keirith saw him on his hands and knees, his body jerked in a convulsive shudder. He controlled himself with an effort as the two men supervising the proceedings directed the guards to lay Gap Tooth on his back at the edge of the slab. Two shoved their hands under the small of his back, while a third placed a thick cushion under his buttocks. The men who had raised him seized his ankles and lifted his legs straight out from his body, while the other pulled his bound wrists over his head. Through it all, Gap Tooth lay limp and unresisting. Spring lambs about to be castrated put up more of a fuss.

"They're given drugs," the Pajhit said. "To keep them from thrashing about."

Of course. In the orderly world of the Zherosi, even a public castration must go smoothly. The hysteria that had bubbled so near the surface burst out in a bark of laughter that he quickly choked off.

The Pajhit gave him a sharp look. "It's still within my power to pardon them."

"Why would you do that? When you've gone to so much trouble to convict them?"

The words shocked him into soberness. He was stretched too thin. The gods only knew what might come out of his mouth next.

The crowd had fallen silent and he realized that one of the supervisors had turned to face the Pajhit, an upraised dagger in his right hand. The Pajhit lifted his hand and let it fall. As his assistant spread himself across Gap Tooth's torso, the man went down on one knee. His left hand reached between Gap Tooth's spread legs. Keirith felt his sac contracting as if his testicles wanted to crawl up inside his body.

A high, thin scream broke the breathless silence. Gap Tooth bucked once before the assistant restrained him. The other man's hands moved between his legs and Keirith fought his rising nausea, glad now he couldn't see the blade. He clenched his teeth, wondering why no one shoved a gag in Gap Tooth's mouth, then realized that the screaming was part of the entertainment. Just as it had been for the men who raped him.

The screams died. Gap Tooth must have fainted. Keirith's nausea returned as the man with the dagger leaped to his feet and thrust a bloody hand into the air to display his prize. He strutted the length of the platform to the crowd's roar of approbation, while his assistant bent over Gap Tooth to tie off the wound.

And it was done. The guards lifted Gap Tooth's unconscious body from the platform and dragged Greasy Hair onto it. He fought a little harder, but was subdued easily enough. The upraised dagger, the signal from the Pajhit, and it was done. Again. Leaving only the Big One.

Perhaps the drugs had worn off or perhaps he finally realized what was about to happen. He fought hard, lashing out at the guards with his fists and feet, knocking one off the platform and sending another staggering backward.

The crowd laughed and cheered him on, just as Gap Tooth and Greasy Hair had chuckled and urged on the Big One. The crowd would have cheered that, too. Just as they would cheer when the man rose to his feet with the Big One's testicles clenched in his bloody fist.

Take him. Cut him. Do it now. Give me the dagger. I'll do it. Let me do it!

"Kheridh. Kheridh! Sit down."

He sank back on the bench, wondering when he had gotten to his feet. He closed his eyes, conscious of the whispers of those around him. He felt the brush of flaxcloth against his ankle as the Pajhit shifted on the bench. Heard the Big One's scream of agony, and then another and another until it seemed one ceaseless bestial roar that was finally obliterated by the answering roar of the crowd. It slowly subsided into the garbled noise of everyday conversation. Those on the dais took leave of the Pajhit and launched into new topics of discussion, chattering like sparrows. He caught the phrases "dreadful wine" and "terrible food" and reflected dully that his grasp of the Zherosi language was improving.

"The litter is here."

The Big One was gone. The platform was deserted. The crowd in the plaza was thinning. For a few days, they would remember the good show that last prisoner put on, but then he would be forgotten. But the Big One would remember. Always. Just as Keirith would. Only death could wipe away his memories of that night or the Big One's memories of this morning. Until then, the two of them were linked forever in a bond of blood and pain and shame.

He crawled into the litter and sank down on the pillows. Neither of them spoke during the trip back to the palace.

He followed the Pajhit into his chamber and accepted a goblet of wine. The bronze clattered against his teeth, and he lowered it without drinking. The Pajhit reached toward him and he jerked away. Wine sloshed over the rim of the goblet, splashing the priest's robe. He was still trying to frame an apology when he felt wine dripping down his legs. When he saw the red stain spreading down the front of his khirta, he gagged.

He barely made it outside before vomiting into the bed of bitterheart. When he realized he was down on his hands and knees, he forced himself to his feet, leaning heavily against the wall. He straightened slowly and turned to find the Pajhit holding out the goblet of wine.

"Rinse your mouth."

His hands shook, but he managed to cleanse the taste of vomit from his mouth. He handed the goblet back. It was just too heavy to hold.

"I'm sorry. I made a mess of your flowers."

"It was my fault. I know you dislike being touched."

Keirith forced himself to meet those calm brown eyes. "They didn't rape a Zhiisto, did they?"

"No."

"You made it all up."

"A crime was committed."

"And no one ever asked to speak with . . . the victim?"

"Oh, yes. I produced a Zhiisto. Told him what he must say. He was quite effective."

"But if anyone questions him—"

"He has returned home. My gift will enable him to purchase a fishing boat and marry the girl he had given up for lack of a bride price."

Everything neat and orderly.

"You arranged all this for me. Why? Did you think I would enjoy watching that?"

"Did you?"

"It made me sick."

"That doesn't answer my question."

"Then answer mine!" His outburst seemed to shock the Pajhit, but he didn't care. "Why did you do it?"

"They deserved to be punished for what they did, and this was the only way to make that happen."

"Because rape isn't a crime when the victim is a slave."

"Because no one cares when the victim is a slave."

Keirith meant his laugh to sound mocking, but he could hear how close it was to hysteria. "I'm supposed to believe you care about me? To be grateful that you raped my spirit and discovered those men raped my body?"

"Believe what you want."

"I will. I do. You don't care about me."

"Not if you're going to behave like a whining child. The world is cruel, Kheridh. Women die in childbirth. Men die of plague. Children starve. Boys are raped."

The words shocked another bitter laugh from him. "You're telling *me* the world is cruel? After what I've suffered?"

"Everyone suffers, boy! Life is suffering."

"I hate you."

"You hate the fact that you were raped. That you reveled in their punishment. And that I was able to exact the retribution that you could not."

"You entered my spirit—"

"And you were helpless to stop me. Just as you were helpless to combat your Tree-Father who deemed you an abomination. Helpless to escape the warriors who attacked your village. Helpless to fight off the men who raped you. But now you have a choice. You can let your hate and your helplessness consume you. You can bewail a world where innocents are raped and dreams are shattered. Or you can learn to live with those realities and understand that only one thing will prevent them from happening again."

Keirith found himself with his back up against the wall, breathing as hard as if he were withstanding a physical assault.

"You have a gift, Kheridh." Although the Pajhit spoke more gently, his voice held the same intensity. "A gift you're afraid to use. But only by using it will you gain power. Today, you learned what a man with power can do. Power protects you. It protects those you love. It shields your spirit from attack and allows you to punish those who hurt you. Without power, you will always be a helpless, terrified boy cowering in the dark."

Keirith stumbled to the doorway and bolted past the startled guards. The Pajhit's words pursued him down the corridor. "You cannot run from yourself, Kheridh. Or from the truth."

"Follow him—but at a discreet distance," Malaq instructed the guards. Then he sank down on the stone bench nearest the door.

He had gambled that honesty would win the boy's respect, but he'd failed to gauge the depth of Keirith's reaction to the punishment. He'd pushed too hard, too soon, forgetting how deeply boys feel things at that age.

Pursuing him now would only drive him away forever. Like a falconer training a hawk, he must demonstrate patience, persistence, dedication, and calm. He had swung the lure. He must wait to see if the boy returned to it.

Chapter 19

KEIRITH ROUNDED A CORNER and careened into the Zheron. The startled priest grabbed on to him to steady himself. Without thinking, Keirith shoved him away. "Please. Forgive me. Must go."

"What is it? Good gods, what's the matter?" The concern on the Zheron's face was at odds with the leer he remembered from his interrogation.

"Please. Let go. Must . . . please!"

"Yes. All right."

The Zheron glanced around as if seeking help. Over his shoulder, Keirith saw Hircha's moon-gold hair. The Zheron spoke rapidly to her.

"The Zheron says you look ill. He wishes to know if he can help."

"Please. Thank the Zheron. I am well. I just . . . oh, gods, I just want to get away from this place!"

Before he could stop her, Hircha was translating. The Zheron frowned—was he going to punish him for that last outburst?—then suddenly smiled. Again, he spoke rapidly to Hircha.

"The Zheron says you've been caged too long. He offers to take you to the beach. To walk. To swim. Whatever pleases you." When Keirith hesitated, she added, "This is a great honor."

Why would the Zheron want to honor him? When they passed in a corridor, the priest responded politely to his bow, but walked on. The thought of having to make conversation sickened him, but how could he refuse without giving offense?

"The Zheron invites me to accompany you as that will make it easier to talk. But he wishes to assure you there is no need for conversation. It is enough to enjoy the morning air and the freedom."

The wistfulness on Hircha's face finally convinced him. "The guards. They'll follow us."

When Hircha translated, the Zheron grinned and made a short reply before walking away. Keirith stared after him, mystified.

"He said, 'Not if we're clever.' "

Three litters were waiting in the central courtyard. It was easy to let the guards see them crawling into one, then slip out the other side and into the adjacent one. The empty litter headed toward the western gate. Theirs followed the Zheron's out the main gate.

He managed well enough when they proceeded along one of Pilozhat's wide streets, but each time the bearers lurched down another flight of steps, he was thrown against Hircha. Her fingers clutched his arm as she tried to steady herself. Her hair tickled his cheek. Her breast brushed his bare arm. She apologized and laughed and said it would have been less bruising to walk. When she tumbled across his lap, a wave of heat shot through him.

He had just seen three men castrated. How could his body react this way?

It took forever to reach the beach. His arms ached from clinging to the frame of the litter. His shoulders ached from the unnatural positions he'd assumed to keep from brushing against her. And his loins ached from the sensations flooding his body.

When the bearers halted, he crawled out of the litter. Mercifully, the bulky folds of the khirta hid any evidence of his arousal.

The Zheron waved the bearers off and they retreated down the beach. To give himself a moment to recover, Keirith walked to the edge of the water. The curve of the shoreline screened them from the city. Only the sound of the waves and the cries of the sea birds disturbed the restful silence. After the noise and the crowds in the Plaza of Justice, it seemed a gift from the gods.

"Would you like to swim?" Hircha asked. "The sea's very warm."

"Nay. Thank you."

She reached down to pull her shapeless gown over her head and he quickly turned away. He heard a squeal and glanced back to find her plunging into the water. Her pale bottom flashed as she dove beneath a wave. Moments later, she bobbed back up, her hair streaming over her small breasts.

"Come in," she called. "It's wonderful."

Shaking his head, Keirith backed away. "I'm fine. Really. I'll just sit over there. In the shade."

"Suit yourself."

Resolutely, he walked toward a tumble of boulders and sat down facing the mountain. Even in the shade, the sand was almost too hot for comfort. The Zheron strolled over to him. "Don't you want to join her?"

"Thank you, no. This is good. Very less sun."

"You can't swim?"

"Yes. But no swim today. Thank you."

The Zheron flung himself onto the sand, folded his hands behind his head, and closed his eyes. "This *is* good. It's never peaceful at the palace."

"Yes. Thank you for to bring me."

"Thank you for bringing me," the Zheron corrected.

Dutifully, Keirith repeated the sentence.

"You learn quickly."

"Thank you. I try hard."

The Zheron propped himself up on his elbow and studied him for so long that Keirith asked, "Please? Something is wrong?" The speech that followed was largely incomprehensible, but it seemed he was apologizing for something. "Forgive me. I do not understand."

The Zheron frowned, clearly frustrated. Then he leaped to his feet and shouted to Hircha.

Keirith kept his gaze on the sand as she approached. The Zheron tossed her gown to her and the two of them chatted easily while she dressed. She perched on one of the rocks, her damp legs next to his cheek, and wrung the water out of her hair. "How may I serve you, my lord?"

The Zheron faced him, his expression earnest, and delivered a short speech.

"The Zheron says I am to translate exactly, not merely give you the essence of his words. He wishes me to do this because he wants to be sure you understand."

Keirith nodded.

"Kheridh. The Pajhit has kept you very close. As is his right. But now that we're alone, I wish to say . . . I wanted you to know I'm sorry for the way I had to speak to you that first day. I know it was humiliating for you. I was shamed by it, too. I don't hold a grudge against you for attacking my spirit. I would have done the same had a man spoken thus. And I hope you hold none against me for obeying the Pajhit's wishes."

Uncertain how to respond, Keirith nodded again.

"Will you clasp arms on it?"

"What does that mean?" he asked Hircha. "Clasping arms?"

"It's a gesture of agreement. Of friendship."

Keirith hesitated, searching the man's face for some hint of what lay behind the earnest expression. The Zheron spoke so impatiently that Hircha could barely keep up with him.

"You hesitate to accept my friendship. I understand. It's just . . ." Hircha perfectly captured the impotent wave of his hand. "I'm not used to being hated. Since I was a boy, everyone has always liked me. I like . . . being liked. I suppose that's silly and weak, but . . . never mind. This is beneath us. I shouldn't have said anything. Forgive me. I hope you enjoy this time away from the palace. I'll go back now so I don't spoil it for you."

The Zheron rose. Keirith knew enough of palace protocol to recognize his bow as one offered to an equal. As the Zheron spun away, shouting for the bearers, he called out, "Wait."

The Zheron slowly turned.

"I did hate you." When Hircha hesitated, he said, "Tell him."

A grimace twisted the handsome features, but was quickly banished.

"I wanted to kill you. But you stopped me. How did you do that?"

"That's just a trick. Something every Zhiisto learns."

"Can you teach me this trick? Without entering my spirit?"

The Zheron frowned, considering. "We've never done it that way. It would be harder—for both of us. But it might be possible. It would mean that much to you?"

Keirith nodded.

"The Pajhit may not like it—you coming to me instead of him for instruction. I'll have to consider the best way to approach him. Or escape his notice. When I have, I'll tell Hircha when we can meet."

"Thank you." After a moment's hesitation, he added, "I'm not sure I can offer friendship, but I can dispense with hatred."

The Zheron broke into a great smile when Hircha translated. Keirith found his forearms seized in a strong grip.

"Friendships aren't built in a day, but we've made a good start." The Zheron stepped back, his smile fading. "And now I have to return to the palace. It's a great honor to be Zheron, but it's not much fun. You and Hircha stay. Not too long—the sun will roast those fair skins. Come back during the midday sezhta. That way, you can sneak into the palace while everyone's resting. If you're caught . . . well, tell them it was my doing. But try not to get caught. Please. The Pajhit will have my hide if he finds out."

Shaking his head at his folly, he waved away the second group of bearers and climbed into his litter. A hand shot through the curtains to wave farewell.

"That was interesting," Hircha said after a long silence. "He's always so . . . wait. I want to go back in the water. We can talk after that."

Her gown slapped against his neck. Keirith pulled it off, folded it neatly, and laid it on a rock. Then he sank down on the sand, wondering what had possessed him to tell the Zheron he'd wanted to kill him.

Hircha was in the water a long time. He'd almost gotten up the courage to join her when he heard her breathless pants. She pulled her gown on and sat down beside him. "You took a great risk."

"I know."

"Just to learn this trick of shielding your spirit?"

"And to find out whether he would agree to teach it to me." He searched her face as intently as he had searched the Zheron's. "Can I trust him, Hircha? Is he . . . is he a good man?"

"He can be reckless. Quick to anger—but equally quick to apologize. When I first came here . . ." She swallowed hard. "I was sold to a pleasure house. I was expected to . . . to lie with strangers. To serve their desires."

"But you were only nine!"

For the first time, he understood the fate of the boys and girls who had been sold to the "great houses." Forced to endure what he had endured—and to smile at their violators.

"Everyone suffers, boy! Life is suffering."

"Xevhan took me away from that. He gave me my life back."

Could gratitude alone account for the softness of her expression, the huskiness in her voice? Or did she love him?

Two tears welled up and spilled down her cheeks. She scrambled to her feet and turned away.

Do something. Take her in your arms. Comfort her.

But after he rose, he just stood there. A helpless, terrified boy—just as the Pajhit had said. Finally, he whispered, "Please. Don't."

With a small cry, Hircha flung herself at him. His arms came around her. His cheek rested on her wet hair. She smelled of the sea and an earthy musk that must be the scent of her body. Through the damp gown, he could feel her heat.

"Thank you. Thank you for being so kind."

Her eyes were as clear and blue as the sky, her kiss as delicate as the brush of butterfly wings. Sand scratched his cheeks as she cupped them between her palms. Her mouth parted under his. Her tongue darted between his lips. He started and felt her smile. Her tongue moved more slowly, caressing his. He groaned and pulled her closer, groaned again when he felt her body pressing against his: the soft breasts, the warm belly, the firm thighs.

He reared back. Her hand snaked up to explore his cheek, the curve of his ear. Then it curled around his neck and pulled his head down again. When she released him and stepped back, he gave a strangled cry of protest, but she just smiled and pressed her fingertips to his lips.

She pulled the gown over her head and this time, he didn't look away. Nor did he stop her when she unknotted his khirta, although he could feel himself flushing hotly when it fell to the ground. He knew he was scrawny and skinny-shanked, but her eyes admired him and her smile told him he was handsome and her hands told him she wanted to touch him and be touched, to fondle and explore.

She pulled him down onto the sand. If it was a dream, he didn't want to wake. He only wanted more of her. At home, there had been dreams that jerked him awake in the night, his seed spurting on his belly, his heart racing as he lay on his pallet, breathless with fear that someone had heard. And the days when he sneaked away to his secret place on Eagles Mount, the sun hot on his belly, his fist moving urgently between his legs. Nothing like the gentle stroking of her fingers, the shock of teeth grazing his nipple, the tickle of damp curls teasing his loins.

Her soft cries maddened him. His ballocks ached with need. He wanted to have what other men possessed. He wanted to bury his shame in her softness. He wanted to take her, fierce and rough and hard, and feel her helpless beneath him, crying out, begging him . . .

He wrenched away and staggered to his feet. His hands shook so badly he could barely wind the khirta around his hips. And all he could say was, "Oh, gods. I'm sorry. I'm sorry. I can't."

Chapter 20

HIRCHA WATCHED KEIRITH stumble down the beach. Before he vanished from sight, one of his guards appeared and led him toward the city.

She listened to the lapping of the waves and the pounding of her heart and thought about fleeing. But he would find her. He always found her. So she pulled on her gown and shouted for the bearers and let them carry her back to the palace.

He was waiting for her in his chamber, sitting motionless on one of the stone benches. His eyes were half-closed and his head rested against the wall. The qiij always left him sluggish, but rarely did the lethargy come on him this quickly.

She kept her eyes lowered as she approached. There was no need to tell him of her failure; she had felt his spirit enter hers, had felt him inside of her throughout the encounter with Keirith, his touch as intimate as the boy's. Felt, too, the painful wrench of his parting.

Pleas would disgust him, excuses rouse him to anger. Without a word, she prostrated herself at his feet and waited.

One sandal tapped the floor. From the chamber above came the dull pounding of more feet and the muffled sound of voices and laughter as the Zhiisti, freed from their morning lessons, converged on the dining hall. A trickle of sweat oozed down her breast. A fly buzzed near her ear. And still the ceaseless tapping of his foot continued, unvarying in its slow, relentless rhythm.

Her knees ached, but she remained motionless. Submissiveness pleased him. She had learned that as a child. One of many things he had taught her.

He might forgive her. Shrug off her failure and offer her a chance to redeem herself. Or he might beat her.

Once, she had known how to please him. Once, she had only to walk into this chamber to see him smile and open his arms and pull her onto his lap. He would ask what she had done that day and laugh delightedly at the things she told him. Silly, simple things like using the new oil he had chosen for her bath or walking to and fro in his chamber wearing the new skirt he had ordered—the blue one that matched the color of her eyes—just to listen to the three flounces swish. And he'd tell her to walk for him so he could hear it rustle and she would, and he would tell her she was beautiful and she'd duck her head shyly, and he would raise her chin between his thumb and forefinger and reach into the bowl that he always kept filled with honey balls just for her and pop one into her mouth. And then he would bend his head and she would open her mouth yet again so he could kiss her and share the sweetness.

It was all sweetness then, before her breasts blossomed and the hair sprouted under her arms and between her legs. Sweet honey in his mouth and sweet oil scenting his body. And so gentle, whether teaching her how to kiss or how to take him in her mouth and suck him like a honey ball.

He was the only sweetness she knew after the raider tore her, screaming, from her mother's arms. And if she had been terrified when he first walked into that tiny room in the pleasure house, he had calmed her with his soft hands and his soft voice.

"Don't be afraid," he told her when old Mother Lashi left them. "I won't hurt you."

He held her as if she were as fragile as a wren's egg. And afterward, when his head fell back and he groaned like a dying man and his lap grew warm and moist beneath her bottom, he kissed the red marks on her arms where his fingers had clenched them and told her he would never hurt her again.

But he had. The first time he had lain with her, she had not been able to stifle her tears. He wept with her and promised it would be better the next time. And it was.

"You are beautiful," he told her, oiled fingers easing between her legs.

"You are perfect," he told her, lying next to her in the dark, stroking her hairless thigh.

"I love you."

When her moon flow began, she hid the truth from him. She'd learned by then that there had been others before her and always, they were sent away when the blood came. For three moons, she kept her secret, claiming a stomach complaint, a spring chill, a nettle rash. But she could not hide the more obvious changes her body was undergoing.

That was the first time he beat her. Worse than the beating was the disgust in his eyes. She begged him to let her stay and serve him in other ways. Grudgingly, he gave his permission.

Then came the night she found him smiling down at another little girl in a flounced skirt. She fled the palace, neither knowing nor caring where she was going. Men with leashed dogs found her and brought her back. That was the second time he beat her. But instead of sending her to the pleasure house as she expected, he took the small dagger he used to slice fruit and cut the tendon behind her right ankle.

He smiled at her after, his eyes bright with excitement, his fingertips bright with her blood. As one slave dragged her out of the chamber, she heard him shouting to another to bring little Emitzia to him.

And so it had been for more than three years. A little girl on his lap was no longer enough to arouse him. A little girl on her knees took too long to bring him to climax. And a little girl screaming as he thrust into her again and again . . .

Qiij fired the appetite at first, only to dull it later. Like little girls who grew up.

His foot ceased its relentless tapping. Now there was only the patter of her heartbeat. She felt a gentle nudge against her forehead. When she raised her head fractionally, the sandaled foot slid beneath her chin. Slowly, he pushed her head back. She tried to remain prostrate but the pressure forced her to fall back on her haunches. That's when she saw the braided leather whip in his lap.

She dared a look at him then. He smiled, one hand stroking the whip.

"Forgive me," she whispered.

He struck her across the face. Before she could prostrate herself, he seized her by the hair. The tiles scraped her knees as he dragged her toward the low table where they had sat, side by side, as he fed her dainties from his plate.

Miko was waiting. It was always Miko who held her down. He smiled as he seized her wrists and dragged her facedown across the table. A ragged fingernail scratched her back as he yanked her gown over her waist.

When the first blow fell, she flinched, but made no sound. At the tenth blow, she bit through her lip and tasted blood. By the twentieth blow, her back and buttocks were on fire and the blood ran down her chin. But she was determined to stifle the cries that would only add to his pleasure.

His breathing grew hoarse, each crack of the whip punctuated by a curse. "Worthless. Bitch. Worthless. Stupid. Ugly. Bitch."

He paused, panting. Miko released her wrists and she let her breath out. She struggled to get her shaking hands under her to push herself up from the table. A hand pushed her back down. Sweat stung her wounded back.

"Take her."

Dazed from pain and exhaustion, she wondered why he would hold her down if he meant for Miko to take her back to the little room she shared with five other girls. Only when rough hands spread her thighs did she understand.

She struggled against the hands, one pair smooth and sweaty, the other rough and dry. She heard Miko spit, felt him rooting between her thighs, one fist bumping against her body, while the fingers of the other bit deep into the flesh at her hip.

His sudden thrust tore a scream of denial from her throat. Even after she forced herself to silence, it echoed inside her head, the high keening cry of a dying creature mingling with the animal grunts of the man behind her and the hoarse panting of the one watching.

Miko shuddered and groaned. She gasped as he collapsed on top of her. Then he pushed himself up, leaving only the warm ooze of his slime on her thighs and the stinging sweat of his belly on her buttocks.

She got to her feet. She pushed her tangled hair off her face. She made herself look at the man who had once claimed to love her. His handsome features twisted with disgust.

"Get her out of my sight," Xevhan said. "And send Xia to me."

Miko knotted his loincloth at his waist and took her arm. She hated herself for needing his support to negotiate the short trip to her quarters.

He pushed her through the doorway and stood there, frowning. "Why don't you scream? When he beats you. He likes it when they scream."

"I know."

He shrugged. "Pride'll only get you bruises."

"Get out."

His face darkened and he stalked into the room. Despite her determination to show no emotion, she flinched and threw up both hands to ward off a blow. Without even touching her, he managed to back her up against the wall.

"You're not his little queen anymore, girl. You haven't been for years now. You should have let him send you back to the pleasure house before he got a taste for hurting you. And it's not just the beatings anymore. He liked watching us. First time in a moon he'll be fit to plow Xia. And that'll make him want to watch again. You treat me nice and pleasant and respectful between times and I'll do you easy instead of rough. Makes no difference to me," he added as he walked toward the doorway, "but it'll save some wear and tear on your honey hole."

She waited until his footsteps receded before stripping off her gown and throwing it on the floor. Her legs trembled as she bent, wincing, to reach for the cloth that hung over the basin they used for washing. She dipped it in the water and dabbed gingerly between her thighs. Jaw clenched, she rinsed the cloth and slowly, methodically cleaned all traces of him from her body. When she was finished, she collapsed onto her pallet of fleece, shivering.

She stared at the wall, thinking of Xevhan, her lover and tormentor, thinking of Keirith, who might have been her friend and whose refusal to lie with her had provoked both the beating and the rape. She didn't know why he had pulled away from her. Perhaps he had sensed that she was unclean. Or with his powers, he had seen into her spirit and knew she was false.

But there had been one moment when he stared at her and his eyes told her she was beautiful, even with her bobbing breasts and the hair between her legs. She'd loved those shining eyes and that soft, trembling mouth. She'd wanted to bask in his admiration and her power to rouse it, to pretend that he was just an ordinary boy and she was just an ordinary girl and that they could touch and kiss as if it were the first time for both of them.

What a fool. Of all the lessons Xevhan had taught her, the most enduring was that you could trust no man. You could only be used by them and then discarded like a dirty cloth.

Unless, she reflected, you used your power to possess them. She had lost her power over Xevhan, but she might still wield it over this boy.

The palace was awash with rumors: he was the Pajhit's illegitimate son, he was the Pajhit's lover, he was the Son of Zhe. More likely, he was just a boy who'd been stolen from his home as she had been.

But he had power and—for now—the protection of the Pajhit. Two good reasons for Xevhan to hate him. And he was afraid and alone—two good reasons for Keirith to trust her.

Miko was right. Whether or not Xevhan had always had a taste for hurting others, he'd discovered the pleasure of it with her. As the qiij robbed him of potency, his need would only escalate. Three years ago, he had cut a tendon. Today, he'd watched another man rape her. Sooner or later, he would kill her.

She had failed to escape before, but with Keirith's help, she might succeed. But before she fled, she would teach Xevhan the meaning of fear. And before he died, she would watch his eyes widen with the shocked realization that his submissive little girl had destroyed him.

Chapter 21

THE GUARD TOLD HIM about discovering Kheridh
on the beach, but Malaq learned of the incident with
the girl from Xevhan.

"I know I should have consulted you. But the opportunity arose, and . . ." Xevhan shrugged. "Anyway, the girl
bungled it."

"He might have escaped."

"Worth the risk, don't you think? To find out if he was
the Son of Zhe. Besides, the bearers were only a shout
away."

Since that morning, he had kept Kheridh close. He'd
ended the language instruction with the girl and taught him
himself. He'd threatened the guards with disembowelment
if they let Kheridh out of their sight again.

Kheridh said nothing about the girl's absence. Indeed,
Malaq could hardly drag anything out of him. He pursued
his lessons dutifully. He was unfailingly polite. But the wall
that he had thrown up after learning his dream had been
breached remained impenetrable.

It was the girl who provided the opening he needed. He
noticed her limping down the corridor, observed the careful
way she moved, and called her name. She flattened herself
against the wall, wincing. Her lower lip was swollen, the
newly-healed cut plain.

After a quick glance to ensure they were alone, Malaq
asked, "How badly did he beat you?"

Her head jerked up. Quickly, she lowered it again, but he had already seen the flash of cold, blue fire in her eyes.

"My lord, it is his right—"

"Answer my question."

"He whipped me." She licked her bruised lip. "Then gave me to his manservant."

"Gave you to him? To serve, you mean?"

"He raped me."

Her voice was flat. She might have been discussing the weather. But her fingers, hidden in the folds of her gown, tightened convulsively, bunching the fabric at her thighs.

"Come to my chamber tonight."

"My lord . . ."

"If anyone stops you, say I have summoned you."

"Yes, my lord."

He watched her hurry away, her limp more pronounced in her haste to escape him. When she appeared that evening, Kheridh flushed but said nothing.

"Tell Kheridh the truth," Malaq instructed her. "All of it."

He waved the guards outside and followed them, resisting the urge to linger in the corridor and eavesdrop. When he returned a short while later, they were still standing opposite each other. The girl's face was swollen from crying, but Kheridh was pale and tight-lipped. As she turned to leave, he lifted his hand as if to touch her, but let it drop to his side.

When she left, he stalked into the garden. Malaq hesitated in the doorway, watching him gulp the night air like a drowning man.

Without turning, Kheridh asked, "You knew?"

"That she was Xevhan's cat's-paw? Of course."

"But you didn't tell me."

"Would you have believed me if I had?"

Instead of answering, Kheridh said, "The man who did this to her. Will he be punished?"

"No."

"Because she's a slave."

"Because the man who raped her was acting on Xevhan's orders."

"And this, I suppose, is another lesson about the danger

of being powerless." At last, Kheridh turned. Moonlight made his face look as ghastly as a corpse's. "What do you want?"

"I want to teach you. And learn from you."

"To what end?" His voice cracked.

"Your gift is a wonder to me. Among our people, only the king, the queen, and the chief priests can access that power at will and only through the use of a drug called qiij. It frees the spirit while enslaving the body. I would free our people from this hunger."

"You don't seem . . . hungry."

"I use it rarely."

"Did you use it to invade my dreams?"

"Yes."

"Do you believe I'm the Son of Zhe?"

He should have suspected the girl would tell him of the prophecy. Hoping the darkness hid his surprise, he said, "I don't know."

"That's why I'm still alive?"

"It doesn't matter to me what you are."

"But it matters to Xevhan. I didn't think he was that devout."

"Xevhan is devoutly ambitious."

"And what does he gain by proving I'm not the Son of Zhe?"

"The queen's approval."

His eyes widened. "She's behind this?"

"If you mean did she suggest that Hircha seduce you, no. But she wants to know the truth about you."

"So do you. Isn't that why you sent the slaves to me after I spoke with the adders?"

"Yes."

"So you and Xevhan aren't so different."

"Believe that if you like. However, I've suggested to the queen that you are of value to us, regardless of your . . . paternity."

"So if she thinks what I know outweighs who I am, she'll keep me alive."

"That is my hope."

Kheridh sank down on the bench. For a long while, he simply stared at the stone flags. When he raised his head, he looked utterly drained. "There's no way I can win, is there? Some people want me dead. Others want me alive. I'm like . . . what's that game? With the ball?"

"Pelinq?"

"Aye. You're on one team. Xevhan's on the other. The queen watches from the seats. And I'm the ball kicked back and forth between the players." His smile was bleak. "The ball never wins."

"Then be a player."

"On your team."

"Yes."

"Even if the queen favors Xevhan's?"

"You could never join Xevhan."

"Because of what he did to Hircha?"

"Because your spirit is clean and uncorrupted. Because you can fly with a bird for the sheer love of it, not for the power you gain over it. Because you are good."

Kheridh took a long, shaking breath and buried his face in his hands. Malaq remained where he was, watching him fight for control. When he lifted his head again, his eyes were dry. "Everything that happened . . ." His voice was a reedy whisper, as if all the life had been sucked out of him. "I thought it was because I was bad."

"No."

His hands clenched and relaxed, then clenched again. "I'll never go home again, will I?"

"I don't know. I don't think it would be permitted."

His throat worked. "May I go to my room, please?"

Malaq nodded.

At the threshold, he paused. "I'll never know if you're lying to me, will I? I'll never know who I can trust."

Malaq fought the urge to cry, "Trust me!" The boy yearned for a friend, might even turn to him for comfort. But later, alone in his room, he would have time to think, to remember, to sift through the events of the last days and realize that in Pilozhat, trust was a commodity more precious than water.

"Trust yourself," he said. "Your instincts. Your observations. Reveal your powers, but not your heart. You are enmeshed in a dangerous game, and your life depends on your ability to play it well."

The blue eyes searched his face. Whatever he found there made his shoulders droop. Exhaustion and tension had etched new lines around his mouth and the skin was stretched tight over his cheekbones. Even if he survived, Malaq wondered if the damage could ever be healed, if he would lose the last shreds of innocence and wonder that still filled his dreams.

Kheridh bowed politely. "Good night, Pajhit," he said in Zherosi.

Malaq returned the bow. "Good night, Kheridh."

Two days later, Malaq invited Vazh to supper. He wondered at his perversity, but decided that the danger to Kheridh was great enough to warrant his friend's inevitable recriminations.

Vazh spent most of the meal complaining about Besul, the weather, the incompetence of the generals conducting the Carilian campaign, and the growing resistance among the Tree People.

"They turned on the garrison at Two Forks. You heard? Damned fools don't even know when they're beaten."

"Perhaps they're not beaten."

Vazh eyed him over his goblet of wine. "You don't approve, of course."

"Of subjugating the Tree People? No. That should hardly come as a surprise."

"A hundred pelts a year. Plus a levy of barley or oats."

"Plus the slaves," Malaq reminded him in a mild voice.

"Four a year. Is that so much to ask?"

"It is if it's your child."

"They breed like rabbits. And don't give me that slit-eyed look. You know it's true. Besides, I was willing to waive the requirement in exchange for timber."

"Hardly a viable offer for people who worship trees."

"Would they rather be overrun? Their villages destroyed? All their children carried off?"

"I imagine they'd rather be left alone."

"Well, that's not going to happen. We need the land and the timber."

"There is such a thing as trade."

Vazh slammed his goblet down on the table. "Gods, I hate it when you talk all mincing and proper."

"Forgive me. I will try not to mince."

"Your mouth purses like a virgin's crack."

Malaq gestured to the slave bending down to proffer a platter. "Try the skewered goat. It's really quite delicious."

"Shove the skewer up your arse. It's really quite invigorating."

As the shocked slave hurriedly backed away, Malaq found himself returning Vazh's grin. After so many years, he was used to the crudeness. Vazh was the one person in Pilozhat he could trust and the only one to whom he could speak his mind.

Niqia leaped onto the low table and picked her way carefully toward the goat meat. With an oath, Vazh scooped her up and deposited her on the floor again. "Damn cat." He waved his napkin at Niqia who ignored him. Only when he half-rose did she abandon her grooming. After favoring him with a malevolent stare, she padded away with slow dignity.

"Haughty as that bitch I named her after." Vazh smiled fondly. "Still living in Oexiak with that rich merchant she left me for. She's a grandmother now. Can you believe it?"

"Of course. None of us are young anymore."

"Speak for yourself. I keep my voracious widow satisfied— she's buried two husbands, drained the life out of 'em, sure as I sit here—and my sword's still lively enough to tickle that pretty slave I acquired last winter."

"May its blade never tarnish."

Malaq sketched a pious sign of blessing and Vazh laughed. He took a deep swig of wine and slapped his belly. "So. Do I get to meet the amazing adder boy, or have you tucked him in for the night?"

If Vazh hoped to discomfit him with the sudden change of subject, he was disappointed. "I'll summon him if you wish," Malaq replied, as if the idea had just occurred to him. He nodded to a slave who hurried out of the chamber.

"You're as transparent as water," Vazh commented.

"You must not have seen the river lately."

"Now you're trying to muddy things." Vazh laughed at his awful joke and took another gulp of wine. "Has he had any more conversations with the adders?"

"No." Malaq leaned forward and lowered his voice. "But he has had one with Xevhan."

Forearms splayed across the table, Vazh listened without

interruption to the tale of the girl's attempted seduction and Xevhan's subsequent visit. "Could be he just wants to get to the bottom of things."

"Yes."

"As the queen commanded."

"Yes."

"Still . . ."

"Yes."

Vazh swore, then abruptly sat back. Without glancing over his shoulder, Malaq knew Kheridh had arrived. He waved him forward, all the while watching Vazh. At first, his gaze held only reluctant curiosity, but as Kheridh came closer, Vazh stiffened. The narrowed gaze flicked toward him, assessing, challenging. Malaq met it, careful to keep his face expressionless.

Kheridh bowed deeply, first to him and then to Vazh.

"Kheridh, this is Khonsel Vazh do Havi, a member of the royal council. Khonsel, this is Kheridh."

"I am honored to meet you, Khonsel," he said in perfect Zherosi.

Vazh studied him, his gaze raking Kheridh from the top of his head to his sandaled feet. Brave men had trembled under that silent scrutiny; he'd squirmed under it himself more than once. But that was long ago.

Kheridh's uncertain smile faded. Straightening his shoulders, he gave Vazh stare for stare. Malaq hid his approval behind his wine goblet.

Vazh scowled and rapped out a series of questions: Where is your village? How long have you lived there? Can you use a bow? A spear? A dagger? How old were you when you made your first kill? Under what moon were you born? How do the adders speak to you? Who is your father?

For the first time, Kheridh hesitated. White-faced but calm, he answered in the northern tongue. Vazh's imperious gaze swung toward him. "Well?"

Malaq delicately applied a napkin to his lips. "He paraphrased one of our sayings: a man may know the womb from which he emerged, but even the great Khonsel cannot say for sure who planted the seed."

Vazh's broad face flushed. Kheridh tensed. Malaq found himself measuring the distance between them. Then Vazh snorted and the tension eased. "Well, he's arrogant enough to be the son of a god. And clever enough to evade a straight answer. Don't translate that."

He didn't need to. Kheridh could understand the tone if not the words. After his perfect greeting, his Zherosi had slipped, conveying an air of bewildered innocence. Malaq wondered how much of it was deliberate. Despite Kheridh's apparent calm, the knuckles of his clasped hands were white. Vazh's gaze lingered on them a moment before he said, "Come here, boy."

Kheridh took one step forward, careful to remain out of reach.

"I said, come here."

Vazh's derisory tone brought a flush to Kheridh's cheeks, but he came closer.

"Give me your hand."

After the briefest hesitation, Kheridh thrust out his right hand. Vazh seized it. So intent was he on Vazh's face, Malaq didn't see the knife until it was too late. Kheridh's breath hissed in, but even when the blood beaded his wrist, his gaze never wavered.

Vazh flung his hand aside. "It seems the Son of Zhe bleeds like an ordinary man."

"The Son of Zhe is not immortal. Or impervious to injury."

"Obviously. His blood is dripping on your rug."

Malaq tossed his napkin to Kheridh who caught it one-handed and pressed it to his wrist. "Thank you, Kheridh. You may go now." Kheridh hesitated, as if he meant to speak, then bowed and turned on his heel.

Vazh picked up his wine goblet with studied casualness. He smacked his lips appreciatively. "I wouldn't trust a Carilian with my dog, but they do know how to make wine."

"I shall have a crate delivered to your quarters tomorrow."

"You're too kind."

"Yes, I am."

Vazh reached for the pitcher and refilled both their goblets. Then he leaned forward, thick fingers engulfing the delicate stem of the goblet as he observed him.

Malaq sighed. "Are we to engage in a staring contest as well? I'm happy to oblige you, old friend, but I'd prefer you to speak your mind." He smiled, conscious of his weariness. "Your bluntness has always been one of the qualities I treasure most."

"We've known each other—what? Twenty-five years now? You were my best commander. Zhe's coils, that day at Berov . . ." Impatiently, Vazh waved away the memory of the battle. "But you always possessed a . . . I don't know . . . call it a romantic streak. And it nearly destroyed your career. Would have if I hadn't stepped in."

"These are old battles."

"It's the same battle!" Vazh's fist came down on the table and the dishes rattled. "First, it was the woman."

"My wife," said Malaq very quietly. "She was my wife."

"Then, after I crack my stones to keep you in my command, you throw it all up to become a priest."

"I discovered my true vocation later than most men."

"And now, this boy."

"Yes. This boy."

Their eyes met. Malaq was the first to look away.

"You don't truly believe he's the Son of Zhe."

Malaq hesitated.

"You won't find the answer in your wine goblet."

"Who can say? Visions manifest in the unlikeliest places." His smile faded. "No. I don't believe he's the Son of Zhe."

"Thank the gods. If you started babbling prophecy at me, I'd have to strangle you. And it's too hot to do murder. Why let the rumors go unchecked?"

"Times are hard. A failed harvest last year. The floods this winter and the drought that followed. Womb of Earth trembles and the people are afraid."

"Harvests fail. Rains cease. Womb of Earth trembles like a palsied grandmother . . ." Vazh made a hasty sign of propitiation. ". . . but life goes on."

"He is . . . special."

"That business with the adders?" Vazh snorted. "Every priest has the power to touch the spirits of others. Or so you're always reminding less exalted folk like me."

"We rely on qiij to . . . never mind." Vazh had little interest and less patience when it came to spiritual matters. "The point is he can touch spirits without qiij. And he's only at the cusp of his power."

"Then he's dangerous."

"He can be taught."

"To use this power better? Are you mad? How long before he turns it against us?"

"I can control him."

"For now, maybe. Not forever. Meanwhile, he sows dissension. Those who think he's the Son of Zhe want to worship him. Those who think he's not want him dead."

"I can protect him."

Vazh opened his mouth and closed it again. He cracked his knuckles with methodical violence and then looked up. "He is not Davell."

Although he had been waiting for it since the moment Vazh first looked upon Kheridh, Malaq's breath still caught. It had been many years since anyone had spoken the name.

"I realize that." He was pleased that his voice sounded so calm.

Vazh toyed with a piece of flatbread. "There is . . . a resemblance. I'll grant you that." There was only the sound of the flatbread, cracking into smaller and smaller pieces. "The hair, of course."

Brown as mud when wet, but streaked bronze and russet in the sun. Like the leaves in the northern forests when the first chill of autumn is upon them.

"And the eyes."

So dark a blue you might think them black. Too big for his face, really. Or his face too thin for those eyes. They always seemed so wide, as if dazzled by the world they beheld. Until the last, of course, when they just stared up at the clouds shadowing his face, all the wonder drained out of them.

"And the stubborn streak."

Which he got from me. Which killed him. Because I loved him too much to shame him and send him home.

"He fought well that day."

Keep talking, old friend. Paint him for me with words. The tilt of his head as he squinted at the battlefield. The eager smile when our eyes met and the quick duck of his head when he realized he was smiling. So proud in his uniform. So much taller than the others. Such an easy target.

"Malaq . . ."

"As you say, there is a resemblance. On longer acquaintance, the differences become apparent."

"Then why not let him go?"

"That would be the stubborn streak, I suppose."

Vazh refused to return his smile. "The queen won't let him live."

"She will if I can prove his value."

"What value? Other Tree People have this power. I wonder we didn't net any in the recent raids."

"We did."

It took Vazh a moment to grasp the implications. "Burn me! You had them sacrificed."

"I took the precaution of making my own investigation before the council meeting."

"Did you even bother to test their power?" When he remained silent, Vazh leaned forward. "Don't do this," he said softly. "Don't risk everything for this boy. When he falls, he'll take you with him. And he will fall, Malaq."

"While I am able, I will protect him."

He looked into the eyes of his oldest friend and waited.

Vazh cursed eloquently; the sheer number and inventiveness of his curses had always impressed Malaq. Still cursing, Vazh shoved himself up from the table. "I'm not promising anything." He stalked away, then turned back. "The boy was right about one thing. Meaning no disrespect to the memory of your blessed mother, she surely copulated with a mule to produce you."

"I think it unlikely," Malaq replied. "Mules are sterile."

"Would that your father had been!"

Malaq remained at the table, watching the light in the garden fade from orange to rose. For all Vazh's curses, Kheridh now had one more person watching over him.

When twilight finally yielded to darkness, he pushed himself up, conscious of the stiffness in his knees. He walked down the narrow hallway to his bedchamber. Niqia's head came up as he sat on the sleeping shelf beside her to unlace his sandals. He removed a pillow from his bed and placed it on the floor before the little alcove.

He knelt before the altar and performed the rites: crumbling fragments of flatbread into the polished black bowl, pouring an offering of wine into the tiny bronze acorn, lighting the cone of incense. He whispered his wife's name and prayed she had found her way to her people's paradise. He lit the fourteen beeswax candles, one for each year of Davell's life. Then, as he did every night before he slept, Malaq closed his eyes and prayed for the spirit of his son.

Chapter 22

SMOKE FROM THE BURNING herbs filled the hut of the three priestesses. Griane sat cross-legged beside Faelia, trying very hard to keep from coughing. She would have preferred that her daughter remain at home, but Muina insisted she come tonight; a girl's first moon blood was especially powerful.

Powerful or not, Faelia had been less than pleased by her rite of passage, complaining that it would be far more exciting to spend a night in the forest searching for her vision mate than to sit in the moon hut for five days. Griane let her grumble, knowing that her lack of enthusiasm stemmed, in part, from the absence of her father and brother who should have shared the celebration with the rest of the family.

At least they were both alive; Gortin had assured her they were not in the Forever Isles. She still had hope to cling to, unlike poor Duba who had sunk deeper into despair when Gortin told her that Owan's spirit had flown there. Although Griane tried not to blame Gortin for his inability to find Keirith or Darak, she couldn't understand why a shaman who could fly to the Forever Isles with his spirit guide could not fly to the land of the raiders. But then, she'd never understood the workings of magic.

Which made it all the more unnerving to sit here tonight. Lisula had suggested a Summoning after Faelia went to the moon hut. Griane had never heard of the rite, but she was so desperate to find out about the welfare of her husband

and son that she'd immediately agreed to join the priestesses at the full moon.

As instructed, Griane and Faelia saved the moss they
had used to absorb their moon blood. The two clumps lay
in separate bowls in the center of their little circle. Two
other bowls held water from the lake. Collected at dawn
the last three mornings, they had carried it, cupped in their
hands, to the priestesses. "It must touch nothing other than
your flesh before it is poured into the sacred bowls," Lisula
had warned.

Griane clutched the tuft of Keirith's baby hair between
her thumb and forefinger. She had turned the hut upside
down searching for a strand of Darak's hair before Faelia
suggested the wolfskins. Cursing her stupidity, she'd
combed through the coarse fur and found a long, dark hair.

All the materials were gathered, all the preparations made.
It remained to be seen whether the Summoning would
work.

Muina leaned back toward the fire pit, using an oak leaf
to waft more smoke around the circle. "Oak-Lord, let your
branches spread wide above the forest. Oak-Lord, let your
roots burrow deep beneath the earth. Oak-Lord, help us find
the lost ones."

All the priestesses looked about as likely to fall into a
trance as Faelia. But Lisula had told her, "We leave flying
to the priests. Women's magic is a thing of earth and water."

Like a woman's body, Griane thought. Solid as earth, yet
shedding blood every moon.

Lisula handed a holly leaf to Muina who addressed the
same chant to the Holly-Lord. Silently, Griane added her
own prayer.

Please, Cuillon. Help me find them.

Muina raised the heart-shaped leaf of speedwell and Griane swallowed hard. When Darak bid Tinnean farewell,
hundreds of the flowers had sprung up at the base of the
One Tree, creating a living blue pathway that led from
brother to brother.

Tinnean. Are you here? Can you see us? Can you see them?

Muina finished the chant to Tinnean Tree-Friend and
cleared her throat. "A priestess must relinquish the title
and responsibilities of Grain-Mother when her moon flow
ceases. But if she can no longer call the earth to fertility,

she can awaken its hidden powers. If she cannot bless the
first sea trout of the year, she can uncover the mysteries
that lie beneath the surface of the waters. That is what we
will attempt tonight."

Faelia caught her breath and Muina gave her a reassuring
smile. "There's no danger to you or your mother. And
although I'm not as strong as I could wish, the magic will
be easier because the three of us share a bond of blood.
My mother's sister was your grandmother, Faelia. My link
to your father's family is more distant, but it's through the
female line as well. That lends power to our Summoning.
That and the moon blood."

"Why moon blood?" Faelia asked.

"It's more powerful than ordinary blood. That's why
women are segregated from the tribe during their moon
flow." Muina's expression darkened. "Some men call a
woman unclean, but that just shows their fear and ignorance of the mystery. How can a woman bleed with no
wound? Why does her body weep blood in harmony to
Gheala's ebb and flow?"

Darak had merely seemed resentful that Griane's moon
flow took her away from him. The first time she went to
the moon hut after their marriage, he had waited outside
the last night so he could see her the moment she emerged
at dawn. Years later, Ennit revealed it to Lisula who
promptly told her. When Griane asked Darak about it, he'd
blushed and mumbled something about killing Ennit. When
she told him it was sweet, he'd turned even redder and
promised to kill her if she ever told anyone.

Although it might only be a woman's fancy, she'd always
been convinced that Callie had been conceived the day of
that conversation with Darak. Just as she firmly believed
that Faelia had been conceived after they had quarreled
and made up.

A sharp pinch on her knee made her squeak in surprise.
As she turned to glare at Faelia, Muina said, "We'll search
for Keirith first. Griane, you will summon him as you share
the closest blood tie."

Lisula placed one of the bowls of water before Muina
who passed her hands over it three times. "Lacha, goddess
of lakes and rivers. Halam, earth goddess, bone mother.
Gheala, moon sister. Lend us your power. Lend us your

strength. Lend us your light. Help us find Keirith, child of our tribe, child of Griane's womb."

Lisula lifted Griane's clump of moss with two rowan twigs and dropped it into the water. Then she passed one twig to Muina who chanted, "From one womb, blood and babe. From one flesh, mother and child." Muina swirled the clump in a slow circle. Then Lisula retrieved the dripping moss and laid it atop the oak leaves Bethia held.

"Stir the water fourteen times with Keirith's hair," Muina said. "Don't let your fingers touch the surface of the water."

The pinkish water barely moved, but Lisula gave her an encouraging nod so she must be doing it right.

"Blood of the mother," Muina muttered. "Hair of the child. Blood and body unite to show us Keirith."

Griane's mouth hurt. It took her a moment to realize she was gnawing her upper lip.

Please, Maker, don't let me drop the hair.

When she finished, she sighed with relief and heard Faelia do the same. Still staring into the bowl, Muina said, "Drop his hair into the water."

Reluctantly, Griane complied. Softer than rabbit fur, she had carefully preserved the tiny tuft since Keirith's birth. As the strands spread across the surface of the water, Muina said, "Call his name, Griane. Three times."

She barely managed a whisper, but at Muina's sharp look, she found the strength to mimic the Grain-Grandmother's voice of summoning. Oddly, just pretending to have the power made her feel as if she did.

They were all leaning forward now, every pair of eyes fixed on the bowl. And so they remained. Griane's knees began to ache from kneeling on the rushes. She forced herself to concentrate on the bowl, willing something— anything—to happen. But only when Faelia's fingers dug into her arm did she see.

Although no earthly power stirred them, the hairs were moving. They circled sunwise around the bowl, slowly at first, then faster as if caught in a whirlpool. An involuntary shiver shook her as the single whirlpool split into two. A third appeared beneath it. The twin whirlpools shuddered. Two blue eyes blinked open. A mouth froze in the act of yawning. The lips moved, forming a single word.

"Mam?"

"Keirith? Keirith, can you hear me?"

Her trembling hands grasped the bowl, and the vision vanished.

"Oh, gods. I've lost him."

"Nay," Lisula said. "It wasn't you."

Muina slumped against Bethia's shoulder, breathing hard, but one hand came up to wave Lisula's hands away. "I'm fine, child. Just tired. I'll need to rest a bit before we try to summon Darak."

As Bethia lifted a waterskin to Muina's lips, Faelia whispered, "I saw him, Mam. It was Keirith. I know it was."

Griane nodded and carefully released the bowl.

"Muina will have seen more," Lisula whispered. "We can ask her when she's stronger."

"I'm strong enough now." Muina took another sip of water and thrust the skin at Bethia. "He was sleeping. I felt stone all around him. But his sleeping place was familiar to him and comfortable. There were others near him—not Darak," she added quickly. "Strangers. I sensed an injury. Nothing life-threatening, but . . ."

"A broken limb? A head wound?"

"Nay. His back, perhaps. It must have happened a while ago. If it were more recent, the color would have been darker."

"His eyes?"

"Nay, child. I see colors in the water. They tell me if a person is hurt. A sound body will look blue or green. Wounds will flare bright red. Keirith . . ." Her frown deepened. "His body is sound enough, but there is something. Perhaps a wound to his spirit. Those I cannot see."

"At least he's not in any immediate danger," Lisula said.

Muina's face remained troubled. "Or he didn't sense the danger. He sleeps alone. I would have expected him to be with the captives taken from the Holly Tribe. Unless . . ."

Unless they had met the same fate as Owan.

"Keirith might have escaped," Lisula suggested. "Or be in hiding. Or have found a protector."

Or the raiders might have discovered his power and removed him from the other captives.

"He's alive," Bethia said in her calm voice. "He is unharmed. The Tree-Father will continue to seek a vision, and when it comes, he will be able to tell us more."

For once, Bethia's serenity made Griane want to shake her.

"The night is waning," Muina said. "And we still must seek Darak."

"Are you strong enough, Grain-Grandmother?"

Muina gave Bethia a withering glance. "I'll manage. Help me up. Faelia, you must summon your father."

"Not Mam?"

"She shares no blood link to him. You do."

As the chanting began, Griane tried to still her turbulent thoughts.

Keirith's safe. For now. That's something. Gortin will keep trying. The vision will come. It must.

She held up her hand so Faelia could untie the precious hair from her forefinger. "How many times?" Faelia whispered.

"What?"

"Fa's age!"

"Oh. Thirty-eight."

Faelia's lips moved as she counted each circle. The hair trailed limply in the motionless water and Griane found herself chewing her lip again. Faelia cleared her throat. Her "Fa!" was loud enough to make them all start.

"His name," Muina said. "You must say his name."

Faelia looked stricken. "Have I ruined it?"

"Nay, child. He is 'Fa' to you, after all. So say that twice more and then his name three times."

Faelia obeyed, crawling forward on hands and knees to stare into the bowl. The water gave a small shiver and subsided.

"Faelia's blood link to Darak is not as strong as yours to Keirith," Lisula whispered. "Give it time."

Instead of swirling in a circle, the water rose into tiny crests, lapping like miniature waves against one side of the bowl. Griane's gaze kept darting from the bowl to Muina's face. Two lines formed between her brows and her lips were pressed together as if in pain.

Please, gods, let him be there. Please let him be all right.

She pictured Darak's eyes in her mind—soft as twilight when he was happy, dark as storm clouds when angered. She willed them to appear in the water, to blink open as Keirith's had. And then the mouth would curve up in that lopsided smile and the deep voice would assure he that he was fine.

"Stop fussing."

For a fleeting moment, she thought Muina was speaking Darak's words. Then Griane looked up and found her leaning against Bethia. When she looked down at the bowl again, the water was still.

"Is he dead?" Her voice sounded utterly calm. How was that possible?

"Nay!" Faelia's cry seemed torn from her throat. "I did something wrong. Please, can we try again?"

"Hush, child." Muina's voice was little more than a whisper. Lines of strain creased her forehead. "Darak lives."

Griane heard a strangled moan, but only when Lisula's arms went around her did she realize it came from her. Her hand reached out blindly for Faelia who seized it with icy fingers.

"Darak lives. But he's sick."

"Darak's never sick. He survived the plague. He's never even had a fever, save for the one after he escaped from Chaos." When Muina remained silent, Griane added, "You all know how strong he is."

"Strong as a boar," Lisula said, patting her hand.

"Stop coddling her." Muina's voice was sharp. "That she can get from any woman. She came to us to learn the truth. Do you want to hear it or not?" When Griane nodded, her stern features relaxed. "His body was aching and exhausted. But his stomach troubles him more."

"His stomach?" She stopped herself from saying that Darak could eat anything.

"It felt . . . raw. And his throat. As if he'd been retching."

Darak was too wise in the ways of the forest to eat something poisonous. A flux of some kind?

"Is he dying?" Faelia's voice sounded so scared that Griane squeezed her hand hard.

"Nay, child. He's taken some food recently and likely the illness will pass. But he's not as young as he once was."

Strong as a boar—and stubborn as a rock. In his anxiety to reach Keirith, he would drive himself hard.

"Do you know where he is?" she asked.

"I sensed stone and turf around him, so he must be in a hut. There were others sleeping there, too."

The village healer could give him something for his stom-

ach, but short of tying him down, Griane doubted anyone—
or any ailment—could keep him from his quest. Urkiat was
too much in awe to try. That was the trouble with strangers;
they knew the Spirit-Hunter, not the man.

"Darak's not a fool," Muina said. "He knows he must
conserve his strength to search for Keirith. That alone will
make him take care of himself."

But he hadn't done that during the quest for Tinnean.
He'd gone hunting when he was injured and exhausted, and
when the hunting was bad, he'd gone without so those who
were weaker could eat. He'd been shouldering a man's responsibilities since he was eleven. If he'd learned to trust
others over the years, that early self-reliance was too deeply
ingrained to be forgotten.

"Isn't there anything else we can do?" Faelia asked.

"Not tonight. But rest easy. You did everything right.
Searching for Keirith wearied me, else I'd have seen more
of your father." Muina's mouth twisted in a bitter smile.
"The magic needs a woman past her moon flow, but I'm
getting too old for it."

"Thank you," Griane said. "Lisula and Bethia, I thank
you as well."

She kissed all three priestesses and left the hut. As soon
as they were outside, Faelia said, "At least they're all right.
That's something."

"Aye. Keirith—wherever he is—is safe. Your father is
wise enough to know the limits of his strength."

And Faelia was young enough to be comforted by the
words. But long after the children had fallen asleep, Griane
lay awake, her fingers digging helplessly into the wolfskins.

Men went off to be tested for courage: at their vision
quests, on their hunting trips, into a strange land or into
the heart of Chaos itself. Women were tested for endurance: for their ability to bear the pain of childbirth, the
anxiety of sitting up with a sick child, or the bone-deep
ache of loneliness while they waited and worried and
watched for a loved one's return.

Men were lucky.

Her mind formed the prayer she repeated every night
before she slept: *Maker, keep them safe. Maker, bring them
home. Maker, give me the strength to endure.*

Chapter 23

B Y THE TIME THEY reached Ailmin's village, Darak was so weak from seasickness that he had to rest for two days. The chief was a hard-faced man about his age, the third the tribal elders had chosen in ten years; the raiders had killed his predecessors.

When he asked for the loan of a currach, Ailmin frowned. "There's a deserted village three days south of here. My men will take you that far. After that, you'll have to go on foot. You don't have the skills or stamina to manage a currach on your own."

Urkiat bristled at his dismissive tone, but Darak knew Ailmin was right. Still, the truth stung as did the realization that the hospitality so prized among the northern tribes was given grudgingly here, even to the man who had rescued the Oak-Lord. In the north, strangers were welcomed for the news and gossip they brought. Here, they were suspect. The raiders were killing more than the children of the Oak and Holly; they were destroying a way of life.

Ailmin's men beached their currachs in the deserted village and remained only long enough for the supplies to be unloaded before launching them again. There were no farewells, no earnest blessings for their safe journey, just sullen faces as closed and hard as their chief's.

"They had no right to treat you like that," Urkiat fumed. "They owe their lives to you."

"Ailmin gave us food and transport. And a map." Darak patted his belly, where the scrap of hide lay safely nestled under his tunic. Crudely drawn with a charred twig, it gave them the location of every village—inhabited or deserted—along the coast.

"All the same, it was an insult. If I ever see them again, I—"

"Let it be, Urkiat. Our enemies are the Zherosi."

They made little progress the first day; scaling a gentle slope was enough to leave him panting and exhausted. But he slowly regained his strength and his appetite, thanks in large part to Urkiat. When he wasn't scolding him for going beyond the limits of his endurance, Urkiat ranged through the forest to bring down squirrels, set snares at night to trap rabbits, and crouched over the fire pit stirring Jirra's restorative herbs into a hot brew to ease Darak's stomach. Although the insistent fussing made him feel like a useless old man, Darak knew he would never have managed alone. One night, after batting Urkiat's hands away as they tucked his mantle under his chin, he told him he was worse than Griane with his fussing and scolding. But he smiled when he said it, and Urkiat blushed like a boy.

He missed Griane, as much for her common sense and good instincts as for the presence of her body nestled next to his at night. And he had no opportunities to seek out Wolf; if he so much as walked away from the fire to piss, he found Urkiat sitting bolt upright, waiting anxiously for his return.

The farther south they journeyed, the steeper the land became and the hotter the weather. A sennight had passed without rain; in the north, there were showers almost every day at this time of year.

Urkiat grew more uncommunicative daily. On the fourth day after leaving the deserted village, he broke his silence to insist that they abandon the coastal route.

"But that makes no sense." Darak spread the map on the ground. "Look. Here's the next village." He tapped the tiny cairn that Ailmin used to depict a deserted village. "And there's the next." He pointed to the circle that indicated an inhabited one. "It's a good ten miles south. If we turn inland now, we'll lose two or three days in the hills."

"They might see us from their currachs."

"If they do, we make for the forest."

"It's too dangerous. I know this land. And I'm telling you we must go inland. Now."

Darak took in the white face, the shaking voice, and the desperate eyes. "It's your village, isn't it?"

Urkiat's shoulders sagged. Silently, he nodded.

"Why didn't you just tell me?"

"I was . . . I didn't want you to think I was a coward."

"There's no shame in wanting to avoid a place that holds so many bad memories. But we've got to be able to trust each other. And we can't do that by keeping secrets."

"I know. I'm sorry."

"Tell me now if you can face this. If not—"

Urkiat's head jerked up, his expression stark but determined. "I can face it."

They reached the village late that same afternoon. Once, it must have been a pretty place, nestled beneath a rocky promontory in the gentle curve of the beach. Scrub pines shaded the circle of huts while farther down the shore, a heron waded through the gently waving reeds of a marsh.

A few huts still retained their walls, although the roofs had long since caved in. The rest had fallen into ruin, mere tumbles of stones, interlaced with a tangle of vines and fallen branches. Seedlings had sprouted among them and in the meadow that must have once been a small field.

The cairn was still intact. When Darak bent to pull a tall clump of salt grass that blocked the entrance to the barrow, Urkiat spoke for the first time. "Let the forest take it."

All the same, Darak placed a stone atop the cairn and whispered a prayer. He looked up to find Urkiat wandering down the beach. Shouldering his pack, he followed.

When Urkiat finally sat on a flat rock, Darak hesitated, wondering if he should intrude on his thoughts. In the end, he approached, but stood a little apart from him. If Urkiat wanted to talk, he would listen, but he would not force him to share his memories. Some tales were better left untold.

Urkiat took a deep, shuddering breath. "I was keeping watch with my brother. He was sitting on this rock and I was next to him—where you are—on the ground. We'd argued about that—him getting the more comfortable spot. Mareth cuffed me. He was fourteen. He'd been standing watch for two years. When I kept watch with a younger boy, then I could take the good spot."

His bleak expression softened. "You wouldn't think you'd remember such things with all that happened later, but I do. Maybe *because* of what happened later. Or maybe because it was my first watch. But I still remember the cuff and the argument. And the cold—gods, it was cold that night."

He jerked his thumb over his shoulder. "Two others kept watch on the headland. That was my father's idea—to have two sets of watchers. But we never even saw them. There was only a little splash. Like fish. And the same kind of creak that branches make when they rub together in the wind. That was the sound of their oars. I didn't know that then. I was still trying to puzzle it out when Mareth grabbed my shoulder. I tried to shout—" His voice caught and he cleared his throat. "All that came out was a whisper. We just stood there, staring at this . . . giant . . . emerging from the mist by the marshes. And then Mareth shoved me and told me to run. He shouted a warning to the village, shouted at me, but by then, they were everywhere. I screamed then and stumbled. That's what saved me." He fingered the scar on his cheek with trembling fingers.

"When I woke up, they were gone. It was quiet. Except for the moaning. The smoke was so thick it choked you. We'd had a lot of rain that autumn and the thatch was damp. The village was empty save for the bodies. I found Mareth. Near me. They'd stabbed him so many times his tunic was in shreds."

Urkiat swallowed hard and swiped his lips with his fist. "I must have passed out . . . my head . . . I could hardly see. When I woke again, I was in our hut. My grandmother was bending over me. She'd fled into the forest with the others. We lost ten that day. Eight dead and two . . . just gone. Stolen. And all our stores."

He was silent so long that Darak finally asked, "But your folk didn't leave?"

"Nay. Even after they came the next autumn and killed eight more, we stayed. The following spring, more ships came. This time, the raiders wanted to talk. And my father . . ." He spat the word out like a curse. ". . . who had buried his firstborn son . . . my father—the chief—

invited the leader of the raiders into his hut and offered him wine and fed him salmon and barleycakes. And when they came out, the council met and we had a new treaty with the men who had butchered our people."

Urkiat leaped up and stalked down the beach, only to whirl around again a moment later. "My father agreed to provide furs and hides every spring and grain every autumn if the raiders left us in peace. My father agreed they could use our village to launch attacks on the tribes farther north. My father agreed they could cut down as many trees as they needed to build their great fortress and repair their ships. And when the leader of the raiders asked for a boy to serve him and run messages to and from the fortress, my father offered me."

Urkiat's voice dwindled to a hoarse whisper. "I thought I'd die of the shame. But you don't, do you? You eat it and drink it and vomit it up like bile."

"Don't." Darak didn't even know if Urkiat heard him for he was staring out to sea again.

"I served him two years."

"You were a boy."

"I was fifteen when I killed him."

After a long moment, Darak managed, "The leader of the raiders?"

"Aye."

"You hated him. Hated what he'd done to your people."

Urkiat laughed, the hoarse croak of a raven. "I loved him."

Darak opened his mouth and shut it again.

"He was kind. And honorable. And fair. He taught me his language. He told me about the great cities of the Zherosi. He told me his people and mine should be friends, that if we tried very hard to learn each other's way, we could live together as we had generations ago."

Urkiat spat. "He was a dreamer. Or a liar. I still don't know which. But I . . . I loved him like a father. That's why I had to kill him. Because I was losing myself and everything I thought I believed in and sooner or later, I would choose him over my people and then I'd be . . . nothing."

Urkiat sank down on the beach as if his legs would no longer support him. "That's when they destroyed the vil-

lage. After I killed him. I didn't plan it. I just . . . it just
happened. And then I ran away. I should have stayed. Then
they would have killed me, too."

He stared out at the sea like a man bespelled. "They
hanged my father," he said calmly, "but the rest were impaled against the walls of the fortress. Even the babes. They
didn't waste spears. They shoved sharpened stakes through
their bellies. A few were still alive when I found them."

"Dear gods . . ."

"They must have taken some as slaves. There were only
fifty-three bodies. I counted. As I dragged them to the Death
Hut. Three days, it took me. They didn't all fit. I had to
lay most of them on the ground. But I folded their hands
across their chests and closed their eyes." His voice had
become as light and high as a child reciting his lessons. "It
was very warm. Like today. And the sea so bright it hurt
to look at it."

Numbed by the horror of the story, it took Darak a moment before he could move. Urkiat's head came up. Although his eyes were wild, his voice was still very quiet.
"Don't touch me, please. If you touch me, I'll weep. And
tears are a privilege I don't deserve."

Darak went down on one knee, careful not to touch him.
"Aye, you do. But if you won't weep for yourself, weep
for your folk. They deserve your tears."

Very slowly, he reached out and laid his hand on the
dark hair. Urkiat's hands came up, whether to push him
away or cling to him, Darak didn't know, because he was
already pulling him into his arms. When Urkiat's sobs finally ebbed, and the sun dipped into the sea, Darak helped
him to his feet. He settled the pack on his shoulders and
took his hand, as if he were a little lad like Callie, and led
him away from the ruins.

Chapter 24

FOR DAYS, KEIRITH did little but go over the events of the last sennight. He felt like an animal caught in a snare; any move would only tighten the noose around his neck. The Pajhit's words, so similar to his father's, echoed in his head: *"Trust your instincts. Your observations."* Words that applied equally well to both the hunter and the hunted.

Perhaps it was because he thought so much about his father that he dreamed of swimming in the lake with him. They dove deep, squinting at each other through the murky water. Hands clasped, they floated together, enjoying the silence and serenity. But then something pulled him to the surface.

He woke to hear his mam calling his name, her voice as clear and strong as if she sat beside him. Still half asleep, he sat up, looking around the hut for her. Only when he saw the walls of stone and the guards, silhouetted in the doorway, did he remember where he was. He lay back on his fleece, hoping they would think his shivering came from cold instead of fear. And in the morning, he walked into the Pajhit's chamber and, with a calm he did not feel, laid out his bargain.

"I'll tell you everything I know about my gift, teach you everything I've learned about the way a shaman works with a spirit guide. I . . . I'll even let you touch my spirit if it's the only way for you to understand. But in return, I want your oath that I may go home."

"To a people who view your gift as an abomination? Who would sacrifice you for using it?"

"Your people would sacrifice me as well."

The Pajhit conceded that with a reluctant nod.

"I want to go home."

"Very well. You have my oath. Once I've learned what I need to know, I'll help you leave Pilozhat. If you still wish to go."

And so he became the teacher and Malaq his student. Keirith taught him the lessons he had learned as an apprentice: stillness, emptiness, control. Every afternoon, they sat together in Malaq's bedchamber while he struggled to master these skills. Without the crutch of qiij, it was impossible for him to slip the bonds of his body, but there were also distractions that broke his concentration: priests calling him to meetings to organize the festival called The Shedding; the Master of Zhiisti wailing about some dispute among his students; or simply the brush of Niqia's fur against his hand.

"It takes time," he assured Malaq. "Be patient."

In the evenings, Malaq became the teacher again. "Shielding will not cast someone out of your spirit, but it will prevent him from searching it. And for two spirits who wish to commune, shielding keeps them from . . . bleeding together."

"Is that dangerous?"

"It can be—if the spirits touch for a long period of time. Think of the shield as a wall. Partners whose spirits are touching can make the wall as strong as they wish. The more permeable the wall, the greater the connection. And the deeper one spirit may probe another."

It raised all Keirith's old fears. Until he mastered the technique of shielding, he would be vulnerable.

"I know you fear what will happen when our spirits touch. But I promise you, I will go no deeper than you permit me."

The first time he felt the delicate brush of Malaq's spirit, he instinctively pushed him away. Although Malaq withdrew immediately, Keirith was too drained by the experience to try again until the following evening. This time, he forced himself to withstand the shock of the initial intrusion. Within moments, Malaq's presence faded until it was barely perceptible.

<Good, Kheridh. Very good.>

It was like sharing thoughts with the eagle, except Malaq's were much fainter.

<Because I have erected the wall. But I left a chink in it through which we can communicate. I want you to try and stop up the chink with your power.>

Instead, he blasted a hole through it. The next night, however, he did a little better. The hardest part was learning to restrain his power, allowing it to unfurl as gently as he had when he touched the eagle. When he apologized yet again for his clumsiness, Malaq looked at him in astonishment. "It takes some Zhiisti a moon to master the rudiments of shielding."

After that, though, they had to stop the lessons; three nights of using qiij sapped Malaq's energy. When he recovered, Keirith resumed his instruction, but Malaq was fretful at his continued failure.

"We just haven't found the right tools to help you," Keirith assured him. "Sometimes, the Tree-Father gazes into the smoke of a fire. Or into a bowl of water."

They gave up on the bowl of water after Niqia began drinking from it.

"A polished stone?" Keirith suggested.

After some hesitation, Malaq removed one from the small altar in his bedchamber, a palm-sized disk of greenish-black stone, speckled with red.

"Concentrate on the red blotches," Keirith said. "Just let yourself fall into them. Become part of the stone."

The first time, the trance lasted only a few moments, but Malaq was as excited as an apprentice, swearing that the specks had formed the shape of two wings. "What does it mean?"

"What do you think it means?" Keirith replied, just as the Tree-Father would have.

"I think it was you. You were the wings. Carrying me to a new realm of knowledge." Then Malaq recovered his customary reserve and added dryly, "Or perhaps it was only the pheasant I had for supper."

They laughed together, giddy with the success and the shared bond of power. Malaq was still chuckling when Keirith rose.

"What is it?"

"Nothing. I'm just tired. Excuse me."

The next morning, he went back to the Pajhit's chamber and told him he wanted to observe a sacrifice.

"May I ask why?"

"I . . . I just need to."

"Very well. I'll have the guards bring you to the temple of Zhe before dawn."

"Nay." Keirith swallowed hard. "I wish to see a sacrifice to Heart of Sky."

All expression fled Malaq's face. "As you wish."

It was still dark when he left the palace, but already the corridors were bustling with slaves carrying platters of food, and anonymous officials ducking into storage rooms. None of them even flinched when they heard the awful blast of the horn, but then they must have heard it thousands of times before.

Torches blazed near the steps of the temple, illuminating the shadowy figures standing at the altar. Behind the temple, Kelazhat's looming mass was black against an azure sky striped with rose and gold clouds.

Malaq stood atop the platform with two other priests. A band of bronze circled his forehead. A shimmering cloak in shades ranging from pink to ruddy red cascaded over his golden robe.

Keirith's guards halted directly before the platform. The guttering torchlight made it difficult to decipher Malaq's expression. He probably knew why he had insisted on coming here today. Perhaps he considered it another test. And it was. Only this time Keirith was testing himself.

It had come to him so clearly in that moment of shared laughter. He liked teaching Malaq and was eager to learn the skills Malaq could teach him. He enjoyed sharing his gift with another who accepted and admired it, who accepted and admired him. He was losing himself in the lessons and the fellowship and the sense of belonging. Today's sacrifice would remind him that he was still a prisoner, still an outsider—always an outsider—among the enemies of his people.

His stomach roiled when the horn bellowed again.

Please, Maker. Don't let it be someone I know.

He had watched the Tree-Father slit the throat of a bullock each Midwinter, the throat of a young ram each Midsummer. He had watched the blood spurt into the sacred bowl, smelled its hot, salty-sweet scent. But he had never watched a man lying helpless on a slab of rock as a dagger carved open his chest.

When he heard the footsteps, he resisted the urge to glance over his shoulder and stared straight ahead. The polished stone of the altar gleamed in the torchlight. It was the same greenish-black color as the stone Malaq had used to help him fall into a trance. Only now, the red blotches looked like spatters of blood.

The captive stumbled up the steps, supported by two guards. The man must be drugged, just like the three who'd been castrated. The guards staggered a little as they eased him onto the stone slab; the man was big and the drugs made him ungainly. The guards pulled his arms over his head and took a firm grip on his wrists. Two others stepped forward to seize his ankles. The man's head turned to watch them and Keirith let out a breath he hadn't realized he was holding: the victim was a stranger.

The Pajhit lifted the bronze dagger skyward. The man hummed a hoarse little counterpoint to the priests' chanting.

Maker, let it be quick. Don't let him suffer.

Keirith never knew if it was the chanting or the billowing smoke or the sweet-scented oil in which the torches had been dipped. All he knew was the sensation of falling and rising at the same time, every sense sharpened by the impending sacrifice that unfolded with dreamlike slowness.

The man's pale skin blushing as the first rays of the sun bathed him. The momentary flash of the dagger as it darted like a swallow, first from breastbone to belly, then across the ribs. Rivulets of blood like tiny red waterfalls. The scent of it, hotter than the summer breeze. The body arching in agonized protest, then collapsing back onto the slab. Two hands reaching into his chest. Another dagger, quick and delicate as the zigzagging flight of a minnowfly. The heart, redder than the newly risen sun, weeping its lifeblood through the fingers that raised it skyward.

But it was no longer a stranger's face that stared open-eyed at the Pajhit. Even as Keirith watched, the features shifted: the nose becoming more prominent, strands of gray sprouting among the dark hair, pockmarks blistering the cheeks.

And then the head turned. His father's eyes, gray as a Midwinter sky, stared down at him. His father's lips, spattered with his heart's blood, moved. And his father's voice, softer than the hiss of an adder, whispered, "You have murdered me."

Chapter 25

GRIANE WAS SCRAPING Faelia's uneaten stew back into the pot when the bearskin twitched aside to reveal Gortin hovering in the doorway. "Forgive me for intruding on your meal."

"Nay, we were . . ." Her voice trailed off. "You've had a vision."

He nodded. His grim face told her it was bad. With an effort, she kept her voice calm. "Faelia, take Callie to Ennit's."

"Is it about Fa?"

"Go to Ennit's."

"I have a right to hear."

"Don't talk back!"

"It's not fair," Faelia muttered, but she tossed her braid over her shoulder and pulled Callie out of the hut, without so much as a nod to Gortin.

"Forgive my daughter's manners, Tree-Father. Please sit down." Mouthing the niceties gave her a chance to reclaim her composure.

"Before I begin, I must warn you that visions are . . . chancy. You can never be entirely certain of their meaning. The best you can do—"

"For mercy's sake, stop dithering and tell me what you saw!" Immediately, she stammered out an apology, but Gortin just shook his head and took a deep breath.

Oh, gods, don't let them be dead.

"I saw Darak. Lying on a slab of stone. An altar . . ."

Gortin's voice droned on. He probably thought his calm would steady her, but somehow, his lack of emotion made the images even more horrifying.

"You think Keirith has killed his father?"

"Nay!" Gortin looked shocked. "Visions—"

"Are chancy. Aye."

"—reveal what might happen as well as what will happen. I might have touched Keirith's nightmare. Or one of his visions. Or it may simply be a warning that Darak will face great danger in the holy city. He couldn't have reached it yet. It's been only a moon since he left."

"Only a moon."

"I know it must seem longer to you, but I beg you not to lose hope. If Darak could walk out of Chaos, he will surely return to us."

"Of course."

"I'm sorry, Griane. Perhaps I should have waited until I had better news."

"Nay. You were right to come. I thank you." She rose on shaking legs. If she had to make polite conversation any longer, she would scream.

Gortin rose as well, quickly tracing a sign of blessing on her forehead with his thumb. "As soon as I see anything more . . ."

"Thank you, Tree-Father. Good night."

Griane waited to leave the hut until she trusted herself to face her children and lie. It amazed her that the earth was still solid beneath her feet, that the western sky still blushed pink. Outside Ennit's hut, she took a deep breath, praying that neither her face nor her manner would betray her. Even before she straightened, Faelia was on her feet.

"It was nothing," she said. Her voice sounded appropriately disgusted. "Just some strange ritual. Even Gortin couldn't make sense of it."

"Was Keirith there?"

"Aye. And a bunch of priests."

"What was he doing?"

"Watching a sacrifice."

"What kind of sacrifice?"

"I don't know, Faelia!" Too sharp, her voice was too sharp. "A lamb, perhaps. I asked Gortin over and over again, but he could only say that visions were chancy, that the things you see often mean something else."

"So what did the lamb mean?" Callie asked.

"That . . . Keirith feels young. And helpless. Maybe the lamb reminded him of home."

"Or maybe Conn was the lamb," Callie said. Then he gasped. "But that means something awful's going to happen to him."

"Nothing's going to happen to Conn," Ennit assured him. "More likely, Gortin had lamb stew for supper and it didn't agree with him."

Thank the gods for Ennit. Callie was smiling now, although Faelia continued to study her. When she opened her mouth to pose another question, Griane said, "It's getting late. Ennit needs to get the girls to sleep."

She shooed Callie and Faelia out of the hut. She could hear Callie chattering about lamb stew and Faelia telling him all he ever thought about was his stomach. Griane closed her eyes, grateful for the ordinary sound of quarreling. Then a hand grabbed her arm.

"Ennit! Good gods, you gave me a fright."

"What did he really see?"

"I told you—"

"And I know you. Was it that bad?"

Try as she might, she couldn't control either her shaking voice or the words that poured out. Ennit's hand tightened on her arm, but all he said was, "Keirith would never stand by and watch someone hurt Darak."

"I know." But she couldn't help remembering that last evening: Keirith, wild-eyed, by the doorway, Darak slumped by the fire pit.

"Likely it's just as Gortin said. A warning. Or something."

"Aye."

"You know how strong Darak is. How determined. If he could escape from Chaos—"

"I know! Every day someone tells me that."

"I'm sorry."

Ennit was only trying to help. Everyone tried to help. But they all seemed to forget that Darak was fifteen years older, a Memory-Keeper instead of a hunter.

Ennit sighed. "Gods, I wish Struath were here. He had a rare gift of vision."

"Gortin tried."

"And visions are—"

"Chancy. Aye. So Gortin said."

"I'm no use to you at all, am I?"

She gave him a quick hug. "Of course you are. If not for you and Lisula . . ." The tears were too close; all she could do was hug him again.

"He'll come back, Griane."

"So now you're having visions?"

"Nay. I know Darak. He'll come back. Just try and be patient. I know it's the hardest thing in the world—especially for you." He flashed her an understanding smile. "Just don't do anything . . . foolish."

"Like what? Pack up my things and go after them?" She patted Ennit's cheek. "I'm not that foolish. Thank you for listening. It does help. Really."

"You know you can always come to me. If you need to talk. Or shout. Or keep from strangling Faelia."

"You're a dear man. Lisula is very lucky."

Gods help her, her voice broke on that. She hurried toward her hut, then veered away. She couldn't face Faelia and Callie. Not yet. She needed a few moments to gather herself.

The familiar sounds of families at supper—talking, arguing, laughing—were too painful. She fled the village and headed toward the lake, but there were too many memories there. In the end, she simply stopped where she was and leaned against an alder.

Visions were chancy. Dreams or reality. Predictions or possibilities. Nothing you could base your life on. Nothing you could trust. Not like you'd trust a poultice of elderflowers to take the fire out of a burn or crushed yarrow leaves to stop bleeding. Of course, there were uncertainties in healing, too. A wound could heal clean or fester. When it healed, you thanked the gods. When it didn't, you knew what steps to take and in what order and if those didn't work, you did your best to ease the pain of this world and the transition to the next. And prayed to the gods for a miracle.

"Try not to worry."

"Try to be patient."

"Don't lose hope."

"Trust in the gods."

Who could determine what was skill or luck or the will of the gods? Had the Forest-Lord led Darak back to the grove of the First Forest all those years ago or had it been the circlets of her hair she'd used to mark the path? Had the Maker saved Darak when his fever raged or had it been her skill? Or Mother Netal's spirit guiding her? Or the magical healing leaves she had brought back from the Summerlands?

The Summerlands—where the Trickster had taken her after he rescued her from Morgath.

"Don't do anything foolish."

Relying on the Trickster was chancier than any vision. It was a measure of her desperation that she would even consider it. Well, she might be desperate, but she wasn't a fool. Fellgair's protection always came at a price. If he had demanded that she give up all hope of returning to the world in exchange for opening a portal to Chaos, the gods only knew what he would ask to keep Darak and Keirith safe.

She must be patient and strong and try not to worry. And banish any temptation to call on the Trickster for help.

Chapter 26

KEIRITH TRIED TELLING himself that he'd simply imagined his father lying on the altar, that it had not been a vision at all. But still he saw those blood-spattered lips and heard that familiar voice saying, "You have murdered me."

Almost as disturbing as the vision of his father was how little thought he had given to the man who had been sacrificed. A true child of the Oak and Holly would be haunted by his death, would protest the injustice of it, or attempt to help the remaining captives. Yet he could barely recall the man's features, and when he heard the horn at dawn, he covered his ears and tried to forget what it heralded.

Perhaps that was the meaning of his father's words: that by abandoning one of his people, he had abandoned them all. Watching a stranger die upon the altar was as damning as if the stranger had been his father.

He had gone to the sacrifice to remind himself of who he was. Instead, he was more adrift than ever. He could see the concern on Malaq's face, but he couldn't confide in him; that would only deepen their friendship. And he couldn't continue with the lessons in shielding for fear Malaq would learn what he had seen. When he'd asked for a scrying stone, Malaq gave him the speckled bloodstone and asked no questions. But even with it, he could not find the stillness and emptiness he needed to reach Natha. Qiij might open his power of vision, but only one person would dare violate the prohibition and give it to him.

So this morning, he rose with the kankh horn and went to the little courtyard. He pretended to admire the rock garden, but all the while he watched the corridor for Xevhan's return from the dawn sacrifice. When Keirith heard his voice, he raced out of the courtyard, accompanied by startled oaths from his guards. Xevhan's steps slowed as he approached, surprise turning to wariness. They had not spoken since the day on the beach.

Keirith bowed. "I am glad to see you, Zheron."

"And I to see you. Are you well?"

"I am, thank you. And you?"

"Very well, I thank you."

"May I speak with you?"

Xevhan hesitated, eyeing the two guards. "I was just going to take a little caja and bread in my chamber. Would you join me?"

"That would pleasure me much."

Xevhan's chamber was far more opulent than Malaq's. Black serpents crawled up red-painted pillars. Multicolored birds circled the gold sun on the ceiling. Thick rugs of red and gold lay strewn on the floor.

One place had been laid at the low table. At Xevhan's command, a slave quickly set another. A man leaned against the wall, arms folded across his chest. When Xevhan addressed him as Miko, Keirith realized he was the man who had raped Hircha. He was surprised at how ordinary he looked. He'd imagined a burly man with muscular arms and a thick chest.

Like the Big One.

It sickened him to sit at the table where Hircha had been raped, but he forced himself to make polite conversation and sip the bitter caja. Xevhan must have noted his reaction to the drink because he smiled. "Caja is an acquired taste."

"Yes."

His shudder drew an appreciative chuckle from Xevhan. It seemed impossible that he could have beaten Hircha so brutally and then ordered his slave to rape her, but Keirith was convinced she was telling the truth.

When he'd told her he understood what she had gone through, she'd shaken her head impatiently. When he repeated the words, he saw understanding dawn. They'd exchanged no hugs, no reassurances of sympathy, but the shared knowledge of their ordeals dispelled some of the taint of that day on the beach.

Resolutely, he put thoughts of Hircha aside and smiled at Xevhan. "It is many days since we speak. Since we spoke."

"The Pajhit was angry about our outing."

"Old people do not understand fun."

"He's not so old," Xevhan reproved.

"He is not so young either," Keirith said.

That provoked another chuckle. "Your studies have been fruitful. You speak very well." Xevhan eyed him over the rim of his cup. "But I can summon Hircha if you'd be more comfortable."

Keirith hoped his shrug conveyed disinterest. "It is better if Hircha is not here. There are things I want to say to you. Alone."

Xevhan slowly set his cup on the table, then turned to Miko. "Wait outside."

Without changing expression, Miko left. Keirith knew he'd still have to speak cautiously; neither the guards nor Miko would enter without Xevhan's invitation, but they could listen. He'd seen few doors in the palace; eavesdropping must be a popular—and informative—pastime.

"The Pajhit makes me teach him the trick of vision. He says if I do this, he sends me home."

"I see."

"I think he lies. I think he wants the trick for nothing. He does not teach me to shield my spirit from another."

Xevhan dipped a fragment of bread in his cup of caja and remained silent.

"You say you can teach me this."

"I said I could try. But I doubt the Pajhit would approve."

"He is not your master, is he?" Keirith tried to look innocent, as if the hierarchy of the Zherosi priesthood remained a mystery.

"Of course not." Xevhan's voice was calm, but Keirith detected a slight flush on the sallow cheeks.

"Always, he is planning The Shedding. He does not teach. Or let me try qiij."

Keirith had to ask Xevhan to repeat his response. Finally, he grasped that Xevhan was telling him qiij was forbidden to the uninitiated. "You, I think, are a man who makes rules."

Xevhan's gaze went to the doorway. "Your guards will tell the Pajhit," he said softly.

"They do not have to know."

"The effects of taking qiij can last all day. And if you should become ill . . ." Xevhan shrugged. "The Pajhit will find out. And your defiance will displease him."

"I am an ignorant tree lover." He'd heard that phrase often enough to know it by heart. "What do I know of such dangers?"

"But I know. Why should I take such a risk for . . . an ignorant tree lover?"

Keirith took a deep breath. "Four days ago, I see—saw—a sacrifice. At the temple of Heart of Sky."

"Malaq permitted you to observe a sacrifice?"

"He wanted me to go to your temple. But I said no. His."

Xevhan patted his lips with a napkin. Keirith wondered if he did it to hide a smile.

"I saw something at the sacrifice. A vision. The man on the altar becomes a Zherosi priest."

"Who?"

"I could not see his face. But the head is shaved." That was vague enough. All the priests shaved their heads. "Since I come here, I see much. Greater visions than ever. This place . . . the mountain . . ." He allowed what he hoped was a dreamy look to fill his face. "It is beautiful, the mountain. Like . . . like home. After the sacrifice, I try to see clearer. But the way is blocked. Qiij, I think, opens the way."

Even if Xevhan didn't believe him to be the god made flesh, he might hope he would reveal something damning under the influence of the drug. Still, it was a dangerous gamble.

"Have you told the Pajhit about this vision?"

"No." Keirith pouted. "He takes knowledge and gives nothing in return."

Xevhan considered and finally shook his head. "I cannot give you qiij." His fingers rose to stroke the tiny vial. "Of course, if you should overpower me . . ."

For a slave to attack the Zheron must be a crime. Even Malaq might not be able to save him.

"I would, of course, swear you meant no harm. And would see to it that you were not punished for your foolishness."

Or condemn him to the altar stone.

Keirith rose and bowed. "As you say, great Zheron, it is foolishness. I thank you for speaking to me. And for your friendship."

He was at the threshold when Xevhan called his name. "Among our people, the host and guest drain their cups as a sign of friendship."

Reluctantly, he took his place opposite Xevhan again and raised his cup.

"To new beginnings," Xevhan said.

"New beginnings."

Xevhan drained his cup and Keirith did the same. The caja settled into his belly with a comforting warmth that almost made up for its bitterness.

"Perhaps I could confer with the Pajhit and the Motixa. Determine if they would permit an exception to the law."

"Thank you, yes."

"And in return, you might teach me the trick of vision."

"Yes. There is much we can learn together. But how can we meet? Without the Pajhit knowing?"

"We can find a way."

Keirith's confidence soared. Of course, they could find a way. The Pajhit was busy. Guards could be bought. It all seemed so easy now. He wondered why he had never realized it before. He laughed, enjoying the unexpected euphoria of feeling in control again. How could he have ever doubted his gift of vision? He would seek Natha. He would find his father—perhaps see his entire family. He jumped to his feet, eager to return to his room and try. A wave of dizziness overwhelmed him; he must have gotten up too quickly. Or perhaps he was simply lightheaded with relief. He found himself clinging to Xevhan, laughing at his giddiness.

Xevhan smiled, too, but his eyes narrowed. "Perhaps you should lie down."

"Nay, I'm fine." He realized he'd spoken the tribal tongue and giggled. "I am sorry. I mean to say that I am well. Wonderful, really. I'm liking caja better and better all the time." He'd slipped into the tribal tongue again. Babbling like an idiot. What was wrong with him?

Nothing. For the first time since arriving in Pilozhat he felt strong and whole. He could fight ten men and emerge unscathed. He could scale Kelazhat without pausing for breath. He could raise his arms and fly like an eagle. He was just having a little trouble staying on his feet.

He reeled and clung to Xevhan. Good old Xevhan. Always there when you needed him. A girl for your pleasure? A friendly cup of caja? Xevhan could provide both.

So helpful, too. Steadying him when he tripped on the rug that rose up like a red and gold wave. Walking him down a hallway that seemed a mile long. Sitting him down on the sleeping shelf. The blankets were soft against his cheek. Lamb's wool. Had to be. Nothing rough that might scratch the Zheron's smooth skin. Only the softest wool from the softest little lambs.

Keirith baaed.

"Be still," someone hissed.

But Natha wasn't there. Perhaps Xevhan was his spirit guide now. But why did he need him? Oh, aye. The vision. He wanted to seek a vision. But he was suddenly tired. The giddy rush of euphoria was fading, leaving a comfortable glow that warmed him like a fire on a winter night.

He reached for his bag of charms. The scrying stone would help him concentrate. If only he could loosen the drawstrings.

"What? What do you want?"

"The bloodstone," he mumbled. "To help me See."

Xevhan slapped his hands aside and fumbled inside the bag.

His body felt as if it had turned to water, his flesh liquid, his bones limp as lakeweed. Yet his senses felt more alive than ever. How else could he hear the slow and steady drumming of his heart? Or feel every thread in the weave of the blanket? Or see every red speckle on the face of the dark disk that suddenly loomed before him.

"Look at the stone," someone whispered.

It seemed as large as the sun. It filled his vision, wobbling a little as it hung there. The wobbling made him dizzy and he closed his eyes.

"Look at the stone, Kheridh."

Obediently, he opened his eyes. Surely the pale things around the edge of the sun were fingernails. Or were they moons? Four little waxing moons and one waning moon circling the dark sun.

"Look into its heart."

He couldn't see the sun's heart, but its face was covered with freckles. Great swatches of them. Faelia's were nothing compared to the sun's. Perhaps that's where freckles came from. Perhaps the sun sweated freckles. Or shed them. That must be what The Shedding was all about. The sun shedding freckles like an adder shed its skin. Or weeping them.

Bloodred tears spattered the face of the sun. Droplets of blood spattered his father's lips.

"Father!"

"Speak Zherosi," the voice demanded. "Tell me what you see."

Bloody tears oozed down the dark face and were caught in a swirling spiral.

"Come back! Please, Fa, come back."

The sun retreated from him. Or perhaps the spiral was growing. He was falling into it, but floating up at the same time. Rising to the ceiling. Scattering the flocks of painted birds. Bursting through stone and into sunlight. Flying like the eagle.

"Like Zhe."

"What about Zhe? Do you see him? Is he speaking to you now?"

"Father? Where are you?"

"Are you the Son of Zhe? Are you? Answer me!"

The sun was blood, dripping gore onto the slopes of Kelazhat. The sun was fire, shimmering on the altar, gleaming on Malaq's bald head, shining on the bronze dagger that appeared over his shoulder. The sun was death, colder than the ring on the priest's forefinger, swifter than the dagger that plunged downward, stooping like a hawk on a pigeon.

"Behind you!"

The sun smiled in benediction and promise. Or was that Malaq?

"What do you see? Tell me!"

The sun shattered and screamed. The blood gushed down

the steps of the altar, flowing like a river, flowing like the adders that surged across the sacrificial ground, flowing like earth, a cataract of earth that groaned like a dying man and swept everything away in its path until only Malaq's eyes remained, twin pools of agony.

"You have murdered me."

He lay in the shadowland between dreaming and wakefulness. Once, he heard the sound of voices raised in argument. Later, he felt something cool and damp on his forehead. Still later, a gentle hand raised his head and a cup swam toward him.

"Nay!"

"It's only tea."

After he smelled the mint, he took a cautious sip.

"A little more," the voice urged.

He managed another swallow.

"Good. Rest now."

The next thing he saw was Malaq. His eyes were as dark as they had appeared in his vision, but held no trace of agony.

"Can you manage a little broth?"

Keirith nodded. He pushed himself into a sitting position, but he had to allow Malaq to spoon the broth into his mouth. It was then he realized he was in Malaq's bedchamber.

"How did I get here?"

"The guards brought you. You collapsed in Xevhan's chamber. That was this morning."

Judging from the flickering oil lamps, it must be evening. A whole day—lost.

"I've been asleep?"

"Yes."

"You've been here with me?"

"Yes. Finish your broth."

"The whole time?"

"Stop talking. You're making a mess."

"You sound like my mam."

Malaq lowered the spoon. "Did you dribble broth on her, too?"

"I meant the scolding."

"I should do more than scold you. I should beat you. I may yet decide to do so. But not until you finish your broth."

Keirith obeyed, swallowing one spoonful after another. And when he had finished, he said, "I went to Xevhan because of something I saw at the sacrifice."

By the time he finished describing his vision at the temple, he was shivering uncontrollably. Malaq opened a wooden chest—the only piece of furniture in the chamber— removed a blanket, and draped it around his shoulders. The scratchy wool comforted him.

"I had to find out if my father was safe."

Malaq didn't ask why he had waited until now to tell him. He simply nodded.

"I tried to find my father—through vision—but I couldn't. So I went to Xevhan."

He frowned, recalling his euphoria. Xevhan must have slipped the qiij into his drink. What a fool not to have realized.

"I asked him to give me qiij."

"I know."

"He told you?"

"He didn't have to. I know the signs."

No questions, no recriminations, just a great weariness in his voice that added to Keirith's guilt. He told Malaq how Xevhan had drugged him. It was hard to describe the vision with those sad, dark eyes watching him, but he did. When he finished, Malaq nodded again.

"It was Xevhan," Keirith blurted out. Although they were speaking the tribal tongue, he instinctively lowered his voice. "I recognized the ring on his finger."

"I see."

"Nay, you don't. It was Xevhan who struck you down."

"I understand."

"What are you going to do?"

"Nothing."

"But you have to. He's dangerous. He wants you dead."

"I doubt it. He would derive much more satisfaction from my disgrace than my death. The fact that I died in your vision is probably due more to your concern about your father than to any actual threat I face. Even the words were the same, were they not?"

Keirith nodded, unconvinced.

"The end of the vision interests me. With the adders streaming across the ground and the earth collapsing. Did you know there was another tremor today?"

Keirith searched his memory, but everything was jumbled up in his mind.

"You cried out in your sleep. Something about the adders. A few moments later, the Qepo rushed in to tell me they were restless. And then the earth shook. A small tremor. It did no damage. But I wondered if you felt it—or felt the adders' fear as you did that first time."

"I don't remember. I'm sorry."

"It doesn't matter." The Pajhit smiled, his expression so similar to the one in the vision that Keirith winced. "You should rest. We'll talk more in the morning."

"But Xevhan . . ."

"Let me worry about Xevhan."

"But you won't!"

"Of more concern to me is the danger you may be in. You'll have to explain the vision to Xevhan. Not the part about him killing me. Make up something else. Don't let him know you told me about it. Tell him I was furious at you for taking the qiij. Stick to the story Xevhan planned, that you took it without his permission. It's a flimsy excuse, but it will have to do. Pretend to be worried that your behavior has compromised further opportunities to meet. Play the innocent. You can do that, can't you?"

Keirith felt himself flushing under that keen-eyed gaze. "He won't believe me."

"But he'll wonder. If he believes you're eager to learn from him—that you'll teach him instead of me—he might not move against you. And that will buy us a little more time."

"Us." As many times as he had disobeyed, Malaq had forgiven and protected him. He had given up his bed, nursed him as tenderly as a mother. Keirith wanted to believe it was just an act, a ploy to keep his loyalty, but instinct told him he could trust this man.

"Why are you protecting me?"

"I'm beginning to wonder that myself," Malaq replied with a rueful smile. "Get some sleep."

"But where will you sleep?"

"I've made up a pallet in the other chamber. Enough," he added as Keirith opened his mouth to protest. "It's perfectly comfortable." He extinguished two of the lamps, but left the third burning. "Good night."

"Forgive me," he whispered.

"There's nothing to forgive."

Keirith pulled the blanket around him and lay back on the fleece. A heavy weight descended on his stomach and he gasped. Niqia kneaded him for several moments, sharp claws making him wince.

"Settle."

She ignored him, continuing her careful kneading until, apparently satisfied, she sprawled across his belly. Keirith stroked the soft fur behind her ears and was rewarded with a contented purr.

The plan to lull Xevhan's suspicions could work if he played his part well, but it would not help Malaq. Was this what it was like for the priests of Pilozhat? Always watching their backs, always courting friends and observing enemies and plotting against both? It was so alien to his life at home—but then everything here was.

As unnerving as all the plotting was, there was something exciting about it. Pitting your skill against another's. Using your power to woo him or destroy him. Risking everything. It was as thrilling and frightening as flying with the eagle.

"You are enmeshed in a dangerous game, and your life depends on your ability to play it well."

And if the vision was true, it was not only his life at risk, but Malaq's as well.

Chapter 27

GRIANE SPRINKLED THE last drops of the elderberry wine on the roots of the heart-oak and rested
her palm against the tree's thick trunk. She should say a
prayer. If only she knew what to pray for.

*Don't be a ninny, Griane. You know why you're here.
Just do it.*

The name stuck in her throat.

"Maker, help me. Show me if this is the right path."

Sunwise, she circled the sacred tree. That's what the priests
always did when they summoned power. But she wasn't summoning power; she was simply delaying. She closed her eyes
and repeated her prayer—and promptly stumbled over a
root.

*Well, that's what happens when you try to walk and pray
with your eyes shut. Any fool would know better. And only
a fool would take that for a sign.*

"Please, Maker. Give me a sign. Something to let me
know whether I should do . . . what I'm thinking of doing."

Nothing happened. The birds still twittered, the morning
sunlight still slanted through the branches of the trees.

*What did you expect? A clap of thunder? A flash of
lightning?*

The glade darkened. She gasped and flicked her forefinger three times against her thumb. She considered spitting
in the four directions, but while she hesitated, the sunlight
returned. It had only been a passing cloud. It would have

shadowed Bel's face no matter what she said. But she *had* said something. She had asked for a sign.

"Bel's blazing ballocks."

Signs were no more reliable than visions. Better to trust your common sense. Of course, if she did that, she would leave right now. Of all people in the world, she knew better than to trust Fellgair.

Damn her indecision. Damn Gortin and his visions. And damn Darak for leaving her here with nothing to do but wait and worry.

"Oh, Maker, I didn't mean it. Especially the part about Darak." This time she did spit. She'd never discovered if an ill-wish counted if you didn't speak it aloud, but now was not the time to chance it.

Impatiently, she swiped at her eyes. She'd never been a weeper, but these days she was always crying. The other day, she'd found a patch of speedwell in the forest and burst into tears; poor Sali just stared at her with her mouth hanging open.

"I'm going home," she announced. And stood staring up at the wide-spreading branches of the heart-oak.

For four days, Gortin's vision had haunted her. Worse were the images she conjured: Darak's body twisting with agony, gouts of blood spurting from his chest, his mouth going slack as the scream faded, the gray eyes glazing in death. Four days and four nights with those images racking her mind and helplessness tearing at her spirit like a carrion crow. And always the fear of the consequences if she asked the Trickster for help.

Even if she called, Fellgair might not come. He might not even remember her. It had been fifteen years since she had seen him. He'd been angry with her for leaving the Summerlands without bidding him farewell. But he had opened the way home for a kiss. And promised—predicted—that she would have many years with Darak. Fifteen years wasn't many. Not as people measured time and certainly not as gods did.

Keirith would never let them hurt his father. Never.

Fellgair had made another prediction that morning—that he and Darak would meet again. Perhaps he'd known even then that she would be standing here, wondering if she should call his name.

In the underbrush, a fox yipped. The hairs on her neck and arms rose. Very slowly, Griane turned.

The fox padded out of the thicket and froze when it saw her. Golden eyes fixed her with an unblinking stare. It lifted one delicate forepaw. Despite the thick mulch of dead leaves littering the glade, it made no sound as it stalked toward her.

The fox paused and cocked its head. Large triangular ears pricked forward. Suddenly, it catapulted high into the air and pounced on a pile of leaves. It nosed through them and emerged with a vole dangling between its jaws. It tossed its head, flinging the vole skyward. The muscles in its hind legs tensed. Just before the unfortunate creature hit the ground, the fox leaped up and snapped it out of the air. Then it settled into a patch of sunlight and proceeded to devour its prey in three quick bites.

A red tongue flicked out to lick the long whiskers. Then the fox yawned, treating Griane to a vivid display of the sharp shears on its upper jaw.

"Is it you?" she whispered.

The fox's ears pricked up at her voice. It rose. And winked.

The sleek body stretched. The narrow rib cage swelled. Back legs straightened. Forelegs pushed off the ground to hang by its sides. Paws tapered into clawed fingers that waggled a greeting. The thick brush grew even more luxuriant. The muzzle widened. Widened still more as the Trickster smiled and strolled toward her.

"As if I could forget you, Griane."

"But I didn't call you."

"I've missed you, too."

"I only thought . . ."

Fellgair shook a reproving finger. "You see? It does count if you only think it." He sighed. "Poor Darak. Poor Gherkin."

"Gortin."

"Whatever."

"I didn't mean it. I wasn't cursing him. Them."

"Of course you weren't."

"So nothing bad will happen?"

"Ever?"

"Please, Lord Trickster—"

"Oh, must we progress to the pleading so soon? Let's sit. Chat. Reminisce about old times."

He flicked a forefinger at some fallen leaves, which arranged themselves into a neat bed between two of the heart-oak's roots. He sprawled full-length, propping himself up on one elbow, and patted a spot in front of him. Griane chose a root out of reach.

"This reminds me of our time together in the Summerlands. You perched primly on your rock. I, lounging at your feet. You were wearing fewer clothes then."

After fifteen years, he still had the unerring power to make her blush. As his gaze roved over her, she resisted the urge to tuck her skirt around her ankles.

"Do you miss the Summerlands?"

She nodded. It was the most beautiful, magical place she had ever known. But she had abandoned it eagerly for the chance to return to the world, little knowing that Struath and Yeorna were already dead, and Darak and Cuillon in Chaos.

"Is Rowan still there? And the other tree-folk?"

"Of course."

"Are they . . . different?"

"How do you mean?"

"More human?"

"That supposes they're changing from trees to humans and not the other way around."

"Aren't they?" she asked, surprised.

"Actually, they are. But that transformation occurs over thousands of years. To your eyes, Rowan would look just the same."

"And to yours?"

"Even to my eyes, the changes are barely perceptible. The slightest softening of the bark. The tiniest hint of eyelashes."

"Do you ever change?"

"You just saw me."

She'd forgotten how difficult he could be. She must remember to phrase her questions more precisely or she would surely end up being tricked by the bargain she made with him. If she made a bargain.

"I meant—"

"I don't age as you do." The golden gaze drifted to her

hair. "All the colors of fox fur now. Just as I predicted all those years ago. Did you curse him for leaving you again after you arrived home?"

Her hand had reached self-consciously to smooth the white streak in her hair. Now she let it drop back to her lap. "I thought you wanted to reminisce about happy times."

"I wanted to reminisce."

His voice was as pleasant as ever, his manner casual. But the threat—however veiled—was always present when you dealt with the Trickster: I establish the rules for the game. Obey them or the game ends.

Heart pounding, she said, "I don't want to talk about that." And waited to see how he would respond to such a deliberate violation of the unspoken rule.

"All right. What shall we talk about? The weather? It's been warm this spring. The barley? Looks like a fine crop. Your health? You have shadows under your eyes because you haven't been sleeping. Your tunic hangs on you because you haven't been eating. You dream of him at night and wake, gasping his name. During the day, you keep busy so you won't notice how frightened you are, but the fear is always there—stalking you like a predator—and when it pounces, you cry. You hate giving in to tears, so you either hug the children too hard or snap at them for pestering you with questions you can't answer. And then you curse your Darak. Whose face is the first thing your eyes seek when they open in the morning. Whose hands are the last thing your body seeks as you drift into sleep at night. Darak, whom you chivvy and chide and scold in the vain hope that he won't realize how desperately you need him."

"Stop. Please."

"You curse him—just as you did all those years ago when he left you to return to the First Forest barely a moon after you healed his body and gave him the will to live and finally, finally brought him home safe. I've missed our little chats, haven't you?"

Griane pressed her lips together tightly. At least she could be proud that she had surrendered without a tear. "I didn't curse him."

"Young love is so beautiful. So you forgave. If not forgot."

"Aye."

"And never spoke of it after?"

"Nay."

"Yet you wondered, didn't you? Every time he went back to the grove of the First Forest. You kissed him farewell and watched him walking across the fields and wondered if it was the last time you would ever see him."

"He gave me his oath."

"Men are fond of giving oaths. They're also notorious for breaking them."

"Not Darak. He never would have left me. Not after . . ."

"Not after Keirith was born." Fellgair's voice was very gentle. "You're right, of course. He would never leave then—no matter how much he longed to. It's ironic, isn't it? That the child who guaranteed he would remain is the same one who took him away from you in the end. Do you hate him?"

"Darak?"

"Keirith. For taking your Darak away."

It's not his fault. It was the raiders. Or fate. Or ill fortune. Darak's fault for leaving him. Urkiat's for not fighting harder. Mine for not insisting that he come with us when his father ordered him to. Why didn't he listen? If he had, none of this would have happened. Keirith would be safe at home and Darak . . .

Lying on the altar stone. His heart clutched between the bloody fingers of a priest.

She stumbled to her feet, gagging. Blindly, she reached out a hand for the heart-oak. Fellgair's fingers closed around hers. She whirled around, flailing at him with her fist, hating him for his truths, hating him for hurting her.

Effortlessly, he swept her into his arms and sat, cradling her against his chest as if she were a child. She slumped against him, breathing in the sharp animal reek that mingled with the sweet aroma of honeysuckle. So perfect for him, that improbable combination of scents. She'd never realized that until now. But for a being in whom order and chaos combined, everything about him was a combination of opposites: cold and warmth, cruelty and kindness, viciousness and charm.

His fur tickled her nose and she sneezed. Hastily, she slid off his lap and blew her nose on the hem of her tunic.

"I made you cry." His voice held wonder rather than regret.

"You've made me cry before."

"I remember." He touched the tip of his forefinger to her cheek, careful not to scratch her. He raised the finger and licked it. His eyes closed. A sensual smile curved his mouth.

"Are they alive?"

His eyes opened. The dreamy expression vanished. "Yes."

Weak with relief, she asked, "Will you bring them home to me?"

"Griane . . ."

"You could just . . . open a portal. Like you opened the portal to Chaos. You could do that."

"I could."

"But you won't. Because that would be interfering. And gods aren't supposed to interfere in the affairs of men."

"Correct."

"But you do it all the time. You told us Tinnean was in Chaos. You opened the portal for Darak. You—"

"I merely fulfilled my part of the bargain."

"Saving me from Morgath wasn't part of the bargain."

His eyes narrowed. "You're better at this than you were fifteen years ago."

"You did that because you wanted to."

"Perhaps."

"So if you interfered then—"

"Saving you had no significant effect upon the game."

"You call it a game? The world was dying!"

"Yes, yes." He brushed aside the deaths of thousands, millions with an impatient gesture. "But it was Darak who had the potential to restore the balance of nature. Because he loved his brother and wanted him back."

"He loves his son and wants him back."

"But the situation is different, isn't it? Your world is in no immediate danger of dying. Your husband and son, perhaps. But not the world."

"The raiders killed twenty-three people in our village."

"Twenty-three. Oh, dear."

"Don't you dare mock their deaths."

"I'm mocking you, not those who died. Twenty-three

deaths or twenty-three hundred. The number is insignificant. We're talking of the possible annihilation of a culture, not the death of the world."

"Annihilation?" she echoed, her voice faint.

"It's a possibility."

"And you don't care? If we're . . . annihilated?"

"I'd prefer if you weren't."

"Of course. Who would worship you then? Who would sing songs and make up tales and bow down before you?"

"I haven't noticed any bowing lately," he responded dryly. "As to the rest, I am worshiped by many peoples. As are the Maker and the Unmaker, Bel and Gheala. Even the Oak and the Holly. Although, for obvious reasons, their cult is limited to those living in arboreal regions."

"It's all a joke to you."

"No, my dear, it's not. That is merely my manner—and the cumulative effect of suffering thousands of these arguments with indignant mortals over the ages. You worry about the fate of individuals, Griane. I involve myself in the fate of worlds."

"Then you won't help me?"

"I said I would not bring them home. After that, you embroiled me in this debate and lost sight of your purpose in coming here today." He winked. "The bit about saving you from Morgath was good, though."

She had hoped to appeal to his affection for her. Now she was reduced to bargaining.

"If you won't bring them home, will you protect them?"

He considered her for a long moment before replying. "I'll protect one. Your husband or your son."

Griane shook her head. "You made Darak do this. Choose between me and Cuillon."

"And he chose the Holly-Lord."

He was watching her closely to see if it still hurt after all these years. She'd never been any good at hiding her feelings. Let him see. "I can't choose."

"You won't choose. There's a difference."

"All right. I won't choose."

"Then we have nothing further to discuss."

When he started to rise, she clutched his arm. "How can I choose one if it means condemning the other to death?"

He simply watched her.

Think, Griane.

"Would I be condemning the other?"

He smiled. "You survived without my protection. After I saved you from Morgath, of course."

"You didn't answer my question."

His smile broadened as he sank back onto his bed of leaves. "You would not be condemning the other to death. Although his odds of survival might diminish."

"Might? Will they or won't they?"

"I cannot predict the future, Griane. There are too many variables."

"Who has the best chance of surviving without your help?"

"You know them better than I."

"But you know where they are. What those people are like."

"They are adequate farmers, excellent forgers of metal, expert seafarers, extraordinary builders, and ruthless warriors. They are ruled by a king and queen with powers similar to Keirith's, although theirs are enhanced by the use of drugs. They worship the usual assortment of gods and goddesses of whom the greatest are the sun, the earth, a winged serpent, and the God with Two Faces. They have a stratified class system, including a caste of priests and priestesses whose primary responsibility is to offer sacrifices—human and otherwise—to ensure the blessings of these gods. And they are utterly convinced of their right to absorb neighboring countries to exploit their people and their natural resources." He yawned, revealing his sharp teeth. "Those, of course, are only the broad strokes."

What chance did either of them stand against such people? Keirith's gift might intrigue the Zherosi, but they were just as likely to view it as a threat. And Darak? His hunting skills had proved invaluable in the First Forest, but in the land of the raiders?

"Oh, yes. I should probably mention the prophecy."

"Prophecy?"

"That one day, the son of their winged god will appear among them and herald a new age. He must be a virgin, possess an interesting assortment of powers, and have red hair." Fellgair tapped a clawed forefinger against his cheek. "Now who does that remind me of?"

"They think Keirith is a god?"

"Son of a god," he corrected. "Some do. Some don't."

Which could mean Keirith was safe or in even greater peril than she suspected.

Her husband or her son. Darak on an altar stone. Keirith treading a dangerous path between the god some wanted him to be and the fragile mortal he was.

"Please, Lord Trickster." She fell to her knees before him. "If you want me to beg, I will beg. If you want my life, it is yours. Take it. And protect them both."

"But I don't want your life, Griane."

"What do you want?"

He leaned forward, so close that she could feel the heat of his breath. The world receded to those golden eyes, twin fires boring into her. Embers sparked and swirled within the slitted black pupils, a dizzying dance of light within darkness, heat within cold. The cold rippled down her spine. The heat filled her belly, her womb, her loins.

And then he blinked, shattering the spell. She framed the question in her mind, but could only manage to gasp out, "Forever?"

"No. A day will suffice."

"But in the Summerlands, you said—"

"I said foxes were monogamous. I'm a god, not a fox."

Fifteen years ago, she had made the stupid mistake of concluding that if she gave herself to him, she would have to give up her family, her friends—her world—along with her maidenhead. She would not make that mistake again.

Shaking off the lingering effects of the spell, she said, "You want me."

"Yes."

"My body."

"Dare I hope to win your heart as well?"

"My body, Fellgair."

He sighed. "As you please."

"For a single day."

"Dawn to dusk."

"In exchange for protecting them."

"In exchange for protecting one of them."

"Nay."

He shrugged. "That is the offer."

"Please."

"I will protect only one, Griane. Choose."

"I can't. Fellgair, I can't!"

He rose and brushed past her.

Darak's name screamed out of her before she could stop it. In shocked disbelief, she clapped her hands over her mouth.

The Trickster walked slowly across the glade and bent over her. Very gently, he pried her right hand free and clasped it. "Return here at dawn of the first full moon after Midsummer." His face was grave, without a hint of his usual mocking smile. He pressed a light kiss to her forehead, then turned abruptly and strode into the trees.

Too late. Too late to take it back. Oh, gods—oh, gods—oh, gods.

She'd let him goad her. She had not even asked him to specify what "protection" meant. She had betrayed her son without even ensuring the life of her husband.

She clutched her arms as she swayed back and forth, as if she were rocking him to sleep. But the song that echoed in her head was not a lullaby, but the lament for the dead.

Keirith, my son, my firstborn, my child.

Forgive me.

Chapter 28

AFTER HIS CONFESSION, Urkiat had watched him uneasily for a day or so. Darak was gentle with him, asking his advice on the route they should take, praising him when he brought down game, dutifully repeating phrases in Zherosi and questioning him about the port city of Oexiak. Urkiat gradually relaxed, glowing with a quiet pride at the confidence placed in him and eager to demonstrate that he was worthy of it.

He could have kept him at a distance, offering the cold advice to let go of the past and concentrate on their quest. But Darak knew how memories could eat away at a man's spirit. So he had opened his arms, offering his strength and compassion and accepting, in return, the weight of Urkiat's pain and his obvious desire for a father figure to replace the two who had died. Not all of those who were lost had been killed or captured by the raiders.

Wolf disapproved. "He is weak," she told him when he sneaked out of camp to visit with her.

"All men are weak."

"A weak pack member endangers the hunt."

"He's trying. He's like . . . a half-grown pup."

"Half-grown pups play at hunting. They watch their elders. Only when they have the proper skills do they join the real hunt."

"I'll teach him," Darak assured her. "In time, he'll grow strong."

"We do not have much time. Soon you will reach the

stone place. I cannot find you there, I am a creature of the forest. So watch him, Little Brother. And be careful."

When he returned to camp, Urkiat was gazing into the fire. "Is it because you can't bear to sleep near me? Is that why you go away at night?"

Hoping to ease his anxiety, Darak told him about Wolf. Urkiat just stared at him as if he'd sprouted fur and claws.

"You could try to reach your vision mate, too."

"I think it's different for you. Because of . . . who you are."

He had expected the journey to wear away the remnants of Urkiat's awe; watching a man heave up the contents of his stomach day after day wasn't especially conducive to worship.

"I still put on my breeches one leg at a time. My legs ache every evening from walking. My bladder aches every morning with the need to take a piss. And I piss urine just like you. Not brogac."

That surprised a smile out of Urkiat. "Good thing. Darak Spirit-Hunter sounds a lot better than Darak Brogac-Pisser."

Laughter dispelled the awe. For the first time since leaving home, Darak felt he had a true comrade.

Their new bond strengthened them as the journey grew more difficult. Villages nestled on the narrow strip of coastline, forcing them into the foothills. The dense forests of oak and ash gave way to scrub pine that offered little shelter from the sun. And it was always sunny. Climbing the steep hills left them both sweat-soaked and exhausted. Their food supplies dwindled and some nights they went to sleep with only a suetcake to ease their hunger.

Then one afternoon, they reached the summit of a hill and came to an abrupt halt. Below them, open fields stretched for miles, as vast as the cloudless sky above them. Here and there through the shimmering haze, Darak could make out clusters of dwellings that must be villages and the meandering path of the river that connected them. But there were no trees on the riverbank. There were no trees anywhere. It was as if they stood at the edge of another world.

Urkiat pointed to a mass of white buildings overlooking the sea. "That's Oexiak. And that's the road to Pilozhat."

Where Keirith was—if the raider had spoken true.

"We should rest now. Better to cross the fields at night and reach Oexiak in the morning."

Curbing his impatience, Darak settled down on the hillside, but sleep eluded him. He stared at the city, glistening in the haze, and prayed that it held the answers he needed.

Nothing prepared him for Oexiak. Until they walked through the northern gate, the Gatherings were the largest confluence of men and animals Darak had ever seen. Oexiak was like twenty Gatherings packed into a sprawling mass of stone houses that perched atop the cliffs like an enormous flock of nesting sea birds. Again and again, they lost their bearings on the stone paths that wandered through the close-packed buildings. Luck and repeated directions from incurious pedestrians led them eventually to something called the Fleshers Market.

Bellowing oxen, bleating sheep, and squawking birds vied with the screeching of buyers and sellers haggling over bloody slabs of meat, braces of pheasants and hares, and heaps of fleece piled high atop the wooden stalls. Dogs slunk between them, lapping up blood and dodging kicks from customers and traders alike.

Darak had feared his coloring and height would make him stand out. Although the marketplace teemed with Zherosi, there were many others who had to be foreigners. Men with skin the color of charcoal and close-cropped black hair as curly as a lamb's. Men with the same hide-colored complexions as the Zherosi, but with luxuriant manes of hair that fell halfway down their backs. Men with beards and men who were clean-shaven. Men who sported tattoos and others who sported bronze necklaces. Men in woolen tunics, men who wore strange half-breeches that seemed to be made of flaxcloth, and men in sleeveless tunics and baggy breeches made of materials that were completely unknown to him.

He saw far fewer women and most of those were barefoot and simply dressed. When he asked about that, Urkiat shouted, "The rich women send their slaves to the market. And the poorer folk can't afford meat."

Chief or shepherd, fisherman or hunter, in his village everyone lived in the same huts, wore the same clothes, ate the same food. But he had glimpsed the taller buildings on the upper slopes of the hill; it wasn't only geography that gave them the appearance of looking down on the sprawling city below.

His height allowed him to pick out the traders dealing with hides and furs. Once he overcame his reluctance to shove people aside, his size helped him bull his way through the press of bodies and clear a space for Urkiat to unroll the furs they had carried from home. Darak stood back, watching uneasily as Urkiat negotiated with the weasel-faced trader. This involved so much shouting, groaning, and fist shaking that he feared they would come to blows, but suddenly the two men spat into their palms and slapped them together three times.

After the trader counted shiny disks into his cupped palms, Urkiat turned to him, sweat-sheened and grinning. "A good trade. Ten serpents and six eagles. Keep your share in your belt pouch. Harder for the coin snatchers to get at them there."

Darak did as he was ordered, although the only part of Urkiat's instructions he'd understood was where he should keep the disks.

"We'll head for the harbor—where the ships are beached. Best place to find out about the captives."

As they threaded their way west, Urkiat educated him about coins and thieves and other aspects of city life, information he had gleaned from the stories of the unnamed Zherosi warrior he had served and loved and killed. Stories that must have seemed as incredible to Urkiat as the legends Darak told the children.

Apparently, the eagle coin had a feather stamped on it and the serpent coin had a spiral, but how thirteen eagles could equal a serpent remained a mystery. "Just remember that serpents are worth more," Urkiat told him. "It's not like the Gathering where you trade pelts for daggers. Here you must have coins to buy what you need."

Coins. Streets. Harbor. He needed an entirely new vocabulary just to make sense of what he saw. For the first time, he understood how Cuillon must have felt, assaulted by strange smells and tastes, alien objects and rituals. At least he could communicate with Urkiat. Standing on the docks, all he could make out was a harsh wash of sound as women haggled over the price of fish, fishermen sang as they repaired their nets, and sailors traded shouts and curses as they loaded bales of fleece, bolts of cloth, and huge earthenware jars of . . . the Maker only knew what.

By midday, they had merely confirmed that the red-haired captives were taken to Pilozhat for the Midsummer sacrifice. Although Darak had lived with the knowledge for more than a moon, he had hoped—foolishly—that the story might be false.

Fear is the enemy.

They still had twelve days. Twelve days to reach Pilozhat, find Keirith, and free him.

Control the fear.

As he had so many times since Keirith was stolen, he found himself conjuring the vision he had seen through the portal in Chaos: the naked boy stretched out upon the stone altar, the priest standing behind him with his dagger upraised, the strange man-woman who had tossed the token through the open portal.

Darak's hand crept up his chest where the sinuous bronze snake lay nestled among his charms. He had discarded it in Chaos, believing it too dangerous to keep, only to discover it clinging to his woolen mantle after he escaped. Fellgair had told him to guard the token, but he'd refused to explain its purpose or importance. Could it help him find Keirith? Did it possess some magical power that could save him from the altar?

Control yourself.

Urkiat seized his arm and dragged him out of the way of a man leading a line of the flop-eared beasts called donkeys. "There are bound to be other people traveling to Pilozhat. They come from all over for the festival."

Despite his eagerness to leave the noise and confusion of Oexiak behind, Darak reluctantly agreed they had to replenish their supplies. Coins bought them smoked fish and dried fruits, but the flat, crisp bread was too expensive. Even water came at a price. They had to line up in yet another marketplace where men dipped wooden ladles into more of those giant earthenware jars and doled it out to women with wooden buckets. The water seller eyed their skins disdainfully, but two eagles got them filled to bursting. Water, he noted, was more precious than food.

And no wonder. The heat was stifling. The sweat dried on his body before it could cool him. Darak eyed the men's loose-fitting half-breeches with longing, but he refused to waste money on clothing. Nor did he want to draw attention to the scars on his back and arms.

As the day waned, Urkiat led him back to the harbor in search of cheap lodging. There were any number of inns there, all identified with signs affixed to the wall that pictured a cup in the upper left hand corner and a fleece in the upper right. Some were too expensive, others already filled. The light was fading when Urkiat popped out of the doorway of one with a blue wave and flying fish on its sign and motioned him inside.

At first, all he could make out was the roaring fire against the far wall. A huge slab of meat roasted over it. As his eyes adjusted to the gloom, he made out other details: a rough stone hearth, tall enough for a man to walk into without stooping; unadorned mud-brick walls; and everywhere, furnishings and implements fashioned from wood.

What looked to be an entire tree trunk, one side planed smooth, ran the length of one wall. Men sat before it on high wooden seats with three legs. Dozens more sat on the wooden benches drawn up on both sides of three long wooden tables. They drank from wooden cups. They speared meat from wooden platters. They used small wooden dippers to scoop stew from wooden bowls. Bad enough that they destroyed whole forests to build their ships, but to mutilate a tree simply to craft a bowl . . .

Swallowing his bile, he followed Urkiat to the tree trunk. It, too, must have a name, as well as the three-legged seats before it. He'd have to remember to ask. Urkiat squeezed between two men to hail another behind the tree trunk. After a few moments of conversation, he dropped coins into the outstretched palm. The man bellowed something to a harried-looking woman who snapped out a reply as she hurried past, slopping wine from a pitcher onto the dirt floor.

"I've arranged for food. He'll sell us sleeping space on the roof for two more eagles. At least it will be cool. Cooler. And safer than sleeping on the street."

The only seats available were at the table closest to the
fire. Grimacing, Darak led the way. Two boys, naked except for the loincloths swaddling their skinny hips, crouched
on either side of the hearth. Their hands gripped something
that they moved in repetitive circles. After observing them
a moment, Darak realized that their efforts slowly rotated
the slab of meat over the flames.

A round-faced man in a violently pink tunic looked up
as they approached. Smiling, he squeezed closer to his
neighbor who scowled at the contact. After a quick glance
at the half-naked man who stood behind him, however, he
slid down the bench.

Darak hesitated, eyeing the big man by the hearth. His
hand rested on the hilt of a long dagger thrust into the sash
that secured his half-breeches. A braid of black hair hung
nearly to his waist and his naked chest gleamed like polished wood. Only his eyes moved, pausing in their survey
of the room long enough to fix him with a keen gaze. Overcoming his reluctance to have a potential enemy at his
back, Darak slid onto the bench while Urkiat seated himself across the table.

In moments, his tunic was drenched. The men around him
seemed oblivious to the heat. A few, like the round-faced
man, appeared to be foreigners; most clumped together at
another table. Sailors from one of the ships, perhaps. The
Zherosi blended into an indistinguishable mass: short and
slender, long black hair tied back with leather thongs, hairless, bare chests. He wondered how they could tell each
other apart.

There was no opportunity for private conversation. He
and Urkiat simply drank the wine the serving woman
poured. Moments later, she returned, bearing a wooden
platter that she thumped down on the table between them.
Blood and grease oozed from the thick slices of meat,
swamping the pile of . . . vegetables, perhaps? The long
orange ones must be some kind of root. The round white
ones tasted like onions, although they looked nothing like
the green shoots he was accustomed to. He guessed the
meat was mutton; it was too highly spiced to say for sure.
It could just as easily be that funny little creature called
goat. A wooden bowl contained some sort of chunky paste
that look suspiciously like vomit. But the men around him

were dipping the orange spears into it and eating with apparent gusto, so he cautiously tried it.

Despite its revolting appearance, it tasted harmless enough, although the grainy consistency was as strange as the spices that lent it flavor. He ate grimly, eager to escape the heat and the noise and the smells. Especially the noise. All day, it had inundated his senses: dogs barking, people shouting, babies wailing. How did they think in this place? Where did they go to find silence?

Throughout the meal, Darak was conscious of the big man standing at his shoulder. Equally uncomfortable—if more obtrusive—was the scrutiny of the round-faced man to his right. When he caught him staring at his maimed hands, the little man didn't even have the grace to look abashed. Instead, he grinned, displaying large white teeth. Then he half-rose from his seat, placed a chubby hand over his heart, and delivered a lengthy and utterly unintelligible speech.

When he finally finished, Urkiat rose and offered the same bow. He'd only managed a few words before the stranger clapped his hands like a delighted child. "I knew it!" he exclaimed in the language of the tribes. He swiveled around, poking his finger into the naked belly of the man behind him. "Didn't I say when they came in, Hakkon, that they had to be from the north?"

His expression unchanged, the big man inclined his head.

"That height, that garb, that rough-hewn, barbarous splendor."

Darak stared pointedly at the agitated forefinger now jabbing his arm, but the little man was too caught up in his triumph to notice. "On such matters, my friends, I am never wrong." He left off his persistent jabbing to signal the serving woman and call out an order in Zherosi before switching back to their tongue without a breath. "In my business, the talent of observation is vital. Indeed, that talent has allowed me to rise to the very height—or very near the very height—of my profession."

He paused, panting slightly. Because he seemed to expect it, Darak asked, "And what is your profession?"

"I, sir, am an entrepreneur. Creator of spectacle, master of revelry, guardian of inspiration, and lodestar of the finer emotions, tragic and comic. I am Olinio." He beamed proudly. "Known professionally as Olinio, the Keeper of Wonders."

Darak glanced at Urkiat who gave a baffled shrug.

"In short, an entertainer. But not, I assure you, one of those ragged players who ekes out a living tramping from one miserable village to the next, pouring out his genius for the peasantry."

"Nay."

"Honesty bids me admit—painful as it is to do so—that I began my career in such circumstances. And in such I might have remained—unknown, unappreciated, unheralded. But I found a niche."

"A niche?"

"Exactly. By birth or accident, my players are disfigured, deformed or—" He seized Darak's hand and squeezed it. "—cruelly maimed. But by nature, by training, by endeavor, they have become performers of the first rank."

Darak carefully removed his hand. "I see."

"In another land, they would be scorned. But in Zheros, they worship a god with two faces, a winged serpent, a flayed god. Here, the unusual, the unfortunate, the otherwise unemployable are greeted with cheers and huzzahs."

"Huzzahs."

"And cheers." Olinio's snub nose disappeared briefly into his cup. "I knew, sir, when I first glimpsed you—"

"In his rough-hewn, barbarous splendor?" Urkiat ventured.

"Indeed. I knew you were a cut above the ordinary. And then I saw your cruel disfigurement—yes, I saw you watching me watch you—you, too, are a skilled observer of the human condition. Well. I knew blessed Zhe—may his wings be ever strong—had guided you to me."

To thwart the chubby fingers reaching for his again, Darak folded his hands in his lap. "I don't understand."

"Of course not. How could you? But you shall. I came here tonight—distressed, distracted . . ."

"Disgruntled?"

Darak glared at Urkiat who quickly took refuge in his cup.

"Exactly. Forsaken by my star performer. On the eve of the most important performance of my career."

"What happened?" Urkiat asked.

"Gutted by a whore." The little man dismissed his star performer with a wave of his hand. "But now you are here and the gods are smiling." He tapped his chin with his forefinger. "It is, I suppose, too much to hope that you have experience."

"Experience?"

"In the performing arts. The comic duel, the lecherous seduction? Oh, how foolish of me. Clearly, you are made for the hero's death. You know the thing—the noble mien, the fearsome war cry, the flourish of the sword, the thrust, the parry, the scream of agony, the hopeless pleas to the gods. The final walk around the perimeter of the arena, stumbling, staggering, falling to your knees only to rise again, too proud to die, too strong to give in—plus it's good for business, sometimes they throw coins but more often, alas, flowers—until at last, the final heart-wrenching moment when your legs buckle and you fall to your knees and then to the ground where you convulse in your extended death throes. Also quite popular. Especially with the ladies."

"Aye. Well. I've killed men."

"Hmm. That's helpful, although the goal of the performance is, of course, *not* to kill—or to die—but to create the illusion that you can—or will. Still, with practice . . ." His hand darted out to squeeze Darak's bicep. "Good musculature. Lovely cold-eyed glint. Soft-spoken—we'll have to work on that. And the specific moves. Do you speak Zherosi? Ah—so it must be the pantomime. Still, I think you will do."

"Do what?"

"Join my troupe. I can only offer food and lodging. This is, in a manner of speaking, an apprenticeship. But the experience you will gain is worth more than money. And the opportunity to perform for the Zheron . . . that, of course, is priceless."

"The Zheron?"

"The priest of Zhe. One of the most powerful men in the holy city. In the entire kingdom. My troupe performed for him last year. He was very pleased. And very generous."

Darak lowered his head to hide his excitement. It would disguise their true purpose in Pilozhat. And a priest would know where the captives were kept for the Midsummer sacrifice.

" . . . a private entertainment inside the palace. But some of the richest lords and ladies in Pilozhat will attend. And the priests, of course."

He didn't know what a palace was, but he might be able to slip away after this entertainment and find Keirith.

" . . . are hesitating. I assure you any actor would kill for the honor." Olinio squirmed. "I could . . . perhaps . . . add the sum of . . . two serpents. For the entire engagement. Naturally, we will have other performances during the festival." He sighed. "Before less exalted audiences."

"Naturally." In one day, they had depleted a third of their coins with no hope of replenishing them. "The arrangement would have to include my friend here."

Olinio actually wrung his hands. "But that is impossible. The scar . . . yes, that is nice. But all my players possess some true deformity." He considered Urkiat, frowning. "If you had a hump. A limp. Something."

"I could wear a patch over one eye."

Olinio stared at him, aghast. "Risk the displeasure of the Zheron for a . . . a charlatan's trick?"

"I only thought—"

"A club foot, now. That might work. With the proper footwear . . ." Olinio's eyes narrowed. "An added expense, of course. Along with the cost of costumes." He hesitated a moment longer, then clapped his hands. "Three serpents for both of you. That's my final offer."

In the sudden hush, Olinio's voice rang out loudly. Darak's gaze followed those of the other patrons to the doorway.

"Gods save us," Olinio whispered.

In disbelief, Darak stared at the apparition he had first glimpsed through the portal in Chaos.

Olinio's fingers dug into his forearm. "For mercy's sake, lower your eyes."

But he could only gaze at the doorway, transfixed. Impossible that she—he?—could have remained unchanged after fifteen years. But every detail was as he remembered. The right half of the head shaved while on the left, glossy black hair fell to its waist. The left side of the face painted, the dusky cheek and swollen lips reddened.

The innkeeper rushed forward, bowing, stammering. The men at the tree trunk slid off their seats and retreated to the far corners of the room. The patrons at the closest table shoved their neighbors aside in an effort to make space. Those on the far end vacated their spots to stand shoulder to shoulder against the mud-brick wall.

The stranger observed all this with a placid smile. Elegant fingers—nails painted blood red—languidly brushed something from the folds of the long robe. One half was crimson, the other, brown.

"The Supplicant of the God with Two Faces," Olinio said in a hoarse whisper. "I've only seen her once. What could she be doing in Oexiak? And in this cesspit? Oh, merciful gods, she approaches."

And still he couldn't look away. It was as if she'd bespelled him.

She glanced over her shoulder to nod at the innkeeper. When Darak spied the bronze snake dangling from her left earlobe, his hand convulsively clutched his bag of charms. The movement caught her gaze. Her steps slowed and Olinio squeaked in terror. Then she passed them, trailed by the innkeeper who hurried forward with a bronze goblet.

Olinio darted a quick glance behind him.

"What is she doing?" Darak asked.

"Stroking the hair of the spit boy. Oh, gods, if she should speak to Hakkon . . ."

"Why?"

"He's a mute. How will I ever find another bodyguard?"

The innkeeper broke in with a long stream of Zherosi. The Supplicant answered in a low murmur. Even with his back to her, Darak could feel those eyes. It took all his control to keep from hunching his shoulders against that penetrating gaze.

Suddenly, the innkeeper was standing next to him, shouting something. Olinio squeaked again. "Move. Now. Quickly."

Darak rose from his place, only to be stopped by the gentle pressure of fingers on his shoulder. As the innkeeper backed away, the fingers traced a lingering path down his back. The Supplicant took one step toward the doorway. Unaccountably, she stumbled. Unthinking, he grasped her arm to steady her.

Every person in the room drew breath in a collective

gasp. Darak looked into eyes as dark and bottomless as that portal to Chaos. You could fall into those eyes, he thought. Fall into them and be lost forever.

She broke the spell by looking down at his hand. When he started to pull away, she clasped it with a strong grip. The nails on her right hand were clipped and free of paint. Even the fingers seemed shorter, but surely that was impossible. As impossible as her presence in this room, looking exactly as she had fifteen years ago.

"I thank you for your kindness."

Her voice was low and husky and she spoke the tribal tongue as if she'd grown up in his village.

"You're welcome. Forgive me if I . . . if my touch offended you."

"If the touch offended, would I seek to prolong it?" Her thumb caressed the jagged scar on the back of his hand and he felt the blood rush to his face. "May I return a kindness for a kindness?"

"I . . . that is . . . of course."

She leaned toward him, close enough for him to smell the faint hint of wine on her breath and the sweet scent that perfumed her body. "Keep my token safe, Darak. Your son might need it."

Stunned, he could only stare as she glided toward the door. Although he reached it only a few steps after her, he found the street deserted—as if she had simply vanished. And that was as impossible as everything else about her.

Chapter 29

IT TOOK KEIRITH three days before he managed to catch Xevhan returning from the morning sacrifice. This time, he merely bowed and whispered, "Meet me in the courtyard," before continuing along the corridor.

Priests drifted in and out of the courtyard all morning. A few stood before the rock garden in silent contemplation. Others chatted together. Despite the covert glances in his direction, none approached him.

They all bowed when Xevhan entered. He wandered from group to group, exchanging pleasantries, discussing plans for The Shedding, commiserating with one about a particularly difficult Zhiisto and with another about a death in his family. For each, he had a quick grin or a sympathetic nod. And each brightened visibly at receiving his attention.

With every evidence of surprise, Xevhan finally noticed him. "Ah, the Pajhit's little slave boy."

"Good morning, great Zheron."

"How are your lessons faring?"

"Not good. The Pajhit is displeased."

Xevhan glanced casually at the other priests. "Really?"

Noticing that the last priest had finally given up his contemplation of the rock garden, Keirith said, "Please to explain to me the meaning of the rocks."

Together, they wandered toward it.

"The spiral in the center represents our sacred adders."

"He knows about the qiij," Keirith whispered.

"The crystals represent Heart of Sky."

"I told him I took it from you. Not that you gave."

"The red stones represent Zhe."

"I said I do not remember my vision."

"And the black . . ."

"But I do."

". . . the black stones are Womb of Earth."

"I saw Malaq. Struck down by Zhe."

"And those . . . the ones placed at random . . . they represent the God with Two Faces."

"The god of changing fortune?"

"Yes." Xevhan gave him a hard look, then bowed his head as if in prayer. "We cannot talk here. Come to my chamber."

"He forbids me to see you alone again."

"Lose the guards."

"They follow me always."

Xevhan glanced up, noting the guards who loitered just outside the courtyard. These two had been assigned to him the morning after he recovered from the qiij. Keirith doubted Xevhan was the sort of man who noticed the faces of guards, but if he did, it would support his tale of Malaq's displeasure.

"I'm hosting an entertainment," Xevhan whispered. "After The Shedding. Find a way to attend."

"But the Pajhit—"

"Find a way to attend."

Out of the corner of his eye, Keirith noticed another priest approaching and bowed to Xevhan. "Thank you, great Zheron, for your teaching."

Xevhan nodded absently and left the courtyard with the other priest without a backward glance. At least, he was intrigued. Whether or not he could keep him intrigued was another matter. Now for the second part of his plan.

"I wish to speak with Khonsel Vazh do Havi," he told his guards.

The older one shook his head. "You don't want to be bothering the Khonsel."

"Yes. Please. I do. Does the Pajhit forbid that I speak with him?"

"No, but—"

"Then please to take me there."

The guards exchanged glances. The younger one shrugged. The older one frowned, but finally said, "All right. But if you try anything foolish, I'll knock you flat, Son of Zhe or not."

"That is fairness. Thank you."

The guards led him up the narrow stairway built into the corner of the palace. He'd never been on this floor. Scribes carrying clay tablets edged past harried-looking men in khirtas who argued vociferously as they strode through the windowless corridor. Rectangles of light from the doorways stretched across the floor. Most of the small rooms held only fleece pallets, lined up with typical Zherosi precision on the floor. A few contained collections of spears and swords. Although there were guards posted outside, he noted their location all the same.

His guards paused outside a chamber where a line of men waited for admittance. Two men complained about the confusion. Another reminded them it was always this way right before The Shedding. Talk turned to the upcoming ceremony, but the men spoke too softly for Keirith to catch much of what they were saying. Clearly, they longed to witness the formal presentation after the rite, but that, apparently, was reserved for those with noble blood or a great deal of money.

When they finally made it to the doorway, Keirith saw the Khonsel bending over a wooden table. Half a dozen men were gathered around him, making the chamber seem even smaller than it was. All were staring with apparent fascination at the hide that lay stretched out on the table. The men wore amulets on their chests and bands of bronze around their biceps. Some bands were wider than others—a symbol of power, perhaps. Certainly, the two with the widest bands talked more than the others.

At one point, the Khonsel looked up. When their eyes met, he frowned and immediately returned to his examination of the hide. He jabbed his blunt finger at several places, talked briefly about "a coordinated assault" and "an overland sweep," which made Keirith wonder if they were planning more raids on his people. Finally, the Khonsel rolled up the hide and thrust it at one of the wide-banded men. They all thumped their chests and bowed. Keirith dodged aside as they marched toward the doorway.

The older of his two guards bowed very low. "Forgive this interruption, Khonsel, but the boy asked to speak with you."

The Khonsel methodically cracked his knuckles. "Leave us," he said at last.

"Forgive me, great Khonsel, but the Pajhit has given us orders never to leave the boy unattended."

"He won't be unattended. He'll be with me."

"Great Khonsel—"

"Zhe's coils, he's not going to fly out the window. Wait outside."

The guards bowed and backed away. The Khonsel nodded to a young man with a patch over his left eye. "That's all, Geriv. Tell the Stuavo what we'll require."

Bundling up the remaining hides that lay strewn across the table, Geriv quickly departed.

"Khonsel do Havi. Please to be listening—"

"Not here."

Keirith followed him into the adjoining chamber. A well-worn rug lay in front of the sleeping shelf. A stool sat in one corner. The small window admitted little light at this time of day. The severity of the whitewashed walls was relieved only by a niche containing a vase with purple flowers. They seemed incongruous in the spartan setting— even more incongruous given what he knew of Vazh do Havi.

The Khonsel seated himself on the sleeping shelf. "All right. Tell me. But keep your voice down."

Keirith took a deep breath, praying his grasp of the Zherosi tongue would be adequate. He told the Khonsel what he had seen at the sacrifice. He told him about the qiij and the vision. He told him about his conversation with Malaq and his subsequent conversation with Xevhan. With such a man, he thought it unwise to try and hide anything.

Years of squinting into the sun had etched deep creases at the corners of the Khonsel's eyes and the heavy lids made him look half asleep, but there was nothing sleepy about the dark eyes boring into his as if they would pierce his spirit.

When he was finished, the Khonsel said, "Tell me again. From the beginning."

This time, when he completed his story, the Khonsel asked, "Why did you come to me with this tale?"

"You are Malaq's—the Pajhit's—friend."

"How would you know?"

"He does not eat with others. Only you. And you speak to him . . . it is different than others. Without the pretending."

The Khonsel grunted. "Did Malaq send you?"

"No. He says there is no danger."

"Stubborn old fool."

"Yes. No. I mean—"

"Why should you care if Malaq is in danger?"

"He is . . . kind to me."

"And he's an important man, isn't he?"

"Yes."

"And you want to stay on his good side."

"Excuse me, please?"

"You think I'll run to Malaq and tell him you came here. So eager to help. So trustworthy."

"I do want to—"

"And then you'll bind him to you so close he'll never be free."

"I do not understand."

The Khonsel rose. "Get out."

"You must watch Malaq. Help him. Then I go."

The Khonsel was on him in three strides. Keirith stumbled back so quickly he slammed into the wall.

"You dare give me orders?" the Khonsel demanded, thrusting his big face close.

"Aye, you great bully!"

The Khonsel reared back. Although he had spoken the tribal tongue, the meaning of his words was probably clear enough. He waited for the blow. Instead, the Khonsel laughed. "You've got stones, boy. I'll say that for you."

Keirith didn't know what rocks had to do with anything, but he nodded politely. "Yes. Thank you. You are a man of stones, too."

"Big enough."

"Please. Malaq is your friend. You are an important man. You can keep him safe."

"Why do you care?" he asked again.

Keirith took a moment to choose his words. He had to make the Khonsel believe him or he, too, would wave aside the danger. "He gives me his bed when I am sick. He feeds me broth. He thinks of the danger to me, but not of the danger to him. He says . . . he says I am good." He swallowed hard, forcing his eyes to meet the Khonsel's. "I am not so good. Oftenest, I am scared and not knowing who is a friend. Malaq says to trust my heart. My head. They say he is good. That you are his friend. And Xevhan is not."

The Khonsel's smile made him look even more menacing. "And do your heart and head tell you that you are the Son of Zhe?"

Even Malaq had never come right out and asked him. He found himself remembering the day he had freed the wounded rabbit from the snare and felt the terrified beating of its heart beneath his fingers. His heart was beating like that now.

Maker, help me.

He could evade the question as he had the first time the Khonsel confronted him, but he doubted a clever proverb would suffice now. "If I answer, I put my life in your hands. Into Malaq's hands, I could put my life. But not—forgive me, please—not yours."

The Khonsel studied him for a long moment. "I didn't think you were," he said, as if he'd just admitted the truth. "Nor does Malaq. He said so the other night."

"He did?" His voice broke with surprise. "But—"

"Enough. Get out."

"What about Malaq?"

"I'll watch his back. Same as I've been watching yours."

"Excuse me?"

"He made me promise. The night I met you."

Malaq knew he was not the Son of Zhe, but far from betraying him, he had asked his friend to protect him.

"Go on. Get out. And don't come to me again. It'll only make Xevhan suspicious."

"But if something happens—"

"Talk to Geriv. The young fellow with the eye patch. He's my sister's son. You can trust him."

"How do I find Geriv if I am needing him?"

"He'll find you."

Keirith got out of the chamber as quickly as his legs

would carry him. The Khonsel's smile left him with little doubt that his actions would be scrutinized more carefully than ever. And if he did anything to arouse his distrust, he'd have an enemy instead of a protector.

Chapter 30

DESPITE OLINIO'S ASSERTION that he did not tramp from one miserable village to the next, that was exactly what they did. Every evening, they unfurled their banner in another dusty town. Olinio's troupe sang, danced, and recited to audiences who were as generous with their applause as they were stingy with their coins. More often than not, they received food and lodging as their payment.

The players were the strangest assortment of people Darak had ever met. In addition to Hakkon, there was Rizhi, a beautiful blind singer even younger than Faelia; Bo and Bep, who had the burly arms and torsos of men but stood only as high as his belly; and Thikia, a hump-backed old woman who cooked their meals, sewed their costumes, and attended to any bruises, scrapes, and ailments that afflicted the company. Like Olinio, she spoke the language of the tribes. Darak wondered if they had been born in the north or simply acquired the tongue in their travels.

"How long have you been with Olinio?" Urkiat asked her as they trudged alongside the cart that carried their possessions.

"You'd do better to ask how long Olinio's been with me." Thikia grinned, showing astonishingly good teeth for one so old. "Forty years, we've been together. Since the day his father—may his cock stand as tall as a tree in Paradise—planted Olinio in my womb." She laughed at their slack-jawed expressions.

Everyone was expected to perform a variety of roles. In addition to serving as Olinio's bodyguard and performing feats of strength for the audience, Hakkon cared for the bullock that pulled the cart, repaired the wheels when they cracked, and erected the cloth that served as scenery for the performances. Thikia supplemented her roles as healer, cook, and seamstress by playing the visionary prophet, the wise grandmother, and the wicked enchantress—often in the same play.

"Change the wig, throw a cloak over your robe . . ." She shrugged. "People are easy to fool."

Olinio quickly decided that Urkiat would assume the heroic role because of his facility with the language. The club foot was abandoned in favor of red paint to highlight his scar. For Darak, he created a new character.

"The Wild Man of the North. You will fight Urkiat—the gallant Zherosi warrior—who will, of course, slay you. You will be fearsome yet farcical, terrifying and tremendous. And it has the added benefit that you needn't say anything—simply wave your club, growl, and die in agony. I don't suppose you could foam at the mouth? Perhaps we can concoct something. Mother! Foam! And fur. The Wild Man needs fur!"

Each midday, while the rest of the company lounged in the shade of the cart, he and Urkiat practiced their battle. "I feel like a fool," Darak muttered.

"It's not so bad."

"Not for you."

Urkiat was clothed in an immaculate khirta and wore a headband of gold-painted leather. He held a wooden sword, also painted gold. Darak was still waiting for Thikia to finish his costume, but his ridiculous "club" looked suspiciously similar to the ones Bo and Bep wielded.

They were the comical performers, juggling everything from fruit and balls to wine flasks and jugs. When a play called for an animal, they donned fleece or fur and crawled about on all fours. They engaged in mock battles with snakelike sacks of grain that they waggled lewdly at each other.

"I'm sure your club won't waggle half as much," Urkiat assured him earnestly.

Although Bo and Bep were ostensibly twins, they shared

little in common save for their diminutive stature. Bo was Zherosi-dark, while Bep was fair-haired and blue-eyed. Bo was as sweet-natured as Bep was sullen. But it was Bep who coached Urkiat on lunges and thrusts, all designed to look terribly menacing without doing any harm. Nevertheless, Darak's ribs were bruised after the first practice session and Urkiat nearly incoherent with apologies.

"Doesn't matter," Darak said, repressing a wince as Thikia slapped a poultice on his side. "I just have to sidestep faster. We'll try it again—on the morrow."

Only Rizhi was immune from the chaffing—good-natured and ill—of the others. Even Bep treated her with surprising tenderness, helping her on and off the cart, refilling her bowl at mealtimes, and shielding her from the boys who crowded around her after a performance. Although Darak couldn't understand most of her songs, her clear, sweet voice could move an audience to tears during a ballad, while her wicked smile made them roar with approval at what he assumed were bawdy songs.

Darak was shocked to learn that her parents had sold her to Olinio last autumn. She seemed perfectly happy with the troupe, making him wonder what kind of a life she had known before—and what kind of parents would sell their child.

By the third day of their journey, the roads were packed with people heading for Pilozhat. Every performance was crowded with folk eager for some respite from the monotony of travel. Olinio announced that the time was ripe for the debut of the Wild Man of the North. After they pulled their cart into the parched field where they would perform, Thikia shoved a handful of fur at him.

"What's this?" Darak asked.

"Your costume."

He dangled the small rabbitskin pouch by its two leather thongs. "Where's the rest of it?"

"That's it."

"It's no bigger than the bag I keep my charms in!"

"It's for holding other charms, Wild Man."

"I can't wear this," he said, scandalized. "My arse'll be hanging out for the whole world to see."

"That's the idea." Thikia licked her lips. "The ladies're going to love you."

"Not when they see the scars on my back."

"Scars? Even better. You wait. After the performance, you'll have to beat 'em off with your club."

"I'll talk to Olinio."

"It was Olinio's idea."

"But . . ." Darak turned to Urkiat who suddenly became very busy knotting his khirta around his waist. "I won't do it," he said firmly.

"You will," Thikia promised, just as firmly. "Or Olinio'll leave you here with nothing but the clothes on your back. Assuming he doesn't take those to pay for all the training you've received."

"Training? Waving a sack of grain and growling?"

"Save your breath, Wild Man. If you want to get to Pilozhat, you'll wear your furry little cock bag and keep your mouth shut."

Thanking the gods Rizhi couldn't see him and Hakkon couldn't comment, Darak ducked behind the painted backdrop to put the damn thing on. If Griane were here, she would be the one howling. As for Keirith, once he got his son safely home, he would remind him every day for the rest of his life how much he owed his father.

He emerged to a loud whistle from Thikia and a coarse laugh from Bep. Bo gave him an encouraging smile and quickly looked away. Hakkon just blinked, but Darak could have sworn he was fighting a smile.

"It's not so bad," Urkiat said.

"Stop saying that!"

"All the important things are covered."

"I warn you . . ."

"Just be sure and double knot the thongs."

Urkiat's serious expression gave way to a grin. Darak swung his club and Urkiat ducked, still grinning.

"I liked you better when you were awestruck."

"I'm still awestruck. It's a wondrous great fur bag. A prodigious . . . ow!"

Olinio's head poked around the backdrop. "Stop this fooling around. Our audience is gathering." His voice dropped an octave as it always did when he referred to the audience. As if they were performing before the king and queen of Zheros and not a crowd of farmers and laborers.

Olinio inspected his fur bag and sighed. "A pity we had

no more fur. I would have liked a hood. With ears. Still.
Very impressive. Imposing. Intimidating. You'll want to be
sure and double knot—"

"I did!"

"Exactly." He fluffed his multicolored tunic and smoothed
his thinning hair. "Let the magic begin!"

When his turn came to perform, Darak stalked around
the backdrop and was met by jeers, boos, whistles, and
enthusiastic applause from the women. Cheeks burning, he
growled and howled and swung his club. He had the pleasure of knocking the great Zherosi warrior on his arse twice
before a sword thrust under the armpit finished him off.
He fell to the ground, refusing to writhe, and lay motionless
throughout Urkiat's lengthy recitation. When it was finished, he got up, glared at the audience, and stalked off to
tumultuous applause.

He was pulling his tunic over his head when he was
clasped in a sweaty embrace.

"Breathtaking!" Olinio exclaimed. "Positively breathtaking. I am thrilled to limpness."

Darak shook him off and reached for his breeches.

"I knew it from the moment I saw you. I am never wrong
about such things. Rizhi. Quick. The final song. Bo, Bep—
the jars for coins. Smile, everyone, smile."

Urkiat appeared a moment later, a little dustier than
usual, but in high spirits.

"If you say one word about my rough-hewn, barbarous
splendor . . ."

Urkiat backed away, hands raised. "Not a word. I
swear."

They collected a lot of coins that evening, although mostly
the copper ones called frogs. And Thikia was right about
the ladies; they crowded around, giggling and murmuring,
as he helped Hakkon pack up the backdrop and costumes.

Darak was so intent on avoiding his female admirers that
he didn't notice the other knot of spectators until he heard
the laughter. A group of youths trailed after Bep. One was
on his knees, waddling back and forth in a cruel imitation
of his ungainly walk. When Bep tried to slip away, two of

the burliest farm boys seized him under the arms and lifted
him in the air. His short legs swung back and forth and
everyone bellowed with laughter. Bep bared his teeth in a
ferocious grin as if he enjoyed the rough play, but one look
at his scarlet face and blazing eyes sent Darak striding
forward.

"Put him down."

The youths hooted. One or two threw back their heads
and howled. Darak shoved past them, seized the free arm
of one of Bep's tormentors, and twisted it up behind his
back. The boy gave a genuine howl of pain and dropped
Bep who tumbled awkwardly to the ground. The laughter
died, replaced by a far more menacing silence.

Darak's hand went to the dagger at his waist, but before
he could pull it free, Bep shouted something in Zherosi
that sounded like "Away, you beast!" and kicked him in
the shins. Darak stumbled backward to renewed laughter,
pursued by Bep who clouted him repeatedly with his grain-
filled club, all the while yelling curses and hopping from
foot to foot like a demented bear cub. Still laughing, the
youths drifted away in search of other entertainment.

"Next time, stay out of it, Wild Man."

Before he could reply, Bep walked away. Only then did
Darak realize he had spoken the language of the tribes.

When it happened at the next town, Urkiat urged him to
follow Bep's advice, but the cruel laughter of the men and
their obvious delight in persecuting Bep was more than he
could stomach. This time, though, he took a lesson from
Bep. He raced through the crowd, howling and grimacing
and waving his stupid club. Even Bep looked startled, then
shouted something back that made his tormentors nod
eagerly.

Bep lowered his head and charged. Even braced for the
impact, Darak's breath whooshed out as Bep butted him
in the belly. He stumbled and fell. Bep leaped on top of
him. Darak winced as a fist caught him on the cheekbone.
He warded off another blow, promising never again to in-
tervene on behalf of the ungrateful little demon. Suddenly,
Bep crawled off him—giving him a good knee in the groin

as he did—and leaped up, waving his fists triumphantly in the air.

"The Wild Man is vanquished!" he shouted, drawing whoops and cheers from the crowd. One man gave him an approving pat on the head, as if the little man were a dog.

Darak picked himself up, watching with disgust as Bep swaggered off with his former tormentors.

"He's not worth it," Urkiat muttered. "Come on. You'd better let Thikia take a look at that eye."

"It'll do."

"You don't want it swelling—"

"It'll do, Urkiat." Softening his voice, he added, "Just leave me be for a bit."

While the rest of the company headed to the inn, Darak wandered into the field. Thick, shorn stalks of the grain they called millet crunched underfoot. The richer farmers disdained it for some reason, preferring to plant barley. This year, they would regret that decision. The millet survived the drought while the barley withered. In some fields, he'd seen lines of people passing water jugs in a vain effort to keep their crops alive. Even if the rains came now, it would be too late; there would be hunger in Zheros come winter.

He sat down with his back against a boulder and drew his sleeve across his forehead. Although the sun had vanished, the heat remained. The sunsets here were spectacular, but he missed the long, gentle twilights of the north. The light faded so slowly around Midsummer, as if the day were reluctant to surrender to night. And when it did, the reign of darkness was so brief that you could still be dozing off when the birds began to sing.

Here, the birds offered a few halfhearted cheeps and gave up. He'd seen hawks soaring overhead, crows and ravens picking over the carcass of a dead animal, but the chorus of birdsong that greeted him in the mornings was missing. Like the trees. And instead of rolling hills, the land was so flat, he woke each morning thinking he was sure to spy the holy city looming ahead of them. But all he could make out was a dark mountain, shimmering in the haze.

I'm coming, Keirith. Wait for me.

The crunch of millet stalks alerted him to an intruder. He craned his head and made out a short, stout figure, silhouetted against the fading colors of the sky.

Bep leaned against the boulder and folded his arms. For once, their heads were nearly level. What must it feel like to stare up at everyone? To be a man in spirit with a body no taller than a child's?

"You're as stubborn as a bullock," Bep said.

That was another difference between the two little men: Bo's voice was soft and lilting, Bep's as musical as two stones grating together.

"Just couldn't keep out of it, could you?"

"I don't like bullies."

"As if you've ever had to put up with them."

"It was wrong."

Bep laughed, a deep bellow that sounded surprisingly friendly. "Right or wrong's got nothing to do with it. This is the world, Wild Man."

"It shouldn't be."

"Stubborn as a bullock," Bep mused. "And stupid as a sheep. Wait. I'm not through insulting you yet."

"Well, I'm through listening."

"Touchy, aren't we?"

"Don't think because you're shorter, I won't knock you on your arse."

"The same arse you were so eager to save these last two nights."

"It wasn't your arse I was worried about."

"Nay. It was the principle of the thing."

Darak opened his mouth and shut it. Finally, he said, "I'm not always so self-righteous."

"Thank the Maker for small blessings."

"It's true, then? You're a child of the Oak and Holly?"

Bep's mouth twisted. "I'm nobody's child, Wild Man. And nobody's friend either."

"Nay, of course not. The man who offers you friendship gets a bruised cheek and sore ballocks."

For a moment, he thought Bep would strike him. Then his face relaxed. "At least you had the sense to make a game of it this time."

"So maybe I'm not as stupid as a sheep. Why . . . ?" He hesitated, then plunged ahead. "Why do you let them treat you that way?"

"Good gods, man. Isn't it obvious? Because they're too big and too many to fight." Bep shook his head, disgusted.

"I spent my youth trying to prove myself with my fists. Now I play the fool. Instead of a beating, I earn laughter and coins. And women. Oh, aye, there's always one or two want to see what the little man's made of. And they find out quick enough that I'm a big man where it counts. I've got one waiting for me now. A farmer's wife whose husband's off to Pilozhat and left her to care for the fields. Tonight I'll be the one doing the plowing."

"I see."

"Do you, Wild Man? Can you imagine what it's like to have your face pillowed between two soft breasts and your cock buried between two strong thighs?"

"Have a care you don't suffocate," Darak said shortly.

Bep laughed. "Skittish as a virgin, aren't you? Naught but blushes and lowered eyes."

"I'm not blushing," he said, furious because he was.

"Are you so skittish with your wife?"

"Nay. And it's none of your concern if I am." He rose.

"I told you why I play the fool," Bep said. "Suppose you tell me why you play the Wild Man for Olinio."

"It's not for him."

"Who, then?"

"Again, that's none of your concern."

"True. But I can't help wondering why the great Darak Spirit-Hunter should join a troupe of traveling players."

Darak froze. The players knew him as Reinek. He'd taken his father's name as a precaution, although both he and Urkiat thought it unlikely that anyone in Zheros had heard of Darak Spirit-Hunter. But a child of the Oak and Holly would know the tale. Even one as far from home as Bep.

"Could be he got bored in that little village of his," Bep speculated. "Wanted another adventure. But the Wild Man of the North? That's a bit lower than I'd expect him to go. So I ask myself, 'Why would the Spirit-Hunter be in Zheros? And in such a tearing hurry to get to Pilozhat?'"

He'd never said anything about wanting to go to Pilozhat. But Bep could have seen him scanning the horizon, could have overheard him asking Olinio how many days before they reached the holy city. Who'd have guessed such innocuous behavior could betray him?

Unless Urkiat had let it slip.

Nay, he wouldn't be so careless.

A satisfied smile lit Bep's craggy features. "I start to wonder if maybe the Spirit-Hunter is on another quest. Last time, he went looking for his brother. Maybe this time, it's his wife. She'd be a bit old for the pleasure houses, though. So maybe it's not his wife he's looking for, but his daughter. Or his son."

"What do you want?"

"Perhaps I'm just curious."

"Perhaps."

"Or perhaps I mean to betray you to the priests in Pilozhat. They might consider the Spirit-Hunter a valuable hostage."

"They might."

"Or perhaps I'm doing you the favor of warning you."

"About the priests?"

"About the world, my innocent Wild Man. Coins loosen tongues and scruples alike. Right or wrong matters less than turning a profit. Your height, your hands, your manner . . . they all make you stand out. That's a good thing when you're just a silly player. But not so good when you've got something to hide. So take the advice of a fool: watch your back, keep your dagger close, and play the Wild Man. He'll survive a lot longer in Zheros than Darak Spirit-Hunter will."

It would be easy enough to take him. Leave his body in the field. Blame his death on thieves or drunks or a jealous suitor. Instead, Darak watched Bep cross the field and disappear into one of the whitewashed houses.

"Wolf?" he whispered. "Can you hear me?"

He had to wait a long while for her to appear and when she did, she was as insubstantial as mist, the stalks of millet clearly visible through her body. But her tail still wagged in greeting as she padded over and lay down beside him.

"Is it too hard for you?" he asked. "I won't call you again if it is."

"It is hard, Little Brother. But good to share the night with you."

When he told her about his encounter with Bep, she surprised him by saying, "His warning was wise. And his behavior that of any pack leader seeking to demonstrate his dominance to a newcomer."

"But he's not the pack leader."

As he described Olinio, her head came up. "That one is weak. The small one is strong. That is why he tests you. To decide whether to accept you or chase you off." She whined softly. "Or kill you. That often happens to a lone wolf seeking a new pack."

"But I'm not alone. And I'm not seeking a new pack. I have you and Urkiat."

"Then tell the young one to be cautious. To watch for any signs of aggression." She lowered her head onto her paws again. "I am sorry I cannot help you, Little Brother."

"But you already have, Wolf."

He stared up at the sky and watched the stars appear. There was the Archer, pointing the way home. And there, the Boar's Tusk, pointing the way to Pilozhat. The road to the holy city was as straight as a spear, but the path to Keirith was full of pitfalls.

"Close your eyes, Little Brother. I will keep watch."

As she stretched and rose, he lay down on the warm earth. His fears would still be waiting in the morning. He would face them then. Tonight, he had Wolf. Tonight, at least, he was safe.

Please, gods, let Keirith be safe, too. And Griane and the children. Please, gods, let me reach my boy in time.

Chapter 31

THE PALACE WAS UNUSUALLY quiet on the day of The Shedding; everyone was expected to spend the morning in contemplation and prayer. Only when the king and queen emerged from seclusion at midday did the celebrations begin. So Keirith had little to do but sit in his room, contemplate the floor, and pray that he was ready for Xevhan's entertainment. Malaq would be busy all day, but they had already discussed how he should behave tonight; it was only a matter of waiting for the interminable day to end.

He flinched when he heard the distant blare of horns; he always associated the sound with death. But when the two guards loitering outside sketched spirals on their chests, he guessed the rite must be over.

As the afternoon wore on, he grew more restless. Finally, he walked to the doorway and suggested a game of dice. The younger guard brightened, but the older one shook his head. "Wouldn't be proper."

"But the praying is done, yes? And this is a day of happiness for your people. And if I just sit here, counting stones in the floor, I think I scream. So dice is good for all of us."

After a moment, the older guard nodded. The younger one raced off and returned with a leather cup and wooden dice. He plopped down on the floor and rattled the cup invitingly. The older one settled himself with a grunt.

The afternoon passed pleasantly enough after that. They played for beans, but the young guard was as excited as if

they were coins. His name was Ysal. He'd grown up in
Pilozhat. His father had served in the palace guard before
him. He had three sisters and two brothers. One brother
was in the army and was certain to go far. The younger
one—the clever one—was apprenticed to a metalworker.
His sisters were all unmarried, but one was betrothed to
the same craftsman who had taken on his brother as an
apprentice. He was old—thirty at least—but very respectable
and had offered an excellent bride price for his sister, who
was no great beauty although she was the sweetest girl in
the world. Another had her eyes on the son of a tanner,
although how she could put up with the stink was more than
he could imagine. He had served in the guards for three
years and it was good, steady work, and he hoped to put
enough money by so that when he was old, he could buy a
house of his own and marry a rich wife and buy a pretty
slave girl.

The older guard's name was Luzik.

It was the first time he'd really talked with a Zheroso
other than Malaq. He couldn't help liking Ysal. He seemed
so . . . ordinary. He loved his family. He dreamed of his
future. He celebrated his people's festivals. Just like a child
of the Oak and Holly.

"Tell me about The Shedding. I know little about the
rite. It honors the adders who shed their skins, yes?"

Ysal nodded. "All night, the priests keep vigil in the
temples. Save for the Pajhit—he stays with the king. And
the Motixa is with the queen. They keep vigil, too. At
dawn, the Qepo milks the adders. Everyone has to pray
and fast until the king and queen Shed."

Ysal grimaced; clearly, neither praying nor fasting ap-
pealed to him.

"At midday," he continued, "the king and queen go to
the throne room to greet the people. Well, the important
people. Just for a few moments, though. Shedding their
skins is very tiring. But everyone else celebrates. The parties go on all night. Dancing, singing. And the food . . ."
He smacked his lips in anticipation.

"Shedding their skins? Their clothes, you mean." Keirith
felt the heat rise into his face as he imagined the queen
standing naked in the throne room.

"Not their clothes. Their skin. Their flesh."

"But . . . I do not understand."

Luzik blew out his breath in exasperation. "They go into seclusion with one set of bodies and come out with new ones."

"Whose bodies?"

"The Hosts."

"The most beautiful man and woman in the kingdom," Ysal added. He tossed the dice, exclaiming with dismay when a frog and an eagle came up. "My cousin was almost chosen last year. She made it all the way to the presentation. But the queen chose another girl." His downcast expression brightened. "But it was still an honor. And it got her a rich husband. A merchant from—"

"The king and queen take the bodies of the Hosts?"

Luzik scowled. "That's what we've been telling you." He rolled two eagles and grunted with satisfaction.

Numb with horror, Keirith could only stare at them. The beautiful queen who had spoken so kindly to him cast out the spirit of another and took the body for herself. Just as Morgath had done with Grain-Mother Yeorna.

"And afterward?" he managed. "What happens to . . . to the Hosts?"

Both guards made the sign of the spiral. "Their spirits fly to Paradise," Ysal said, "where they live among the green hills and the flowing rivers. They're honored above all mortal men and women. It's your turn, Kheridh."

Yeorna's spirit didn't fly to the Forever Isles; it was cast into Chaos. He remembered the sickly king, lolling on his throne. Now he possessed the body of a beautiful young man. He was strong again and revitalized. Until next year when it happened all over again. No wonder Malaq had brushed aside his questions about The Shedding.

"Roll the dice," Ysal urged. "You need two serpents to beat Luzik."

Keirith strode to the doorway.

"Where are you going?" Luzik demanded.

"The kitchen."

"But what about the game?" Ysal called plaintively.

The Master was screaming at the First Cook who had dared change the special herbs he used to season his seaweed pottage. The Fish Cook was screaming at an undercook for overcooking the eels. The Meat Cook was beating the spit boys for falling asleep and allowing the mutton to char on one side, and the Sauce Cook was clouting the sauce boy with a ladle for allowing the cream for the rabbit stew to curdle.

Hircha kept a wary eye on the senior cooks as she chopped leeks and onions. The heat from the open fires was so intense that sweat dripped off her forehead onto the table. Between the screaming cooks and the crying boys and the clatter of pots and pans and utensils, she couldn't even hear what the Wine Keeper was shouting. His assistant rushed forward to placate him and skidded on the spot where a flask of olive oil had shattered earlier. He flailed, knocking the Wine Keeper into a pot girl, and all three went down amid a shower of cutlery.

It was always chaotic here. During the seven-day festival that began with The Shedding and climaxed with the Midsummer rite, there were simply more tantrums, more screaming, and more beatings. Last year, one of the undercooks stabbed his senior with a carving knife. After a brief struggle, a pot boy seized a frying pan and bashed the undercook over the head. Until the guards appeared, everyone simply stepped over the unconscious bodies and took extra care not to slip in the blood.

When she'd first arrived in the kitchen, she'd been given the most unpleasant and backbreaking tasks. They all knew she'd been the Zheron's favorite and delighted in making her life miserable. Now, they mostly ignored her.

Hircha swiped her wrist across her forehead, flinging droplets of sweat into a tureen of mussels. If it were only the feasts, it might not be so bad, but of course, the kitchen had to continue to supply food for the ordinary folk as well. Feeding two hundred people was a chore at any time, but during the festival, the population of the palace swelled as noble families and rich merchants traveled from as far away as Oexiak.

And it wasn't only the great feasts in the royal hall that required special attention, but the smaller, private gatherings. They shouldn't have to prepare lavish dishes for those, but who would dare refuse the Zheron?

Once, she had attended those little gatherings, sitting on his lap, laughing at the performers he had paid to entertain his guests. One year, there had been a troupe with animals: a bear that danced on its hind legs, a goat that could beat a drum with its hoof, little dogs that jumped over clay pots and skittered through barrels. She liked the dogs best. When the performance was over, the Zheron summoned the trainer so she could hold one in her lap and pet it.

Hircha swept the leeks and onions into one bowl as an undercook slammed another down in front of her. Wiping her hands on her gown, she picked up her knife to slice the kugi.

"Not too thick," the undercook snarled.

"Yes, Master." He didn't deserve the title, but she'd learned to be lavish with compliments—as long as the Master himself was out of earshot.

She'd been nervous when she received Xevhan's summons yesterday, but when he smiled and spoke to her as if nothing had happened, fury welled up inside of her. Miko handed her the clothes she was to wear while serving at the entertainment. His fingers lingered on her wrist and it took all her strength not to snatch her hand away. After she was dismissed, she went back to the kitchen and was quietly sick. She cleaned the bowl before anyone could shout at her and returned to her work.

Her determined slicing slowed. She found herself staring at the knife. It was too large to steal. But one of the smaller ones used for paring fruit . . . that she could slip unnoticed into her gown. She'd be killed, of course. But as long as she had the satisfaction of seeing the blood gushing out of his throat, it would be worth it.

She heard a fresh commotion and glanced up. Keirith was standing in the doorway, arguing with one of the undercooks. The Master strode forward, scowling, but his expression changed to one of obsequious politeness when he saw Keirith. Clearly, he'd heard the rumors about the captive from the northern tribes and was taking no chance of offending the boy who might be the Son of Zhe.

When Keirith spied her, he stalked past the Master, seized her arm, and led her out of the kitchen. Hircha shot a pleading look at the Master and resisted the urge to shake Keirith off. Didn't he realize she could get a beating for this? Or didn't he care?

Once they were safely in the corridor, she waited for a young soldier with an eye patch to pass before twisting free. "What are you doing here?" She kept her voice low, eyeing Keirith's guards who hovered nearby.

"Is it true? About The Shedding?"

"What about The Shedding?"

"That the king and queen cast out the spirits of the Hosts and steal their bodies."

He was very pale. And although his voice was low, it was shaking. His whole body was shaking. She stopped herself from snapping out the obvious answer. This was the first time they had spoken since their encounter in the Pajhit's chamber. He had come to her for the truth, but she doubted he wanted to hear it.

"The priests help them," she said. "The Pajhit and the Motixa. But aye. It's true."

He looked so shocked and lost. Like a little boy who had found out his best friend had betrayed him. She felt a flash of sympathy and ruthlessly suppressed it.

"I should have told you. During our lessons."

"It's not your fault."

Whose, then? The Pajhit's? He had taken over the lessons after her dismissal. Would it help her plans to try and turn Keirith against him?

"It is . . . shocking. The first time you realize. And understand what these people are capable of."

"They say the spirits of the Hosts go to Paradise."

"If they said they were cast into the Abyss, do you think anyone would volunteer?"

"But still, it's a . . . a willing sacrifice."

"What does that matter?"

"Tree-Father Struath told my . . . he said the greatest sacrifices are made willingly. That those find the most favor with the gods. So perhaps their spirits do go to Paradise."

"Perhaps." She glanced toward the kitchen. "I must get back or I'll get a . . . I'll be punished," she finished. For good measure, she bit her lip.

"I'm sorry. I didn't mean to get you in trouble."

"It's all right. It's not every day a kitchen slave gets a

visit from the Son of Zhe." When she received no answering smile, she said, "Why don't you ask the Pajhit? He'll be able to tell you more."

Keirith's eyes flashed. The bewildered expression vanished. "If he tells me the truth."

So he did believe the Pajhit had betrayed him. They must have grown close during the last half-moon.

"You can't believe anything they tell you. I should know." Her voice trembled with genuine emotion. What an innocent she had been. Even more innocent than poor Keirith.

"I wanted to see you," Keirith said. "After we talked. I didn't mean to . . . to abandon you."

"You didn't." She touched his arm and felt him tremble. "I never blamed you." Another quick glance at the kitchen. Another bite of the lip. But this time, she was surprised to feel shame at her blatant manipulation.

Don't be a fool.

"You've only to send for me and I'll come. Even if it does mean a beating."

She kissed him lightly on the cheek and hurried back to the kitchen. The stupid pot girls whispered and giggled, but the Master regarded her thoughtfully. She had already returned to slicing up the kugi when she felt him beside her.

"Things are well in hand here. You may return to your chamber."

"Thank you, Master." Flashing a smile of gratitude, she reached for a discarded cloth. She swept the small paring knife under it and wiped her hands. "You are very kind to this slave." She dropped the cloth on the table. Her right hand remained hidden in the folds of her gown, the knife a hard, comforting presence against her thigh. As she sidled past the Master, she allowed her arm to brush lightly against his. Like a pig, he grunted with pleasure.

All men were the same. They wanted a warm body in their beds and a warm sheath for their cocks. Except Keirith.

She wished now that he'd never revealed what had happened to him on that ship. She didn't want to be drawn into his pain. She didn't want to feel sympathy for him. She frowned, recalling his horror at learning the truth about The Shedding and that nonsense about a willing sacrifice.

Willing or not, you were still dead. And she doubted Paradise awaited you afterward.

Despite all the betrayals, he still believed he could understand these people—and worse, trust them. Poor, stupid boy. They'd break his heart if they didn't kill him first.

Chapter 32

PILOZHAT SHIMMERED IN the afternoon sunlight. Darak eyed the palace where they would perform, wondering how he would ever find Keirith in such a huge place.

They were camped in the parched fields to the west of the city, along with hundreds of others too poor or too thrifty to pay for lodging during the festival. All morning, people had streamed into Pilozhat, leaving friends behind to guard their possessions.

"They'll get their turn," Urkiat had assured him. "The inns and pleasure houses will be open all night."

During the heat of the day, those in the fields sought a patch of shade, some under carts, some in the lee of boulders, others simply shoving two sticks in the ground and draping a cloth over them. Now that the afternoon was waning, they were beginning to stir.

None of the players had ever witnessed the Midsummer rite. So while Hakkon accompanied Olinio to the palace to make final arrangements for the Zheron's entertainment, he and Urkiat wandered from camp to camp, hoping to gather information while they advertised the players' public performances. Darak listened eagerly as Urkiat translated the accounts of those who had seen the rite before.

"A hundred men," asserted one man. "I counted."

"Did you see the Pajhit cut their hearts out?"

"Sure as I see you. Got there two days before to stake out my place. And there was already a crowd, let me tell you. I was too far back to have any blood splatter on me, though."

Darak's stomach roiled when Urkiat translated. Judging from the expressions of those listening, they sympathized with the speaker's misfortune.

"I'm too old to be sitting in the sun for six days," he continued. "And if you want to feel the hot blood on your face, that's what it means. But don't worry. There's plenty to be had after."

"Be sure and bring your own cloths," another man interjected. "Or jars if you're looking to carry home enough to sprinkle on your fields and livestock."

"I thought the priests sold those at the temple," a young man said.

"And charge a year's income for them."

"But they're blessed."

"So they say." The first expert shrugged. "It's the blood that's sacred, not the jar you put it in."

"My wife screeched like a gull when I bought one last year," another man confirmed with a rueful grin. "So this year, I packed two—and didn't I leave home with her screeching at me that I should have brought more?"

Urkiat said something that provoked a lively discussion. Only later, as they were walking away, did he explain. "One man claimed the captives were held in a separate compound. There."

"That building nestled in the slope of the hill?"

"Nay, that's the temple of the God with Two Faces. See that section of the palace that juts out? That's it. They march the captives to the temple of Heart of Sky. You can't see it from here."

"Could we free Keirith during the procession?"

"Too many guards. And the captives are roped together."

"How reliable is the information?"

"Everyone who'd seen the sacrifice agreed about the procession. And the guards."

"So we'll have to get him out of the compound." When Urkiat remained silent, Darak gave him a sharp look. "What?"

"Look at those walls. And there are guards inside. You

can't just walk in, snatch Keirith out from under their
noses, and walk out again."

Darak's hand went to his bag of charms where the token
from the Supplicant lay. "I might."

"There's something else. I asked whether the captives
ever tried to escape. And the man laughed. He said they
all stood in line, meek as lambs, waiting to climb the steps
to the altar. He took it as a sign that they were glad to
offer their lives to the sun god."

"More likely they're drugged."

"And that will make it even harder to free Keirith. If he
doesn't want to come—"

"Of course he'll want to come!"

"I mean if he doesn't understand what's happening." Urkiat shrugged helplessly. "I don't know. It just seems so
impossible."

"You expect me to give up now? After coming all this
way?"

"Nay. But—"

"Good. First thing we need to do is get a look at the
place where they're holding Keirith. If I can get inside—"

"How?"

"Let me worry about that. We've got the performance
tonight. That'll give us an opportunity to see a bit of the
palace. Maybe pick up some more information."

The first flaw in his plan was revealed after Olinio and
Hakkon returned. "A small change," Olinio announced.
"Nothing important." And he launched into a long speech.

"What?" Darak whispered as Urkiat's face fell.

"We're to perform on the beach."

As soon as Olinio finished speaking, Darak stalked over
to him. "You said we'd be performing in the palace."

"The Zheron decided the beach would be more festive.
He's arranged a special pavilion for his guests and a tent—"

"We won't be anywhere near the palace."

"It's not the setting that's important, but the audience.
Some of the finest families in the kingdom will be in
attendance."

"What about the other priests?"

"I imagine some of them will be invited, too."

"You imagine?"

"Well, I could hardly ask to see the guest list, could I?"

"You promised we would perform in the palace. Before the priesthood."

"Well, the situation has changed!" Olinio snapped. "The money's the same, no matter where we perform or who attends. Trust me, we are far better off showcasing our talents to the nobility. They, at least, understand that artists do not survive on prayers. We're certain to garner any number of offers for additional appearances. It's a coup, I tell you! You should be elated, excited, ecstatic." He bustled off, shouting instructions.

Darak found Bep watching him with a sardonic smile. "Maybe it's a good thing there won't be any priests. Those rich folk probably couldn't care less about the legend of the Spirit-Hunter."

Darak strode over to the cart and worked out his frustration packing up their supplies.

The site selected for the entertainment was a secluded cove east of the city. Sweating slaves worked through the afternoon, erecting canopied shelters, arranging rugs and cushions beneath them, and setting torches in the sand. Others trudged down from the palace, laden with baskets and platters, crates and jugs. Judging from the sheer number of supplies, they could be entertaining a hundred people, not the forty the Zheron had told Olinio to expect.

Olinio insisted they practice their mock battle twice. The shifting sand made the footwork tricky and each time one of them slipped, he clutched his head, moaning. Only when Urkiat suggesting using the difficult terrain to create drama did he brighten.

"Dear Urkiat, you may have a warrior's face, but you possess the spirit of an artist."

Urkiat solemnly agreed. Darak just kicked at the sand, disgusted.

The sun was touching the horizon when Hakkon spotted the litters coming down the beach. Darak counted ten before Olinio hustled everyone into the tent. He remained outside, offering obsequious bows to each guest. The performers took turns peeping through the tent flap.

"Is that the Zheron?" Darak asked Thikia, eyeing an older man, littered with bronze jewelry.

"Nay. That's him. Over there. Talking to the woman in blue."

"He's so young."

"But rich. Which probably accounts for his rise. Doesn't look very pious, does he?"

In fact, he looked like most of the men there: smooth-faced, handsome, laden with jewelry, quick to laugh. He broke off a cluster of grapes from a platter held by a slave girl and offered it to the woman in blue, leaning close to whisper something that made her smile.

The slave girl gave Darak a start. With that long blonde hair—so pale it looked almost white—she could be a child of the Oak and Holly. She looked completely out of place among the Zherosi, but none of the guests spared her a glance.

Something jabbed him in the small of his back.

"My turn," Bep said.

Darak relinquished his position and ducked out the back of the tent where the air was less stifling. The feast would go on all evening. Olinio had sternly warned them to stay out of sight lest they ruin "the magic." There was still too much light to allow him to wander, unseen, down to the sea and dare a refreshing plunge in the surf. So he simply sat in the shade of the tent, arms folded atop his knees, and tried to come up with a plan to rescue Keirith.

The Supplicant's token might get him into the slave compound, but he had no way of guessing whether it would allow him to free his son or simply lead to his own imprisonment. He could seek her out at the temple of the God with Two Faces, but for all he knew, she was still in Oexiak. Even if he did find her, how did he know if she was trustworthy?

Too many questions and far too few answers. But he could not allow himself to believe—to even admit the possibility—that he had come so far, only to stand by helplessly while the Zherosi sacrificed his son.

Keirith clung to the sides of the litter. He was shaken enough from his quarrel with Malaq without this lurching journey to the beach.

He had returned to his room to dress for Xevhan's entertainment. It gave him the time he needed to calm himself
before confronting Malaq. But he must not have been calm
enough; as soon as he began questioning him about The
Shedding, Malaq turned on him in a fury.

"Yes, I might have told you. But if I had, you wouldn't
have heard one other thing I said. And I have other things
to do than constantly reassure you."

Keirith had been too stunned by his vehemence to respond. Malaq had immediately apologized, pleading the difficulty of the king's Shedding. Observing his pallor and
obvious exhaustion, Keirith hadn't pressed him. It was Malaq
who had promised they would talk again on the morrow.

The litter thumped to the ground and Keirith crawled
out. He wished Ysal and Luzik were escorting him instead
of the men who guarded him at night. It would have been
comforting to have someone he knew—other than Xevhan.

He smoothed his khirta nervously. He'd dressed with
care: scrubbing his body with the soap and cloth Malaq
provided; perfuming his hair with oil and tying it back with
a gold thread; fastening his khirta with a bronze pin instead
of simply knotting it. But compared to the other guests, he
knew he looked as out of place as he felt.

He was eyeing the crowd with misgiving when he realized
what was nagging at him: this was the same cove where
Hircha had tried to seduce him. Was that Xevhan's not-so-
subtle way of unsettling him? Perhaps he simply liked this
place. It was a perfect setting for the feast. The sky was
tinged pink from the setting sun. The waves rolled gently
onto the beach. Dozens of multicolored cushions lay scattered beneath the three scarlet canopies. On the third side
of the square, a large blue cloth hung between two poles.
Crude trees and mountains had been painted on it. It must
have something to do with the promised entertainment.

The gold and bronze of the guests' jewelry flashed in the
torchlight, as did the bowls and platters and goblets passed
by the slaves. They were all young and beautiful, the boys
dressed in skimpy loincloths, the girls wearing skimpier
bands of cloth around their breasts and short skirts that
revealed their slender legs. He saw one guest fondle a girl's
breast before accepting a goblet of wine, without pausing
in his earnest conversation with another man. A woman

reclining beneath a canopy boldly reached between a slave boy's legs. He smiled uncertainly as she giggled with her companion.

But most of the guests ignored the slaves completely. Their animated voices vied with the soft shushing of the waves and the sounds of flute and drum and lyre. It surprised him to see how many of the men wore daggers; perhaps they merely wanted to display the jewels studding the sheaths. As for the women, they fluttered from group to group like brilliantly colored butterflies.

"So you have come at last."

Heads turned to see whose arrival had prompted Xevhan's hearty greeting. Conversation ebbed, then rose again in feverish speculation.

Xevhan's smile dimmed fractionally when he saw the guards. "Help yourself to food and drink," he told them. "You may sit with the litter bearers. Don't worry—your charge won't be going anywhere." As soon as they were out of earshot, he whispered, "There was no problem with Malaq?"

"At first, he was angered. Then he says, yes, yes—you must go."

"He wants you to spy on me."

"I can say enough to make him easy in his mind. And to make him want us to meet again. And then we talk and teach and learn together, yes?"

Instead of replying, Xevhan turned to his guests. "My friends. This is Kheridh, the boy I was telling you about. But I warn you. He's more accustomed to speaking to our sacred adders than to Zherosi nobility, so keep your words simple or you'll turn his head."

Amid the laughter, Keirith did his best to look awestruck and nervous. In such glittering company, it wasn't difficult.

As Xevhan led the way toward one of the shelters, a woman pushed forward and said, "You must tell us all about the adders. We keep two in our household, of course, but they've never said a word to me."

"No wonder," the man at her side replied. "They can't get a word in edgewise."

The woman slapped his arm. "Don't pay any attention to my husband."

This provoked more laughter. Keirith smiled politely,

wishing she would not walk quite so close. Xevhan sat down and waved him to the cushion next to his. To his dismay, the woman promptly took the cushion on his left. Her fingertips played along his arm. "Such pale skin. Isn't it really the palest skin you've ever seen?"

"I don't know," her husband replied. "This pretty little creature looks like she was dipped in moonlight."

Keirith looked up, startled to find Hircha standing behind them clutching a bronze pitcher. A rigid smile twisted her lips as she stepped out of reach of the man's hand. "Wine, noble lord?"

"That'll do for a start." He winked at her. His wife laughed.

Keirith felt himself flushing, ashamed that Hircha should have to endure such treatment. He wondered how much worse it would get as the feast progressed and the wine flowed freely. Xevhan just watched it all with a small smile that made Keirith shudder in spite of the warmth of the evening.

Bep had gotten hold of a pitcher of wine. By the time Darak reentered the tent, he was draining it. When Bep tossed the pitcher aside and tried to pull Rizhi into a dance, Darak grabbed him and shook him hard.

He never saw Bep move. He simply felt fingers fumbling between his legs and then a shocking pain as they squeezed. He roared and punched Bep in the head. Bep staggered into Bo, knocking him into Urkiat's wooden sword. Bo yelped, Bep laughed.

Olinio chose that moment to shove back the tent flap, his face nearly as red as his tunic. Bep stopped laughing. Turning his head away, he vomited between Hakkon's bare feet. Olinio launched into a stream of Zherosi and swept out again.

Darak started laughing, but he had to stop because it made his ballocks ache even more. In a moment, they were all laughing. Bep wiped his eyes and apologized profusely to Rizhi. Her fingers fumbled for Bep's face. Cradling it between her hands, she kissed him lightly on the forehead and whispered something that made him blush.

While poor Hakkon cleaned up the vomit and Thikia inspected Bo's arse for damage, Bep sidled over to him. "Sorry about your ballocks. No hard feelings?"

"I doubt I'll be feeling hard for a number of days, thank you."

Bep grinned. "Maybe we can work it into the act."

"Only if we use your ballocks."

"Nay, Wild Man. It's much funnier when I do it to you."

"That's your opinion."

"That, my friend, is the essence of comedy."

It might only be the wine that made Bep so friendly, but Darak was glad to put aside suspicion for one night and enjoy the fellowship.

A drum sounded outside. Olinio launched into his opening speech. Thikia snatched up her wise grandmother's shawl. Hakkon led Rizhi forward. Bo and Bep retrieved their clubs. Carefully adjusting his fur bag, Darak plucked his wooden sword from the pile of accessories near the tent flap.

The magic was about to begin.

They started snickering as soon as the chubby man began his speech. Although he looked silly in his scarlet tunic and sky-blue breeches, Keirith couldn't help feeling sorry for him. Sweat plastered his thin hair over his scalp and ran down his jowls. His hearty voice grew more tremulous as the snickering turned to open laughter.

"What a ridiculous man." His dinner companion casually rested one hand on his bare knee as she leaned across him to speak to Xevhan. "Where did you find him?"

"His troupe of oddities performed for me last year. If you think he's ridiculous, wait until you see them."

"I hope it's soon," someone called. "Can't you make him shut up?"

Something flew through the air and struck the man on the chest. His speech stuttered to a halt. With a sickly grin, he swept his arms wide and shouted, "Behold the amazing half-men!"

Two small men raced out from behind the blue cloth and circled the torchlit performing area, waving limp-looking things that resembled clubs. They ran smack into each other and somersaulted backward, only to rise to their feet and begin exchanging blows amid the laughter of the audience.

The woman cooed delightedly. "Oh, how perfectly ugly they are. Don't you think so, Kheridh?"

He nodded politely and took a deep drink. He was as much an oddity as the poor little men, but at least he didn't have to perform to the jeers and laughter of these spoiled rich people.

The crowd fell temporarily silent while Rizhi sang, but the mood turned raucous again when Olinio announced the epic battle of the great Zherosi warrior and the Wild Man of the North.

"They're drunker than I am," Bep said, struggling with the thongs that secured the moth-eaten fleece.

Thikia glanced around the circle of performers. "Urkiat—translate for me so Reinek understands. All right, everyone. They'll laugh at us no matter what we give them, so we might as well make it a comedy. We'll cut my wise grandmother's recitation and start with the shepherdess scene. Bep, Bo—play up the sheep. Reinek, we'll need a lot of howling. Chase Bo and Bep around. Tear at their fleeces. Hakkon—wave your staff, shake your fist, smack Reinek on the arse. Rizhi . . . just look sweet, dear. Urkiat—lots of eye rolling and gestures during your opening speech. Make it a parody of the ones they're used to hearing from their heroes."

"Olinio will kill me," Urkiat muttered.

"Olinio is a professional. He'll understand. As for the battle, make it as ridiculous as you can. No sword tonight, Reinek. Urkiat—chase him around the arena, swat him with your sword, pick your nose. Anything. After you're defeated, Reinek, let's have a lot of staggering and groaning. Go right up to the pavilions. Curse the men. Wave your fur bag at the ladies. Then get back to the center of the arena and die."

"What about the speech afterward?" Urkiat asked.

"Cut it. Hakkon will bring out Rizhi and give you her hand. Bo, Bep . . . oh, you know what to do. I'll waft on

and say something about good triumphing over evil and
then we'll go right into the final song." She flashed a grin.
"Smile, everyone, smile. It may not be magic, but it's a
living."

Keirith's head ached from the wine and the smoke and the
braying laughter of the woman next to him. When the
chubby man announced some sort of a battle—dodging a
rain of kugi and grapes—he struggled into a sitting position.
Merciful Maker, let this be the end.

They had been here half the night. A few men were snoring. Those who remained awake were thoroughly drunk.
As the little blind girl stepped forward, flanked by the two
half-men in what he guessed were sheep costumes, the
woman's husband groaned. He rose on unsteady feet,
seized the hand of a startled slave girl, and pulled her into
the darkness.

His wife took this opportunity to snuggle closer. She
rested her cheek against his shoulder. Her breast brushed
his arm. Her wandering hand settled on his knee.

Keirith cast a quick glance at Xevhan but he was staring
at the blind girl, a rapt expression on his face. Everyone
else was roaring at the antics of the sheep-men. The roar
grew louder when a naked man leaped out from behind
the blue cloth and howled. Mercifully, his appearance made
the woman next to him lean forward. The Wild Man's hair
hung over his face, but no one was looking at that, least of
all his dinner companion.

"Your vision," Xevhan whispered. "Tell me."

After a quick glance at the woman, Keirith whispered,
"I feel the earth shaking. There are adders everywhere."

The crowd roared. The Wild Man had lifted his leg and
was pretending to piss on one of the sheep-men.

"Go on," Xevhan urged.

"I see Malaq. Smiling. But then the sun turns dark. A
shadow comes down."

A loud cheer made him look up again. The Wild Man
was chasing off the big shepherd. The little blind girl sank
into a graceful faint. The Wild Man strutted toward her,

shaking his fur-clad penis. A few people shouted warnings, but more cheered him on. "Give it to her," the woman cried, her face flushed with excitement.

"The shadow," Xevhan prompted.

"The shadow covers Malaq. I see feathers. Big, black feathers. And Malaq falls. I think it is Zhe who strikes him down."

Loud boos accompanied the appearance of another man, clad in a khirta and holding a sword. Clearly, the crowd was more interested in seeing the Wild Man ravish the helpless girl. The warrior made a rude gesture that turned the booing to applause. He flung his head back and flashed a triumphant grin.

"Was I there?"

Keirith just stared at the warrior. It was the man his father had brought home. The one he had fought beside. Urkiat. Good gods, what was he doing here?

"Did you see me in the vision?"

"Once."

Keirith lowered his head. It was dark under the canopy. Urkiat had the torchlight in his eyes. He would never see him. He would never even notice one person among so many.

"What was I doing?"

"You . . . you rise. Like Zhe at dawn."

He dared a look at Urkiat who was chasing the Wild Man. Disbelief turned to horror as Keirith watched them.

"Rise. You mean flying? I was flying?"

"Flying. Yes. Flying. Over Malaq."

It couldn't be. He was drunk. He was tired. He was imagining things. Many men were tall and dark-haired and powerfully built. That was not his father shaking his head and snarling. His father was at home with his mam and Callie and Faelia.

He found himself leaning forward, searching for the telltale scars on his back, craning for a glimpse of his hands, but the Wild Man moved so quickly that he couldn't be certain.

Urkiat issued his challenge. The Wild Man fell to his knees and flung up his hands in pretended terror. Even in the uncertain light of the torches, Keirith could see the stumps of the missing fingers. Just as he could see his fa-

ther's sharp profile when the Wild Man threw back his head
and howled.

Darak lunged at Urkiat, who squealed like a girl and fled,
obliging him to chase him around the perimeter of the performing area again. He stopped in front of one of the canopied shelters to catch his breath. He snatched a bunch of
grapes away from a man and ate them slowly, all the while
grinning like an idiot. A woman held out a goblet of wine
and called out something. He drained the goblet and tossed
it over his shoulder, then whirled around in pretended terror at discovering Urkiat creeping up on him. He flung the
grapes at Urkiat's face, enjoying his startled expression.

"That's for making me chase you. Twice."

Urkiat brandished his sword and bellowed something in
Zherosi that provoked enthusiastic cheers.

"Can we finish this, please?" Darak added a howl for
good measure. "I'm too old for this."

"As you wish, Wild Man."

Urkiat lowered his sword and ran right at him. Darak
sidestepped and Urkiat careened past. Darak jumped up,
jeering and pointing. Another pass, another sidestep. Urkiat hacked at him and he ducked. Then, just as they'd
planned, he dove for Urkiat's legs. He knocked him on his
arse and they rolled over a few times. Both of them were
spitting sand by the time Urkiat shoved him away. Darak
fell onto his back.

"I give up."

"About time."

With a hideous cry, Urkiat raised his sword and drove it
into the sand near his armpit. Darak screamed and writhed
as Urkiat twisted the blade back and forth. Finally, Urkiat
straightened to tumultuous applause.

Coughing and clutching his side, Darak staggered to his
feet. He lurched toward the nearest shelter and was greeted
by a number of feminine squeals. He bared his teeth at the
men and winked at an older woman who winked back.
Then it was off to the next shelter for more of the same.

The smoke from the torches made his eyes water and
the light was too blinding to see the faces of the people

under the canopy. But Olinio had said the Zheron was
seated near the middle of this one and had begged him to
pass close. Fine. He'd give the priest a quick snarl, a nice
growl. After that, he was going to die.

He fell to his knees, peering at the occupants, but his
eyes were too dazzled by the torchlight to see more than
shadowy forms. He gave a genuine groan as he got up
again. Hoping for the best, he stumbled into the shelter.

He went down on all fours. He snarled. He lowered his
head and growled. And then he looked up into his son's
eyes.

He couldn't move. He couldn't think. All he could do was
stare back at his father. Already, the squeals and laughter
and exclamations were giving way to surprised muttering.
He could feel Xevhan's eyes on him. He had to do something, say something before he put his father in danger.

"What's the matter with him?" the woman demanded.
"Go away, you nasty beast."

Her words brought Keirith out of his daze. "Go away,"
he repeated. He seized the cushion he was sitting on and
hit his father in the face with it. "Go away, Wild Man.
Go away."

His father fell back on his haunches, his face terrible.
Others took up the cry. Cushions struck his father on the
head, the chest. The woman tossed the contents of her goblet at him, giggling as the dregs dripped down his cheeks.
In a moment, kugi and flatbread were flying toward him.

"Get away!" Keirith screamed in the tribal tongue.

Mercifully, Urkiat appeared at that moment. His face
went blank with shock and then he seized his father's arm.
The crowd cheered as he dragged him back to the center
of the arena. His father lay there, chest heaving, while the
old woman launched into a speech.

"That was odd," Xevhan said.

"Yes. Very scaring."

"It was almost as if he knew you."

Think, Keirith, think.

"He is a tree lover. Like me. But why is he here?"

"I was hoping you might tell me."

"Well, he certainly acted strange enough," the woman interjected. "And those awful hands. Did you see them, Xevhan? Like some animal had gnawed off his fingers."

"What did you say to him?" Xevhan asked.

"What?"

"At the end. You screamed something at him."

"I say, 'Go away.' He maybe does not understand Zherosi, so I speak in my tongue."

"Very clever."

"Look, Xevhan. It's your little blind girl. I saw you ogling her before, you wicked man. She is a pretty child. If only someone would dress her decently."

Xevhan's gaze slid briefly to the performing area. "A dull ending to the battle."

"Yes. Not good. Not good at all." He was talking too fast, acting too strange. Xevhan would never believe he was simply unnerved by the Wild Man. "One man with sword. Another like wolf. It is no fight at all."

Stop babbling, Keirith. Have a drink of wine. Talk to the woman. Anything.

His father was still lying on the ground while the other performers danced around him, singing.

Why isn't he getting up? Did the shock of seeing me kill him?

"You're right," Xevhan said.

Jolted out of his thoughts, he could only stammer, "Excuse me, please?"

"It wasn't much of a fight at all."

Xevhan's chilling little smile sent a wave of nausea through him. Before he could speak, Xevhan rose and strode out of the pavilion. The chubby man darted forward, bowing and babbling something, but at Xevhan's glance, his voice trailed off.

"Friends, I hope you have enjoyed tonight's entertainment." Xevhan held up his hands, forestalling the applause. "Young Kheridh thinks the fight would have been better if the Wild Man had wielded a sword against his opponent. I know it's late, but what do you say to a real battle? The Wild Man of the North against the great Zherosi warrior. This time with real swords instead of wooden ones."

The crowd screamed its approval.

Chapter 33

URKIAT WAS ARGUING with Olinio, but like the frenzied shouting of the guests, their voices seemed to come from a great distance.

Keirith is alive.

Keirith is safe.

Keirith thinks the fight would be better with swords.

Darak had been too shocked at seeing Keirith to move, to speak. After Urkiat dragged him away, he'd recovered enough to feel relief that his son had acted so quickly, pride that he had averted suspicion by pretending to attack him. Then Urkiat translated the Zheron's speech, and relief and pride leached away.

Keirith, drinking and feasting with the Zherosi. Keirith, screaming at him to go away. Keirith, suggesting a fight with real swords. Nay, that was the Zheron's doing. It had to be. He didn't know what Keirith was doing here, but his son would not betray him.

Darak felt oddly calm, as if this were all a dream and he would wake and find Griane lying next to him, Faelia grumbling about getting up so early, Keirith shaking Callie awake. But of course, it wasn't a dream. It was all happening.

Keirith had risen to the challenge. So must he.

He sat up, smelling the salt from the sea and the smoke from the guttering torches. He got to his feet, staring at the eastern sky, just beginning to lighten with the promise of a new day. And then he walked toward Urkiat.

"It's all right."

"What? Darak, do you understand what's happening? They want us to fight."

"I understand."

"Well, I won't do it! No matter what the Zheron threatens. Good gods, you can barely stand."

"I'm fine."

"You can't—forgive me, but you can't even grip a sword properly."

Darak frowned at his hand. "Lash the hilt to my wrist."

"It won't—"

"Let's get this over with before their mood turns even uglier."

Two of the guests supplied the swords. They were lovely weapons. Fine balance. Not much heavier than the wooden ones they were used to. And the same length as well, about as long as his forearm. The edges were wickedly keen, though. He gripped the hilt, thumb and little fingers falling naturally into the shallow depressions in the leather made by its owner. With the sword lashed to his hand, he should manage well enough. He was more worried about his legs, which were shaking from exhaustion.

Thikia supplied a thin strip of rawhide. When Urkiat fumbled with it, Bep shoved him aside. "I'll do it. Your hands are trembling like a virgin's on her wedding night."

Olinio kept up a steady stream of instructions about thrusts and parries until Darak told him to be quiet. Bep's advice was more practical.

"Hakkon and Bo are trying to sweep the performing area so it'll be more even, but steer clear of the backdrop. The sand's churned up there and we don't have time to do anything about it. Go easy. Get the feel of the swords. But you'll have to land some genuine blows or the crowd'll get nasty. Urkiat? Are you listening?"

Urkiat nodded. He looked like he might vomit.

"You'll be fine," Darak told him. "It'll be just like we practiced."

The drum pounded an imperious beat. Darak looked around the circle of anxious faces. "Smile, everyone, smile. It may not be magic, but it's a living."

When Bep translated, wan smiles blossomed on all faces except Urkiat's. He just hefted his sword and whispered a prayer.

Keirith's hands clenched into fists as they circled each
other. Even in a performance, feet could stumble, an arm
could come up too slowly to block a thrust. Even in a
performance, blood could be shed.

His father looked relaxed and alert, balancing on the
balls of his feet like a dancer. Keirith remembered standing with his mam, watching him walk through the village.
Her face had lightened with one of her rare smiles.
"Look at the man. Loose-limbed and graceful as a wolf
on the prowl." And then she'd scowled and smacked him
lightly on the head and asked him what was he thinking,
idling around the house when there were chores to be
done?

His father lunged with a swiftness that made Keirith
catch his breath. When Urkiat feinted, he clamped his lips
together to prevent another telltale reaction.

The crowd was restless. A scatter of boos and catcalls
came from the pavilions as they went back to their circling.
His father's lips moved. Urkiat nodded.

Another lunge. Urkiat caught the blow and threw it off
with a screech of metal. Then he attacked. His blow
knocked the sword out of his father's grasp, but the leather
thongs kept him from dropping it. The crowd screamed at
Urkiat to move in, but he ignored them.

His father hefted the sword with both hands and charged.
Urkiat rolled beneath the blade and landed in a crouch.
His father paused to shake his hair out of his eyes and
nearly missed a low lunge toward his thigh. He stopped it
close and flung Urkiat's sword back.

Urkiat staggered, thrown off balance. Feral shouts of
"Take him! Gut him!" rang out. Urkiat ducked under his
father's blade, which sliced the air with a great whoosh.
The movement spun him past Urkiat, his blade following
his body in a sweeping circle that barely missed ripping
open Urkiat's belly. And then they were both moving so
quickly Keirith could scarcely follow them as they whirled
and sidestepped and slashed at each other.

They broke apart. His father was breathing in open-
mouthed pants, the wolf's grace abandoned for flat-footed

plodding. Urkiat circled, giving him a chance to recover. He finally darted in and his father spun away. The crowd screamed when they saw the trickle of blood oozing down his left arm, screamed louder when Urkiat lowered his blade.

"It's a scratch," his father shouted. "Come on!"

Urkiat's charge drove him across the arena. Even with both hands gripping the hilt, each blow beat his sword lower. His arms were losing their strength. His legs were wobbling, his feet clumsy in the loose sand. He warded off a downward thrust, but the tip of the sword opened a new cut on his shoulder.

Urkiat sidestepped a clumsy blow and deliberately turned his back. He strutted away, punching the air with his sword, shouting taunts in Zherosi. It was pure showmanship and the crowd loved it. And it gave his father a few precious moments to recover.

He advanced on Urkiat who spun around at the last moment and blocked the blow. Thrust. Parry. Lunge. Retreat. He could hear his father's hoarse pants. He was winded, his strength gone. Why didn't Urkiat stop? Why did he keep pressing him?

His nails dug into his palms. And then his father went down and Keirith bit his lip to stifle a cry.

His father scuttled backward, right arm raised to fend off Urkiat's slow, deliberate blows. He kept trying to find a foothold in the loose sand, but instead of rising into a crouch, he ended up on his knees. Urkiat advanced, the tip of his sword pointed at his father's throat.

Xevhan would end the fight now. He had to.

The crowd was shouting, men and women alike on their feet, shaking their fists, screaming for blood. Screaming for his father's death.

"Your lip is bleeding, Kheridh."

He didn't trust himself to look at Xevhan. He picked up a napkin, dabbed at his lip, and tossed it aside before Xevhan could notice his shaking hands.

"What do you think? Should I let him kill the Wild Man?"

"He is brave. He fights well. Why kill him?"

Xevhan gestured to the screaming men and women. "It seems my guests demand it."

Urkiat wouldn't kill his father, no matter what Xevhan ordered. But if he refused, Xevhan could have them both killed. The crowd didn't care as long as blood was shed.

"Great Zheron. They are tree lovers. Like me. I ask this. As a greatest of favors. Stop the fight now."

"Dear Kheridh. I would so like to oblige you. But I fear my first obligation is to my guests."

Slowly, Xevhan rose and walked into the arena.

Keirith heard Hircha's voice, whispering in his ear. "There's nothing you can do. Except help me kill Xevhan when this is over."

Killing Xevhan later wouldn't save his father. Was he strong enough to cast out his spirit now? If Xevhan had taken qiij, he would be able to shield himself. He didn't seem drugged. Gods, why hadn't he observed him more closely before he got up? Why hadn't he watched him all night? Watch. Observe. Remember. That's what he was supposed to do.

If he guessed wrong, his father would die.

Gods, forgive me.

Keirith closed his eyes and summoned his power.

"The Zheron's coming out," Urkiat said. "What do you want me to do?"

"Finish it now. Before he gets in the way."

Urkiat nodded. Darak tightened his grip on the sword. They'd practiced the move a dozen times. More. Olinio called it breathtaking. It had better be. Otherwise, this bloodthirsty crowd would have both their heads.

He took a deep breath, signaling his readiness, and lunged upwards, his sword driving toward Urkiat's heart. But instead of spinning away, Urkiat remained motionless.

Darak had only a heartbeat to glance up and see his frozen look of abstraction. He screamed Urkiat's name, hoping to shock him into action, but even as he did, he knew it was too late to stop his body's momentum, too late to avert the thrust.

The sword drove up and under his breastbone. Urkiat's sword fell from his nerveless fingers. Darak flung out an arm to catch him, the weight of Urkiat's body dragging them both to the ground. His right hand, bound to the sword, was useless. All he could do was cradle Urkiat in his left arm while the blood gushed out of his chest. In Urkiat's eyes, he saw the reflection of his own shock and disbelief. And all he could say was, "Gods, man. Gods. What happened?"

Urkiat's mouth opened as if he might speak, as if he could explain what had gone so horribly wrong. Then his back arched in an agonized spasm and his heels dug into the sand. Darak tightened his grip, his breath coming in the same deep, ragged gasps as Urkiat's. He buried his face in Urkiat's damp hair, then jerked his head up again.

Let him have the face of a friend before him. Let that be the last thing he sees.

He hoped Urkiat would want that. He hoped his face would give him comfort instead of reminding him that it was his friend—the man he trusted and respected as a father—who had killed him.

"I'm with you, lad. I'm right here."

The world narrowed to the man in his arms, to the struggling body and the staring eyes, to the feel of bone and flesh under his arm, to the warmth of blood soaking his hand. It was so quiet. As if the world were dying with Urkiat. No birds sang. No men shouted. His mind was screaming, "Why did this happen?" but his voice continued its ceaseless murmur, offering words of comfort, of friendship, of love.

The dark blue eyes were glazing. The struggle was nearly over.

"Go easy, lad. I'll be with you. Always. To the Forever Isles and beyond."

Urkiat's chest rose and fell. Rose again. Slowly sank as the breath left him. Moments passed. Darak's heart thudded, a painful testament to life. Urkiat's chest rose once more. His eyes darkened. His head lolled. And he was gone.

Through the receding haze, Keirith heard a clear, high voice singing. He lifted his head. No one seemed to have noticed him slumping across the cushions. They were too enthralled by the spectacle in the arena.

It was the blind girl, her sorrowful face tilted skyward. He was too exhausted to try and make out the words, but the slow, mournful melody made it plain enough that it was a lament. To Keirith's amazement, some of the Zherosi joined her. A moment ago, they had been screaming for death and now they mourned it. Who could understand them? Who would ever want to?

He pushed himself into a sitting position. One of the little men was kneeling beside his father. As he reached for the thongs binding the sword, his father's head came up, his mouth twisted in a snarl. Then he saw who it was and allowed the little man to free his hand.

His father tried to ease the sword from Urkiat's chest, but in the end, he had to wrench it free. He flung the sword away and pulled Urkiat closer, rocking him like a babe. And then his head came up again. He seemed to be listening to the lament. The little man bent closer, questioning him, but his father just kept shaking his head.

"Not one of their songs!"

His chest heaved. He shook the hair out of his face. And then he closed his eyes and sang.

> *The sun hides his shining face*
> *And the moon shrouds herself in darkness.*
> *The winds scream upon the hilltops*
> *And the waters of the rivers swell with tears.*

One by one, the Zherosi fell silent, until there was only his father's halting voice, choking on the tears that coursed down his face.

> *The branches of the trees echo my moans*
> *And the earth falls away beneath my feet.*
> *The clouds cast shadows upon my face*
> *And the bitterness of winter fills my spirit.*

His voice broke. The little man took up the lament in a voice rough as sand.

> *I seek but cannot find you.*
> *I call but receive no answer.*

Oh, beloved, beloved.
Would I had died for you.

His father's voice fell to a whisper on the last words. He closed Urkiat's eyes. Brushed a damp strand of hair off his forehead. Bent to kiss him softly on the mouth.

As Xevhan started toward his father, Keirith struggled to rise. He swayed and nearly fell; the magic had taken the last remnants of his strength. He staggered past Xevhan and faced the silent crowd.

"It is time to go." His voice was little more than a whisper. He repeated the words again, raising his voice so that everyone could hear. "No more killing. Please."

The little man clutched his father's arm, whispering urgently. Xevhan must have seen death in his father's eyes, for he backed away, beckoning the chubby man. "Come to my chamber at midmorning for your payment. Bring the blind girl."

He strode toward his litter, shouting at the bearers to hurry. For of course, it was nearly dawn. And time for another sacrifice.

His father's gaze followed Xevhan. The little man grabbed his face, forcing him to look at him. The performers drew closer. The one who had played the shepherd held his staff at the ready, but he didn't need it. As Keirith watched, the tension drained out of his father's body.

"I'm sorry," Keirith whispered.

His father looked up at him, his eyes dull. "You didn't kill him."

Only because I wasn't strong enough to cast out his spirit. I just distracted him—and left you to kill your friend.

"You can't stay here," Keirith said. "It's too dangerous."

His father's expression hardened. "I haven't gotten what I came for."

"Please . . ."

Someone was tugging at his arm. Hircha, her face even harder than his father's. "Leave. Now. Before you condemn them all. And you should leave, too, Wild Man. Whatever you came for, it's not worth another death."

The little man stepped in front of his father. One by one, the other performers closed ranks, forming a circle around his father and Urkiat. Y*ou are not one of us,* their actions said. *You don't belong. We don't want you here.*

Keirith let Hircha lead him to a litter. He let her help him inside. And when she crawled in next to him, he didn't even shrink away.

"The Wild Man. He's Darak Spirit-Hunter. I may have been a child when I was stolen, but I know the tale. How many men possess such hands? And such scars?"

Keirith closed his eyes.

"And he's your father. Isn't he?"

In Hircha's voice, he heard sympathy and understanding. But the voice in his head drowned hers out. His voice, fervently proclaiming his good intentions when he touched an animal's spirit. The words mocked him now: *"I don't hurt them. I would never hurt them. I'm not like Morgath."*

But he was. He was Keirith the False. Keirith the Destroyer. Keirith the Eater of Spirits.

Chapter 34

EXHAUSTION ALLOWED MALAQ to sleep. When he rose before dawn and learned that Kheridh had not returned, he chided himself for his anxiety. Xevhan's entertainments could last all night; there was no cause for alarm. Then he returned from the sacrifice and found Kheridh waiting for him.

He had seen men staring up at the dagger that would cut out their hearts, women sitting beside the rubble of their homes. Kheridh's face had that same dazed look. Malaq took his hand and led him to a bench in the garden. That Kheridh should permit the touch frightened him even more than his expression.

It took all Malaq's control to remain silent while Kheridh told him what had happened. That the Spirit-Hunter should be in Pilozhat, that this man—of all men—should be Kheridh's father, and most stunning of all, that Kheridh should trust him enough to reveal it. . . . The revelations made it hard for him to focus on the rest of the story. And yet, it made sense; only an exceptional man could have fathered such an extraordinary son. But extraordinary or not, Kheridh was still a fourteen-year-old boy who, in one night, had discovered his father had come after him, had watched helplessly while his father was injured, and had used his power to lead a man to his death.

When he finished, Malaq asked, "Does Xevhan know?"

"He suspects . . . something. Hircha knows."

"You told her?"

"Nay. She guessed."

"Do you look so much alike?"

"I don't know. I never thought so." For the first time, Kheridh looked at him. "Will you help him?"

Malaq's mind was working furiously. Xevhan would go to the queen with his suspicions. At best, the Spirit-Hunter would be held for questioning. If they tortured him, he would talk. All men talked sooner or later.

Too anxious to sit, he rose and paced. He would have to act quickly. Get the Spirit-Hunter out of the city. And the players; some of them might know his true identity. Then it would only be Kheridh's word against Xevhan's.

"Please."

He turned to find Kheridh on his knees.

"I'll do anything you ask. Teach you everything I know. I . . . I will stay here. As long as you want me. Only please. Don't let them kill him."

And there it was. Everything he had ever wanted: Kheridh's trust, his cooperation, and—if he agreed to help—his gratitude. Gratitude that might be transformed to love in the course of time. All for doing what he was planning already: to get his father away from him.

Very gently, he pulled Kheridh to his feet. "Of course I will help."

Darak cleaned Urkiat's body himself, but the others helped carry him to the cart and carve a shallow hole in the hard earth. Even Olinio gathered stones for the cairn. They buried him on a small rise that was sheltered on three sides by steep hills. Although the mountain was visible, the city was not; at least Urkiat would not lie within the shadow of Pilozhat.

When he laid the last rock on the cairn, they all looked at him expectantly. He chanted the death-song for Urkiat. He repeated the words from the rite of Opening, although only a shaman could free a spirit to fly to the Forever Isles. He prayed that Urkiat's would find its way there. Spirits severed abruptly from their bodies became lost. Like Tinnean and the Oak-Lord, they drifted into Chaos. Perhaps in those last moments, Urkiat had understood what was happening. Perhaps the Maker had guided his spirit. But he would never know until he walked onto the shores of the Forever Isles himself.

After the burial, he removed his tunic and breeches and, for the second time that morning, plunged into the sea. The first time, he had rinsed Urkiat's blood off his body, unwilling to conduct his final rites covered in gore. Now, he sought to cleanse his spirit. But he knew he would always carry the stain of this death and the guilt of causing it.

Again and again, he went over his actions. Had he moved too suddenly? Had he failed to give Urkiat sufficient time to prepare? Always, it came back to the same thing: Urkiat had simply stood there as if bespelled. His face had a faraway expression, as if he were looking into other worlds, hearing voices no one else could discern. But Urkiat was no shaman. He was just a young man carrying the burden of too many deaths, seeking retribution and forgiveness. These last days, he'd seemed easier in his mind, happy even, shedding a little of the guilt and darkness that shadowed his spirit to caper like a child during their performances or tease him about his ridiculous fur bag.

"Oh, gods."

Naked, Darak sat on the sand. At least Urkiat's bones would lie near the sea. And his spirit—please, gods—would live on in the Forever Isles. He hoped there was good fishing there and a sleek currach to carry him over the waves.

He heard a grunt as Bep sat beside him. For a long while, neither of them spoke. Finally, Bep said, "That was your boy."

Darak nodded.

"What will you do?"

"I don't know."

His plans had involved freeing Keirith. He hadn't expected him to be an honored guest of the people who kidnapped him.

"He might come to you. If they let him."

"Aye."

"I could sniff around the palace."

Darak looked up. "You're going there?"

"Olinio's taking Rizhi. To perform for the Zheron." Bep spat.

"Alone?"

"Not if I can help it. I wouldn't trust a dog alone with that man."

"And after?"

"Olinio's agreed to leave the city. After what happened, he thinks we should make ourselves scarce." Bep shifted awkwardly. "It's probably best . . ."

"If I don't come with you? I wasn't planning to."

"No offense. You'd put us in danger. And if you stay, you'll put your boy in danger, too. He seems well enough. Don't start bristling, you know what I mean. For whatever reason, the Zheron has taken him under his wing. Else he'd be with the rest of the slaves."

"Are you suggesting I leave him here?"

"I'm suggesting you watch your step. You stand out in a crowd, Darak. And you don't have the language. How will you manage without . . . on your own?"

"I don't know."

"Well, think about it."

"I just buried my friend. I haven't slept. Can't I just—"

"You've got the rest of your life to mourn Urkiat. And to sleep. If you're not careful, the rest of your life could be awful short."

The brief flare of anger died.

"Do you want my advice?" Bep asked.

"Do I have a choice?"

"Nay. First, put on your clothes."

He rose, obedient as a child, and slapped the sand off his body. He pulled on his tunic and breeches, but when he started to lace his shoes, his hands shook so badly that Bep had to tie them. He stared at his hands, bemused. They had cleaned the blood off Urkiat, carried him to the cart, dug out a grave, and piled stones above it. Throughout it all, they had been utterly steady.

"Get your share of the money from Olinio now. While he's feeling guilty. Trust me, that won't last. Then find a place to hide. Maybe where we camped last night. You'll be harder to find in a crowd than if you're alone."

Darak gazed down the beach. "There's only one flaw in that plan."

"What?"

He nodded at the men marching toward them. "Seems they've already found me."

Chapter 35

MALAQ WAVED THE SLAVES away and surveyed his chamber critically. Satisfied, he placed the small clay disk on the table and wiped the few specks of red dust off his hands with a napkin. The other two disks remained in his bedchamber; he hoped he would not need them.

When he'd asked for the safe conducts, Vazh had inundated him with questions.

"Don't ask why. Just do this for me. For friendship's sake."

It was the first time in his life he had ever seen fear on Vazh's face.

Perhaps there was no need for fear. But twice, Malaq had gone to the queen's chamber, requesting permission to speak with her, and twice, he had been turned away. She was still recovering from The Shedding. She had a tiring reception this afternoon and the formal banquet this evening. Likely, she was saving her strength. Likely, she was seeing no one. But no matter how many explanations he found, the anxiety remained: what if Xevhan had already given her his version of the events?

He'd been disturbed to learn that the leader of the players would be meeting with Xevhan. In the end, though, he decided it was better to let him keep his appointment. The blind girl would sing. Xevhan would drool over her. And the revolting Olinio would add Xevhan's payment for last night's performance to the fat purse of serpents Malaq had given him to speed him on his way.

Barely midday and he was already weary. And he would need all his energy and concentration for this meeting.

When the guard respectfully requested permission to enter, he took a deep breath. The players were taken care of. Now, he must ensure that Kheridh's father left Pilozhat.

"Enter."

Darak Spirit-Hunter strode through the doorway. His astonishing pale gaze flicked over him in brief assessment before surveying the room. Searching for Kheridh or examining his escape routes? Both, probably. And looking for Xevhan whom he clearly had expected to find.

Malaq was relieved to discover that Kheridh had gotten his coloring from his mother. Still, a perceptive observer would notice the similarities: the slanting cheekbones, the knife-edged nose, the square chin. The height, too, although Kheridh had yet to fill out his gawky frame. When he did, he would be as imposing as the man before him. If he lived that long.

The guards gripped the Spirit-Hunter's broad shoulders. He made no sound as his knees hit the floor, but the frown deepened.

"Enough. Wait outside."

The guards bowed and backed out of the chamber.

"Please. Rise."

If the Spirit-Hunter was surprised by the tribal tongue, he gave no indication. He rose with easy grace, although he must be close to forty summers. Gods, the man was a giant. He kept his hands lightly clasped in front of him. Did he always hide his maimed hands from strangers or did he fear his identity had been discovered?

Malaq kept his face impassive, but excitement made his heart beat faster. Darak Spirit-Hunter. How much of the tale was true? How much the usual exaggeration of the storytellers?

"Please." Malaq gestured to the table. "Let us sit."

After they were seated, he clapped his hands once. The Spirit-Hunter tensed, then relaxed as the slaves filed in. Malaq had deliberately ordered a lavish meal. Let him see how a priest lives in Pilozhat. Let him note the opulence of the surroundings, the plethora of food. Let him realize that his son had been living like this, not as a prisoner or a slave. And let him wonder how easily a boy—abandoned by his own people—might be seduced by such splendor.

Try as he might to look disinterested, the Spirit-Hunter studied each platter they laid on the table, taking in the roasted squab, the mussels swimming in oil and spices, the steaming slabs of bread, the bowls of jhok and avhash. Expressionless, he examined the thick napkins, the pottery plates painted with brilliant spirals of green and gold.

"I thought you might be hungry," Malaq said with a deprecating shrug.

"I am."

The voice was as he'd imagined, deep and resonant, but the admission surprised him. He would have expected the man to deny it, to proudly refuse any food offered by his enemy. Instead, he tore off a piece of bread.

"Try the jhok," Malaq said, nodding toward the bowl. "It tastes better than it looks."

"I know."

"Would you care for wine?"

"Water, please. If you have it. I'd like to keep a clear head."

He was obviously exhausted, but there was keen awareness in the bloodshot eyes and even dry humor in the voice.

Malaq poured the water into a cup rather than a long-stemmed goblet. The Spirit-Hunter took it between both hands and drained it in a few thirsty gulps. Malaq refilled his cup and set the pitcher down. "If it's all the same to you, I prefer not to test your patience—or mine—by prolonging this exchange of pleasantries."

He actually smiled. "I would prefer that as—" He broke off, his expression suddenly wary. "Is it possible that . . . a wildcat could have gotten in here?"

Malaq laughed and swiveled around. "Yes. But she's quite tame." He sliced off a strip of squab and held it out. Niqia pulled it daintily from his fingers and dropped it onto the floor.

The Spirit-Hunter half-rose from his place, leaning on the table to watch her.

Dear gods.

He'd seen the same boyish wonder on Kheridh's face

when they studied magic together, the same delighted smile when they were successful.

"She's small for a wildcat."

Still dazed from the revelation, Malaq struggled to gather his thoughts. "You mean you've seen one? In the wild?"

"Only once. And only for a moment."

"Niqia is a mixed breed. Very beautiful, but—" Failing to receive another treat, Niqia leaped onto the table, prepared to help herself. Malaq pulled the platter away. "But very spoiled."

"Or hungry."

The Spirit-Hunter reached for the knife resting on the platter of squab. Malaq tensed. The maimed hand hovered above the knife. The smile vanished. The pale eyes met his. "I'm not that foolish."

He was surprisingly deft with the knife; remember that, Malaq cautioned himself. After he sliced off a sliver of meat, he grasped it between his thumb and little fingers and held it out. Niqia picked her way through the platters, ostentatiously ignoring the outstretched fingers, then stalked back. Malaq watched the interplay of the two hunters, the one patient, the other wary. Finally, Niqia deigned to accept his offering. The Spirit-Hunter let his upturned hand rest on the table. When Niqia was finished, she sniffed his fingers cautiously and proceeded to lick them.

"She's taken a liking to you. She's fond of Kheridh as well."

The fingers twitched once and went still. Malaq scooped up Niqia and deposited her on the floor, deliberately prolonging the moment. "That's what we call your son. You, I believe, are called Spirit-Hunter by some, although your tribal title is Memory-Keeper. You came to Pilozhat in search of Kheridh. Last night, you found him."

Other than the muscle twitching in his jaw, his face remained impassive. "You know a lot about me. May I ask who you are?"

"Forgive me. I am Malaq, the Pajhit—priest—of Heart of Sky. Kheridh has been under my protection since he arrived here. This morning, after—"

"Why?"

"I beg your pardon?"

"Why is he under your protection?"

"Because of his gift."

"His gift?"

Malaq pushed his wine goblet aside and leaned forward. "There is a prophecy among our people. That a boy will come to us. A boy with hair the color of the setting sun and the gift of speaking with our sacred adders. And he will lead our people into a new age. For generations, we have awaited the coming of the Son of Zhe."

The Spirit-Hunter's features relaxed. "You think Keirith is the son of your god?"

"No. Any doubts I might have had on that subject vanished when I saw you."

The frown returned. Was he unaware of the resemblance? Or was he worried that others might notice it as well?

"Perhaps I see what others do not. But your behavior— and his—during the Zheron's entertainment aroused . . . speculation. I can protect Kheridh. But I cannot protect you. You must leave Pilozhat today."

"Not without Keirith."

He put the slightest emphasis on his son's name. Malaq made a mental note to use his Zherosi name more frequently.

"You have come many miles to rescue Kheridh. And if he were in danger, I would send him away with you. Believe it or not, I want what is best for him."

"You have no idea what's best for Keirith."

"And you do?"

"Aye. He belongs at home. With his people."

"The same people who regard him as an abomination?"

Did the fingers tighten on the cup or was that wishful thinking?

"What future does Kheridh have in your village? At worst, he will be sacrificed for using his gift. At best, he will have to hide it the rest of his life."

"He'll learn to control it."

"And who will teach him that? You? Forgive me, but you don't understand it. Your Tree-Father? He was the first to compare Kheridh to the shaman who mutilated you."

"You know nothing about . . ."

In a quiet voice, Malaq finished the sentence. "Morgath."

"I know his name." The Spirit-Hunter had banished the

savage edge from his voice, but for the first time, the effort at control showed.

"And I know this man also possessed an extraordinary ability to touch the spirits of others. That he used his power for evil. With my help, Kheridh will learn to understand his gift, to use it wisely. Here it will be revered. In your village . . ." Malaq shrugged. "He has some ability to shield himself from other spirits, but how long do you think it would be before he's provoked? Or succumbs to temptation? A wounded creature, screaming in pain. An eagle, begging him to fly once more. A tribe mate, threatening him or his family. Kheridh *will* use the gift, Memory-Keeper. Just as—in a moment of fear and anger—he used it against you."

That shook him. It had shaken Malaq when Kheridh revealed it to him earlier while they formulated their strategy for this meeting.

"I may not understand this power," the Spirit-Hunter said, "but I know my son. He would never choose to live among the murderers of his people."

"Our land is as harsh as our gods. To ensure its fertility, we offer the ultimate gift of human life."

"And what about the thousands of our people who weren't offered up as sacrifices but slaughtered by your raiders or carried off into slavery?"

Malaq adjusted the folds of his napkin. "These are difficult times in Zheros. Pestilence has decimated the ranks of our workers—"

"Slaves."

"—and drought has destroyed our crops. We require wood for our ships, land to feed our people. Your forests are rich, your soil fertile. In the past, we have offered . . . accommodations."

"What? To sell our children? To destroy the trees who are our brothers?"

"Some of your southern tribes accepted this compromise."

"And those that didn't were slaughtered."

Malaq sighed, appreciating the irony of championing a policy he had always despised. "We will never agree on religion. Or on politics."

"Or what's best for my son." A grim smile twisted his

mouth. "Did you really think you could convince me that Keirith would be better off here? That I would agree that he should turn his back on his people, his beliefs, his gods? Would any father agree to such a choice?"

"You love Kherith. I understand that. He's the kind of boy . . ." Malaq hesitated. "Kheridh has a gift for inspiring love."

Idly, he allowed his fingers to caress the stem of the goblet. Up and down. Up and down. From under his lowered lashes, he watched the Spirit-Hunter. Only his eyes moved, flicking from the fingers stroking the goblet to the knife lying on the platter and finally to his face.

This is the last thing Morgath must have seen—those cold gray eyes boring into his.

"Choose your weapons more carefully, priest. If I thought you were bedding my son, I'd kill you, but I wouldn't abandon him."

"That was unpardonably crude. And a lie. Forgive me."

"So your taste runs to girls?"

"My tastes are none of your concern," Malaq snapped. He took a deep breath, annoyed that he had allowed the Spirit-Hunter to provoke him. "For a man of my position to take Kheridh as a lover would be an unforgivable abuse of power."

"Which you would never stoop to."

Malaq answered the heavy sarcasm with a short laugh. "Are you really so narrow-minded that you see yourself as the personification of all things good and decent while I—perforce—am the opposite? That you are absolutely right about absolutely everything? For a man who has witnessed miracles and spoken with gods, your arrogance is not only astonishing but dangerous. The world—and the people in it—are a bit more complex than that, Memory-Keeper." He shook his head. "I pity your son. And I finally begin to understand the burden he faced growing up with such a father."

The Spirit-Hunter pushed himself to his feet. "We have nothing more to say to each other."

"One thing only. You claim to know your son's mind. You're certain he would never choose to remain here. Shall we ask him? Shall we allow Kheridh to choose his path freely and without coercion?"

"Freely? When he knows you need only clap your hands to have me killed?"

"I am not your enemy!"

"You have my son. I want him back. That makes you my enemy."

"Yes, I want Kheridh to remain. But if I kept him against his will or used you to ensure his cooperation, I would lose him more surely than if I sent him away. I can offer no proof of my sincerity . . . except to say that I do understand how you would feel to lose him."

"Only a father could understand that."

"Yes."

His eyes widened. Malaq couldn't bring himself to say more, not even to win the man's support. "Would you sit, please?"

He sat, surprise changing to wariness.

Malaq pushed forward the clay disk. "This will provide you safe passage through our lands. It's marked with my seal."

The Spirit-Hunter barely glanced at it. "You know I can't read what's written on it."

"Actually, you can. So can any illiterate guard who might stop you. The disk has a simple picture—a man missing two fingers of each hand."

The narrowed eyes flicked from the disk to his face.

"And yes, this might be a trap. The disk might direct a guard to execute you on the spot. But it doesn't. If Kheridh chooses to go with you, I'll provide another safe conduct for him. I give you my oath—on the gods that I worship—that you may both leave Pilozhat with no fear of pursuit or retribution."

"Not on your gods. Swear on your son's life."

Malaq's breath caught. Rage blinded him. But, of course, it was the clever move. He should have anticipated it.

"My son is dead." His voice sounded foreign to him, thick and clogged as if he were choking. "Shall I swear on his spirit's hope for rebirth?"

Their gazes locked. Finally, the Spirit-Hunter said, "Nay. I accept your oath."

Damn you for your gentle voice and your understanding eyes. And damn me for allowing you to see my pain.

"Your wife—she was a child of the Oak and Holly, wasn't she?"

Even Vazh never called her that. Just "his woman."

"That's why you speak our tongue so well. And know the legends."

He would not give the man the satisfaction of nodding.

"I'm sorry for your loss. And for reminding you of it."

"I don't want your sympathy." Despising his weak, pathetic voice, Malaq cleared his throat. "I want you to leave Pilozhat."

"On that, we both agree."

"Even if it means losing Kheridh, I am willing to let him choose his own path. Are you willing to risk the same?"

Another endless pause before the Spirit-Hunter gave a short nod.

Malaq rose and walked to the doorway to instruct the guards. After they left, he turned back. "You and I will not meet again. Would you permit me to ask you something?"

This time, the nod was cautious.

"Did you really speak with your Trickster-God?"

The Spirit-Hunter hesitated, considering the implications of his answer. In the silence, Malaq said, "I've been a priest for fifteen years. The gods have never shown themselves to me. It would be a relief to know they actually exist."

That they hear the prayers of men, even if they don't always answer them. That my life has not been dedicated to a lie.

"Even if the gods aren't yours?"

"If your gods exist, mine must as well. Who knows? Perhaps all gods are the same. Perhaps they merely show different faces to those who worship them."

"They exist."

Strange, the comfort those two words gave him. "And did you travel to Chaos?"

"Aye."

"And witness the . . . transformation of your brother?"

This time, the Spirit-Hunter only nodded.

"Thank you." Malaq offered the deep bow only bestowed upon equals. "When you and Kheridh have finished speaking, the guards will escort you out of the palace. The road to Oexiak leads west."

"I know it."

"Then fare you well, Memory-Keeper. May your path be
smooth, your journey swift, and your homecoming joyous."

"I . . . thank you."

He frowned. Malaq wondered if he had offended him by
offering the Tree People's traditional blessing for travelers,
but that didn't account for the odd hesitancy.

"If it makes any difference . . . I don't think I'm absolutely right. About anything. I just . . ." He looked away.
"He's my son."

"Yes. You are a fortunate man."

Weary beyond words, Malaq walked away. If the gods
could hear a man's prayers, perhaps his son could, too.
After all, the man before him was proof that miracles
could happen.

The priest disappeared down the narrow hallway at the far
end of the room. Darak watched him go, still stunned by
the knowledge that the man had been married to a woman
from the tribes. He tried to shake off the questions that
filled his mind and the disbelief that a man who knew their
culture so well could countenance its destruction.

He might have been lying. Clearly, he was skilled at manipulation. But when he spoke of his son . . . those emotions were genuine.

Darak drained his cup and refilled it with wine. It was
pale and gold and as cool as the water. He wondered how
they managed to keep wine cool in a place so unbearably
hot, then frowned and gathered himself.

In a few moments, Keirith would walk in. They hadn't
spoken—really spoken—since the night before the raid.
The priest knew about that night. What else had Keirith
told him? Surely, he would know better than to trust him.
He was young, but he wasn't stupid.

*Just scared and alone. Never knowing when he went to
sleep if he'd survive another day.*

He heard footsteps behind him and spun around.

When he'd first glimpsed Keirith at the entertainment, it
had been too dark to see him well. Later, he'd been too

stunned by Urkiat's death to study his appearance. It was a shock to see him wearing the baggy half-breeches of the Zherosi. Had he been wearing those last night? His unruly hair was oiled and tied back. He hadn't noticed that either. He'd only seen the stark face, the staring eyes. The face was calm now, if strained, and the eyes met his steadily enough, although he hesitated in the doorway as if reluctant to come closer.

"Keirith."

"Father."

Belatedly, he realized he was still clutching the cup of wine. He bent down and placed it on the table so he could embrace his son, but by the time he straightened, Keirith was already walking around the table. Gods, he even moved differently. The sudden spurt in height last year had left him awkward, yet after little more than a moon, he carried himself with the careful grace of a heron picking its way through the reeds, leaving him feeling like the awkward one—too big and too clumsy for this beautiful room.

"I'm sorry," Keirith said. "About Urkiat."

"Aye." Darak forced down the surge of emotion. "You look . . . well."

"I am. Thank you."

They might have been strangers. Or worse, acquaintances meeting after a long absence and taking refuge in meaningless pleasantries.

"I've come to take you home."

Keirith grimaced and the breath rushed out of his lungs as if someone had punched him.

He knows the priest is listening. He's just being cautious. Remember Tinnean. Remember how you failed at the thorn tree because you were too impatient. Go slow. Fear is the enemy.

"Let's sit down, Father."

With an effort, he resisted the impulse to shout, "Nay, let's not. Let's thrash it out—all that lies between us—and settle it once and for all." Instead, he simply nodded; time enough later to deal with the past.

"The priest—Malaq—said you could come with me."

Keirith twirled Malaq's cup by its long stem, refusing to meet his eyes.

"Keirith?"

His fingers continued their restless, repetitive motion. Darak reached across the table and they went still.

"Talk to me, son."

Instead, Keirith pushed himself up and retreated to the far corner of the room. Immediately, Darak went after him, but as he approached, Keirith held up a hand, warding him off. His son hunched forward, his breath coming in harsh, quick pants. The bones jutted from his naked shoulders, sharp and terribly fragile.

Control the fear.

"What have they done to you?"

Keirith shook his head.

"Have they hurt you? Threatened you? Is it the priest? Is he forcing you—?"

"Nay!"

As Keirith brushed past him, Darak grabbed his arm. They both froze. Keirith stared down at his fingers until Darak dropped his hand.

"You shouldn't have come, Father."

"Did you think I would simply let them take you? That I would abandon you?" When Keirith hesitated, he knew the answer. Shaken, he could only blurt out, "Merciful Maker, you're my son."

"Not here. Here I am just . . . myself."

"Nay. Here you are Kheridh." He spat out the name. "Or the Son of Zhe. But you aren't Keirith."

"And who is Keirith? The son of the great Darak Spirit-Hunter. The abomination who should be sacrificed at the heart-oak."

"I would never allow—"

"If I go back, I'd be going to my death. We both know that."

"Not if you refuse to use this power."

"But I want to use it! Don't you understand? I love the power, and I love using it." Keirith's voice cracked as he laughed. "I may not be the Son of Zhe, but when I touch the spirit of another, I feel like I am. In those moments, I *am* a god."

Darak's hand came up and Keirith flinched. Fingers clenched, he lowered it. "He's poisoned your mind."

"He's opened my mind. He's taught me more in a moon

than Gortin could in a lifetime. He understands me better
than . . ."

"Better than I do," Darak said softly.

Keirith took a deep breath. "Please, Father. If we go on,
we'll only hurt each other more."

How could anything hurt more than hearing that his son
believed a stranger—an enemy of their people—knew him
better than his own father? Had the priest cast a spell over
him? Surely, Keirith couldn't have changed so much.

Control yourself.

"This priest may understand your power. And he may
cultivate it. But have you asked yourself why? How many
questions has he refused to answer? How many times have
you caught him in a lie? He's using you, son. If you cross
him—if you threaten him or any of these people—how long
do you think it'll be before you're lying across their sacrificial stone?"

"You don't know him."

"Neither do you." The uncertainty in Keirith's face made
him add, "You and I . . . we may not always agree. We
may . . . say things, do things to hurt each other. We're
both stubborn and strong-willed."

*"We were too much alike, you and I. Maybe that's why
we were always butting heads."*

His father's words. And now, despite all his efforts, he
seemed to be repeating the pattern with his son. Keirith
watched him, wary and confused, waiting for him to continue.

"No matter what lies between us, we come from the
same roots. We worship the same gods. We are children of
the Oak and Holly, who have lived all our lives in the
village our ancestors founded when they fled from these
people."

Tentatively, Darak raised his hand and, although Keirith
drew back, he laid it gently on his son's shoulder. A fine
vibration coursed through Keirith's body. His fingers tightened. "Please. Come home with me."

Please, Maker. Don't let me lose him as I lost Tinnean.

Keirith wrenched free. "I'm sorry, Father."

Shocked, Darak could only stammer, "He's threatening
you. He must be. Otherwise—"

"He is not threatening me. I want to stay. I want to learn

from him. I'm sorry you had to come. That I put you in danger. But you can leave—you must leave. Take this and go."

Keirith scooped up the disk and held it out. When he didn't take it, Keirith seized his hand and thrust it into his palm.

"Please. Just . . . go."

Darak stared at the disk, as useless as Struath's tiny crystal that had failed to retrieve Tinnean's spirit. Nay, *he* had failed, not the crystal. Just as he had failed now. And not just now but for years, or Keirith could never reject him so easily.

Of course, he had made mistakes. Every father did. The night of Keirith's attack, the day of the raid—those were the worst. But did they wipe out everything else? The summer days when he taught him a hunter's skills? The winter nights when they sang songs together at the fire pit? He was there to catch him when he'd taken his first steps, to embrace him when he'd returned from his vision quest. And he was here now. What greater proof could he offer of his love?

The smell of the food choked him. The oil scenting Keirith's hair sickened him. The immaculate breeches, the neatly laced sandals, the perfectly trimmed fingernails . . . they had stolen his son and left this copy behind as surely as if they had cast out his spirit and invested the empty body with a stranger's.

"And what am I to tell your mother?" Keirith winced, and he was savagely glad. "And your brother and sister? That after a mere moon in this cursed place, you've chosen to abandon them to become a Zherosi priest? To take your place before the sacrificial stone and cut out the hearts of your own kinfolk? To feel like a god?"

"Tell them whatever you want! Tell them . . ." Keirith took a deep breath and turned away. "Tell them I am dead."

"Better that you were. Better that you had died when the raiders attacked. Then we could mourn you and remember you in our prayers and hope to meet you again in the Forever Isles."

Keirith's shoulders hunched as if he had struck him.

"Look at me. Look at me!"

Slowly, Keirith turned. Unshed tears made his eyes bright, but his mouth was pressed into a tight, hard line.

"Tell me that you're abandoning us of your own free will."

Keirith's mouth worked. He swallowed hard and whispered, "Go home, Father."

"Tell me—"

"Aye!"

"And if I don't believe you?"

"Then believe this. I killed Urkiat."

"What . . . what are you talking about?"

"Oh, it was your hand that drove the sword into his chest. But have you wondered what made him stand there, waiting for the blow? That was me, Father. I tried to cast out his spirit. I wasn't strong enough to do it, but I did manage to distract him. Just long enough for you to strike the blow that killed him."

His mind realized the truth, but his heart and his spirit shrank from accepting it.

"But why? Urkiat would never . . . I wasn't in any real danger . . ."

"Xevhan had decided on a fight to the death. One of you was going to die. I chose Urkiat. That is what the power gives you. The ability to choose."

"But not the right!"

"And if I hadn't? What then?"

"I would have done . . . something."

"You'd be dead."

There was no emotion in his son's voice. None at all.

"Last night, I gave you your life. Now you must give me mine." For just a moment, Keirith hesitated. Then he shook his head impatiently. "I can't go home, Father. Not now."

"No one has to know."

"You know. I know. I've already struck out at you. I led Urkiat to his death. Sooner or later, I'll cast out the spirit of a man. As Morgath did."

"You could never become as evil as Morgath."

Keirith made a sound, halfway between a laugh and a sob. "Dear gods, Father. I already am."

Darak stared at this stranger who wore his son's face and his son's body, unable to speak.

"Good-bye, Father."

Perhaps it was the lack of emotion in his voice or the confidence of his stride that made Darak call out, "Kheridh!"

His head came up at the name. Darak fumbled in his bag of charms until his fingers found what he wanted. He flung it across the floor and watched it slide to a halt next to Keirith's foot. "It was a gift. From the Supplicant of the God with Two Faces. You'll find better use for it than I will."

Damning his shaking voice, he strode out of the chamber, startling the guards. For once, he was grateful for their presence; he would never allow himself to weep in front of them.

❧

Keirith sank to his knees. The tears in his eyes made the little snake shimmer. His hand groped for it. The bronze was still warm from his father's body.

He fell forward. His mouth opened, but no sound emerged. All he could do was rock back and forth, slowly and deliberately striking his forehead against the floor again and again and again, as if the physical pain could banish the deeper agony.

Strong arms enfolded him. Not his father's arms. He would never know their touch again. Gentle hands stroked his hair. Not his mother's hands, those clever, nimble fingers that could stitch together a man's flesh and ease the burn of a child's skinned knee.

"I'm so sorry. I know it was hard. But you had to speak to him that way. Otherwise, he never would have left and that would have put you both in jeopardy. Now he'll be safe. I promise you that, Kheridh."

He shuddered, remembering his father's bitter voice. How could one word cut so deeply?

"In time, he'll accept your decision."

And he will hate me and curse my name and never, ever understand.

The bile rose in his throat. He shoved Malaq away and retched helplessly, as if he could cleanse himself of the evil things he had said, vomit up every awful part of himself until he was clean and whole. But he would never be clean, or whole, again.

He'd done the only thing he could to ensure that his father left before anyone discovered his identity. But still he had expected the determined footsteps to slow. He had waited for that, praying he would feel the warm hand descend on his shoulder and hear the deep voice announce that they were leaving together, that nothing else mattered, that everything—somehow—would be all right.

But his father's footsteps never faltered.

How could he fail to see through his pretense? How could his father believe he had changed so much? Unless, in his heart, this was how he had always seen him—a cold, power-hungry, ruthless creature. Like Morgath.

Exhausted, he lay on the floor while Malaq wiped his face and cleaned up the mess he had made. It astonished him to think that the Pajhit of the Zherosi would shame himself by performing such an ugly, menial task rather than shame him by summoning slaves.

"You are the only one who can convince him," Malaq had said. And he had. His father had repudiated him. His family was lost. His gods would never hear his prayers. There was no going home. There was only this new life among strangers, stretching ahead of him in an endless succession of empty days and spirit-draining nights.

But he was not alone. He had Malaq. The friend he had never expected to find, the mentor whose knowledge and wisdom would guide his path. The father of his spirit, if not his body.

Chapter 36

NUMBED BY HIS ENCOUNTER with Keirith, Darak stumbled after the two guards. Only when sunlight blinded him did he realize they were standing at the western entrance of the palace. One of the guards seized his arm and pulled him out of the way of a litter. The other pointed to something in the distance and repeated "Oexiak" several times. When Darak nodded his understanding, they left.

He slid down the wall. An endless line of litters streamed past him. From behind their swaying curtains came the sounds of laughter and excited conversation. Even the litter bearers wore eager looks, despite the sweat running down their faces. So did the women, straggling toward the gate. Some had babes strapped to their backs, others, small children clinging to their legs. All clutched bowls like the beggars he'd seen squatting in the streets of Oexiak.

He was the only beggar in Pilozhat who wasn't celebrating. Despite his pleas, Keirith had rejected him—just as, fifteen years ago, Tinnean had defied him to choose the path of the shaman. His journey through Chaos had taught him the danger of trying to control the lives of others. But how could he simply walk away from his son?

"I killed Urkiat."

The horror surged anew. It was one thing to attack in a moment of anger, but to do so coldly, without provocation . . .

"You could never become as evil as Morgath."

"Dear gods, Father. I already am."

But he wasn't. He couldn't be. No matter what Keirith said, no matter what he had done, Darak refused to believe he was evil. But left among these people, he would be seduced by the terrible gift he possessed. Whether they killed him or not, the Zherosi would destroy him.

If it had been his father in the arena, would he have sacrificed another to save him? Aye. And to keep him safe, he would have used any argument, even if it meant risking his hatred and driving him away. But his father would have recognized the desperation that prompted the bitter words. He would have suppressed his pain and resisted the urge to lash out. And he would have stayed in that chamber—just as he had remained beside him throughout his ordeal in Chaos.

He could not bring back Urkiat, but there was still time to save his son. He must go back. If reason and pleading couldn't convince Keirith to leave this place, then by the gods, he would drag him away by force.

Darak stuffed the clay disk into his belt pouch and rose. A shiver raced down his spine. At his feet, a tiny bronze snake lay atop a clump of parched grass. It was the twin of the one he had given Keirith—unless somehow it had returned to him, just as it had when he'd discarded it in Chaos.

He snatched it up, craning his neck to see if Keirith was among those near the gate. Instead, he spied the tall, robed figure, looming above the growing crowd of beggars. First, the Supplicant appeared in Oexiak, now here. This time, he would not let her escape. Whoever she was, he was certain she could help him—and Keirith.

She slipped in and out among the beggars, always just within view, always just out of reach.

Like the Forest-Lord, leading me back to the grove after I escaped from Chaos.

At the edge of the hillside, he paused to get his bearings. The path led down the hill past a pillared courtyard. It must be the temple of the God with Two Faces. But the Supplicant was nowhere to be seen.

Ignoring the curses of the bearers, he zigzagged through the line of litters and hurried down the steps. He almost missed the bronze chain, casually draped over a stubby bush, its tiny medallion still swinging back and forth. At the base of a pillar, he found a bracelet. Each of the circular gold pieces bore a face. On half, he made out the smiling countenance of a young woman, on the others, a skull.

First she mimicked the Forest-Lord, now Griane who had left circlets of hair to mark his way back to the grove. Just as surely, the Supplicant had led him to the entrance of her temple.

It seemed to have been built directly into the hillside. The low doorway only enhanced the feeling that you were entering a cave. He hesitated a moment, then ducked inside.

He saw a rectangle of light just ahead, although his sun-dazzled eyes missed the shadowy figures flanking the inner doorway until he was nearly on top of them. The guards—or priests—bowed politely. Voices exclaimed from within. Two robed figures fell to their knees. The Supplicant laid her hands on their heads, then glanced over her shoulder, watching him and waiting.

He hadn't come this far to turn back now. With a confidence he didn't feel, Darak strode inside.

The brightness was misleading. Half of the chamber was illuminated, while the other lay in shadow. There were more people than he had thought, all of them on their knees. The Supplicant led him deeper into the chamber, across woolen rugs as soft and thick as mulch. Tiny flames flickering from the hanging bowls made it seem as if the place was lit by a swarm of fireflies. Shadows danced among the paintings, barely visible, that decorated the walls.

He smelled the sweet fragrance of honeysuckle before he saw the flowers. Huge bunches spilled over a stone table—or altar—that appeared to be carved from the same stone as his tribe's ritual vessels. They might have sprung from different cultures, worshipped different gods, but at one time, his people and the Zherosi had some things in common.

"Who knows? Perhaps all gods are the same."

He backed away as new worshippers approached. He could only make out a few words of their chant, but there was no mistaking the joy on their faces. Clearly, the Supplicant was beloved if her appearance was greeted with such fervor.

Gauzy draperies billowed as she slipped through them. Still clutching her discarded jewelry, he followed.

The room was small, but far more opulent. And it was very cool, perhaps because it was built under the hill. A slender girl crawled around the low table on her hands and knees, pausing to plump cushions of red and brown. Other servants—all young and beautiful, even the boys—scurried past with platters and pitchers. Did they know she was coming? Or where she had gone? Although there were no other doors in the chamber, she had vanished—just as she had that night in Oexiak.

The spicy aromas of the food vied with the fragrance of honeysuckle from the vases adorning niches in the walls. Paintings of trees covered one wall of the chamber, an autumn forest of gold and brown and scarlet. Not for the first time, he longed for the sight of something green.

He carefully placed her jewelry on the table. The servants bowed and left. The chanting continued in the outer room, augmented by the sweet trills of a flute. And still, there was no sign of her.

"Welcome, Darak."

His greeting died when he turned to discover her emerging from the painted forest on the wall. There was no door. She simply . . . walked out of the trees. But even her entrance—incredible as it was—paled in comparison to her naked body.

"Don't gape, dear. It's unbecoming."

The words conjured up a memory, but he simply couldn't grasp it. All he could do was stare at her, his gaze shifting between the heavy breasts and the thick penis jutting from the black thatch of hair.

"How sweet. You can still blush." She advanced on him slowly. "And do you still think I'm beautiful?" Her lips pursed in a pout when he failed to reply. "If you don't find me beautiful, I shall be hurt. You don't want me to be hurt, do you?"

Numbly, he shook his head.

The scent of honeysuckle wafted toward him as she approached. Her eyes were level with his. In the dark depths, gold flecks swirled. He could feel himself falling into them, just as he had when Fellgair's golden eyes first bespelled him.

A hand brushed his cheek, the palm as rough and spongy as a dog's pads. Two long shears sprouted from her upper jaw. A red tongue lolled out between them.

"Have you missed me, Darak?"

He could feel his mouth moving, but no words would emerge.

"Welcome to my temple."

"Your . . . ?" And then he realized. The God with Two Faces.

"I told you I had many worlds. This is one of my favorites. They treat me so well here. A lovely temple, devoted followers . . ." The Trickster strolled toward the table. "The finest food. Shall we eat?"

"Put some clothes on first."

"It's too hot for clothes."

"Fur, then."

Fellgair shuddered. "Far too hot for fur. Don't you like me like this? My followers find me quite impressive."

"I don't doubt it. With that . . . spear hanging between your legs."

Fellgair heaved an exaggerated sigh. "A heavy burden, indeed. As are these." He hefted the full breasts. The coolness of the room had caused the plum-colored nipples to tighten into tiny buds. "Come. Sit."

Darak collapsed onto one of the cushions. Fellgair seated himself far more gracefully across the table. "You're staring," he chided. "I always thought your taste ran to small-breasted women. With red hair."

"Leave Griane out of this."

"But she's already involved. Who do you think requested that I look in on you? Well, you know how persuasive she can be. And when she wept—"

"She . . . she wept?"

"Or perhaps that was me. I can't remember."

"Is she all right? Are the children safe?"

Fellgair leaned forward, proffering a bowl. "Jhok?"

"Why did Griane come to you?"

"Try the lamb, then. It's rolled in spices, then roasted on skewers."

"Damn the skewers." Darak shoved the platter aside, sending it crashing into a pitcher. He leaped up to steady it, cursing himself for losing control in front of Fellgair. "I'm sorry. That was . . ." His voice trailed off.

Fellgair glanced up from grooming his brush. "Rude? Petulant? Childish?" He gave the white tip of his brush a final lick, smoothed the fur on his ruff, and settled himself on the cushions again. His black whiskers twitched as he grinned. "You seem more comfortable with me in this guise."

"Fox or man—or woman—I'm never comfortable with you."

"Very wise. Mortals should always quail in the presence of a god. Speaking of which . . ." Fellgair held out another platter. Three golden-brown quail lay atop a nest of leafy vegetables.

"Did you make some sort of bargain with Griane?"

"I don't wish to discuss that."

Darak turned on his heel and stalked toward the doorway.

"But I am prepared to discuss your son. The interview didn't go especially well, did it?"

Of course, Fellgair would know what had happened. After fifteen years, he'd almost forgotten how exhausting it was to try and keep up with the Trickster. Slowly, he turned. "What do you want?"

"A conversation. Why don't you begin with, 'I'm delighted to see you again after all these years.' You *are* delighted, aren't you?"

"Surprised."

"Then you might also be surprised to learn that your dull little Tree-Father—what's his name?—had a disturbing vision in which your heart was cut out. Keirith was there at the time. Watching attentively. You look pale, Darak. Perhaps you should sit."

He remained where he was, grateful for the wall at his back. "Did you send Gortin that vision?"

"You always think the worst of me. If my nature weren't so forgiving, I might take offense."

"If your nature weren't so devious, I wouldn't think the worst of you."

Fellgair grinned. "Very good. Thrust and parry. Oh. My condolences about Urkiat. Was it terrible for you?"

"We were talking about Gortin's vision."

"Your verbal skills have improved. It must be your training as a Memory-Keeper. Who'd have thought it?"

"You predicted it."

"It was one possibility."

"And did you see the possibility that my son would be kidnapped by the Zherosi? Is that why you gave me your token all those years ago?"

"Only when a child is conceived is the pattern of his life spun," Fellgair replied, deftly avoiding a direct answer.

"But later?"

"Later? Yes, of course, I saw the possibility."

"And didn't warn me?"

"Oh, forgive me. I hadn't realized that my role in the universe was to avert your family crises."

"I only meant—"

"A role better suited to a father than to the Trickster." That silenced him. "I tried to find him."

"After you drove him from your hut or after you abandoned him to the mercy of the raiders?"

As many times as those same words had echoed in his head, it was still shocking to hear them spoken aloud.

"To answer your earlier question, I did not bring the Zherosi to your village. I did not encourage you to abandon your son to seek the pleasure of the kill. And I did not make the raider club Keirith over the head and drag him back to his ship. Men set those events into motion. Just as, fifteen years ago, a man came through a portal from Chaos into the grove of the First Forest."

"You're . . . are you saying Morgath is behind this?"

"Morgath is dead, Darak. Even the most powerful shaman has difficulty recovering when a dagger is driven into his eye. Or should I say her eye? It was, after all, the Grain-Mother's body he inhabited at the time. There were so many. It's hard to keep track. An owl, a bear, a wolf, a wren. The lovely Yeorna. Do you still dream about her beautiful blue eyes, Darak?"

"Nay."

"Or Morgath cutting away your flesh?"

"Nay."

"Or poking around inside your spirit?"

"Nay!"

"I'm glad. I'd hate to think he had broken you."

"He didn't."

"Then why have you never spoken of what happened? Why did you return home with Griane only to abandon her—setting the pattern early, weren't you?—and flee back to the First Forest?"

"I didn't . . . I had to . . ."

"Decide whether you wanted to live or die."

"Decide what to do with my life."

"Yes. One gets so tired of the 'gallant but crippled hero' role. Still, it's more fulfilling than the 'great hunter who cannot hunt.' Or the 'Memory-Keeper who cannot free himself from memories.'"

The onslaught was as relentless as it was true.

"Griane knew. Such a wise woman, your wife. She saw the possibility that you would not be able to face the world. That her love—great as it was—was not strong enough to hold you. And yet she allowed you to go back. She waited—one long moon—while you decided between life and death. And her beautiful red hair turned white."

The pain in his gut radiated up into his chest. The mere act of breathing hurt so much he could only take in air with shallow pants. Oddly, his fingers hurt, too. It took several moments before he realized they were splayed against the wall behind him, fingertips scraping stone.

"You're much crueler now than you were fifteen years ago."

"We'd only just met," Fellgair replied with a mocking smile. "I was on my best behavior."

"Why are you doing this?"

"Being cruel?"

"Bringing up the past."

"Because the past influences the present. The things that happened in the First Forest and in Chaos still affect you today. And everything that affects you affects your son."

It's my fault, then. All of it.

"You are his father," Fellgair replied as if he had spoken aloud. "So you deserve some of the fault—and the credit—for Keirith's life. But there are other forces at work. Mortal life is a series of possibilities, stretching from the moment of conception to death."

Fellgair traced a line in the air. A trail of creamy light

shimmered in the wake of his claw. "Before a child is born, a single thread connects him to his mother." The creamy light separated into two strands of intertwined white and gold. "After birth, other threads are woven into the pattern: father, brother, sister." He sketched new lines in as he spoke: red, green, blue, each thread branching in many directions. "Outside forces may disrupt the pattern: disease . . ." He twisted a blue thread and its light dimmed. "Death." With a quick slash of his claw, he severed the thread. The blue branches vanished. The other colors flickered uncertainly.

Dear gods, had something happened to Callie? Or Faelia? Or were the blue threads the babe they had lost?

"The child grows older. The pattern widens to include his tribe mates." With quick gestures, Fellgair sketched in dozens of new threads that stretched out from the white in a spiderweb of color and light. Almost like the wards Struath and Yeorna had erected to protect them from Morgath.

"The child begins to make choices." Dozens of smaller strands of white light shot out in all directions. "He chooses an eagle's feather instead of a hawk's to add to his bag of charms." One tiny strand flared and vanished; another grew brighter. "He knocks down the older boy who is bullying him." As an orange thread vibrated wildly, Darak searched his memory for a time Keirith had gotten into a fight. "He hones his skills so that he can surpass his father as a hunter."

Not Keirith's life, he realized, but his own, shimmering before him.

"And when his father dies . . ." Red threads flickered and vanished, leaving a gaping hole in the pattern. ". . . he chooses to becomes surrogate father to his brother—teaching him, shaping him, channeling his life into the path he wishes him to follow." Green threads unwound from white. "By the time the boy is a man, the web of his life has been snipped and spun and reshaped a thousand times. For most, the shaping is small. For others, a single decision can alter their lives forever. Like Tinnean's decision to defend the Tree. And yours to go in search of him."

Green threads snapped, their ends waving wildly until only one slender strand remained intact, thickly cocooned by the threads of white.

"I know about my life. Show me Keirith's."

A casual wave of Fellgair's hand erased the spiderweb
of his life. "This is Keirith's pattern before he was kidnapped." Moving too fast for him to follow, the claws created an intricate new pattern, dominated by threads the
deep blue of the Midwinter sky at dusk. "And this is Keirith's pattern afterward." Fellgair flicked a finger and half
of the threads vanished. "The pattern of his life is still
being rewoven." One by one, the branching strands of blue
disappeared, until only one remained.

If Fellgair's pattern was true, Keirith's chances of survival were as slender as the trembling thread that repre-
sented his life. He forced himself to examine the
shimmering pattern more closely. Crossing Keirith's
thread were strands ranging in hues from dusky rose to
that of dried blood. The colors of the Zherosi, surely. Just
as surely, the web of white threads branching out between
them belonged to him. And the brilliant ones that shifted
from red to gold as he watched—those must be the Trickster's. But where were Griane's? The light blue, so closely
intertwined with his white, perhaps. Yet those barely
touched Keirith's.

He had to swallow several times before he trusted himself to speak. "Will you save him?"

"No."

"Can I save him?"

"Yes."

The surge of relief left him weak. "How?"

The Trickster merely smiled.

"Please."

With infinite care, Fellgair plucked a strand of white between two lethal claws. Darak's heart gave an odd little
flutter. As Fellgair lifted the thread, his heart missed a beat.

"What do you want?"

Under Fellgair's claws, the thread stretched into a tiny
white peak. Darak reeled, dimly aware of smooth stone
sliding past his fingertips, of the jolt of pain as his knees
hit the stone flags, of the duller pain that blossomed in his
chest and swelled until he felt his heart must burst. He
gasped for breath. Black dots danced in front of his eyes,
obliterating the web, obliterating everything except those
two claws grasping the peak of the taut white thread. If
Fellgair broke it, he would die.

And then he realized that was the bargain Fellgair offered: his life in exchange for his son's.

Flames erupted at the edge of his vision, brilliant bursts of red and gold. Or perhaps those were Fellgair's threads. Or Griane's hair, the way it used to look before the white had stolen in. The way it had looked that morning in the grove, fiery spikes framing her white face.

Forgive me, girl.

His vision blurred. Something warm and wet ran down his cheek. The world tilted. He had fallen like this when Fellgair first bespelled him, as slow and steady as if he were sinking into the waters of the lake.

Griane.

Callum. My sweet boy.

Faelia. My fierce wolf pup.

Wolf. Am I dooming you, too?

Keirith . . .

Never to see them again. Never to touch them. Never to say farewell.

Summoning his strength, he choked out, "Take me."

The pain in his chest eased, surprising him. Perhaps Fellgair meant to give him a quick death. He sucked in great gulps of air, helplessly staring up into the golden eyes that would be the last thing he would see. He closed his eyes, trying to conjure Griane's face. For just a moment, he captured it—the smattering of freckles, the pointed chin, the frown she kept in place to hide her true emotions. And with it came the awareness that she was with him.

He opened himself to her presence, his spirit reaching out for hers. Only then did he realize the truth: it was not Griane's spirit but Fellgair's. Inside of him. Invading him. Just as Morgath had invaded him all those years ago.

His eyes flew open and met Fellgair's calm gaze. He flailed uselessly at the restraining arms, as if by thrusting them away he could somehow rid himself of the god's spirit.

<Hush.>

Fellgair's voice, the scolding tone as familiar as if he had spoken aloud. He could feel his presence, hovering at the edge of his consciousness.

Why?

<Your words, Darak. Your bargain.>

He heard mocking laughter, but the Trickster's face was grave. It was Morgath's laughter, echoing in his memory.

Panic constricted his chest. A giant fist squeezed his heart. His vision narrowed to those two golden eyes above him. His body convulsed as he fought for air. But there was no air.

<Darak. Stop.>

Stop breathing? Stop fighting?

<Stop.>

Something pressed against his chest, but instead of crushing him, his breathing eased. Relief made him sag in Fellgair's arms. So strong, those arms. On that final journey to the grove, he had yearned for the Forest-Lord to cradle him like this, but there had only been that one fleeting touch, a warm paw cupping the back of his neck the way his mam used to. Now, instead of Hernan's leaves ticking his cheek, there was Fellgair's fur. And the scent of honeysuckle filling his nostrils. And music . . . why did he hear music? And a heartbeat. He'd never imagined that gods possessed hearts, but surely that was Fellgair's.

His heart slowed its frantic pattering to match that steady beat. As if he were back on the tree in Chaos again, feeling that other heartbeat keeping vigil with him, leading him away from Morgath, guiding him through the dream-forest and deep into the cavern where Tinnean and the Oak dwelled within the World Tree.

The music.

<Yes.>

His heartbeat raced again as the word sounded inside of him. What new trick was Fellgair trying by conjuring up the song of the World Tree?

Impatience lanced through him, but before he could panic, Fellgair had withdrawn to the periphery of his consciousness again.

What game is this?

<A very important one. For Keirith.>

Keirith?

<He was the reason you made the bargain.>

I know, but . . .

It was so hard to think clearly, to move past the terror of Fellgair's presence inside of him, even if he made no attempt to penetrate deeper.

<Nor will I. It is for you to let me in.>
Denial made his body spasm helplessly.
<Then Keirith will die.>
He struggled to rise, but Fellgair held him fast.
I offered my life.
<No, Darak. You said, "Take me.">
And Fellgair had. Because he had been foolish enough—
and frightened enough—to speak without clearly stating the
terms of the bargain.
I meant my life. You know that's what I meant.
<But I don't want your life. I want your spirit.>
What?
<Open your spirit.>
But you're already inside of me.
<Open your spirit, or Keirith will die.>
Please! You cannot kill my boy!
<Open your spirit—>
Why are you doing this?
<Because it's a greater sacrifice than your life.>
So simple, really. And so true. Dying would be far easier
than opening his spirit to Fellgair—to anyone. But only by
making that sacrifice could he save Keirith. Of course, the
Trickster knew that. He knew everything. He would never
have accepted the lesser price. His hasty offer had just
made it easier.
The very thought of opening himself to Fellgair made his
spirit shrink, closing like a clenched fist. Immediately, he
felt Fellgair drifting away.
Wait.
<You are unwilling.>
Nay. I'm— please!
His mind refused to acknowledge the truth, but the Trickster could sense his fear as easily as he could feel the terrified racing of his heart under his hand and the harsh rasp
of his breath ruffling the fur of his chest.
With shaking hands, he tried to sit up, but he was ridicu-
lously weak. In the end, all he could do was shift his head
to stare up into Fellgair's face. Silly to think he could read
the Trickster's expression. Sillier still to hope he might find
something in it to reassure him.
His head drooped against the furry chest. Fellgair surprised

him by taking his hand. The gesture was comforting. Then he noticed the claws curving across the back of his hand.

Tinnean, help me.

Darak opened himself.

Expecting the power of the god to flood his spirit like the song of the World Tree, he was surprised to feel only the slightest probing. As gentle as Struath's touch the morning he had returned from his vision quest.

The memories filled him: Struath's eye staring down at him; the shaman's fingers cupping his cheeks; the shaman's smile when he called out, "Today, a man walks among us." His kinfolk pouring out of their huts, shouting and cheering. His mam—laughing, crying, hugging him. So young . . .

He lifted her wasted body.

Oh, gods . . .

A child's weight in his arms. Her body cold. Her hair lank and streaked with gray. Her merry face sunken and empty. Muina had bathed and dressed her, but he had closed her eyes. Just as he had closed Maili's.

It took all his control to stop himself from pushing Fellgair away as new images flooded him. Maili's face, thoughtful and frowning, when he asked her to marry him. "I think we'd suit each other. I think we should wed." Maili's nervous smile as he pulled her away from the wedding feast. Maili's averted eyes as he undressed. He had to hurry. Mam and Tinnean would come soon. He wanted their first time to be private.

Maili's fingers, fumbling with her braid, freeing her hair to tumble over her shoulders and breasts. Maili's quick gasp as he pulled her bridal tunic over her head. Another as he eased her onto the furs.

Her skin, creamy in the firelight. Her hands, shielding the dark curls between her legs. His fingers pulling them away, too rough, too eager. Her inadvertent flinch when he touched her there. Her huge eyes when he lowered himself onto her, so dark in the dimness of the hut they looked black. Her scream . . .

He heard a moan and knew it was his.

Fellgair saw it all, felt it all: his groan of completion, Maili's muffled weeping, his useless apology, her body turning away from him, curling into a ball.

And still the god sought more, probing deeper, sifting
through memories of happy times and bad. His life poured
out like water from a broken flask. Tinnean's small fingers
clutching his the first time they watched the Northern
Dancers weave their pattern in the night sky. Tinnean's
body flinching as the belt struck him. Tinnean's eyes peeping through the tangle of leaves sprouting from his face.

Remember his eyes, blue as speedwell.

Callie's eyes, that same blue. His chubby fingers fumbling
with Tinnean's flute. Faelia's skillful ones whirling a sling
over her head, shouting in triumph when she brought down
a wood pigeon . . .

"Oh, Fa. It screamed."

Keirith's face, tear-streaked and stark. Keirith's voice,
shaking as he shouted his accusations. Keirith's body, heaved
over the side of that giant boat.

*"You'll never be able to shield him from pain or guard
him close enough to keep him from harm."*

Lisula holding out the small, naked creature that was his
firstborn son. The red face, screwed up in a fierce squall of
protest. The ten tiny fingers, each of them perfect. The
smooth skin, so impossibly soft . . .

Griane's smile as she left the birthing hut with Keirith
in her arms and discovered him waiting for her. Griane's
eyes, the blue that lived at the heart of a flame. Griane's
voice, scolding, bullying, easing his fears, crooning a lullaby.
Griane's hands, binding wounds, patting a babe's bottom.
Stroking his hair. Touching his body. Placing his ruined
hands on her small breasts. Shivering with delight at his
tentative touch.

"I don't want to hurt you."

"You won't."

Hands and mouths exploring. The wonder of it. The joy.
Laughter in the night instead of tears. Whispered confidences instead of silence. Her legs wrapped around him. Her
fingers digging into his buttocks, urging him on, both of them
heedless of his newly healed wounds. Pain and pleasure . . .

*"Morgath enjoys both in equal measure. You're very
much like him in that respect."*

Morgath humming as he wove his severed fingers into
Yeorna's hair. Morgath oozing through his spirit, relent-

lessly stripping away his defenses. Morgath laughing with
delight at each failed attempt to escape.

*"I can read every thought. Feel every fear. Uncover all
your dirty little secrets."*

Darak fled, desperately seeking a place where he was
safe, where neither memories of Morgath nor the spirit of
the Trickster could reach him. Somewhere, he would find
that calm he had experienced during the first moments of
communion with the World Tree. Somewhere, he would
find the music.

The vibration coursed through him, as slow and steady
as it had been in Chaos. But it was not the World Tree. It
was Fellgair's heart, beating beneath his cheek. He scarcely
had time to realize it before it vanished, along with the
god's presence inside of him.

"Nay!"

Fellgair eased him out of his arms.

"Please." He stared up into Fellgair's face, at once stern
and sorrowful. "I can do this."

Fellgair shook his head.

"Let me try again." He pushed himself onto his knees.
"I beg you . . ."

The Trickster vanished.

Darak covered his face with shaking hands. He would
not weep. Weeping would not help his son.

He staggered out of the chamber, ignoring the surprised
glances of the worshippers. He still had time. He would
find Keirith. He would get him out of this place. The Trickster could not stop him. Or the Pajhit. Or even Keirith
himself.

The afternoon sunlight blinded him. His heart fluttered as
if a tiny bird were trapped in his chest. When the guards
marched toward him, he felt such joy he was afraid it would
fail him. One of them pulled his dagger from its sheath, but
he made no move to stop him. It was all he could do to cling
to the arms of the two who helped him up the steep hillside.

Only when they turned away from the gate did he realize
that Keirith had not changed his mind, that these guards
were not the ones who had come for him before. He struggled feebly. Something struck his head. After that, they
dragged him.

Through the whirl of his vision, he made out another gate in another wall. Men dozed under canopied shelters. When the guards shoved him into one, the man he jostled stirred long enough to mutter a curse in the language of the tribes. With bitter irony, Darak realized he had managed to get inside the slave compound after all.

"No more today. Come back tomorrow."

The undercook's third assistant shooed the last of the women away and muttered a curse. "All right, you girls, back to the kitchen. We've done our charity work for the day and we have an important feast to prepare. Hircha! Stop dawdling, or I'll have you whipped."

Hircha picked up the empty basket, murmuring an apology. The undercook's third assistant cuffed her anyway. "Just because you served at the Zheron's entertainment last night doesn't mean you can shirk your duties today."

The other girls tittered. The undercook's third assistant grinned. Hircha followed them back to the kitchen. The pot boys struggled with a sack of grain, but in her mind, she saw the Zheron's men dragging the Spirit-Hunter to the slave compound.

Chapter 37

FOR AN ENTIRE AFTERNOON, Malaq had stood beside the king, a fixed smile on his face, as an endless parade of nobles, merchants, and officials from every town in Zheros expressed their heartfelt joy that, once again, their beloved rulers had Shed their old bodies and emerged in reborn glory to guide their people. The queen had waved away his request to speak privately, assuring him there would be time to talk at the council meeting following the reception.

All afternoon, he'd been conscious of Xevhan's covert glances. Although he looked haggard from lack of sleep, there was no mistaking the glitter of triumph in his eyes. Once again, he told himself that Xevhan's accusations couldn't harm him. The Spirit-Hunter was gone. So were the players. Kheridh knew what to say if questioned. He only hoped the poor boy would remember the story they had agreed upon; he'd been so dazed with grief that Malaq was forced to repeat it twice.

As yet another noble lord prostrated himself, the king slumped in his throne, a sullen expression on his face. Clearly, the effects of the qiij were wearing off. Malaq had urged him—as he did every year—to exercise restraint now that he had a fresh, strong body, but the habit was so ingrained it was probably impossible to break.

He envied Eliaxa; she merely maintained a connection to the queen's spirit throughout The Shedding to be sure nothing went wrong. But the king was so weak that Malaq had to cast out the Host's spirit himself and then ease the king's into the lifeless body. It was an exhausting ordeal; this year, he'd nearly lost the king.

The queen leaned forward, smiling at the nobleman. She seemed perfectly at ease in her new body. If she lacked the willowy grace he had admired for the last year, the shimmering gown of gold she had chosen for today set off her darker skin perfectly.

Malaq shifted his weight and stifled a yawn; that he could even consider the queen's clothes with everything else on his mind proved that the tedium of a royal reception overcame all fears.

They resurfaced as soon as the kankh announced the end of the reception. As he followed the king and queen into the private chamber, Vazh appeared at his elbow.

"What's this meeting about?"

"I don't know."

"Are you in trouble?"

"Possibly."

Even if there had been time to say more, he must keep his distance; if anything went wrong, he didn't want Vazh implicated.

He sank onto the cushion with a grateful sigh; his legs ached from standing so long. He caught a faint whiff of honeysuckle as the Supplicant lowered herself onto the empty cushion to his right. Perhaps it was merely coincidence that she had chosen to attend today's meeting, but he doubted it. He hoped his polite smile covered his dismay.

A strand of black hair fell forward to tickle his shoulder as she whispered, "Rumors are flying. Has the Son of Zhe come to earth at last?"

"If so, it would be the greatest miracle of our age."

"Second only to my appearance at a council meeting."

She had the disturbing gift of divining the thoughts of others—and she loved demonstrating it. Even after so many years, he was always taken aback by the strange man-woman duality. There were times he could swear he saw not only the swell of breasts beneath her robe but the bulge of a penis as well. Appearances, of course, could be deceiving. He had only to look at Xevhan's handsome face to be reminded of that.

"Let us begin," the queen said. Her voice was higher now, lacking the familiar breathiness. "We have only a short time before we must prepare for the formal banquet."

"And I'm worn out from that reception," the king muttered.

If his body was reborn after The Shedding, his personality remained unchanged.

"Some of you might be aware of the events that have transpired, but for those who are not, I'd like to ask the Zheron to speak."

Xevhan's recitation held no surprises, although Eliaxa was clearly disturbed when he mentioned the resemblance between "The Wild Man" and Kheridh and proclaimed them father and son. The queen's expression was utterly unreadable. When Xevhan concluded, she said, "Pajhit? Can you shed any light on these events?"

"Yes, Earth's Beloved."

Calmly, he countered all of Xevhan's points. Yes, Kheridh knew the man; he had once belonged to his tribe. No, he had not told the Zheron; he was shocked into speechlessness at his unexpected appearance, and after the other man's death, the Zheron had to hurry away for the dawn sacrifice. As to the resemblance, Kheridh said the man was a relative—but of course, everyone in those tiny villages was related.

"A relative," the queen said. "Not his father."

"No, Earth's Beloved."

"Did you note a resemblance?"

She might be guessing, but if her spies—or Xevhan's—had reported that he'd spoken with the Spirit-Hunter, it was better to admit it than be caught in a lie. "The coloring is altogether different," he replied evenly. "But there are similarities in the bone structure. Again, not uncommon when the bloodlines are such a tangle."

"And when did you speak with this man—what is his name?"

He froze, trying to remember what name the dreadful Olinio had used. "Urnek? Renek? Forgive me, Earth's Beloved. It's been a long day, and I simply cannot remember."

"Reinek," Xevhan said.

"Ah, yes. Thank you." So he'd taken time from ogling the singer to make inquiries. "I had my guards bring the man to me for questioning after Kheridh informed me what had happened at the Zheron's . . . entertainment. I did try to inform you of my intentions, Earth's Beloved, but you were resting."

"Oh, very good," the Supplicant murmured.

Distracted, Malaq paused to take a sip of wine. "I thought the man might have information that would prove useful on future raids. Unfortunately, he left his tribe several years ago, so I'm not sure how accurate it is."

"And afterward?" the queen asked.

Malaq shrugged. "I released him. He'd committed no crime. The death of the other man was clearly an accident. An investigation would reveal that the Zheron had instigated the fight, and I was loath to have a senior member of the priesthood implicated in such a sordid affair."

For some time he had been aware of Xevhan's restiveness. Now he shoved himself to his feet. "He is the boy's father. Before I could question him, Malaq spirited him out of the city."

"Releasing him is hardly the same as spiriting him out of the city."

Xevhan's smile chilled him. "Nor is it the same as providing him with this."

The safe conduct disk clattered onto the table.

"My men discovered it after they took him to the slave compound. Unlike you, I took the precaution of having the man detained. Would you care to explain how he got it?"

"Obviously, I gave it to him." Malaq hoped he sounded bored, but his stomach was churning.

"And why would you do that?"

"To get him away from Kheridh."

"Because he's the boy's father!"

"Because he upset him!" He was on his feet now, too. "I will not have him distracted by the fate of a tribe mate when he should be focusing his attention on teaching us about his gift."

"Teaching *you*, Pajhit. The rest of us have learned nothing."

"Perhaps you might have—if you weren't plying him with qiij."

Xevhan's head snapped back.

"You gave him qiij?" the queen asked sharply.

"He came to me. Demanding it. When I refused, he took it."

Malaq shot him a scornful look, but remained silent, allowing the others to picture Kheridh attempting to rip the vial of qiij off Xevhan's neck, remove the stopper, and swallow the drug before Xevhan could prevent him.

"Merciful gods," the Supplicant said. "The boy must be a brute. I hope you weren't too badly injured."

If I survive this meeting, I will place two cartloads of flowers on your altar.

"He's not permitted to take qiij," the king noted. "He should be punished."

"I am the one who should be punished," Malaq insisted, "for failing to make it clear to him."

"He knew," Xevhan said. "I told him."

"Before he overpowered you?" the Supplicant asked.

Besul rapped the table impatiently. "We are straying from the subject. Pajhit. Zheron. If you would sit, please. Now. As I see it, there are several issues to consider. One: the incident with the qiij. Troubling, yes, but with time so limited, we can surely afford to delve into the matter later. Two: the propriety—or impropriety—of the Pajhit giving this man a safe conduct. And the Khonsel for providing one. Again, troubling, but . . ."

The queen cut off Vazh's bellow of protest with a peremptory gesture.

". . . but only worth exploring as it relates to issue three: the relationship of this man to the boy Kheridh. The boy claims they are distantly related. The Zheron claims they are father and son. If true, the boy clearly cannot be the Son of Zhe."

"It is true," Xevhan asserted.

"The man confessed?" Vazh asked.

"He will."

"A man will say anything under torture," the Supplicant noted. "In a day, we could make him swear to being Eliaxa's father. May his spirit dance forever through the green hills of Paradise," she added piously.

"Then let us consider issue four," said Xevhan. "The Pajhit's obvious affection for all these tree lovers. For years, he has protested against our raids. He has protected this boy since he arrived. He even got a son on one of their whores. Furthermore—"

The Supplicant's hand gripped his forearm. But Vazh was already on his feet, his shouts overriding Xevhan's voice. "Bury you! Slander the Pajhit further and I'll challenge you, priest or not."

"Enough! Sit down, Khonsel. Zheron, you will moderate your tone."

"And furthermore," Xevhan continued in a softer voice, "the man in question is not merely a performer. He is considered a hero among his people. The leader of the players recognized him. Are we to believe that the Pajhit—with his extensive knowledge of these people—did not?"

Malaq laughed. He kept on laughing until he had mastered the overwhelming desire to rip Olinio's flapping tongue from his head and batter Xevhan's triumphant face with his fist.

"Forgive me," he said, still breathless. "Of course, I know the legend of Darak Spirit-Hunter. But that's all it is. A legend. About as plausible as their belief that the man's brother turned into a tree. To believe that a man could march into the Abyss and free the spirit of a god makes about as much sense as . . ."

"Believing the Son of Zhe could come to earth?" the Supplicant asked.

Eliaxa gasped. "That is blasphemy."

"His hands are maimed," Xevhan pointed out. "Just as the Spirit-Hunter's are supposed to be."

"I've got scars on my back," Vazh said, "but that doesn't make me the Flayed One."

"Then we must probe the man's spirit," Xevhan said. "And the boy's. Today. That's the only way to learn the truth."

The queen shook her head. "I'm not yet recovered from The Shedding. Neither are the Pajhit and the Motixa."

"Then at least hold them prisoner until you're stronger."

"All this talk is giving me a headache," the king whined. "Why don't we just execute them now?"

"Sky's Light, the boy might be the Son of Zhe!" Eliaxa exclaimed. "We cannot—"

"Well, execute the man then." The king grinned. "Or better still, sacrifice him to Zhe."

"But he is maimed," Eliaxa protested. "It would not be fitting."

"That's what makes it so perfect. Was not Zhe maimed as well? His feathers blackened and burned?" The king sat back on his throne, sickeningly proud of his reasoning.

"How wise you are, Sky's Light." Xevhan was practically purring with satisfaction. "What gift could please Zhe more than the living personification of his pain?"

"The Motixa is right." Malaq fought to keep his voice level. "Earth's Beloved, you cannot permit this sacrilege."

"It's not sacrilege," the king insisted. "Not if I say it isn't. I want him sacrificed. I am the king and I say we shall. Oh, let's do it, Jholianna. I know it would please Zhe. And it would please me, too."

Before she could answer, a guard tentatively asked permission to enter.

"What is it?"

"Forgive me, Earth's Beloved. Sky's Light." The guard ducked his head. "It's the Qepo. He says there's a problem with the adders."

The queen frowned. "Very well. Send him in."

The Qepo trotted forward and prostrated himself.

"Speak."

"Forgive me, Earth's—"

"Speak!"

"The adders. They are restless."

"That's all? We're dealing with important matters here."

"Yes, Earth's Beloved. Forgive me. But the last time they were so restless, Womb of Earth shook."

The queen's frown deepened. "You believe an earthquake is imminent?"

"I don't know, Earth's Beloved. I only know the adders are restless."

"More restless than they were before the last tremor?"

"Well . . . it's hard to say."

"Yes or no."

"No, Earth's Beloved."

"Then we have no reason to suspect anything more than a mild tremor."

"I cannot say, Earth's Beloved. But we've already had two in the last moon. In the past, a series of mild tremors preceded a more serious one."

"Only once," Besul said. "Ten years ago. During the Milk Moon."

"What does the season matter?" Vazh demanded.

"I simply noted—"

"The boy is apparently on cordial terms with our sacred adders," the Supplicant interjected. "Why not let him speak to them?"

"Yes," Eliaxa agreed eagerly. "If the adders are uneasy, he will surely find out why."

The queen considered and finally nodded. "Take the boy to the pit. If the adders tell him that a serious earthquake is imminent, we will evacuate the city. Khonsel—"

"The plans are already in place, Earth's Beloved. They were drawn up ten years ago. During the Butterfly Moon." Besul's strangled sound of protest drew a smile that immediately faded. "But evacuating the entire city requires time."

"I realize that. Qepo, we thank you for your diligence. Report the boy's findings directly to me. You may go."

After the Qepo had withdrawn, Xevhan cleared his throat. "As to the cripple . . ."

Everyone began speaking at once, but the queen only had eyes for her brother.

Forgive me, Spirit-Hunter. I did try.

"We have allowed him to distract us long enough. Sacrifice him. Tomorrow at dawn. The boy is not to know. After he has spoken to the adders, I want him confined to his chamber. No one is to speak to him."

The queen's eyes demanded his obedience. Malaq could only nod.

"Since none of my priests has been able to ascertain this boy's identity, it falls to me to do so—even if that means invading his spirit."

"But that would be a sacrilege!" Eliaxa exclaimed. "The prophecy makes clear—"

"Prophecies are never clear. If he is the Son of Zhe—a fact of which I am very much in doubt—he will understand our need for proof." The queen's gaze swept across the face of each priest and lingered on the Supplicant. "Your counsel is too often absent from our meetings. And your assistance this last moon was sorely needed."

"My god is a demanding one, Earth's Beloved. In fact, he summons me now. During your seclusion, he showed me many signs—good and bad—that suggest great changes are coming. But with so many signs to interpret—and so many possible interpretations—it has been difficult for me to advise you. So I have remained silent, communing with the god and hoping for revelation. But no matter what may befall our people, you have my assurance that I will always love those who worship the god I serve."

The supplicant rose and bowed, first to the queen, then to the king, and quietly left the chamber. For a moment, they all stared after her.

"Zheron."

Out of the corner of his eye, Malaq saw Xevhan start.

"While we appreciate your diligence in attempting to discover the boy's identity, allowing him to take qiij was a grave error. Neglecting to mention it to us, a worse one."

"Forgive me, Earth's Beloved."

"After Midsummer, you will retire to the sanctuary of Avhilat for a moon to reflect on your shortcomings."

A miserable eyrie in the most forsaken part of Zheros. Where he would be cut off from his supply of qiij.

"I will appoint another to carry out the duties of Zheron during your absence."

And that would hurt even more than the loss of qiij.

"Motixa." The queen spoke gently. "Instead of probing the boy's spirit yourself—or pressing the Pajhit to do so—you allowed your hope for the coming of the Son of Zhe to blind you to the possibility that the boy is a fraud. We do not chide you for your faith, but in the future, we hope you will leaven it with skepticism."

"Yes, Earth's Beloved."

"Pajhit."

No gentleness in the voice now and none in the face that regarded him.

"You have allowed your affection for this boy to take precedence over your duties to your people. We must reflect on whether your past service to us outweighs your divided loyalties. After we have examined the boy, we will decide whether you are fit to continue as Pajhit. Until that time, you are relieved of your responsibilities and confined to your chamber."

Malaq bowed his head. "Yes, Earth's Beloved."

Chapter 38

HIS ROOM FELT LIKE a cairn. Malaq's chamber held the memories of his encounter with his father. So, despite the relentless sun, Keirith took refuge in the garden.

He sat in a small patch of shade, knees drawn up to his chest. The air was almost too hot to breathe. His head ached. His eyes felt gritty from lack of sleep, but he didn't dare close them for then he might dream. If the Big One didn't pursue him, his father would. Or Urkiat.

Niqia had fled indoors, irritable from the heat. Malaq was at the reception. Ysal kept poking his head through the draperies, trying to tempt him with a game of dice, a plate of food, a cup of cool water.

His worried face appeared again. "That girl is here. Hircha. I told her I didn't think you'd want to see her, but she won't go away."

Before he could reply, the draperies were flung aside. Ysal gave a startled yelp as Hircha pushed past him.

"I told you to wait—"

"I need to talk with you."

She seemed tense and agitated. Her fingers kept plucking at her gown.

"It is all right, Ysal. Thank you."

Ysal shot a pained look at Hircha. "I'm only trying to do my duty, you know. It wouldn't kill you to be polite." Still muttering, he left them alone.

"What is it?" Keirith asked. "Is something wrong?"

She hesitated a moment, then blurted out, "I saw something. When I took the kitchen scraps to the gate. For the poor. We do that during the festival. After the sezhta. We take food to all four gates—"

"Aye. And?"

"I was at the western gate. I saw the Zheron's guards coming up the path. Your father was with them."

"That's impossible. My . . . the Spirit-Hunter's gone. He left the city."

"It was him. He stood head and shoulders above the guards." She refused to look at him, just stared at the stone flags while her fingers creased her gown and smoothed it again. "They were headed toward the slave compound."

All he could do was shake his head.

"I couldn't come before. I only just finished in the kitchen. I wasn't even sure if I should tell you. But . . . he's your father. And I thought you should know."

Finally, he managed to move, but as he pushed past Hircha, she grabbed his arm. "What are you going to do?"

"I have to go to him!"

"You'll only make things worse."

"Then I'll find Malaq."

"Only the queen can help him now."

"Then I'll go to her!"

"Xevhan probably ran to her while the blood from this morning's sacrifice was still warm." Hircha grimaced. "Unless he waited until he was finished with the blind girl."

The thought of what Xevhan might have done to the little singer only fueled his bloodlust. His mouth filled with saliva and he swallowed hard, refusing to give in to the overwhelming urge to find Xevhan and kill him.

He shook off Hircha and began pacing Malaq's chamber. He had to do something. He couldn't just wait here while they tortured his father to get the truth from him. Then he saw the snake earring, lying on the table. He scooped it up and was heading toward the doorway when Hircha said, "If you're looking for me, I can save you a hot, dusty trip."

It took him a moment to realize it wasn't Hircha's voice, another to turn and discover the apparition, lounging in the doorway of the garden. Part of his mind registered her strange appearance; the other was trying to imagine how she had scaled the wall to Malaq's garden in her long robe.

"We can talk more privately outside."

He exchanged a quick look with Hircha before following her.

They found her lolling on the bench at the far end of the garden. "In a few moments, the queen's guards will arrive to take you to the adder pit, so I fear we must dispense with pleasantries. I am the Supplicant of the God with Two Faces. How I got here is unimportant. Your father will be sacrificed at dawn tomorrow on the altar of Zhe. And if you're going to faint, I suggest you put your head between your knees and breathe slowly."

The scorn in her voice brought his head up. "I'm not going to faint."

"I'm relieved."

"And I *was* coming to you. You gave my father this. He gave it to me."

"I'm aware of the chain of events."

"Can you help him?"

"I've already given Darak the help he requires."

Keirith stumbled toward her and went down on his knees.

"First your father, now you. It's obviously a day for begging. To save time—and your knees—let us consider your anguished pleas completed. I refuse."

"But . . . he's going to die. You can't let that happen."

"I can. But it would mean breaking a promise, which I am loath to do. Besides, I'm fond of Darak."

"How do you—?"

"I have neither the time nor the inclination to enlighten you as to my relationship with your father. Nor do I have the patience to listen to you plead. It seems to me you do very little else. 'Supplicant, help my father.' 'Malaq, help my father.' When are *you* going to help him?"

Keirith got to his feet, anger overcoming his shock. "I tried to help him!"

"Oh, yes. Urkiat. That did show initiative. Now it's time to show a bit more. For years, you've complained about being in your father's shadow. Here's a marvelous opportunity to step out of it." Her expression grew stern. "You have power, Keirith. Far more than your father possessed when he destroyed Morgath. Why don't you use it?"

"How?"

"That, I'm afraid, you'll have to figure out for yourself." She smiled brightly. "It's been lovely meeting you. I hope we shall see each other again, but that's rather difficult to predict at the moment. Oh, and Hircha. You showed initiative in bringing Keirith the news of his father's arrest. That sort of behavior will serve you far better than limping about, nursing your resentment."

The draperies billowed as she stepped into the chamber. In the time it took him to rip them aside, she had vanished; there was no possible way she could have reached the doorway so quickly.

Hircha flicked her forefinger against her thumb three times, then smacked her palms together four times in the Zherosi sign to banish evil.

Forget about how she comes and goes. Think about what she said.

He must use his power. But how? To convince the queen to be merciful? To kill Xevhan before he could sacrifice his father?

Think, Keirith, think.

He'd never be able to sway the queen. If he killed Xevhan, another priest would simply take his place as Zheron. Short of killing every guard in the slave compound, he wouldn't be able to free his father. And regardless of the Supplicant's mockery, he doubted his power alone could save him.

"Hircha? Will you help me?"

"I . . . what do you want me to do?"

"Go to the place Xevhan held the entertainment. If the players aren't there, see if you can find them."

"They could be anywhere in the city!"

"I know!" Quickly, he lowered his voice. "Just try. Find the little man. The fair-haired one who sang with my father. He might help."

"Do what?"

"Free him."

"You'll never get him out of the slave compound."

"Nay. The only time will be right before the sacrifice."

"He'll be guarded."

"Aye. But they won't be expecting an attack."

"An attack? It's suicide!"

"Just ask the fair-haired man to be there. And to bring

the big shepherd. If he'll come." Hearing voices in the corridor, he pulled Hircha to the far end of the garden, buying a few precious moments of time. "Try to get to Malaq. I'm not sure they'll let me see him. Tell him what we're planning."

"I don't even know what we're planning!"

"Neither do I. But I'll come up with something."

Someone called his name.

"Please, Hircha."

She scowled. "All right. I'll try. I must be as crazy as you are."

He squeezed her hand and walked forward to meet the queen's guards.

It was close to sunset before Hircha found the players. The grooves left in the sand by their cart led her to the fields west of the city. It would have taken her until midnight to search every camp, but few could afford the luxury of a bullock.

Only the big man was there. She quickly discovered he couldn't tell her anything about the fair-haired dwarf's whereabouts, and his closed expression made her doubt he'd do so even if he could speak. So she told him what had happened to Darak and the fate that awaited him at dawn. She took care to call him "The Wild Man." But she did admit that Keirith was his son and that he had sent her to ask for their help.

At first, he stood there with his arms folded across his chest, staring toward the city as if she didn't exist. She wondered if he was deaf as well as mute. Then he frowned and looked at her and she knew he understood. He made a circling motion with his hand as if he wanted her to repeat the story again.

"I'm just going to have to tell it all over again when the dwarf comes."

When the mute turned away to contemplate the city again, she sighed. Now she had offended him. "He *is* coming back, isn't he?"

The mute inclined his head.

"Any time soon?"

He shrugged.

Hircha sat down and leaned against the cart. The mute stood over her, as silent and unmoving as a pillar. And very nearly as tall.

If she were smart, she'd go back to the palace now and get some sleep and get on with her life. Better still, she should set out west and find a new life. She wasn't expected back in the kitchen until midnight to help clean up after the banquet. Assuming it was over; sometimes, these formal affairs lasted all night. Even if the Master noticed her absence, no one would have time to look for her until dawn. She could be free of Pilozhat and free of Xevhan.

It was all Keirith's fault. Ever since that first interrogation. Reminding her of the tongue she used to speak, the home she used to have, the girl she might have been. Seeking her sympathy with his sad eyes and trembling hands.

The Supplicant had praised her for showing initiative in telling Keirith about his father. If only she'd shown some last night. The knife had been strapped to her thigh. Each time she'd passed behind Xevhan, her fingers had trembled with the urge to plunge it into his back. She might have managed it during the fight. With all eyes fixed on the men in the arena, she might even have slipped away unnoticed.

With one blow, she could have killed Xevhan and severed her bond to Keirith. But she had hesitated. Later, she tried to convince herself that she had been caught up in the battle, but the truth was she had allowed her emotions to rule her reason. Because she had feared Keirith would be accused in her place. Because she had seen how desperate he was to save his father. Because the Spirit-Hunter had come hundreds of miles to save his son, and no one had ever risked so much for her. She envied their love and hungered for a little piece of it—even more than she hungered for Xevhan's blood.

It was pathetic. She would count to one hundred. If the dwarf hadn't returned by then, she would leave.

She'd reached one hundred and fifty-five when the mute grunted and pointed toward Pilozhat. His eyes were better than hers. In the fading light, it took a while before she picked out the players among the small clusters of people returning from the city. They straggled up to the cart. The fair-haired dwarf's eyes were bloodshot as if he'd been drinking or crying. The others looked equally gloomy.

"You were there," the dwarf said. "Last night."

"Yes, I—"

"Did the Zheron send you to spy on us?"

The mute grabbed his shoulder and shook his head. Ignoring them both, Hircha addressed herself to the leader of the troupe, choosing her words with care. "The Zheron has arrested the Wild Man. He means to sacrifice him tomorrow at the temple of Zhe."

"Sacrifice him?" The leader splayed his fingers over his heart. "Merciful gods. First Urkiat. Then Rizhi. Now this."

"Rizhi?" For the first time, she realized the blind girl was missing. Had Xevhan decided to keep her? "Where is she? What's happened?"

"She's dead." The fair-haired dwarf turned his malevolent gaze on the leader.

"He said he wanted to hear her sing. That was all."

He spoke eagerly, as if trying to convince the others. Or perhaps he only wanted to convince her; judging from their expressions, the players had heard it all before.

"She was fine when Hakkon and I brought her back. A little distant perhaps, but I thought she was tired. We all thought she was tired. She'd gotten no sleep last night, after all. And she'd spent half the morning performing for the Zheron. I could never have anticipated it. One moment, she was sitting beside the cart. And the next, she had a knife in her hands. She couldn't even see. How could she grab the knife so quickly? How could I have stopped her?"

"How could you let her bleed to death?" the fair-haired dwarf demanded savagely.

"I tried! But the wounds were . . ." He shuddered. "You all saw me. I bound her wrists myself. With cloth cut from my own tunic. I didn't hesitate a moment, even though it was brand new and the cloth cost me two eagles. Oh, it's a tragedy. A terrible tragedy."

Presumably, he meant Rizhi's death, not the mutilation of his tunic.

"At least, the poor child got a decent funeral."

"Only because I insisted," the dwarf said. "If you'd had your way, you would have shoved her in a hole the way we did Urkiat."

"Bep." The old woman rested her hand on his shoulder. "It's done. Blaming each other isn't going to bring Rizhi back. Or Urkiat." She managed a weak smile. "Thank you for coming to tell us about poor Reinek. He was a good man. Quiet but dependable. And although I always suspected his heart wasn't in his work, he was an exceptional Wild Man. We will pray for him."

"After we leave Pilozhat," the leader insisted. "Hakkon, hitch up the bullock. If we break camp now, we can—"

"No."

To Hircha's surprise, the leader wilted at the old woman's voice.

"But we can't stay. Not after all that's happened."

"We've been two days and a night without sleep, Olinio. We've buried two of our comrades and another is dying tomorrow. We'll leave when the sun's up."

"You're not suggesting we witness the sacrifice?"

"No. But we should at least lay an offering on the altar of the God with Two Faces afterward. Perhaps that will encourage him to smile on us again."

"But, Mother . . ." As he launched into a volley of protests, the old woman walked away. Still protesting, he trotted after her.

"I'm sorry about the little girl," Hircha said. "She had a beautiful voice."

"She had a beautiful spirit, too," Bep said. "Until the Zheron crushed it."

The dark-haired dwarf sat slumped against the wheel of the cart, either exhausted or disinterested, but she didn't want him listening. Hircha jerked her head away from the camp. After a moment, Bep and Hakkon followed her.

"Keirith—the boy who spoke to the . . . to Reinek last night—he sent me."

"And you're a good friend of Keirith's, of course. And the Zheron's slave."

"Look. The last thing I want is to get involved in this crazy scheme. But Keirith asked me to come to you, and I agreed. He wants to try and help Reinek escape right before the sacrifice. After the procession leaves the palace. But he can't do it alone. Not with four guards around Reinek. Keirith's still working out details—"

"Well, that's reassuring. So far, it's worse than the plot

of one of our pantomimes." Bep slapped his forehead. "Wait! I've got it! I'll pretend to be a dog and bite one guard, while Hakkon beats another to death with his staff. That'll just leave one each for Reinek and the boy."

It took all her self-control not to slap him. "If you want to help, fine. If not, I've delivered the message." She tried one last time. "I know freeing Reinek isn't as good as killing the Zheron, but it's . . . it's something."

She was walking away when Bep called, "Girl!" He walked toward her slowly, his eyes hard. "Why are you so eager to help?"

"I have my own reasons for wanting to hurt the Zheron."

"And those are?"

"None of your business!"

Bep spat. Hakkon just watched her. Silently, she cursed them. And Keirith for getting her into this. And his father for getting caught. Most of all, she cursed herself for foolishly following her heart instead of her head.

"I was one of the Zheron's little girls, too. Does that satisfy you?"

The shock on their faces was answer enough.

Chapter 39

The first thing Darak saw were his charms, scattered on the dry, cracked earth. Tears came to his eyes when he saw the pieces of the fire-blackened twig.

After all that has happened, how can I weep over a broken charm?

He forced himself to sit up. Was it the blow to his head that made him so groggy or the aftereffects of his ordeal in Fellgair's chamber? The sun had disappeared behind the wall of the slave compound. It seemed impossible that he could have slept the afternoon away. Then he saw the bulging waterskin lying beside him. He remembered the guards holding it to his mouth, forcing him to drink. He'd been too grateful for the water to protest.

Carefully, he returned the charms to his bag and tied it around his neck. His belt pouch was empty; they'd taken the coins and Malaq's safe conduct disk. He couldn't believe Malaq had betrayed him. This had to be the Zheron's work. Which meant that Malaq's promise to protect Keirith might be worthless now. But if the Zheron had ordered his arrest, why had the guards brought him here? Unless the Zheron meant to question him later.

He learned little from the men sharing his shelter. Most simply rolled over with a groan or stared at him in confusion. They could barely mutter their own names, never mind recognize Keirith's. Force of habit made him repeat the names; if he managed to escape, he could bring word to their families. But the news would be grim: nearly all had red hair, which meant they would be taken to the altar of the sun god in a matter of days.

Simply walking to the next shelter made his heart flutter. The few men who acknowledged him spoke an unrecognizable tongue, but in the third, he discovered men from Keirith's ship. The only ones who were alert enough to respond were a hunter named Temet and a Memory-Keeper named Brudien. It was a shock to hear the names, part of the long list he had carried in his head for so many days.

"There were twelve ships," Temet said. "I think. They put most of the red-haired captives in ours." He fingered a dirty, blond braid. "Brudien and I have a bet. He says the fair-haired ones like us will make it till Midsummer. I'm wagering they'll take us before."

"The next few days should tell," Brudien said with a small smile.

Darak found their calm chilling, a combination of hopelessness and the effects of the drugs the Zherosi must be giving them. Surely, the heat couldn't account for the lassitude of those in the compound or explain why even Brudien and Temet tended to drift off in the middle of a sentence.

At sunset, Darak followed them to the long table where the guards dispensed food. The first one frowned when he held up his empty hands, then thrust out two bowls. Darak slung the waterskin over his shoulder and held out his bowl to another guard who ladled a thick fish stew into it. The next dished out a mixture of meat and dried fruit. Awkwardly cradling the bowls against his chest, he walked back to the shelter.

"You're lucky," Temet whispered. "Until yesterday, it was only a watery soup. They must be fattening us up for the sacrifice."

The stew smelled delicious, but he followed Temet's example and dribbled it into the circle of bowls held out by the other men. Then he passed the other bowl around as well. Each man took only a tiny handful; drugged and hungry and enervated from the heat, they still preserved the ways of hospitality in the slave compound.

"It's probably in the water, too," Temet said. "But you can't do without that."

Grimly, Darak determined to try. "Is there any way out?"

"The gate you came in and that door over there. Unless they want to sell you, you won't be leaving by the gate." Temet's gaze lingered a moment on his hands. "The guards select two men before dawn. Once, they took three. Don't know why. But those who go out the door never come back."

He nodded to the guards who were hauling ladders onto the narrow walkways near the top of the walls. "They pull the ladders up at night. You'd have to scale the wall like a squirrel. Or fly over it."

"There are more than a hundred men here. And . . . what? Twenty guards?"

"On the walls," Brudien said. "But you saw how many more arrived when they fed us."

"Still, if we all attacked at once . . ." Darak's voice trailed off as he scanned the sleeping men.

"We waited," Temet said. "That was our mistake. If we had tried to escape when we first arrived . . ."

"Nay. The first sennight, we were so drugged, we could scarcely move." Brudien leaned back against the wall and closed his eyes. "They're very thorough, the Zherosi."

"A man alone—on his way to the sacrifice. He might break away."

Temet shrugged. "*You* might. The drugs haven't fuzzled your brain or your body." A dreamy expression came over his face. "I was the fastest runner in my village. Won every race at the Gatherings. Swift as the wind, I was. Swift as the wind."

When the light began to fade, Darak realized no one would come for him until the morrow. Whatever the Zherosi planned for him, he needed to be strong. He stretched out on the ground, whispering the names of those who had already gone to the altar stone and those who still remained from Keirith's ship. Then he said a prayer for Keirith and fell into a deep, dreamless sleep.

Keirith lay in the pit, staring up at the night sky. Even with Natha's help, the adders had been too frenzied to send him more than a few disjointed images: stones tumbling into the pit, earth crumbling beneath their bodies. It took their combined power to calm them.

He had been too caught up in the events of the day to pay much attention to his headache or to Niqia's behavior. Now it seemed clear another earthquake was coming, but he didn't know how soon. Nor did he know if the adders' terror foretold a stronger tremor than the last.

A few toppling walls wouldn't devastate the city. And if the walls of the slave compound fell, his father might be able to escape in the confusion, along with all the other captives. If he gave the Qepo a definitive answer, the guards would take him back to his room and he'd be helpless to save his father. If he stalled for time and the earthquake struck, he risked being buried in the pit—and dooming hundreds of people to similar deaths.

Keirith sat up. The guttering torches on the viewing platform revealed the Qepo and two of the queen's guards. "The earth shakes. Soon, I think. But I do not know how bad."

"They're quieter now," the Qepo observed.

"Yes. I will talk to them again. But first I must rest."

The Qepo nodded his reluctant assent.

"May I speak with the Pajhit? With his magic and mine, we can learn more, faster." When the Qepo hesitated, he asked, "He is not ill?"

"No."

The Qepo shot a furtive glance at the two guards. Apparently, they intended to remain, replacing the two—why had he never bothered to learn their names?—who usually took over from Ysal and Luzik at night. Finally, he said, "The Pajhit cannot speak with you."

Had Malaq been arrested, too? Had Xevhan turned the queen against him? No one would tell him. At least, Malaq had the Khonsel watching out for him. His father was alone. He couldn't rely on the players; even if Hircha found them, there was no guarantee they would help. And the Supplicant would do nothing. It was up to him.

Keirith closed his eyes, seeking stillness and emptiness and inspiration. The night drifted by and he drifted with it. Once, he heard a woman speaking with the Qepo, but he ignored them. Moments later, the Khonsel's voice demanded to know what was happening. The Qepo's whispered reply provoked a series of oaths that gradually faded as he stomped out.

Stillness shattered, Keirith pulled his bag of charms from around his neck and laid each out on the ground. Even without the single torch in the pit, he could have recognized them by touch. The eagle's feather, the first one he'd collected. The strand of lakeweed, the green fronds hard now but still delicate in design. The stone, as round and red as Bel at sunset. The crooked quickthorn twig. And the last of his charms, the polished bloodstone Malaq had given him.

One by one, he returned the charms to his bag. He wondered if his father was keeping vigil tonight, too. The thought that they were together in spirit comforted him, as did the weight of his bag of charms against his chest.

He pulled memories of home from his mind, examining them with the same love and tenderness with which he had examined his charms: the day he and Conn made their blood oath; the morning he returned to the village from his vision quest and heard the Tree-Father proclaim him a man; sitting in a circle with the other children while his father related the ancient legends; sitting around the fire pit with his family while Callie blew a halting melody on his flute; sitting in the Tree-Father's hut, learning to empty his mind and still his thoughts.

"You have power, Keirith. Use it."

Smoke rose from the four braziers.

"Power protects those you love. And it allows you to punish those who hurt you."

Thin tendrils drifted skyward, as if the spirits of the adders were ascending.

"Perhaps they are frightened of us. That is good."

The tendrils curled like beckoning fingers.

"His power shall burn bright as Heart of Sky at Midsummer. His footsteps shall make Womb of Earth tremble."

"Come," the smoke whispered with Natha's voice. "Come with us."

His brothers wriggled around him, forming a circle of protection. Like the players with his father.

"You are one of us," the smoke whispered. "You belong with us."

Fluid as water, ethereal as smoke, the adders danced.

Their eyes were the fiery glow of the rising sun. Their voices were Zhe's blackened feathers, dispersed by the breeze. Their bodies were waves, bearing the fallen god home. And he was the fire-haired god made flesh, bright and terrible and strong.

Far away, a voice called, "What is it? What's happening?"

The smoke whispered its reply. "The coming of a new age."

Chapter 40

A PERSISTENT PRODDING woke Darak—a guard, poking him with the butt of his spear. Gheala hovered over the western wall, a pale fingernail of light in the dark sky. Somewhere in the distance, dogs howled.

He crawled to his feet and stumbled toward the cluster of men in the center of the compound. Another captive swayed slightly as the guards bound his hands. Darak's stomach lurched. Temet gave him a bleary smile and accepted the cup a guard thrust toward him.

Two men. Every morning.

He was not going to be questioned. He was going to the altar stone he had first seen through the portal in Chaos.

Obeying the guards' gestures, Darak removed his tunic, then held out his hands and allowed them to bind his wrists. They left his feet free; clearly, they thought he would be too stupefied to run. When a guard shoved a cup toward him, he hesitated. If he didn't drink, they would force it down his throat.

A sudden burst of song shattered the predawn stillness. The guards' heads jerked toward Temet. A quick slap silenced him, but it gave Darak the precious moment he needed to twist his wrists and let the water splash onto the ground. When the guards looked back, water was dripping from his chin. One peered into the cup and thrust it back at him, forcing him to drain the dregs. It tasted as musty as it smelled. He prayed a swallow wouldn't impair him.

His gaze sought Temet, who shrugged and offered that same bleary smile. Just a moment of recognition, of thanks given and acknowledged before the guards moved in.

Darak's hope for escape sank as four surrounded him, all armed with swords. Even if he knocked one aside, he doubted he could outrun the others. The one who must be the leader muttered a few words in Zherosi and pointed to him. When Darak caught the word "Zhe," he wondered why he hadn't realized his destination immediately. Of course, the Zheron wanted the pleasure of sacrificing him. But at least Temet's gesture had not been made in vain. If there was no escape, there was still the possibility of revenge.

They would have to free his hands before the sacrifice. He would have only a moment, but the Zheron would be unprepared. He might be able to wrest a weapon from one of the guards. Or take the dagger out of the Zheron's hand and slaughter him on the altar of the god he served. Or simply reach up, twist the man's head between his palms, and break his neck.

Darak pictured the Zheron's look of astonishment. He heard the satisfying snap of bone. The bloodlust surged and he tamped it down until the flames were mere embers.

Soon.

His hands were utterly steady, just as they had been during the raid. Steady and strong and whole. They had killed for him that morning; they would kill for him again today.

Very soon.

His lips were numb. The effect of the drugged water. All the better. It would prevent a smile from betraying him. Slack-jawed and shambling, Darak let the guards lead him across the compound.

Nelkho roused him before dawn, lighting the lamps and laying out his robe and cloak just as he always did. Either the old slave didn't know of his fall from grace or he simply assumed that he would follow his usual routine.

Malaq stood quietly while Nelkho slipped the chain over

his head. The queen had not demanded he surrender his vial of qiij. In name, he was still Pajhit. But for the first time in five years, another would stand at the altar of Heart of Sky at dawn.

Dully, he wondered what would happen if the queen dismissed him. Vazh would loan him enough money to get a new start somewhere. But what could he do? He was unsuited for trade, too old for the army. A provincial priest, perhaps, serving out his remaining years in a run-down temple. If they would have him. Even his relatives might be reluctant to welcome him, fearing the queen's displeasure.

Impatiently, he shook off selfish concerns. All he faced was disgrace and poverty. Kheridh faced death. Unless he could shield himself from the queen, she would discover the truth. And once she did, he would die on the altar as surely as his father.

They would be taking the Spirit-Hunter to the temple now. The man who had bargained with one god and rescued another would die under the dagger of a man unworthy to speak his name. Malaq waved Nelkho away and knelt before his shrine. The least he could do was pray that Darak's spirit found sanctuary in the Forever Isles.

A commotion outside disturbed him. He rose and walked to the doorway where he found one of his guards arguing with the queen's men.

"What is it?"

"Please, Pajhit." It was the young one who guarded Kheridh during the day. "Something's happening in the adder pit."

"What?"

"I don't know. I . . . I went there." He shot a worried look at the queen's men. "To make sure . . . to see if Kheridh was . . ."

"Yes, yes. And?"

"The guards were gone. And the Qepo. But I looked into the pit . . ." He shuddered.

Malaq seized his shoulders. The sharp stink of the guard's fear only heightened his.

"The adders. They were swarming all around him."

The fingers of the other guards flew as they sketched spirals on their chests.

"Yes. It's frightening the first time you see it, but there's nothing—"

"They were following him. To the door. Like . . . like dogs obeying their master."

Malaq's hands fell to his sides.

"The Son of Zhe," one of the queen's men whispered. "It's true."

As Malaq started out the doorway, the other guard stepped forward. "Forgive me, Pajhit. But the queen gave orders—"

"I must go to the pit."

"But my orders—"

"Damn your orders! Let me pass, or I will cast your spirit into the Abyss."

The guard hesitated, his hand on the hilt of his sword. Malaq didn't wait for his decision. He shoved past him and raced down the corridor, pushing through a knot of startled priests on their way to morning prayers.

A few Zhiisti had gathered in the central courtyard to watch the procession of sacrificial victims. Their shocked faces blurred past him; Malaq imagined the delight they'd take in describing the oh-so-serious Pajhit with his robe hiked up to his knees as he ran up the steps to the throne room.

When he heard another set of footsteps echoing behind him, he glanced back and discovered the young guard hard on his heels. Malaq pushed through the draperies at the far end of the chamber and bolted into the corridor that led to the royal apartments. He'd barely flung open the door to the viewing platform when he heard the scream.

Please gods, don't let him be dead.

He clattered down the stairs and found the Qepo pressed against the far wall. Kheridh walked toward him, his face serene, his eyes unfocused. Malaq spoke his name softly, but he was too deep in trance to hear. As he passed the stairs, Malaq extended a hand to touch his shoulder, only to draw back, instinctively flattening himself against the wall like the Qepo.

Kheridh walked among a living tide of adders, a writhing mass of slender bodies that surged past the step on which he stood and spilled over the feet of the terrified Qepo. Ignoring them both, ignoring even their natural instinct to

flee. Moving with one mind and one intention—to follow
the boy who led them through the anteroom and into the
corridor beyond.

"The coming of a new age."

It must have been the young guard who spoke; the Qepo
had slid down the wall, shaking uncontrollably.

Malaq lurched around the corner after Kheridh. His
shoulder scraped stone and he winced as he flung out a
hand to push himself forward. His legs moved reluctantly
and his feet rose and fell as if weighted with heavy stones.
He remembered wading waist-deep through the river that
flowed beside his village, ponderous as a bullock as he
fought the swift, icy current. He'd been frightened then,
too, but elated by the battle. And now, just as in the battles
he had fought, time seemed to slow and tiny details impressed themselves on his senses: the laces of his sandals, snapping against his ankles; a drop of sweat trickling down his
forehead; his giant shadow capering grotesquely on the opposite wall.

He rounded one corner and caught a glimpse of Kheridh
disappearing around another. Where was he going? There
was nothing on this level save for storage rooms and
slave quarters.

He heard a scream. The clatter of bronze. Passed a slave
boy huddled against the wall. A girl, sprawled in the doorway of her chamber. Terrified faces peeped out at him as
he rushed past. Other slaves poured in from adjoining corridors, blocking his way, ignoring his shouts and curses. The
young guard edged past him and used his sword to clear a
path. After that, Malaq had only to follow the new eruption
of screaming to see Kheridh heading toward the central
courtyard.

When he reached it, he drew up short. A crowd had
already gathered. Torches illuminated fleeing figures, but
most stood transfixed, watching the boy who strode with
awful majesty through the courtyard and the tide of adders
that streamed after him.

Someone grabbed his arm. He started to shake off the
restraining hand when he saw it was Hircha, her sullen face
transformed with wonder.

"Where is he going?" Malaq demanded. "Do you know?"

"To the temple of Zhe. To free his father." Her smile was radiant. "And kill Xevhan."

Before Malaq could react, a woman cried, "He comes! He comes!"

He saw the white hair first. Then the crowd parted to reveal Eliaxa hurrying toward Kheridh, her face alight with joy. She had clearly been on her way to the temple of Womb of Earth; her arms were still filled with bitterheart, although the chaplet crowning her head was askew.

"Behold the fire-haired god made flesh! Behold the Son of Zhe!"

In the terrified silence that followed, another voice spoke. "Behold the Son of Zhe who brings a new age to Zheros and death to the unrighteous."

He thought he knew Kheridh's voice. Halting at times, defiant at others, broken with anguish, wooden with shock. Only rarely—very rarely—had it possessed the eagerness or excitement that should be the right of every boy on the cusp of manhood. This was the deep, resonant voice of prophecy, the unforgiving voice of doom. And everyone acknowledged it with moans and gasps and muttered prayers. Men and women fell to their knees. Eliaxa chanted the prophecy, her voice as strong as the boy's despite the tears streaming down her cheeks.

As if scripted by the gods, the Motixa led the Son of Zhe and his escort of adders forward. Malaq trailed behind, the lone acolyte who passed among the kneeling figures who wept and prayed and rocked back and forth in terror and ecstasy.

He heard shouts behind him and turned to see guards clearing a path for the queen. Even in her nightdress, she was a commanding figure. She shouted Kheridh's name and demanded that he stop.

His inexorable stride slowed. He turned to face her. His hand came up. An accusing forefinger stabbed the air. "Eater of spirits, eater of life. Womb of Earth will destroy you and all who obey you."

Screams drowned out the prayers. Malaq saw the queen's mouth move. Guards edged toward Kheridh, their swords drawn, but their eyes were on the adders, seething around his feet. Ignoring the chaos, Kheridh strode into the passageway that led to the eastern gate. Again the queen shouted. A guard hefted his spear.

Malaq raced forward. There was a blur of movement: a flurry of white, a shower of red, the spear arcing through the air toward Kheridh's unprotected back.

Eliaxa's hands came up, clutching the shaft of the spear protruding from her chest. Her dark eyes flew wide, but—dear gods, have mercy—she was smiling as she crumpled to the ground.

Her spirit had already fled by the time Malaq knelt beside her. Sprays of bitterheart—bright as Eliaxa's blood—lay scattered around her body like an offering. He closed the staring eyes and sketched a spiral on her forehead before rising.

"No one touches him!" he shouted over the uproar. "No one! Or I will call the wrath of the gods down upon this city."

His gaze met the queen's. She shook her head. In disbelief? Disappointment? She seized the arm of the nearest guard. A moment later, the man sprinted toward the administrative wing.

Already, people were pushing past Eliaxa's body to pour into the passageway after Kheridh. He would never get through. He told Kheridh's guard to find the Khonsel and bring him to the temple of Zhe. Then Malaq ran for the northern gate.

Darak emerged from the dark passageway into chaos. Figures dashed madly through the open area, while others were on their knees, moaning and wailing. The guard in front of him thrust out an arm to stop a fleeing man. Between sobs, Darak caught the word "Zhe." The hands gripping his arms tightened convulsively; the fear on his captors' faces was obvious.

The dawn sacrifices couldn't have generated all this commotion. Had something happened to the Zheron? Or Keirith? Malaq had said some believed him to be the Son of Zhe.

The guard in front shouted a command. Shouted again when the others refused to move. Temet and his guards marched left. Swords drawn, his guards led him straight ahead. Men darted past, clutching makeshift bundles that leaked coins and bronze jewelry; others followed in their wake, stooping to snatch up the discarded treasure. Women hugged screaming babes to their breasts; others dragged sleepy-eyed children by the hand. He searched the crowd for a glimpse of auburn hair, but he'd never be able to spot Keirith in this mob.

Something scuttled over Darak's foot. A moment later, the guard on his left cried out. Screams broke out all around.

That was when he saw the rats. Gods, they were everywhere. Scurrying across the compound, drawing screams and exclamations from the people who jumped aside to avoid them. All except the robed priests who knelt calmly at the base of a wide stone staircase, singing. With mounting horror, Darak heard "Kheridh" repeated over and over again.

Calling on his limited Zherosi, he stammered out, "Kheridh. Zhe-boy. Where?"

The guard on his left just stared at the steady stream of people pushing past the priests into a passageway. Had Keirith gone that way?

"Kheridh. Zhe-boy." The drug made the words sound thick and garbled. "Zhe-boy. He comes here?"

The guard in front whirled around, hand upraised for a blow. Another shouted a warning and pulled him out of the path of a careening litter. They collided with one of the bearers who dropped his pole. The litter lurched sideways, spilling its screaming occupants to the ground.

Darak wrenched his arms free. Staggering away from the guards, he raced toward the passageway.

Malaq stumbled and cursed. Glancing to his right, he saw Kheridh, moving with that same inexorable pace along the walkway. A few people followed at a careful distance. He saw no sign of the Spirit-Hunter; perhaps he'd escaped in the confusion.

He had to reach the temple before Kheridh. His only hope of saving him was to play along with this pretense that he was the Son of Zhe. The other two priests might be sufficiently cowed by the boy's appearance, but he doubted Xevhan would be. Nor would he simply stand there and wait for the adders to swarm over him. Kheridh must be planning to cast out his spirit, but if Xevhan had taken qiij this morning, he would be able to shield himself.

Malaq's steps slowed. He clawed at the stopper of the vial, his eyes darting from Kheridh to the temple. Grimacing at the bitter taste, he swallowed the undiluted qiij.

An unearthly yowl made him glance behind him. Niqia crouched low to the ground, her tail lashing back and forth. Good gods, had she followed him all the way from his chamber? She yowled again, but he had no time to ease her distress.

The sharp stitch in his side returned after only a few steps. He judged Kheridh's distance from the temple and fell into a trot. The guttering torches revealed movement behind the altar. He doubted the priests could see the adders, but they had clearly seen Kheridh and realized he was not the sacrifice they were expecting.

Nor will he be.

Malaq smiled, knowing it was the qiij that gave him confidence. He slowed to a walk and cleared his throat. He'd spent half his life in the priesthood and the other half on battlefields. He knew how to pitch his voice for all men to hear. Sweeping his arm in Kheridh's direction, he called out the ancient words.

"By these signs shall you know him. His power shall burn bright as Heart of Sky at Midsummer. His footsteps shall make Womb of Earth tremble. Speechless, he shall understand the language of the adder and wingless, soar through the sky like the eagle."

One priest clutched the serpentine pillar. The other traced a spiral on his chest. Xevhan gave an inarticulate cry of rage.

"No pageantry shall attend his arrival. No poet—"

"It's a lie!"

"—shall sing his name. No mortal woman shall know his body. No mortal man shall call him son."

"He is not the Son of Zhe!"

Standing before the altar, Malaq intoned the final words of the prophecy. "Hail the Son of Zhe, the fire-haired god made flesh. Welcome him with reverence and with dread. For with him comes the new age."

"You fools! Don't believe him. He's protected the boy all along. He's a traitor to our people. A traitor to our gods!"

The other priests were staring past him, their eyes wide. Xevhan's voice trailed off. They all stood there, dumb-struck, watching the boy arrive amid a seething flood of adders.

"Behold the Son of Zhe!" Malaq called.

"Behold the Child of Serpents," Kheridh replied. "Be-hold the Destroyer of the Unrighteous."

Malaq laughed, the qiij singing through his body. Kher-idh's expression remained as distant as if he *were* the De-stroyer of the Unrighteous. Could the trance still be holding him? If not, he should take his place among the premier performers in the kingdom.

One priest fled, then the other. Malaq glanced over his shoulder and smiled at Xevhan. "We were wrong. And the proof of our error is before us."

Kheridh stood motionless before the altar. The adders writhed wildly around his feet. A few attempted to wriggle up the steps. Malaq was too exhilarated to care. They wouldn't strike him. Kheridh wouldn't permit it.

"Welcome, Kheridh. Son of Zhe. Son of my heart. Wel-come to your temple."

Kheridh's expression changed, the dazed look replaced by shock and—incredibly—horror. Puzzled, Malaq took a step toward him. "Kheridh?"

Agonizing pain ripped through his back, as if Heart of Sky had pierced him with a molten shaft of sunlight. Dis-tantly, he heard a scream but knew it had not come from his mouth. He flung out a hand, groping for the altar, but his fingers slid down the side of the stone. So smooth, so cool. Already, the fire was lessening, the shaft of sunlight oozing warmth down his back.

Cold hands grasped his. He looked up into his boy's eyes.

Heart of Sky's first rays bronzed his pale face and turned his hair to fire. His mouth was moving, but Malaq couldn't understand the words. A delicious chill crept through him. Clouds gathered over Kheridh's head, although Heart of Sky still illuminated his face. But even Heart of Sky seemed to be dimming.

Rain would feel wonderful.

He wished he could pat Kheridh's face and assure him that everything would be all right, but his arms were so heavy. He'd hardly slept the last few days and now, it was catching up with him.

The clouds grew thicker, obscuring the beloved face. Thunder rumbled, echoing through the air above him and the earth below.

Malaq smiled. He'd always loved thunderstorms.

The earth groaned as if Halam protested the coming of dawn. Like everyone else at the gate, Darak froze, awaiting another sign from the earth goddess. The sky to the east smoldered with red and orange clouds. Naked tree trunks loomed up, dark against the flaming sky. Nay, not trees. Pillars flanking a walkway.

Darak raced down it, weaving between clusters of people who stood as still as the pillars looming above them. The ground trembled again, and he staggered sideways. He heard a roar like an angry bull, but before he could puzzle it out, the earth convulsed.

He went down hard, knees cracking against stone. When he tried to get to his feet again, he sprawled headlong. The earth goddess bellowed like Taran the Thunderer. She rolled like the waves of the great sea. Stone scraped his naked arms as he slid sideways. Another wave heaved him up and slammed him against a pillar. The small part of his mind that still functioned registered wood beneath his fingers instead of stone. The massive tree trunk shuddered as if it shared his terror.

Most of the people he had passed had flattened themselves on the ground, but a few men lurched down the path, staggering from pillar to pillar. As he watched, Halam flung them to the ground as a child might discard an unwanted toy. One inched forward like a crawling bug before collapsing. As if tired of the game, Halam heaved a final sigh and became still.

Cautiously, Darak pushed himself to his knees. A few heads came up, but most of those on the walkway remained prone. Although it had seemed to take forever, the shaking of the earth could only have lasted mere moments; Bel was barely peeping over the horizon.

As he got to his feet, a figure leaped out from behind a pillar. Darak stumbled backward, only to find himself seized by Hakkon's strong hands. Before he could ask what he was doing here, Bep scurried toward them.

"Hold out your hands and listen." Bep sawed at the ropes binding his wrists. "Your boy. He's up ahead. But he's—"

Another tremor, stronger than the first, hurled them all to the ground. By the time Darak recovered, he found Hakkon collapsed at the base of a pillar and Bep scuttling sideways across the path like a crab.

All along the walkway, the giant pillars swayed. In Bel's dawning light, they looked red as blood. A fissure ripped open and snaked across the earth, leaving a trail of cracked paving stones heaved up like huge, broken teeth. Earth poured into the fissure, sending up a cloud of dust. A pillar rocked back and forth, mesmerizing him. How could something so big move so gracefully? Then the pillar tottered uncertainly. Its top knocked against another and they both lurched like drunken men. The second pillar began to topple. He rolled out of the way, only to see the first looming above him—a red giant that blotted out the sky as it slowly descended. He flattened himself next to the fallen pillar and prayed.

The crash reverberated through his body. Gravel, earth, and pebbles rained down on him. Choking, he buried his face in the crook of his elbow. Above the thunderous noise, the high, shrill shrieks of terrified men and women echoed the earth goddess' agony.

He dared a look up and stared at the palace in horrified fascination. The wall seemed to be . . . dancing. A block near the top teetered and hurtled to the ground, crushing a man beneath it and scattering those nearby who rolled, crawled, and dragged themselves away. Another block cracked and fell, and then another, as if some malevolent god were gleefully ripping apart the wall and tossing it at the hapless people below. And then the wall collapsed with a roar that made him cover his ears.

In the aftermath of the shock, everything went still. The ground ceased shaking. Dust drifted earthward. Even the screaming faded into weak cries for help.

Darak cautiously flexed his legs, then his arms. Finally, he raised his head. The second pillar had fallen crosswise atop the first. An arm's length away and he would have been crushed.

Shaking, he eased out of his tiny grotto and used his teeth to pull the rope from his wrists. Hakkon rose unsteadily, lifting one hand in weary acknowledgment. Darak peered through the gloom, searching for Bep.

"Oh, gods!"

Incredibly, he was still alive, although his belly and legs were surely crushed by the pillar. Darak knelt beside him and brushed the dirt from his face.

Bep's eyes fluttered open. His mouth twisted in a semblance of his mocking grin. "What an ending."

"Just lie still."

"Listen." Bep gasped for air. His free arm flailed. Darak caught his hand and squeezed hard. "Your boy. The temple. Go. Now."

Bel poured soft golden light on the altar. It turned the snakes wriggling away from the stone steps into tiny waves. It painted the feathers in the Zheron's headdress the colors of fresh blood and birch leaves in autumn. It sent sparks flashing from the bronze dagger between the two struggling figures.

Darak leaped up, screaming his son's name—in warning, in denial, in a ceaseless prayer to keep the dagger from descending, to stop the deathblow from falling, to let him get there in time.

Maker, help me.

His legs were so heavy, so slow. His feet tripped over upended paving stones.

Maker, don't let him kill my boy.

The feathered headdress bent lower as the Zheron forced Keirith down.

Keep fighting, son, keep fighting, just a few moments more.

Keirith's back arched over the stone. Keirith's hair streamed over the edge of the slab. Keirith's upraised fists locked around the priest's wrist, but—oh, gods—his arms were bending under the strain, his fists inching toward his chest as slowly and relentlessly as the point of the Zheron's dagger.

Please, Maker, don't take my boy. Please, Fellgair, take me, take me, take me!

Chapter 41

THE INITIAL BURST of agony was already ebbing
when Xevhan's face suddenly disappeared. The sunlight burned his eyes. More painful was the sense that he
had failed. Malaq was dead. Xevhan had won. And his
father . . . he could only hope his father had escaped in
the chaos of the earthquake.

But even his failures leached away, like rain into soft
earth, like blood into sand. There was only the sun, bright
and remorseless, yet incapable of driving away the cold that
crept up his legs, stealthy as Niqia stalking a butterfly.

He closed his eyes. Behind his lids, the crimson sun faded
as if a cloud had passed overhead. From far away, he heard
the voice, calling him. Felt the hands, gripping him.

Keirith opened his eyes and saw his father's stark face,
stubbled with a day's growth of beard. He was always so
meticulous about shaving, but of course, so much had happened. He smiled and his father's face crumpled and disappeared. Then it bobbed back. Calloused fingers brushed the
hair off his face. Cracked lips moved, but a sudden breeze
snatched away the words.

He was flying. Not the soaring flight he had known with
the eagle or the jolting disorientation of emerging too
quickly from a trance. He was drifting skyward, like a wisp
of smoke rising through the venthole of their hut. But like
his flight with the eagle, his eyes were keener than they
had ever been as a boy.

There were the adders, wriggling toward the mountains

and freedom. There was Xevhan, fleeing in the opposite direction. And there was Hircha, standing on the ruined path he had just walked, shading her eyes against the glare of the rising sun as she watched Xevhan.

I'm sorry, Hircha. I might have killed him if the earth-quake had come a moment later.

Two men were dragging the Khonsel away from the crumbling hillside overlooking the city. The slender man reminded him of Ysal. The other glanced up, shouting at the column of soldiers trotting toward them. When Keirith saw the eye patch, he recognized Geriv who had shadowed him since that morning in the Khonsel's chamber. But today, he must have had other responsibilities. No one would bear witness to Malaq's murder.

His regret faded as he drifted higher. He saw Temet, leaning against the ruined altar of Heart of Sky, bellowing out the hunter's song. He saw dozens of people fleeing the palace. Among the dark heads was a cluster of color. The newly risen sun made their hair shimmer like the fires licking through the palace. Perhaps that fair head belonged to Brudien. Perhaps the red one beside it was Sinand's, but he was too high now to discern their features.

Pilozhat was a pile of tiny white blocks that lay tumbled one atop the other at the bottom of the hill. The sea rose and fell like a panting bosom, tossing the ships about, but even as he watched, her anxiety began to subside. Soon she would be placid again; Womb of Earth could no more destroy the sea than she could tear a hole in the limitless sky.

The sunlight was everywhere, but now it bathed him in peace. This was how the sun must shine in the Forever Isles, soft and radiant and eternal. He wondered if it shone that way in Malaq's Paradise. Perhaps Paradise and the Forever Isles were the same. He hoped so. He would like to see Malaq waiting for him on those sun-drenched shores.

A terrible howl shattered the silence in which he drifted. The sunlight retreated as if affronted. He felt himself floating earthward again and resisted the pull. But the howl came again—a hoarse, animal cry of pain that tugged him away from the sea and the sky and the sun, pulling him back over the ruined city, back to the altar.

He didn't want to go there. There was only pain at the altar. Pain and failure.

A third time, the howl rent the air. And this time, he knew it was not the cry of a wounded animal, but the grief-stricken scream of a man.

Three times for a charm. Everyone knew that.

Reluctantly, Keirith answered his father's call. He hovered over the temple. Malaq's body sprawled on the steps. His body lay on the altar. There was so much blood. He hadn't realized that. The big man from the troupe of players was bending over his father. Hircha was there now, too. And Niqia. At least Fa wouldn't be alone. That was good.

But his father seemed unaware of that. His head was thrown back, his face contorted with grief. Keirith wished he could tell him that everything was all right now. His father's pain made him ache, pulled him farther from the welcoming sunlight.

The earth was sliding into the gorge behind the temple, just melting away. Soon, the temple would melt with it. They had to leave. Hircha tugged on his father's arm. Even in the midst of disaster, she knew what to do. Cool, clever Hircha. She would keep them safe.

But Fa wasn't listening. He was still clinging to that body. His body.

I'm not there, Fa. Let go.

"Come into me. Keirith! Please. Come into my body."

Suddenly, Keirith understood. He had to reassure his father that all was well. Then he would cease his grieving and allow him to fly away.

Without the distraction of his body, it was so easy. His spirit flowed toward his father, gently seeking, gently touching.

"There's no time for this!" Hircha shouted. "Pick him up. Drag him if you have to."

Before Hakkon could move, the Spirit-Hunter reared back, his eyes huge. He crumpled onto the steps of the altar, then began convulsing. Hakkon heaved him into his arms to keep him from striking his head, but big as he was, he couldn't restrain him. The Spirit-Hunter writhed. His legs jerked in helpless spasms. His eyes rolled back in his

head and his back arched. For a heartbeat, he remained
frozen in agony. Then he collapsed.

Hircha seized his limp arm, frantically searching for a
pulse. "He's alive. Whatever happened, he's alive."

A rumble behind her warned of another rockslide.

"You'll have to carry him."

East held death at the bottom of the gorge. To the north,
there was only wilderness, to the south, only the sea. Hakkon heaved the Spirit-Hunter over his shoulder, grunting
with the effort. Without waiting for her, he strode west.

Hircha paused. With a trembling hand, she lifted Keirith's head and pulled his bag of charms free; his father
should have some token of the son he had lost. Then she
gently closed his eyes.

"I'm sorry. For everything. But I'll see your father safe.
I swear it on my life. So you can fly away. Fly to the Forever Isles. You're lucky to be out of this miserable world."

Niqia yowled. She turned to find the cat sniffing the Pajhit's face. When the pink tongue darted out to lick his
cheek, Hircha burst into tears.

The Spirit-Hunter had lost his son. Hundreds of people
must have seen their loved ones die this morning. And she
was crying because a cat had lost its master.

She bent down to pick up Niqia, but the cat arched her
back, hissing.

"Fine. Stay here. I can't be responsible for you, too."

Angrily swiping the tears from her cheeks, she limped
after Hakkon.

PART THREE

I seek but cannot find you.
I call but receive no answer.
Oh, beloved, beloved.
Would I had died for you.

Lament for the Dead

Chapter 42

LIKE A NIGHTMARE, random images and sounds impressed themselves on Hircha's consciousness: the horrible chorus of human and animal cries that came from the palace, echoed by others, faint but clear, from the city below; a lone priestess, rooted before a gaping wound in the ground where the temple of Womb of Earth had stood; a man crouched beside a fallen pillar, lifting the hand of the person crushed beneath it to his mouth. His head shook back and forth in a frenzy of grief. Only when she got closer did she realize he was trying to work a ring free with his teeth.

The clouds of dust had settled, revealing the capricious devastation the earthquake had wrought. Pillars rose up between those that had toppled. The eastern wall of the palace had collapsed, but the others still stood. However, smoke billowed from the north wing, smearing the pale blue of the sky with black.

Men and women clawed through the rubble. Others streamed through the south gate, most with only the clothes on their backs. A few dragged carts behind them, hauling whatever was left of their belongings, only to abandon them with wails and curses when they reached the edge of the plateau.

The steps that led to the city were gone. All that remained of the houses that had clung to the hillside was a heap of debris. The buildings closer to the shore had escaped destruction, but they were threatened by the flames licking eagerly at the thatch of the collapsed roofs. Lines snaked from the sea; people must be passing buckets to control the flames before they engulfed the entire city.

She could not worry about Pilozhat's fate. She had to consider hers and Hakkon's and the Spirit-Hunter's whose head dangled limply against the big man's shoulder.

Incredibly, the stairway that led to the temple of the God with Two Faces was still intact, but it was clogged with refugees, shouting and shoving as they fought their way to lower ground. Amid the chaos, a woman stood immobile, barely covered by the shreds of her nightdress. As they passed, she called out, "Have you seen my little girl? She was right beside me at the gate."

All the way down the steps, above the shouts and the curses and the weeping and the prayers, Hircha could hear that high-pitched voice calling, "Have you seen my little girl? Have you seen my sweet Shevhila?"

The temple of the God with Two Faces appeared unscathed. Outside, the tall figure of the Supplicant moved calmly through the crowd. A word, a touch, and the seething mass quieted. People paused to accept a dipper of water from her acolytes. In spite of her raging thirst, Hircha scuttled past with her head down, hoping Hakkon's bulk would shield her from the Supplicant's gaze.

It seemed like half of Pilozhat had taken refuge in the western fields. Some were dazed, some cradled the limp bodies of loved ones in their arms, but many were ripping up khirtas for bandages, tending to the wounded, sharing food and water. Squads of soldiers rounded up able-bodied men and women and marched them toward Pilozhat, probably to help fight the fires and dig out those trapped in the rubble. Hircha had to marvel at the efficiency of the Zherosi; it was almost like they knew the earthquake was coming.

As they neared the road to Oexiak, Hircha spied a pink tunic, incongruously bright among the dusty grays and tans. Olinio's querulous voice rose above the cacophony of shouts and moans. Soldiers tossed costumes, scenery, and sacks of belongings out of the cart, ignoring his shrieks of protest.

"My mother is dead. Must you steal from me, too?"

"We need the cart to carry the dead," a soldier explained patiently. "Shall we take them?"

Only then did Hircha notice the two bodies. Apart from a small cut on her forehead, the old woman looked unhurt; perhaps she had simply died of fright. The smaller body was covered with a bloodstained cloak.

"My mother was an artist. You expect me to allow you to throw her into a mass grave with . . . with nobodies?"

"The bodies will be burned. But if you want to bury her, that's your business. As long as it's done soon." The soldier shrugged apologetically. "The heat. You understand."

Olinio's wail turned into a cry of astonishment when he finally noticed them. He exclaimed again when Hakkon lowered the Spirit-Hunter to the ground. "Oh, Hakkon. Thank the gods you're alive. And Reinek, too. If only Mother had been spared. And poor Bo. The bullock went wild and . . . oh, it was terrible, terrible. It trampled him. No, don't look. It's too awful. And Bep is missing."

Hakkon shook his head, his grim expression testifying to Bep's fate. Olinio threw up his hands and wailed again.

"Stop that noise!" Hircha ordered. Olinio broke off, his mouth hanging open. Before he could recover, she said, "The soldiers are waiting. Do you want them to take your mother or not?"

Olinio sniffed. "Take Bo. The little man there. But not my mother."

Two soldiers lifted the small body and laid it in the cart with surprising gentleness. As they dragged the cart away, Olinio stared down at his mother. "Why didn't she listen to me? If we had left last night . . ." His voice trailed off in a sob.

"Your mother is beyond pain. I know you don't want to leave her, but Hakkon and I have to get the . . . Reinek out of the city. We didn't save him from the Zheron's knife to have him recaptured."

Olinio gasped. "You disrupted a sacrifice? Are you mad? The Zheron will have your heads."

"The Zheron has other things to worry about."

For now. But the Spirit-Hunter had witnessed Keirith's murder and possibly the Pajhit's. Xevhan could never allow him to live.

Olinio drew himself up. "I must arrange a proper rite for my mother. With a priest to officiate. And chanting. She'd like that." He turned to Hakkon, his jowls quivering. "I am shocked—shocked!—that you would tarnish the reputation of this company by engaging in criminal activities. And after all I've done for you! I shouldn't even permit you to remain in my employ. But given these uncertain times, I am willing to—"

He fell to his knees, his expression ghastly. Mystified, Hircha looked over her shoulder and saw the Supplicant moving steadily through the crowd. Although she stretched out her hands to touch those she passed, her gaze remained fixed on them.

Olinio babbled prayers under his breath; even stoic Hakkon seemed nervous. Hircha just stood there, frozen, as the Supplicant approached. Her dark gaze swept over them to rest on the Spirit-Hunter.

"He is injured?" she asked quietly.

"He collapsed. After Keirith . . ." Hircha's voice cracked and she took a deep breath. "He's dead, lady. Keirith is dead. And Reinek . . ."

"Bring him to my temple."

"But we have to leave the city. At once."

Two small lines appeared between the Supplicant's brows. "Perhaps you misunderstood. That was not a request."

"Yes. Of course. Instantly," Olinio stammered. "You do us great honor, lady. Inexpressible honor. I am—"

"Speechless?"

Olinio pressed his lips together and nodded. The Supplicant turned to Hakkon. "You risked much to help him. I thank you. And I am sorry for the death of your friend."

Hakkon's mouth trembled as he nodded.

"Bep will receive a hero's welcome in the afterworld. He will eat of the finest fruits and drink of the finest wines. He will lie on the softest fleece, beneath a bower of the sweetest honeysuckle, beside a stream that flows with the purest water. And large-breasted beauties with skillful hands and knowing mouths will vie with each other to pleasure him."

The Supplicant winked. After a moment of stunned surprise, Hakkon nodded again.

"And when your turn comes to take that flight, you, too, will receive a hero's welcome. And there will be large-breasted beauties should you desire them. But your mother will be the first to welcome you. And when her hand clasps yours to lead you into the sunlight, you will finally be able to speak aloud the words of love you have carried in your heart these many years."

The tears filling Hakkon's eyes spilled over, carving pale tracks in his dirty cheeks. The Supplicant pulled his head down to her shoulder and held him while he wept. When he finally raised his head, she gave him a lingering smile and slowly walked away.

Olinio wiped his forehead, leaving grimy streaks on the sleeve of his tunic. "She must have taken a fancy to you when she saw you in Oexiak. If only I'd known. I could have arranged a special performance for her. Oh, well. Take Reinek to the temple. Be polite. Do whatever she asks. And smile, Hakkon, smile! You must learn to take advantage of unexpected opportunities when they— Here. You. Girl! What are you doing?"

Without interrupting her rummaging, Hircha said, "I'm looking for Reinek's pack." She dug a battered hide bag out of the pile of discarded supplies and held it up. "Is this it?"

"Yes. I think so. Urkiat's is there, too. Somewhere. Yes, that's it. I don't suppose you could take the rest of the things . . . ? Oh, never mind. I'll manage." His eyes gleamed. "The God with Two Faces is smiling on me again. Just as Mother predicted. And I didn't even have to spend money for an offering."

Chapter 43

HE FLOATED IN A SEA of honeysuckle. Dimly, he sensed another presence, but it was too far away to trouble him. The summons disturbed his peace and he retreated deeper into the restful sea. When the summons came again, he bent his will on resisting it. A faint throb of resentment emanated from the other; it, too, preferred the peace and comfort of the honeysuckle sea. The third summons pulled him upward, overriding his desire to drift, overriding even the nameless terror he sensed lurking at the surface.

The sea disgorged him. His chest heaved with the effort of breathing. His muscles ached. And that was wrong. Frantically, he sought the sanctuary of the sea, but the voice commanded him to open his eyes.

The face of the Supplicant filled his vision. "Welcome back, Keirith."

A wave of nausea heaved him up. Cool hands grasped his arms, steadying him. As the nausea faded, memory returned. The piercing joy from his father's spirit when he first touched it, followed by the violent shock that threatened to shatter them both. The helpless terror of dissolution and the ferocious wrench as he was pulled back from the brink. And then plummeting into an abyss, as dark and bottomless as the Supplicant's eyes.

He tried to shake his head, but the effort was beyond him. The Supplicant eased him back on the fleece and took his hand. As she raised it, he squeezed his eyes shut.

"You must look."

Against his will, his eyes opened and he saw what he had feared. The antler tattoo, branching across the thick wrist. The scar, puckering the dust-grimed skin of the palm. The swollen stumps of the forefinger and middle finger that Morgath had sawed off in Chaos.

He had tried to comfort his father. Instead, he had killed him.

Grief roared through him and then an echoing surge of terror. He had only a moment to realize the terror was not his, another to recognize the other presence. Then his new body was torn from his control.

His father's spirit fought with mindless desperation, insensible of everything except his horrified belief that Morgath had taken possession of his body as well as his spirit. Keirith knew he should calm him, but the instinct for survival overwhelmed reason. Even the Supplicant's command failed to restrain him. His body convulsed as they battled. Desperate, he summoned his power.

"No! You will cast him out!"

Keirith's heart slammed against his ribs. The power continued to swell, as wildly uncontrolled as his thrashing body. Too late, he tried to call it back. A bolt of pure agony pierced him and he screamed, then screamed again as he felt the aftershock rip through his father's spirit. He was still screaming when his father vanished.

<Be still.>

The Supplicant's voice spoke inside him. His body went limp. His scream faded. A shrill voice shouted something, but it came from outside his spirit and he could identify neither the speaker nor the words. He groped for his father and met an impenetrable wall. He battered against it, a butterfly assaulting stone.

<Stop that. He is safe. I'm shielding him from you.>

His whimper of relief sounded loud in his ears.

<You must relinquish control of his body.>

The whimper crescendoed to an animal cry of fear.

<I know you're frightened. But he is terrified. Hard enough for your father to wake with another spirit inside of him. Imagine what he feels when he discovers that this alien spirit controls his body and will destroy him to maintain possession.>

Guilt filled him, overwhelming the fear.

<You can apologize later. Now pay attention. Opening his spirit to receive yours was the hardest thing Darak has ever done. To lose control of his body will push him to the brink of madness. I can wrest control from you, but I prefer not to cause you additional pain. All you need do is let go. I'll keep you safe. Just as I'm keeping your father safe.>

Why are you helping us? You're a Zherosi priestess.

<I am far more than a priestess.>

Who are you?

<Your father calls me Fellgair.>

His spirit shuddered and shrank away.

<You may call me Lord Trickster. Come, Keirith. Every moment you delay only increases your father's terror. I don't have time to reason with you and calm him. If I must take control, I will.>

Why should I believe you?

He felt something that might have been exasperation.

<Very astute.>

There was a pause and then he felt the voice again, still soft, but far more gentle and unquestionably masculine.

<Hush. Hush and listen. Darak! Listen to me. You are safe. I'm holding you. You know me. Say my name. Yes, that's right. Again. Good.>

The wall prevented him from sensing his father's responses. Unless it was a trick.

<Be quiet, Keirith.>

It was as if the Trickster kept them isolated in separate rooms, able to hear and speak to both of them, while they could only communicate with him.

<Yes, Keirith is here. No. Darak! Listen to my voice. You must be calm and you must listen. Keirith is safe.>

There was a brief pause.

<Because I'm shielding you from each other.>

Another pause, longer than the first.

<You're not strong enough—>

Another flash of exasperation, this time directed at his father.

<All right. But only for a moment. I'll open the gateway just a little so that you can feel him. Keirith? Your father is frightened. Do not reach for him. Let him come to you.>

How could the Trickster shame his father by revealing his fear?

<Because the Trickster used his wondrous powers to keep him from sensing what I just said to you. Credit me with some sensitivity. And stem your turbulent emotions. I'm going to open the gateway.>

The tiniest chink cracked open in the wall. For a panicked moment, he felt nothing and wondered if his father refused to touch him. Obeying the Trickster's instructions, he quelled his anxiety, remembering how it had been when he and Malaq shared a connection. But instead of Malaq's gentle probing, a wild torrent of emotions and thoughts poured through the gateway. He touched uncertainty and fear and a tremulous determination, but stronger than any of these was the sense of delirious relief.

I'm here, Fa. I'm all right. I didn't mean to hurt you.

That was all he managed before his father disappeared. Although he knew Fellgair had simply closed the gateway, his panic resurfaced. Again, he mastered it, but the effort left him exhausted. With his remaining strength, he willed himself to surrender his father's body.

He drew his breath in. His father let it out. Keirith could feel the heaving chest and the beating heart, but the sensations came from a great distance. It was stranger still to hear his father's voice murmuring his name, feel his father's fingers clenching and unclenching in the fleece, and be helpless to make the sound or the movements.

<As long as I maintain the wall between you, this is how it will feel. When I remove it, your will must prevail against the natural urge to use his body. And your power must keep your two spirits from bleeding together.>

Panic surged again; he'd never managed to erect a shield himself.

<You've done it all your life. Malaq merely deepened your understanding of the process. You will not be strong enough to keep him out altogether. When the strain gets too great—for either of you—you must retreat deeper into yourself.>

And will my father . . . will he know what I'm feeling?

<Yes.>

Before he could prevent it, the emotions flooded him: the helpless terror of the rape, the sickening joy of the castration, the guilt of Urkiat's death, and the growing horror of the half-life that stretched ahead of him. Only now did he begin to grasp the implications of his rescue. The endless vigilance required lest their most private thoughts and emotions be laid bare to each other. The impotence of being locked in a body he could never possess—feet moving without his volition, mouth opening to receive food he couldn't taste. Every private act of his father's exposed—when he pissed, when he moved his bowels, when he . . . dear gods, what about his mam? His father's lips kissing her, his father's hands touching her, his father's . . .

<Stop.>

The Trickster's presence filled him, bathing him with the calm and peace of the honeysuckle sea. But instead of retreating into that restfulness, Keirith fought.

Let me go.

<And negate your father's sacrifice?>

What about my sacrifice? I was willing to die. I wanted to die. I only came back to ease his grief.

<Your choice, Keirith. And his to open his spirit to you.>

I didn't mean to stay!

<A spirit cannot help rooting itself in a body. It's as basic an instinct as breathing. That's why the Holly-Lord's spirit remained inside Tinnean's body all those years ago. Even a god desires a form.>

Please. Let me go. I can't do this.

<In this matter, I cannot interfere.>

Desperation made him bold.

You're always interfering.

He felt a flash of amusement.

<Now you sound like your mother.>

Then do it for her. Or you'll destroy us.

<Enough.>

He recoiled under the lash of the god's displeasure.

<I'm sorry.> The Trickster's voice was gentle now, as it had been when he spoke to his father. *<You've endured a great deal of pain and I'm asking you to bear more—your father's as well as your own. I'll tell him what to expect, but it won't be easy. For either of you. Can you do this?>*

What choice did he have? If the Trickster wouldn't free him, he would have to protect his father—and himself.

<Don't think about the future. Even I cannot see how this will end. Just survive one moment and then the next.>

And the next and the next and all the endless days and nights that stretched ahead of him. Nay, that was an invitation to madness. The Trickster was right. He must survive from moment to moment. He must maintain his vigilance, no matter the cost to him. And when his father was safe, he must find a way to free himself and end the suffering he was causing them both.

Fellgair shooed the fair-haired slave girl—Hircha, he'd called her—out of the chamber, but he allowed Hakkon to remain. Together, they washed him and dressed him in his spare clothes. When one of Fellgair's attendants reached for his breeches, Darak snatched them back. That was Keirith's blood splashed on the doeskin, the only tangible part of his son's body he still possessed.

Fellgair refused to allow him to return to the temple of Zhe. Nor would he send one of his attendants to bring Keirith's body here. Darak might have challenged him, but Hakkon and the girl had risked much to protect him and he could not repay their courage by bringing the Zherosi down on them. He would never be able to kiss his son good-bye or cut a lock of hair in remembrance. He could only sit here, well-fed, well-clothed, and well-tended, and picture the Zherosi desecrating his son's body as Urkiat had mutilated the raider.

When he wasn't imagining that gruesome scene, he was seeing Keirith sprawled across the altar—the dagger's hilt between his ribs, the blood pulsing out of his chest. He'd watched the life fade from those blue eyes and thought only of preserving him. Now that the first shock had worn off, he wondered if it would have been kinder to let his spirit fly to the Forever Isles.

Fear is the enemy. Control the fear. Control yourself.

Those were the words he must live by in the coming days if he was to spare Keirith the tumult of his emotions. But his determination failed him when Fellgair opened the gateway again. When his spirit collided with Keirith's, he panicked and fled. Each successive encounter, however, proved a little easier. Although Keirith's barrier was far weaker than Fellgair's, it was strong enough to dilute the impact of his thoughts and emotions. It was like sleeping on the beach, hearing the constant ebb and flow of the surf. When the strain of maintaining the barrier grew too great, Keirith's presence crashed in upon him. Then his son retreated and Darak had to fight the urge to follow.

If the effort of controlling his thoughts and emotions tired him, it was exhausting Keirith. Each time they came together, it was harder for his son to shield himself. Finally, he asked Fellgair to keep the barrier closed so Keirith could sleep.

That was when the girl stormed back into the chamber to plead with Fellgair to allow them to leave the city. When Fellgair demurred, she announced that she would go alone. In a few short sentences, Fellgair explained what had happened. The small amount of color in her face leached away.

"When Darak and Keirith are able to exist in the same body, they will leave," Fellgair announced. "Until then, you will all remain here. Rest. Eat. Chat. Hakkon and I will have to forgo the chat, he for obvious reasons, and I to attend to other matters."

"It's on your head, then," she called as Fellgair left the chamber. "If the Zheron discovers him here—"

"He's still alive?" Darak reached up to grab her wrist. Ignoring her wince of pain, he dragged her down beside him.

"Aye. I think so. I saw him running away."

He was alive. The man who had ordered him to fight Urkiat. The man who had planned to sacrifice him. The man who had murdered his son. He was alive.

The killing lust sang, hot and hungry. He wasn't aware that he'd released Hircha or gotten to his feet until he saw her backing away. Hakkon gripped his shoulder, pleading silently for calm. He banked the hunger until it sang with the icy fire of frostbite.

"Let him come."

"Do you think he'll come alone?" Hircha demanded. "He'll bring guards. If you touch him, they'll cut you down. And then Keirith will die, too."

Darak swallowed down his disappointment and tasted

blood; in his eagerness for the kill, he must have bitten his lip. The taste lingered in his mouth, sour and stale.

Denied the pleasure of contemplating the Zheron's death, he sought information. The soft venom in Hircha's voice told him she'd be happy to see the Zheron die. Prying information from her about Keirith was more difficult, getting her to talk about herself nearly impossible. Although she possessed Griane's boldness and strength, he found little evidence of a warm heart. It was hard to tell whether she was simply hiding her feelings or whether her years of captivity had hardened her. When he pressed her too hard, she turned sullen and silent. He had to be content with her version of the events that had led up to Keirith's astonishing display of power.

He wished he possessed some way to reach Tinnean. Of all men in the world, his brother understood how two spirits could survive within the same body; he had dwelled with the spirit of the Oak for more than a moon. The experience had changed him, certainly, but the essence of his brother remained intact—the quiet strength, the flashes of humor, and the wonder. Perhaps it was different when you dwelled with a god; he scarcely noticed Fellgair's presence now.

The thought prompted a resurgence of the familiar power.

<I'm just a comfortable old shoe.>

I didn't mean that and you know it. Where are you?

<I am succoring my people. There was a small catastrophe recently. I suppose you scarcely noticed that either.>

We can't stay here much longer. When will you open the gateway again?

<Whenever you like. I'm quite capable of opening the gateway and succoring my people at the same time.>

I know. I just . . .

He wanted Fellgair to be in the chamber with him. To his astonishment, he found the god's physical presence comforting.

<How sweet. As it happens, I was planning to return soon.>

Since he walked in moments later, he was probably lurking in the outer chamber.

"I never lurk. I appear. Creating wonder and amazement. Are you ready?"

Both Hakkon and Hircha looked startled, then uneasy. Darak quelled the inevitable flutter of panic and nodded. Braced for the impact of their joining, he felt only the gentle brush of Keirith's spirit against his.

<He's sleeping.>

He must be utterly exhausted if the opening of the gateway failed to rouse him. Fellgair's presence vanished. They were on their own now.

Darak closed his eyes; one of the most difficult parts of this enforced union was the inundation of sensations from without as well as within. He saw a younger Conn—perhaps eleven or twelve—down on all fours, pretending to munch grass. Conn raised his head, shook it in apparent resignation, and baaed. Amusement rippled through Keirith, followed by a bark.

Keirith was dreaming, Darak realized, and he was seeing the dream through his son's eyes. Conn looked far too old for this sort of game, yet he could feel the boys' shared delight and rejoiced in it; in his dreams, at least, Keirith could find happiness.

Conn winked and crawled toward a rock. Keirith's gaze swung away to follow an eagle soaring overhead. Dejection mingled with awe, as if Keirith was observing his dream as well as experiencing it.

Something growled and his gaze swung back to the rock. Callie was perched upon it. He couldn't be more than three summers. His snarl turned into a fit of giggles as Conn crawled around in circles, bleating madly. He was still giggling when Keirith raced toward him, barking.

Up he went, high in the air, his laughing face looking down into Keirith's. Conn interrupted his bleating. "The dog's supposed to chase the wolf off, not pick him up."

"He's not a wolf anymore," Keirith said. "He's an eagle."

"Fly, Keiry, fly!"

Keirith raced across the hillside, Callie's legs bumping against his chest. Their happiness tumbled over Darak, fresh and pure as a stream. As soon as Keirith set him down, Callie poked him. "You be the wolf. I'll be the dog."

"Why am I always stuck being the sheep?" Conn asked plaintively.

"Because you're so baaed at barking."

A clump of grass hit Keirith in the belly. He picked it up and hurled it back. Soon, they were tussling with each other, with Callie shouting encouragement. Conn demanded that Keirith play the sheep, but he refused. The playfulness of the dream-Keirith warred with a growing anxiety from the dreamer.

Keirith's power surged as he pushed Conn away. Although it was just an echo of what he had experienced, the memory made Darak recoil. Revulsion tore at Keirith as his dream-self directed the power at his tormentor.

Conn cried out and collapsed. To Darak's horror, Keirith turned toward Callie. His little boy's scream tore through him. Like the wood pigeon, he thought, then realized the thought had come from Keirith.

Keirith's dream-self went down on his knees, shock and guilt radiating from him. Then he looked up. It took Darak a moment to recognize himself. Gods, was this how Keirith saw him, this stern-faced, accusing stranger? He was as helpless to stem his shock and denial as Keirith was to keep his self-loathing from battering them both.

It's only a dream, son. You would never hurt Conn or Callie.

Voices from the outer chamber pulled his awareness away. He opened his eyes to find Hakkon staring at the doorway and Hircha with her back against a wall. Only Fellgair's expression remained placid.

Darak heard a deep chuckle. It came from Keirith's dream. When he shut out the external distractions, he found only darkness and a fear so pervasive it made his heart race. Sensations flooded him from within and without: whispers in the dark; shouts from the outer chamber; the grittiness of the cloth shoved in his mouth; the tramp of booted feet, growing louder by the moment.

Darak opened his eyes and found Fellgair watching him. "It seems you'll have that confrontation, after all."

Palms and knees scraped against wood. A hand yanked back the draperies across the doorway of Fellgair's chamber. Soft doeskin brushed his back. Armed men marched toward him.

"Stop. It's too much."

Cruel fingers dug into his buttocks.

"Nay. Oh, gods. Keirith!"

A man shouted something in Zherosi.

Keirith jolted awake. Terror, pain, and humiliation crashed into Darak's unprotected spirit. He tried to rise and fell to his knees, reeling from the horror of Keirith's violation and the desperate need to conceal it lest he wound his son further.

Someone seized his groping hand. Amid the babble of voices, he heard Fellgair's, calm and commanding. He concentrated on that, only that, and felt a new wave of shock emanate from Keirith as he became aware of what was happening.

The contending voices fell silent. The dusty hem of a red robe appeared before him. Darak raised his head and stared up into the smiling face of his son's murderer.

Chapter 44

STUNNED BY XEVHAN'S arrival and the horrifying certainty that his father knew about the rape, the violent surge of hatred nearly overwhelmed Keirith. He felt the muscles in his father's legs tense.

Nay, Fa! The guards will kill you.

He felt reluctant acquiescence, but beneath it, the bloodlust simmered.

Once his father backed down, Xevhan's smile returned. Despite his obvious elation, he looked ill. Perspiration beaded his forehead. His fingers trembled as they smoothed his robe. His eyes were bloodshot and heavy-lidded.

Fellgair seemed unsurprised by Xevhan's arrival. But why should he be? He had betrayed them.

<Nay. Not Fellgair.>

Keirith couldn't understand why his father trusted the Trickster, but the onslaught of shared emotions and thoughts made it difficult to think clearly.

<It's my fault. I'll try harder.>

His father's effort at control helped. At least Keirith was able to concentrate on what Xevhan was saying. Fellgair finally interrupted the torrent of invective to ask, "Are you well, Zheron?"

"Yes, Supplicant. Very well. Now that I've found the man who murdered our Pajhit."

<What are they saying?>

As Fellgair gasped, Keirith translated quickly. It was hard to see anything of the fox-faced god his father had described in the tall, graceful priestess. The moan of distress was so heartfelt that the closest guard thrust out his hand, clearly fearing the Supplicant might faint. Fellgair clung to the proffered hand and favored the guard with a smile that made his expression glaze over in slack-jawed adoration.

"I am grieved to learn of our beloved Pajhit's death. This is a sorrowful day for our people."

"Yes. Terrible. But his murder will be avenged and his killer brought to justice."

"I am certain of it." Fellgair's smile caressed Xevhan, but the dark eyes glittered.

Keirith was still translating—and trying to understand the Trickster's game—when shouts from the outer chamber interrupted him. As if ten guards weren't sufficient, Xevhan had sent for more; he was taking no chances on an escape.

Khonsel do Havi strode into the chamber. Even with a bloodstained bandage around his head, he retained his air of authority. When he saw Geriv, Keirith wondered if his shadow had witnessed Malaq's murder after all. Nay, he'd been nowhere near the altar. But the Khonsel would surely remember his vision. If only he could talk with him, convince him of the truth. There had to be a way.

"Stop! Gods, I can't stand it!"

He'd been too caught up in his own excitement to pay attention to his father's growing agitation. The outburst made the Khonsel break off his greeting to Fellgair.

"What's wrong with him?"

"He's been subject to these fits since he was brought here."

"Who brought him?"

"The girl and the man beside him."

"You—what's your name?"

"He cannot speak," Fellgair replied. "The girl claims his name is Hakkon."

"This is the man!" Xevhan exclaimed. "The one I spoke of in the council meeting."

"The mute?"

"The cripple! The father of the false prophet. The one called the Spirit-Hunter. The one who murdered our Pajhit."

<What? Tell me.>

Keirith translated Xevhan's meandering account of what had happened at the temple. The Khonsel seemed taken aback by Xevhan's growing frenzy and eyed him narrowly.

"Zheron. You are not yourself."

"Forgive me." Xevhan managed a weak smile. "It's the qiij. And the strain of helping the queen."

"She's still alive?"

"One of her ladies offered her body for The Shedding. But it was . . . difficult. Coming so soon after the first Shedding. The healers are with her. They assured me she was out of danger."

"Thank the gods. If we had lost them both . . ."

No wonder Xevhan seemed on the verge of collapse. Eliaxa and Malaq had always performed the rite. And if the queen was badly injured, the strain must have been enormous.

Fellgair intoned a prayer for the spirit of the dead king. Keirith felt more grief for the ordinary folk who must have awakened in terror to find the walls and roofs of their houses caving in on them. Ordinary folk who might have been saved if he had confided his suspicions to the Qepo.

<Don't blame yourself.>

It's hard not to.

<Did you know how bad it would be?>

Not for sure. But—

<Then let it go, Son.>

Fellgair droned on; even the Khonsel was shifting his feet.

<He's giving us time.>

For what?

<So I can get hold of myself.>

Shame accompanied his father's thought and was banished by renewed determination. Gods, he was strong.

<Nay. Not like you.>

Pride swelled, filling his father's spirit, flowing into his. His father was proud of him, even after the awful things he had said and done.

They both retreated before the intensity of the emotions. This time, his father recovered first.

<This Khonsel. You trust him?>

Malaq did.

He had no time for more; Fellgair had no sooner finished

the prayer before Xevhan began speaking again. "We can be thankful for one thing: Malaq's murderer has been caught. He took refuge here. As if a barbarian deserves the right of sanctuary."

"How did you find him?" the Khonsel asked.

Xevhan smiled and gestured to one of his guards. "Bring him in."

The chubby leader of the troupe of players slunk in between the guards. His father's rage surged and was ruthlessly suppressed. The name surfaced in Keirith's mind, but he couldn't be certain if the thought was his or his father's.

"This is the man who identified the Spirit-Hunter. When Olinio discovered he was still in the city, he came to the palace at once to inform me."

"How much did he pay you?" his father demanded.

Keirith prepared himself to seize control of his body again and felt impatience ripple through his father.

<Leave me be!>

You can't attack him.

<I won't! But I can't talk to them and you.>

Intent on each other, they paid no heed to Hakkon until he sprang forward with an inarticulate cry. Too late, his father rose. He was still reaching for Hakkon when the Zheron's guards moved in. The Khonsel shouted at them to sheathe their swords, but the thrusts caught Hakkon in the back. For a moment he stood frozen, his hands at Olinio's throat. Then he slowly crumpled to the floor. Olinio shrank away, wheezing.

Don't, Father. Don't!

"Let me go."

An icy calm descended over his father, but anguish roiled beneath it. He could not attack Olinio; he would not be so foolish.

"Nay."

He needed to speak, Keirith realized. The effort of remaining silent taxed his control too much.

His father moved toward Hakkon. Geriv's sword rose until the point hovered at his chest. Without even glancing at it, he knelt and pulled Hakkon into his arms.

Thoughts of Urkiat swirled between them. And Malaq, stabbed in the back just like poor Hakkon. How many more must die before Xevhan was stopped?

"If my testimony is not enough, here is more proof."
Xevhan's voice sounded exulting, triumphant.

The killing lust stirred.

"The mute was going to kill the only man who could
testify to the murderer's identity."

Blood, it whispered.

"This is holy ground," Fellgair said. "And your men have
polluted it by committing murder."

Retribution, it promised.

"If your temple is unclean, so is mine. For on its holy
altar, this man murdered our beloved Pajhit."

Their head snapped up.

"I demand his immediate execution."

Their eyes watched him.

"Give me a sword. I'll do it myself."

The killing lust sang, drowning out the contending voices.
It thundered through flesh and bone, driven by the wild
pounding of their heart. It shattered the fragile barrier between their spirits, uniting them in the single, overwhelming
desire to destroy.

If death was the price for revenge, they would welcome
it. Death brought release. Death brought freedom. Freedom from memories and nightmares. Freedom from shame
and fear. Freedom to hunt with the wolf pack and fly with
the eagles. Death was easy. Death was sweet.

They rose, smiling. With one mind, they formed the
words. With one voice, they spoke them.

"Vazh do Havi. Remember Kheridh's vision. Remember
the dagger in the Zheron's hand. That dagger drips with
Malaq's blood and Kheridh's. Their blood cries out for justice. For the death of this unholy priest who profanes this
temple with his lies."

"He is the liar! A liar and a madman!"

His fear was delicious, as potent as the song coursing
through them, as sweet as the death that awaited them.

"Water cannot cleanse you. Fire cannot purify you. Earth
cannot hide you."

Xevhan shouted orders that the Khonsel countermanded.
Xevhan turned on him in a fury and Geriv stepped forward,
naked sword at the ready. He, too, was shouting and at his
command, more men poured into the chamber.

The bloodsong echoed off the walls, surrounding them,

consuming them. Only the Khonsel seemed immune, but he had fought in many wars. He knew the lure of the blood-song and could resist its seductive call.

Their gaze swept the chamber, savoring the communion of thirsty spirits, and found Hircha. She had neither spoken nor moved since the Zheron entered. She was watching them, her eyes huge in her narrow face. Defying the blood-song, they backed away from the two groups of men to shield her from the swords; someone must survive to tell the tale.

"False priest. Murderer. For you, there is only death. And an eternity in the bottomless Abyss."

Xevhan's gaze darted toward the guard on his left. He licked his lips, eyeing the sword with longing.

The bloodsong's rhythm slowed. *Patience and control,* it sang, *stillness and calm.* The song of the shaman seeking the gods-given vision. The song of the hunter stalking his prey.

"Can you take us, murderer? Are you strong enough?"

Xevhan's fingers clutched the vial of qiij. The ring on his finger shone with the bright beauty of fresh-spilled blood.

"Come to us," they crooned, drawing the words from their shared memories of that first encounter with him. "You want to. You want it so much you're shaking."

Even then, they had sensed what this man was, but in the days that followed, they had allowed themselves to be deceived because they were so lonely, so frightened. They should have recognized his cruelty, his delight in hurting others.

"We can feel your fear," they whispered, drawing the words from their shared memories of Morgath's torture. "We can read every thought. Uncover all your dirty little secrets." A wolf's growl rumbled in their throat. An adder's hiss caressed their tongue. "Come to us, assassin."

Although they were expecting Xevhan's spirit to attack, the force of his assault shattered their union. The world tilted as his father reeled. Keirith heard him cry out as he fell. Dimly, he was aware of a commotion in the chamber. Golden flames burned in the depths of Fellgair's eyes, but before Keirith could decipher their meaning, Xevhan's shocked recognition radiated through him. Confronted by two spirits, he hesitated, torn between his hunger to destroy him and his desire to pursue his father, so much weaker, so much easier to cast out.

Go, Father! Now!

His father's spirit fled, desperately seeking a hiding place. Keirith fled after him, flinging up barriers to protect them. Xevhan obliterated them all. Exhausted as he was from helping the queen Shed, he was still so much stronger than Keirith had imagined.

<Stronger than you will ever be, boy.>

The lingering effects of qiij fed that relentless pursuit. Its heat licked at Keirith's spirit, threatening to annihilate him.

<I will annihilate you. And I'll cast the shreds of your spirit into the Abyss.>

Scattered like the ashes of a bonfire. Scattered and forgotten.

<But I'll leave your father alive. I'll parade what's left of him through the streets of Pilozhat, a drooling, gibbering idiot. What an end for the great Spirit-Hunter.>

Xevhan's delight oozed through him like malignant sap. This is what his father had experienced when Morgath attacked, this hopeless realization that there was no place to hide, no barrier strong enough to shield him. And the boundless terror of that malevolent spirit savoring his fear and prying into his memories.

<I can read every thought. Uncover every secret.>

Summoning his power, Keirith attacked, driving Xevhan back. His momentary surprise gave way to a ripple of pure pleasure.

<If you'd fought that hard on the ship, you might have gotten away.>

Again, Keirith attacked, shame as potent as qiij.

<But you didn't want to get away, did you? Those sailors gave you what you needed. Punishment. Pain. That's what all unnatural creatures desire—and deserve.>

The upwelling of wrath surprised them both. His father's spirit lashed out; even Xevhan, powerful as he was, retreated before the furious assault. It was hopeless; his father knew it. He possessed neither the skills nor the strength to sustain the attack, but it was fueled by something more potent than qiij or shame or hatred.

Fierce and protective, his father's love flooded Keirith.

Once, he had been blind enough to resent his strength, believing it somehow diminished his. Only now did he realize that it only made him stronger.

Was it that knowledge that made Xevhan falter? Or was the strain of The Shedding finally taking its toll?

Keirith summoned his power, drawing energy from unyielding stone and honeysuckle-scented air, from the shuddering fire of the torches and the pool of Hakkon's blood. He summoned his power for Hircha, for Urkiat, for the nameless men who had died under the Zheron's dagger. For Malaq, his friend and mentor. And for his father who loved him.

He summoned the power and held it while the bloodsong swelled, eager yet controlled, hungry yet calm. The song of the hunter closing in for the kill. With heart and mind and spirit, Keirith hurled the coiled energy at Xevhan.

Shock turned to disbelief, disbelief to fear. And when the relentless power continued to surge, the fear changed to terror.

It was Xevhan's turn to flee and his to pursue, carried effortlessly on the tide of his power. He was an eagle swooping in for the kill, deadly talons seeking fur and flesh and bone. His father cried out a warning, but he could no more allow Xevhan to escape than he could harness the power he had unleashed. All he could do was ride the torrent that connected him to Xevhan.

His spirit ripped free of his father's body. For a moment, he drifted, observing the shock of those below who watched Xevhan totter backward. The familiar peace stole over him. The thread connecting him to Xevhan was as slender and fragile as the spinneret that had connected him to the eagle. If he severed it, he could fly away forever.

Hunger for vengeance overrode the desire to escape. He channeled that hunger into the thread, spinning it thicker and stronger. His father cried out his name, but already the power was pulling him forward, carrying him down.

The world lurched as he rooted himself in Xevhan's body. Lurched again as Xevhan slammed into a wall. Colors exploded before him—russet, gold, brown—all the colors of autumn. Trees filled his vision—slender birches, thick-trunked oaks. He was home and it was harvest time and he was flying through the forest.

He blundered into a tree and pushed it aside. Another rose in its place and he burst through it, scattering evanescent shards of wood that flickered like embers in the night sky. He ripped through an interwoven barrier of saplings that screamed as his power shredded them. Nay, not saplings. Shields. Erected by the man who had murdered him.

His power surged, feeding on the terror. This was what Morgath had experienced: the dizzying invasion, the intoxicating arousal of battle. Xevhan fought hard and that only made it sweeter. Brutal and relentless, Keirith pressed the attack, thrusting at his opponent's spirit, penetrating it, savaging it. Xevhan's scream echoed through him and he quivered with anticipation. Xevhan's body convulsed and he shuddered with pleasure.

He was close now, so close. He could feel Xevhan's hold on his body weakening. It required only a final push to expel him. But he was tiring. The battle was draining them both. He sensed a tiny crack in his enemy's spirit and gathered himself for one last assault.

For Malaq.

Xevhan's spirit shattered. A cascade of discordant emotions inundated Keirith—denial, hatred, terror—and with them, random thoughts and memories: a bloody, pulsating heart, a child's laugh, a man's reproving voice. Keirith flung off the contamination, casting out the shreds of Xevhan's spirit, flinging them into the void.

Somewhere, a scream was fading into silence. His strength was fading, too. So tired now, too tired to fight. The brilliant colors of the forest dimmed. He looked up to find his father struggling helplessly in Fellgair's arms. The world shrank to their faces—his father's contorted, Fellgair's calm. He tried to speak, to bid his father farewell, but he could only lie there, caught by the golden fire dancing in the Trickster's eyes.

Abruptly, the fire went out. The dance vanished, leaving two dark pools that grew larger and larger until they filled his vision. Gratefully, Keirith allowed the welcoming darkness to claim him.

Chapter 45

HE WOKE TO FIND himself staring up at a white-washed ceiling. The scrape of sandals alerted him to another presence. He turned his head to see a figure retreating through the doorway.

Keirith reached for his father's spirit and felt nothing. He bolted upright. Bracelets clattered against his wrists. A scarlet robe fell to his ankles. A ring with a red stone adorned his right forefinger. Black tattoos snaked up his slender, swarthy forearms.

With a tentative finger, he touched the tattoo on his left arm. Involuntarily, his hand jerked back. He forced himself to touch it again, running his trembling fingers down the length of the twisting snake. Again and again, he traced the snake's shape until he was rubbing it with mindless ferocity as if to scrub it off. His fingernails scored four red marks in his flesh. The snake slithered through them, mouth agape, laughing at him.

In the flickering light of the oil lamps, the ring winked. He wrenched it from his finger and hurled it away. He tore the bracelets from his wrists and heard them clatter dully against the tiles. But the snakes remained, jeering at his pitiful attempt to obliterate them.

The wave of nausea made him double over. Dully, he noted that Xevhan's second toe was longer than the big one. He covered his eyes to shut out the sight of them. Helplessly, his fingers played over his face, feeling the clammy forehead, the smooth cheeks, the small cleft in the chin.

Xevhan was dead.

Xevhan was gone.

And now he possessed his body.

"Oh, gods . . ."

He flinched at the sound of that voice. His voice. Deeper than it should be, breathy with horror. He should feel triumphant instead of sick. He had killed his enemy. He had won. He was Keirith the Destroyer. Keirith the Eater of Spirits.

"Feeling better?"

His head jerked up. Khonsel do Havi stood in the doorway, observing him. Belatedly, he realized this was the Khonsel's chamber. Thin cracks snaked up the whitewashed walls. A thick layer of dust covered the stool. A broken vase spilled wilted bitterheart onto the floor. Judging from the light outside the tiny window, it must be close to nightfall—or dawn.

"How long have I been sleeping?"

"A night and a day."

"Thank you for bringing me here."

"Your quarters were damaged."

Stupid, Keirith. The Khonsel thinks you're Xevhan.

He took a deep breath. "Khonsel do Havi, I am not the Zheron. I am Kheridh. My father—"

His father would only know he was gone. He would believe he was dead. He would suffer that same lacerating grief all over again.

"Please. My father. The Spirit-Hunter. Is he alive?"

"The Spirit-Hunter's alive."

Keirith covered his face with trembling hands. Then, ashamed at displaying such emotion in front of the Khonsel, he pretended to smooth his hair. He started when he touched the bare scalp. Of course, he had no hair. Xevhan shaved his head; all the priests did. His stupidity made him chuckle, then laugh. He fell back on the fleece. Even when he heard the rising note of hysteria, he couldn't stop the helpless shrieks of laughter. The Khonsel's grim expression finally sobered him.

"My father took my spirit in when I was dying."

"Took your spirit in?"

"Yes. We are together. One body. Two spirits." His Zherosi was fracturing under that narrow-eyed stare. He knitted his fingers together to make his point clearer. "Hircha and Hakkon took us to the temple of the Supplicant. You must talk to her. The Supplicant. She knows the truth."

"I did talk to her. She didn't mention anything about 'one body, two spirits.' Perhaps it slipped her mind."

It was typical of the Trickster—one moment, helping them, and the next, putting them in jeopardy.

"You were saying?" the Khonsel prompted.

"We wake—woke up. In the temple. And then Xevhan came. And you. And the performer—Olinio. And Xevhan says my father kills Malaq. But it is not so. It is just like the vision. I see the dagger in Xevhan's hand . . ."

He gasped, as if reliving that moment when the dream state had shattered, leaving him standing among a sea of fleeing adders, watching the dagger descend.

"Too late . . ."

Malaq slumping against the altar. Xevhan bending to wrench the dagger free. The earth convulsing beneath his feet as he staggered up the steps.

"I fight . . . I try . . ."

He could feel the delicate bones of that wrist under his fingers, the strain in his arms as he tried to hold off death. And then the shock of the blade driving into his flesh.

He fell back against the wall. His hand clawed its way up his chest to grasp the hilt of the dagger. Instead, his fingers closed around the vial of qiij. He was panting now, his heart pounding as wildly as it had during those last moments of life. But he had to make the Khonsel understand. He had to make him believe.

"We see him—my father and I. In the temple. Laughing. Happy. And we want to kill. We make him angry so he will attack. And he does. He is inside us. He tries to cast us out. But I fight. He runs away and I follow. Into his body. And this time, I win."

The Khonsel nodded thoughtfully and relief washed over him. Slowly, the big hands came up. Palm slapped against palm, steady as a drumbeat at first, and then faster and faster until the Khonsel's applause echoed in the small chamber.

"You missed your calling. Perhaps your friend Olinio can find a place for you among his players."

"No. Please. You do not understand."

"You've even got the boy's mannerisms and speech down. Very impressive. You were impressive in the temple, too. All righteous indignation and wrath. Until the man mentioned the vision."

The Khonsel bared his teeth in a feral grin and Keirith shrank back.

"You nearly pissed yourself, didn't you? Pity you didn't know he spoke Zherosi. Still, you might have pulled it off if you'd kept your head. Was it the qiij that pushed you over the edge? Malaq always said you couldn't handle it."

"You must believe . . ."

In a few long strides, the Khonsel was on him. He seized him by the front of his robe, yanked him off his feet, and shoved him up against the wall.

"I told Malaq the boy would be the death of him. Well, Malaq paid for his stubbornness. And the boy paid as well. That leaves you."

The Khonsel's face was so close he could see the dust caked in the deep lines that age and exhaustion had carved around his eyes. But exhausted or not, the meaty fingers that encircled his throat were very strong.

"I thought about killing you last night. But I wanted you awake. I wanted to see your eyes go wide—yes, just like that—and smell the stink of fear on you and listen to you beg for your life."

"Please . . ."

"Good. Beg some more, and I might kill you quickly."

He was going to die. After twice evading Xevhan, he was going to die at the Khonsel's hands. Fury welled up in him—and just as quickly faded.

The Khonsel wanted to kill Xevhan. He'd never even know that he was giving him the release he sought. Relief made Keirith smile.

The fingers around his throat relaxed slightly. Two lines appeared between the Khonsel's heavy brows.

"Do it," Keirith whispered.

The Khonsel's expression cleared. "Yes. You first. And then the Spirit-Hunter."

"No!"

"Why not?"

"He . . . he is not the Spirit-Hunter."

"So you lied about that."

"Yes. Yes, I lied. He is just a cripple." He had to fight to keep from wincing when he said those words. "A worthless cripple," he repeated, injecting scorn into his voice.

"And why do you care about a worthless cripple?"

Desperately, he sought a reason why Xevhan would want to protect the very man who had accused him of murder. It was no good. He should have simply agreed when the Khonsel proposed killing his father, but the denial had sprung to his lips without thought. And now he was trapped. He couldn't save his father. He didn't care about saving himself.

"Do what you want. It does not matter. Malaq is dead."

"And you killed him."

Malaq had come to the altar for him, had died because of him. Xevhan merely wielded the dagger that struck him down.

"Yes. I killed him. Your best friend. Your oldest friend. You fought battles together. You ate together, drank together. You even named his cat."

"His cat?"

"Niqia."

"I know her name. Why do you think I gave it to her?"

He was too tired to wrangle. He just wanted the Khonsel to stop playing with him and finish this. "I do not remember."

"Try."

"He said . . ."

Malaq staring up at him, apparently unperturbed to find him standing on a bench in his garden. Delivering his lecture on breeding wildcats in the dry tone he always used during those first days. It was only later that either of them risked speaking from the heart.

"It was the fur," he said wearily. "Or the body. I forget. Soft body. Sharp claws. Like the lady." The Khonsel just stared at him. Had he spoken the tribal tongue? "Soft body," he repeated. "And—"

"Sharp claws. I heard." Both the Khonsel's expression and voice were noncommittal. "And did Malaq tell you about Davell, too?"

Keirith closed his eyes and leaned his head back against the wall. "No."

"You've never heard the name?"

"No!"

"Or the name of Malaq's wife?"

"Priests cannot marry."

"Before that. When he fought with me. She was one of the Tree People."

Keirith opened his eyes. Perhaps the Khonsel thought he would be shocked by the revelation, but he was beyond shock. Malaq had loved a woman of the tribes. It explained his facility with the language, his knowledge of the legends, his eagerness to find similarities between their peoples. She must have died. Malaq would never have left her. His wife died, and Malaq became a priest. It all made sense now.

"Malaq had a wife," he murmured to himself.

"And a son."

He was not beyond shock after all. "Malaq has a son?"

"Had. Davell is dead."

A strange undertone of excitement lurked in the Khonsel's voice. Keirith waited for him to continue, but the man just watched him.

"How did he die?"

It must have been the question the Khonsel desired. At any rate, he smiled. "He was killed in battle. When he was fourteen."

His age. Davell had been his age when he died.

"I thought it would kill Malaq, losing him so young."

Keirith saw again the terrible grief that had contorted his father's face at the temple of Zhe and tried to imagine such emotion twisting Malaq's smooth features.

"He was tall for his age. Stubborn like Malaq. They butted heads more than once."

His mam's voice, scolding, "Broody like your father. And stubborn as a rock."

"Had his mother's coloring, though. The dark blue eyes."

The same color as his.

"And the hair, of course."

The words hung there until Keirith forced himself to ask, "The hair?"

"Auburn." The Khonsel's smile widened. "A deep, rich auburn."

The same age. The same eyes. The same hair.

It wasn't him. It had never been him. From the first moment, Malaq had only seen the son he had lost.

He wasn't aware the Khonsel had stepped back until he felt himself sliding down the wall. He pulled his knees up to his chest. His father had warned him that Malaq was using him; he'd believed it himself during the early days of his captivity. He'd tried so hard to push Malaq away, to keep him at a distance. But Malaq wouldn't let him go. And in the face of that persistence—and his own desperate need to trust someone—he had let down his guard. That had been his mistake, allowing himself to feel genuine affection for the man and deceiving himself into believing that the affection was returned.

Malaq laughing with him in the excitement of sharing knowledge and power. Malaq spooning broth into his mouth, scolding him for making a mess. Malaq holding him in his arms while he crouched on the floor, gentle fingers stroking his hair, gentle voice assuring him that he had done the right thing by sending his father away.

Nay, that was real. Malaq had held *him,* comforted *him,* not some replica of his son.

"I don't care."

"What?"

His head jerked up. He blinked furiously to clear his vision. "I said . . ." He cursed and switched to Zherosi. "It does not matter. Malaq is dead. I never . . ." Damn his voice for breaking. "I do not care about him. Not now, not ever. Do you hear me?"

"If you don't lower your voice, the whole palace will hear you."

He launched himself at the man, hating him for his mockery, his satisfaction, his supreme self-possession. The Khonsel caught him easily and held him as he struggled. And when he finally stopped struggling, the Khonsel sat him down on the sleeping shelf and watched with that same satisfied expression as he wiped his face with the back of his hand.

"Are you through?"

"Yes."

"Good. Geriv!"

Geriv was there in a moment; he must have heard everything.

"Bring us some food. And wine. And while we're waiting, boy, you tell me everything you remember from the moment you started herding the adders to the temple."

"Leave me alone." Then the words sank in. He raised his head to find the Khonsel waiting patiently for understanding to dawn. "You believe me? But why?" He could feel his face growing warm. "Because I acted like a fool. About Malaq's son."

"Mostly. The bit about Niqia helped, too." The Khonsel leaned back against the wall and folded his arms across his chest. "There were other things, of course. You expected to find hair on your head. You were concerned about your father. And you still gnaw your thumb when you're nervous."

"You knew who I was? When you came in?"

"Sit down. I questioned your father. After he calmed down. A strong man, your father. Took four men to pull him off the Zheron. Off you. Cursing and shouting and calling me a fool for not listening. The girl—what's her name?"

"Hircha," he murmured.

"She translated. And filled in a few of the missing pieces. But they couldn't know who'd won the battle any more than I did when I came in. Xevhan was clever enough to pretend to be you. But even he couldn't muster tears for Malaq."

Unable to face the penetrating stare, Keirith fastened his gaze on the floor. The wilted sprays of bitterheart were the color of dried blood. He closed his eyes and saw Malaq offering him the scarlet blossoms. A gift of flowers to celebrate the Ripening. A gift he must have given his wife and his son when they celebrated the festival with him.

"It wasn't just the resemblance." The Khonsel's voice was flat and unemotional. "In the beginning, maybe. But he wouldn't have risked so much if that's all it was."

When he trusted his voice, Keirith said, "Thank you. For saying so."

"The stubborn old fool would come back and haunt me if I let you think otherwise." A brief smile, surprisingly tender, softened the lined face. It vanished as he cocked his head, listening. "That'll be Geriv with the food. We'll eat here. Too many people coming and going. It would be better if they thought the Zheron was still ailing."

Geriv arrived with a platter. After he laid it on the floor, he left, only to return moments later with cushions. In his wake, a familiar figure slunk along the wall.

"Niqia!"

At the sound of his voice, her ears went back and her mouth opened in a soundless hiss. She skittered under the stool and crouched there, tail lashing furiously. Keirith swallowed down the lump of disappointment; of course, she wouldn't know him anymore.

"I found her at the temple. Nearly shredded me when I tried to pick her up." The Khonsel scowled at the scratches on his arms, then settled himself on a cushion with a grunt. "As if I don't have enough to do without playing nursemaid to a damned cat." Gingerly, he picked a piece of meat out of one bowl and tossed it toward her. "Sit, Geriv. Even you have to eat. And pour us some wine. Thank the gods that was spared." He drained his cup in a few thirsty gulps and refilled it from a dented bronze pitcher. "Now. Start at the beginning."

"What about my father?"

"Later."

"But—"

"Later."

His tale was interrupted a dozen times by the endless stream of visitors coming to see the Khonsel: soldiers making reports, slaves bearing messages from someone called the Stuavo; healers arriving with updates on the queen's condition. Keirith eavesdropped shamelessly on their conversations and grew increasingly impressed with the Khonsel's efficiency; no wonder Malaq admired him.

"How bad is it?" he asked after the Khonsel returned from yet another interview.

"Only three hundred dead. So far. We're still digging bodies out of the rubble."

Only three hundred.

"It would have been worse if I hadn't had the district

closest to the palace hill evacuated." The Khonsel smiled wearily. "I came to the pit that night."

"I know. I heard your voice."

"The Qepo said he'd never seen the adders so wild. I didn't want to wait and see what you learned." He started to spit, then restrained himself. "Never been much of a man for magic. The queen refused to evacuate the palace, but I took a few precautions on my own. Ordered the ships out to sea. Moved the oil and flammable supplies out of the storerooms. Had the fires in the kitchen put out." This time he did spit. "If the damned priests didn't insist on lighting incense and candles when they pray, we might have prevented more fires. Still . . ."

He waved away the priests and their rituals impatiently and gulped more wine. "The palace district was pretty much destroyed. What the earth didn't take, the fires did. But at least some of the wells were spared. And none of our other cities suffered major damage, thank the gods. I've sent birds requesting food, water, supplies, but it'll be another day before the first shipments arrive. Womb of Earth, spare us from more aftershocks."

"More?"

"You were asleep. Just a bit of a rumble. But it gave people a scare." He broke off as Geriv came in to murmur something. "No other incidents of looting? Good. Commend your brother. And then come back. We have other matters to discuss."

"What happens now?" Keirith asked after Geriv left.

"We rebuild."

"But the king . . . and Malaq . . ."

"The queen lives. New priests will be appointed to replace those who were lost. We still have the Supplicant." The Khonsel shook his head in wonder. "Hers was the only temple undamaged in the earthquake. The God with Two Faces looks after his own."

Certainly, Fellgair wouldn't tolerate any damage to his beautiful temple.

"But the adders . . . without them, you cannot make qiij."

"We'll capture more. As we've done in the past. An earthquake topples buildings, boy. Not kingdoms." The Khonsel shot him a keen look. "Does that disappoint you?"

Keirith took advantage of Geriv's return to gather his

thoughts. "I did not want people to die. Good people. Innocent people. But—"

"Like the Motixa."

Keirith winced. "Yes. She was innocent. But my people
are innocent, too. You steal them, sacrifice them, turn them
into slaves."

"Is that why you didn't tell anyone the earthquake was
coming?"

"But I do—did—tell the Qepo."

"Not when. Not how bad."

"I only knew soon. Not how bad." The Khonsel watched
him, waiting. "Not . . . so bad as this."

"And would you have said anything if you'd known it
was going to be 'so bad as this'?"

He started to say, "Of course." The words died under
the Khonsel's relentless stare.

He could protest that his father was going to be sacrificed, that he hoped he might have a chance to escape when
the earthquake struck—that all the captives might have a
chance. He could claim that, even if he had spoken up, the
queen would have sacrificed his father and then sent him
to the altar stone as well. But why tell the Khonsel what
he must already suspect?

"I do not know if I would have said anything. I
think . . . no."

The Khonsel refilled his goblet. "So. What would you do
with him, Geriv?"

"Kill him," Geriv replied, his voice devoid of emotion.
"He's dangerous."

And no one would ever know. Only Geriv and the
Khonsel had seen him.

The Khonsel leaned forward. "You wanted to die.
Earlier."

Nothing escaped the man. "Yes."

"Does it sicken you so much to be in his body?"

The snakes on his forearms sneered at him. "Yes. But . . .
it is more than that. Among my people, it is a crime to cast
out the spirit of another. A terrible crime."

"And what would your people do to a man who had
committed such a crime?"

"Kill him." His voice sounded as emotionless as Geriv's had.

"There's another choice," the Khonsel said. "Everyone thinks you're the Zheron. You could become him. Quite a rise in fortune. You might even fulfill Malaq's dream of peace between our peoples."

"First you want to kill me. Now you want me to stay and be the Zheron?" He waited for the Khonsel to smile, but his expression remained serious.

As impossible as it sounded, he realized it might work. A head injury would explain his fractured Zherosi. He could cite the earthquake as a sign of the gods' displeasure, use it to halt—or at least decrease—the sacrifices. But could he stop the raids? As long as the Zherosi needed slaves to work their fields and timber to build their ships, their eyes would turn north.

Together, he and Malaq might have been able to do it. But alone?

The seductive song of power whispered through him. He could change the policies of a kingdom. He could protect his people. He could use his gift for good. But the song also carried the memory of the triumph that had coursed through him as he battled Xevhan, the pleasure of eradicating his defenses, of destroying his tenacious hold on life. That was his power, too.

He had cast out the spirit of a man. The village elders might accept that he had done so to protect himself and his father, but Morgath had been sentenced to death for less.

His fist pressed against his chest as if that could stifle the yearning that rose up in him. Even if it meant his death, he wanted to see the eagles soaring over the lake and breathe the scent of peat smoke in the air. He wanted to walk into the village of his birth, where every hut was familiar, every face known. More than anything, he wanted to see his mam again, and Faelia and Callie and Conn. He wanted to go home.

"Thank you, Khonsel. But the Zheron is dead."

The Khonsel nodded once as if satisfied.

"Another test?" Keirith asked, unable to keep the bitterness from his voice.

The Khonsel shrugged.

"And if I failed?"

"I would have been forced to break my promise to Malaq," the Khonsel replied evenly.

"Even if he came back to haunt you?"

"Yes. Geriv is right. You are dangerous. And because of you, Malaq is dead. But I made him a promise and as long as you don't pose a threat to my people, I intend to keep it."

"Then . . . you will help us? My father and me?"

The Khonsel's expression hardened. "Tell me something first. Did he suffer?"

Keirith flinched. "The first moment . . . when the dagger goes in . . . that is bad. But after—"

"Not Malaq."

And then he understood.

"He knew he was going to die. That nothing could save him—not power or pleading or qiij. I ripped his spirit apart and shredded it and hurled the pieces of him into the Abyss. He felt it all. And he died screaming."

The Khonsel let out his breath slowly. "Thank you."

Chapter 46

FELLGAIR HAD DESERTED him. Hakkon was dead. And Keirith . . . gone. The Zheron had been alive when they took him away, but Darak had no way of knowing who had won the battle. He'd tried to tell the man in charge—the Khonsel—everything that had happened, but it was impossible to tell whether the man believed him. And now, more than a day had passed and he'd heard nothing.

The Khonsel hadn't forgotten about him, though. His guards still lingered in the temple. After a day of enforced inactivity, half of them sprawled on the floor, sleeping. The rest slumped against the wall, barely glancing in his direction.

Hircha had retreated into silence, but she'd watched him all day and half the night. Finally, he'd told her to get some sleep. She was lying near him with her eyes closed, but the tension in her body revealed her wakefulness.

Grief and rage had faded, leaving him numb. He ate to keep Hircha from nagging him. He drank—more than he should—to numb himself further. And waited, disinterested, to learn what his fate would be.

Since taking in Keirith's spirit, events had spiraled out of his control. His feeble efforts to help his son repel the Zheron had been worthless, his attempt to keep Keirith from pursuing the man even more so. He could not help Keirith now, but he might be able to intercede for the girl.

The guards stirred, kicking their comrades awake. Only

then did Darak hear the tramp of feet. By the time the
Khonsel strode through the doorway, the guards were
standing at attention.

Hircha shot him a wild look before she managed to com-
pose her features. The Khonsel rapped out a command and
the guards saluted and withdrew. As soon as they were
gone, two others marched in, grim-faced and silent. They
took up positions on either side of the doorway as the
Khonsel strode toward him, his expression equally grim.

Darak rose. If he was going to be sentenced to death, he
preferred to receive the news on his feet. The Khonsel
glared at him, but his voice was very soft.

"The Khonsel wants no outbursts." Hircha's voice shook
as she translated. "Nor displays of emotion."

Keirith was dead.

"You are to listen to what he has to say and obey his
orders without question. Do you understand?"

His boy was dead.

"Darak. Do you—"

"Aye."

The man's eyes held his. He spoke low and fast. The
only emotion he betrayed was a frown at Hircha's sudden
intake of breath.

"The Khonsel says . . ." Her voice cracked. "Keirith
is alive."

The Khonsel began speaking again, but Hircha's translation became a meaningless flow of words. Alive. Merciful
Maker, he was alive. Hircha was shaking his arm. He knew
he must listen to her, but his mind was adrift in joy. No
outbursts? No displays of emotion? Dear gods, did the man
think he was made of stone? His boy was alive.

He covered his face with a shaking hand and fought for
control. "Wait. Please. Start again."

Slowly, patiently, she repeated what she had just told
him. This time, though, he found himself recalling Keirith's
words: *"Sooner or later, I'll cast out the spirit of a man. As
Morgath did."*

From the moment they had carried the Zheron out, he
had known it was a possibility. Gods, he had even prayed
for that outcome. Keirith was his son. The Zheron had
meant to destroy him, to destroy them both. But still an

instinctive shudder of revulsion raced through him at an act that was the ultimate subversion of nature.

An act I drove him to. For didn't I subvert nature when I called him back from death? At that moment, I sentenced him to committing this sacrilege—or remaining trapped inside my body until he could bear it no longer and fled into oblivion.

Hircha's urgent whisper brought him back. "I'm sorry. I . . . what were you saying?"

"I said Keirith is dressed as an ordinary priest. He's waiting with Geriv—the man with the eye patch—in a cove west of the city where a fishing boat will take you to Oexiak. The two guards by the door know the place. They are Geriv's brothers, but they don't know the truth. You are just a valuable slave who must reach his master before he sails. Do you understand?"

He had to make her repeat it all again. The words made sense, but he simply couldn't believe them.

"Darak. There's little time. The boat leaves at dawn."

It could be a trap. But why would the Khonsel craft such an elaborate lie when he could simply execute him?

"I understand. But . . . why? Ask him why he's doing this?"

Irritation crossed the Khonsel's face as he replied.

"He says . . . it doesn't explain anything, but he said, 'Because I'm a sentimental fool.' "

It was not the face of a man given to sentimentality or foolishness. A determined face and—if he was reading it right—an honest one. The kind of man he'd have welcomed during the quest: stubborn and fearless and strong.

"Darak? Will you go?"

Only when he heard the tremor in Hircha's voice did he realize the Khonsel's bargain failed to mention her. "Tell him I'll go. If you're allowed to come with me."

Her breath caught. Her head came up, the incredible blue eyes huge in her thin face. For a moment, he thought she would cry, but she quickly controlled herself and translated his reply. The Khonsel blew out his breath in exasperation and answered her shortly.

"He said, 'Of course.' " Her expression was dazed. " 'I thought that was understood.' "

"Thank you, Khonsel." He knew he couldn't clasp the man's hand, so he offered a jerky bow instead. "Thank you for our lives. We will remember you in our prayers."

A tremulous smile lit Hircha's face as she listened to the soft but vehement reply. "The Khonsel says, 'Better you should reimburse me the forty serpents I had to lay out for the boat.'"

Still scowling, the Khonsel turned on his heel, shouting orders to the guards.

They headed west, skirting the open field where he had camped with the players. Dozens of small fires lit up the plain like fireflies, but once these were behind them, they had only Gheala's thin sliver of light to guide them.

After the incessant noise of Pilozhat, the stillness was eerie, broken only by the rustle of dry grass and Hircha's labored breathing. Twice, she missed her footing and sprawled headlong, but picked herself up without a word. After that, though, she permitted him to take her hand and help her over the rough terrain.

The sky to the east was just beginning to brighten when the guards slowed. Ahead, he could make out the dark expanse of the sea. Single file, they zigzagged along the top of a cliff, careful to keep a safe distance from the edge. The guards were clearly looking for a path down, but much of the cliff had fallen away during the earthquake; piles of rocks and debris littered the shoreline.

Finally, the guards halted, their uneasy glances alternating between the sky and the shore below. After a muted discussion, one of them turned and spoke softly. Hircha nodded, but made no attempt to translate; no doubt, the slaves of the rich merchant's son were expected to understand Zherosi.

One guard started down the slope. Darak seized Hircha's hand and followed. He slipped once on the loose pebbles, scraping his free hand raw as he caught himself. When they finally reached the bottom, he breathed a thankful prayer to the Maker.

The boat looked like a miniature version of the ones that had raided the village. Men were moving about onboard;

others stood on the beach. Before he could search for Keirith, Geriv strode toward them and nodded to their guards. Without a glance, the three started back up the cliff. He wished he had thought to ask for the names of Geriv's brothers; like it or not, they, too, would be remembered in his prayers.

An older man gestured for them to hurry. As Darak scanned the men again, a sharp command rang out. He flinched when he recognized the Zheron's voice. Flinched again when he found him standing on the deck of the boat.

It's not the Zheron. It's Keirith. That is my son.

He strained to see Keirith's expression, but all he could make out was a slender figure in a yellow robe. Despite the heat, he was wrapped in some sort of mantle. His arms were folded across his chest, the very picture of a rich young man who had been kept waiting by his dilatory slaves.

He's pretending. Just as he did the night of the performance. He can't show any emotion or it would give everything away.

Hircha was staring at Keirith, too. The gods only knew what the Zheron had done to her; it must have been something awful to arouse the hatred she had shown earlier and now, this naked fear. She recovered before he did, though, seizing his arm and dragging him to his knees beside her. Bowing her head, she offered what must be an apology for their tardiness, but he couldn't take his eyes off the robed figure looming above them. He searched for something—anything—that would prove this was his son. Keirith stared back at him, hugging himself as if he was cold. When the older man spoke to him, he nodded impatiently and barked out another order in Zherosi.

Hircha rose and walked toward the boat. Two men pulled her over the side, then extended their hands to help him. Darak was reaching for them when their expressions changed. He whirled around to see the Supplicant walking across the sand. The fishermen fell to their knees. Fellgair smiled pleasantly at them before crooking his finger at Keirith.

After a moment's hesitation, Keirith jumped onto the sand. As he passed, their gazes met again. The shadows under his eyes looked as purple as new bruises. Sweat glazed his forehead. Despite the confidence of his stride, he was trembling, fighting hard for control. The urge to touch him was overwhelming. Before Darak could succumb to it, he ducked his head.

I have to help him. I have to play my part. Later, there will be time to talk, to hold him. To make things right.

In a low voice, Keirith said, "Come."

It shocked him to hear the tribal tongue coming from the Zheron's mouth. Keirith's mouth. And this was Keirith's voice, this light baritone made harsh by emotion. What had it been like to wake up in that body? To hear that voice for the first time? Had he been terrified? Triumphant? Or simply numb, as he had been when he had awakened to discover himself lying atop Morgath's corpse?

The same numbness seemed to possess him now as he trailed after Keirith. Fellgair regarded them with a complacent smile. "You neglected to say good-bye," he chided.

With difficulty, Darak dragged his gaze from his son. "Aye. I'm sorry. You were gone. I wanted to thank you for all you did."

"Yes. Everything's turned out quite well, hasn't it?"

"Malaq is dead," Keirith said. "And Urkiat. And hundreds of others." Although his voice was quiet, it sounded raw and hoarse. As if he had been shouting—or screaming. "And I will spend the rest of my life wearing the body of the man who murdered me."

"It's a delicious irony, isn't it? Although I doubt Xevhan would appreciate it."

"Neither am I."

"If you dislike this body, you can always acquire another. You could live forever, skipping from one to the next like our beloved queen."

"Never!"

"After all, what's a body? It gets old. It dies. Spirit is what matters. Ask the beloved but bark-encrusted Tinnean."

Keirith opened his mouth and shut it again. Fellgair bestowed a beneficent smile upon him, then sighed. "Our intrepid sailors grow restless. The tide waits for no man. And tempted though I am to hold it while we linger over our farewells, such an act would be far too ostentatious. Even for me."

Fellgair leaned forward and kissed him lightly on the forehead. "I hope we shall meet again, Darak." A shadow darkened his expression, but it was gone in a moment. "But I'll certainly encounter you, Keirith. Won't that be fun?"

Keirith turned on his heel and stalked back to the boat. Fellgair sighed again. "He reminds me of you—rude and impetuous. Let's hope he improves on future acquaintance as you did."

"He'll be safe?" Darak asked. "The fishermen won't recognize the Zheron?"

"Xevhan didn't mingle with common folk."

"Men don't just disappear."

"Dozens have since the earthquake," Fellgair reminded him. "The Khonsel's a resourceful man. He'll think of something. Or perhaps I'll make my own arrangements. They're still pulling bodies out of the ruins. Imagine the Khonsel's surprise when he discovers one of them is the Zheron."

"But how . . . ? Nay, I don't want to know. As long as we're out of this place forever." Darak eyed the dark mass of the mountain looming behind Fellgair; even here, it dominated the sky with malevolent watchfulness. "Thank you. For helping me. I wish I'd known—when you entered my spirit—that you were preparing me to save his."

"But that would have ruined the fun."

"Did you know then what would happen?"

Fellgair's expression grew solemn. "His chance of surviving was small. The odds that he would acquire the Zheron's body were smaller still. Until the oleaginous Olinio entered the fray."

"*You* sent him to the Zheron?"

"I didn't have to. His greed was motivation enough. Peace, Darak. Olinio will get the reward he deserves—in this life or the next. Now kiss my hand like a devoted worshipper and run along."

Darak bent over the delicate hand. Fur brushed his lips. But when he jerked his head back, he saw only the slender fingers of the Supplicant.

Someone shouted. The fishermen shoved the boat into the water. Darak scrambled aboard. The men settled themselves on the four wooden benches and bent their backs over the long paddles. Oars. Urkiat called them oars.

Maker, carry his spirit to the Forever Isles. He got so little happiness in life; he deserves a little after death.

His stomach lurched as the boat crested the first of the breakers. Two men tugged on ropes, laboriously raising the tall spar bearing the wind cloth. Keirith stared out to sea, but Darak clutched the spar, watching the robed figure on the beach grow smaller and smaller until it vanished from sight.

PART FOUR

*These acts are offenses against the creatures
  of the world:
To cut a limb from a living tree
  without a sacrifice offered in return.
To pull a fish from the waters
  without a sacrifice offered in return.
To kill a bird or animal
without a sacrifice offered in return.
To kill without provocation
  any man or woman or child.
The punishment for one who commits such offenses
  is to be cast out of the tribe.*

*These acts are offenses against the gods:
To raise a weapon against the One Tree,
  in which dwell the spirits of the Oak and the Holly.
To raise a weapon against the heart-oak of our tribe.
To seek power through unnatural communion with a
  creature of Chaos.
To subvert or subjugate the spirit of any creature.
The punishment for one who commits such
  abominations is death.*

The Forbidden Acts

Chapter 47

THREE DAYS LATER, they were retracing the route Darak had taken half a moon before with Urkiat. They had acquired supplies in Oexiak, purchased with more of the Khonsel's coins. Keirith exchanged his priest's robe for the long breeches and tunic worn by the raiders. When Darak pulled Keirith's mantle from his pack and handed it to him, Keirith stroked the wool with trembling hands and quickly turned away.

The tunic hid the snake tattoos on his forearms and the mantle would cover his shaven head, but there was no disguising his swarthy complexion and dark eyes. Few would accept him as a child of the Oak and Holly, and no one who knew the tale of the Spirit-Hunter would believe this grown man was his son. Illait and Girn would be wise enough not to ask too many questions, but in the other villages, he would have to pretend Keirith was a man he'd met in Zheros.

Each day, he grew more accustomed to Keirith's new form. After a sennight, he no longer started when he heard the voice. But the unexpected gesture could still undermine his control—to see him gnawing his thumb or compulsively rubbing his head. Or to look up and discover him tracing the lines on his palm or the curve of his chin or the swell of a bicep. Exploring his new body with the same fear and fascination that Cuillon had shown when he woke to find himself in Tinnean's body. Whenever that happened, Darak would ask a quiet question to bring him back, taking care to look away before he spoke so he wouldn't see Keirith's guilty start of surprise.

Even after they left Zheros behind, Keirith maintained a wary distance. At first, Darak thought he was reluctant to speak openly in front of Hircha, but it soon became clear he didn't want to talk at all. He rebuffed every attempt to draw him out, sometimes with a gentle refusal, but more often, with a sudden flare of anger, quickly followed by a mumbled apology.

After all Keirith had been through, Darak could understand why his moods swung from anger to depression. His son's physical condition troubled him more. Just walking along the beach made him break into a sweat. At night, he huddled under two mantles, shivering. He ate little and when he did, he barely managed to keep the food down.

"It's the qiij," Hircha confided in one of their rare conversations. "A drug that Xevhan took. His body still craves it." But even Hircha didn't know how long the symptoms would last.

The nightmares began within days of leaving Zheros. When they grew more violent, Darak risked another rebuff to reach out to his son.

"Talk to me, Keirith. Let me help."

"You had nightmares after Morgath."

"Aye."

"And they went away?"

"In time."

"Then give me time. Just . . . give me a little time."

The same words he'd said to Griane all those years ago. And like Griane, he didn't press Keirith, although it hurt to see his son's pain and be helpless to alleviate it.

As he had after his own quest, he reflected bitterly on the shortcomings of the tribal legends. They were filled with heroic deeds and fierce battles. They taught the lesson that good triumphed over evil, that balance was restored through sacrifice and selflessness. But they failed to speak of what happened after the battle was won, after the goal of the quest had been achieved. They never spoke of the wounds—physical and emotional—that had to be endured, the sleepless nights, the lingering doubts. Old Sim would probably say no one wanted to hear about those, but they were as much a part of the quest as everything that came before.

He had bent all his energy on finding Keirith and freeing him, refusing to contemplate the possibility of failure. He had warded off thoughts of home lest they weaken him. Only now did he allow himself the luxury of loneliness. He longed to hold his son—as much for his comfort as for Keirith's. But only in the moments when Keirith fought off a nightmare did his son permit such contact.

He hadn't realized how starved he was for companionship until he sought out Wolf. Her joyful greeting brought tears to his eyes. Now that they were back in tribal lands, she was fully restored. If he missed the reality of her rough tongue against his cheek and her thick fur under his fingers, he took comfort in her strength and her wisdom.

"My pup is wounded, Wolf. And I don't know how to heal him."

She cocked her head, considering. "Do you keep him warm at night? And lick the wound to clean it?"

"It's a wound of the spirit, not the body."

"Those are harder to reach. But they, too, must be cleaned or they will fester. You know this, Little Brother."

In shame and fear, he had buried the memories of his ordeal in Chaos. The events of the last moons had unearthed them. Wolf was right; he could not let Keirith make the same mistake.

He wondered if Keirith's adder could offer the same comfort Wolf gave him. Natha was both vision mate and spirit guide; surely, that made the bond doubly strong. But when he suggested it, Keirith shook his head. "I'm too tired to seek a vision."

"Maybe you don't have to. I can speak to my vision mate—and the gods know, I'm no priest."

"But how?"

"I call her name. I picture her in my mind. And she comes to me."

Keirith nodded thoughtfully. "That's where you go. When you leave camp. I wondered."

"Aye. She'd come here, but you wouldn't be able to see her. And I didn't want you to think I'd lost my mind and was talking to myself."

"After everything that's happened, you'd have reason enough." Keirith's smile failed to hide the bitterness in his voice.

"After my vision quest, I never saw her again until Chaos. Maybe that . . . changed our bond. Made it stronger somehow. But it's worth trying, son."

He never knew if Keirith followed his advice. Perhaps the very fact that Natha was an adder conjured too many painful memories.

They continued their silent journey north. Each step brought them closer to home—and to the inevitable confrontation with the council of elders. Keirith seemed unconcerned about his fate; he simply wanted to see his family again. But the thought that he was leading his son to his death haunted Darak.

Could he convince the elders that Keirith had acted in self-defense? Would they be able to separate the boy from the act? Or would they simply remember Morgath and recoil in horror when they saw him?

Even Hircha, who'd hated the Zheron, could scarcely bring herself to look at Keirith. Finally, Darak took her aside and reminded her that Keirith needed kindness and friendship. He spoke gently enough—Griane would have been proud—but Hircha shot him a murderous look and told him to mind his own business.

If her attitude infuriated him, he had no complaints about her stamina. Despite her limp, she never asked them to slow the pace. She helped gather deadwood for their fire every evening and insisted on carrying an equal share of their supplies every day. And through it all, she maintained a stubborn silence as impenetrable as Keirith's.

Only once did she show any emotion. They had been traveling up the coast for a sennight. When she cried out, he froze, reaching for the dagger he had purchased in Oexiak.

"What? What is it?"

"It must be the same. There can't be two."

"Two what?"

"The Old Man."

His gaze followed hers to the top of a promontory, but he saw no one. Then he understood. With a little imagination, you could see the shape of a face in the rocks: a high forehead, a jutting nose, a pointed chin. Before he could stop her, she was lurching down the beach. He shouted at her to stop, knowing what she would find, but she ignored him. Cursing, he raced after her and saw her steps slow.

The village had been abandoned more recently than Urkiat's; although most of the roofs had caved in, the walls were still standing and the forest had yet to reclaim the field. Tufts of seagrass sprouted in the doorways. Inside, he found only the stones of the fire pits. Either the raiders had stripped everything or these folk had left of their own accord. For Hircha's sake, he hoped it was the latter.

She ducked into one hut and remained inside a long while, emerging with a tight mouth and red-rimmed eyes.

"They might have fled deeper into the forest," Darak said. "Other tribes have. We'll ask at Ailmin's village."

Her mouth quirked in a bitter smile. "It seems you're stuck with me."

He'd never realized his resentment was so palpable. Apologies would be useless; this girl valued truth, no matter how painful. Finally, he said, "And you're stuck with us. I'd say you got the worst of the bargain."

Something that might have been surprise flashed in her eyes. Her expression softened, reminding Darak of how young she was—and how vulnerable—beneath her tough exterior.

She shrugged. "I'd say we're about even."

And with that grudging acknowledgment, he had to be content.

Keirith's cry startled Hircha out of sleep. She waited for Darak's soft murmur to calm him. Hearing nothing, she rolled over.

Keirith was tossing restlessly, but Darak was gone. Perhaps he had to relieve himself; even the great Spirit-Hunter must piss sometimes. She shook Keirith gently, but he just moaned.

"Harder," he muttered. "Make her squeal."

More astonishing than the words was the fact that he had spoken Zherosi. She shook him hard and he bolted upright. His eyes were wild, his lips twisted in the snarl she'd seen so often when Xevhan was in one of his rages. Instinctively, she scuttled backward.

Keirith blinked. His mouth relaxed. "Hircha?" The voice was Xevhan's, of course, but the tentative note was Keirith's. "I'm sorry I scared you."

"You were dreaming."

He hugged his knees to his chest, staring at the glowing embers of the fire.

"Do you want some water?"

He shook his head.

"Shall I fetch Darak?"

Keirith seemed unsurprised to find his father gone. "He'll be back soon."

He kept his face half turned from her as if ashamed of his outburst. Or perhaps he wanted to spare her the sight of it. Darak had seen how she avoided looking at Keirith. Keirith would have noticed, too. A hot wash of shame flooded her face. Poor boy. Hard as these last days had been for her, they were a hundred times worse for him.

"Do you want to talk about it? The nightmare, I mean?"

She expected him to say no. He always brushed off his father's attempts to draw him out and after the way she'd behaved, he had no reason to confide in her. He surprised her by saying, "I was dreaming of the blind girl."

"The . . . you mean the one with the players?"

He nodded. "She sang for him. And then he watched Miko rape her."

His words transported her back to Xevhan's chamber. Her body shuddered as if she were once again absorbing those brutal thrusts. She could hear Miko's grunts and Xevhan's labored breathing, hoarse with excitement.

"Hircha?"

Keirith went down on his knees before her, careful not to come too close or touch her. He knew the instinctive lurch of fear when a hand reached out unexpectedly. Even one offered in friendship carried the memories of others that had brought only pain.

"Forgive me," he said. "I didn't think."

With an effort, she pushed the memories away. "You can't blame yourself for what they did. You have to put Pilozhat behind you."

"Like you have?"

"I'm . . . trying."

"So am I," he whispered.

Impulsively, she held out her hand. He seized it eagerly.

"It's . . . I suppose it's natural," she said, searching for something that would ease his misery. "For us to think about him. About the things he did. And it's hard—gods, Keirith, I know how hard it must be. In his body."

"It's mine now."

"Aye."

"He's gone."

"Aye."

"I'm not him!"

His grip was so tight, she could barely keep from wincing. "I know. I'm sorry if I've been . . . unkind."

"You loved him, didn't you?"

Her breath caught. She let it out slowly. "Once."

Before the blind girl. Before all the other little girls. Before qiij and ambition stole the last shreds of decency he possessed.

"But that was a long time ago. And the man I loved . . . the man I thought I loved . . . he never really existed." She squeezed his hand. "He's gone, Keirith. He'll never hurt us again."

Only later, as she was drifting off to sleep, did she wonder who had told him what Xevhan and Miko had done. Perhaps one of the guards. Or a gossiping slave. How else could he have known what had happened to the poor girl?

Chapter 48

THREE DAYS AFTER HIS conversation with Hircha, they reached Ailmin's village. When his father introduced them as captives rescued from the Zherosi holy city, Ailmin's gaze lingered on him. He probably wondered why a Zheroso needed to be rescued from his own people. His father's reputation won them hospitality, but it was grudgingly given. No feast was prepared to welcome them. No stories were shared around the fire. Ailmin's wife served them in silence, and in silence, they ate. And when the grim meal was finished, they curled up beside the fire pit with their weapons close at hand.

Dreading a nightmare among strangers, Keirith waited until everyone was asleep and made his way to the beach. The evening thunderstorm had washed the air clean. The sand was damp and cool under his bare feet. Seaweed and broken shells littered the beach, but the sea was calmer now, the soft shushing of the breakers and the hiss of foam the only sounds in the world.

His bag of charms rested against his chest. The reminder of his past—his true self—comforted him and he was grateful Hircha had preserved it. He spread his mantle on the sand and emptied the bag onto it, touching each of the charms, just as he had the night before the earthquake. Malaq's bloodstone warmed quickly in his palm. He let his thumb glide over its smooth surface as he stared out to sea.

For days he had tried to convince himself that his dreaming mind was simply weaving nightmarish images into his memories. But how could he know what had happened to the blind singer? How could he experience everything about that encounter so intensely? The skin, soft as a rowan petal. The surprised flinch when Miko seized her wrist. And the screams that went on and on until her sweet voice became hoarse and broken and finally fell silent.

Even the Tree-Father sometimes failed to make sense of visions. And what were dreams but sleeping visions? But there were other images, other memories, too many to dismiss. Xevhan's spirit had shattered before he cast it out. What if those shattered pieces remained inside him, lost to his waking mind but emerging while he slept?

One by one, he gathered his charms and slipped them back into his bag. The dagger lay against his hip. He drew it from its sheath, remembering the shock of Xevhan's blade driving into his flesh. He didn't think he could bear that again. Better to walk into the sea and let the water close over him. He thought of his family waiting at home, considered the possibility that his imagination had conjured the nightmares, weighed the horror of carrying Xevhan's spirit with him to the Forever Isles against the possibility of escape.

Twice, he had tried and failed to reach Natha. He told himself that snakes were not wolves, that his father's bond to his vision mate had endured for years. But secretly, he feared Natha no longer recognized his spirit.

"Please, Natha. Please come."

Gheala's light cut a wavering swath across the dark waters. Lulled by the sound of the surf, he drifted, as once he had floated in the honeysuckle sea. The night waned. Gheala's reflection moved slowly westward. It rose and fell with the ceaseless motion of the waves. It slithered across the water, riding the crest of the breakers and vanishing in the foam. It wriggled onto the shore.

The creamy color faded. Clad in his familiar green and black, Natha glided toward him. Tears stung Keirith's eyes as he felt the brush of scales over his bare toes.

"Why did you seek me that other way? I could not reach you."

"I didn't have the strength for trance."

Natha hissed in irritation. "You did not try."

"I . . . I'm sorry."

Natha hissed again, but this time his tongue flicked out to kiss his ankle. "You taste different."

"I wear another body."

"I have eyes. Why did you shed the old one?" At his inadvertent flinch, Natha's head reared up. "Ahh. You did not wish to shed."

"Nay."

"Well, it is done now. This body is strong. It will serve you well."

"I want *my* body! My real body!"

"You speak like a child. I wonder why I bother with you."

Keirith sighed. "Because you are patient and wise."

"Yes. And you are impatient and foolish. The gods should have sent you a squirrel for a vision mate. Or a rabbit."

"Or an eagle," Keirith retorted, hurt by Natha's coldness.

A sharp pain stung his ankle as Natha struck. "Then fly with your eagle and leave me in peace."

"Wait! Don't go. Please, Natha. I'm sorry."

Natha slithered back, but remained out of reach.

"I'm scared, Natha. I think . . . the man whose body I wear . . . I think his spirit still lives inside me."

Natha wriggled over his ankle, up his leg. As he slithered higher, Keirith fell back as if pressed down by a heavy weight. Slow as sap rising, Natha wound his way up his chest, his throat, his chin. The tongue flicked out to kiss his lips. The head butted against his mouth, forcing it open. He choked as the slender body slid over his tongue, but then Natha's physical being vanished, leaving only the sensation of something flowing down his throat. It warmed him like his mam's hot apple cider as it filled his belly, warmed him in another way altogether as it gushed into his loins.

His arousal subsided, leaving him as flushed and spent as if he had climaxed. Natha spiraled through him, as ceaseless as the waves, as refreshing as a stream. When that soothing presence vanished, the sense of loss made him want to weep.

"Remember," Natha whispered. "Follow the path I took when you seek sleep. Or when you feel the man stirring."

"He's there? He lives?" Keirith couldn't keep the panic from his voice.

"Fragments only. Rid yourself of them."

"How?"

"Are you a hatchling? They must be disgorged or digested. Excrete him as you would feathers or fur."

"I'm not an adder!"

"No, you are a foolish boy. The principle is the same whether the fragments are those of a man's spirit or a nestling's body. If they remain too long inside of you, they will putrefy."

Already, he seemed to feel the taint spreading through his spirit. Natha's tongue caressed his cheek, calming him. "We will take the path together. Seek out the fragments and expel them."

Keirith didn't ask how or when. It was enough to know that Natha would be with him, that Xevhan would be rooted out, that—please, gods—when death came for him, he would not carry the taint to the Forever Isles.

"The wolf lover comes. You must wake now."

With an effort, he pushed himself up. Where Natha had lain, he saw two large bare feet. His father's gaze rested on the dagger that lay forgotten on the mantle. As Keirith reached for it, he swooped down and seized his wrist.

"It's all right," Keirith said. "I wasn't going to . . . I spoke with Natha."

His father's grip eased just a little. The strength he possessed with only three fingers always astonished Keirith.

"It's all right," he repeated.

His father released him, but only when he sheathed the dagger did the tension leave his body. "May I sit with you?"

Keirith slid over, making space on the mantle. His father's thumb beat a nervous tattoo on his thigh. Before Keirith could reassure him again, he said, "Tinnean said I must speak of Morgath or he would live in me forever. He was right. You bury the memories. Forget about them for days, moons at a time. But they're still there. You can never bury them deep enough."

"And if they remain inside too long, they putrefy." When his father's head jerked toward him, he added, "Natha's words."

His father nodded. He took a deep breath and let it out slowly. And then he began to speak of what had happened to him during his quest.

Every Midwinter, Sanok told the tale of Darak Spirit-Hunter, the hero. This was the story of the man: the agony of having pieces of his body cut away; the horror of Morgath's invading spirit stripping away his defenses; the hope and terror and, ultimately, understanding that arose from his communion with the World Tree; and those final shattering moments when, surrounded by the love of his brother and father, he had faced up to the darkest parts of himself and conquered Morgath.

Even when his father described Tinnean's transformation, his voice remained calm. Only when he spoke of what had happened after he returned to the village did Keirith detect the first tremor of emotion.

"I didn't believe I could ever hunt again. I didn't know what to do. Who to be. I was lost. And . . . and scared. The nightmares were bad. As if he were still inside of me."

Almost the same words I spoke to Natha.

"I . . . I left your mam. I told her I needed time. And I went back to the First Forest. I sat under the tree—Tinnean's tree—and I thought about dying. Not killing myself so much as sitting there and letting the life drain out of me. A slow death, but a peaceful one. No more nightmares. No more memories. No more wondering what to do with my life."

The fingers clenched around his knees and relaxed.

"But there was your mam. I loved her. It was . . . a gift I'd never expected. I thought about her sitting in our hut, waiting, wondering . . . and I got up and came home. Well, Lisula fetched me, actually. She'd had a dream that I was ready. I suppose you can guess who sent it."

Keirith offered a silent prayer that the Trickster would never take such an interest in him.

"I begged your mam's forgiveness. And told her some of what I've told you. But not all."

Once it would have shocked him to imagine his father keeping secrets from his mam; they seemed so much a part of each other. Now he understood.

"I think you already knew most of this. Two spirits dwelling together . . . there's little you can hide from each other.

Whether it's what happened to me on that tree—or what happened to you on that ship."

He forced himself to meet his father's eyes and nod.

"Since that morning at the altar, I've wondered if I did wrong. If I should have let you go. Maybe that would have been kinder. But I . . . I couldn't. I didn't think about the consequences. I didn't consider what kind of life I was bringing you back to. I just knew I couldn't let you go. So maybe all that happened after is my fault—for being selfish."

When Keirith made a sound of denial, his father shook his head fiercely. "You cast out his spirit and took his body. According to our laws, that's a crime. But I can't see it that way. You fought him as an equal with the only weapon you had."

"I don't regret casting out Xevhan's spirit. It's . . ." He had to take a deep breath before he could say the name. "It's Urkiat I keep thinking about."

"Aye. We'll always bear the burden of his death."

"It's my burden, not yours."

"Don't."

"Sometimes, I wish I *had* cast out his spirit. That would have been better than leaving you to—"

"Don't!"

His father shoved himself to his feet. "We both bear the guilt. There's nothing we can say or do to change that. You were trying to save me. You made a choice. I understand."

But he would never forgive him. And Urkiat's death would always lie between them.

His father sank down beside him again. Keirith wondered if his expression had betrayed his thoughts or if his father had simply sensed them. Ever since their spirits had dwelled together, each of them seemed to know without words what the other was thinking and feeling.

"Urkiat had committed an act that he thought was unforgivable. And I made him confront it. I didn't realize what I was asking of him. If I had . . ." He shrugged helplessly. "Facing his past was one of the hardest things Urkiat ever did. But I think it gave him peace. Sometimes it helps to speak of the things that haunt you. Bring them into the light. Look at them plainly. If you're lucky, the thing you fear shrinks down to a size you can handle. But even if it still scares you, at least it's out in the open, not lurking in the shadows. Or in your dreams."

His father sounded so tired and so old. As if the weight of his life would crush him.

"Urkiat died because of us. But he also died *for* us. If we waste our lives in guilt and shame, we dishonor his death. You and I—we've both felt . . . tainted by the things that have happened to us, the choices we've made. We've looked at the future and wondered if we could bear it. Dying is easy, son. You know that now. It's living that's hard. But as long as there are those who love you, it's worth the struggle. And no matter what, I'll be here."

His father's fingers groped across the mantle, then stopped. Slowly, Keirith reached out and covered them with his. And then he began his tale, from those first moments of terror on the ship to his last conversation with Natha.

When he was finished, his father whispered, "I wish to gods it could have been me. That would be easier to bear."

Keirith squeezed the clenched fist.

In the same fierce whisper, his father said, "We'll get through this. We will."

After that, they sat together in silence, watching Bel's dawning light chase away the shadows.

Chapter 49

FOR GRIANE, MIDSUMMER passed in a numbing haze of fear and recrimination. While the rest of the tribe offered sacrifices to ensure the Holly-Lord's victory, she could only wonder if her son had been sacrificed to appease the hungry gods of the raiders. Waking and dreaming, she pictured Gortin's vision, only now it was Keirith's eyes staring up at the priest's dagger, Keirith's blood drenching the altar stone, Keirith's body convulsing in its death throes.

A few of her kinfolk still spoke of Darak and Keirith as if they were alive, but most avoided mentioning them at all. Others filled their places now. At Midsummer, Othak stood beside Gortin, wearing the brown robe of the initiate. Sanok still recited the legend of the Oak and the Holly, but he stumbled over the words so often that Nemek had to finish the tale. Although no one said so, it was clear that Nemek was Memory-Keeper in all but name.

Callie went daily to the lake with offerings for Lacha. Faelia disappeared into the forest. And every night, Griane turned her face to the night sky, watching Gheala grow fat and counting the days until she must fulfill her bargain with Fellgair.

To avert Faelia's suspicions, she began going to the glade every morning at dawn to pour an offering of water over the heart-oak's roots. To her surprise, the ritual soothed her, allowing her to voice her fears to the sacred tree and giving her the strength to face another day. Perhaps the

Maker heard her prayers as well, for the nightmares abated; she even managed to sleep soundly the night before she was to meet Fellgair.

She dressed quietly that morning and slung a waterskin over her shoulder. As she made her way through the village, the scent of peat smoke filled the air and the occasional cry of a babe broke the silence as other mothers built up their fires and hushed their fretful children.

The gray half-light faded to darkness under the thick canopy of the forest, but she knew the path too well to stumble. She made her offering to the heart-oak and said prayers for the safe return of her husband and son. Only when she asked the Maker to guide her did her voice falter.

She had lain with only one man in her life. The mechanics must be similar with a god. But what if it was . . . better? Even after fifteen years, she could remember the gentleness of Fellgair's touch. She prayed today's memories would not intrude each time Darak reached for her, but if they did, she would bear them in silence.

She heard a twig snap behind her. Taking a deep breath, she turned to greet Fellgair.

Jurl rested his bow against a birch and eased the quiver of arrows off his back. "So this is where you sneak off to every morning."

"I leave sneaking to you," Griane managed when she recovered from her surprise.

"When did you become so pious?"

"When the raiders stole my son. What do you want, Jurl?"

His smile was more unpleasant than usual. "We've got unfinished business."

Chinks of blue peeped through the leaves. Fellgair would arrive any moment.

"Whatever business we have can wait."

"I've waited long enough." He advanced on her slowly, the smile gone. "I didn't tell anyone you freed that boy. It's just you and me, so don't bother denying it. I kept my mouth shut. I let everyone think I was a fool. The way I see it, you owe me."

"I don't owe you anything. You were drunk then and you must be drunk now to talk like this."

"Besides, you're the kind of woman who needs a man between her thighs at night."

"It's morning. And my thighs are just fine, thank you."

They were shaking, in fact, but she wouldn't let Jurl know that. Like all bullies, he would give this up if she refused to back down. To her dismay, he kept walking toward her, forcing her to back away. Gods, he'd be chasing her around the heart-oak soon.

"When Darak comes home—"

"Darak's dead."

"He's not."

Jurl shrugged. "Dead or alive. Doesn't matter to me. I'm not talking marriage. I need a young girl for that. A breeder to get sons on. Real sons, not miserable little whiners like Othak. But you'll do fine in the meantime."

"I'll do nothing in the meantime."

"You will. Else I'll tell the whole tribe about the boy. And I'll tell your precious Darak that you offered yourself to me to shut me up."

"You wouldn't dare."

"You think I'm afraid of him? The great Spirit-Hunter?" Jurl spat. "I'll tell him. And I'll make him believe it. I'll describe every mole and freckle on your body."

He moved even before he finished speaking, and although she'd been expecting it, she reacted too slowly. Still, she might have gotten away if she hadn't tripped over an exposed root. He was on her in an instant, shoving her facedown across the root, trapping her hands beneath her. She grunted in pain as his heavy body fell on her. When she screamed, he left off fumbling with her skirt long enough to press her face into the soft mulch. She twisted her head, gulping for air, choking as leaves and earth filled her mouth.

The weight on her back and thighs suddenly eased. She shoved herself up and kicked out with a bare foot. Although she struck empty air, she heard a thud behind her and a horrible wheezing. Scrambling to her knees, she reached for the dagger at her waist.

Her hand froze. Jurl was tearing at the neck of his tunic, his mouth opening and closing like a landed fish. Griane hesitated, then dropped to her knees beside him. She peered into his open mouth, but saw nothing stuck in his throat. Knowing he was too heavy to turn over, she clenched her fists together and pounded his chest. It only made him gasp harder.

Could it be an attack like the one Old Dren suffered last

summer? But Dren hadn't appeared to be suffocating as Jurl surely was. She tried breathing into his mouth, but he was thrashing too wildly.

His face slowly darkened to the color of raw liver. His heels gouged great furrows in the mulch. His bulging eyes pleaded with her, but all she could do was kneel beside him and squeeze his hand.

A foul smell assaulted her nostrils as he voided his bowels. His convulsions grew weaker. His legs slowly relaxed. The tortured gasping ceased, and the blue lips went slack.

Griane closed the staring eyes, but could not bring herself to whisper a prayer that his spirit should fly to the Forever Isles. All his life, Jurl had been a brute and a bully. His first wife had died of childbed fever; the second had fled back to her family. His only surviving child was terrified of him. At least poor Othak was safe from his father's beatings now, although he would probably carry the emotional scars forever.

A sudden whiff of honeysuckle drove away the stink of death. Black-clawed feet appeared before her. Golden eyes regarded Jurl's body. The long nose wrinkled in distaste.

"You did this?"

"It's past dawn. Today you were promised to me." Fellgair shrugged. "Besides, I never liked him. Shall we go?"

She had witnessed many of Fellgair's moods—mocking, seductive, stern, even sorrowful—but she had never seen him so ruthless. For the first time in their long acquaintance, she was truly afraid of him.

His face softened. "Do you think I would ever deal with you like that?"

She hesitated only a moment, but it was long enough. His expression became remote. "Do you wish to rescind our bargain?"

"Nay."

He studied her a moment, then nodded. She clasped his outstretched hand and clung to it tightly as the glade of the heart-oak melted into a smear of color and light.

Even with her eyes closed, she knew where he had taken her. For fifteen years, she had preserved the sensations in her memory: the crispness of the grass between her bare toes, the gentle splash of the waterfall, the heady aroma of the air, richer than any that existed in her world. But memory failed to capture the brilliance of the colors that burst upon her when she opened her eyes: the lush greens and vivid reds, the bold blue of the sky, and the rich browns of the tree trunks. As if the Maker had splashed the colors across the Summerlands that very morning.

The pool was exactly as she remembered, the water cascading over ledges carved with otherworldly precision into the hillside. A mere swallow of that water would slake her thirst for the entire day. The plants she had named still grew beside the pool: silver-leafed heal-all that could seal a wound with a touch, broad-leafed heart-ease that could soothe the most troubled spirit. They had kept Cuillon strong during that long journey back to the grove of the One Tree and helped Darak survive the damage Morgath had inflicted on his body.

She shaded her eyes, gazing across the grasslands, but the clumps of trees seemed firmly rooted in the earth.

"Would you like to see her again?" Fellgair asked.

She hesitated, wondering what that pleasure would cost her.

Fellgair's lips pursed in exasperation. "Not every gift I offer has a price. If it would please you to see Rowan again, I will take you to her. Give me your hand."

"Can't we just walk?"

"Waste our day plodding through the Summerlands? What an extraordinary idea." He thrust out his hand, but still she hesitated.

"I'd like to see Rowan, but I would give it up if you'd tell me . . . if I knew for certain . . . is Keirith alive?"

"Yes."

In spite of her best effort at control, she burst into noisy, foolish tears. At least Fellgair had the decency not to comfort her. He simply sat on a rock, the model of patience, while she choked and gasped and finally gave up and sat on the ground at his feet and allowed herself to weep. Only when her sobs subsided into hiccups and her hiccups to moist sniffles did he hold out a scrap of cloth. She smoothed the delicate white square with her fingertips.

"It's called a handkerchief," Fellgair said. "One day—in

the not-so-distant future, I hope—the best people will use these instead of sleeves to wipe their faces."

She did as he suggested, although it struck her that sturdy doeskin would do a much better job than this lacy little cobweb. Still, it was very pretty; perhaps the best people's noses didn't leak so much when they cried.

When she held it out to him, he examined the crumpled mess with obvious distaste. "Keep it. Please. Perhaps you'll start a trend in your village." He shifted his examination to her face and sighed. "You're not one of those women who weeps beautifully, are you?"

"If the sight offends you, you may rescind our bargain."

"On the contrary, I find red noses erotic." He waggled his long tongue at her in such a parody of lewdness that she had to smile. "Much better."

"Thank you."

"You do have a low threshold for compliments."

"I meant for telling me about Keirith."

"Ah. Well. It pleases me to please you."

And that, of course, was why she was here: to serve his pleasure. Before sunset, she must lie with him. Allowing her to see Rowan, telling her about Keirith . . . these were simply his form of foreplay. He would never be so crude as to throw her to the ground and mount her. He wasn't Jurl. But it surprised her that he should think such gestures necessary. He was a god, after all. He could make her desire him, just as he had all those years ago. Knowing that Keirith was safe, knowing that he would protect Darak, she would offer herself willingly and consider the price cheap.

"Why do you want me?" Her face grew warm under his scrutiny, but she forced herself to add, "You could have any woman in the world. Younger women. Prettier women."

The kind of women who knew instinctively what handkerchiefs were for. Women who looked beautiful when they wept. Women with soft voices and softer bodies, their bellies unmarred by stretch marks, their breasts high and firm.

Instead of mocking her, his expression became thoughtful. "I admire your courage and your fierceness. The marks on your belly testify to the pain of childbirth. Your breasts, to the children you've suckled. Your fingertips . . ." He took her hand and turned it over, one claw lightly caressing the green-tinged tips. ". . . to the years of handling the plants that heal your people. And if your hair is streaked with white and occasionally less than tidy . . ." The dexterous claws moved. A leaf fluttered to the ground. ". . . it bespeaks the battles you have fought and survived."

The golden eyes filled her vision, as hot as the Summerlands sun. And then they vanished as he pressed a gentle kiss to her cheek. His whiskers still tickled.

"Come. We'll find Rowan. And later, I'll show you other sights. There are many wonders in the world, Griane. I am only one."

The mocking smile returned. Before she could reply, he tightened his grip on her hand. Again, the world dissolved, only to re-form moments later as time and space stuttered to a halt. The blur of color and light solidified into images: a circle of trees around her, bare earth beneath her toes, and in front of her, a massive wall of wood that she recognized as the trunk of the great oak under whose roots she had once slept.

The shadows were as deep as ever beneath the oak's branches, the leaves fluttered as gently in the slight breeze. But there *was* something different: the luminosity of the runneled bark, the shimmering intensity of the green leaves. The spirit of the Oak-Lord now dwelled within the tree, sheltering here after his defeat at Midsummer. A living, immortal presence imbuing the tree with his power, filling the clearing with an energy so vital it made her skin prickle. Warmth suffused her as if she'd drunk too much elderberry wine. Nay, not wine, but the water of the Summerlands, filling her with strength and peace.

She rested her cheek against one of the roots that arched high over her head, wanting to be closer to the source of that peace. Then she heard the rustle of leaves and the creak of branches and looked up.

Fellgair was right. They looked just the same to her, that strange amalgam of tree and human, their faces grooved and rough, their green hands serrated like leaves. Her gaze flitted from the spiky needles that capped the pine-man's head to the mottled silver of the birch-woman's belly to— Maker spare her blushing face—the large acorns that swung between the oak-man's legs.

And then she spied two eyes of Midsummer green. Smooth

gray lips pursed in a knothole of surprise. A thick bead of
sap hung suspended on one cheek. Nine delicate fingers
reached out to touch her hair. Among the fading white
blossoms at her wrist, Griane spied a circlet of bright red
hair. Laughing in spite of the tears that blurred her vision,
she flung herself into Rowan's strong arms.

There were advantages to traveling with a god. Fellgair
interrupted her clumsy sign language to interpret for her.
To her ears, he spoke the tribal tongue, but his words apparently made sense to the tree-folk. There was much leaf
fluttering during the tale of her journey through the First
Forest, but when she told them about Tinnean, it was as if
a great storm blew through. She had to describe his transformation twice before they calmed.

Of course, the story of the boy who became a tree had
more impact than her endless chatter about Darak and the
children and her life in a village they had never seen. But
they listened attentively and Rowan, at least, seemed to
understand her anguish when she explained what had happened to Keirith.

When her voice finally ran down, Rowan touched her
hair again. Lounging against a root, Fellgair said, "She's
wondering about the white streaks. Why this change happens now instead of in the autumn when leaves change
their color." His brief explanation of aging provoked more
leaf fluttering. "Rowan asks what you are becoming."

"Becoming?"

"Aging is not a process they understand. Change is. Rowan is becoming more human. So she wonders what the
nature of your change is."

"What should I tell her?"

Fellgair shrugged. "Tell her what you like."

"But if the tree-folk are becoming more human, won't
they die one day? I wouldn't want to frighten them."

"Here, there is no death. There's a slight dimming of the
life-force when the Oak-Lord returns to the One Tree, but
only if he was destroyed—or if the balance of nature was
irreparably damaged—would the creatures of the Summerlands die."

"But the Oak-Lord's spirit is immortal. He's a god. He can't die."

"Who told you that?"

"I don't know. Struath, I suppose."

Fellgair rolled his eyes. "Ah, the beloved shaman. Strong, secretive, and woefully misinformed. We're immortal in the sense that we neither age nor change, but we are not indestructible. Anything that is created can be destroyed. Even me."

In a few sentences, he had changed her entire conception of the world. Yet it had existed thus since the Beginning. And would continue to exist as long as nothing happened to—how did Fellgair put it?—irreparably damage the balance of nature.

"How should I answer Rowan?" Fellgair asked.

"Tell her that I'll continue to change. My hair will grow whiter and my face will become grooved like an elder. And one day, my . . . my heartwood will become a butterfly and leave the cocoon of my body and fly to a place like the Summerlands. And I'll live there forever. Unless I want to spin another cocoon."

"What an appalling mix of metaphors," Fellgair murmured.

"Well, I'm not a Memory-Keeper, am I? Tell her whatever you want."

"Very well."

"Except that I'm going to die."

"Fine."

"Or become infirm."

Fellgair closed his eyes. His lips moved. She was quite certain he wasn't praying. But he simply told Rowan that the changes she had observed were natural to humans and occurred more quickly in their kind than in the tree-folk. When Rowan accepted his explanation with a small nod, Fellgair rose, licked the tip of his brush twice, and announced, "Now we must leave you."

"So soon?"

"It's nearly midday."

She hadn't realized so much time had passed. Much as she wanted to linger, she was wary of testing Fellgair's patience.

The tree-folk moved closer. She patted a barky arm,

stroked a drooping catkin. When they turned their backs,
she feared she had offended them. Then she realized they
were forming a protective circle that excluded the Trickster.

She peered between Rowan and the oak-man. Fellgair
still wore a pleasant smile, but his brush swished back and
forth with more vigor than usual.

"Griane?"

Of course, she would go with him. He held Darak's life
in his hands. But it puzzled her that he would ask so politely when he had the power to force the tree-folk to stand
aside. Perhaps the Summerlands hindered his ability to
make mischief. She doubted this place would encourage visits
from the Unmaker's son.

"Griane."

"I'm coming."

She hugged Rowan hard, repeating all the useless things
people say when they don't want to say good-bye. Even
if they couldn't understand the words—Fellgair refused to
translate—she hoped they would understand the sincerity
of her voice and her gestures.

Rowan touched her cheek. Griane took the delicate hand
and kissed the nine fingers one by one. Then she slipped
out of the circle to take her place beside Fellgair. The last
thing she saw before the clearing melted away was Rowan
pressing her fingertips to her lips.

Fellgair was true to his promise. He showed her many wonders, both within the Summerlands and without. He allowed her to peep through portals at snow-clad mountains
that extended from horizon to horizon, their peaks so high
they were obscured by windswept clouds. She looked into
deep canyons of rock striped all the colors of sunset, across
endless hills of golden sand that rippled like waves. She
hovered over sprawling cities of stone and tiny villages of
snow and ice. She saw women dressed in cloth so sheer it
revealed every curve of their bodies, and others bundled in
so many furs that only their dark eyes were visible.

And then he gave her still greater joy by leading her
through the Summerlands and teaching her about its plants.

He pointed out ones she recognized like sundew and red-shank, without ever realizing they could be used to dye wool. He gently uprooted unfamiliar ones and offered them to her with an explanation of their healing properties. She repeated his instructions out loud to imprint them on her memory and darted from plant to plant, demanding information that he always provided with an indulgent smile.

When her hands overflowed with her bounty, he conjured another handkerchief, much larger than the first, so she could carry her precious sprigs. When she grew weary of walking, he whisked her back to the waterfall so she could drink and be restored. And when she clasped his white-ruffed cheeks between her palms and kissed him soundly on the lips, he pressed one hand to his heart, groaned ecstatically, and collapsed on the grass at her feet.

"Oh, Fellgair, I never expected . . . it was more than I ever . . ." She dropped to her knees beside him. "Thank you."

"You're welcome." He raised himself on his elbow, squinting against the brilliance of the afternoon sun. "There is something else I would show you. But I'm not certain it will please you."

Her smile faded. "Darak. Is he ill? Or hurt? Or—"

"It's not Darak I planned to show you, but Faelia. But if you wish to see him—"

"What's happened to Faelia?"

"Nothing. Yet. Stop spluttering. She's fine. But something might happen today that will . . . change things."

"What? What will happen?"

With one claw, he sliced open the air in front of her. She caught a glimpse of brown and green before he grasped both edges of the sky and peeled it back, revealing a dense forest that hung suspended between the summit of the waterfall and the pool. A thin mist obscured the vista, yet bright shafts of sunlight slanted through the trees.

"The mist is my doing. It allows us to watch without being seen, to speak without being heard."

"But where . . . ?" The words trailed off. At first, she thought it was one of the Watchers, but the trees were far smaller than those of the First Forest. Then she saw a flash of red among the greens and browns.

Faelia took three steps forward and froze. Griane stifled

a cry at the sight of the bow. Was it Keirith's old one or had she crafted it herself? And why, why had she flouted the tribe's law to hunt with it?

Her daughter's face was intent, her eyes fixed on something Griane could not see. As she watched, Faelia took three more steps and froze again, as motionless as the trees around her. In one fluid movement, she brought the bow up, drew the bowstring back to her cheek, and released. In a blur of motion, she drew another arrow from her quiver, nocked it and released again.

Her triumphant shout broke the stillness. She raced out of sight, but with a quick gesture, Fellgair shifted the scene to follow her. Faelia knelt beside a small doe, fingers stroking the long neck, lips moving in a prayer too soft for Griane to hear. The doe's flanks heaved once, twice, and fell still.

Why had Fellgair shown her this? So she could put a stop to Faelia's hunting before anyone else found out?

Something moved in the shadows behind Faelia. Griane tensed, but Fellgair's hand came down on her shoulder. "Wait."

A large paw rested against the trunk of a birch. The tree's branches drooped, yellow catkins reaching out to return the caress. The leaves of the neighboring trees fluttered as if they, too, sought the creature's touch. Faelia's head came up and her hand moved to the quiver. She scanned the trees but apparently saw nothing for she turned back to the doe.

A dark form emerged into a shaft of sunlight. Griane gasped as she beheld the wide-spreading antlers, the green leaves cascading over a chest as massive and furry as a bear's.

Hernan. The Forest-Lord. Protector of wild things and lord of the hunt. Darak claimed the god had led him back to the grove, but he'd been out of his mind with fever and she had never really believed it. The delicate feathers on his legs trembled with every step, a shivering display of blue and brown, tawny and gold. Darak had said nothing about those or the large, webbed feet that moved silently through the thick mulch of dead leaves. But he had described the feel of Hernan's warm paw cupping the back of his neck. Those paws looked strong enough to break

Faelia's neck like a twig, but the Forest-Lord seemed content to observe her.

"Why can't she see him?"

"Because he doesn't wish her to. She's too young for such a vision."

She had warned Darak about encouraging Faelia. How would they ever turn her from this path now?

A giant paw rose and Griane's breath caught, but the Forest-Lord simply laid it atop Faelia's head. She moaned, a woman's sound of pleasure. Then her eyes went wide. She scrambled to her feet and whirled around, but the god had already blended into the shadows. A hot blush stained her throat and cheeks. She muttered something under her breath and drew her dagger to butcher the doe.

Fellgair pulled the portal closed and held up a hand to forestall her furious questions. "He would not have harmed her. But he has offered his blessing."

"I don't want his blessing. I want him to leave my daughter alone."

"It's too late for that. Faelia is a hunter like her father. To try and turn her from this path would be as cruel as . . ."

"As what? What?"

"As attempting to turn Darak from his," Fellgair concluded, his voice gentle.

"But I didn't . . . Darak chose to become a Memory-Keeper. Even you encouraged him."

"I sent a dream to Old Sim. Who offered Darak a choice. Which Darak accepted. It's taken him nearly half his life to understand that he made the wrong choice. No man who abandons his life-path can be truly happy."

Vehement denials rose to her lips and died. She had seen Darak bring down a doe in the First Forest with one shot to the heart, remembered the fierce joy on his face, the exuberance of his embrace. When, in all his years as Memory-Keeper, had she ever seen such exultation?

"Has he been so . . . so miserable all these years?"

"You know he hasn't."

It helped to hear Fellgair confirm that. Darak loved her. And the children. He'd been happy with them—and unhappy with himself. A part of her had always recognized the truth, but she had thrust it away, fearing that if he went back to the forest, she would lose him.

"They will need more than your love when they return, Griane. They will need your acceptance."

She nodded, her heart pounding. Not "if" they returned but "when." They were both coming back to her.

"There's more."

"Is it . . . bad?"

For a long moment, Fellgair hesitated. Then he sliced open the sky once again. This time, she saw two men standing on a beach. Although their backs were turned to her, she recognized Darak at once. A soft whimper escaped her as he turned toward the other man. He looked exhausted. His clothes hung on him. But he was alive, thank the Maker. Alive and unharmed.

The other man continued staring out to sea, his shoulders slumped. Compared to Darak, he looked positively frail. Although he wore the tunic and breeches of a raider, his hair was very short, little more than a cap of dark fuzz.

Darak was speaking with some urgency, and she longed to hear what he was saying. But it was the hunger on his face that shocked her, a naked longing that he masked immediately when the other man glanced up at him.

"Who is he?" she whispered.

His sparse hair had made her conclude the man was Darak's age, but he was young and smooth-cheeked. He kept shaking his head until Darak seized his shoulders. Then his eyes squeezed shut and an expression of despair came over his face. Darak pulled him close. Slowly, the younger man's arms came up and he rested his cheek against Darak's chest.

They were still standing there, locked in each other's arms, when Fellgair pulled the portal shut.

"Tell me who that was."

"That was Keirith."

"Don't be ridiculous. I know my own son."

And then Fellgair told her what had happened.

❦

At some point, she must have sat down, for the grass was much closer. And Fellgair must have stopped speaking, for there was only birdsong and the ceaseless splash of the waterfall. The sun was low in the sky. She could still feel its heat on her face, but she was shivering.

The sun still shone. The birds still chirped. The waterfall splashed. The Summerlands took no heed of her son's murder. It neither grieved for the loss of his body nor rejoiced at his spirit's survival. Nor did it condemn her for the choice she had made, the choice that had led Keirith to the altar she had seen so many times in her nightmares.

"Is he alive?" she had asked the Trickster. And he had told her the truth. But he lived in the body of the man who had murdered him. He saw with his eyes, moved with his body—transformed like Tinnean into something new.

If she had chosen differently, would it be Darak returning to her in the body of a stranger? Or would they both be dead? She would never know. But every day, for the rest of her life, she would look into her son's eyes—dark now instead of blue—and wonder.

Did I make the right choice?

Was the right choice not to have chosen at all?

Can I ever make it up to him?

Dry-eyed, she stared up at the one who had offered her the choice, but even a god couldn't give her the answers.

Keirith, my son, my firstborn, my child.

Forgive me.

Fellgair knelt before her, his hands cupped. "Drink, Griane."

The cold water burned her throat. Fellgair gently stroked her face with the back of his hand. The fur was soft against her cheek.

In time, she would feel again, instead of merely noting sensations. In time, the numbness would give way to pain and grief and anger. Dully, she wondered why Fellgair had allowed her to see Keirith. It was hardly the best way to seduce a partner, unless he wished her to be numbed to compliancy.

He pressed his damp hand between her breasts. Obediently, she tried to lie back, but his left arm came up to circle her shoulders and hold her still. So she simply sat there and waited for his next command.

The hand on her chest was warm. It eased the shivering and she was grateful, for her muscles had begun to ache.

The warmth moved up into her shoulders and neck, down into her arms and hands. Her head lolled against his chest. Her fingers unclenched. Her hands lay limp in her lap.

The warmth flooded her belly and loins. Not the moist heat of desire but a subdued glow as if a tiny fire had been kindled inside of her. But this fire was a molten stream that flowed gently through her legs. Her bent knees relaxed. Her heels slid through the grass. Her toes flexed once, tingling with sensation.

She could have floated there forever, suspended between the curve of Fellgair's arm and the hand still resting between her breasts. But the hand demanded more. It seemed to grow heavier until it became a great weight that threatened to crush her. Heat radiated from the fingers, no longer a gentle stream but five white-hot shafts of energy penetrating her. She struggled feebly, her heart clenching into a small fist that protested the intrusion with every beat.

The fingers between her breasts massaged her gently. The fingers inside her body encircled her heart, cradling it. The spasm of pain made her gasp.

"Call his name, Griane."

Her heart was a stone in her chest. She fought, lips clamped together, but she had no strength left to resist the inexorable pressure that squeezed the stone and shattered it.

Grief and loss, self-hatred and fury—every bitter emotion she had carefully locked inside burst free. The scalding torrent raged through her and she was helpless to stop it. Only the voice could do that, the voice that kept repeating, "Call his name, Griane."

And as she had in the glade of the heart-oak, she heard herself scream it.

"Darak!"

The bolt of heat shot through her chest, another white-hot flash that radiated through her body, singing through flesh and blood and bone, easing the bitterness of grief, cleansing the lacerating guilt, filling her with light and peace. And in its wake, came the tears she had not been able to shed.

When she finally raised her head, she discovered sadness in Fellgair's ancient eyes. In that moment, she loved him. Not as she loved Darak—nothing could supersede that love—but for giving her this day, so full of sorrow and joy, pain and hope. When he bent his head to hers, she lifted her mouth with a willing heart, but instead of kissing her, his lips brushed her damp cheeks and his rough tongue scoured away the last traces of tears.

He undressed her quickly and laid her down on the cooling grass. With his hands and mouth, he offered her pleasure and, true to his nature, he was by turns gentle and fierce. She never knew if she was still beguiled by the spell he had woven earlier or if her desire was simply created by his skillful fingers and teasing mouth.

Twice, she murmured his name, once in affection, and then, more urgently, as she sought release. Only then did he move between her legs, spiky-soft fur tickling her body, whiskers tickling her cheeks. She tried to hide her face in his chest, but he pulled back, golden eyes fathomless and rapt. She was as helpless to look away as she was to control the sensations flooding her body. When she locked her legs around him, urging him to move faster, he smiled and obeyed her silent command, and all the while, his eyes held hers, savoring the frenzy building inside her.

Then he froze abruptly and reared back. Still awash in the sensations he had aroused, she whispered, "Please," not knowing if she meant "enough" or "go on" or "tell me what's wrong?"

"Fellgair?"

With a sound that was almost a groan, he thrust deep inside her, once, twice, three times, a fierce, bruising invasion that penetrated to her womb. She cried out as the climax roared through her and the hot flood of his release filled her.

He rolled away from her and rose. "We've overstayed our welcome. Please dress. We must leave."

She rose and pulled on her clothes, wondering at his sudden coldness. Although her body still pulsed with the satiated afterglow of sex, her mind could not reconstruct exactly what had happened. The same mist he had created to shield her from Faelia seemed to have fallen over her memory. Confusion gave way to shame. What could she have done to displease him so?

Without looking at her, he proffered the knotted handkerchief that held the healing plants. Then he thrust out his hand. She took it, closing her eyes against the inevitable dizziness of the journey. When she opened them again, she found herself on the lakeshore, far enough east of the village to be out of sight of any fishermen returning home. At least she would not have to see Jurl's body again.

"What have I done?"

"Nothing." He bent and pressed his lips to her forehead. "Forgive me, Griane."

"I don't understand. It's only a little after sunset."

He shook his head, a pained smile twisting his lips. Finally, he met her eyes. His expression became so fierce that she involuntarily took a step back. "If you ever need me, just call my name. Three times." Again, that strange, pained smile. "Three times. And I will come to you." He waited until she nodded and then vanished.

Slowly, she pulled off her clothes and draped them over a rock. The water was shallow at this end of the lake and still retained a little of the day's warmth. Her hand came up once to touch the sticky wetness between her thighs. It felt the same as a man's. It looked as milky. But the scent was different—sharper and more acrid.

She scrubbed between her legs, then used handfuls of sand to scour her body. Shivering, she emerged from the water and dried herself with her skirt. She didn't dare bring the healing plants home, but neither could she discard them. In the end, she found a secluded place to plant them. Nearby, she dug another hole to bury Fellgair's handkerchief.

She washed her hands and turned slowly toward the village. The bargain was fulfilled. Darak was safe. Keirith was . . . alive. And no matter what her need, she would never call on the Trickster again.

Chapter 50

ALTHOUGH KEIRITH WAS grateful for the currachs that carried them from village to village, he worried about his father's seasickness. Some days, he ate little more than an oatcake. At night, he fell asleep, exhausted. But no matter how tired he was, he always took time to speak with the Memory-Keeper and recite the litany of names.

He'd gathered the names during his brief time in the slave compound. But most of the captives had been taken elsewhere. They must be scattered throughout Zheros now. Their families could only hope they might escape someday, like those who had fled after the earthquake. Some would be recaptured and others would perish in the wilderness, but Keirith hoped a few would find their way home. If any could survive, it would be Temet and Brudien—the one strong in body, the other in spirit. All he could offer them—and all the lost children of the Oak and the Holly— were his prayers.

As they traveled north, more names were recognized by the Memory-Keepers and more villages welcomed them, although most of the inhabitants still eyed him uneasily. Only in Illait's village did his father introduce him as "Keirith, my son." There were surprised murmurs from those who had gathered to greet them. As Illait's keen gaze swept over him, Keirith held his breath, waiting for the inevitable questions.

" 'Twas the same with me," Illait finally said. "My father, tall and broad as an oak. My mam, near as fair as you,

girl. And me, small and skinny as a weasel with a face
to match."

Tolerant smiles blossomed on the faces of his kinfolk;
clearly, they'd heard the story dozens of times.

" 'Course it's hard to see much of a resemblance with
your fa's face as green as summer leaves. Terrible seafarer,
your fa. Me, I love it. Riding a wave up and up, and then
plunging down, down, down, so fast you think your stomach's still hanging in the air above you. Where are you off
to, Spirit-Hunter?"

His father strode behind a hut and reappeared a few
moments later. He wiped his mouth and glared at Illait.
"Holly-Chief, you are cruel."

"Never. But it does comfort us lesser men to know that
the great Spirit-Hunter's got one weakness."

"More than one, I assure you."

"Well, come along to my hut. And while Jirra brews up
something for that tender stomach of yours, you can tell
me about the others."

Once they were alone, Illait dismissed his father's thanks
for their welcome. "As long as I'm chief, you and yours
will always find one here. Now. Tell me what's happening
with the gods-cursed raiders. We get nothing but rumors."

While the women served food, Illait plied his father with
questions about fortifications and weapons. A look of grim
satisfaction crossed his face when they described the earthquake, but it faded when Keirith assured him the Zherosi
would rebuild.

"Maker curse them. If Halam cannot swallow their holy
city, how are we to stop them?"

"By standing together," his father said. "And fighting off
every encroachment."

"Begging your pardon, but 'tis us will be encroached on
first. I'm thinking we should do what Girn did and relocate
farther inland."

"But maintain your watches on the coast. Light signal
fires on the hilltops as soon as a ship is spotted. That way,
no village will be taken by surprise."

"What if the Tree-Fathers could work out a way to communicate with each other?" Keirith suggested. "Spirit to
spirit?"

"They can do that?" Illait asked.

"I don't know. But a Tree-Father knows the spirit of every member of his tribe. So if your daughter married into a tribe to the north, your Tree-Father could still find her. And maybe warn her if the raiders were spotted." He grew more excited as he thought about the idea. "You've said yourself, Father, that the tribal bloodlines are all tangled together. There must be a way to use that to our advantage."

"If the Tree-Fathers can't do it, the Grain-Mothers can."

They all looked at Jirra.

"What are you talking about?" Illait demanded.

"Women's magic," she said calmly.

"And what do you know about that?" Illait's face was growing red.

"I hear things."

"What kind of—"

"Things that don't concern men. Even chiefs. Now stop bellowing and eat your stew before it gets cold."

Illait's face got even redder, but whatever he muttered was lost in his cup of brogac.

It was only when the meal was over that his father glanced toward the little boy sleeping atop a pile of rabbitskins. "I take it Hua is no better."

Illait and Jirra exchanged a quick, pained look.

"Is he sick?" Hircha asked.

"Spirit-sick," Jirra replied. "He saw the raiders kill his parents. The Tree-Father has done everything he can, but . . ." She shrugged helplessly. "Every day he grows a little weaker. Soon there will be nothing left of him."

"The gods know I love the boy," Illait said, "but it'll be a blessing when his spirit flies to the Forever Isles."

Keirith became aware that both his father and Hircha were watching him. Suddenly, the air in the hut was stifling. He mumbled an apology and got to his feet so abruptly he collided with Illait's daughter.

"Forgive me. I . . . I need to go outside. To . . . relieve myself. Forgive me."

"No need for forgiveness, lad. When you've got to piss . . ." Jirra cleared her throat loudly and Illait's voice trailed off.

He was headed toward the beach, gulping great lungfuls of salt-scented air, when he heard his father call his name.

Conscious of the folk sitting outside their huts, enjoying the cool of the evening, neither of them spoke until the village was behind them. Then Keirith flung up his hand and said, "Nay."

"I haven't said anything."

"You want me to try and help him."

"You heard Jirra. The boy's dying."

"I haven't the skill. And even if I did, I don't have the right."

"Your power gives you the right."

"You didn't think so when I tried to cast out Urkiat's spirit."

His father winced. "This is different."

"It's the same power!"

"Used to heal, not to destroy. If the power was inherently evil, every Tree-Father in every village would be condemned. Struath used the power to try and reach Tinnean's spirit. Illait's Tree-Father has used it to try and save Hua. You used it to help the ewe birth her lambs."

"That's not the same as reclaiming a boy's spirit."

"I know."

"I'm not a shaman. I'm not even an apprentice."

"I know!"

"I'd be hauled before the tribal council."

"The council would never know."

"Illait—"

"Loves his grandson. So does Jirra. They can be trusted."

Keirith looked up into that calm, stubborn face and repressed a curse. "Fine. So I somehow manage to save Hua rather than kill him. How do we explain his sudden recovery? A miracle?"

"Why not? It's close enough to the truth."

"Why do you want me to risk so much for a boy you don't even know?"

"Think about it. That's all I ask. No matter what you choose, I'll understand."

After his father left, Keirith paced the beach angrily. He had his own battles to fight. With Natha's help, he had cast out a few fragments of Xevhan's spirit, but more were buried inside of him. If he couldn't reach them, how could he reach this poor boy? Didn't his father understand that he could hurt Hua, cause even greater damage? His newfound faith in his power was as foolhardy as his apparent belief that they would return home and life would go on as if nothing had happened.

"You're not Morgath," his father had told him when they first discussed the tribe's reaction. "You didn't destroy the Zheron for the love of it, but to save us. We just have to make the elders understand that."

His father was so relieved that they had survived the ordeal in Pilozhat that he simply could not understand that his existence was an affront to everything their people believed. Hircha knew better; he saw the knowledge of his doom in her eyes. But there was no pity there. If anything, she seemed to admire his determination to return home and meet his fate.

Like Hua, he was ready for death. It would be a sweet release for both of them.

"You bury the memories. But they're still there. You can never bury them deep enough."

But Hua had. Whether his spirit had simply shattered when his parents were murdered or whether he had deliberately retreated into himself rather than face their loss, he had escaped the memories. It would be cruel to force him to confront them now.

Yet when he had told his father all that happened to him, he'd felt as if a great weight had been lifted. Like his father, he'd needed to tell his tale. Perhaps Hua did, too. But he still didn't know if he could reach him.

"I didn't have the strength for trance."

"You did not try."

Natha's voice and his father's battered him. By the time he returned to the hut, he had banished them and made his decision. Then he saw Jirra crouched beside Hua's pallet, dribbling water between his lips, and Illait's genial face shadowed by misery. And heard himself saying, "I might be able to help."

He sat beside Hua and clasped his limp hand. Flesh dry as birch bark covered the delicate bones. Knobby wrists protruded from the sleeves of a tunic that hung on arms little thicker than sticks.

If he were a shaman, he would have a spirit catcher, a crystal he had shaped with his own hands. With it, he could recapture the fragments of a wandering spirit and bring it home, just as his father carried the spirits of the Oak and Tinnean back to the grove. But tonight, *he* was the spirit catcher and he had only his power to help him reclaim Hua.

Keirith closed his eyes, but behind him, he felt the weight of all the other eyes that watched him. Deliberately, he shut them out, along with the hiss of the fire and the smell of the stew, until there was only his heart, beating a slow tattoo within his chest, and his breath, rising and falling with Hua's.

In darkness, he waited for Natha. In darkness, Natha came, filling him with the same sinuous warmth he had first experienced that night on the beach. Keirith let the energy pass from his hand to Hua's. It seeped into wasted flesh and hard bone, flowed into blood, and surged through the boy's body with the faint but relentless beat of his heart. The energy reached for Hua's spirit as naturally as a flower turned toward the sun—and found only a dark void.

Slowly, carefully, Keirith probed deeper. It was like diving down into the lake at home with still, silent waters all around him. He had never touched such emptiness. If not for the beating of Hua's heart, he would have thought the boy was dead.

As he sank deeper into the darkness, he felt a faint pulse of energy. Eagerly, he followed it, only to be pushed away. At first, he thought Hua was doing it. Then he realized it was Natha, urging him to go back. He remembered the allure of the elemental dance in the adder pit, the freedom of floating above his body after death. The deeper he went, the more tenuous his connection to his body. But Hua was so close; if he retreated now, the boy's spirit would be lost.

Keirith hesitated. He attuned himself to the rhythm of his heartbeat, to the pressure of his hand clasping Hua's. Then he dared to probe a little deeper.

Immediately, he encountered fierce resistance. His joy in discovering the strength of Hua's spirit was tempered by the realization that the barriers he'd erected were even stronger than Xevhan's. Born of his determination to keep the painful memories at bay, they would also shut him out. If he pushed too hard, he risked shattering that frightened spirit.

He and his father had taunted Xevhan into attacking them, but even if it meant losing Hua, Keirith couldn't bring himself to hurt him. He cradled Hua's spirit, sensing the terrible fragility beneath the hard shell.

As he did, an image rose before him: his mam seated beside the fire pit, rocking a fretful Callie in her arms, crooning a lullaby to ease him into sleep. Unbidden, the words filled him.

> *Hush, my little one.*
> *Hush, my own.*
> *Don't be frightened.*
> *You are not alone.*
> *Gheala lights the night.*
> *Father guards your dreams.*
> *Mother will—*

The violent outpouring of pain and denial ripped through Keirith. Images buffeted him: a man racing out of a hut, clutching a spear, a woman screaming for him to come back. And Hua's terrified thoughts and emotions as he watched.

He didn't know why everyone was shouting or why Grandfa and Fa had run out. He wanted his mam, but when he reached for her, she pushed him away and ran after Fa. He mustn't cry. He was a big boy now. He had to be brave like Fa and Grandfa. He had to go with them. But Grandmam wouldn't let him. She grabbed his hand and pulled him out of the hut so fast he tripped and fell and skinned both knees. And he did cry then, but only a couple tears. Grandmam didn't take him in her arms like she used to when he was little. She just pulled on his arm hard and Auntie Sariem pulled on the other and they dragged him to his feet and told him to run, run, run, fast as a rabbit, into the trees, and don't look back.

So he ran, fast as a rabbit, and didn't look back. Not even when he heard the roar. Not from a wolf or a wildcat or any animal he knew. It must be some awful creature the Unmaker had sent from Chaos.

All around him, people were running. Behind him, people were screaming. The beast was eating them and if he didn't run faster, it would eat him, too.

Abruptly, the images vanished, leaving only the wail of Hua's spirit.

<I won't look back! You can't make me.>

I won't.

<I don't want to see it, I'm safe in the forest, it can't get me here.>

You're safe. But it's still with you, isn't it? No matter how hard you try and shut it out.

<It's not, it's not, it's not!>

I know because the beast came after me, too.

<You're lying.>

You know I'm not. You can feel me, same as I feel you.

The touch was featherlight and gone at once. Keirith opened himself, allowing the boy to sense the pain and fear that haunted his recent memories, while shielding him from a barrage of images that would only frighten him more. Again, Hua reached for him, as wary as the eagle when he had first tried to touch its spirit.

<You touched an eagle?>

Little boy wonder. Little boy awe. It made Keirith ache.

Aye. He let me fly with him.

Suspicion tainted Hua's touch, but it faded as Keirith shared the memories of that flight. So long ago, it seemed, but through Hua, he experienced the joy again and the giddy, breathless excitement.

<Who are you?>

My name is Keirith.

<I know but . . . who are you?>

A boy. From another tribe.

<By that little sea?>

The little . . . Aye, the lake. The eagles live on that mountain you saw. And I live in the village. With my sister and brother and my mam and my—

Hua thrust him away with a wail. Again, Keirith surrounded his wounded spirit, holding it close.

I know you don't want to come back. But your grandmam is here. And your grandfa. And your aunt Sariem. They miss you. They want you to leave the forest and come live with them again.

<I can't! The beast is there.>

But I am, too. I've fought the beast. And if you fight it with me, we can make it go away.

<It'll eat me!>
Please, Hua, if you just try—
*<Nay! I won't do it. You can't make me. Go away, I hate
you, you're a bad man, just like the ones . . .>*

Hua shrieked as the memories burst free, inundating
Keirith with the terror of that morning.

The beast was behind him, ready to snap him up with its
huge, awful fangs. He had to look back. He had to see how
close it was. But when he did, there was no beast, only men
with long daggers and fishing nets and spears and clubs.

I'm holding you. I'll keep you safe. They won't hurt you.
<Not me!>

Mam. Running. Her hair streaming behind her. Sunbright,
Fa called it. Mam's sunbright hair tangled across her face
when she looked back. They were chasing her. They were
going to catch her. He screamed, loud as he could, but Mam
couldn't hear him. He had to help her. He had to chase away
the bad men. So he yanked his hands away from Auntie
Sariem and Grandmam and ran, fast as a rabbit.

Fa was running, too, running toward the men chasing
Mam. He would kill the bad men and make the others go
away and never come back. But Fa had to go faster, fast
as a rabbit, else he'd never get there in time.

<I don't want to see!>

Fa was walking sideways, like he did after the Midsummer feast and didn't Mam shout at him that night when
she took away the jug? But Fa wasn't laughing now. He
just fell to his knees and onto his face with the . . .

<Nay!>

. . . arrow sticking out of him. Get up, Fa, please get up!
But he just lay there. Grandmam and Auntie Sariem were
pulling him away, but not before he saw Mam pick up the
spear. Not before he saw her charging toward the bad men.
Not before he saw her sunbright hair whipping around her
neck and her legs bending and her body falling, just like
Fa, but oh gods, oh gods, oh gods . . .

The scream ripped through Keirith, bringing with it the
image of the severed head, rolling over and over on the
ground, sunbright hair trailing behind it.

Hua screamed again and all Keirith could do was hold
his fragile spirit, drawing on his strength and Natha's to
absorb the awful images. He took them all in—the arrow

in his father's back, the bloody stump of his mother's neck—and with them, the shock and the horror and the agony of loss that Hua had not allowed himself to feel before. Felt his spirit tremble with the effort to hold them, heard his scream mingling with Hua's, and thought he could never be strong enough to hold this much pain, his spirit would shatter along with Hua's, both of them lost, oh gods, I'm sorry.

Natha coiled around them, holding them safe. He flowed through their spirits, carrying memories to comfort them— a father's strong arms hugging them, a mother's hand reaching out to steady them as they took their first awkward steps.

Sariem's laugh banished the screams. Faelia rolled her eyes and the raiders fled. Callie's giggle sent a shaft of sunlight blazing through the shadowy forest. Grandfa bellowed and uprooted the thorn bushes and vines obscuring the path. And there was Grandmam, squatting down at the edge of the trees—she shouldn't be doing that, not with her knees so bad with the joint-ill. Grandmam's face, creased in a great smile, Grandmam's arms, flung wide to welcome him home.

Natha released them, dissipating like mist before the sun. Keirith touched Hua's spirit in farewell and gently withdrew. He found himself lying on the pallet, his arms flung around Hua's shoulders. As he eased free, he looked at the circle of anxious faces hovering above him.

Jirra's eyes went wide with shock. Her hand flew to her mouth. Keirith turned to find Hua blinking uncertainly. His mouth moved, but the words were too soft to hear. With a hoarse cry, Jirra pulled her grandson into her arms, laughing and weeping and rocking him just like she used to when he was little.

Keirith accepted Jirra's tearful thanks, Sariem's kiss, and Illait's bruising hug. He lingered beside Hua a moment to whisper, "There's no shame in crying when you're sad. Or in grieving for your mam and fa."

Tears welled up in Hua's eyes and oozed down the wasted cheeks. Keirith gently wiped them away. "You've got your grandmam and your grandfa and your aunt to help you."

Hua's lips moved. Keirith had to put his ear to the boy's mouth to catch the words.

"Your grandfa's going to move the village to a new place—a secret place that the bad men won't find. And if they come in your dreams, remember my friend Natha. Pretend that he's coiled around you again, keeping you safe, even while you're sleeping. Someday, you'll have your own vision mate to protect you. Maybe you'll find an adder, too. Or an eagle."

He stumbled on his way out of the hut and his father's hand came up to steady him. The village was asleep, the long twilight beginning to fade into darkness. Together, they walked down to the sea.

"Are you all right?"

"Aye. Just . . . very tired."

"And Hua?"

"He'll need time to heal, but he's strong. Else he couldn't have held back the memories so long."

"You're strong, too. Else you couldn't have reached him. You're a healer. Like your mam."

Keirith shook his head.

"It's true. Only you heal spirits, not bodies. That's your gift. And you must use it."

It was as impossible as dreaming that the council of elders would welcome him back into the tribe. Yet Keirith wanted to believe it could happen, that he could use his power for good as he had tonight.

"When I came back from the First Forest, when I thought I'd never hunt again . . ." His father took a deep breath. "What I was really afraid of was that I couldn't be the best. Not the best in the tribe but as good as I once was. So I became a Memory-Keeper."

The disgust in his father's voice made Keirith wince. "Did you hate it that much?"

"Nay. But the forest always called me. For fifteen years, I tried to ignore it. I don't want you to make the same mistake. I'm a hunter, Keirith. And you're a shaman. Maybe not the same kind of shaman as Gortin or Struath, but that's your life-path. And no matter what anyone says, you must follow it."

That was why his father had wanted him to help Hua—not only to reclaim the boy, but to reclaim himself.

Although exhaustion shadowed his father's eyes, there was no mistaking the eagerness on his face as his gaze swept over the village to linger on the trees beyond. The gods only knew how long it would take him to learn to draw a bow with those hands. He might never again bring down a deer with one shot to the heart. But his instincts were still keen and his desire keener. After so many years, his father had found his path again.

But can I really find a place with my tribe?

The resurgence of hope left him breathless—and terrified. It was easier when he had given up. His father was right. Living was hard. Even harder than he had imagined.

His father's hand came down on his shoulder. Keirith looked up into that calm, stubborn face and found the courage to smile back.

Chapter 51

GRIANE DUCKED OUT of the birthing hut and found herself surrounded by people. Elathar's sons had abandoned their nets to get a look at the new member of their family. She carried the squalling infant up the hill, her progress slowed as more of her kinfolk joined the throng. The whole tribe had awaited this birth with special eagerness; it was the first since the raid.

The old women scraping hides insisted she stop and show them the babe. They still sat outside Jurl's empty hut; until his bones were safely interred in the tribal cairn, the council of elders would not risk his spirit's displeasure by bestowing his home on another family. Some still shook their heads over his mysterious death, but most accepted that his quick temper had brought on the fit that killed him.

She smiled automatically as the old women pronounced the child a fine boy and left them discussing the labor pains and birthing ordeals they had endured. Nemek had obviously heard the shouts of congratulations; he paced impatiently outside the hut. Only Nionik's hand on his arm kept him from sprinting toward her as she approached.

She smiled at Mirili and Nionik and held the babe out to Nemek. "I bring you Catha's son."

"A son? I have a son?" With a dazed expression, he looked from the infant in her arms to his father. "I have a son."

"Not until you accept him from Mother Griane," Nionik reminded him with a smile.

Nemek extended shaking hands, balancing the child on his palms with such trepidation that Griane and Mirili both reached out to settle the poor mite securely in the crook of his arm.

"He's so small." He peered more closely at the wriggling bundle. "Is he supposed to be that red?"

"Your face was redder," Nionik said. "And wrinkled as a withered apple."

"He was not," Mirili protested. "He was beautiful. As beautiful as my grandson."

Nemek shot his mother a grateful glance. He bent his head over his son, crooning sweet nonsense. Suddenly, his head jerked up. "Catha. How is—"

"She's fine. And we counted four pops when we threw the afterbirth in the fire, so it seems I'll be presenting you with four more babes."

Mirili exclaimed with pleasure but Nemek turned pale. "Four . . . more?"

"I don't know why you're looking so queasy," Griane said. "Your part is done in a moment."

Nemek bristled. "My part lasts a good deal longer than a moment, thank you." Then blushed when his father laughed.

"Will you come inside and share a cup of elderberry wine?" Nionik asked.

"Later, perhaps. Now I must return this little one to his mother. He's hungry."

"That's why his face is so red," Nemek told his father.

Nionik nodded gravely. Griane shared a smile with Mirili. No need to fear for this child's future; he would be surrounded by love.

She was starting back to the birthing hut when a shout stopped her. Everyone froze as Conn raced into the village. Callie trailed behind him, his face nearly as red as the babe's.

"Three coracles," Conn said between pants. "Coming up the river."

"It's Fa!" Callie tugged at her skirt. "Fa and Keirith. I know it. Lacha brought them home."

Three coracles. That must mean the girl was with them. The one Fellgair had told her about. Quickly, she thrust the Trickster from her mind as she'd done every day in the half-moon since returning from the Summerlands.

"Come on, Mam! We have to go down to the lake. We have to be there when they come."

The coracles could just as easily contain visitors from another village, but she could scarcely breathe for hope.

Maker, let it be them.

Already, people were streaming out of the village. Callie's excitement had infected everyone. All around her, Griane heard eager speculations that Darak and Urkiat were returning with Keirith. They didn't realize Urkiat would never return, that his body was lying in foreign soil. She could only hope his spirit heard the prayers she offered.

She glanced around, searching for Faelia. She had entrusted her daughter with the truth about Keirith, had even revealed that the Trickster had told her. Despite her youth, Faelia could be counted on to keep a secret; the gods knew she had enough of her own. But Griane had said nothing to Callie, fearing he would spread the tale to the entire village.

Failing to spy her daughter's bright hair, she walked quickly to the birthing hut and found Lisula and Muina waiting outside. They were the only others who knew about Keirith. Neither had offered much comfort when she had shared the tale with them, both of them worried about the reaction of the tribe. Griane had bristled when Muina reminded her of the law.

"Keirith is not Morgath!"

"I know that without you shouting at me," Muina replied. "But others will only see the power and the potential for destruction."

Judging from their worried expressions, both priestesses were recalling that conversation, but there was no time to speak. Sali ducked out of the birthing hut and held out her arms for the child.

"You go, Mother Griane. Bethia and I will stay with Catha." Sali hesitated, darting anxious glances at all of them before blurting out, "I hope it's them. I know how much you've missed them. I've prayed every night for their safe return." Then, as if appalled by her speech, she darted back inside.

Muina stared after her in astonishment. "I don't think

I've ever heard that many words come out of the child's mouth in all the years I've known her."

"Whatever happens," Lisula said, "you know we'll stand by him."

"Where's my stick? I won't stand at all without that."

Lisula produced Muina's quickthorn stick and they made their way slowly down the hill. Griane trailed after them, telling herself not to build up her hopes in case the visitors were strangers. Like the others, she shaded her eyes against the late afternoon sun, watching the coracles move out of the long shadow cast by Eagles Mount.

"Mam! Mam!" She turned in the direction of Faelia's voice and found her pushing through the crowd. "Is it them?"

"We don't know."

Faelia surprised her by throwing her arms around her neck. "What do we say? If it's Keirith?"

She'd discussed that very question with Muina and Lisula without arriving at an answer. All she could think to say was, "Follow your father's lead."

Over Faelia's shoulder, she spied Ennit striding toward her. He kissed Lisula on the cheek before turning to them. "It looks to be two men and a woman. One of the men might be Darak—I couldn't be sure—but the other . . ." His face crumpled. "It wasn't Keirith. I'm sorry, Griane. He had almost no hair at all and what there was of it was black."

Griane hugged Faelia hard, praying that no one would guess that she and her daughter were sobbing with joy.

As he drove his paddle deep into the water, Keirith stared at all the people lined up along the shore. Somewhere in the crowd were his mam and Faelia and Callie. Conn, too, perhaps. He'd looked for him as they passed Eagles Mount, but tears reduced the scene to blurred smears of white and green.

It will be enough to see them all again. After that, it doesn't matter what happens.

As they drew closer to shore, his father glanced back and flashed a smile. Always, when they discussed this homecoming, his father insisted all would be well, but Keirith sensed the doubts lurking beneath that confidence. Only once had his father voiced them.

The morning after Hua's recovery, his father took him aside. To Keirith's surprise, he included Hircha in their conversation as well.

"Illait wanted me to ask . . . he would have spoken to you himself, but he thought it might be better coming from me. He's invited you to stay. Both of you. If you want."

"Stay?" Hircha echoed.

"He said no matter what had happened in Pilozhat, you'd restored his grandson."

"You told him?" Keirith asked in shocked disbelief.

"Nay. But Illait's no fool. I don't know how much he's guessed, but he's offering you a home here. You'd live in his hut. Be part of his family."

"I have a home," Keirith said. "And a family."

"Aye. Always. But . . . it's a risk. Going back. You know that."

"Do you want me to stay?"

"I want all of us to be together. But I also want you safe. I can't guarantee what the council will decide. And I'll not ask you to pretend to be some stranger I found in Zheros."

"I couldn't do that. It's just . . . too hard."

"Besides," Hircha said, "that's my role. Unless you want to claim me as your long-lost daughter."

His father frowned as he always did when Hircha turned her acid humor on him. For some reason, she enjoyed pricking him, probably because her father didn't know what to make of it. And because, despite her bravado, she was a little afraid of him.

"Aye. Well. Think about it. Both of you."

Keirith shook his head. "I want to go home, Fa."

"I've come this far," Hircha said, humor gone. "I'll see it through to the end."

Keirith shuddered now, recalling her words. Then he remembered his father's, fierce and soft: "As long as I live, they will never take you to the heart-oak."

His father had meant to comfort him. Instead, he'd convinced him that if the council voted for death, he must end his life rather than let his father sacrifice his.

A great cry rose up from the shore. Obviously, they'd
recognized his father. Keirith scanned the crowd again.
When he spied the two bright heads side by side, he caught
his breath. Merciful Maker, Faelia was as tall as his mam.
And there was Callie, jumping up and down, waving. They
were all there: the Grain-Mother and Grain-Grandmother,
the Oak-Chief and the Tree-Father, Ennit and . . . aye,
there was Conn, shading his eyes, searching for him.

His father was still splashing to shore when Ennit
plunged into the water to embrace him. The Tree-Father
made the sign of blessing over him. The Grain-Mother kissed
his cheek. Callie pushed past them and his father caught
him up in his arms. But Faelia and his mam just stood
there, staring past his father at him.

He leaped out of his coracle to help Hircha. A few of
his kinfolk glanced at him, frowning, but most were too
excited by his father's return to pay much attention to the
strangers he'd brought with him.

His father set Callie down so he could hug Faelia. His
mam watched them. She was very pale, her cheeks damp
with tears, her body rigid with tension. His father must
have noticed, too. When he said her name, his voice was
soft and hesitant, as if uncertain of his welcome.

The sound of his voice broke his mam's strange stillness.
She stepped into his arms, turning her cheek over and over
against his as her fingers clutched his tunic in a white-
knuckled grip. His father sought her mouth as a flower,
withered by the unrelenting sun, might seek water.

Around them, folks smiled and murmured, but it was too
intimate a moment for Keirith to watch. His gaze drifted
to Faelia, who stared back at him with disturbing intensity.

She knows. Somehow, she and Mam both know.

His mam whispered something to his father that made
him start. After a long moment, he nodded. He turned to
face the crowd, but before he could speak, the chief raised
his hands for silence.

"We're glad to have you home, Darak. And we welcome
your friends. There will be time later to hear what happened, but for now, perhaps the Tree-Father would say a
prayer in thanks for your safe return."

In less than three moons, the Tree-Father seemed to
have aged years. Pouches beneath his eyes bespoke sleep-

less nights and the hand pressed to his father's forehead in blessing shook with a visible tremor.

"Maker, we thank you for hearing our prayers and bringing Darak home to us. This very day, we shall offer a sacrifice at the heart-oak in thanks for his return. And we beg your mercy for the other son of our tribe. Wherever Keirith may be, keep his spirit safe until we meet him again in the Forever Isles."

"Thank you for your welcome and your prayers," his father said. "But we shall not have to wait to meet Keirith." He paused, looking around the circle of happy faces and Keirith held his breath. "I bring you a tale of wonder. A miracle vouchsafed by the Maker." His father's voice held the deep cadence of the Memory-Keeper now. "I saw my son sacrificed by a Zherosi priest. I saw the dagger in his chest, his blood spilling onto the altar."

Gasps and moans accompanied this statement. The Tree-Father looked so stricken, Keirith automatically took a step toward him. Then he noticed Othak sidling forward. Othak wearing the brown robe of the initiate. Othak squeezing the Tree-Father's arm and murmuring words of comfort. Othak who had slipped into the position that should have been his as easily as he slipped through the crowd. Keirith told himself it would have happened even if the raiders hadn't captured him, but resentment still burned within him.

His father waited for the commotion to subside. "As my son lay dying, I called to him. I opened my spirit to his and sheltered it. Just as Tinnean's body sheltered the spirit of the Holly-Lord during our quest."

Amid the whispered speculation, fingers sketched the sign of blessing.

"But the priest who murdered my son pursued us. He attacked our spirits. And together, we drove him out."

Keirith glanced sharply at his father; that was not what they had discussed. By claiming that he helped drive out Xevhan's spirit, his father could be held equally culpable for the crime.

"The Zherosi priest is dead. A man who sacrificed hundreds of our people. But my son lives." His father slipped behind him and put his hands on his shoulders. "This is Keirith, son of Darak and Griane."

Stunned silence greeted his pronouncement. All eyes were fastened on him, some with disbelief, some with horror.

"It's true."

Heads swung toward his mam as she strode forward to stand on his left. Without hesitation, Faelia took up a position on his right. Only Callie remained where he was, his face puckered in a frown.

"The Maker sent me a vision." His mam gazed defiantly around the crowd, as if daring anyone to contradict her. "This is Keirith, the son of my body. Reborn through the Maker's mercy. Come home to us at last."

In the uproar that ensued, his father remained calm, assuring the chief that he would relate the entire story to the elders. The Grain-Grandmother shouted down those who called for the council to meet at once, insisting that the family deserved a night together to celebrate their reunion. The Grain-Mother stepped forward to kiss him on both cheeks. Then, with his father's arm around his shoulders, they made their way through the crowd and headed home.

Once inside the hut, an awkward silence arose. "This is Hircha," his father finally said. "I should have introduced her before." He shrugged apologetically. "Without her, we would not have escaped."

"Welcome to our home, Hircha." His mam's voice was strained, but her smile seemed genuine. "Your home," she corrected herself. "It's little enough to thank you."

"I didn't do much."

After another awkward pause, Faelia gave him a quick kiss. Then she pushed Callie forward. "Kiss your brother."

"That's not my brother."

Although Keirith was expecting it, the words still hurt.

His father knelt beside Callie. "Did you hear what I said down by the lake?"

Callie stared at the rushes and nodded.

"A bad man killed your brother. I took Keirith's spirit inside mine. I kept it safe. And when the bad man died, Keirith took his body. You remember how the Holly-Lord took uncle Tinnean's body when his spirit left it?"

"But he didn't keep it. He went back to his tree."

"Aye. Because that was his true form. But Keirith is a man. So he had to have the body of a man."

Callie squinted up at him suspiciously. "How do we know?"

"Know what?" his father asked.

"That it's really Keirith. That it's not the bad man."

"Because the bad man's spirit is gone. It's gone," his father repeated in a gentler voice. "This is just his body. But Keirith's spirit is inside. I know because I've talked to him. And once you've talked to him, you'll know, too."

"Say something Keirith would say," Callie demanded.

They all looked at him expectantly. To save his life, he couldn't think of anything. Tears welled up in Callie's eyes. "I told you! He's not Keirith. Keirith's dead!"

Keirith realized he was gnawing his thumb and quickly dropped his hand. His mam always scolded him for that. When he was little, she'd smeared a foul-tasting ointment on his thumb to keep him from sucking it, but even that failed to break him of the habit completely.

His mam and Faelia were both watching him with wide, tear-glazed eyes. As if only now, seeing the familiar gesture, they truly believed who he was. Yet neither had hesitated to stand by him on the beach. His father and Hircha had had a moon to grow used to his appearance; he couldn't expect the rest of his family to overcome their shock in a few moments.

"You used to call me Keiry," he said to Callie. "When you were little. And you and Conn and I played wolf among the flocks. And Conn always got mad because he had to be the sheep. Because . . . it was a stupid joke . . . I said he was . . . baaed at barking. Do you remember?"

Callie nodded slowly.

"And . . . and before the raid, you lost your quartz charm. The one shaped like a fish. And I found it. But I didn't give it to you."

When Callie frowned, Keirith nudged the rushes with his foot. The light from the fire was too dim to see anything, so he got down on his hands and knees. It had to be here. He remembered that moment so clearly. "I did see it. The night before the raid. It was here—by the doorway." He clawed through the rushes, ripping up great handfuls and tossing them aside, but the charm was gone. Defeated, he sank back on his haunches.

A small, grubby fist appeared before him. The fingers opened to reveal the charm. "We found it," Callie whispered. "When Mam and Faelia put down fresh rushes."

Callie flung his arms around his neck. Keirith wished he could freeze this moment: the warmth of Callie's body pressed against his, the mingled odors of grass and earth and sheep.

Too soon, Callie squirmed free. "How come if you're a man your face is so smooth?"

"The raiders don't have a lot of hair on their faces."

"Why?"

"I don't know."

"Don't you have to shave at all?"

"Nay."

"Will you ever?"

"Probably not."

Callie considered this. "Do you have hair in your crotch now?"

"I had hair in my crotch before!"

Faelia giggled. Then Hircha. Keirith felt himself flushing, but then he laughed. In a moment, they were all laughing except Callie, who just looked puzzled. "What about the hair on your head?"

"That'll grow in." Keirith took Callie's hand and drew it back and forth over the soft stubble. "The priests there shave their heads. A moon ago, I didn't have any hair at all."

"It feels like the sheep. After the shearing. I know! I'll shave my head, too, and then we'll both look the same."

Keirith pulled him back into his arms and buried his face against the soft, warm neck.

Griane took refuge in preparing supper. She had to do something to keep from staring at Keirith. Before she could ask Faelia to help, Hircha picked up a knife and began skinning the rabbits Faelia had snared that morning.

"I worked in the kitchen," she said with a hesitant smile.

"Kitchen?"

"Where the food was cooked."

A place just for cooking. It was as inconceivable as Darak's claim that you had to purchase water. With half her mind, she listened to the stories they told Callie—silly tales about the strange group of performers Darak had fallen in with and incredible descriptions of the place Keirith had lived. An enormous building of stone with more rooms than there were huts in the village. Painted tree trunks that held up the roofs or simply marched alongside a path for no reason whatsoever. A tame wildcat that took food right from your fingers.

Callie interrupted with dozens of questions, but whenever he asked about the bad man, Darak or Keirith steered the conversation to another topic. Since she was prepared for Fellgair to enter the tale, she could listen with the same wonder as the children when Darak revealed that the raiders worshiped the Trickster, too.

It was harder to hear how Fellgair entered Darak's spirit. She knew how much pain his brief account hid and found it hard to forgive Fellgair for choosing that method—of all the ones in the world—to help Darak. Still, it had worked. Darak had saved their boy. It was more than she had done.

She doubted Fellgair had told him about their bargain; despite his time with the players, Darak was not a good enough performer to hide his feelings. Yet each time Fellgair's name came up, she could feel his eyes on her, gauging her reaction. It would be just like the Trickster to hint that a bargain existed without revealing the details.

Then Callie asked why Urkiat hadn't come home with them.

"He died, son. He was pretending to fight with me. But we were using real swords—they're like long daggers. And Urkiat . . . he didn't move when I expected him to."

"You killed him? You killed Urkiat?"

"Callie!" Her voice sounded too shrill, too sharp. Even Hircha was staring. "It was an accident."

"The bad man made Fa and Urkiat fight," Keirith said. "Urkiat was . . . distracted. Just for a moment. Fa didn't mean to hurt him."

Fellgair had told her much the same story, but the bitterness in Keirith's voice proved there was more to it than a simple accident.

To her surprise, Hircha squatted down beside Callie. "He died in your father's arms."

"You were there, too?"

"Aye. I saw it all. And I think—at the end—he must have been glad to have your father with him. Holding him. Easing him on his way. Helping him . . . drift off."

Griane saw the looks Darak and Keirith exchanged, but Callie was intent on Hircha's face. "Like when Fa rocks me to sleep? Safe like that?"

"Aye. Just like that."

She let her palm rest against his cheek a moment, then abruptly turned away as if embarrassed by her show of affection.

"Jurl died, too," Callie said.

"Jurl?" Darak's shock was obvious. "What happened?"

"He threw a fit. And he fell over by the heart-oak and his eyes bulged out and—"

"That's enough," Griane said.

"Well, they did."

"We're not going to discuss it tonight."

When talk turned to happier news, Griane gratefully allowed Faelia to carry the conversation. She couldn't help sneaking glances at Keirith, looking for familiar gestures and expressions. When he caught her at it, she smiled brightly. His answering smile was so eager it made her ache. Then the smile would slip and he would fall silent, staring into the fire pit or glancing around the hut as if seeing it for the first time. And then catch himself with a quick, guilty start before picking up the thread of the conversation again with a stranger's apologetic laugh.

Darak saw it all, of course. His hands betrayed his anxiety, reaching out too often to pat Keirith's knee or squeeze his arm, bringing him back from the shadows with a gentle touch or a soft word. Only as the evening wore on did she realize that Darak touched him as much for his comfort as for Keirith's. And that something unspoken flickered between them, as if each knew exactly what the other was thinking and feeling. Perhaps they did. Their spirits had dwelled together. They knew each other intimately. More intimately than she could hope to know either of them.

The sudden stab of jealousy shocked her. She must have made a sound, for every face turned toward her. "Forgive me. I'm being stupid and sentimental. I'm just . . . I'm so happy you're home."

Grateful tears welled up in Keirith's eyes. Darak smiled across the fire pit, but his gaze lingered on her too thoughtfully.

Muina's arrival helped dissipate the tension. Keirith's face lit up when Lisula and Ennit followed her inside, but the light died when he realized they'd brought only the younger children.

"Blame Ennit," Lisula said, quick to notice Keirith's disappointment. "He made poor Conn stay with the flock so he could visit with Darak."

"Poor Conn will have his turn on the morrow," Ennit announced, too heartily. "Uncle Lorthan's too old to be scrambling about the hills at night. And with Trian gone, that just leaves Conn and me."

"And me!" Callie shouted.

Keirith smiled with the rest of them. He seemed to enjoy the company and as the evening wore on, some of the shadows retreated from his face. But now and then, Griane caught him watching the doorway as if expecting Conn to appear.

One by one, the children fell asleep. When Hircha struggled to hide a yawn, Muina said, "You should be ashamed of yourself, Lisula. Keeping these poor folk up half the night so you could hear their stories."

Lisula smiled; after so many years, she was used to Muina's humor. She hugged Darak hard. "It's so good to have you home. But you need feeding. You're skin and bones." Then she turned to Keirith. "And you—you are a gift from the Maker. My blessings on you, Keirith. Tonight and always."

Once they were gone, Darak bundled Callie into bed while Faelia and Hircha helped her clean up. Keirith stood uncertainly by the fire pit. He looked so lost. Before she could speak, Darak said, "Tired, son?"

"Aye."

"It's been a long day."

The broody look descended again; strange how the expression could be so similar in a face altogether different.

"Try not to worry about the council meeting," Darak said, then shrugged awkwardly as if he understood how impossible that was.

Keirith just nodded and started unlacing his strange foot-

gear. Why bother to wear shoes at all if your heels and
toes hung out? On the morrow, she'd trim down his old
shoes; they'd be too large for his feet now.

"I'm afraid you and Faelia will have to share a pallet,"
she told Hircha.

Hircha shot Faelia a shy glance. "I don't mind. If you
don't. I don't snore." She frowned and glanced over her
shoulder at Keirith. "Do I?"

"Nay. But Faelia does."

Faelia stuck her tongue out, then looked abashed.

"Merciful Maker, Faelia, it's me!" Keirith looked even
more abashed than Faelia. "I'm sorry."

"Nay, it's my fault."

"It's no one's fault," Darak said. "It'll take us a while
to get used to each other again." His gaze drifted toward
her, then back to the children. "But no matter what's happened, we're still the same people we always were. Aye?"

"Aye, Fa." Faelia kissed his cheek, then glared at Keirith. "And I don't snore." When Keirith rolled his eyes, she
snatched up his discarded shoe and threw it at him. He
ducked, grinning.

"Stop that," Griane ordered. "You'll wake Callie."

"A portal to Chaos could open up and Callie would sleep
through it," Keirith said. "Even Faelia's snoring doesn't—"

The second shoe hit him in the head.

"Enough. Both of you. Hircha will think we're savages."

Hircha shook her head, her expression almost wistful.
Faelia flopped down on the wolfskins and ostentatiously
turned her back on Keirith. Despite the warmth of the evening, Hircha slipped under the furs. Faelia rolled over to
whisper something that made Hircha smile.

Griane smoothed Callie's hair and hesitated beside Keirith. "Good night, son."

"Good night, Mam. It's . . . it's good to be home." His
hands rose, then fell back. Quickly, she opened her arms.
She could feel him trembling and realized this was the first
time she had touched him.

Gods forgive me. How could I have failed to hug him?

His body was still slender, but broader through the shoulders. A man's body now. It was hard to guess the priest's
age with that smooth skin and unlined face. Older than

Urkiat, probably. Keirith had not only lost his body but years of life, too. She hugged him fiercely, wishing she could restore those lost years and protect him from the council of elders and the stares of their kinfolk and all the pain he would endure in the coming days.

"I'm just so glad you're home. And I'm sorry . . ." Her voice broke.

"It's not your fault, Mam."

But of course, it was.

Darak's hands came down on her shoulders and she started. "I was thinking of going to the lake," he said. "I've so much salt crusted on me, I might crack." His smile was as hesitant as Keirith's. "Will you come?"

She nodded, equally shy. "I need to wash out these clothes."

Through the indeterminate gray of twilight, they walked to the lake. Griane wondered if it was mere chance that led them along the beach to the place where they had made their peace after the interrogation.

Darak pulled off his clothes and waded into the water. While she scrubbed her birthing skirt, she stole covert glances at him and caught him doing the same. Fellgair's presence loomed between them as tangibly as if the god were standing there.

Only when Darak was drying himself with his mantle did she slip off her birthing tunic. Just as quickly, she pulled the other over her head and kept on with her scrubbing. She could feel him behind her, watching. And all she could do was squat like a fool, rubbing Catha's blood from her tunic.

"Talk to me."

She babbled something about Faelia's rite of woman-hood.

"Nay. Griane. Talk to me."

He'd pulled on his spare tunic and was sitting on the same rock he'd sat on after washing the raiders' blood from his body. She'd been the one to reach out that day. Now he was doing the same.

She abandoned her scrubbing and rose. "Fellgair killed Jurl."

"What?"

"He was threatening me. About the boy. The raider."

"He didn't hurt you?" He was off the rock, but froze when she backed away.

"Nay. Fellgair appeared. Before anything could happen."

"He just . . . appeared."

She took a deep breath. "I was waiting for him. In the glade of the heart-oak. I asked him for help."

Darak sank slowly down on the rock.

"You don't know what it was like! Gortin had a terrible vision. He saw you being sacrificed. And when I went to Muina, she said you were sick—" She broke off as Darak's head jerked up. "It was a rite. With all the priestesses. I saw Keirith. He spoke to me. But I couldn't see you. Muina hadn't the strength by then. I only knew you were sick. So . . ."

"You went to Fellgair."

"I was alone. I had no one to help me." She couldn't keep the bitterness out of her voice. "At least Fellgair . . ."

"What? At least Fellgair didn't desert you?"

"I didn't say that."

"Nay, but you meant it." He stalked toward her, then abruptly veered away. "He hinted that you'd come to him. And then today, when we landed, and you said that he'd told you about Keirith . . . I was just glad it wouldn't be such a shock. I should have expected such trickery from Fellgair, but . . . good gods, Griane, what were you thinking—asking him for help?"

"I wasn't thinking! I was out of my mind with fear and worry. Just as you were when Tinnean was lost."

The anger drained out of his face, but he stared at her so intently that she winced. "And what did he ask in return?"

"He . . . wanted me to go to the Summerlands with him."

"And what else?"

"And spend the day."

"And what else?" When she didn't answer, he crossed to her in three strides and seized her arms. "What else did you give him in return for saving us?"

She shoved him away. "He wouldn't save you both! He made me choose."

His eyes widened in stunned disbelief.

"He made me choose," she repeated in a broken whisper. "Just as he made you choose between me and Cuillon

all those years ago. And I . . . I chose you. And now
Keirith—"

"Nay."

"If I had chosen him, then—"

"It's not your fault."

"He's my son. My son! Any mother would choose her
child. Any wild creature would protect her young. But I
didn't. Fellgair pushed and pushed and I just called out
your name and then it was too late."

He shook her, his fingers digging painfully into her arms.
"Look at me. Look at me! We cannot know, Griane. We'll
never know. We're alive, girl. We're alive and we're home.
That's all that matters."

"Is it?"

She saw the terrible uncertainty on his face, the desire
to believe that nothing had happened in the Summerlands
warring with the helpless fear that it had. He would not
ask her again. She knew that. But should she tell him?
Would the truth be easier to bear than the lingering doubt?

"Darak . . ."

He seized her face between his hands and kissed her, his
mouth hard and demanding. Without thought, her arms
came up, her hands tangling in his wet hair, her body pressing against his, needing the reassurance of his love as much
as he needed hers.

He jerked away, but only to grab her wrist and pull her
down onto his discarded mantle. He bore her back, pinning
her beneath him, spreading her thighs with his knee. She
lifted her hips to receive him, but he reared back. His eyes
filled her vision, daring her to look away.

"You're mine."

He sheathed himself with a single hard thrust that made
her gasp. His teeth clenched, but he couldn't prevent a low
groan from escaping. As if to deny it, he gripped her tighter.

"Mine. Now. Always."

With each word, he moved inside of her. She tried to
pull his head down, but he captured her wrists and pinioned
them at her sides. And when she closed her eyes, unable
to look at his ravaged face, the calloused palms came up
to clasp her cheeks.

"Look at me."

His eyes were as gray as the twilight. Wide and tearless,

they held her captive as surely as his body. Neither of them was permitted the escape of tears, the oblivion of release, only this relentless imprisonment of body and mind and spirit.

"One blood. One body. One life."

The words of the marriage ceremony. The words that bound them together forever.

His breath came hot and fast, his body demanding the renewal of the pledge they had given to each other so many years ago. And her body answered, hips rising to meet his, fingers digging into the scarred back. She cried out his name, desperate to possess him, to be possessed by him, to expunge the memory of Fellgair, to blot out the grief and pain she had brought him and Keirith both. And when he cried out hers, his voice was so fierce and full of longing that she wanted to weep.

The pleasure built until she could no longer contain it. Her body shuddered as the first wave engulfed her. Only then did his lips seek hers. Her cry mingled with his as they lost themselves in a final surrendering of self.

They clung to each other in wordless communion, each offering strength to the other and receiving it in turn. Just as they always had, as they always would. Nothing could change that—not distance or death, not even the Trickster.

"One blood," Griane whispered. "One body. One life."

Darak's hands cupped her face. "Always."

And then there was only the sweetness of their mouths and the rhythm of their hearts and the warmth of the summer night enfolding them.

Chapter 52

NIONIK ARRIVED AT the hut shortly after dawn to tell them he wanted the council to meet immediately. "I know you've only just returned, but it would be better to deal with this matter at once." Darak agreed; the sooner the council could settle things, the better.

Griane fussed over them while they dressed, as if their appearance could possibly determine the outcome of the meeting. "Just tell the truth," she advised them. "They'll believe you. And mind your temper, Darak."

"My—?"

"You're going to hear things you won't like, and it won't help matters if you start snapping at the council members."

"I don't snap."

"Nay. You shout." She smoothed his braids, brushed a speck of oatcake off his tunic. When he captured her fluttering hands, she went still. He waited for her to look up at him, watching the color rise up her throat to stain her cheeks. Finally, the blue eyes lifted and she gave him a tremulous smile.

He smiled back and pulled her close. Last night had confirmed their love, but the shadows were still there. In time, it would grow easier. In time, he would stop tormenting himself with images of Fellgair smiling at her, stroking her hair, touching her body. The Trickster might have been content to make her choose between her husband and her son. He might not have demanded anything more.

And if he had . . .

His arms tightened around Griane.

"Darak. I can't breathe."

He released her. He even managed to laugh as she
shooed them out of the hut. "We'll be waiting," she promised. "Unless I decide to sneak over to the longhut and
listen outside."

"Can we?" Callie asked.

"Nay! I was teasing."

"It won't help matters if your mam charges into the
council meeting like a mad bullock."

Griane punched him. He grabbed her fist and kissed it.
Hircha smiled along with the children. Only Keirith's smile
seemed unnatural, as if he sensed the undercurrents. With
an effort, Darak thrust aside those concerns; today, all his
energy must be focused on the council meeting.

The rest of the elders were gathered in the longhut when
they arrived. They all nodded politely and tried not to stare
at Keirith. Darak chose a place next to Muina, and Keirith
sat down beside him. Elasoth nodded to him and he nodded
back. He was a natural choice to join the council. All of
Elathar's boys were good, steady lads, although Elasoth had
always seemed shyer than his younger brothers. He didn't
know whether that would hurt Keirith or help him.

Nor could he predict how Lorthan would respond to
their revelations. Ennit's uncle was a sweet, soft-spoken
man, but easily swayed by the opinions of others, especially
Strail who never hesitated to speak his mind.

Ifrenn's presence was a blow. Darak had counted on Sanok's support and had been shocked to learn how feeble
he'd become. To his shame, he had not even noticed Sanok's absence on the beach, but he promised himself that
before the day was over, he would visit him.

"Darak. Stop daydreaming and answer the girl."

He looked up to find Nionik's daughter leaning toward
him, a waterskin cradled in her arms.

"Thank you, Oma." He held up the cup, eyeing her
swelling belly. "Not long now."

She straightened, one hand on her back. "By the full
moon, Mother Griane says. Elasoth swears it'll be a boy
from the way he kicks."

"What do men know?" Muina shook her head dis-
missively. "Use the needle on a thread, child."

"I did. It swung round and round no matter how many times I did it. Another girl for sure." With a sigh, she continued around the circle. Elasoth looked flustered when she poured his water; obviously, this was his first council meeting and he wasn't sure how to behave.

Nionik had no such reservations; he kissed Mirili's cheek and thanked her for the basket of oatcakes. As soon as she and Oma departed, he called for silence.

"The first order of business is to ascertain that it is, indeed, Keirith's spirit inside this man's body."

"Good gods, why would I make that up?" Darak exclaimed. "Do you think I'd pass off some stranger as my son?" He subsided under Nionik's quelling stare. The council had barely begun and already he'd forgotten Griane's warning. "Forgive me. I just never expected a test would be required."

He saw the panic in Keirith's eyes as he rose. Saw, too, how quickly he suppressed it. Gortin rested his hands lightly on Keirith's shoulders and closed his eye. For the first time, Darak was grateful for his limited gift; Struath would have sensed the remnants of the Zheron's spirit immediately.

Two deep creases formed between Gortin's brows. His eye flew open.

"What is it?" Nionik asked.

"Nothing. This is Keirith." The tremor in Gortin's voice was plain. "His spirit . . . has changed . . . but it is Keirith."

"Changed? How?"

"A man's spirit is not fixed. It reflects the things that happen to him. The joys he has experienced. The suffering he has endured. Keirith's spirit has endured . . . a great deal." Gortin bowed his head. "I'm sorry. I'm so sorry."

Keirith's hand came up to cover Gortin's. Even hard-bitten Ifrenn seemed moved.

Maker, let them remember this moment. If they do, they can never condemn my boy.

Nionik waved Gortin and Keirith back to their places. "We must now decide whether the Holly Tribe should be invited to share our deliberations."

This time, he managed to keep his voice level. "The Holly Tribe?"

"Morgath was brought before the combined councils for

casting out the spirits of animals. Keirith—by your account,
Darak—has cast out the spirit of a man. There is a precedent."

He resisted the urge to shout, "Damn the precedent!"
Instead, he asked calmly, "Will Keirith get a fair hearing
from the Holly Tribe? The elders hardly know him."

"Forgive me, Memory-Keeper, Oak-Chief . . ." Elasoth
glanced around the circle uncertainly.

"Go on," Muina ordered. "You've as much right to
speak as anyone else."

"I just thought . . . since the elders of the Holly Tribe
don't know Keirith, they would not be swayed by sentiment."

"What's wrong with sentiment?" Lisula demanded. "We
are surely judging not only the act but the man who committed it. We who know Keirith best are best able to judge
his character."

Elasoth wilted visibly. The rest of the council began de-
bating the point until Muina interrupted. "If you call the
elders of the Holly Tribe in, you might as well take the
boy to the heart-oak now and have done with it."

"They're not fools," Strail rumbled. "Well, most of them
aren't. Can't say I think much of their new chief."

Ifrenn hawked a gob of phlegm into the fire pit. "He's
a sanctimonious stick. How else could he have lived with
my sister for so many years? She's so pious, she pisses
honey."

Nionik cleared his throat. "Your point, Strail? About the
Holly Tribe."

"Oh. Aye. Just that wise men—women too, I suppose—
would keep their minds and ears open and not rush to
judgment until they'd heard the whole story."

Muina's voice overrode Lorthan's murmur of assent. "As
soon as they hear Morgath's name, Keirith is a dead man."

Darak flinched, but Keirith accepted the brutal words
without changing expression.

"I agree with the Grain-Grandmother," Gortin said. "It's
too easy to draw parallels between Keirith's power and
Morgath's without taking into account their natures."

"A good point," Lorthan said.

"Besides," Muina added, "this is our business. Must we
run to the Holly Tribe every time we have a difficult prob-

lem to resolve? Bad enough that we have to discuss how many fish we can take from the lake and whether a hunter can cross the river in pursuit of a deer he's stalking."

Gods, she was clever. The two councils had argued both issues only this spring and there was still a good deal of acrimony about the outcome of that debate—especially among hunters like Ifrenn and Strail.

"Is there any more discussion? Then I call for a vote. Those in favor of inviting the elders of the Holly Tribe to our council?"

"Nay," Elasoth said loudly. Lisula leaned toward him and whispered something. "Oh. Forgive me, Oak-Chief."

"Never mind," Muina said. "Despite Nionik's vote-calling and all-in-favoring, we're not very formal here."

"All in— Does anyone wish to invite the elders of the Holly Tribe? Fine. Then we'll settle this matter ourselves."

Darak breathed a quiet prayer of thanks to the Maker and another to Muina. The first battle had been fought and won.

Muina poked his knee. "Control your temper," she whispered.

"I'm trying. But it's hard—"

"I don't care how hard it is. If you start arguing with everyone, you'll condemn the boy as surely as the Holly Tribe. Forgive me, Oak-Chief," she said in a normal voice. "I was reminding Darak of his manners."

Good-natured chuckles greeted her remark, as much over his discomfiture as Muina's bluntness. He couldn't risk alienating the council members, especially Ifrenn and Strail; they had always been jealous of his hunting skills. Keirith's fate could be determined by such personal issues, no matter what Strail said about wise men who would keep their minds and ears open.

For the rest of the morning, he kept his mouth shut. Keirith gave his account of what had happened in Pilozhat and answered the exhaustive questions that followed. Darak had insisted that neither of them reveal his part in Urkiat's death. It was one thing to cast out the spirit of an enemy, another to attack a child of the Oak and Holly.

When it was his turn to speak, he simply supported Keirith's story, taking care to emphasize the Zheron's determination to destroy them both. He also told them how Keirith brought Hua back from the brink of death. His words provoked shocked exclamations and dozens of new questions for Keirith to answer. Darak had been certain the story of Hua's reclamation would show the elders that Keirith could use his power for good, but while Lisula proclaimed it a miracle, the expressions of the others ranged from doubt to awe to fear.

By midday, the questioning was finally over. "Thank you for appearing before the council," Nionik told Keirith. "And for your thorough, honest answers. We'll excuse you now so we can consider what you've told us. Before you go, is there anything you'd like to add?"

Keirith rose. "I just want to thank the elders for hearing me. And to say that I'll abide by your decision." He hesitated a moment; for the first time, he looked uncertain. "I don't know why I have this power. It's not something I wanted. It . . . scares me. I understand how a man . . . like Morgath . . . could abuse it. Maybe I have, too. I don't know. But if I had to choose—if I could go back to that moment when the Zheron attacked us—I would still cast him out. He meant to torture my father, strip away pieces of his spirit until he was mad." Keirith looked down at him. "I didn't tell you before. It was after you had . . ."

"Fled."

"Nay."

"I fled! When the Zheron attacked, the great Spirit-Hunter hid and left his son to fight for him."

"You didn't know how to fight him! I did. And when he was close to breaking me, you came back. Without you, I couldn't have defeated him. He would have cast out my spirit and then he would have found you and taken you apart piece by piece. I couldn't let him do that. That's what I wanted to say. To all of you. My father is the bravest man I've ever known. And I couldn't let the Zheron destroy him."

Keirith placed both hands over his heart and bowed very low to him. The gesture stunned Darak. Similar to the genuflection Malaq had made when they parted, it was, at once, utterly foreign and completely natural. The others would see it and wonder if this was evidence of the changes Keirith's spirit had undergone.

He wanted to embrace his son, to tell him how proud he was of him. Instead, he rose and offered the same genuflection to Keirith. One by one, the other members of the council got to their feet. They remained standing until Keirith left the longhut.

All afternoon, the debate raged. As Memory-Keeper, it fell to Darak to recite the law that might condemn his son. He stumbled only once, when he reached the last of the acts deemed offenses against the gods: "to subvert or subjugate the spirit of any creature. The punishment for one who commits such abominations is death."

A lengthy discussion followed. Had a crime been committed? If so, was it justified? In the case of murder, the law was clear: anyone who killed without provocation would be cast out of the tribe. But the law didn't specify whether subversion or subjugation of a spirit could be justified—as could murder—if the act was committed in self-defense.

"As elders, it's our duty to interpret the law as well as enforce it," Lisula insisted.

"Of course," Lorthan agreed.

"Why is it so vague?" Elasoth asked.

"Because it was only set down after Morgath's sacrilege," Muina replied. "Until then, no one could imagine anyone would subvert the spirit of another creature."

"Or possess the power to do so." Strail glanced at Ifrenn who nodded.

"Struath did," Darak interjected.

"What Struath did—or didn't do—has no bearing on our deliberations," Gortin said.

"I believe it does. Struath was a great shaman, but he told me that he had cast out the spirit of a wren. He didn't mean to. He was young. Just a few years older than Keirith. And under Morgath's influence."

"I will not sit here and listen to you vilify Struath!" Gortin exclaimed.

"I saw Struath use his power to try and cast out Morgath's spirit."

"He was fighting for his life!"

"So was Keirith!"

"Stop shouting, both of you." Nionik's glare swung from him to Gortin. "Struath is dead, may his spirit live on in the Forever Isles. Whatever . . . mistakes he might have made, he paid for. We will not debate his actions here."

He couldn't belabor the point without risking the censure of the entire council, but he had to make them understand that the tribe's greatest shaman had used the same power as his son. You could not revere one and condemn the other.

"Struath once told me that magic was not evil," Lisula said, "only those who misused it."

Lorthan nodded thoughtfully. "Very wise."

"Tree-Father, you know Keirith well," she continued. Better than any of us. Except Darak, of course. When you dismissed him from his apprenticeship, did you believe he had misused his gift?"

Darak didn't trust himself to look at Gortin. What a fool to provoke him by bringing up Struath.

"I was afraid of his power. And the potential to abuse it. Naturally, I thought of Morgath."

Darak's hands clenched into fists.

"But Keirith is not Morgath. It was my duty as Tree-Father to help him understand his gift, to teach him to use it wisely. Instead, I acted out of fear. And . . . jealousy."

Slowly, Darak raised his head.

"Keirith sought communion with the eagle, not power over it. He would never touch any wild creature with the intent to harm it. In casting out the spirit of this foreign priest, I believe he acted in self-defense. If Keirith had killed him with a dagger, we would exonerate him. He had to use another weapon—the only one he possessed."

Once again, Gortin had proved himself the better man. And all Darak could do was nod his thanks.

By late afternoon, they were all exhausted, but Darak was confident that Muina, Lisula, Gortin, and Nionik would stand with him. Lorthan, too, probably; he always voted with the chief.

Nionik held out two small bowls. One contained black pebbles, the other white. "No one should be swayed by another's choice. For that reason, we will cast our votes anonymously. When I pass the bowls, please take four pebbles—two black and two white."

He waited for the bowls to return before continuing. "The first vote will determine if Keirith was justified in casting out the spirit of this man. If you believe he was, place a white pebble in this." He held up a small deerskin pouch, not much larger than the bag of charms each man wore around his neck. "If you believe Keirith's act was not justified, place a black pebble in the bag. Is that clear?"

After receiving nods from everyone, Nionik added, "If there are more white pebbles than black, Keirith is exonerated and our deliberations are over. If not, Keirith will be deemed guilty of a crime and we must vote on his punishment."

"What . . . ?" Elasoth faltered. "What punishment will we vote on?"

"I'm coming to that," Nionik replied. His ill-concealed impatience made Elasoth flush. "Forgive me. I'm tired. We all are. You're right to seek clarification. We're deciding a young man's fate today and there must be no confusion as to our proceedings. For a crime of this nature, there are only two punishments: casting out or death. If you place a black pebble in this bag, you are condemning Keirith to one of those punishments. Is that clearly understood?"

Nionik's gaze moved slowly around the circle and lingered on him. Darak wanted to believe it was Nionik's way of showing his support, but it was hard to read anything other than exhaustion in his face.

Gortin got to his feet stiffly and closed his eye. "Maker, guide the heart and mind of each person sitting around this circle. Oak and Holly, give us wisdom and help us to judge this boy—the child of our tribe—as we would wish to be judged."

As Gortin sat again, Lisula rose. "Lacha, soothe our hearts with your eternal waters. Bel, fill our minds with the light of truth. Halam, earth mother, guide the hands that hold Keirith's fate. Taran, Thunderer, proclaim the path we must follow. Eternal elements of life, bless this council and bless Keirith, who needs our wisdom. And deserves our mercy."

Nionik frowned at Lisula who glared back at him defiantly, Maker bless her.

When Darak's turn came to vote, his hands betrayed him and he fumbled the bag. Both Elasoth and Muina reached out to help him, but he shook his head and carefully slipped a white pebble inside. Lisula gave him an encouraging smile as she passed the bag to Nionik who poured the pebbles out.

Darak could only make out a spill of black and white among the rushes. Lisula's sharp cry told him the outcome.

Nionik looked up. "Keirith has been judged guilty."

He could feel Muina's fingers gripping his knee. He could hear Lisula's soft murmurs of distress. But all he could do was stare at Nionik and shake his head.

"I'm sorry, Darak. Truly sorry."

They had condemned his boy. His own folk had condemned him.

"The council has decided that Keirith committed a crime."

"Nay."

"We must now vote to determine whether he will be cast out of the tribe—"

"Nay!"

"Or sentenced to death."

Darak's gorge rose and he staggered outside. He barely made it behind the longhut before his legs gave out. He fell to his knees, fighting the urge to vomit. He could scarcely breathe for the hard knot in his chest. It was like Fellgair was holding his heart again, squeezing it between remorseless fingers. When he felt the hand on his shoulder, he looked up, surprised to find Lisula kneeling beside him instead of the Trickster.

She pulled his head down to her breast. Something damp and warm oozed down his face. Lisula's tears, he realized. Why couldn't he weep for his son?

He should never have allowed Keirith to come home. He should have forced him to stay with Illait. But he had been so sure . . .

"Darak. Dear. They're waiting for you."

He shoved himself upright with such force that Lisula fell back on her elbows. "You expect me to vote on whether my child's heart should be cut out of his chest or whether he should be driven from his home?"

"Darak, please . . ."

"Get away from me."

He leaned against the longhut, his fist pressed against his chest. It had all been for nothing—the endless journey, the terror of opening his spirit, Keirith's battle to defeat the Zheron. Urkiat's death. And Bep's and Hakkon's and Malaq's.

"What future does Kherid have in your village? At worst, he will be sacrificed for using his gift. At best, he will have to hide it the rest of his life."

In his arrogance, he had refused to heed Malaq's warning, assuring him that Keirith belonged with his people. The same people who were now deciding whether to kill him or cast him out of his tribe forever.

He heard footsteps in the grass and turned.

"The council has voted for a casting out," Nionik said.

Instead of relief, the rage burned hotter. He had only to look at Nionik's face to realize the truth. "It was you."

"What?"

"Muina. Gortin. Lisula. They voted with me. It was you." Nionik met his gaze without flinching. "Aye."

"He's my son."

"You think it was easy for me? Good gods, Darak, I have a son, too."

"How could you do it?"

"I had to vote my conscience."

Darak bit back the curse that rose to his lips.

"He could have stopped," Nionik said.

"What?"

"After he drove the man's spirit from your body. Instead, he pursued him. He cast out his spirit and took his body. He could have stopped, Darak. But he didn't."

"The Zheron meant to sacrifice me on his altar. He drove a dagger into my son's chest. You think he would have stopped? Ever?"

When Nionik shook his head wearily, Darak grabbed him by the front of his tunic and shoved him up against the wall of the longhut. "If Keirith had stopped, we would have died. But that would have been all right. Because then, Keirith would have paid for his mistake—as Struath did."

Nionik pushed him off. "I don't know! But I do know this power is dangerous. And so do you. And one day, Keirith will turn it on someone else."

"Then why not kill him?"

"Because . . . none of us could bear the thought of it."

"He's fourteen years old. He can't hunt for fear he'll hear the screams of the animals he kills. Casting him out *is* killing him. You've just offered him a slow death instead of a quick one. Can you bear the thought of that?"

"Darak . . ."

"Let go of me."

Nionik dropped his hand. His shoulders drooped, but when he finally raised his head, he wore the face of the chief once more—stern and emotionless. "The council has voted. The law must be upheld."

"You think I'll stand by while you drive my son from the village?"

"Then you'll be violating the law and you, too, will be punished." Nionik rubbed his eyes. "I know how hard this is. But without the law, we are savages."

"And with the law, you are murderers. May the gods forgive you, Nionik. I never will."

Numbly, he walked home. He could hear the sounds of families inside their huts, but no children lingered outside to play, no old folks chatted together, enjoying the last rays of sunlight. Perhaps word had already spread and everyone wished to avoid him, uncertain of what to say, unwilling to face his bitterness—or fearful they might be tainted by association.

Even before he reached his hut, he knew what he had to do, but he still needed a moment to gather himself before going inside. To his surprise, he found Gortin there with Muina and Lisula. Muina was hushing Lisula whose cheeks were wet with tears. Griane was dry-eyed but very pale. Callie clung to her skirt, sucking his thumb; it had been years since he'd done that. Somewhere behind them, he could hear Faelia sobbing and Hircha murmuring comfort.

Keirith stepped forward. Incredibly, he smiled. "It'll be all right, Fa. Really. It will."

Between them, no words were needed. But even if Keirith understood his intentions, he was clearly fighting for calm. As much as Darak wanted to hold him, he knew such a gesture would shatter his son's control. In the end, all he could do was smile back. "Aye, son. We'll get through this. Together."

Before he could say more, the bearskin was drawn aside. Darak recoiled when he saw Nionik. He remained in the doorway, wise enough to know he was not welcome.

"I came to inform you of the council's decision, but I see that's unnecessary. Believe me, Keirith, this was not easy for—"

"What do you want?" Darak interrupted.

Ignoring him, Nionik said, "Nemek and Mintan are waiting outside to escort you to Jurl's hut. You'll remain there until the sentence is carried out on the morrow."

"Nay!" Griane exclaimed. "For mercy's sake, let him spend this night at home."

"Post a guard." Darak made no effort to keep the bitterness from his voice. "If you're afraid he'll run off."

"You don't need a guard," Keirith said. "I won't run away. But please . . ."

His voice broke. Damn Nionik for making his boy beg.

"I'm sorry. Your family is free to visit you, but the law requires—"

Darak started for Nionik, only to be pulled back as Keirith seized his arm. "Don't, Fa. It doesn't matter." He turned toward the others with that same forced smile. "We'll talk later. But now, I . . . I'd better go."

Again, his voice broke. Before Darak could stop him, Keirith pushed past Nionik. The chief bowed formally, once to him and again to Griane, and left without speaking.

"I'll speak with the elders," Gortin said. "Perhaps I can convince them to change their votes."

"They won't," Darak said. "But I thank you. All of you. Your friendship means a great deal. Lisula . . . the things I said before . . ."

"Hush. I know."

Finally, he forced himself to meet Griane's eyes. "I'm sorry."

"It's not your fault."

"I shouldn't have let him come back."

"It was Keirith's choice and he made it. Just as the elders made theirs. There's no time now for regrets or recriminations. We must prepare ourselves."

Although her voice was quiet, she seemed to blaze as she had the morning he had awakened in the grove of the First Forest. Her fiery hair. Her bright eyes. Slender and pale as a birch, but stronger than any oak. When he'd fled with Tinnean, she had chased after them through the cold and dark of Midwinter. Even then, she had known without words what was in his heart. The hard knot of pain in his chest eased.

"Aye. We must prepare."

Chapter 53

KEIRITH SHOOK HIS head when Nemek brought in the bowl of stew. "I'm not hungry."

"I know. But you should try and eat."

And because Nemek looked so miserable, Keirith took the bowl and thanked him. Nemek lingered a moment as if he meant to speak, then rushed out. Keirith heard Mintan say, "There, lad. Get hold of yourself. It won't help poor Keirith to hear you making such a fuss." Mintan probably thought he was whispering, but deaf as he was, his softest comment always came out as a shout.

He knew he should eat—the gods only knew when he'd have hot food again—but after choking down one bite, he put the bowl down. At least he'd kept Fa from attacking the chief. He just hoped he wouldn't do anything foolish like trying to free him. He'd seemed calm enough when he'd first entered the hut. It was all an act, of course. Just as he'd been trying to act calm so he wouldn't upset his family further. Perhaps that's why the law said a condemned man had to spend his last night alone. As hard as it was to be away from his family, it was a relief to abandon the pretense of calm.

He had never witnessed a casting out, but every child knew what was involved. Worse than the shame of the ceremony itself was the thought of his family witnessing it.

Unwilling to think about that, he rose and paced. Five strides across the hut. Five strides back. There was nothing here to remind him of Jurl or Erca. Someone had placed

a pile of rabbitskins near the fire pit, along with a waterskin
and a stone bowl in case he needed to relieve himself. He
might almost be back in his little room in the palace; he
even had his two guards outside.

He felt no bitterness toward the elders; he was merely
angry that he had allowed himself to hope. But anger was
as fruitless as clinging to the belief that none of this would
have happened if he had resisted the temptation to fly with
the eagle. Long before then, his power had set him apart.
He wished he knew why the gods had chosen him. Perhaps
it was one of the games the Trickster enjoyed playing on
hapless mortals.

Oddly, it was the Trickster's words that helped calm him:
*"Don't think about the future. Just survive one moment and
then the next."*

He forced himself to sit. He picked up his bowl of stew.
He finished every bite. As he was setting the bowl down,
he heard a commotion outside: Conn demanding to see
him; Mintan protesting that there was no need to push;
Nemek murmuring something too soft to hear.

The bearskin was flung back. For a moment, Conn's
stocky figure stood silhouetted against the soft twilight.
Then he stepped inside and let the bearskin swing shut
behind him.

Keirith endured the silent scrutiny as long as he could.
Then he said, "Hullo, Conn."

His milk-brother flinched.

It was as if Conn had slapped him. Last night had been
hard enough—waiting, hoping Conn would come to welcome him home. But this . . .

Conn took one step toward him, shaky as a newborn
lamb, then sank down on the rushes and covered his face
with his hands. His shoulders heaved as he sobbed.

"Don't."

Conn's head jerked up. Fat tears oozed down his cheeks.
"I should have come! You're my best friend. And I didn't
even come see you. And now . . ." His voice broke and he
covered his face again.

Keirith knelt beside him. "You can't cry. You can't! Because then I'll start. And if I start . . ."

Conn raised his head and dragged his sleeve across his

nose. "I'm sorry." His face crumpled and he shook his head angrily. "I won't."

They sat side by side, neither daring to look at the other. Conn took long, heaving breaths until he got himself under control. "I was watching the flock. When Fa came and told me." He slammed his fist against one of the stones of the fire pit. "How could they do it?"

"I cast out a man's spirit."

"I don't care! It's still you."

Keirith swallowed hard. His hand groped toward Conn who nearly crushed it in his grip.

"We'll run away," Conn said. "After dark. I'll pack food and weapons. I'll hide them down by the lake and come back for you. I'll . . . I'll knock Mintan down. Nemek, too. And we'll steal a coracle and go . . . somewhere. Downriver, maybe. Or up. It doesn't matter. We can live off the land."

"You're a shepherd."

"So what? I'm good with a sling. Better than you. And I've got a bow and arrows."

"Aye, but you can't hit anything with them."

Conn opened his mouth and closed it again.

"And The Ferocious Scowl won't change that," Keirith added.

After a moment, Conn's face relaxed. "That was The Mutinous Glare. It's new."

"It's good. Really."

Conn punched his arm. He punched Conn back. They both laughed. And then the laughter caught in their throats and they just stared at each other.

"What will you do?"

He thought about his father, sitting under Tinnean's tree, contemplating death. Perhaps he should find a tree. One with a view of Eagles Mount. And just sit there until the end came. A slow death, but a peaceful one. And then he remembered his father's plea: *"Death is easy. It's living that's hard. But as long as there are those who love you, it's worth the struggle."*

"I don't know," he finally said. "I guess I'll just have to figure it out as I go along."

"Well, that's a piss-poor plan."

"I know. Sorry."

" 'Figure it out as I go along.' Gods, Keirith."

"Sorry!"

Conn sighed. "Is there anything I can do?"

"This is good. Just . . . talking. Like normal."

"Do you . . . do you want to tell me about it? What happened? You don't have to. I can understand if you don't want to."

"I don't. But you're my milk-brother. You should know."

Griane directed the preparations. Choosing what to take was easy; they had little enough in the way of possessions. Packing them was another matter.

Darak left once, to visit Sanok and to inform Nionik of their decision. "Sanok thought I was my father," he said when he returned. "He kept calling me 'Reinek' and asking after the boys."

"And Nionik? He didn't try to change your mind?"

"He simply reminded me the law must be carried out. And told me we were entitled to our share of last season's harvest."

"Good."

"I'll not take anything from him!"

"It's our right. And we'll need the food."

And he swallowed his pride and agreed.

Their kinfolk began arriving as the gloaming gave way to darkness. Some came and went furtively. Others announced their presence boldly. Just like the night before Darak and Urkiat left, word of their plans had spread throughout the village. Tonight, though, far fewer came to bid them farewell; clearly, many people supported the council's decision. But those who slipped into the hut brought gifts: spare clothes, packets of food, flints and arrows, axes and firesticks.

"We'll never be able to carry it all," Faelia whispered.

"Aye, we will," Griane replied with grim determination.

Sali brought three charms. "This one wards off tiredness," she explained to Faelia. "This one protects you from wild beasts. And this one brings true love." When Faelia eyed the last charm skeptically, Sali gave her a weak smile. "Well. You never know."

Griane patted her cheek. "You're a good girl. And you'll make a fine healer. Don't be afraid to shout at people, though. It makes them think you know what you're doing."

"Aye, Mother Griane," she said in her usual meek voice.

"Sali . . ."

"Aye, Mother Griane," she repeated with more spirit.

"That's better."

Muina brought a flask of elderberry wine and laughed when Ennit produced a jug of brogac. "After a few drinks," he promised, "you'll be able to drive off the wild beasts just by breathing on them."

Somehow, she managed to say farewell to Ennit and Lisula without crying. "We're best friends," Lisula whispered fiercely. "Nothing changes that. And someday, perhaps, you'll come back." They both knew that would never happen, but neither wanted to believe this was the last time they would ever see each other.

Muina's eyes were bright when she offered her blessing. "It's a hard path, child, but if you could manage in the First Forest, you'll manage now. The gods bless you and keep you safe."

Ennit and Darak embraced, both of them fighting to keep their emotions under control. Ennit was the only friend Darak had ever had—save for Cuillon—and now he was losing him. But they were all losing friends; that was the only way they could keep their family together. She just wished Keirith could be here to share the farewells with them.

She hated to think of him sitting alone in Jurl's hut, but there was so much to do before dawn. Darak assured her that Keirith understood what they were planning and once their preparations were complete, he promised to remain with him until the casting out. Even so, this night must be lonely for him—and long.

When the last of the visitors left, she tucked Callie into bed and picked up two waterskins, a handful of nettle-cloths, and the basket she used to collect herbs. Darak looked up from his packing, but all he said was, "Don't be too long."

She had nearly reached the far end of the lake when she
realized she was being followed. Even in the thin light of
the waxing moon, she recognized Hircha's fair hair.

"I thought I could help."

Griane hesitated, then thrust out the waterskins. "You
can fill these. There are some plants I want to dig up."

"Now?"

"There won't be time on the morrow."

She dampened the nettle-cloths and knelt down, guiding
herself with her fingertips. Carefully wriggling her fingers
into the soil, she freed the roots and wrapped the first plant
in one of the cloths.

"What is that?" Hircha asked, peering into the basket.

"It's called heal-all."

"I've never heard of it before."

"You wouldn't have. It's from the Summerlands."

Hircha caught her breath. With one forefinger, she gently
brushed a slender leaf. "Are they beautiful? The Summerlands?"

"Oh, aye. More beautiful than any Memory-Keeper
could describe." Griane bent closer to the heart-ease. "I
should have come before the light went."

"Let me."

"Be careful not to bruise the roots. Or pull too hard."

"I know." After a moment, Hircha added, "My mother
was a healer."

Griane watched her to be sure she knew what she was
doing. "You've a gentle touch."

"She let me help her gather plants. And tie them up for
drying. I even helped make infusions—simple ones. But
then . . ." Hircha's voice trailed off.

"Then the raiders came. How old were you?"

"Nine."

She groped for Hircha's hand and squeezed it. After that,
they harvested the plants in silence, lulled by the chorus of
frogs and night insects. When Hircha finally spoke, her
voice startled Griane.

"I liked knowing what each plant was used for."

"Aye. There's a comfort in plants."

"Does . . . does Faelia help you?"

"Faelia wouldn't know Maker's mantle from mugwort.
She's a hunter."

"Lots of girls snare rabbits and birds."

"Aye. But Faelia's brought down a deer."

Hircha digested this in silence. "My tribe didn't allow women to hunt with a bow."

"Nor does mine."

Another silence, longer this time. "Does Darak know?"

"There hasn't been time to tell him. Everything's happened so fast. Nay, leave the rest. I must remember to tell Sali about them before we go."

Together, they walked back toward the village. It was a soft, warm night. The smell of peat smoke mingled with the faint odor of decay from the Death Hut. By habit, Griane paused outside the birthing hut, listening for sounds, but both Catha and the babe must be sleeping.

She paused again beside the tribal cairn and rested one hand on the rocks. She had barely finished her prayer when Hircha blurted out, "Did Darak tell you he'd asked me to come with you?"

"We discussed it beforehand. Have you made up your mind yet?"

"I don't want you to take me just because you feel . . . obligated."

She peered at the girl, trying to read her expression. Finally she gave up and said, "I told you when you first arrived that our home was yours. And I meant it. We haven't had much time to get to know each other. I see someone who is young and strong and tough-minded. A little free with her tongue. A bit like me, I suppose. I'd like to have another woman around. Especially one who knows something about healing. And you get on well with the children." With them, at least, Hircha could let down her guard and dare to show affection. "Both Faelia and Callie seem to like you."

"Darak doesn't."

They did seem uncomfortable with each other, but Darak would never have suggested that Hircha come with them if he disliked her.

"He's afraid I'll hurt Keirith."

"Will you?"

"I don't know! I don't want to hurt him. It's not like I'll try to."

"Good."

There was a long silence. Griane curbed her impatience and waited.

"I hated him," Hircha said in a low voice. "Keirith. I didn't want him getting too close. Because if you let people in . . ."

"Sometimes, they'll hurt you. Even the ones you love. If you're afraid of people getting close, you should stay here. Even in a village this small, you might be able to manage that way. But not with five other people. We'll need to trust each other. And we'll have to risk far more than our hearts if we're going to survive." Griane hesitated, then decided to ask the question that had been on her mind since Hircha had arrived. "Do you love Keirith?"

Hircha's head jerked toward her. "Nay."

"Does he love you?"

"I . . . I don't think so."

"But you're friends."

Hircha considered. "Aye. I guess we are." She sounded surprised but not displeased.

"I think you can help each other. You both understand what it was like in that place."

"Darak—"

"Is his father. Keirith still needs a friend. And so do you."

The gods only knew what the raiders had done to the girl. She still wasn't sure if it had been wise to ask her to join them. But she'd seen the longing in Hircha's eyes when she listened to them arguing and weeping and laughing together. Hircha needed a home and a family and a place to belong.

Griane bent down to pick up a rock and placed it atop the cairn. "The bones of my mother and father are inside. And my sister. My aunt and uncle. My son. Aye, I had another boy. He only lived a few moments . . ."

And only after a moon could a child of the tribe receive a name. But she had named him in her heart and that was how she remembered him in her prayers. Rigat.

"I'm sorry I won't lie with them. But a body is just flesh and bone and blood. It's the spirit that matters. And the heart."

Darak might understand that, but understanding and accepting were very different.

"It's hard . . . when the body is before you every day."

Lost in her thoughts, it took Griane a moment to realize Hircha was talking about Keirith—and the man whose body he now wore.

"I know it's Keirith inside," Hircha said. "I can see that. Not just in what he says but the way he walks, the gestures he makes. His kindness."

She must have known the other man well. Darak claimed she had feared and hated him, but Griane suspected there was more to it—and that Keirith knew what it was. There may not be love between them or desire, but there was a bond. The kind that formed when people shared tremendous adversity and survived. And that could only help them both in the hard times ahead.

"None of us can wipe out the past," she said quietly. "No matter how much we might want to. All we can do is acknowledge it—for better or worse—and move on."

"Aye. But it's not easy."

Griane brushed a wisp of hair off Hircha's face. "I know."

Chapter 54

CONN BROKE DOWN only once, when he told him about the rape. After that, he never made a sound. By the time Keirith finished, the faint slivers of light seeping through the chinks in the walls were gone. And no one from his family had come to see him.

"It's late, Conn. And I . . . I guess I should try to sleep."

"Aye. But first, we need to make a new oath."

Conn unsheathed his dagger and stared down at his shaking hand.

"Try not to cut my wrist," Keirith said.

Conn managed a weak smile. His fingers found the place at the base of his thumb. There was a quick, sharp sting as the dagger bit into his flesh and then the warm swell of blood. Conn passed him the dagger. Keirith was surprised to discover how steady his hand was as he made the cut for Conn.

"To be friends in this life," Conn said as they clasped hands. "And brothers in the next."

"Spirit linked to spirit."

"Heart bound to heart."

Conn cut two strips from the bottom of his tunic and they bound each other's wounds. They got to their feet, neither of them willing to say good-bye. Then they heard the voices outside and embraced, a hard fierce hug that promised they would always remember their oath. Conn paused at the doorway, his expression fierce. And then he was gone.

Expecting to see his family, Keirith tried to hide his disappointment when Ennit and Lisula ducked inside. Although he was grateful to them for coming, he just didn't have the strength for another emotional encounter. The Grain-Mother was the first to realize he wanted to be alone. Before she left, she promised his family would be along soon.

Drained and exhausted, Keirith sat down beside the fire pit. He kept glancing at the doorway, waiting for the sound of footsteps. But none came. Even without the Grain-Mother's promise, he knew they wouldn't desert him.

As the night wore on, he feared something had happened. But the village was very quiet. Everyone was asleep. Even old Mintan was snoring.

Abruptly, his droning snores turned to a surprised snort. The bearskin moved. His father stepped inside. "I'm sorry I couldn't come earlier. Are you all right?"

He looked very tired but calm. Relaxed, even. As if they had all the time in the world.

"Aye. I . . . I saw Conn."

"I'm glad."

"Ennit and Lisula came, too."

"Gortin would have, but he's been going from hut to hut, trying to convince someone on the council to change his vote."

His father's expression was proof enough that no one had.

"Where's Mam? And Faelia and Callie?"

"Your mam and Hircha went to the lake. How they can see to gather plants at this time of night is beyond me."

Gathering plants? The night before the tribe was going to cast him out?

"Faelia and Callie are asleep. I thought of waking them, but they'll have a long day on the morrow and they need the rest."

Numb with disbelief, Keirith just stared at him.

"You don't mind?"

A horrifying suspicion was forming, but he couldn't find the words to voice it.

"Oh, gods." His father looked stricken. "I'm sorry. I thought . . . since there would be time on the morrow . . . never mind. I'll fetch them now."

He was halfway to the door when Keirith grabbed his arm. "What are you talking about? What have you done?"

For a moment, his father's face was perfectly blank. "I'm talking about leaving the village." He spoke slowly and carefully, as he might to a child. "All of us. After the casting out." Whatever his father saw on his face made him take a step back. "You said yourself . . . you said everything would be all right. And I thought you understood. I thought you knew. Gods, Keirith! Did you think we'd abandon you? Stand by and do nothing?"

"I only meant . . . when I said that, I meant I'd accepted the council's decision."

"Well, we didn't!" His father stared at him as if he were a stranger. "You sat here—all night—thinking we weren't even coming to say farewell? You believed I could do such a thing? After all we've been through together?"

"Nay. I . . . I just thought you were giving me time. With Conn. And later, I thought . . . I wondered if you would try and free me. Take me away like you did Tinnean. But not the whole family. You can't drag Callie and Faelia into the wilderness."

"I'm not dragging them. We all voted."

"I didn't!"

"I voted for you. You were the only one opposed. I made all the arguments you're going to make now, so you may as well save your breath."

His father's implacable calm—nay, arrogance—turned his shock to anger. "You have no right—"

"I'm the head of this family. That alone gives me the right!" His father's shoulders heaved as he fought for control. "We all discussed it. And we all agreed. I'm sorry you don't, but the decision has been made."

"Then you'll have to unmake it. I won't permit it!"

"By the gods, you will!" He paced, a caged beast in the tiny hut. "I expected you to be relieved, at least. That we intend to stand by you."

The hurt in his father's voice kept Keirith from shouting back. "I am. But you can't do this."

"Your mother and I survived in the First Forest for

nearly a moon without fire or friends—and me half dead on top of it. We have time to find a place. To build a home."

"And how are you going to feed everyone? With a Memory-Keeper's tales?"

His father's head snapped back. "I'll hunt," he said, a savage edge to his voice. "And so will Faelia. We'll set snares. We'll gather roots and berries. In the spring, we'll plant barley—"

"Where are you going to get—?"

"From our share of the tribe's stores. Nionik has agreed."

"You've told the chief?"

"The whole village knows. Folk have been coming all night. Bringing supplies. Wishing us well. Wishing you well."

He didn't trust himself to speak. As if sensing his weakness, his father added, "Not everyone agreed with the council's decision."

"And what about the tribe?" His voice was too tentative. He had to strengthen it. He was fighting for his family's survival. "Sanok is failing. And Sali's too young—"

"Nemek's been filling Sanok's shoes for two moons. And Sali's older than your mam was when she became healer. The tribe will manage. So will we."

He had only one argument left and he used it without hesitation. "You'll never see Tinnean again. There won't be anyone to open the way to the First Forest."

His father's breath caught. He let it out slowly. "Aye. I'd forgotten that. But whether or not I go to the One Tree, I'll always carry him here." He laid his palm on his chest. "Those were his last words to me."

Stubborn as a rock? Gods, he was stubborn as a boulder and just as unmovable.

"Why are you doing this?"

His father went rigid with shock. "You have to ask?"

"There are limits to love."

"Are there? I haven't found them yet."

"You've done enough. Suffered enough."

"It's got nothing to do with suffering! You're my son."

"I know!"

"Nay. You don't. You can't." His father dragged his hands through his hair as he paced. "My father tried to explain and I listened to the words and they all made sense.

But I didn't understand. Not until Lisula carried you out of the birthing hut and put you into my arms. This red-faced, red-haired scrap of flesh. I was scared to death I was going to drop you, me with my clumsy hands."

He held them out, staring at them as if he'd never seen them before. "That's when I began to understand what it meant to be a father. The love. The pride. The fear. That, most of all. What if something happens to him? If he should take sick? Or drown in the lake? Or fall out of a tree? Knowing I could never shield you from every danger. Or unhappiness. Or just the pain of growing up and wanting to be a man while you're still little more than a child. To see you pulling away and knowing I had to let you, even though every step terrified me. And made me proud."

It was too hard. He couldn't bear this.

"You and I . . . we know the best and the worst of each other. And the best of me is my love for my family. And maybe the worst is my stubbornness, my determination to hold on to all of you."

"But you'll only lose us all, Fa. Can't you see that? Isn't it better to lose only me? If anything should happen to Callie or Faelia . . . to any of you . . . I couldn't live with myself."

"Any more than we could live with ourselves if we let you walk away."

He backed away, putting the fire pit between them. This was the final test and the hardest. He could not allow love to sway him from doing what was right. If he'd been stronger, he would have done it before. Now he had no choice.

"I'm sorry," he whispered.

"It's all right. I know you're just trying to—"

His father broke off as he unsheathed his dagger.

"I love you, Fa. But I won't let you destroy everyone in the family just to protect me."

"Son. Listen to me."

"You know I'll do it."

"Aye. But if you do . . . I don't think either of us will survive it."

The pain in his father's voice nearly unmanned him. He tightened his grip on the dagger. "Please, Fa. Let me go."

For a long moment, his father stood there. Then, slowly, awkwardly, he knelt on the rushes.

"Nay."

"I've gone down on my knees—willingly—only three times in my life."

"Get up."

"Once, to your mam, to beg her forgiveness for leaving her. Once, to the Trickster, to ask for his help in finding Tinnean. And again to the Trickster, to ask him to help me save you."

"Don't."

"Now I'm begging you. On my knees. Please, Keirith."

"You're killing me!"

The dagger fell from his fingers. His hands came up to cover his face. He knew he must find the dagger. He must finish it now. He must be strong enough to do this. But his father's hands were grasping his shoulders, his father's arms were holding him, his father's voice was murmuring his name over and over. And gods forgive him, he could only cling to him, feeling the gentleness of the hands stroking his hair, the strength of the arms cradling him, the hoarse, broken longing of the voice that spoke his name like a prayer.

He didn't know how long they remained locked together. In the end, he was the one who found the strength to let go. He swiped at his nose with the back of his hand. His father was more direct; he raised his tunic and blew his nose on the hem.

"It'll be dawn soon. Could you sleep, do you think?"

Keirith shook his head.

"Then we'll just sit together until . . . until it's time. Your mam's going on ahead—with Faelia and Callie. They'll leave before the ceremony."

Relief washed over Keirith. He could manage if he didn't have to see his mam's stricken face.

"I invited Hircha to come with us. And she said yes. Well, what she really said was she'd promised to stay till the end, and clearly, it wasn't over yet. So. She's coming. You don't mind?"

"Nay." His face grew warm under his father's scrutiny; at least with his darker skin, no one would notice when he blushed. "We're not . . . we're just friends. And I know she can be difficult. But she'll be all right. You'll see."

"Aye. Well." His father shook himself as if beset by deerflies. "Anyway, they'll all be waiting for us. After the ceremony. But I'll be with you. The whole time. Just keep your eyes on me."

They spent the rest of the night talking about anything other than the upcoming ceremony. When the ram's horn sounded, their gazes locked. They rose together. His father hugged him hard. The ram's horn sounded again and his father's arms tightened, as if to shield him from the sound and all it meant. Then he drew back, but kept his hands on his shoulders.

"It'll be hard, son. There's no point in denying that. But it'll be over quickly. And then we can leave. Together."

Keirith swallowed hard and nodded.

Their kinfolk were already gathered. The Tree-Father blew the ram's horn a third time and handed it to Othak. No one spoke as they took their places in the circle, but all eyes watched him. He sought out Conn and found him standing beside Ennit. Both gave him a quick nod of encouragement. The Tree-Father looked as exhausted as the Grain-Mother. They stood on either side of the chief, the Grain-Mother with the sheaf of barley that symbolized her power, the Tree-Father with his blackthorn staff.

"Keirith."

He started a little as the chief spoke his name and his father's hand came down on his shoulder.

"Step forward."

Slowly he walked into the center of the circle.

"Keirith, son of Darak and Griane. You have cast out the spirit of another creature. The council of elders could not excuse this act, but neither could it condemn you to death for defending yourself and your father. It is the sentence of the council that you be cast out of the tribe forever. Do you understand this judgment?"

"Aye."

"Do you wish to say anything?"

He shook his head; what could he say now that he hadn't said before?

"As long as I've been chief, there has never been a casting out. And I perform this one with no joy." The chief's gaze lingered a moment on his father who refused to look at him. "But the law is the law," he continued in a stronger voice, "and it will be upheld."

Keirith nodded his acceptance.

"Naked you came into this tribe and naked you must leave it."

He removed his shoes. He unfastened his belt. He pulled his bag of charms over his head and then his tunic. As he dropped it to the ground, he heard gasps. Someone spat. A man cursed. His father took a step forward, but froze as the chief silenced the muttering with a sharp command.

Hircha and his father had seen the tattoos, but the tunic's sleeves had hidden them from everyone else. His hands came up to cover them, then slowly went to the waist of his breeches. He fumbled with the drawstrings, but finally worked them free. Before his courage failed, he slid his breeches down and stepped out of them. The heat rose in his face as he cupped his hands over his genitals.

He stared at the grass, too ashamed to raise his head. Then, as clearly as if he had spoken aloud, he heard his father call his name. He looked up then and found strength in his father's fierce gaze. He held it until the three figures blocked it from view.

"Keirith. I cast you out of the tribe." The chief touched his chest with the hilt of his dagger.

"Keirith. I cast you out of the tribe." The Tree-Father's voice shook as he touched him with the tip of his blackthorn staff.

"Keirith. I cast you out of the tribe." The Grain-Mother's barley brushed his chest. Before she stepped back, she kissed his cheek, drawing murmurs from the rest of the tribe.

"From this day forward," the chief said, "no member of the tribe may offer this man food or shelter. No one may speak his name. His existence is wiped from the bloodlines. His bones shall not be interred in the cairn of our ancestors."

"He is dead," the Tree-Father intoned. "He is forgotten. He is cast out." He thumped his staff three times. The Grain-Mother raised and lowered her sheaf of barley.

After a moment, Keirith realized it was over. No one would order him away because he no longer existed.

Before he could gather up his clothes, his father bent and retrieved them. Of course. The law said he must leave with nothing. He couldn't even use his discarded garments to cover his nakedness.

The circle opened so they could pass. He concentrated on taking one step, then another. Each step reminded him that he would never again walk through the village. He would never swim in the lake or hear the breeze rustle through the barley. Never watch the eagles circling their nest. Never see the faces of his kinfolk or hear their voices.

Another step and another after that. And now he heard the footsteps behind him. His father drew up to him and gave him a quick nod, but he didn't speak. Keirith had to lengthen his stride to keep up. It was then that he heard the Grain-Mother's voice, high and tremulous.

> *However far we must travel,*
> *However long the journey,*
> *The Oak and the Holly are with us.*
> *Always, forever, the Oak and the Holly are with us.*

The Tree-Father's voice joined hers and others as well, a ragged chorus singing the song of farewell, the song Brudien had sung when the ship carried them away, the song their ancestors had sung when they left their homeland.

> *In the heart of the First Forest,*
> *In the hearts of our people,*
> *The Oak and the Holly are there.*
> *Always, forever, the Oak and the Holly are there.*

His steps faltered. His father appeared before him, thrusting out a bundle. His clothes, he realized. He could not resist squeezing his bag of charms after he pulled it over his head. His eyes, his skin color, the tattoos on his arms . . . those would always set him apart, but his charms would remind him of who he really was.

Treading carefully between the rows of barley, they made their way across the fields. His family was waiting, their expressions anxious. One by one, he hugged them. His eyes widened when he noticed the bundles of supplies, but his mouth fell open when he saw the three sheep.

"Our share of the flock," his father said.

"We're going into the forest—on trails even you haven't traveled—and we're dragging sheep behind us?"

His father's mouth twitched. "Ennit assured me they would frolic at our heels."

The laughter surprised him. "This is absurd."

"No more absurd than venturing into the First Forest in search of Tinnean and the Oak-Lord," his mam said. "There were five of us that time, though, not six."

"No sheep either," his father added.

They grinned at each other. Then their expressions softened. Their gazes held, intimate as a touch.

"I think they're sweet," Callie said. It took Keirith a moment to realize he meant the sheep.

Faelia rolled her eyes. "Sweet or not, you prod them in the arse if they get stubborn."

"Nay. We'll let Keirith talk to them. Spirit to spirit. Then they'll understand." Callie's face lifted to his, shining in earnest appeal.

"Better keep a stick handy," Hircha said. "In case they're not listening."

His father divided up the supplies; even Callie had a small pack to carry. Only then did Keirith look back. His kinfolk stood at the edge of the fields. Here and there, hands rose in silent salute: the Grain-Mother and Grain-Grandmother, Conn and Ennit. The Tree-Father traced a circle in the air, blessing him. He raised his hand and returned the blessing.

As he was turning away, he saw the eagles gliding in a slow circle above their nest and caught a flash of movement under the overhanging shelf of rock. He had to squint before he made out the fledgling, teetering on the edge of the nest. Its wings flapped with ungainly desperation. Twice, the young one sought to rise and each time, settled back onto the sticks. Then, in a blur of movement, it took flight.

The fledgling's wings flapped frantically as it sought equilibrium. A current of air caught it and lifted it up. The wings flapped again, more slowly, as the young eagle circled the nest in a wobbly parody of its parents' grace.

Come the harvest, it would fly away, north probably, where the open moors offered good hunting. One day, it would mate and build a nest on a rocky crag like Eagles Mount. And if its eyrie overlooked a village, another boy might stare skyward and wonder what it would be like to fly.

Keirith took a deep breath and turned his back on the place of his birth. His family waited in the shadows of the trees, taking their last look at the village. His mam and Faelia hid their trepidation behind identical scowls. Callie hopped from foot to foot in excited anticipation of the journey. And Hircha inspected her new tribe with a small smile.

His father was the first to look at him. His face was tranquil, his body relaxed, as if he were coming home instead of leaving it. But his eyes held a question.

The gods only knew what lay ahead. Danger, certainly. Hunger. Loneliness. An endless struggle to survive. Another danger lurked inside him: the remnants of Xevhan's spirit. Yet for the first time in a long while, he wasn't afraid.

With a firm nod to his father, Keirith strode forward into a new life.

C.S. Friedman

The Coldfire Trilogy

"A feast for those who like their fantasies dark, and as
emotionally heady as a rich red wine." —*Locus*

Centuries after being stranded on the planet
Erna, humans have achieved an uneasy stale-
mate with the fae, a terrifying natural force with
the power to prey upon people's minds. Damien
Vryce, the warrior priest, and Gerald Tarrant, the
undead sorcerer must join together in an uneasy
alliance confront a power that threatens the very
essence of the human spirit, in a battle which
could cost them not only their lives, but the soul
of all mankind.

BLACK SUN RISING	0-88677-527-2
WHEN TRUE NIGHT FALLS	0-88677-615-5
CROWN OF SHADOWS	0-88677-717-8

To Order Call: 1-800-788-6262

DAW 18

Tanya Huff

The Finest in Fantasy

Tad Williams

THE WAR OF THE FLOWERS

"A masterpiece of fairytale worldbuilding."
—*Locus*

"Williams's imagination is boundless."
—*Publishers Weekly*
(Starred Review)

"A great introduction to an accomplished
and ambitious fantasist."
—*San Francisco Chronicle*

"An addictive world ... masterfully plays
with the tropes and traditions of
generations of fantasy writers."
—*Salon*

"A very elaborate and fully realized setting
for adventure, intrigue, and more
than an occasional chill."
—*Science Fiction Chronicle*

0-7564-0181-X

To Order Call: 1-800-788-6262

Kristen Britain

GREEN RIDER

As Karigan G'ladheon, on the run from school, makes her way through the deep forest, a galloping horse plunges out of the brush, its rider impaled by two black arrows. With his dying breath, he tells her he is a Green Rider, one of the king's special messengers. Giving her his green coat with its symbolic brooch of office, he makes Karigan swear to deliver the message he was carrying. Pursued by unknown assassins, following a path only the horse seems to know, Karigan finds herself thrust into in a world of danger and complex magic....   0-88677-858-1

FIRST RIDER'S CALL

With evil forces once again at large in the kingdom and with the messenger service depleted and weakened, can Karigan reach through the walls of time to get help from the First Rider, a woman dead for a millennium?   0-7564-0209-3

To Order Call: 1-800-788-6262

DAW 7